Prince A. Morrow

Atlas of skin and venereal diseases

Prince A. Morrow

Atlas of skin and venereal diseases

ISBN/EAN: 9783742818959

Manufactured in Europe, USA, Canada, Australia, Japa

Cover: Foto ©Andreas Hilbeck / pixelio.de

Manufactured and distributed by brebook publishing software
(www.brebook.com)

Prince A. Morrow

Atlas of skin and venereal diseases

ATLAS

OF

SKIN AND VENEREAL

DISEASES

COMPRISING ORIGINAL ILLUSTRATIONS AND SELECTIONS FROM THE PLATES OF

Prof. M. KAPOSI, of Vienna; Mr. J. HUTCHINSON, of London; Prof. I. NEUMANN, of Vienna;
Profs. A. FOURNIER and A. HARDY; and Drs. RICORD, CULLERRIER, and VIDAL, of Paris;
Prof. LELOIR, of Lille; Dr. UNNA, of Hamburg; Dr. SILVA ARAUJO, of Rio Janeiro;
Dr. P. A. MORROW, of New York; Dr. E. L. KEYES, of New York;
Dr. J. NEVINS HYDE, of Chicago; Dr. HENRY G. PIFFARD,
OF NEW YORK, AND OTHERS.

WITH ORIGINAL TEXT BY

PRINCE A. MORROW, A.M., M.D.,

CLINICAL PROFESSOR OF VENEREAL DISEASES, FORMERLY CLINICAL LECTURER ON DERMATOLOGY, IN THE UNIVERSITY OF THE CITY OF NEW YORK;
SURGEON TO CHARITY HOSPITAL, ETC.

NEW YORK

WILLIAM WOOD & COMPANY

PREFACE.

The great usefulness of pictorial representations of diseases of the skin as an efficient aid in their study is generally recognized. For purposes of differential diagnosis, flesh tints and colors are often quite as important as the form and grouping of the eruption, and colored plates in which all these essential elements are combined, if faithful and true to nature, are scarcely secondary in value to the clinical study of these diseases in the living subject.

The large majority of the profession is practically debarred from opportunities for clinical observation which exist only in large centres of population, and familiarity with the characteristic features of a disease, as portrayed in a life-like picture, will render its recognition easy when met with in practice.

A complete atlas of skin and venereal diseases comprehends a vast number of clinical forms, the most typical examples of which cannot be furnished by the observation of any one individual, no matter how extensive and varied may have been his experience. Appreciating this fact, the author, in the preparation of this work, enlisted the co-operation of the leading dermatologists and syphilographers in this country and abroad, and he has selected from these various sources and his own collection of cases what are believed to be the best and most characteristic delineations of these diseases that have ever been drawn.

In writing the text, the essential facts relating to the symptoms, etiology, pathology, diagnosis, and treatment of the various diseases have been kept in view. Especial prominence has been given to practical details relating to diagnosis and treatment, and no pains have been spared to bring the therapeutical part of the work up to the latest advances made in this department.

Acknowledgments are due Dr. Charles W. Allen, of New York, for most valuable assistance rendered in the preparation of the text of Parts XI., XII., and XIII. during the author's temporary illness

66 West 40th Street, June 1st, 1889.

INTRODUCTION.

THE DOCTRINES OF UNITY AND DUALITY.

In a work designed to be essentially practical, little space can be devoted to the consideration of the theoretical question of the unity or duality of the virus of venereal sores.

The determination of this question has little clinical value except from a prognostic point of view. As most of the plates in this Atlas illustrating the various forms of venereal sores are reproduced from the work of Kaposi, who is an avowed unicist, it is proper to give a brief resumé of the views which have been entertained respecting the identity or non-identity of the contagium of chancroid with that of the syphilitic virus.

Up to the middle of the present century, a belief in the unity of the species and cause of all venereal sores was universal. Although Ricord and other observers were aware of the fact that some sores remained local, while others were followed by constitutional manifestations, it was taught that they all originated from the same virulent principle, local or constitutional effects being determined by conditions inherent in the soil in which the virus was implanted.

In 1852, Bassereau created a revolution in syphilography, by demonstrating that there was a radical difference in the generating source of the two species of sores. He showed by numerous confrontations and artificial inoculations that contagion from a soft sore always produced a local sore, which never affected the general system, while infection from a hard sore was invariably followed by symptoms of constitutional syphilis. By farther investigations the essential characters of the two species of sore were thus formulated.

The simple chancre originates from a soft sore, it develops without incubation, it remains a local disease, it furnishes a pus which is inoculable in generations, both upon the bearer and upon others, whether syphilitic or not.

The syphilitic chancre originates from a hard sore, it develops only after a well-marked period of incubation, it shows a characteristic induration, and is followed by constitutional syphilis; its secretion is not inoculable upon the bearer or other syphilitic individuals.

Upon these results was based the French dualistic theory—a theory which assumes the existence of two distinct poisons—the chancre poison and the syphilitic poison, and has for its fundamental doctrine the proposition that each sore propagates only its own kind.

This new theory was advocated in 1858 by Ricord, and, sustained by the weight of his high authority, was soon very generally adopted.

Unfortunately for the unqualified acceptance of the doctrine of dualism, certain clinical facts were observed in apparent contravention of the theory of the distinct individuality of the two forms of sores; for example, it was noted that a soft sore, developing immediately after infection, later became indurated, and was followed by constitutional symptoms. An explanation of this was furnished by Rollet's hypothesis of a "mixed chancre," viz., that there had been an inoculation of the two viruses at the same spot, the resulting lesion exhibiting the physical characters and potentialities of both the soft and the hard chancre. It was claimed that there might be a simultaneous or successive inoculation of the two viruses. In the former case, the evolution of the soft chancre, owing to its absence of incubation, first took place, while later, after the classic period of incubation, the sore became indurated and impressed with the specific characters of the initial lesion. Or a dual infection might take place at different times, the virus of the soft sore might be implanted upon an initial lesion, or a hard chancre might be engrafted upon a soft chancre, each virus impressing the tissues in a manner peculiar to itself.

The ingenious hypothesis of Rollet accounts for certain anomalous cases of infection not otherwise explicable, as, for example, where two men cohabit with a woman, one receives soft chancre, while the other contracts syphilis, the inference being that the woman possesses a mixed chancre which contains both species of virus. On the same hypothesis may be explained the clinical fact that one individual may have multiple chancroids, all developed simultaneously, or some, secondarily, from auto-inoculation, one of which takes on the specific characters of the initial lesion, while the others preserve their local character.

It was soon evident that, owing to the hasty generalization of the clinical and experimental facts upon which the doctrine of dualism was based, the lines of demarcation between the soft and hard chancre had been too finely drawn. Too much stress was laid upon the form and other characters of the sore, which were regarded as constant and invariable. For example, it had been asserted that induration was the specific sign and seal of the initial lesion, and its presence or absence constituted an infallible test of its syphilitic character. It was found, however, that in very exceptional, but, nevertheless, well authenticated cases, induration is not absolutely peculiar to, or pathognomonic of, the syphilitic chancre. An indurated sore is not invariably followed by syphilis; on the other hand, a sore may run its course without appreciable induration, and yet syphilis follow.

As regards the first case, it is obvious that the induration may be inflammatory, and thus have a deceptive significance. The second case, where syphilis follows a sore in which induration is entirely absent, is regarded as the chief clinical proof of the doctrine of unity. As to its significance, it may be said that specific induration varies in degree from a parchment-like to a cartilaginous hardness, depending somewhat upon the anatomical peculiarities of the tissues upon which it is seated. Upon the female genitals, induration is often indistinct, and but rarely typical. Its appreciation depends largely upon the tactile sense of the observer. It is well known that the induration of a chancre may be entirely obliterated by a rapid ulcerative action; it is almost always wanting in a phagedænic chancre. But, even admitting the entire absence of induration in a sore, it does not necessarily disprove its syphilitic character. Analogy with other specific diseases shows that one clinical characteristic may fail without destroying its individuality.

Again, it was found by experimentation that auto-inoculability was not, as had been claimed, the exclusive attribute of the soft chancre. While it is true that in the enormous majority of instances the inoculation of the syphilitic virus upon the bearer or other syphilitic subjects is abortive, yet Clerc successfully inoculated the secretion of hard chancres upon the bearers, and produced a sore resembling the soft chancre and likewise inoculable in generations. He regarded it as an abortive chancre, which he termed chancroid, due to the fact that the patient was already protected by his syphilis from a second inoculation, and bearing the same relation to syphilis as does the false or spurious to the true vaccinia.

Clerc claimed that the origin of the chancroid or soft chancre was "the syphilitic virus modified in passing through a syphilitic soil," and this view has been adopted by others.

Numerous experiments made by others in this direction were almost invariably failures, until it was discovered that when the chancre was excited to copious suppuration by artificial irritation its pus was readily auto-inoculable. It is well to bear in mind, however, that it is not the syphilitic virus which is inoculated in these cases, only the pus which does not contain the germs of syphilis.

It was also proven by successful experiments in inoculating the pus of acne, scabies, herpes, and other simple inflammations, that ulcers resembling chancroids and furnishing a pus inoculable in generations may thus be produced.

The conclusion has, therefore, been drawn that the chancroid may be generated *de novo* from the products of common and syphilitic inflammation, and without the intervention of the syphilitic virus.

While the results of these experiments have by no means definitely settled the question of the origin of the chancroid, they have tended singularly to modify or rather amplify our conception of its possible sources. The generating principle, instead of being the exclusive product of a chancroid, may have a multiple origin—the pus of chancroidal, syphilitic, and, possibly, simple inflammations. This conclusion could lead, practically, to the rejection of what was considered a cardinal point in the dualistic doctrine, viz., that the chancroidal contagion is a *specific* virus, incapable of being generated *de novo*, and that the supply of infectious material is kept up only by propagation from one chancroid to another.

It is not, of course, possible within the narrow limits assigned to this study of the unity or duality of the virus of venereal sores to critically examine the details of the cases which have been brought forward as affecting the truth or falsity of either theory. Certainly, it may be said that the clinical facts are more readily reconcilable with the doctrine of the dual origin of chancroid and chancre than with the theory of their etiological unity

Practically the doctrine of unity means that there is but one venereal poison which may produce, indifferently, either a local or a constitutional disease; in other words, that both chancroid and chancre originate from the same source of infection—"infection from the secretion of a soft chancre may be either followed by a soft chancre again or by induration and constitutional syphilis; and on the other hand, an infection from the secretion of an induration or other syphilitic local affection may be followed by a simple, soft chancre." Opposed to this theory, that the chancroid and the chancre are convertible, the one into the other, is the clinical fact that inoculation with the secretion of a soft sore, which was clearly chancroid and not syphilis, has never, in a single instance, been followed by syphilis. There is no clinical or experimental evidence upon which to base a belief in the identical and interchangeable nature of the chancroidal and syphilitic contagion.

The theory most in accord with a correct interpretation of the facts developed by clinical experience and experimental pathology has nothing in common with the doctrine of the unity of all venereal poisons. It may thus be formulated :

There is but one syphilitic virus which is invariably derived from the specific secretion of a syphilitic lesion, and is propagated in a continuous series from one syphilitic individual to another.

The contagious principle of chancroid is a pathogenetic agent, entirely distinct and independent of the syphilitic virus; instead of being the exclusive product of the chancroid, it may be generated *de novo* from the products of simple or syphilitic inflammations which do not contain the germs of syphilis.

Leaving theoretical considerations aside, the clinical lines which separate the two diseases are sufficiently broad and distinct to furnish a safe guide for therapeutics. The chancroid is a local ulcer, which is neither the cause nor the consequence of blood-poisoning. The chancre is the initial expression of a constitutional disease which permeates the entire organism.

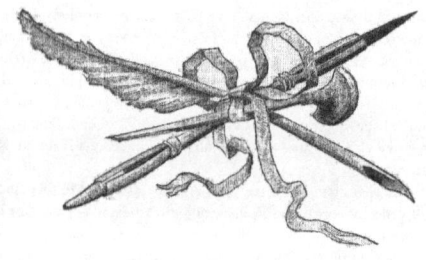

CHANCROID.

ITS NATURE AND SOURCE.

The term chancroid has been generally adopted in this country for the designation of the simple venereal ulcer, and this nomenclature will be employed in this work. In the description of the Plates which have been reproduced from Kaposi, chancroid has been substituted for its German equivalent, "soft chancre" or simply "chancre."

Chancroid may be defined as a local venereal ulcer, essentially inflammatory in its nature and destructive in its action. It is especially characterized by its development without incubation, its tendency to the production of suppurating buboes, and its almost unlimited capacity for inoculation both upon the bearer and upon other individuals.

The contagious elements of the chancroid reside in its purulent secretion; experiments having shown that if the secretion be free of its pus globules, it is no longer contagious.

The contagiousness of the chancroid is its most distinctive characteristic. Whenever its purulent secretion is brought in contact with an abraded surface, it develops at the point of its implantation an ulcer which in turn furnishes a pus capable of reproducing itself, and so on indefinitely. The auto-inoculability of the chancroid furnishes a valuable but by no means absolute diagnostic sign which serves to differentiate it from chancre. Experiments in this direction show that the skin manifests a gradually decreasing capacity for the reproduction of typical chancroidal ulcers, until finally only abortive pustules are produced. After the susceptibility of the skin to suppurative action is exhausted, it may be regained after a period of repose.

Experiment has settled in the affirmative the question of the possibility of the transmission of chancroid to the lower animals, although the soil is less favorable than in the human species to the production of typical ulcers.

While the contagion of the chancroid is in the vast majority of cases effected by direct contact in the exercise of the genital functions, it may be communicated mediately. As examples of the latter mode of contagion may be mentioned the transference of the poison by means of surgical instruments, the fingers, towels, clothing, etc., soiled by the chancroidal secretion.

The admixture of the chancroidal pus with other pathological secretions does not affect its contagious activity. It may be transmitted with the matter of gonorrhœa or with the syphilitic virus, resulting in what has been termed the "mixed chancre." In this latter case, there is no union of the two viruses; each impresses the tissues in a manner peculiar to itself.

The action of the chancroidal pus is purely local. The range of its pathogenetic influence is limited to the lymphatic circle which surrounds its point of origin. The virus may enter the lymphatic vessels proceeding from the ulcer, but its farther progress is arrested by the nearest glands; it never infects the general system, or proves the starting-point of syphilis.

The common sources of the chancroidal virus from which, in the vast majority of instances, it may be directly traced, are the chancroidal ulcer, the virulent lymphitis and the virulent bubo developed in connection with it.

Experiment, as well as certain facts observed in its clinical history, would seem to indicate that exceptionally the chancroid may be derived from the secretions of the indurated chancre and secondary syphilitic lesions. In these cases, the inflammatory products of the irritated lesions, not containing the germs of syphilis, are transmitted. Numerous experiments which have been made in the successful inoculation of the pus of acne, scabies, herpes, etc., the resulting ulcers exhibiting all the characteristic of chancroid, would seem to afford proof that the chancroid may originate *de novo* from the pus of simple inflammations under conditions of uncleanliness and impaired nutrition. This hypothesis is strengthened by the clinical fact that chancroids are much more common among the lower and depraved classes, where such favoring conditions prevail.

Social and sanitary conditions undoubtedly exert an important influence in the etiology of chancroid. As a rule, its prevalence progressively decreases as we rise in the social scale.

SEAT OF THE CHANCROID.

The chancroid has been termed the most venereal of all venereal diseases, because it is most commonly propagated by sexual intercourse, and has for its almost exclusive seat the genital or peri-genital region. No portion of the general integument or the accessible mucous surfaces resists its contagious activity. The genital surfaces are most commonly affected, because they are most frequently brought into inoculative contact.

The most common seats of chancroid in the male are the sulcus coronæ glandis, the internal surface of the prepuce, the frænum, and the sheath of the penis; in the female, the internal surface of the labia, the fourchette, and the introitus vaginæ, very rarely upon the vaginal mucous membrane. Extra-genital chancroids are commonly situated around the anus and the inner surfaces of the thighs, and are much more frequent in women. This is explained by the exposure of these parts to the contact of the vaginal secretions with which the chancroidal poison is mingled. A chancroidal ulcer of the anus often presents a stellate form, caused by the inoculation of the grooves or folds of the anal mucous membrane.

The chancroid may be single or multiple; a number of abraded points may be inoculated at the time of contagion, or the secretion from the original ulcer may successively inoculate a number of points with which it comes in contact. Multiple chancres are the rule in women, as the anatomical conditions of the parts favor the inoculation of contiguous surfaces.

CLINICAL FEATURES AND COURSE.

Chancroid has no period of incubation; the action of the virus begins immediately upon its implantation beneath the epidermis, although the pathological phenomena may not be at once manifest. The rapidity of its development depends upon the conditions of its implantation. When the pus is deposited upon a sound surface, a certain time is requisite to erode the epithelium and gain access to the tissues beneath. A chancroid from contagion in sexual intercourse or from artificial inoculation exhibit essentially the same characteristics. If deposited upon an abraded surface in coitus, or introduced beneath the epidermis by inoculation, ordinarily within twenty-four to forty-eight hours, there is developed around the reddish point of inoculation an acuminated papule, which soon becomes converted into a pustule. The pustule soon breaks, and underneath is found a cup-shaped depression filled with pus, which rapidly extends in circumference and depth.

A typical chancroid is a crater-like ulcer, circular or oval in outline, its edges abrupt, perpendicular, or undermined, its floor uneven, as if pitted or worm-eaten, its borders somewhat thickened, and surrounded by an inflammatory areola. The entire surface of the ulcer secretes an abundant thick, greenish-yellow pus, sometimes sanguinolent or chocolate colored. Its floor is occupied by a sloughing, pultaceous mass, consisting of the *débris* of disintegrated tissues. The sore rests upon a somewhat swollen base, soft and supple to the feel, usually without hardness or rigidity. Sometimes there is an œdematous engorgement of the underlying tissues; the thickening is not sharply defined, but diffuse, gradually merging into the surrounding tissues. The form of the ulcer is modified by the accident of location; when a rent or wound is inoculated, it assumes a corresponding shape; when two or more contiguous ulcers have united, its circular contour is lost, and there is presented an irregularly outlined ulceration.

Multiplicity is a characteristic feature of the chancroid, and serves as an important sign in differentiating it from chancre.

The time required for the evolution and cicatrization of the chancroid varies from four to eight weeks, which may be increased or diminished by complications, the state of the patient's health, irritating treatment, etc. Its course may be conveniently divided into three stages, the progressive, the stationary, and the reparative.

During the progressive stage, there is a more or less rapid extension of the ulcerative process. The stationary stage is characterized by a cessation of the active destructive process, and the ulcer undergoes no appreciable enlargement. The reparative stage is marked by a drying up of the secretion, the floor of the ulcer becomes covered with healthy granulations, and cicatrization gradually takes place, resulting in a thin, smooth, and not pigmented scar, which corresponds in dimensions to the area of the tissues involved in the ulcerative process.

VARIETIES OF CHANCROID.

Clinically, we find that deviations from the typical chancroidal ulcer are sometimes met with, depending upon anatomical peculiarities of the tissues upon which the disease is located or upon the condition of the patient's constitution.

The follicular or acneiform chancroid results from the deposition of the virus at the mouth of a follicle, which burrows down, and may produce considerable destruction of tissues before it opens. Externally, it presents the appearance of an acuminated pustule which on breaking discloses a conical, deep-seated, excavated ulcer. Follicular chancroids are most frequently found on the external surface of the labia majora.

The ecthymatous chancroid, instead of an open ulcer, remains scabbed over, the dried secretion forming a thin blackish crust. It most frequently occurs upon the integument, as the sheath of the penis.

The exulcerous chancroid (ulcus ambustiforme, Kaposi) is a comparatively rare form which presents the appearance of a superficial excoriation or burn. Only the superficial layers of the skin or mucous membranes are involved, although it may be of considerable area. Its edges are sharply defined, its surface smooth and raw looking, and only slightly depressed. It is most frequently seen on the glans penis and foreskin. The *ulcus elevatum* is formed by the exuberant overgrowth of granulations, in consequence of which the surface of the ulcer is elevated above the niveau of the surrounding skin or mucous membrane.

A marked deviation from the course and clinical characteristics of the chancroid is caused by phagedæna. Two distinct varieties of phagedæna are recognized, the sloughing and the serpiginous; the former is more acute and deeply destructive in its process, the latter is more chronic and superficial. Phagedæna is not an inherent property of chancroid; its cause resides in peculiarities of individual constitution.

The sloughing phagedenic chancroid is characterized by the formation of a brownish-gray

PLATE I.

Fig. I.—Multiple chancroids of the foreskin. Consecutive phimosis.

Fig. II.—Multiple chancroids of the phimotic preputial orifice. Œdematous swelling of the integument. Lymphangitis dorsalis penis.

Fig. III.—Chancroid with hardish base upon the right surface of the glans penis, near the urethral orifice.

Fig. IV.—Prepuce drawn backward, partial paraphimosis. At the place of constriction, viz., at the edge of the preputial ring, a deep-seated sore. A second chancroid on the right occupies the furrow and the adjoining portion of the inner preputial layer. The rest of the foreskin puffy.

Fig. V.—A large number of chancroids in different stages of development. The seven more recent are pin-head sized, follicular chancroids on the inner surface of the retracted prepuce. Two, the size of a lentil, are of older date and formed by the confluence of several smaller follicular sores, the contour of which is still discernible. Two confluent follicular chancroids on right side of corona glandis.

Fig. VI.—Chancroids of different ages, the original sore on the inner surface of the foreskin near its edge, pea-sized with hardish base. These chancroids are developed by auto-inoculation from the first. The one on the right side of the frænum, lentil-sized, has almost undermined it. The other two chancroids of the glans are follicular, two to three days old, and are still separated by a hair-line partition wall.

or blackish slough, which is at first firmly adherent to the tissues beneath. It is attended with severe pain and marked constitutional disturbance. The secretion is scanty, thin, and sanious, the edges are undermined, and the ulcer becomes irregular in outline. After the slough separates, it may leave the parts in a healthy condition, or the process may be repeated. The sloughing phagedæna respects no tissue; it destroys all the constituent elements of the skin and subcutaneous tissues, often causing severe hemorrhage from erosion of the vessels. The glans penis, the labia, and the perineal structures may be entirely swept away. In rare cases, it causes death from hemorrhage and exhaustion.

The serpiginous chancroid is much more sluggish in its course and more superficial in its ravages. It rarely causes much local pain or constitutional reaction. In this form, the ulcerative process advances at one side, undermining the skin and dissecting up the tissues, while an attempt at cicatrization is made at the other. This mode of progress gives its path a sinuous or serpentine outline. In this manner it may undermine the integument of the penis to the pubes, extend down the thighs or over the trunk. This process may be interrupted and then begin anew, and may thus continue for months or years, creeping over large areas of surface.

PECULIARITIES DEPENDING UPON LOCATION.

Chancroid is modified in its development and course by the accident of its location and by the occurrence of complications.

Chancroids upon the glans, the sulcus, and internal surface of prepuce are at first usually small and exulcerous, although they may become excavated and penetrate deeply. In this situation they are apt to be multiple from auto-inoculation. They are not infrequently complicated with phimosis or paraphimosis; they may take on a phagedenic action and cause extensive mutilation.

Chancroids of the frænum occasion much pain from the repeated tension to which the parts are subjected; they usually involve the bridle in its entire extent, assuming a linear form, and rarely heal before the frænum is destroyed. The ulceration may perforate the urethra, giving rise to penile fistula.

Chancroids of the meatus usually involve the entire circumference of the orifice, and extend some distance within the urethral canal, producing a funnel-shaped excavation. On healing, the orifice may become strictured from cicatricial contraction.

Chancroids upon the female genitals present certain peculiarities. The ulcerative process is stimulated by the irritating uterine and vaginal liquids, causing a more profuse secretion of auto-inoculable pus, while the anatomical conditions favor the production of multiple sores from inoculative contact.

Extra-genital chancroids are incomparably more frequent in women, especially about the anus. They may occur from unnatural coitus or from auto-inoculation with the secretions of vulvar chancroids. A chancroidal ulcer of the anus often presents a fissured, sometimes a stellate form, and may extend some distance up the rectum.

Chancroids of the rectum are apt to be complicated with painful fissure, cause extensive loss of tissue, and result in stricture of the rectum. They may take on a phagedenic action and destroy the recto-vaginal wall.

Chancroids upon other portions of the general integument are exceedingly rare. They may develop upon the finger of the patient from auto-inoculation. On the face and head they are apt to become phagedenic.

COMPLICATIONS OF CHANCROID.

Since the action of the chancroidal virus upon the lymphatic system is by no means constant or invariable, implication of the vessels and glands occurring only in a certain proportion of cases, it is proper to characterize bubo as a complication.

PLATE II.

Fig. I.—Under surface of penis. Foreskin retracted. On the place of the destroyed frænum, and in the base of its contour a chancroid which terminates near the lips of the urethra. A pin-head sized inoculated chancroid is seen on the right near the large sore upon the inner surface of the foreskin.

Fig. II.—The foreskin retracted. On the right two, on the left six half-bean sized pus-covered sores, with their entire base elevated above the niveau and with abruptly sloping, distinctly defined edges (*ulcera elevata*). Two of the larger groups are seated upon the corona and the glans, all the others upon the inner surface of the foreskin. Almost directly behind upon the outer surface of the foreskin are found three isolated pin-head sized follicular chancroids, which are only a few days old, and have been auto-inoculated from the larger elevated sores.

Fig. III.—Under surface of the penis. The foreskin removed by circumcision. On both sides of the wound, the edges are swollen and converted into large chancroidal surfaces. The confluent chancroids occupy the seat of the destroyed frænum, close up to the orifice of the urethra, and extend along the corona and into the furrow. A few isolated pin-head sized chancroids on the under surface of the glans on both sides of the ulcerated base of the frænum. On the raphe of the penis are seen three chancroids with undermined edges.

Fig. IV.—Upon the right side of the retracted foreskin an oval chancroid, the base of which is somewhat hard, partly infiltrated with hemorrhage, the edges are covered with pus.

Fig. V.—Upon the glans, in the coronal furrow, and on the inner surface of the retracted foreskin, chancroids. On the left are four, large and confluent, upon the inner surface of the foreskin on the right and upon its reflected surface behind are pin-head sized follicular chancroids of more recent date, developed by auto-inoculation. The base of the sores moderately hard.

Fig. VI.—A large-sized chancroid upon the pubes, with deep reaching destruction of tissue at its bottom. Upon the inner surface of the foreskin, on the left near the coronal furrow, an elliptical-shaped fresh cicatrix.

Inflammation of the lymphatic vessels occurs only exceptionally in connection with chancroid. It may terminate either by resolution or in suppuration, and the production of one or more abscesses. If the lymphitis is due to absorption of the chancroidal virus, the abscesses show the characteristics of the chancroidal ulcer.

In chancroidal bubo, one or more glands in both groins may be affected, or only on one side; it may be simple or virulent. Simple inflammatory bubo is due to sympathetic irritation, while virulent bubo is caused by absorption of the chancroidal virus through the intervening lymphatic vessels. Simple bubo may terminate by resolution, while the virulent bubo always ends in suppuration. A definite distinction between the two can only be made after they are opened; the pus of the simple bubo is laudable, and the wound heals up as after an ordinary abscess; the pus of the virulent bubo possesses all the properties of the chancroidal virus—the edges of the wound become inoculated, and the bubo is converted into an ulcer which exhibits the same clinical behavior as a chancroid in other locations. It may take on a phagedenic action, and cause extensive destruction of the tissues of adjacent regions. The ulceration often assumes the serpiginous form, extending down the thighs and laterally and upward upon the abdomen, and may be almost indefinite in extent and duration.

Inflammatory phimosis and paraphimosis developing in connection with chancroid are generally due to the same cause. The ulcers upon the glans or prepuce cause swelling with œdematous infiltration of the foreskin, preventing its free gliding over the glans.

Phimosis is usually due to a sub-preputial chancroid. As this cannot be exposed by retraction of the prepuce, the retained secretion inoculates new points and the ulceration rapidly spreads. The high grade of inflammation not infrequently causes strangulation of the tissues, and more or less extensive sloughing of the glans and both layers of the prepuce takes place.

Phimosis frequently results from the swelling produced by ulcers situated around the preputial orifice. The contraction which takes place in the process of cicatrization often produces a condition of permanent phimosis.

In paraphimosis from chancroid, gangrene is apt to take place along the line of constriction, and may result in sloughing of the portion of prepuce lying in front, together with the glans.

DIAGNOSIS OF CHANCROID.

The physical characters of the chancroidal ulcer, its clinical history and source, and the peculiar property of its secretion often admit of its easy differentiation. The auto-inoculability of chancroidal pus, which was formerly regarded as an absolute and infallible test, has been shorn of its diagnostic significance since it has been found that the purulent secretion of other lesions possesses this property.

The confrontation of patients, when practicable, throws light upon the diagnosis. If the infecting source be clearly a chancroid and not syphilis, the nature of the resulting lesion would admit of no doubt.

There are a number of simple lesions occurring upon the genitals with which it may also be confounded. An abrasion acquired during sexual intercourse, especially when irritated by caustics or otherwise, may present a striking similitude to chancroid. The diagnosis is, however, soon cleared up by abstention from treatment and simple cleanliness, under the influence of which the simple sore promptly heals.

Herpes progenitalis may also be mistaken for chancroid, especially when the vesicles have ruptured and become superficially ulcerated before the patient comes under the physician's observation. Diagnosis is rendered more difficult when the herpetic ulcer is solitary or when contiguous lesions have become confluent, forming irregular cup-shaped ulcers. Here, too, the diagnosis is cleared up by the simple expedient of employing only a protective dressing, which is followed by the ready cicatrization of herpetic erosions.

PLATE III.

Fig. I.—The prepuce removed by circumcision. The edges of the operating wound, the remainder of the inner lamella of the prepuce, the coronal furrow are converted into a chancroid encircling the penis and the glans, which, in many places, especially on the corona glandis and extending over the glans, has eaten deep into the tissues.

Fig. II.—Penis of a four-months-old child. Chancroids upon the glans, the furrow, the inner reflection of prepuce, the urethra, and the urethral lips are developed as the result of ritual circumcision.

Fig. III.—Penis of nursing infant, same age and observed at same time as Fig. II. Chancroid healing at orifice of urethra, a second near the frænum upon the foreskin, likewise resulting from ritual circumcision. The portion of the foreskin which forms the base of the larger sore is in its greater extension thickened and rigid.

Fig. IV.—Prepuce shoved back, upon its under surface four isolated, flat, partly crust-covered ulcerating sores, the bases of which feel moderately hard and rigid. Scales and thin crusts upon glans and foreskin.

Fig. V.—Foreskin removed by circumcision. The solid outer wound edges chancroidal. The substance of the glans necrotic, covered with pitted depressions, here and there red and slightly bloody. The shaft of the penis swollen, its integument inflamed.

Fig. VI.—Paraphimosis of an otherwise healthy penis, the glans red and swollen on account of an existing gonorrhœa.

Fig. VII.—Paraphimosis with linear gangrene at the place of constriction; penis otherwise healthy.

AFTER KAPOSI.

A history of previous attacks of herpes in the same individual, the invasion stage being marked by itching and burning sensations, with a grouped configuration of the vesicles, will indicate the probable herpetic character of the lesions.

Mucous patches situated upon the genital or peri-genital region, especially when ulcerated, may be mistaken for chancroids, especially the variety known as the *ulcera elevata*. A broken-down gumma occurring upon the glans penis may closely simulate chancroid in appearance, as well as in its destructive perforating character. Ordinarily, however, the history of the case, the coincident development of other specific eruptive lesions, and the clinical behavior of the sore under the influence of treatment will indicate its true character.

The affection with which chancroid is most likely to be confounded, and the differentiation from which is clinically the most important, is the initial lesion of syphilis. The differential characters of these two lesions will be considered in connection with the diagnosis of chancre.

PROGNOSIS.

The prognosis of the uncomplicated chancroid is always favorable. Experiments in its artificial propagation have made us familiar with its clinical history, and shown that it has a spontaneous tendency to cicatrization in the course of four to eight weeks, under the influence of simple cleanliness and freedom from irritation.

When complicated with phimosis and paraphimosis, gangrene may occur, and more or less mutilation of the prepuce and glans, and damage to other important structures may result.

When complicated with phagedæna, it may spread indefinitely and cause extensive and profound destruction of tissue. The serpiginous form may be exceedingly protracted in its duration, travelling over large areas of surface.

ANATOMY OF THE CHANCROID.

Kaposi has made a most careful study of the pathological anatomy of the chancroid, and his description,[*] with the cuts representing the microscopical appearances, will be introduced here.

Microscopical examination of a perpendicular section including the margin, the inflamed neighboring parts, together with a portion of the floor of the ulcer and its inflamed base (Fig. 1), shows that the portion of the skin occupied by the chancroid consists of two parts which have evidently undergone different anatomical changes.

From the surface of the ulcer, *cd*, there is a uniform and abnormally thick cell infiltration extending to a considerable depth in the corium. Here it terminates sharply defined in the line *fg*. This cell infiltration is continued underneath the intact papillæ of the margins of the ulcer, *el*, and laterally far beyond the limits of the upper surface of the ulcer. The tissues bordering on the cell-infiltrated parts, *fg*, *hi*, is composed of loose meshes, and exhibits scattered cells with a large nucleus which is well seen when colored with carmine.

In the formation of the swollen margin of the ulcer, *ab*, there is a group of enlarged papillæ, two of which, *e*, lying nearest the surface of the ulcer are thickened and uniformly infiltrated with cells. Above and between these papillæ, the layer of Malpighian cells is thickened. These, *b*, prominently overhang (undermining) the walls of the ulcer.

The surface of the ulcer is formed by the exposed cell-infiltrated corium and is destitute of papillæ. Both the corium and papillæ, wherever infiltrated with cells, exhibit numerous and evidently enlarged vessels, most of which are blood-vessels, a few, however, are lymphatics.

With a higher magnifying power (Fig. 2), the cell infiltrated portion, *ab*, *cd*, is seen to consist of a close network of partly narrow, and partly broad bundles of fibres with faint contours, in

---

[*] " Die Syphilis der Haut und der Angrenzenden Schleimhäute." Wien, 1881, p. 42.

PLATE IV.

FIG. I.—Upon the posterior margin of the vaginal entrance two confluent deep-extending sores. Upon the right upper part of the vaginal introitus three isolated chancroids, elevated above the niveau in their entire extent, the edges sharply defined, the sores covered with pus (*ulcera elevata*).

FIG. II.—The labia majora and minora, and the prepuce of the clitoris studded with numerous chancroids, the left labium minus puffed up in folds, enlarged and prominent, hard and rigid to the feel.

FIG. III.—The inner surface of the female labia majora pressed outwards; upon either surface nine flattened pea-sized chancroids, the greater number of which rest against each other in the natural position of the labia. The most of these have been developed successively by auto-inoculation.

FIG. IV.—Upon the outer surface of the right labium majus is an elongated chancroidal sore. Its sinuous, convex outline indicates its development from several small chancroids situated in a row. The base is soft. Upon the upper part of the front edge of the same labium, a small sore covered with a crust; its base is hard.

FIG. V.—The labia majora separated from each other, the posterior commissure drawn downward. Two hard, confluent chancroids of the mucous membrane of the vestibule and the under fimbriated margin of the vaginal introitus. Upon the left labium majus some excoriations.

FIG. VI.—The left labium majus protruding in front of the right feels quite hard (sclerosis). Upon the upper part of its front surface a lentil-sized sore covered with a crust. In the middle portion along its edge two large chancroids. Underneath these, two pin-head sized pustules.

which is deposited an abundance of nucleated and evenly distributed cells, some of them very large, resembling lymph-corpuscles, others smaller. The cells lying free upon the floor of the ulcer and the neighboring tissues are for the most part small and irregularly formed, with scattered nucleoli, through which the nucleus is but faintly visible. Near these described cells are found free nuclei and nucleoli in large numbers.

In the deeper tissues, the cells have generally the character of inflammation cells, but there are also many smaller in appearance.

Of great interest is the remarkable thickening of the walls of the vessels *g, d, f,* which

FIG. 2.

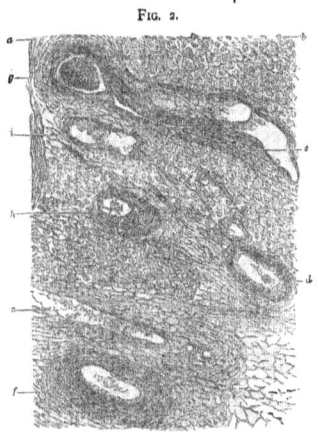

FIG. 1.

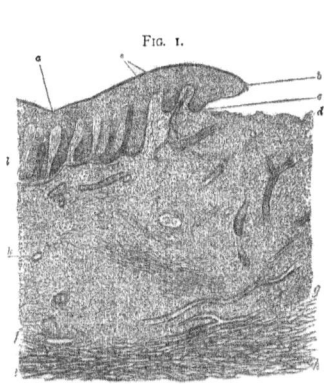

FIG. 1.—Section of soft chancre (chancroid) (Hartnack Oc. 3, Obj. 4). *ab,* wall-like overhanging border of the ulcer; *cd,* base of the ulcer (chancroidal surface; *bc,* epidermis, undermined edge; *cd, fg,* cell-infiltrated tissue (perpendicular depth of the chancre base) penetrated by numerous dilated vessels; *fg, hi,* tissue wide-meshed (œdematous) and free from cell infiltration beneath the base of the chancroid; *e,* enlarged cell-infiltrated papilla, to the left of which a series of elongated partly œdematous papillæ; *k,* continuation of the cell-infiltrated tissues underneath the normal papillæ of the edge of the ulcer.

FIG. 2.—Section of chancroid (Hartnack Oc. 3, Obj. 7). A part of the object Fig. 1, representing the deepest portion of the cell-infiltrated basal tissues of the chancroid and a part of the non-infiltrated œdematous tissue lying immediately beneath; *ab, cd,* deepest part of the cell-infiltrated base of the chancroid, partly close, partly wide-meshed; everywhere uniform and thick cell stratifications; *gr,* dilated blood-vessel; within it, at *g,* an aggregation of red blood-corpuscles; at *e, d, f, h* marked dilatation of the walls of the blood-vessels; at *i* and *c* probably lymphatic vessels.

appear to be imbedded in an abundant network of tissue proliferation due to adventitious fibrous deposits running parallel to them. In this network cells with large nuclei are found.

The lumina of the vessels are everywhere apparent throughout this cell-infiltrated tissue as they are kept dilated by the surrounding œdema.

The degeneration of the tissues and of the infiltrated cells takes place only in the upper portion, and in a degree which is only limited by the extent and depth of the infiltration. But the degeneration always begins and proceeds from the surface to the deeper parts. Interstitial abscesses are found as seldom in the microscopic examination as in clinical observation.

We have not found any characteristics which would enable us to distinguish the cell infil-

PLATE V.

Fig. I.—Gangrenescent bubo, right-sided inguinal bubo, its covering completely removed. At its base, red knotty bunches of glands are exposed. The tissues of the sides of the wound, and partly of its base, are of a greenish-yellow color, fungus like, corrugated, tough (gangrene). The gangrenous bubo is surrounded by an intensely red and swollen integument. To the inner side, a roundish protrusion covered with reddish integument forming an evident continuation of the bubo.

Fig. II.—Upon the right side a gangrenous inguinal bubo.

AFTER KAPOSI

tration of the corium and papillæ, and the subsequent degeneration in the chancroid from inflammatory and suppurative processes provoked by simple causes.

PROPHYLAXIS. TREATMENT.

The marked diminution in the number of chancroids in our large centres of population, where police regulation of houses of prostitution has been systematically carried out, and its comparative infrequency among the better classes would seem to indicate the possibility of its complete extinction under improved material and sanitary conditions.

The precautionary measures which have been recommended as a preventive after exposure are of doubtful efficacy. Thorough washing of the exposed surfaces, the use of aromatic wine, chlorinated soda, acids, etc., with the view of neutralizing the virus at the point where it is deposited, cannot be relied upon. The only sure means of prevention is the avoidance of exposure to the source of the contagion.

The treatment of the chancroid varies according to its stage of development, its seat, and the complications present. Chancroid has been compared to an animal parasite which should be immediately destroyed, and its contagious elements annihilated. If the destruction of the ulcer be thorough and complete, the virulent sore is transformed into a healthy granulating wound with a tendency to heal. This is quite possible when the chancroid has existed only a short time, but as it advances in its evolution the virus infiltrates the tissues surrounding the base of the ulcer, or may be taken up by the lymphatics, and its complete destruction becomes impracticable.

Clinical experience proves that the old rule, that any chancroid, no matter where found or what its stage of development, must be immediately destroyed, should be restricted in its application.

ABORTIVE TREATMENT.

The abortive measures generally employed consist of excision or destructive cauterization. Excision is only practicable when the chancroid is limited in extent, and so situated that the incision can include the entire ulcer and the diseased tissue underlying its base. Even under the most favorable conditions, and when the operation is conducted with all care and under antiseptic precautions, the results of excision are far from satisfactory, the line of incision may become inoculated and a larger virulent surface is substituted for the original ulcer.

Destructive cauterization constitutes the most efficient treatment at our command when the chancroid is in the formative stage and favorably situated. It is not indicated in all cases of recent chancroid for obvious reasons. It is, of course, impracticable in sub-preputial chancroids when complicated with phimosis, or in other situations where they are not readily accessible, as within the meatus, or when situated directly over the urethral canal or upon the vaginal walls, for fear of establishing fistulæ. It is not indicated when multiple chancroids exist, all of which cannot be thoroughly destroyed. Cauterization of an ulcer on the preputial orifice would be worse than useless if other chancroids existed under the prepuce which could not be reached, as the secretion of the latter would certainly reinfect the cauterization wound, and the spread of the disease would thus be promoted.

A variety of caustic agents have been employed for the destruction of the chancroid, as the actual cautery (the hot iron, the Paquelin, and the galvano-cautery), the Vienna paste, Canquoin's paste, the carbo-sulphuric paste, acid nitrate of mercury, nitric, chromic, carbolic, pyrogallic, salicylic acids, etc.

The actual cautery is probably the most energetic in its action, but the sight of the hot iron usually frightens the patient who naturally shrinks from contact with so formidable an appliance. The pain caused by the caustic pastes is usually severe and of prolonged duration, and the depth of destructive action cannot be accurately limited.

Nitric acid, from the convenience of its application and the rapidity and ready limitation of its action, is preferable to any other agent for the purpose of cauterization. The best mode of its application is by means of a glass rod or a piece of soft pinewood, as a match. The surface of the ulcer should be first cleansed of its secretion with a pledget of absorbent cotton, and the acid should then be thoroughly applied to every inequality or crevice of the ulcer and underneath its edges. The pain, which is usually quite intense at the moment of cauterization, may be lessened by the preliminary application of a five to ten per cent solution of cocaine, or the anæsthetic properties of carbolic acid may be utilized by allowing a drop or two of the pure acid to flow over the surface.

After the fall of the slough, if the cauterization has been sufficiently thorough, the wound rapidly granulates. In many cases, however, it will be found that the destructive action has not been carried beyond the sphere of diffusion of the virulent principle, and when the slough separates, the parts beneath still exhibit the characteristics of the chancroidal ulcer.

When, for any reason, a less energetic cauterization than is effected by nitric acid or the acid nitrate of mercury is indicated, carbolic acid may be substituted.

Various other agents, some of comparatively recent introduction, have been recommended in the treatment of the chancroid. Hans von Hebra claims remarkable results from the application of pure salicylic acid in powder over the surface and edges of the sore, which is repeated once or twice a day. A sufficient escharotic effect is usually obtained in two or three days, and an emollient ointment is then applied to favor the fall of the slough, which leaves a healthy surface, healing within five or six days. My own experience with this agent does not corroborate his testimony as to the rapidly curative action of this treatment.

Pyrogallic acid is another agent which is highly recommended in the treatment of chancroidal ulceration, from its supposed selective action upon the diseased rather than the sound tissues. It may be used pure, or combined with bismuth or starch, in the proportion of one part to four, and powdered over the sore; in the form of an ointment, ten to twenty per cent, or in traumaticin or collodion. After the surface of the sore assumes a more healthy, granulating appearance, iodoform or some other less irritating application may be substituted.

METHODIC TREATMENT.

In cases where the abortive method is not practicable on account of the situation of the chancroid, or may not be available by reason of its advanced evolution, the objects of treatment should be to limit ulceration, to protect the surrounding parts from fresh inoculation, and to stimulate reparative action. These objects are best promoted by rest, cleanliness, and astringent and stimulating applications. The patient should avoid all movements attended with friction or irritation of the parts, and special care should be observed in changing the dressings.

Cleanliness is to be promoted by frequent change of the dressings, which should be of lint or absorbent cotton. These readily absorb the discharge which would otherwise overflow the surrounding parts.

Of all the agents which have been employed in the treatment of chancroid, iodoform is perhaps the most efficient and universally applicable. It modifies the ulcerative tendency of the sore, diminishes the secretion, and stimulates a healthy action, while its anæsthetic properties admirably adapt it for the treatment of inflamed and painful chancroids. Unfortunately, its extremely disagreeable, penetrating, and persistent odor render it objectionable to most patients, especially in private practice. Various expedients have been suggested with the view of masking the disagreeable odor of this drug, which have proved only partially successful. An admixture of iodoform with equal parts of tannin, balsam of Peru, finely pulverized, freshly roasted coffee, etc., has been recommended. Combinations with various essential oils, as the oil of peppermint, oil of thyme, oil of erigeron, oil of sassafras, disguise the objectionable odor for a time, but it soon reasserts itself. Combination with coumarin, the odorous principle of the Tonka bean, is probably the best means of correcting the odor. The iodoform may be dusted over the surface, and over this a layer of lint moistened in a solution of coumarin is placed. Iodoform may be applied pure, or triturated with sugar of milk and dusted over the surface, in the form of an ointment, or by suspending it in ether, traumaticin, or benzoated collodion (six to ten per cent). This solution is painted over the surface of the sore, and, upon drying, leaves a coating of iodoform.

Various powders may be used in the place of iodoform, as calomel, oxide of zinc, bismuth, etc., or astringent lotions, as the black or yellow wash, solutions of nitric acid, chlorinated soda, tannin, chloral, permanganate of potash, potassio-tartrate of iron, etc. They should not be used sufficiently strong to cause pain or irritation. Lotions are best applied by means of pieces of lint or charpie moistened with the solution, and renewed as often as they become soiled with the discharge. If the dressing is found dry and adherent, exceeding care should be taken in its removal, since every abrasion of the surrounding surface would be inoculated, and the area of the sore thus extended.

When the chancroid takes on a phagedenic action, constitutional as well as local measures should be employed, since phagedæna is not an inherent property of the chancroid, but a product of constitutional peculiarities. In conjunction with the local treatment, ferruginous tonics, among which the best is the potassio-tartrate of iron, should be given. Nutritious food, good hygienic surrounding, and all measures calculated to build up the general health are indicated.

The most efficient local means we can employ is cauterization. For this purpose the Paquelin or galvano-cautery is preferable; the dead tissue should be removed with scissors, the fluid *débris* washed away, and the cauterization should be energetic and thorough over the entire ulcerated area. Should it afterward manifest evidences of virulent action, the cauterization must be repeated. Spillman treats phagedæna by first scraping thoroughly with the sharp spoon or curette, excising the undermined edges with scissors, cauterizing with the thermo-cautery, and dressing with diluted liquor of Van Swieten.

The caustic pastes above enumerated, nitric acid or the acid nitrate of mercury may also be employed for this purpose.

When the destructive process is more sluggish, the use of iodoform, pyrogallic acid, resorcin, powdered camphor, or a solution of permanganate of potash or the potassio-tartrate of iron often gives excellent results. I have also employed with advantage a spray of the peroxide of hydrogen.

Prolonged immersion of the phagedenic parts in hot water constitutes a most efficient means for combating phagedæna. Under the continued influence of the hot bath, the pain ceases, phagedenic action is checked, healthy granulations form, and the ulcer heals.

The application of bromine is sometimes found effectual in checking the phagedenic process.

What will cure phagedæna in one individual may prove inoperative in another. The management of each case will require special modifications of treatment, depending upon constitutional peculiarities.

The situation of chancroids and the existence of complications may require certain modifications in treatment Chancroids of the meatus, or within the urethral canal, are most conveniently treated by the introduction of tents smeared with ointments, pencils of iodoform, or narrow strips of iodoform plaster, rolled in such a way that the medicated surface may come in contact with the sore.

Chancroids of the frænum, on account of the proximity of the urethral canal, must be cauterized with caution; if the bridle becomes perforated at one or more points, it should be completely divided and the cut edges cauterized, since chancroids involving the frænum rarely begin to heal until after its complete destruction.

The treatment of subpreputial chancroids, when complicated with phimosis, presents many difficulties from their concealed and inaccessible situation. The parts should be kept cleansed of the secretion by frequent injections of tepid water, employing a flat-nozzled syringe. An astringent injection, consisting of a solution of nitrate of silver, chlorinated soda, or permanganate of potash, should then be thrown up. If there is much pain and inflammatory swelling, soaking the penis in hot water or the lead and opium wash, applying compresses continually, saturated with alcohol and hot water, will be found to reduce the congestion in a marked degree. If the inflammation reach a high grade and there be imminent danger of gangrene from strangulation of the tissues, the patient should be circumcised, or the glans exposed by a free dorsal or lateral incision. In either operation, the line of incision will become inoculated and form a chancroidal ulcer, but this is a lesser evil than the extensive mutilation which might otherwise result.

In the treatment of chancroids of the anus and rectum, and of the vaginal walls and neck of the uterus, iodoform is the most efficient application. If cauterization becomes necessary, the Paquelin cautery should be employed in preference to potential caustics.

Since it is not possible to determine the simple or the virulent nature of a bubo developed in connection with chancroid before it is opened, the treatment of both varieties must be essentially the same in the formative stage. Abortion of simple bubo may sometimes be effected by rest, the application of counter-irritants, as tincture of iodine or nitrate of silver, compression, the use of resolvent ointments, etc. When the inflammatory symptoms are marked, the application of ice-cold compresses, or a rubber bag or bladder filled with ice, often relieves pain and diminishes inflammation.

When suppuration occurs, the pus should be evacuated; if the bubo be simple, the pus is devoid of contagious properties, and the opening should be treated as a simple wound. If the bubo be virulent, the pus will be found to possess all the properties of the chancroidal pus, and the cavity will be converted into a chancroidal ulcer.

Instead of a free incision, the bubo may be opened by multiple punctures, by the point of a thermo-cautery, or by a sharpened stick dipped in nitric or carbolic acid, as recommended by various authorities. Le Pileur aspirates the pus, and then throws in an antiseptic fluid, with the view of neutralizing or destroying the virulence of the secretions from the walls of the cavity.

The ganglionic chancroid should be treated on the same general principles already indicated. Should it take on a phagedenic action, the walls should be thoroughly curetted, the undermined edges cut away, and active cauterization employed.

Lymphangitis rarely requires special treatment. If abscesses develop along the course of the lymphatic vessels, they are to be opened, and, if virulent, treated as chancroids.

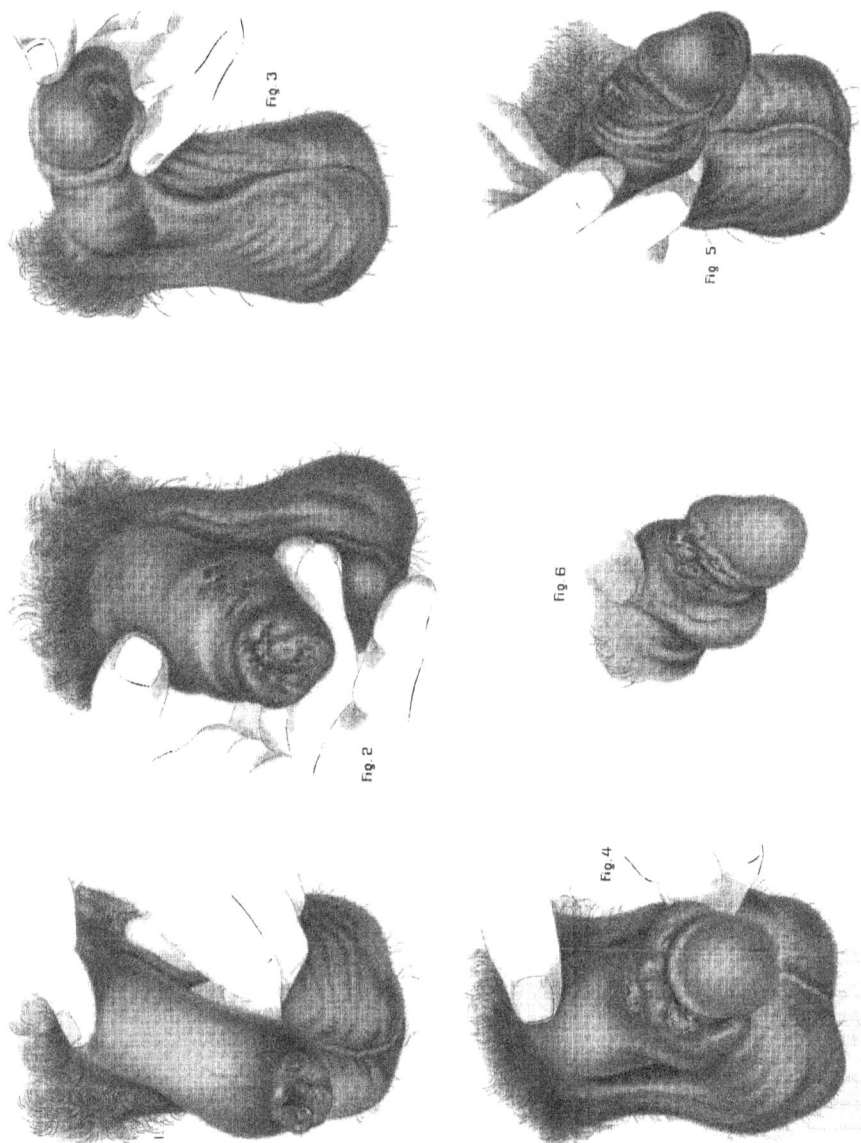

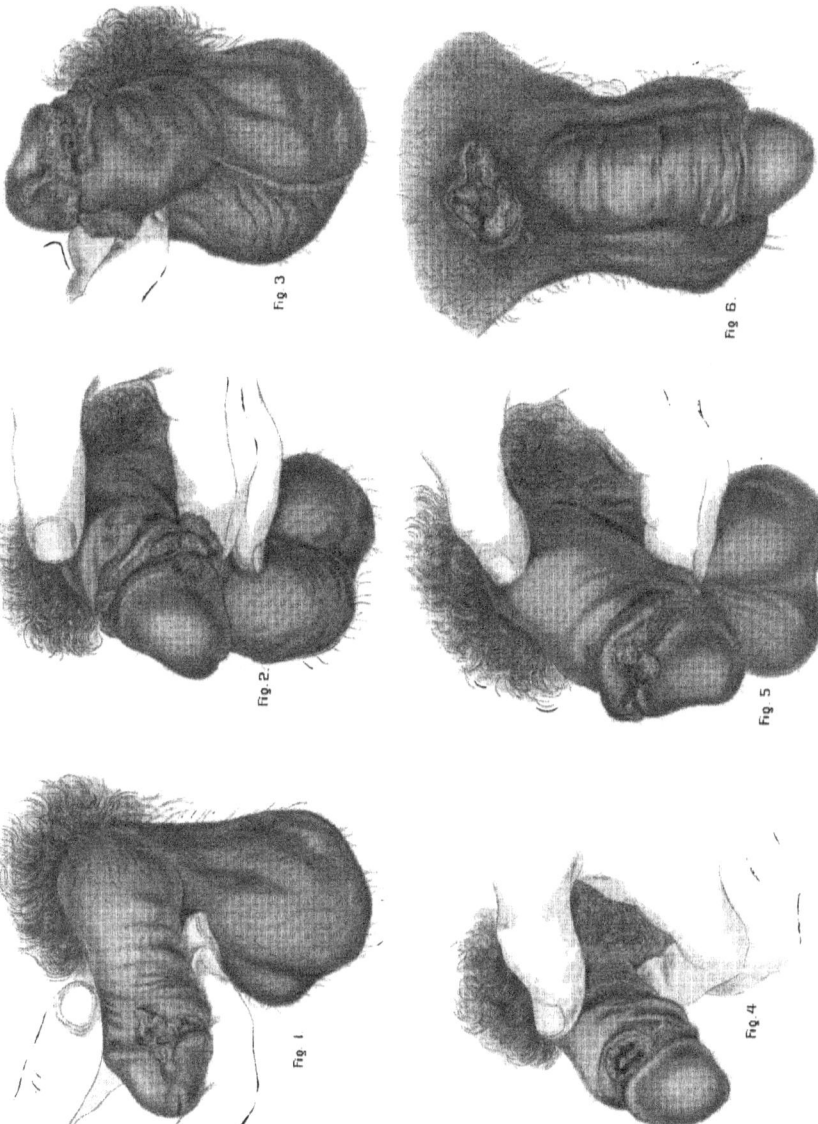

Fig 1

Fig 2.

Fig 3

Fig 4

Fig 5

Fig 6.

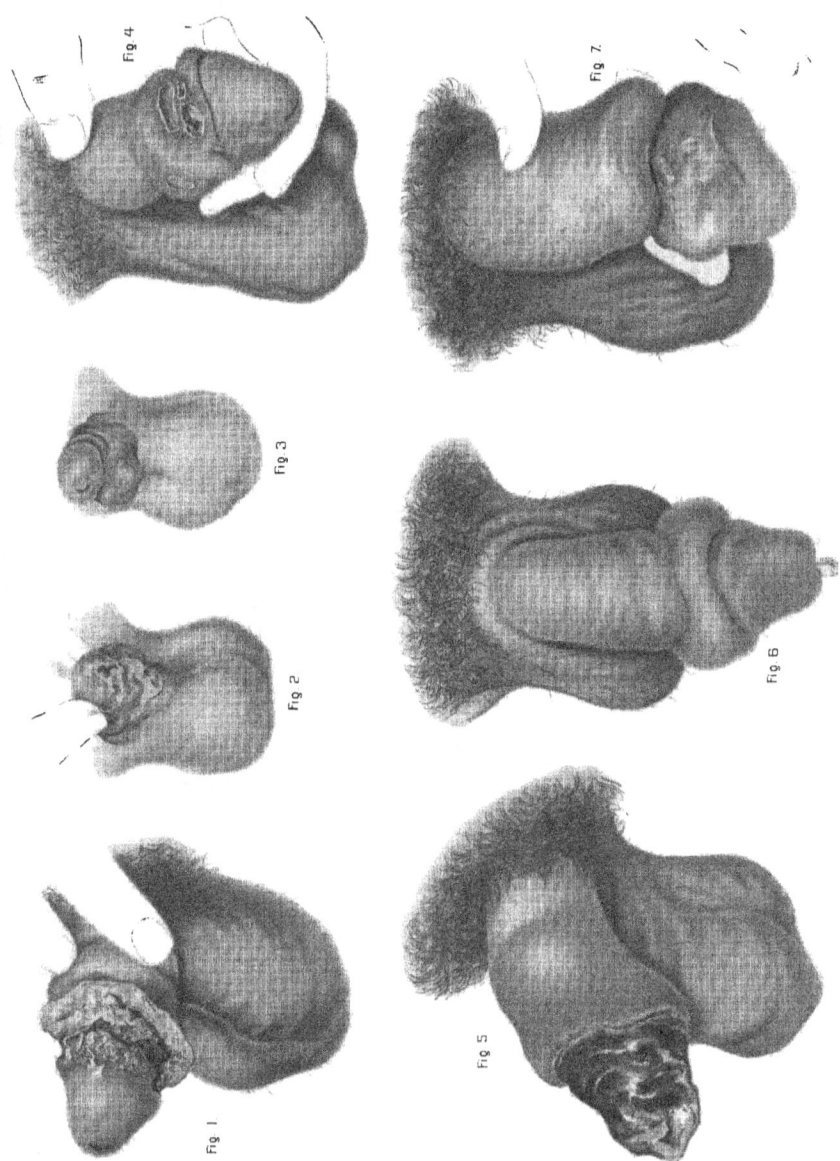

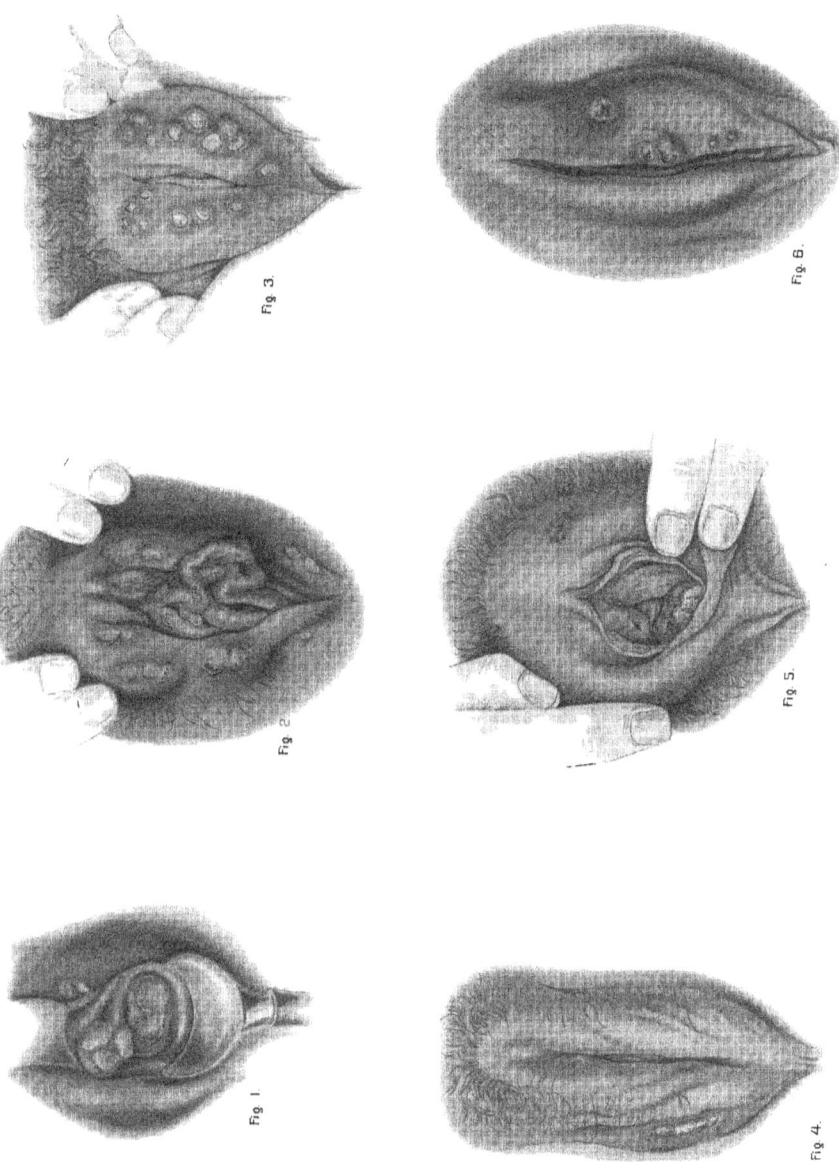

Fig 1.

Fig 2.

Fig. 3.

Fig 4.

Fig 5.

Fig. 6.

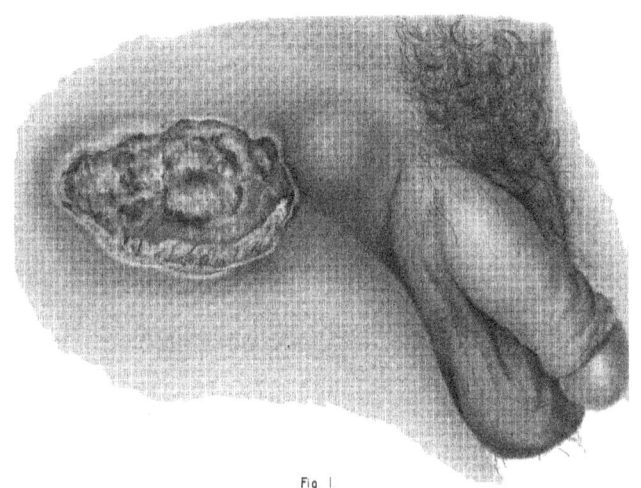

Fig 1.

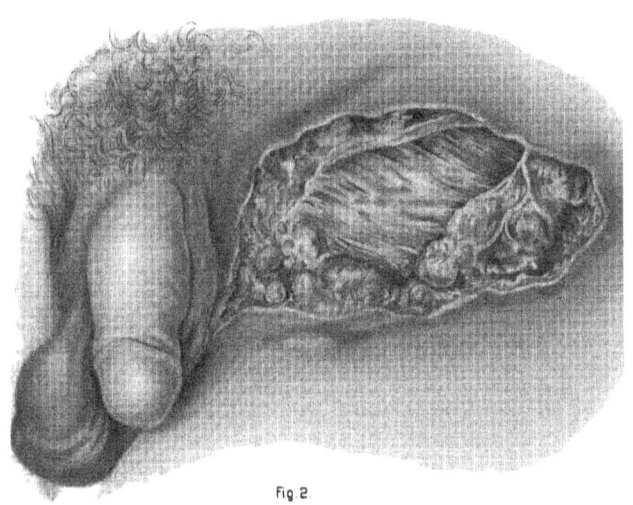

Fig 2.

Plates VI-X missing

Pages 21-36 missing

ATLAS

OF

VENEREAL AND SKIN

DISEASES

COMPRISING ORIGINAL ILLUSTRATIONS AND SELECTIONS FROM THE PLATES OF

PROF. M. KAPOSI, OF VIENNA; DR. J. HUTCHINSON, OF LONDON; PROF. I. NEUMANN, OF VIENNA;
PROFS. A. FOURNIER AND A. HARDY; AND DRS. RICORD, CULLERRIER, BESNIER, AND VIDAL, OF PARIS;
PROF. LELOIR, OF LILLE; DR. P. A. MORROW, OF NEW YORK; DR. E. L. KEYES, OF NEW YORK;
DR. FESSENDEN N. OTIS, OF NEW YORK; DR. J. NEVINS HYDE, OF CHICAGO;
DR. HENRY G. PIFFARD, OF NEW YORK, AND OTHERS.

WITH ORIGINAL TEXT BY

PRINCE A. MORROW, A.M., M.D.,

CLINICAL PROFESSOR OF VENEREAL DISEASES, FORMERLY CLINICAL LECTURER ON DERMATOLOGY, IN THE UNIVERSITY OF THE CITY OF NEW YORK;
SURGEON TO CHARITY HOSPITAL, ETC.

NEW YORK

WILLIAM WOOD & COMPANY

1888

ATLAS

OF

VENEREAL AND SKIN

DISEASES

It is with special satisfaction that the publishers announce that this large and important work, which they have had in contemplation since 1883, is now ready for publication. It has long been recognized by them, from wide observation and acquaintance with similar works published in this country and abroad, that it is impossible for any one author to furnish, from his own collection of cases and illustrations, the most typical and at the same time the best and most lifelike pictures of the many peculiar forms of these diseases. Appreciating the defects and disadvantages arising from this cause, it was determined from the outset to enlist the co-operation, in the making of this ATLAS, of the leading dermatologists and syphilographers of the world. Prominent among them are Profs. M. Kaposi and I. Neumann, of Vienna. The atlas of the former, of venereal diseases, just completed, and that of the latter, of skin diseases, now being issued in parts, will be largely drawn upon in the preparation of this work, the sole right to reproduce them having been granted us by the authors.

Among other distinguished gentlemen who have engaged to contribute selections from their collections of original illustrations may now be mentioned Dr. J. Hutchinson, of London; Profs. A. Fournier and A. Hardy; and Drs. Ricord, Cullerrier, Besnier, and Vidal, of Paris; Dr. P. A. Morrow, of New York; Dr. Edward L. Keyes, of New York; Dr. Fessenden N. Otis, of New York; Dr. J. Nevins Hyde, of Chicago; Dr. Henry G. Piffard, of New York.

Other names will be added to this list as the work progresses.

The Editor of the work is Dr. Prince A. Morrow, of New York, who, in addition to plates contributed from his own remarkable collection, will write the treatise on skin and venereal diseases, which constitutes, besides the description of the plates, the text accompanying them.

In this treatise, it is aimed to include chiefly those features which are the most practical, omitting in great measure pathological and other considerations which would be more properly treated of in extended writings, rather than as the adjunct to an Atlas.

In regard to the character of the plates, it may be said, they are believed to be superior to anything of the kind heretofore produced—as accurate in drawing as photographs, and far more distinct, while the coloring faithfully represents nature.

The text is printed from new type, large, clear, and handsome, and the paper is heavy, with a highly finished surface.

Altogether, considering the reputation of the authors of the plates, the ability of the editor, the superb execution of the plates, the excellence of the presswork, the high quality of the paper of both text and plates, the large size of the page, etc., etc., this ATLAS OF VENEREAL AND SKIN DISEASES will be the most superb work in medical literature ever published in the English language.

The ATLAS OF VENEREAL AND SKIN DISEASES will be published in fifteen monthly parts, each containing five folio, chromo-lithographic plates, many of them containing numerous figures, all printed in flesh tints and colors, together with descriptive text for each plate, and from sixteen to twenty folio pages of a practical treatise upon venereal and skin diseases; the whole forming, when complete, one magnificent thick folio volume with seventy-five plates, containing several hundred figures, exquisitely printed in colors.

☞ The ATLAS OF VENEREAL AND SKIN DISEASES will be sold by subscription only, at the very moderate price of $2 per part.

WILLIAM WOOD & COMPANY, *Publishers,*

56 AND 58 LAFAYETTE PLACE, NEW YORK.

DIFFERENTIAL DIAGNOSIS OF CHANCRE AND CHANCROID.

In the vast majority of cases, when a patient presents himself with a sore upon the genitals, the diagnosis lies between chancre and chancroid. The differentiation between these lesions possesses a capital importance from a prognostic point of view; the one is a purely local affection the range of whose pathological action is limited to a narrow lymphatic circle, the other is the local expression of a constitutional disease, the first in the series of a long train of pathological phenomena.

In order to bring the clinical features of chancre and chancroid into prominent relief for purposes of contrast and comparison, their distinctive characteristics may thus be formulated:

Frequency.—As a rule the chancre occurs but once in the same individual, conferring upon the bearer an immunity almost absolute; the chancroid may occur an indefinite number of times in the same person.

Origin.—The chancre may originate from the secretions of a chancre or syphilitic lesion, from syphilitic blood or serum, and probably from certain pathological secretions, not in themselves syphilitic, but occurring in a syphilitic subject; the chancroid is derived from the pus of a chancroid, a virulent bubo or lymphitis, and probably from the products of simple or syphilitic inflammation, not containing the germs of syphilis.

Incubation.—Chancre has a well-marked period of incubation, on the average twenty-six days, rarely less than ten or more than forty days; the chancroid has no incubation, the inflammatory reaction is usually manifest within twenty-four to forty-eight hours.

Seat.—The chancre occurs most commonly upon the genital parts, but it is frequently found upon other portions of the cutaneous and mucous surfaces; chancroid has for its almost exclusive seat the genital regions and neighboring parts.

Number of lesions.—Chancre is generally single; when multiple, they appear simultaneously; chancroid is rarely solitary, most often multiple, especially in women, new ulcers develop successively from auto-inoculation.

First appearance.—Chancre makes it first appearance as a papulo-tubercle, which may afterward become eroded or ulcerated; chancroid begins as a vesico-pustule or open ulcer.

Form.—The chancre is usually round or oval, with sloping or adherent edges; the chancroid at first round or oval, afterward becomes angular or irregular in outline with abrupt, undermined, or jagged edges.

Surface.—The chancre is smooth, red or livid, sometimes dry and scaly, often covered with false membrane; the floor of the chancroid is uneven, worm-eaten, pultaceous, covered with the débris of disintegrated tissue.

Ulceration.—Ulceration of the chancre is rarely active, most generally absent; it is superficial, flat, sometimes excavated and funnel shaped; active ulceration is an essential condition of the chancroid; it involves the entire thickness of the skin or mucous membrane, and the destruction of tissue may be considerable both in extent and depth.

Secretion.—The secretion of the chancre is scanty, serous, or sero-sanguinolent, rarely purulent, except as the result of irritation; the secretion of the chancroid is abundant and purulent.

Inoculability.—The discharge of the chancre is not inoculable upon the bearer or upon other syphilitic individuals; it is not transmissible to animals; the pus of chancroid is readily inoculable both upon the bearer and upon other individuals; it is also inoculable on animals.

Induration.—The base of the chancre is usually firm, nodular, cartilaginous, and distinctly circumscribed, like a hard body set into the skin, sometimes parchment like and not sharply defined; it is usually persistent for weeks or months; the chancroid has a soft, supple base, the inflammatory engorgement, sometimes factitiously developed by irritation, is not circumscribed, but shades off into the surrounding tissues, and is of temporary duration.

Sensibility.—The chancre rarely gives rise to subjective sensations, when situated upon the female genitals it may pass unperceived by the patient; the chancroid is usually sensitive, the pain is often sharp and severe.

Adenopathies.—The bubo of chancre is almost invariable; the glands, several in number, are hard, indolent, and movable, and rarely suppurate; the bubo of chancroid is not constant; the gland, usually but one, is inflamed, painful, often suppurates, and may furnish a chancroidal pus also inoculable.

While it would seem that these salient points of contrast in the form and characteristics of the two varieties of venereal sores should render their differential diagnosis extremely easy, yet in practice, unfortunately, these typical characters are often obscure or entirely absent, and the lesion may present nothing absolutely pathognomonic. While it is easy to determine the syphilitic nature of a lesion which develops only after the classic period of incubation, and takes on a characteristic induration, yet we cannot say with absolute certainty that a soft sore, developing without incubation, will remain such and not be followed by constitutional syphilis. The situation is always complicated by the possibility of "a mixed chancre," and time is necessary for the recognition of the syphilitic element.

In cases where there has been a simultaneous inoculation of the two viruses, it must be borne in mind, in appreciating the time for the appearance of secondary accidents, that the sore does not take on the character of the chancre until after three or four weeks, and this period must be added to the six or seven weeks which intervenes between the appearance of the chancre and the outbreak of general symptoms. However strongly the clinical features point in favor of the simple character of a venereal sore, the prudent physician, bearing in mind the possibilities of error, will hold his opinion in reservation; he is not justified in positively assuring his patient that it will not be followed by constitutional syphilis.

PROGNOSIS.

The prognosis of the chancre, viewed in the aspect of a local lesion, is almost always favorable. As a local process, the chancre rarely gives rise to pain or other subjective symptoms; it is limited in extent and duration, with a tendency to spontaneous resorption, and heals ordinarily without a cicatrix. When complicated with phagedæna, gangrene, phimosis, or other inflammatory conditions, the local consequences may be more serious, resulting in more or less extensive destruction of the tissues, sometimes mutilation of the glans, urethral fistulæ, etc.

Considered as the first visible manifestation of a disease permeating the entire organism, capable of causing the most profound lesions, and practically indefinite in duration, the prognosis is of much graver import. The relations between the source of the virus, the period of incubation, the induration and other anatomical characters of the chancre, and the ulterior evolution of the disease are most interesting from a prognostic point of view.

As regards the source of the contagion, it may be very confidently asserted that it exerts no appreciable influence either upon the character of the chancre or of the constitutional accidents; whether the contagion be derived from a primary or secondary lesion, whether from a simple erosion or a deep ulceration is immaterial; it does not affect either the activity of the virus or its effects upon the system. It was formerly thought that the virus of a phagedenic chancre carried with it a more intense infective capacity, a greater potentiality for mischief; but we now recognize that phagedæna is not a characteristic of the chancre; it is a property of the individual and is, therefore, not transmissible.

In reference to the period of incubation, certain authorities have formulated the rule that the longer the incubation the milder the syphilis, and the shorter the incubation the severer the syphilis. This theory would seem to rest on a rational basis, since the more prompt invasion of the system would indicate a feebler capacity of resistance on the part of the individual. Such a relation between the period of incubation and the effects of the virus upon the system is by no means constant. Clinical experience furnishes so many exceptions to this rule that its prognostic significance is of little value.

The next element of prognosis is to be sought for in the lesion itself, its induration, ulceration, and other specific characters. Chancre has been termed the "touchstone of the constitution," and the local action of the virus upon the tissues revealed in the primary lesion constitutes, it is claimed, a correct criterion by which we may estimate its general effects upon the system.

In general, it may be said that the more benign the chancre, the greater the probabilities that the earlier eruptive accidents will be superficial and of mild type; but this correspondence does not always extend to the later manifestations; the initial benignity of the disease confers no guarantee against the malignity of tertiary accidents. It has been observed that severe tertiary syphilis, with determination to important central organs, as the brain, cord, and viscera, frequently follows a primary lesion so insignificant as to pass unperceived by the patient. On the other hand, a severe primary lesion with a voluminous induration may be followed by general accidents of mild or medium severity.

It may, however, be very positively asserted that a phagedenic chancre always portends a bad type of syphilis in its bearer, since the phagedæna is an expression of a depraved state of the patient's constitution, which will be reflected in the character of the general accidents. The prognosis of chancre occurring in persons in the extremes of life, in the intemperate, in persons exposed to privation and bad hygienic surroundings, in lymphatic and scrofulous individuals, is always of grave import.

TREATMENT OF THE CHANCRE.

The various agents which have been recommended as prophylactic measures against the risks of contagion are deceptive. There is no preservative against the contagious activity of the syphilitic poison when brought in contact with an abraded surface. When a patient presents himself with a chancre, the only question to be considered is, whether it is possible by destruction of this lesion to prevent constitutional contamination.

The opinion is held by many authorities that it is possible, by excision of the initial lesion, to destroy the virus at its point of entrance, and thus abort syphilis. It is further claimed that, even when total destruction of the syphilitic virus is not effected, by removing the mass of infected material contained in the chancre, the severity of its constitutional effects is materially modified.

The local or constitutional nature of the primary sore, and the time at which generalization of the virus takes place, have an important bearing upon the determination of the value of the abortive method. If, as has been assumed by the advocates of ectrotic treatment, the virus remains localized for a time at its point of entrance, its first effect being limited to the development of the chancre, from which, as an infecting source, general contamination gradually takes place, it would seem rational to suppose that, by removal of the depôt of the virus, the diffusion of its germs through the system might be prevented.

If, on the other hand, the chancre be the local expression of a general blood-poisoning, the evidence of an already accomplished infection, complete destruction of the initial lesion will not arrest or modify its effects upon the system. Without entering into the pathology of syphilitic infection, it may be said that deductions, drawn from analogies with the action of the contagious principles of other infectious diseases—of the vaccine virus, animal poisons, etc.—give support to the theory that absorption of the syphilitic virus begins immediately upon its introduction beneath the epidermis. According to this view, the chancre is not the source, but the sign of constitutional syphilis, general infection has taken place before its appearance.

Leaving aside the theoretical consideration of the precise time at which generalization of the virus takes place, it may be safely asserted that the value of the abortive method has been settled by the test of clinical experience; the practice of excision of the chancre has been condemned by its results. In numerous cases in which the operation has been done under the most favorable conditions, within a few hours after the first appearance of the chancre, constitutional symptoms have followed in regular order. Excision of the inguinal glands in connection with the chancre has been practised in a number of cases, but the results have not been sufficiently favorable to warrant the recommendation of this operation.

While excision of the initial lesion cannot be relied upon to prevent constitutional infection, or to materially modify the intensity or severity of the general symptoms, yet in certain exceptional cases, in marital syphilis for example, when conjugal relations demand the speediest possible suppression of a local source of contagion, its employment is indicated.

The alleged advantages of destructive cauterization of the primary sore are purely illusory; the use of caustics almost always tends to increase the volume of the induration and retard the healing of the ulcer.

The chancre has a tendency to heal spontaneously, and, in the majority of cases, the treatment should be mainly expectant. The indications of treatment may be summed up as follows: rest, cleanliness, the removal of local causes of irritation, and a simple protective dressing. When there is a tendency to suppurative action, mild astringents, dusting with iodoform or calomel, or the black wash may be employed. When the chancre is painful, the use of sedative lotions, as the lead and opium wash, will be found beneficial. Mercurial or other ointments should rarely be employed, especially when the chancre is situated upon a mucous surface.

When complicated with phimosis or paraphimosis and inflammatory conditions with a tendency to gangrene, the more active measures recommended in the treatment of the complications of chancroid may be instituted; resort to the actual cautery is, however, rarely necessary.

Chancres in peculiar situations, as the meatus or anus, are best treated with bougies of iodoform. The voluminous indurations which sometimes remain, even after cicatrization, undergo spontaneous involution which may be hastened by the internal employment of mercury. The induration of the lymphatic ganglia rarely requires treatment. When the glands become painful from periglandular inflammation, the use of mercurial ointment to induce resolution is of service.

THE SYPHILIDES.

PERIOD OF SECONDARY INCUBATION.

The action of the syphilitic virus upon the organism during the primary stage is limited to the production of purely local phenomena. Its only visible manifestations are the chancre with its concomitant adenopathies. During this stage, the virus multiplies in the system until its accumulated force and energy culminate in the explosion of eruptive accidents. With the advent of secondary symptoms, the disease is said to become constitutional, although it is probable that contamination of the blood takes place long before their appearance.

The period of secondary incubation comprises the interval which elapses between the appearance of the chancre and the eruption of generalized accidents. Its duration varies within certain limits; on the average, it is six or seven weeks; the receptivity of the organism, specific treatment, and other conditions may exercise a modifying influence.

PRODROMAL SYMPTOMS.

The eruptions upon the skin and mucous membranes are generally preceded or accompanied by changes in the blood, febrile reaction, various algias, and other evidences of constitutional trouble. One of the first constitutional changes which follows the introduction of the syphilitic virus into the system is a change in the blood. A microscopical examination discloses the fact that there is a diminution in the number of the red corpuscles, with a corresponding increase of the white corpuscles and the albuminous constituents of the blood. This modification in the relative proportion of the corpuscular elements is not due to the direct action of the syphilitic virus upon the globules, but rather to its poisonous influence upon the hematopoietic organs. It is not definitely known at what precise time in the evolution of the diathesis this alteration in the constituents of the blood begins. It has been observed before there were any visible manifestations upon the skin and mucous membranes, but becomes more marked during the early secondary period. The symptoms do not differ essentially from those of chloro-anæmia from other causes.

Although in its chronic course and other characters syphilis conforms to the type of an apyretic disease, yet not infrequently the outbreak of eruptive accidents may be announced by the occurrence of febrile reaction, which may be attended with headache, pain in the back and limbs, and other signs of constitutional disturbance. Syphilitic fever is much more common in anæmic women and in persons of a delicate and highly wrought organization. It is probably due to the impression of the poison upon the nervous system.

The febrile reaction of syphilis has no well-defined characters which can be considered as specific; it varies in type, intensity, and duration. It may present itself with the characters of an intermittent, remittent, or continued fever; it most commonly affects the quotidian type of intermittent fever, with evening or nocturnal exacerbations. When accompanied with pain in the muscles and joints, the symptoms may simulate very closely those of acute articular rheumatism. Syphilitic fever rarely possesses much clinical importance; it is usually of short duration and subsides spontaneously with the appearance of the cruptive accidents; it responds readily to the influence of specific treatment, while proving refractory to the use of quinine and other antiperiodic agents.

There are numerous other symptoms of a subjective character, such as pains in the muscles, tendons, bones, etc., which are liable to occur in the early stage of syphilis. These pains are remarkable for their capricious development, their tendency to shift from one part to another, their paroxysmal character, but chiefly for their tendency to nocturnal exacerbation.

It is plainly within the sphere of the nervous system that we must look for an explanation of these subjective phenomena, probably from the direct action of the poison through the blood upon the nerve centres.

Prominent among the prodromal symptoms are the various algias, such as cephalalgia, sternalgia, arthralgias, etc. They are incomparably more frequent in women and in persons of a nervous temperament. Cephalalgia is one of the most common symptoms, it may occupy the entire cranium, or it may be circumscribed in the frontal, temporal, or occipital region; it usually develops towards evening, persists during the night, and ceases towards morning. It is usually accompanied with insomnia. Arthralgias are especially marked in the large articulations, as the shoulder, elbow, and knee joints: the pain is superficial rather than deep seated.

Rheumatoid pains, varying in intensity and duration and affecting principally certain groups of muscles, giving rise to torticollis, pleurodynia, lumbago, pains at the tendinous insertions of the large muscles, are common at this period. Osteocopic pains along the prominent parts of the bony skeleton may mark the period of invasion of syphilis. They are seated rather in the fibrous than the osseous structures: the true osteocopic pains are more pronounced at a later stage and accompanied with the objective signs of periostitis or ostitis.

In a large proportion of cases, the prodromal symptoms above enumerated are entirely absent, the general health of the patient suffers no disturbance, and the first appreciable symptom of constitutional trouble is manifest in the secondary eruption.

GENERAL CHARACTERISTICS OF SYPHILIDES.

Under the general term "syphilides" are comprehended the eruptions produced by syphilis upon the skin and mucous membranes. These cutaneous manifestations are important, not only as constituting the first visible evidence of the complete saturation of the system with the poison of syphilis, but also as comprising, chiefly, the symptomatology of the disease during all its periods. While syphilis permeates the entire organism, determining functional and organic lesions of the internal organs of the most varied character, yet its principal pathological phenomena are projected upon the external surface. The surface accidents are most important from a diagnostic point of view, enabling us to recognize the specific nature of co-existent visceral lesions inaccessible to our ordinary means of investigation.

The clinical features of the syphilides are so characteristic and well marked that they may be readily differentiated from the ordinary dermatoses. While the lesions consist of the same cruptive elements as are met with in other cutaneous diseases, yet they possess certain peculiarities which are pathognomonic, and which enable the practised physician to recognize, often at a glance, their specific origin and nature. These peculiarities relate to their polymorphism, color, pigmentation, configuration, symmetry, the character of the scales, crusts, ulcerations, cicatrices, absence of pain, or other subjective symptoms.

Polymorphism constitutes a distinctive feature of syphilitic eruptions; in no non-specific disease of the skin is this peculiarity developed to the same extent and with the same frequency. Most dermatoses are characterized by a typical eruptive form, while in syphilis there may be a multiplicity of eruptive elements present at the same time. The frequent co-existence of macules, papules, pustules, etc., side by side is determined by the chronic, sluggish character of the syphilitic process, permitting the development of new crops of eruption before the involution of he old ones, the tendency to repeated occurrences of the same form of lesion, and the modifications which it undergoes in the different stages of its development and disappearance.

The color of syphilitic eruptions is highly characteristic and has been variously described as yellowish-red or dirty-brown, a raw ham or coppery color; it varies with the age of the lesion, the texture of the skin and complexion of the individual, and other circumstances. In the earlier, more acute stage, the efflorescence often presents a bright red or pinkish color; at a later stage of its evolution, it takes on the raw ham or coppery tint. As the spots are disappearing they become greenish-yellow or grayish, exhibiting the changes in pigmentation that characterize superficial ecchymoses. This specific hue of the syphilides is not so pronounced in the later lesions, and is entirely absent in eruptions of the mucous surfaces. In the blonde, the syphilitic tint is brighter; in the brunette, the brownish tint predominates; in the cachectic, the coloration is apt to be livid or bluish-red.

The pigmentation left by a syphilitic lesion possesses little diagnostic value, it is due to the escape of the normal pigmentary matter of the blood into the Malpighian layer and its subsequent metamorphosis. The same result may follow long-continued congestion of the skin from various morbid conditions.

The symmetry of the earlier syphilitic eruptions is a most characteristic feature, the lesions on either side of the median line forming an exact counterpart of those of the other. As the diathesis advances in its evolution, this tendency to symmetrical disposition becomes less marked. The lesions of the tertiary stage, though frequently both-sided, are rarely symmetrical.

The configuration and grouping of syphilitic eruptions is distinctive. Not only do the individual lesions assume a round or circular form, but they manifest a tendency to develop in curved lines, forming circles, arcs, or segments of circles, the annular configuration being determined, no doubt, by the anatomical arrangement of the cutaneous capillaries. The crescentic, serpiginous, and horseshoe shapes of the ulcerative lesions constitute a characteristic feature.

Location.—The earlier syphilides, like the exanthemata of the eruptive fevers, may be distributed over the whole surface of the body, yet each eruptive form seems to manifest a predilection for certain regions.

The erythematous syphilide is most characteristically developed upon the chest, trunk, and flexor surfaces, rarely upon exposed parts; the papular syphilide upon the face, brow, margin of hairy scalp, back of neck, trunk, and limbs; the squamous variety upon the palmar and plantar surfaces.

The pustular syphilide of the acneiform and impetiginous varieties have a preference for the hairy part of the face and scalp, and other parts of the body abundantly supplied with sebaceous and hair follicles; the ecthymatous and rupial syphilides affect the limbs, principally the lower; tubercular lesions are found everywhere. Mucous patches have a preference for the natural orifices, the commissure of the lips, the isthmus of the throat, the entrance of the nares, the integument of the genital and anal regions. Other regions of the body often enjoy a remarkable immunity from eruptive disturbance; the dorsal surfaces of the hands and wrists, the clavicular and sternal regions are perhaps most rarely involved.

The scales and crusts of syphilitic lesions are peculiar in their construction. The scales are usually of a dirty or grayish-white color; they are thinner, more superficial, less abundant,

PLATE XI.

Fig. I.—Indurated chancre of the female nipple. Upon the hard, intumescent, prominent nipple a penny-sized, irregularly circular, sharply defined flat lesion, its floor brownish-red, light bloody, covered with thin, gummy-like crusts. Upon the general integument of the breast and the trunk lentil to penny-sized, pale brownish-red, uniformly tinted spots (Roseola).

Fig. II.—Chancre of the first phalanx of the forefinger of the right hand of a female (nurse), penny-sized, brownish-red, the surface elevated, round, very hard; the centre of which shows a shallow, regularly desquamating depression. Upon the volar surface of the palm, the flexor and lateral surfaces of the finger, lentil-sized and larger, sharply defined, round, brownish-red, partly smooth, partly desquamating spots (Psoriasis Palmaris).

AFTER KAPOSI.

less adherent than in analogous cutaneous diseases. They never present the glistening, silvery-white appearance of the scales of psoriasis, for example.

The crusts of syphilitic sores are grayish, greenish, brownish, or black; they are thicker than the crusts of non-specific lesions of corresponding dimensions; they are often rough and laminated, not so firmly adherent to their base, but rather, as Zeissl says, "swim upon the pus beneath them." The conical stratified crusts of rupia are met with in no other disease.

Ulcerations.—The reniform, horse-shoe shape of the later lesions has already been referred to as characteristic of syphilitic ulceration. This peculiar form results from the centrifugal extension of the wall of infiltration, the ulcerative process advancing at the convex margin, while healing takes place in the centre and along the concave border. The margins of the syphilitic ulcer are usually distinctly circumscribed, its edges perpendicular, its floor grayish or pseudo-membranous, secreting a thick greenish-yellow, sanious pus.

The absence of pain and itching.—The apruriginous character of syphilitic eruptions is a distinctive feature and constitutes a valuable differential sign; the patient may be unconscious of the existence of the eruption so far as subjective sensations are concerned. This absence of pruritus is supposed to result from the slow, indolent character of the syphilitic process, but it is by no means an invariable condition. In certain syphilides characterized by a precocious, rapid development, the pain and other subjective symptoms may be considerable. In syphilides of the scalp and mucous patches of the genital region, pruritus is frequently quite pronounced. Syphilitic lesions in certain localities exposed to motion and constant irritation, as the angles of the mouth, between the toes, about the anus, etc., are apt to be quite painful.

CLASSIFICATION OF THE SYPHILIDES.

In the division and grouping of the syphilides, the classification of Willan has been adopted by most authorities, with modifications in detail rather than in essential principle. This classification is based upon the anatomical alterations in the skin, and indicates the evolution of syphilis by the successive implication of one layer after another of the cutaneous envelope, and the gradual extension of the syphilitic process from the superficial to the deep structures. While the pathological characters of the elementary lesions are chiefly considered in this classification, it also assumes a chronological regularity in the date and order of development of the different eruptive forms.

While, in the large proportion of cases, the different eruptions develop at different epochs and in a definite order of succession, so that there is a certain correspondence between the anatomical characters of the lesions and the age of the syphilis, yet, clinically, this regularity of development often fails, and the type of the lesion does not conform to its position in the chronological scale. There may be a precocious development of the deep ulcerative lesions, while superficial lesions may continue to recur long after the chronological completion of the period to which they have been assigned.

The following classification has been adopted in this work:

1st. Erythematous Form.　Macular syphilide.　Erythemato-papular syphilide.
2d. Papular Form.　　　Miliary syphilide.　Lenticular syphilide.　Papulo-squamous syphilide.　Moist papular syphilide.
3d. Pustular Form.　　Acneiform syphilide.　Impetiginous syphilide.　Varicelliform syphilide.　Ecthymatous syphilide.　Rupia syphilide.
4th. Tubercular Form.　Tubercular syphilide.　Gummatous syphilide.

While the erythematous, the papular, the pustular, and the tubercular forms represent the four fundamental types of syphilitic lesions, the combination or blending together of elementary lesions has led to the necessity of using compound names, as maculo-papular, papulo-pustular,

PLATE XII.

Macular syphilide of the anterior surface of the thorax and the right upper arm of a woman. Rosy red to pale violet, finger-nail sized, roundish spots, which are distributed without regular order, and are seen thickly disseminated, but nowhere confluent.

AFTER KAPOSI.

papulo-tubercular, pustulo-crustaceous, tuberculo-ulcerous, etc., in order to more correctly define their anatomical characters.

The chief obstacle to the construction of a satisfactory classification is the polymorphous character of the eruptions. The same lesion may be modified in its objective characters by the structural peculiarities of the part upon which it is situated, there may be a simultaneous development of different eruptive forms, there may be a mutation of one form into another, so that it may be difficult to decide in which of the above divisions a given eruption shall be placed.

As regards the relative frequency with which the various eruptive forms occur, the following statistics, embracing nine hundred and thirty-one cases of general syphilis, taken from the table of admissions into the Royal Naval Hospital at Plymouth (quoted by Hill and Cooper), afford indications more or less valuable in estimating this point:

Roseola, 225. Papular, 141. Squamous, 112. Pustular, 159. Tertiary ulcerations, 44.

THE ERYTHEMATOUS SYPHILIDE.

The erythematous syphilide is the earliest, the most common, and at the same time the most benign of the cutaneous manifestations. This eruption, variously designated as the macular syphilide, roseola syphilitica, erythema syphiliticum, etc., probably occurs in all cases, yet, since it gives rise to no subjective sensations and is habitually seated upon parts covered by the clothing, it may entirely escape observation.

The date of its manifestation is usually from seven to eight weeks after the appearance of the initial lesion; its development may be retarded or even suppressed by specific treatment.

Two varieties of this eruptive form are recognized, the macular and the papular. Macular roseola appears in the form of rounded or oval hyperæmic spots, with more or less sharply-defined borders, one-eighth to one-third of an inch in diameter; the color at first bright red or pink, and disappearing upon pressure, but later it deepens into an ecchymotic yellowish tint which is not effaced by pressure. On disappearing, they leave a brownish-gray mark.

The spots vary in number, dimensions, and degree of coloration. In some cases, they are few and scattered, in others thickly disseminated like the macules of measles. They may be pale and only faintly visible, giving the skin a marbled aspect, or they may be vividly apparent. When the surface of the body is suddenly chilled, the spots emerge into distinct prominence from contrast with the surrounding white surface. In watching for the appearance of a roseola after a suspicious sore, it is well to expose the surface examined to the air several minutes in order to bring into relief the hyperæmic spots.

The seat of the eruption is usually the front and sides of the chest and abdomen, arms and thighs; the face is rarely affected. It usually lasts several weeks, exceptionally it may disappear after two or three weeks, sooner under the influence of specific treatment, or it may gradually merge into the papular form.

In the papular variety, the spots, instead of remaining smooth, become slightly elevated, seated upon an erythematous base and covered with fine desquamating scales. The papular form of the eruption represents an exaggerated development of the macular; its position is intermediate between the macule and papule, and it may co-exist with either.

Syphilitic roseola may occur a number of times in the course of the first year, or even during the second year of the disease; with each recurrence the spots are larger, fewer in number and somewhat paler. Papular roseola has a tendency to assume an annular arrangement; this circinate grouping, forming circles and fragments of circles, is quite characteristic.

Coincident with the erythematous efflorescence, small scaly papules or papulo-pustules may be found upon the scalp, forehead, or elsewhere. Not infrequently, one or more large, quite voluminous papules appear in the centre of an erythematous patch.

PLATE XIII.

Large papular syphilide of the face; scaly syphilide of the neck; small papular syphilide of the trunk, arranged in groups and clusters (Lichen syphiliticus, Syphilide *en grappe* [Alibert], Syphilodochthus confertus [Fuchs]).

AFTER KAPOSI.

DIAGNOSIS.

The diagnosis of syphilitic roseola is not usually a matter of much difficulty. The location of the eruption upon covered parts, the exemption of exposed surfaces, as face and hands, the absence of heat and itching, the presence of enlarged lymphatic glands and, as is frequently the case, the existence of induration at the point of contagion, enable us to recognize the nature of the eruption. The erythematous syphilide may, however, be confounded with rubeola, scarlatina, with the erythema of mercury, copaiba, and other drugs, with tinea versicolor, etc.

In objective characters, the macular syphilide most closely resembles the eruption of measles. The first appearance of the latter upon the forehead, the suffusion of the eyes, with catarrhal and bronchial symptoms, are sufficient for purposes of differential diagnosis. The scarlatinal eruption may be distinguished by its punctate character, its bright redness, with the accompanying high temperature, and characteristic condition of the tongue and throat.

The erythematous eruption which sometimes follows the internal or external use of mercury is localized in certain regions, rather than disseminated; a close examination of the reddish patches reveals a multitude of minute vesicles, the eruption is itchy and disappears promptly after the cessation of the medicine.

Roseola balsamica, which may follow the ingestion of copaiba and cubebs, has been mistaken for syphilitic roseola. The former consists of rounded or irregular rosy red patches, separated from each other by interspaces of perfectly normal skin, sometimes coalescing, forming patches of considerable size. It usually appears first upon the dorsal surfaces of the hands and feet, its favorite seat is around the articulations. Upon the erythematous surface wheals are often developed; it is attended with intense burning and itching. Other drugs determine a dermatitis which may closely simulate the roseola of syphilis. .All drug eruptions manifest one distinctive, characteristic feature, they disappear promptly upon the discontinuance of the exciting cause.

The yellowish or brownish stains which mark the decline of syphilitic roseola may be mistaken for pityriasis versicolor. The pigmentation of the latter is situated in the epidermal cells and may be removed by scraping or washing, while the syphilitic stains are unaffected by these means. The color, configuration, and grouping of the spots are different. An examination of the epidermal scales under the microscope will resolve all doubt.

PROGNOSIS.

The erythematous syphilide represents the most benign expression of the cutaneous accidents of syphilis: it is habitually seated upon parts covered by the clothing, the face and exposed parts are exempt from the eruption, its presence is neither disfiguring nor compromising to the patient, it is spontaneously resolutive and promptly responds to the influence of specific treatment; its prognosis, therefore, is always favorable.

So far as the ulterior manifestations of syphilis are concerned, the erythematous syphilide has little prognostic significance; the first crop of eruptive accidents does not foreshadow the character of succeeding crops. When, however, the disease continues to recur during several months in the form of an erythema, unaccompanied by severe lesion, it constitutes a favorable prognostic sign, since it indicates a stronger capacity of resistance on the part of the individual, and therefore a milder type of syphilis.

PLATE XIV.

Papular syphilide of the lenticular variety, thickly disseminated over the entire surface of the body, also upon palms and soles, with precocious superficial ulcerative lesions of the lower extremities.

AFTER MORROW.

THE PAPULAR SYPHILIDE.

The papular syphilide, in the extent of its distribution, the variety of its lesions, its prolonged continuance, and its pathological significance, is the most important of the group of secondary eruptions.

The date of its appearance is usually from the fourth to the six month after infection ; it may immediately succeed or develop coincidently with the erythematous form ; it often merges by insensible gradations of papulo-tubercles into the tubercular form ; it may continue to recur during the entire secondary stage, and may lap over into the tertiary stage. While this syphilide is generalized, superficial, and resolutive, it is often at a later stage limited to the production of isolated groups of papules, the lesions involving the whole thickness of the derma, and disappearing by a process of ulceration and loss of substance.

The papules consist of distinctly circumscribed, solid elevations from the size of a pin's head to that of a lentil, sometimes very much larger, seated upon an erythematous base. The color of the syphilitic papule is at first bright red, afterward brownish-red, paling as it subsides ; it is covered with a dry, glossy skin, at first smooth, afterward desquamating, forming a sort of collar of broken, partly-detached epidermis around the periphery.

The syphilitic papule represents the type of neoplastic lesions ; its minute anatomy will be described farther on, but in order to appreciate the clinical features presented by these lesions in their development and course, it may be well to briefly indicate the pathological conditions present.

The three phenomena which constitute the simple characteristic of all the lesions of this group have been thus formulated by Jullien :

1. Infiltration of the derma and of the mucous layer of the epidermis with small cells.

2. The inevitable destruction of these cells which are incapable of organization.

3. The centrifugal course of the neoplasm, both in its development and in its retrogression.

The clinical signs presented by the papule in its evolution and the ulterior alterations which it undergoes admit, therefore, of an easy interpretation. " The papule is prominent because there is a cellular infiltration ; hard, because this infiltration is dense ; it is brilliant because the epidermis is tense over the summit ; surrounded by a collarette, because the horny layer breaks under the effect of this tension ; it is red, because the coloring matter of the blood furnishes an extravasation, and, finally, when resorption takes place, the epidermis wrinkles at its surface and is eliminated by an ephemeral desquamation."

The papular syphilide may be distributed over the entire surface of the body, but it manifests a predilection for certain regions, upon which it is most characteristically developed. The lesions are modified in their objective characters by the structural peculiarities of the tissues upon which they are situated, and their stage of development. Upon the general integument, the papules are dry and desquamating ; upon the hairy scalp, they appear scabby ; where the skin is in folds and opposing surfaces are maintained in contact, as about the mammary gland and the genital and anal regions, the papules are moist, and often take on an exuberant development, sometimes attaining large dimensions ; where the epidermis is thick and corneous, as the palmar and plantar surfaces, they assume a peculiar scaly form which has been compared to that of psoriasis, and given rise to the designation of psoriasis palmaris or plantaris.

According to their form, volume, and other objective characters, the lesions of this syphilide have been 'classified as follows : The Miliary Papule, The Lenticular Papule, The Squamous Papule, and The Moist Papule or Mucous Patch. This division does not imply four distinct varieties, but indicates, rather, the varying form which the papular type of eruption assumes according to its location. Not infrequently they may all be found co-existent on the same subject.

PLATE XV.

Papulo-pustular syphilide, millet-seed to lentil-sized papules of the trunk, partly dry, partly pustulating or superficially exulcerating in the centre, distinguished by its polymorphism and the arrangement of the efflorescence in groups and circles.

AFTER KAPOSI.

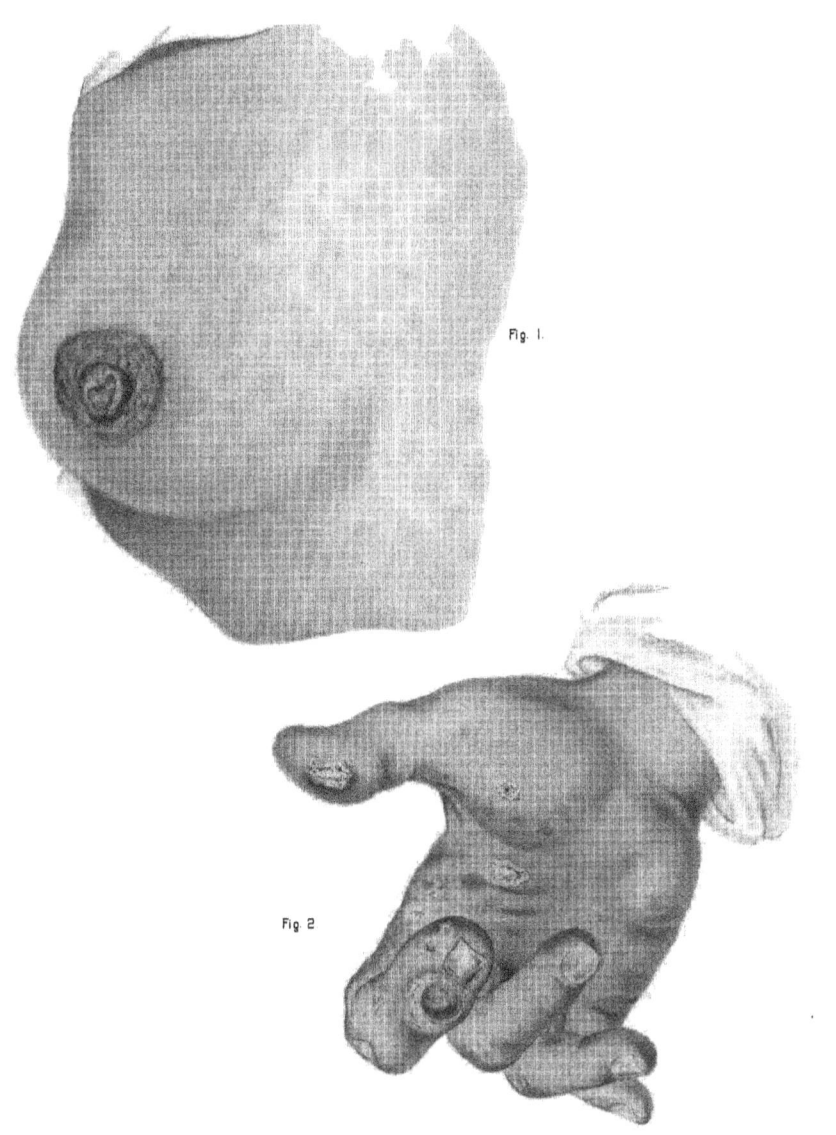

Fig. 1.

Fig. 2

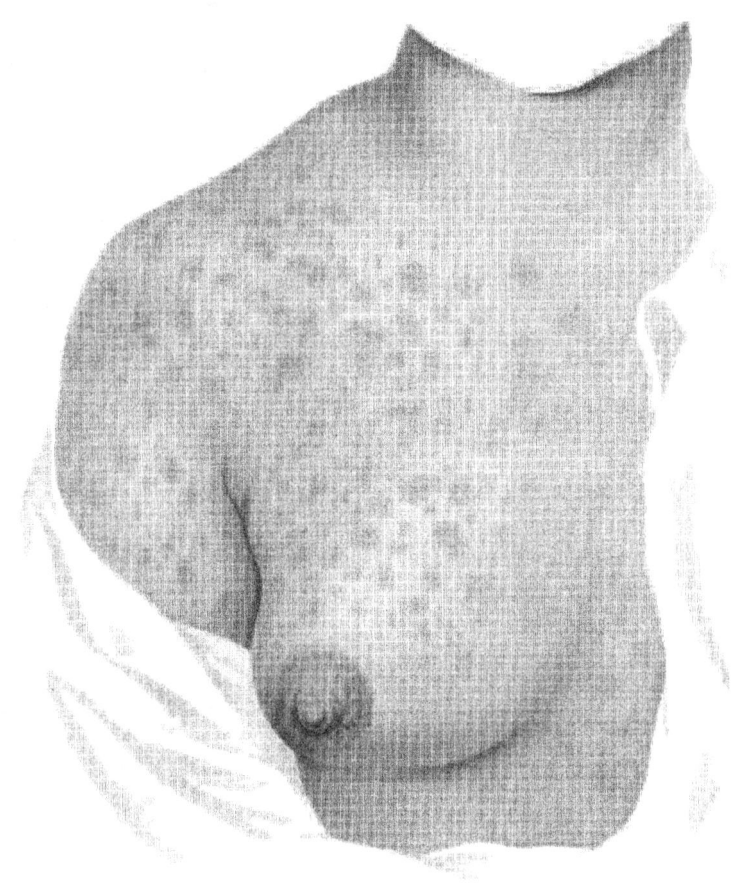

LINDNER, EDDY & CLAUSS, lithog.

WILLIAM WOOD & COMPANY.

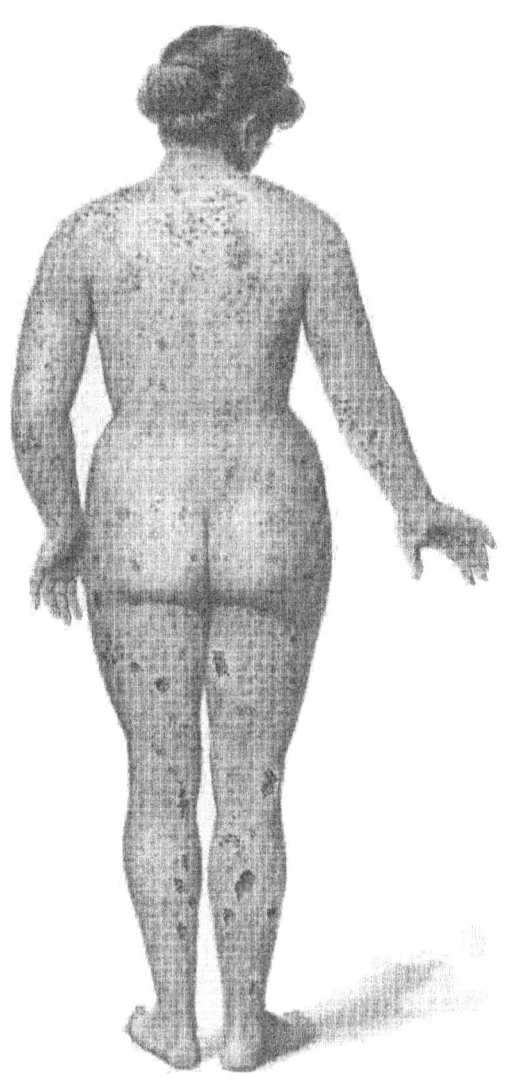

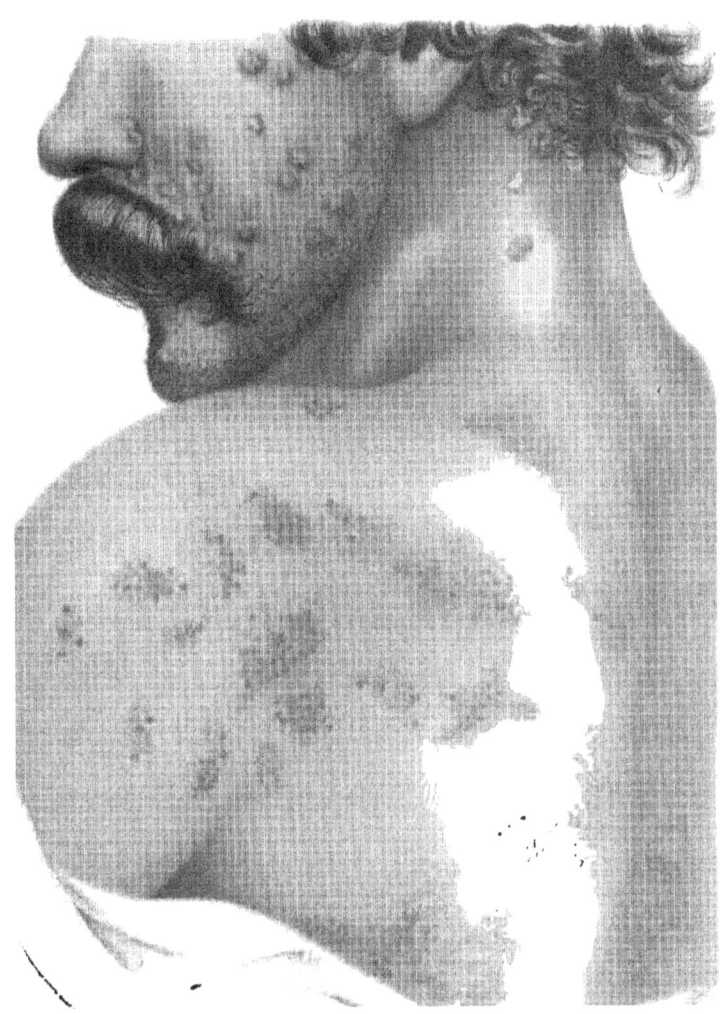

Plate XV.

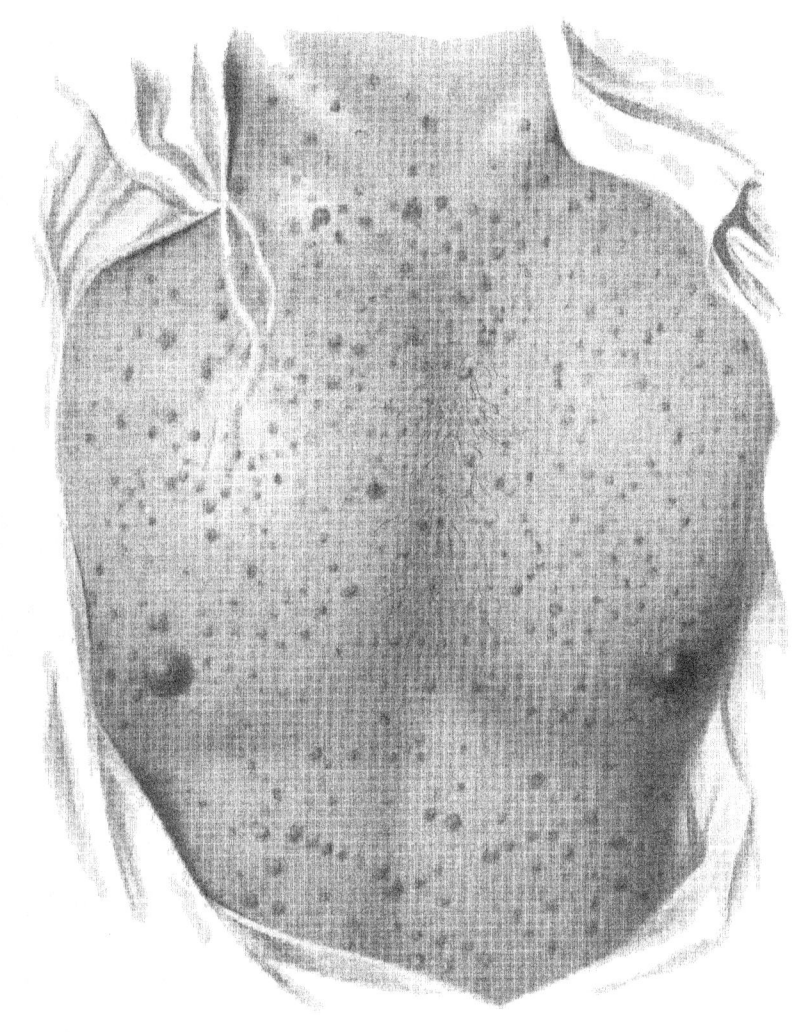

ER. EDDY & CLAUSS. Lithers.

WILLIAM WOOD & COMPANY, Publishers, NEW YORK.

ATLAS

OF

VENEREAL AND SKIN

DISEASES

COMPRISING ORIGINAL ILLUSTRATIONS AND SELECTIONS FROM THE PLATES OF

PROF. M. KAPOSI, OF VIENNA; DR. J. HUTCHINSON, OF LONDON; PROF. I. NEUMANN, OF VIENNA;
PROFS. A. FOURNIER AND A. HARDY; AND DRS. RICORD, CULLERRIER, BESNIER, AND VIDAL, OF PARIS;
PROF. LELOIR, OF LILLE; DR. P. A. MORROW, OF NEW YORK; DR. E. L. KEYES, OF NEW YORK;
DR. FESSENDEN N. OTIS, OF NEW YORK; DR. J. NEVINS HYDE, OF CHICAGO;
DR. HENRY G. PIFFARD, OF NEW YORK, AND OTHERS.

WITH ORIGINAL TEXT BY

PRINCE A. MORROW, A.M., M.D.,

CLINICAL PROFESSOR OF VENEREAL DISEASES, FORMERLY CLINICAL LECTURER ON DERMATOLOGY, IN THE UNIVERSITY OF THE CITY OF NEW YORK;
SURGEON TO CHARITY HOSPITAL, ETC.

NEW YORK

WILLIAM WOOD & COMPANY

1888

ATLAS

OF

VENEREAL· AND SKIN

DISEASES

It is with special satisfaction that the publishers announce that this large and important work, which they have had in contemplation since 1883, is now ready for publication. It has long been recognized by them, from wide observation and acquaintance with similar works published in this country and abroad, that it is impossible for any one author to furnish, from his own collection of cases and illustrations, the most typical and at the same time the best and most lifelike pictures of the many peculiar forms of these diseases. Appreciating the defects and disadvantages arising from this cause, it was determined from the outset to enlist the co-operation, in the making of this ATLAS, of the leading dermatologists and syphilographers of the world. Prominent among them are Profs. M. Kaposi and I. Neumann, of Vienna. The atlas of the former, of venereal diseases, just completed, and that of the latter, of skin diseases, now being issued in parts, will be largely drawn upon in the preparation of this work, the sole right to reproduce them having been granted us by the authors.

Among other distinguished gentlemen who have engaged to contribute selections from their collections of original illustrations may now be mentioned Dr. J. Hutchinson, of London; Profs. A. Fournier and A. Hardy; and Drs. Ricord, Cullerrier, Besnier, and Vidal, of Paris; Dr. P. A. Morrow, of New York; Dr. Edward L. Keyes, of New York; Dr. Fessenden N. Otis, of New York; Dr. J. Nevins Hyde, of Chicago; Dr. Henry G. Piffard, of New York.

Other names will be added to this list as the work progresses.

The Editor of the work is Dr. Prince A. Morrow, of New York, who, in addition to plates contributed from his own remarkable collection, will write the treatise on skin and venereal diseases, which constitutes, besides the description of the plates, the text accompanying them.

In this treatise, it is aimed to include chiefly those features which are the most practical, omitting in great measure pathological and other considerations which would be more properly treated of in extended writings, rather than as the adjunct to an Atlas.

In regard to the character of the plates, it may be said, they are believed to be superior to anything of the kind heretofore produced—as accurate in drawing as photographs, and far more distinct, while the coloring faithfully represents nature.

The text is printed from new type, large, clear, and handsome, and the paper is heavy, with a highly finished surface.

Altogether, considering the reputation of the authors of the plates, the ability of the editor, the superb execution of the plates, the excellence of the presswork, the high quality of the paper of both text and plates, the large size of the page, etc., etc., this ATLAS OF VENEREAL AND SKIN DISEASES will be the most superb work in medical literature ever published in the English language.

The ATLAS OF VENEREAL AND SKIN DISEASES will be published in fifteen monthly parts, each containing five folio, chromo-lithographic plates, many of them containing numerous figures, all printed in flesh tints and colors, together with descriptive text for each plate, and from sixteen to twenty folio pages of a practical treatise upon venereal and skin diseases; the whole forming, when complete, one magnificent thick folio volume with seventy-five plates, containing several hundred figures, exquisitely printed in colors.

☞ The ATLAS OF VENEREAL AND SKIN DISEASES will be sold by subscription only, at the very moderate price of $2 per part.

WILLIAM WOOD & COMPANY, *Publishers,*

56 AND 58 LAFAYETTE PLACE, NEW YORK.

NOTICE.—We regret to have to call attention to an error through which the descriptions of Plates XIII and XIV (Fasciculus III) have been transposed by the printer, the one accompanying Plate XIII belonging really to Plate XIV and vice versa. Subscribers will please make corresponding changes in the numbers on the plates.

WILLIAM WOOD & COMPANY

THE MILIARY PAPULAR SYPHILIDE.

The Miliary Papular Syphilide (Lichen Syphiliticus) is the most infrequent variety of the papular form, representing a proportion of less than ten per cent. The eruption consists of minute, pin-head sized, conical or pointed projections, grouped in circles or segments of circles. These groups of efflorescences, consisting of collections of ten to forty lesions, are distributed over large surfaces, principally the back of shoulders, chest, and face, the intermediary skin being free from any eruptive disturbance. Upon their first appearance, when closely examined, the summit of each papule is seen to be surmounted by a minute vesicle which, upon drying, forms an epidermic scale. When this drops off, it leaves a minute depression corresponding to the mouth of the excretory duct of a sebaceous or hair follicle.

In another variety of the miliary syphilide, the papules are larger, less numerous, and not so characteristically or distinctly grouped. The epidermal covering exfoliates and is detached from the summit, forming a white collarette around the base of the lesion.

Sometimes the groups of papules coalesce at their bases, forming circumscribed patches which, when desquamation is abundant, are suggestive of psoriasis, but the contour of each individual lesion is preserved, and there is not that thickening of the skin observed in psoriasis. Although the miliary syphilide is often rapid in its development, giving rise to the designation of the "acute papular syphilide," it is chronic in its course and slow in its involution, often persisting for several weeks without notable modification. It does not seem to be so readily amenable to the influence of specific treatment as other forms of the papular syphilide. When relapses occur, the lesions are usually of the papulo-pustular type.

In connection with the small papules upon the trunk, there is frequently a coincident eruption of large papules scattered here and there. In Plate XIII., it will be observed that there are large papules upon the face and squamous papules upon the neck co-existing with the clustered groups of small papules upon the back of the shoulders.

THE LENTICULAR PAPULAR SYPHILIDE.

The Lenticular Papular Syphilide is the most common and characteristic variety of the earlier eruptions of syphilis. The papules are rounded or oval, with distinctly limited margins, and but slightly elevated. Compared with the projecting miliary papule, the lesion gains in superficial extent what it loses in height. The surface, at first smooth and flattened, may present later a depression in the centre. As in the miliary papule, the epidermis desquamates, forming a fringe around its periphery. The color, at first bright red, afterwards assumes a more sombre brownish-red tint; in no other lesion is the specific syphilitic tint so characteristically displayed.

The distribution of this syphilide is very extensive; it may be disseminated over the entire integument; its regions of predilection are about the forehead, along the margin of the hairy scalp, the back of the neck and shoulders, the bend of the elbow and knee; it affects rather the flexor than the extensor surfaces of the limbs. The development of papules upon the brow and margin of the hairy scalp constitutes a peculiar feature known as the "Corona Veneris."

The papules, appearing in large numbers upon the face about the alæ of the nose, around the lips, and upon the brows, and becoming tumefied and hypertrophied, impart to the features the peculiar expression seen in leprosy, and have led to the designation of this facial syphilide as "syphilitic leontiasis."

The invasion of the lenticular variety of syphilide is not so rapid as that of the miliary form, requiring from ten to fifteen days for the lesions to attain their complete development. The eruption comes out in successive crops, and may continue to recur during the first eighteen months or two years of syphilis. One crop may be succeeded by another before the former has undergone complete resolution, and hence it is common to observe at the same time, on the same subject, papules of different ages and stages of development.

In the earlier months, the entire surface of the body may be thickly studded with the eruption, the papules sometimes confluent, and spreading in a continuous sheet over a large surface; but with each successive outbreak they are less numerous, more circumscribed, and finally limited to the production of a few papules upon predilected regions which have a tendency to assume a circular configuration.

The lenticular syphilide responds more promptly to the influence of mercurial treatment than the preceding variety. Under its use, the cellular elements undergo degeneration and resorption, the papule flattens and disappears, leaving a brownish-red pigmentation which is often quite persistent. This process is usually effected without loss of substance or atrophy of the skin; sometimes, however, minute depressed cicatrices may result.

In cachectic or debilitated subjects, the infiltration, instead of being resolutive, may be eliminated by the softening and breaking down of the skin in which the cell elements are imbedded, and the production of ulceration. Plate XIV., reproduced from the photograph of a patient under my charge in Charity Hospital, represents a papular syphilide in which some of the lesions are undergoing spontaneous resorption; others, on the lower extremities, have taken on a superficial ulcerative action.

THE LARGE PAPULAR OR NUMMULAR SYPHILIDE.

Under the designation of the large papular or nummular syphilide, another variety is described, in which the papules, while preserving their circular outline, color, and other characteristics, are distinguished by their larger dimensions, often attaining the size of a silver quarter or half a dollar.

The lesions are flat with distinctly defined edges, their margins elevated, oftentimes with a depression in the centre which gives them an umbilicated appearance, quite characteristic; the epidermis, desquamating and partly detached from the central surface, forming a peripheral fringe.

The chronological place of this syphilide is towards the decline of the secondary stage, and it has therefore been classed by some authorities as an "intermediary syphilide." It generally succeeds the small flat syphilide. Not infrequently small and large papules co-exist in the same patient. It may, however, appear early, representing the first of the cutaneous manifestations of syphilis. It is most characteristically developed upon the brow, the neck, the genital parts, and the palmar and plantar surfaces.

Sometimes the nummular papule undergoes a transformation into what is termed the annular papule. The tendency to umbilication has already been referred to as a characteristic feature in the retrogressive stage. This feature becomes more accentuated by an absorption of the central portion of the lesion, which gradually disappears, while the peripheral margin or rim remains hard, elevated, and scaly, resulting in a ring-shaped, coppery wall of infiltration, inclosing a macular centre. This same circinate configuration may result from the linear contact of numerous small papules which have developed in the form of a circle.

As a rarer variety may be mentioned, the development of two or more concentric rings encircled by a larger ring, forming a polycyclic arrangement. Figs. 1 and 2, Plate XXI., afford an admirable representation of both varieties of the annular or circinate syphilide.

The intricate and eccentric forms which the papular syphilide may exhibit in its development by the intersection or interfusion of the circular, crescentic and elliptical patches are quite remarkable. Instead of the characteristic circular or discoid form, the papules may be arranged in sinuous or serpentine rows, giving the eruption a peculiar gyrate form. This configuration is most characteristically seen upon the prepuce or sheath of the penis in the immediate neighborhood of the primary lesion. It may appear precociously before there is any other eruption upon the general surface. Fig. 3, Plate XIX., furnishes a good illustration of the gyrate syphilide.

Still another eruptive form results from the grouping of small papules in a circle around a large papule as a centre. The satellite papules are of uniform size, disseminate, separated from each other by normal skin, and disposed in a system with almost geometric regularity. This form is termed the stellate syphilide or the *syphilide en corymbe*.

THE PAPULO-SQUAMOUS SYPHILIDE.

One of the most important modifications of the papular type of syphilis is represented by the papulo-squamous form. Its essential feature consists in a marked proliferation of the epidermal elements of the surface of the papule. Any one of the varieties of papular syphilide already described may undergo this modification, which imparts to the eruption a striking similitude to psoriasis, and has hence led to the designation of this syphilide as syphilitic psoriasis. This nomenclature is objectionable, since psoriasis represents a distinct idiopathic disease, which in its origin and nature has nothing to do with syphilis, and the retention of a term indicating a combination of the two diseases leads only to confusion.

A papular eruption may present this psoriatic physiognomy from the first, or it may be impressed upon the lesions secondarily. It is observed that papules of the late secondary stage, which are ordinarily of large size and more deeply seated, are more apt to exhibit a tendency to epidermal thickening and exfoliation, so that the chronicity of a lesion is an important factor in the production of this morphological feature. Again, locality exercises a certain influence in determining this peculiarity; upon certain regions, such as the palms of the hands and soles of the feet, the squamous element is rarely absent. Upon the face, the margin of the hairy scalp, especially about the bearded chin, the naso-labial and the naso-jugal furrows, the papules manifest this tendency to scaliness.

Unquestionably a predominant importance must be attributed to idiosyncrasy, or structural peculiarity of the individual skin, as a predisposing influence, since it has been observed that in certain persons all papular lesions, irrespective of their age, dimensions, or locality, are characterized by an excessive scaliness. By many authorities the scaly syphilide is regarded as the expression of a psoriatic diathesis, or rather a syphilis modified by its development in a psoriatic subject. This view is probably incorrect, since many syphilitics in whom the squamous type of eruption is most pronounced have never had an attack of psoriasis.

The mildest expression of the squamous process, and one which has but clinical importance, is termed syphilitic pityriasis. It consists essentially in desquamation of minute furfuraceous scales from large, irregularly rounded, slightly elevated surfaces, which may be generally distributed.

As before intimated, the squamous element is most pronounced and characteristically developed in the larger and more persistent papules of the late secondary or intermediate period, it may continue to develop after the accession of the tertiary stage. It generally occurs in the form of circinate patches, covered with dry, adherent scales, more or less thick, friable or compact, sometimes even of a horny consistency. By the contact and intersection of the circles, it may form festooned and gyrate figures, as described in the evolution of the large papular syphilide; the color, configuration, and other objective characters rendering it quite indistinguishable from *psoriasis figurata* or *gyrata*. In other cases, there is an agglomeration of papules, forming large nappes or solid infiltrated patches of considerable dimensions, the surface covered with fine powdery scales.

Upon certain regions, as the dorsal surface of the trunk, the back of the neck, the face, but more especially about the upper lip and the alæ of the nose, there is often a papillary hypertrophy in addition to the epidermic proliferation, which gives to the lesions a warty, vegetating

PLATE XVI.

FIG. I.—Papular syphilide of face and neck disposed in groups. Massed groups about the angles of the eyes, mouth, and nose Isolated papules upon the forehead, with exulcerated summits, bearing crusts.

FIG. II.—Papulo-squamous syphilide. Lentil to penny-sized papules, with raised, sharply defined infiltration. The older ones, larger, with abundantly desquamating centre.

AFTER KAPOSI.

character. Upon the bearded portions of the face, the papules may present the appearance of a thin crust rather than a scale.

ANATOMY OF THE SYPHILITIC PAPULE.

The following description of the anatomical structure of the syphilitic papule is taken from Kaposi:

On vertical sections through a recent syphilitic cutaneous papule, comprising also a portion of the adjoining healthy skin, we observe:

Within the confines of the syphilitic papule the epidermal and the mucous layer are preserved. The latter is thinned over the centre of the papule (*b c*), and only here and there it is

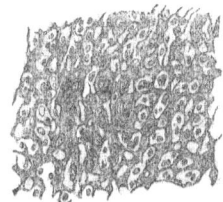

FIG. 5.—Vertical section of a syphilitic papule, from the skin of the back of living patient. (Hartnack, oc. 3, obj. 5.)
a b, Marginal portion of the papule, with distinct cones of the rete and papillæ; *b c*, central, depressed (atrophic) portion of the papule, the demarcation between rete and papillæ obliterated ; *a d, e f*, dense cellular infiltration corresponding to the papule and sharply limited in the depth at *d f; d e*, healthy corium tissue of the immediate vicinity.

FIG. 6.—Cellular infiltration and network of the syphilitic papule. (Hartnack, oc. 3, obj. 10.)

sharply demarcated from the corium. At other points its lower limit is indistinct because a close-meshed network present in the corium seems to continue into the outlines of the rete. The conical processes of the rete Malpighii are absent, and are merely indicated by scattered moderate protrusions of the mucous layer. Over the peripheral portion of the papule the papillæ and the rete (*a b*) are preserved in a nearly normal condition. Under a higher power the cells of the rete appear furrowed, and many of them vacuolated.

The papillæ are indicated only by occasional moderate indentations of the mucous layer. In the central portion, the corium is demarcated from the mucous layer only faintly by a wavy line.

The papillary layer and the upper part of the corium are traversed by a dense network (high power, Fig. 6), whose meshes are roundish and of varying size. The fibres of the net are partly filiform, partly broader and more bandlike, with delicate outlines, and readily take the carmine stain. Coarser trabeculæ, likewise stained by carmine, cross the network at greater intervals in various directions, and run uninterruptedly for considerable distances, thus inclosing the dense network in its larger divisions.

The close-meshed network is almost regularly interspersed with roundish formed elements partly resembling leucocytes, partly much smaller, and partly similar to the nucleus of a white blood-corpuscle. They stain very irregularly in carmine; many are almost filled with dark granules in their protoplasm and in the nucleus. These formed elements lie partly singly, partly numerously within each mesh, and some lie directly in the course of the trabeculæ of the net. Many cells in the meshes are connected by one or more processes with the delicate fibres of the network.

Besides, the network contains some peculiarly shaped formed elements (Fig. 6), cells whose body and nucleus are two or three times the size of the normal, whose nucleus has a bis-cuit-like constriction, and whose appearance resembles the elements found in syphilitic roseola; finally there are others which are almost completely divided into two, lying closely together within the same mesh. At some points there are larger meshes inclosing a heap consisting of from six to eight roundish, lustrous, crowded corpuscles resembling cell-nuclei.

In the section, the blood-vessels do not appear altered in their lumen; their walls are pro-vided with lustrous, roundish nuclei.

The above-described alteration of the skin, which is markedly characterized by the network with its cellular infiltration, is pretty sharply demarcated laterally and inferiorly; being immediately surrounded at the sides by normal papillæ (Fig. 5, *a b*), and both there and in the deeper layer of the corium (Fig. 5, *d, e, f*) by a perfectly normal corium tissue which is free from cells, not œdematous, and has normal follicles.

According to these findings, the syphilitic papule presents itself as the result of a cellular infiltration which is pretty sharply demarcated toward the papillary layer and the upper stratum of the corium both laterally and inferiorly. In its nature it resembles most closely those infiltra-tions which are present in new-formations, such as lupus. The process can hardly be interpreted as an "inflammation" in its more restricted sense. Against such an interpretation we have the relatively slight implication of the vessels, the moderate infiltration of the diseased portion, and the absence of pathological alteration, especially of œdema and cell-proliferation in the corium im-mediately adjoining the morbid focus.

DIAGNOSIS.

The diagnosis of the miliary papular syphilide is rarely attended with much difficulty. Not infrequently vestiges of induration of the primary sore still remain at the time of its development, and it is usually accompanied with other signs of syphilis, as the characteristic glandular enlarge-ments, alopecia, sore throat, etc.

The same may be said of the lenticular syphilide. The earlier eruptions are so typical in their generalization, their symmetric character, the size, shape, and color of the papules, the absence of subjective sensations, etc., that the diagnosis is generally easy. When the eruption is sparsely developed, or in a later stage, when relapses occur in the form of large papules, which become scaly and assume the configuration and distribution peculiar to psoriasis, the diagnosis may be difficult. In all doubtful cases, the history should be inquired into; the existence of a chancre within a specified time, the presence or absence of certain symptoms which commonly characterize the early evolution of syphilis, the co-existence of other specific lesions, will throw light upon the nature of the eruption.

There are a number of papular eruptions of non-specific origin with which the miliary syphilide may be confounded. In the size of the papules and their grouped arrangement, it bears a certain resemblance to lichen scrofulosorum. In the latter affection, the papules are uni-formly of a hempseed-size, either of a pale yellow color or of the same tint as the normal skin.

The eruption is almost always confined to the trunk, rarely appearing upon the limbs; it is very chronic in its nature and may last for years.

Lichen planus may also be mistaken for a papular syphilide. There are, however, marked differences in the structure of the lesions, the order of their arrangement, and course. The papules of lichen planus are more solid, angular, with flattened shining or glazed surfaces, often distinctly umbilicated. They are of variable size and often coalesce at their bases, forming large plaques from which a scanty desquamation may take place. They are chronic in their course, attended with extreme itching, and upon disappearing leave large irregular pigmented stains.

Herpes circinatus has also been mistaken for the efflorescence of the papular syphilide when it assumes an annular or circinate configuration. The vesicles of the former are quite transitory, drying up into small scales, forming a circle of scales upon a slightly inflamed base. The microscopical examination of the scales, revealing the presence of the characteristic spores, would resolve all doubt. Herpes tonsurans, either of the hairy scalp or bearded portion of the face, could hardly be mistaken for a syphilide, since in these localities the circinate form of syphilide is rarely seen. When syphilitic papules occur upon the scalp, the scales are mixed with scabs and crusts, giving them the appearance of pustules.

The papular form of iodic eruption may be confounded with syphilis. Tilbury Fox says: " I have been often consulted for a supposed syphilis when the disease has been simply an iodide rash." The iodic papules are commonly localized upon the face, neck, and back of hands and wrists. They are more elevated, shotty to the feel, and intensely itchy. They come out suddenly, and undergo rapid involution when the exciting cause is withdrawn.

Acne has been mistaken for the papular syphilide, especially when seated upon the back of the shoulders. The lesions of acne are clearly follicular in character; they have for their almost exclusive seat regions rich in sebaceous glands, as the face, upper part of chest and back of shoulders, and are most characteristically developed about the time of puberty.

The cutaneous disease with which certain forms of the papular syphilide present the closest resemblances and with which they are most liable to be confounded is psoriasis, especially when they become the seat of the marked epidermic proliferation described in connection with the scaly papule. The miliary papular syphilide may resemble psoriasis punctata ; the lenticular syphilide, psoriasis guttata ; the larger papular syphilide, psoriasis nummularis. Usually, however, the differences in the minute objective characters of the lesions and in their topographical distribution are sufficient for purposes of differentiation. Thus the miliary papules, when closely aggregated and the seat of abundant desquamation, may suggest a diffuse patch of psoriasis, but a minute examination will disclose that the papules have not coalesced, but are simply coherent at their bases, the contour of their summits perfectly distinct, and covered with small scales, while the surfaces of psoriatic patch is uniform and covered with large flaky scales. Psoriasis may appear upon the hairy scalp and ears, where the miliary syphilide does not occur.

But it is especially the larger papulo-squamous syphilides of comparatively late development which, by their contact and coalescence, assume a configuration so strikingly suggestive of the figurate and gyrate forms of psoriasis that the resemblance is most deceptive. When we come to examine the lesions minutely, differences in the character of the scales and the condition of the subjacent parts will be at once appreciated. The syphilitic scales are smaller, less abundant, of a dirty gray or yellowish color, more adherent and often do not entirely cover the lesion. The scales of psoriasis are larger, thicker, distinctly imbricated, of a whitish or silvery appearance, and completely cover the surface of the lesion. When the scales are stripped off from a syphilitic papule, there is revealed a neoplastic infiltration, dry and of a reddish-brown or coppery color ; when the scales are detached from psoriatic patch, there is presented a reddish surface with a number of hyperæmic bleeding points. In a psoriatic eruption, there are frequently to be found, mingled with the older patches, recent lesions which are so characteristic that a mistake as to their real nature is impossible.

In addition, the localization of psoriasis, with its predilection for certain regions, as the

PLATE XVII.

Scaly syphilide of trunk and right arm. Upon the chest, partly elevated, pea-sized papules, as seen in face (Fig. I., Plate XVI.), partly lentil-sized flat elevations, desquamating in centre, as seen in Fig. II., Plate XVI.

Upon the arm irregularly shaped, variously sized, sharply defined scaly patches, surrounded by raised, brownish-red firm borders.

Below the elbow, upon anterior surface of forearm, large and irregularly shaped surfaces, surrounded with flat, red borders.

AFTER KAPOSI.

extensor surfaces, more especially of the knees and elbows, is in contrast with the preference of syphilis for the face, neck, trunk, and anterior surfaces of the limbs. Upon the hairy scalp the syphilitic lesions are usually discrete, scabbed or encrusted, resembling pustules and presenting a totally different appearance from the heaped up, mortar-like scales of psoriasis. Finally, an inquiry into the history of the psoriatic patient will frequently disclose the fact that he has suffered from a number of preceding attacks of the same form of eruption.

PALMAR AND PLANTAR SYPHILIDES.

Upon the palms and soles the papular syphilide presents such marked modifications, due to anatomical peculiarities of the structure of the epidermis in these localities, that it has been distinguished by certain observers as a separate eruption, under the designation of psoriasis palmaris and plantaris. While the thick and corneous scales which cover the papule give it a certain resemblance to psoriasis, yet the term, though generally employed by continental authorities, is objectionable for the reasons already indicated. The palmar and plantar syphilides are characterized by their tendency to frequent recurrence, their continued development in an advanced stage of the disease, and their obstinate and refractory character, being little influenced by specific treatment. They have a special clinical importance and interest, from the fact that they bear such a close resemblance to the lesions of other constitutional diseases in these localities that it is difficult to differentiate them.

Syphilitic lesions of the palms and soles are modified in their objective characters by the firm adherence of the cutis to the subjacent fascia, and the thickness and non-distensibility of the corneous layer. On account of the resistance of the epidermis, the papules are flat, with a scarcely appreciable elevation. They appear as dull red spots from the size of a hempseed to that of a split pea or finger nail, which soon fade into a reddish-brown hue. The epidermal covering is gradually lifted up and broken, and is detached in lamellæ, leaving in the centre a bright red circular spot surrounded by a border of undermined skin. The circular loss of tissue corresponding to each papule may give it the appearance of being punched out with an instrument.

In another variety, described by French writers as the corneous syphilide, which is much more common upon the palm than the sole, the pathological process seems to be centered in the corneous layer which is elevated in the form of extremely hard, minute conical projections of the epidermis. These hard epithelial concretions may be dug out of the skin, leaving small crateriform depressions.

Under the designation of syphilis cornea, Zeissl describes "a diffuse affection of the epidermal strata of the hands and feet, which consists of a uniform, diffused, rapid degeneration of the most superficial layers of the skin, whereby the affected places look as if the epidermis were transformed into a fine whitish-silver brocade."

The papules, instead of remaining discrete, may coalesce, forming diffuse patches which are usually crescentic or circinate in form, with a tendency to heal in the centre, while advancing by the development of new papules in the periphery. The fusion of the papules may convert the entire palm into a continuous lesion, the sombre red base corresponding to the infiltrated, parchment-like derma. In the natural furrows of the palm and fingers, cracks and fissures are apt to form, sometimes extending deep down into the true skin and occasioning much pain and inconvenience. The persistence of syphilides in this region is, no doubt, largely due to the fact that these lesions are constantly aggravated by pressure, friction, and other causes of irritation to which the parts are exposed.

Syphilitic lesions of the soles, while somewhat less frequent, often co-exist with those of the palms, and present essentially the same objective characters. The epidermis of the sole may

PLATE XVIII.

Fig. I.—Pin-head to lentil-sized, sharply defined, brownish-red, flat, or flat elevated efflorescences in large numbers, and dispersed without regular order upon the volar surface of the hand and fingers, as well as upon the forearm, some of them slightly depressed in centre and scaly (beginning stage of psoriasis palmaris).

Fig. II.—Variously sized, roundish, sharply defined, brownish-red spots on the palm, especially upon the wrist. The larger of them depressed in centre, and partly covered with dry, thick scales, partly showing a brown-red infiltrated corium. In some of them there is observed, between the central overlying crust and the surrounding normal skin, a sharply limited, brownish-red border (the peripheral remains of the papule).

Fig. III.—Diffused palmar psoriasis. The palmar surface in its entire extent brownish-red, and covered with thick, dry, and numerously fissured scales.

The diseased surface demarcated in curved lines from the surrounding healthy tissues. These correspond to the contours of the papules, for the most part lying in their periphery, by the confluence of which the extensive morbid patch is formed. Toward the wrist and the ball of the thumb, the scaling does not extend to the edge, which appears as brown-red, firm, sharply defined margin of the peripheral (the most recent) part of the syphilitic infiltration (the papule).

Within the apparently uniformly diseased area are to be seen isolated, lentil-sized and larger, quite distinct, brownish-red spots which correspond each to an excoriated papule, and also in their turn demonstrate the formation of the diffuse disease from isolated papular discs.

Fig. IV.—Psoriasis plantaris cornea. The epidermis of the sole thickened, callous, dry, with numerous fissures, lifted up in the central parts, exposing here the brownish-red infiltrated corium.

The callous parts are well defined in certain places (on the sole of the foot near the inner border), bow shaped, with a brown-red, thick, infiltrated margin. Upon the plantar surface of the toes are lentil to penny-sized, sharply defined spots depressed in the centre, and desquamating toward the periphery.

AFTER KAPOSI.

become enormously thickened, the brittle horny layers cracking and fissuring, forming deep, painful rhagades which are extremely obstinate to cure.

The earlier palmar and plantar syphilides are usually symmetrical, but in a more advanced stage, only one palm or sole may be affected.

DIAGNOSIS.

The designation of syphilides of the palms and soles as palmar and plantar psoriases would indicate a marked resemblance or identity in the objective characters of the lesions of the two diseases in these localities. This, however, rarely introduces an element of difficulty in the differential diagnosis, since, as a matter of fact, true psoriasis occurs with such extreme infrequency upon the palms and soles that it may be practically excluded from consideration. Indeed, it may be said that it never occurs upon these surfaces except when generally distributed over the body, while, on the other hand, these regions are a favorite seat for syphilides; palmar and plantar lesions may represent the sole signs of the disease for years.

The dermatosis with which syphilis of the palms is most apt to be confounded is eczema. Like syphilis, eczema is frequently localized upon the palms, and is often extremely chronic in its course. When the syphilide occurs in the form of discrete papules, a mistake is not liable to be made; the dry, red, smooth spots deprived of epidermis, with a papular infiltrated base, are quite characteristic; but when the lesions coalesce, forming large patches of infiltration with a sweeping circinate border, the resemblance to certain forms of chronic scaly eczema is most striking. The following differential marks may be indicated: syphilis generally begins in the middle of the hand, and spreads by the development and fusion of new papules; the coppery wall of infiltration which marks its advancing border is therefore scalloped and uneven, its outer edge sharply defined and terminating abruptly against the healthy skin. Eczema oftener attacks the ulnar and radial margins of the hands, and spreads peripherically by the gradual extension of the inflammatory process. The margin of the eczematous patch is more regularly curved, and the infiltration does not terminate abruptly, but shades off into an erythematous redness of the surrounding skin.

Syphilis is usually confined to the palm; it does not extend over the sides upon the dorsal surface of the hand and fingers. Eczema, on the contrary, frequently creeps along the sides and over the dorsal surfaces of the fingers and hand. Finally, itching of the affected parts is absent in syphilis, the only subjective sensations result from the accidental cracking and fissuring of the skin; in eczema of the palms, the sensation of itching is ordinarily most violent and pronounced.

In some long-standing cases, however, the sharp differential signs which distinguish these two affections are lost, and a positive diagnosis is not possible. Even the test of specific treatment is slow, tedious, and oftentimes disappointing in establishing the diagnosis, since palmoplantar syphilides are exceedingly refractory to its influence.

THE MOIST PAPULE.

This form of the papular syphilide derives a special clinical importance from its frequency, its marked tendency to relapse, the subjective symptoms it occasions, and, further, from the fact that it constitutes one of the most common sources of the contagion of syphilis.

The moist papule represents a metamorphosis of the ordinary papule, which is determined by the accident of situation and other local conditions. Its development is favored by fineness and delicacy of the skin and consequent thinness of the epidermis, warmth, friction, the rubbing of adjacent surfaces, and contact with secretions or exudations. It is found at the junction of the skin and mucous membranes of the natural orifices and in the natural folds or creases of the skin where contiguous surfaces come in contact, as, for example, around the genital and anal orifices,

PLATE XIX.

Fig. I.—Papilloma non-syphiliticum. Small agminated to mulberry-like heaps of aggregated excrescences in large number, occupying the inner surface of the reflected prepuce, a few, isolated, upon the glans.

Fig. II.—Condylomata acuminata (non-syphilitica), moderately hard, irregular, superficially smooth, scar-like excrescences upon the foreskin, the glans, the scrotum, the indurated and hypertrophic base showing acuminate warts.

Fig. III.—Syphilis cutanea annulata et gyrata. The integument of the penis in its entire extent seen with delicate, garland-like, clear brown-red delineations.

They are formed by small, brown-red, firm, glazed, partly moist, ridge-like prominences of the skin which surround smaller and larger circles, and combine with each other in manifold fashions.

The circumscribed superficial circles of the skin are of brownish pigmentation.

The foreskin phimotic, thickened, hard (sclerosis). Upon the scrotum, lentil to penny-sized papules, with shallow depressions in centre and excoriated surface.

Fig. IV.—Psoriasis vulgaris (non-syphilitica). Variously sized, red, flat discs upon the penis and skin of the neighboring parts; part of them covered to the extremest limit of their red margin with white glistening scales, partly scaleless and uniformly red (upon the glans).

Fig. V.—Condylomata Lata and Chancre. The inner surface of the prepuce thickened in one place and hard (sclerosis). Upon the dorsum of the penis, four isolated pea-sized, roundish, prominent hard nodules encrusted in the centre. Upon the under surface of the penis one, upon the integument of the scrotum two, sharply-defined, flatly elevated (club-shaped), firm papules, the size of a cent, their centres superficially depressed and scaly. In the pubic region numerous pea-sized, firm nodules.

AFTER KAPOSI.

the breast, the navel, the axillary, inguinal and genito-crural regions, and in the interdigital spaces, more especially between the toes. It is well to bear in mind that the chancre, instead of undergoing a normal process of involution, may be transformed *in situ* into a mucous patch. It is much more frequent in women than in men, and in the former often attains an exaggerated development.

The moist papule begins as a small, flat elevation, irregularly rounded or discoid in form; its dimensions vary from one-eighth to one-half inch in diameter; instead of being flat, the lesion may exhibit a depression in the central parts, with elevated margins. Instead of the formation of a scale upon the surface, as in the dry papule, the epidermal covering is macerated by moisture and transformed into a grayish-white, easily detached membrane. After this is cast off, there remains a grayish or flesh-colored plaque, soft to the feel, with a moist, secreting surface, like mucous membrane, whence the name *mucous patch* given to the moist papule. The papules may become covered with a grayish-white diphtheroid layer, giving them a chalky appearance; they may become superficially ulcerated, presenting an uneven, verrucose aspect. Coincident with these surface changes, there is almost always a marked hyperplasia of the papillary body, imparting to the papules a distinct vegetating character, and has led to their designation as *condylomata lata*. This feature is doubtless determined by the local irritation from the pressure of contiguous surfaces, and the contact of physiological and abnormal secretions. Instead of remaining discrete, there is commonly a coalescence of several contiguous lesions, forming irregularly shaped flattened masses, the surface being broken up by longitudinal or polygonal fissures, which channel the mass in every direction.

Around the anus a number of lesions may be grouped in a longitudinal line on either side, like a row of buttons. Owing to the incessant friction and pressure to which the papules are subjected in this location, combined with the macerating action of the secretions, the papules may become enormously tumefied and hypertrophied, and are attended with more or less itching, burning, and spasm of the sphincter ani muscle. In the radiating folds, deep fissures are frequently formed which may occasion the most violent pain, especially during the act of defecation. From the anus they often spread along the perinæum in irregularly grouped patches.

Upon the scrotum, the lesions are rounded, nummular, of a reddish-gray tint, and generally discrete.

About the female genital parts, moist papules are most abundant, and often take on an exuberant development. In women they are commonly precocious, constituting the first and, in some instances, the sole manifestation of secondary syphilis. They may be either isolated or confluent, forming by their aggregation warty or nodular patches of considerable size, the lobulated surface covered with a profuse, extremely offensive secretion. Zeissl asserts "that moist papules, especially those on the edges of the labia and around the anus, are due to implication of the sebaceous glands." In this region moist papules are attended with considerable itching, and, when ulcerated, occasion much pain and soreness of the parts. Mucous patches of the genital region are frequently complicated with dermatitis, inflammation of the glands of the vulva, œdema of the vulva, etc. The labia majora may become enormously infiltrated, giving rise to a sclerosed, rigid condition which, in pregnant women, becomes a serious obstacle to parturition.

In the interdigital spaces, between the toes, as the fingers are rarely thus affected, mucous patches may occasion great pain and inconvenience, interfering with locomotion, the patient being unable to bear the weight of the body on the feet. The papules, instead of being simply erosive, may become the seat of ulceration, which often extends along the articular fold, upon the dorsal and plantar surfaces. The surfaces secrete a thin, brownish or yellowish fluid, the odor of which is most foul and offensive.

Upon the breast, the papules are large, smooth, slightly eroded or covered with a thin impetiginous crust, and grouped within or about the areola. In fat women, with large, pendulous breasts, a favorite location is the integument underneath the mammæ. Moist papules about the

PLATE XX.

Fig. I.—Confluent moist papules (plaques muqueuses). Pea to kidney-bean-sized, isolated and confluent papules upon the free edges of the labia majora and minora, the raphe of the perineum, and the fold of the thigh. Some of them, the more recent, are dry ; others are moist, and covered with a yellowish-gray suppuration. Round, pigmented patches upon surfaces of thighs.

Fig. II.—Condylomata lata. Variously sized, roundish, flat elevated, sharply defined intumescences, with steep edges upon the posterior surface of the scrotum and both sides of the anal furrow.
   Their superficies is plane or moderately depressed in centre, dry and slightly scaly.

AFTER KAPOSI.

female nipple have a most important etiological relation with the syphilis of nurslings, constituting, as they do, by their ultra-contagiousness and the frequent exposure of the mouth of the child in nursing, the most common sources of infection in infantile acquired syphilis.

At the commissure of the lips, the papules frequently occupy both the cutaneous and mucous surfaces, and are frequently complicated with fissures of the angle of the mouth, more or less painful. In such situations the mucous portion of the papule exhibits the characteristics of the mucous patch, while the cutaneous segment is covered with a grayish or brownish crust.

Moist papular syphilides may continue to recur during the entire secondary stage. Relapsing papules may reappear upon their former site, but the later lesions are apt to be fewer in number, and of less rapid and exuberant growth. If abandoned to themselves without treatment, they may persist for many months, forming large papillomatous masses resembling frambœsia. Sometimes the entire neoplastic growth disappears by a process of ulceration which, however, does not involve the tissues upon which it is implanted. They generally undergo rapid resolution under the influence of appropriate general and local treatment, cicatrization taking place without loss of tissue. The readiness with which they yield to treatment is, however, counterbalanced by the facility and continued pertinacity with which they recur.

ANATOMY OF THE BROAD CONDYLOMA.

According to Kaposi, an examination of the minute structure of the broad condyloma reveals the following characteristics.

In broad condyloma, as in the syphilitic nodule, there is present a cellular infiltration throughout the papillary layer and the corium, which occasionally extends into the subcutaneous cellular tissue and appears to be pretty sharply demarcated laterally towards the adjoining, perfectly normal tissue (Fig. 7).

The limits of the papule are indicated by the portion whose morbid condition is marked by the cell infiltration which is rather sharply demarcated from the surrounding, perfectly normal corium (*fg*, Fig. 7).

The papillæ are considerably enlarged, mainly in their longitudinal diameter, terminating above in two or three branches, frequently with club-shaped ends (Fig. 7, *a*).

In the more recent condylomata, as well as in the peripheral part of moist papules, the mucous layer is considerably thickened, its conical processes are elongated and broadened (Fig. 7, *b*), and is pretty sharply differentiated from the tissue of the papillæ. Only through the central portions of suppurating, ulcerating papules this distinction becomes obscured because the granular, almost dusty appearance of the infiltrated papillæ continues into the cells of the mucous layer. At the same time the latter is thinned or absent at the ulcerated portions; the mutilated papillæ or the suppurating corium with its vertically ascending loops of papillary vessels being freely laid bare.

Under a higher power it can be recognized that the papillary tissue and the corium corresponding to the extent of the papule are uniformly altered by the cellular infiltration (Fig. 7, *a*, *e*; Fig. 8, *c*).

The cells vary in size and shape; most of them are the size of a white blood-corpuscle, some are almost twice as large, many represent only a cell nucleus. Among the cells some are roundish, oval, irregular in shape, and some provided with tail-like processes.

Both the cell-bodies and the nuclei are without exception very granular.

The granular appearance of the cell-body continues also into the processes where these are present.

Cells may be found whose nucleus seems constricted in the centre. Others attract attention by their size which is more than double that of a white blood-corpuscle; in these the pale gray, glossy nucleus constitutes the major portion of the cell which exceeds it only by a narrow zone of the cell-body. This nucleus is sometimes found completely split into two. At other points we find within a circular space resembling one of the latter cells five or six bodies, similar to small cell nuclei, which are grayish, have a dull lustre, are infiltrated with granules, and packed close together, seemingly inclosed in a common envelope.

The above-described cells constituting the infiltration are imbedded in a network composed of meshes varying in size and shape, but mostly close, and extending throughout the infiltrated tissue, *i. e.*, the entire papule. One or more cells lie in each mesh, or the latter may be filled by one of the larger cells described above, or by a heap of nuclei (five or six), presumably due to the breaking down of a cell; partly, however, the cells are imbedded in the trabeculæ of the network.

The network is subdivided into larger segments by coarser diverging fibres from the old connective tissue of the corium which run without interruption for considerable distances; within

FIG. 7.   FIG. 8.

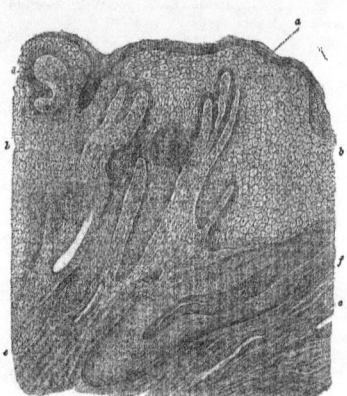

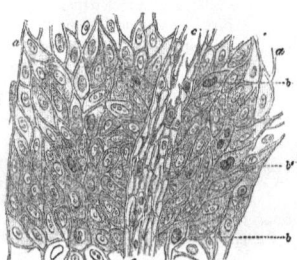

Fig. 7.—Broad condyloma (excised intra vitam). Vertical section. (Hartnack, Oc. 3, Obj 5.)
a, club-shaped, branching, and thickened papillæ with cellular infiltration ; *b*, greatly developed mucous layer ; *c*, corium with cellular infiltration ; *e*, hair with hypertrophic external root sheath ; *f g*, normal corium tissue, histological limit of the broad condyloma ; *d*, transverse section of an infiltrated papilla.

FIG. 8.—Broad condyloma, vertical section. (Hartnack, Oc. 3, Obj. 10 immersion.)

these the finer and closer fibres and trabeculæ of the network become visible. The latter increases in density toward the border of the vessel wall and merges with the network of that structure.

The vessels appear unaltered in their lumen. Their adventitia is widened and interspersed with numerous cells and nuclei which separate it into a network; the nuclei of the capillary wall seem enlarged and multiplied.

The cells of the rete Malpighii (Fig. 8, *a*) are striated, many exhibit vacuoles, constricted or double nuclei (Fig. 8, *b*, *b'*). Over the disintegrating portions of the papule they appear, where still present, in a state of granular opacity, irregular in outline, and broken down.

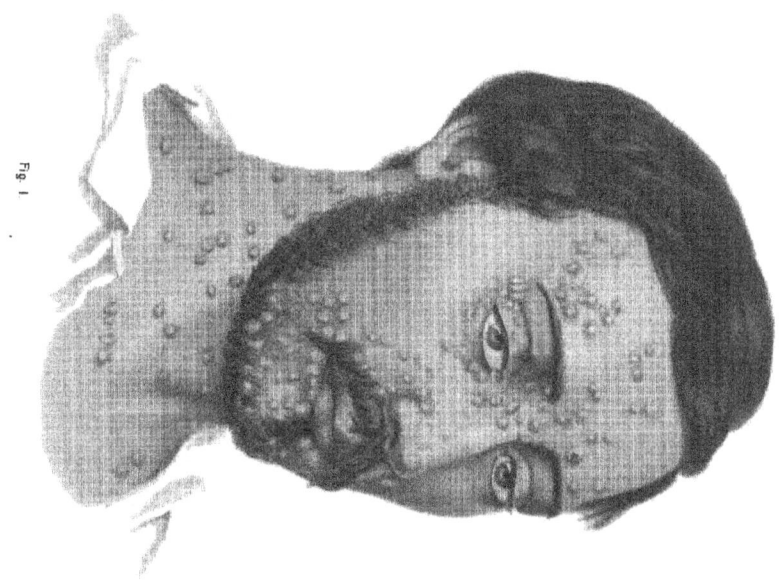

Fig 1

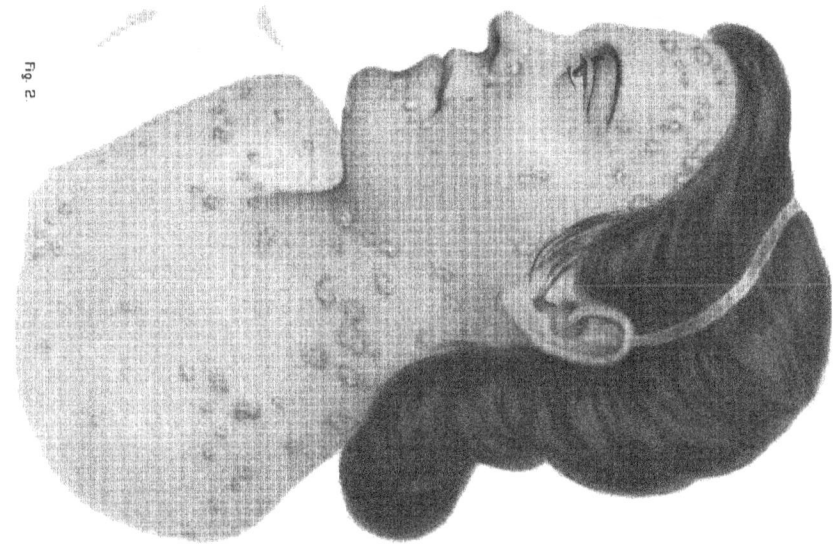

Fig 2

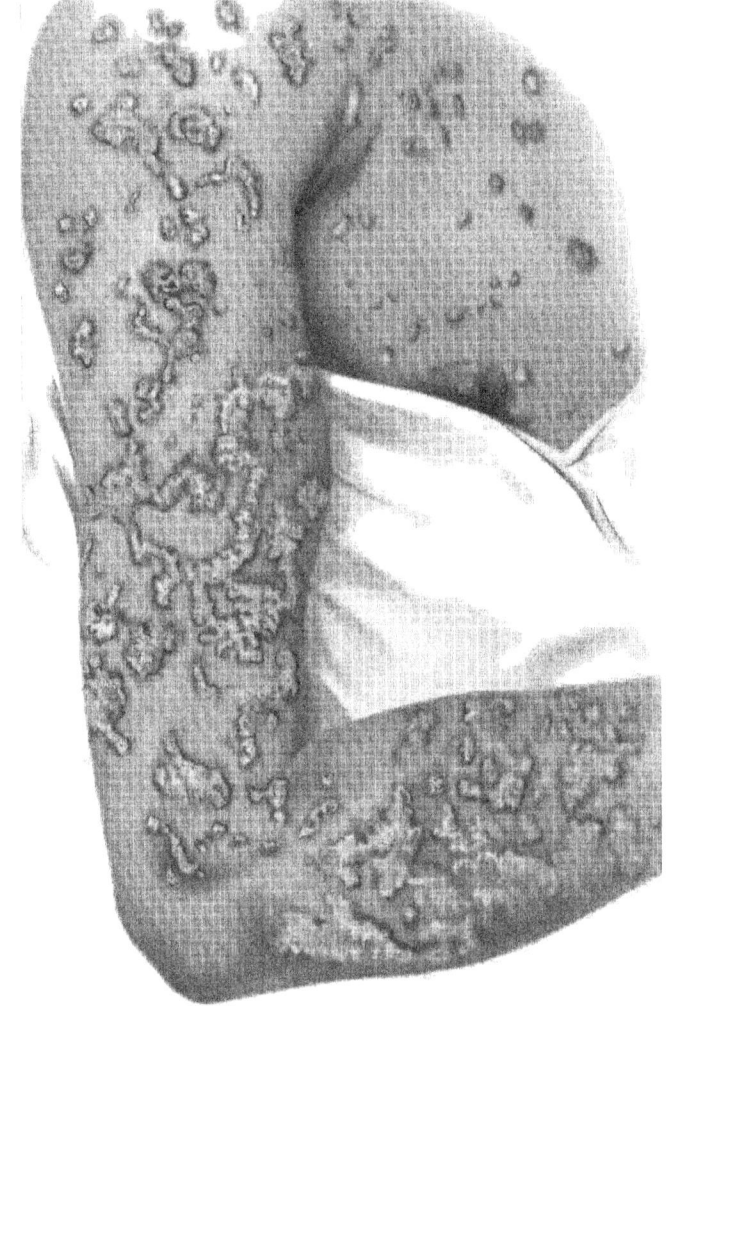

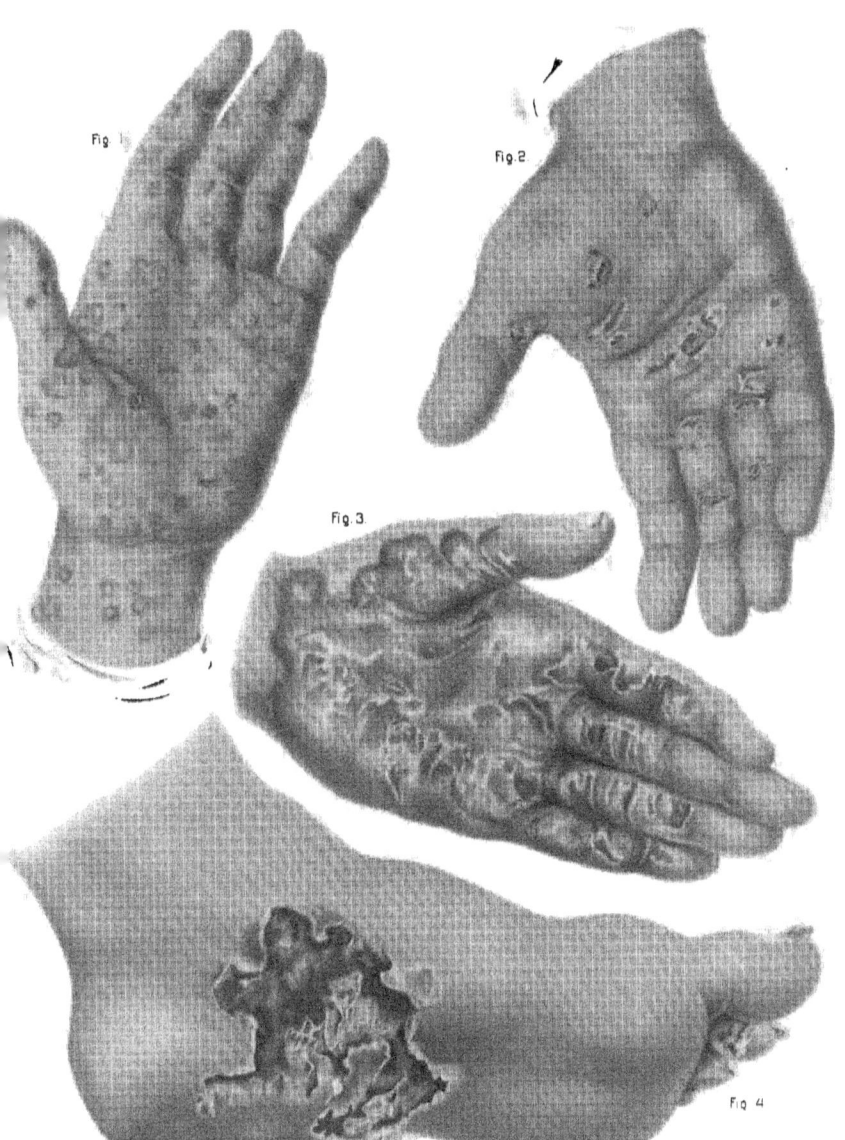

Fig. 1

Fig. 2

Fig. 3

Fig. 4

Plate XIX.

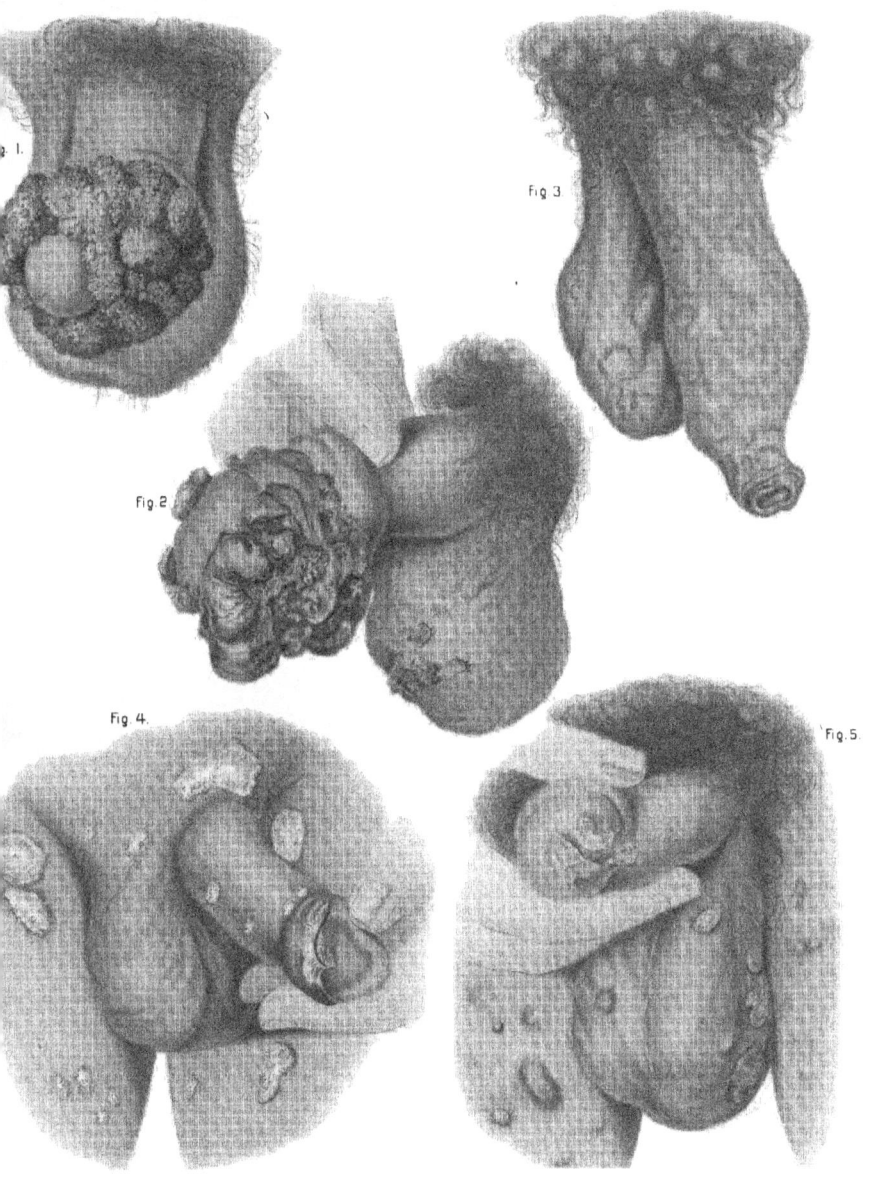

Fig. 1.

Fig. 2.

Fig. 3.

Fig. 4.

Fig. 5.

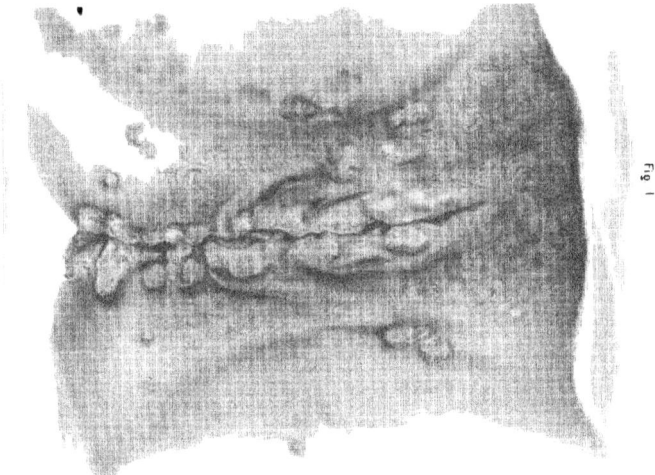

Fig. 1

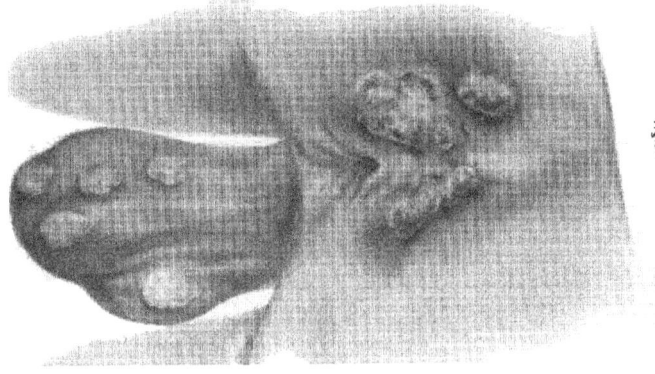

Fig. 2

FASCICULUS V

ATLAS

OF

VENEREAL AND SKIN

DISEASES

COMPRISING ORIGINAL ILLUSTRATIONS AND SELECTIONS FROM THE PLATES OF

PROF. M. KAPOSI, OF VIENNA; DR. J. HUTCHINSON, OF LONDON; PROF. I. NEUMANN, OF VIENNA;
PROFS. A. FOURNIER AND A. HARDY; AND DRS. RICORD, CULLERRIER, BESNIER, AND VIDAL, OF PARIS;
PROF. LELOIR, OF LILLE; DR. P. A. MORROW, OF NEW YORK; DR. E. L. KEYES, OF NEW YORK;
DR. FESSENDEN N. OTIS, OF NEW YORK; DR. J. NEVINS HYDE, OF CHICAGO;
DR. HENRY G. PIFFARD, OF NEW YORK, AND OTHERS.

WITH ORIGINAL TEXT BY

PRINCE A. MORROW, A.M., M.D.,

CLINICAL PROFESSOR OF VENEREAL DISEASES, FORMERLY CLINICAL LECTURER ON DERMATOLOGY, IN THE UNIVERSITY OF THE CITY OF NEW YORK ;
SURGEON TO CHARITY HOSPITAL, ETC.

NEW YORK

WILLIAM WOOD & COMPANY

1888

ATLAS

OF

VENEREAL AND SKIN
DISEASES

It is with special satisfaction the publishers announce that this large and important work, which they have had in contemplation since 1883, is now ready for publication. It has long been recognized by them, from wide observation and acquaintance with similar works published in this country and abroad, that it is impossible for any one author to furnish, from his own collection of cases and illustrations, the most typical and at the same time the best and most lifelike pictures of the many peculiar forms of these diseases. Appreciating the defects and disadvantages arising from this cause, it was determined from the outset to enlist the co-operation, in the making of this ATLAS, of the leading dermatologists and syphilographers of the world. Prominent among them are Profs. M. Kaposi and I. Neumann, of Vienna. The atlas of the former, of venereal diseases, just completed, and that of the latter, of skin diseases, now being issued in parts, will be largely drawn upon in the preparation of this work, the sole right to reproduce them having been granted us by the authors.

Among other distinguished gentlemen who have engaged to contribute selections from their collections of original illustrations may now be mentioned Mr. J. Hutchinson, of London; Profs. A. Fournier and A. Hardy; and Drs. Ricord, Cullerrier, Besnier, and Vidal, of Paris; Dr. P. A. Morrow of New York; Dr. Edward L. Keyes, of New York; Dr. Fessenden N. Otis, of New York; Dr. J. Nevins Hyde, of Chicago; Dr. Henry G. Piffard, of New York.

Other names will be added to this list as the work progresses.

The Editor of the work is Dr. Prince A. Morrow, of New York, who, in addition to plates contributed from his own remarkable collection, will write the treatise on skin and venereal diseases, which constitutes, besides the description of the plates, the text accompanying them.

In this treatise, it is aimed to include chiefly those features which are the most practical, omitting in great measure pathological and other considerations which would be more properly treated of in extended writings, rather than as the adjunct to an Atlas.

In regard to the character of the plates, it may be said, they are believed to be superior to anything of the kind heretofore produced—as accurate in drawing as photographs, and far more distinct, while the coloring faithfully represents nature.

The text is printed from new type, large, clear, and handsome, and the paper is heavy, with a highly finished surface.

Altogether, considering the reputation of the authors, the ability of the editor, the superb execution of the plates, the excellence of the presswork, the high quality of the paper of both text and plates, the large size of the page, etc., etc., this ATLAS OF VENEREAL AND SKIN DISEASES will be the most superb work in medical literature ever published in the English language.

The ATLAS OF VENEREAL AND SKIN DISEASES will be published in fifteen monthly parts, each containing five folio, chromo-lithographic plates, many of them containing numerous figures, all printed in flesh tints and colors, together with descriptive text for each plate, and from sixteen to twenty folio pages of a practical treatise upon venereal and skin diseases; the whole forming, when complete, one magnificent thick folio volume with seventy-five plates, containing several hundred figures, exquisitely printed in colors.

☞ The ATLAS OF VENEREAL AND SKIN DISEASES will be sold by subscription only, at the very moderate price of $2 per part.

WILLIAM WOOD & COMPANY, *Publishers*,

56 AND 58 LAFAYETTE PLACE, NEW Y.

DIAGNOSIS.

Of all the manifestations of syphilis, condylomata lata are the most characteristic, both in their objective characters and in their restriction to certain localities, so that their diagnosis is correspondingly easy.

When the papules are but slightly elevated and confluent, with more or less hyperæmia and redness of the surrounding skin from the discharge, they may be mistaken for eczema rubrum. The eczematous patch does not present the peculiar dirty-gray appearance and the other characters already described as peculiar to the moist papular lesions. In eczema, the itching is more intense, while around the borders of the patch will be seen outlying vesicles or papules.

A mucous patch may become indurated at its base and present a most deceptive resemblance to the primary lesion. The occasional transformation of the chancre *in situ* into a mucous patch has already been alluded to. The differential diagnosis, is not, in this instance, a matter of much practical importance, since both lesions are manifestations of the same poison, pursue the same course, and are amenable to the same treatment.

Condylomata lata should not be mistaken for condylomata acuminata, which are caused by gonorrhœal and other secretions, uncleanliness, and a variety of conditions, but are never of syphilitic origin. Their objective characters are entirely different, as will be observed by reference to Plate XIX. In this Plate, both varieties of condylomata are figured. The acuminate, crested, cauliflower-like excrescences shown in Figures I. and II. are altogether different in appearance from the broad, flat, fig-shaped papules in Fig. V., and also more characteristically shown in Plate XX. A closer examination will reveal marked differences in anatomical structure; the condylomata acuminata are often distinctly pedunculated, with a branched, dendritic character of growth.

These salient points of difference may, however, be obscured or effaced under certain conditions. If the groups of acuminate condylomata are subjected to pressure, as in certain situations from the constant contact of opposing surfaces, the acuminate projections may be flattened out, assuming a mushroom shape with a comparatively smooth surface; on the other hand, local causes of irritation may determine a marked hypertrophy of the papillæ of the flat condylomata, giving to the lesions a decidedly acuminate form, *condylome thymique.*

The history of the case, with the presence of concomitant syphilitic manifestations, will clear up the diagnosis.

PUSTULAR SYPHILIDES.

The pustular type of syphilide, with the various phases which it exhibits in its development and combinations with other forms, represents a large and most important group of the cutaneous manifestations of syphilis.

A reference to the older writers would seem to indicate that the pustular form was formerly a far more frequent expression of syphilis than at present, as a much larger number of cutaneous lesions were grouped under this head. By modern authorities, the proportion is placed at about twenty-five per cent.

No little confusion has been introduced into syphilography by the numerous divisions and subdivisions of the eruptive forms, and the complicated and redundant nomenclature adopted by different authorities to describe the same lesion in different stages of its development. Distinct varieties of syphilides have been recognized according to the resemblance of the specific lesions to those of the simple dermatoses. Thus we have described herpetiform, eczematous, varicelliform, varioliform, acneiform, impetiginous, ecthymatous, rupial, and pemphigoid syphilides. According to the combinations of the elementary forms, the lesions have also been classed as papulo-vesicular, papulo-pustular, vesiculo-pustular, pustular, and pustulo-crustaceous. While

PLATE XXI.

FIG. I.—Syphilis cutanea orbicularis (psoriasiformis). On the skin of the nucha two isolated circles, the size of a dollar, consisting of an uninterrupted, firm, elevated ridge, one and a half lines broad, and brownish-red in color. The skin inclosed within this ridge forms a slightly depressed cicatrix, pigmented faintly in the centre and more darkly toward the periphery. Toward the inside, the ridge is bordered immediately by atrophic skin ; toward the outside, it is separated from the healthy skin by the brownish-red, firm, infiltrated border, above which the epidermis remains unaltered.

Toward the right inferiorly, the ridge is interrupted for a short distance. This gives the diseased surface some resemblance to a kidney shape.

FIG. II.—Syphilis cutanea annularis (psoriasiformis). The circles are partly isolated as in Fig. I., partly joined in groups of twos and threes with serpiginous outlines, some of which become obliterated at the points of contact (right and left shoulder), some (on the neck) run in triple helical curves around each other.

There are, besides, lentil-sized, isolated, brownish-red papules, over which the epidermis is raised (on the trunk) or appears scaly.

In the picture we can trace the developmental steps from the last-named primary efflorescences to the large, isolated and confluent circles.

AFTER KAPOSI.

these names are convenient to express the various forms which the eruption may assume in different cases, it is well to bear in mind that the lines of demarcation between them are sometimes almost imperceptible, and there is often a transition of one into the other.

By most authorities, vesicular syphilides have been distinguished as a separate class. While some lesions may unquestionably present a distinct vesicular appearance at some period of their evolution, the vesicular element is, as a rule, exceedingly transitory, and soon undergoes a pustular transformation. The pustule represents the acme or completion of the pathological process, while the vesicle is only a stage in its development, the same as is exemplified in the mode of evolution of the small-pox pustule.

Most of the lesions of this group are primarily papular; they may at once become converted into pustules, or they may pass through a preliminary vesicular change, which is often so rapid as to be practically indistinguishable. In other forms of pustular syphilide, the lesions are not formed by a purulent metamorphosis of papules, but are distinctly pustular from the first.

Since there is no essential difference between vesicular and pustular syphilides, either in the character of the pathological process or in the subsequent changes, their division into two groups seems quite superfluous. For the sake of simplicity, all the cutaneous lesions of syphilis, whose essential and distinguishing feature consists in an elevation of the epidermis by a fluid exudation, will be classed under the general division of pustular syphilides.

All the lesions of this type originate either from an elementary papular base or from a hyperæmic coppery spot. They may be acuminate, rounded, or flat; they vary in size and in the extent and depth of the purulent softening. The purulent metamorphosis may involve only the apex of the papule or the papular infiltration in its entirety, it may affect only the superficial structure of the corium or it may involve the subcutaneous tissues as well as the true skin.

Pustular lesions may occur among the earlier lesions, the more superficial varieties are ranked among the secondary accidents, while the deeper and more destructive forms may be prolonged into the tertiary stage, and develop coincidently with tubercular and gummatous lesions. Pustulo-crustaceous lesions are the most frequent expressions of malignant precocious syphilis.

The production of pustular lesions is determined rather by the character of the soil than by the element of time. They are much more common among the debilitated and cachectic; individuals whose general health has been undermined by privation, want, and misery are most exposed to this form of eruption. Unquestionably, a local as well as a constitutional predisposition may exist; the skin of certain individuals exhibits a much more pronounced pyogenetic proclivity than that of others, any cause of irritation awakening this tendency to the formation of pus. In some persons, the cutaneous manifestations may exhibit a pustular type from the beginning. Plate XXII. represents a generalized eruption, distinctly pustular, occurring in a woman whose chancre is not yet healed.

From a prognostic point of view, the early occurrence of severe pustular lesions indicates a bad type of syphilis, since it is an expression of a depraved constitutional condition, which will be reflected in the character of the subsequent manifestations. This gloomy prognostic picture is deepened by the fact that mercurial treatment is much less potent in its influence upon pustular than papular lesions. The deep, ulcerative lesions are slow in their involution, and little affected by specifics.

THE ACNEIFORM SYPHILIDE.

Of the entire group of pustular eruptions, the acneiform syphilide is the earliest in its development, the most benign and superficial in character, and the most rapid in its involution.

The anatomical site of the lesions is in the sebaceous glands and hair follicles, and they bear a more or less marked resemblance to those of acne vulgaris. They have a predilection for regions rich in sebaceous glands, as the scalp, face, back of neck and shoulders, and hairy portions

PLATE XXII.

Chancre of the lip, with generalized pustular syphilide.

AFTER NEUMANN.

of the chest. They may, however, have a more general distribution upon the extensor surfaces of the limbs, the buttocks, and the trunk.

The lesions consist of small, conical papules, which soon become surmounted by a pinhead-sized pustule; the suppurative process involves only the apex, and not the totality of the papule.

The pustule is ordinarily of short duration, its contents desiccate, forming a thin scab or crust, which is more or less persistent. After its fall, the surface of the papule becomes the seat of desquamation. The papular infiltration gradually undergoes involution, leaving a small grayish or brownish ecchymotic spot, which is slow in disappearing. Ordinarily this form of syphilide leaves no cicatricial trace; exceptionally, minute depressed scars remain.

The lesions are usually discrete; they may be disseminate or grouped. When the eruption is abundant, it may be preceded by constitutional symptoms of a febrile character. Its duration is about eight weeks, and it does not so readily respond to specific treatment as the papular form. Relapses are prone to occur, but with each recurrence the lesions are less numerous, more apt to assume a grouped configuration with a special localization. The earlier eruptions of this syphilide often develop coincidently with erythematous or papular lesions, mucous patches, etc.; the later outbreaks are often associated with ecthymatous lesions.

DIAGNOSIS.

As the name implies, the acneiform syphilide presents certain analogies, both in its follicular seat, the mode of its development, and its objective characters, with acne vulgaris. In syphilitic acne, the pustular transformation is more superficial, affecting only the summit of the papule, the involution of the pustule is more rapid, the crusts not so deep-seated nor so adherent, the papular base is more dense, distinctly defined, and presents the characteristic coppery coloration. After the elimination of the pustular apex, the syphilitic papule desquamates a number of times, and disappears without scarring. The acneiform syphilide occurs upon the limbs and other parts of the body where simple acne is never seen, and is frequently accompanied with other signs of syphilis.

In acne vulgaris, the lesions are of different sizes, interspersed with comedones, and have an inflamed, non-indurated base; the purulent softening often penetrates to the bottom of the follicle, and may affect the perifollicular structures; it is more furuncular in character, slower in involution, and often leaves permanent scars. Acne vulgaris is most characteristically developed at the period of puberty, and is restricted to certain localities.

The same points of distinction will serve for the differentiation of bromic and iodic acne. In the artificial forms, as in acne vulgaris, the lesions are variously sized, and manifest a special preference for regions rich in sebaceous and hair follicles, but, unlike ordinary acne, they often surpass these habitual limits, and are found upon the hairy portions of the thighs and legs. They are not associated with comedones, and not limited to the young. I have observed a number of cases in which iodic acne has been mistaken for a syphilide.

THE VARICELLIFORM SYPHILIDE.

In this, the rarest variety of the pustular syphilide, the lesions do not have a follicular origin; they may be found upon the palms, where sebaceous glands do not exist; they show a predilection for the forehead, face, and parts where the skin is tender, as upon the flexor surfaces of the limbs and sides of the trunk.

The lesions begin as small, red, infiltrated spots, the epidermis of which becomes elevated by a thin purulent fluid, forming round pustules, surrounded by a well-defined coppery areola. In a day or two, the pustule becomes flattened or depressed in the centre from the partial

PLATE XXIII.

Large pustular syphilide (varicella syphilitica) upon the face, the neck, and the adjoining region of the chest. Near the millet-seed-sized papules are found numerous pea-sized nodules, bearing crusts, disseminated, and crowded in groups. Upon the thorax isolated nodules, the central part of which is depressed below the niveau, covered with a dirty-yellowish crust.

AFTER KAPOSI.

absorption of its contents. The epidermal covering gradually shrinks, and with the dried secretion forms a thin, brownish, closely adherent crust. The fall of the crust shows a dark-red depression corresponding to the slightly exulcerated surface; the loss of substance is rarely so deep as to leave permanent scars. This syphilide is exceedingly chronic in its course, ordinarily one crop of lesions succeeding another during a period of several months; they are exceedingly refractory to the influence of mercurial treatment.

The lesions are usually discrete and scattered, sometimes grouped, exceptionally they may run together, forming by their confluence large pemphigoid lesions (pemphigus syphiliticus adultorum). The rarity of this condition may be judged from the assertion of Zeissl, that he has seen it but once in thirty thousand cases.

DIAGNOSIS.

The occurrence of this syphilide in the form of vesico-pustules, which are distinctly umbilicated and surrounded by an areola, gives it a marked resemblance to varicella and varioloid. It may be distinguished from the non-specific eruptions by the absence of prodromal symptoms and high temperature, the absence of general redness and tension of the skin, and its slower involution. The eruption of varicella appears in successive crops, the lesions are fuller and more tense; they are more numerous and shorter in duration, and there is more heat and itching of the skin. In varioloid, in addition to the headache and backache, the lesions are at first distinctly papular, hard, and shotty to the feel, and appear upon the backs of the hands and wrists, in which location the varicelliform syphilide is not liable to occur.

THE IMPETIGOFORM SYPHILIDE.

In this variety, the lesions are peri-follicular, the infiltration affecting the intermediate spaces between the follicles. The impetiginous syphilide originates from a superficial infiltration, the epidermis becomes elevated by a cloudy, puriform exudation, forming roundish or oval flat pustules, surrounded by a dull-red areola. The pustules soon rupture, and the escaping contents dry into amber-colored, yellowish, or brownish crusts which cover the entire infiltrated surface. Another mode of development is by the confluence of a number of small pustules grouped upon an erythematous base. The pustular element soon disappears, but the crusts are more persistent. The ulceration is usually quite superficial, and does not involve the entire thickness of the corium. After cicatrization, the coppery-red pigmented surface is often the seat of continuous desquamation for a long time, but finally becomes smooth and white.

The impetiginous syphilide does not always pursue this benign course; not infrequently new pustules form at the periphery, and the lesion presents the appearance of an annular elevation of pus around the crust; this purulent ring is soon converted into a crust, and the lesion may continue to enlarge by the development of these concentric zones of ulceration. Instead of this circular mode of extension, the lesion may heal in the centre and at one side, while new foci of ulceration are developed at the other, giving it a reniform or serpiginous shape. In the form which is termed *impetigo rodens* there is not simply an erosion or superficial ulceration, but the destructive process involves the entire thickness of the skin. The removal of the crust reveals an excavation with cleanly cut, abrupt edges, and an uneven pultaceous floor secreting a pus which rapidly concretes into a crust.

By the fusion of contiguous serpiginous lesions, the ulceration may involve extensive surfaces several inches in diameter, and leave large, irregular cicatrices, presenting a great similarity to the ulcero-crustaceous lesions which characterize the tertiary stage of syphilis.

The milder form of impetiginous syphilide has a predilection for the face, scalp and beard, the commissure of the lips, the naso-labial furrows, and the genital region; it may occur upon the

PLATE XXIV.

Syphilis cutanea ulcerosa, representing different lesions of the pustular type (acne syphilitica, impetigo syphilitica, ulcerous syphilide).

AFTER NEUMANN.

arms and trunk, rarely upon the lower extremities. It is not followed by permanent scars, but when attacking the scalp and beard, it frequently destroys the hair follicles and causes alopecia. The occurrence of the severer ulcerative forms always indicates a depraved condition of the general health; they are little influenced by mercurial treatment, and frequently persist for many months. They do not differ essentially in their effects from the deep ecthymatous lesions; they constitute the most frequent expression of malignant precocious syphilis.

DIAGNOSIS.

The impetiginous syphilide may be mistaken for impetigo vulgaris. The objective characters of the lesions are almost identical in certain cases. The lesions of the specific disease are, however, slower and more indolent in their evolution; the crusts do not form so rapidly, they are more dirty or blackish, more porous, more circular in configuration and are not so adherent, the areola persists after the formation of the crusts. In simple impetigo the invasion of the eruption is more acute, and is attended by more or less heat and itching of the skin; the purulent exudation does not so rapidly concrete, and the inflammatory areola disappears when the pustule dries. The crusts are lighter in color, more dense, more brittle, and intimately adherent to their bases. Besides these differential features, the history and the concomitant existence of other signs of syphilis will usually make the diagnosis clear.

Impetigo syphilitica affecting the beard may be mistaken for sycosis. In sycosis the lesions are more deeply seated, often of a furuncular character, and attended with more or less infiltration or brawniness of the skin. In syphilitic impetigo, the hairs fall out and do not grow again. Sycosis rarely leaves permanent bald spots. In syphilitic impetigo, the hairy scalp may be affected at the same time as the beard, which is not the case in sycosis.

Confluent syphilitic impetigo may also be mistaken for impetiginous eczema. In eczema the periphery of the patches is not sharply defined, but indistinct with outlying lesions, the discharge is thinner and the crusts are more yellowish, and the eruption is attended with intense subjective symptoms.

THE ECTHYMATOUS SYPHILIDE.

The ecthymatous syphilide, in its frequency, its long continuance, and its pathological significance, is by far the most important of the pustular group. According to the depth and extent of the ulcerative process, the character of the crusts, etc., it has been divided into two varieties, the superficial and the deep. The superficial form may occur as early as the sixth month and develop coincidently with other secondary manifestations. While it most commonly occurs upon the lower extremities, it may occur upon the brow, the back, and sides of the neck, the inguinal and gluteal regions, trunk and about the anus. The deep variety is usually a late manifestation, except in malignant precocious syphilis. It exhibits the characteristics of the late syphilides in being localized, non symmetrical and destructive in its effects, and is often associated with gummatous lesions. Its favorite location is upon the legs below the knees, but it may occur upon other portions of the body.

The lesions of the ecthymatous syphilide develop from a reddened infiltrated base, in the form of a small round pustule filled with a turbid, puriform fluid, sometimes tinged with blood, surrounded by a sombre red zone. After a few days, the covering of the pustule collapses in the centre, and the desiccated contents form a thin dark-brown scab, beneath which ulceration more or less extensive both in area and depth takes place.

In the superficial variety, the erosion or ulceration is quite superficial and limited in area, it rarely exceeds the dimensions of a ten-cent piece, and the erosion affects only the upper layers of the derma. The crust remains thin, flat, and shows no tendency to develop in the conical stratified coverings which are so marked a feature in another syphilide of this group.

PLATE XXV.

Fig. I.—Rupial syphilide.

Fig. II.—Pustular syphilide of the rupial type, showing vesico-pustules, pustules, and pustulo-crustaceous lesions.. Upon the back and arms is seen a pustular eruption in different degrees of development. Upon the arms especially may be observed the manner in which the eruption progresses from the centre to the circumference. The crusts are set in a circle of epidermis raised up by the pus, this circle itself surrounded by a red areola, the epidermis of which is in process of elevation.

Behind the posterior border of the axilla, the fall of the crusts discloses a group of superficial ulcerations.

At the base of the jaw, near the angle of the inferior maxilla, there is seen a deep ulceration. with prominent perpendicular and slightly everted borders.

FIG. I. AFTER NEUMANN.
FIG. II. AFTER RICORD.

In the course of its involution, the crust becomes raised from its peripheral edges, but remains for a longer time intimately adherent in its central portion. When it is detached, there is seen an eroded or granulating surface upon which a thin crust may re-form, which, upon falling, leaves a smooth, brownish, pigmented spot.

In the deep variety, the primary infiltration is more marked, often papular in character; the ulcerations are more extensive and profound, involving the skin and subcutaneous tissues, sometimes assuming a serpiginous form. If the crust be removed, there will be found a deep punched out or excavated ulcer with an uneven grayish or livid, sometimes gangrenous floor, covered with the débris of disintegrated tissues; the cavity secretes copiously a purulent fluid mixed with blood, which condenses into greenish or blackish crusts. Frequently the crust does not entirely cover the entire ulcer, but is surrounded by a purulent ring. According to Mauriac, "The borders of the ulceration in their centrifugal course surpass those of the crust, which, without being detached, becomes mobile, and seems to float upon the ichorous pus superabundantly secreted beneath it." While the deep ecthymatous lesions are usually discrete and restricted in number and location, they may be numerous, and several ulcers merge together, resulting in a vast surface of ulceration.

The reparative process is marked by a thinning and lessening of the secretion, the thickened borders of the ulcer become effaced, the floor clears up and becomes covered with healthy granulations, and cicatrization advances from the centre to the circumference. After healing of the ulcer, there remains a pigmented brownish spot which is, for a long time, surrounded by a coppery areola, and finally fades into a thin, white cicatrix, more or less depressed. The cicatrices of ecthyma are peculiar and characteristic; when the lesions have been discrete, they are regularly circular in outline; when extensive surfaces have been involved by the confluence of lesions of uneven depth, causing in some places a partial, and in others a complete destruction of the skin, they present the appearance of irregular patches of brown pigmented skin, with remains of its follicular structure, relieved here and there by perfectly white and smooth cicatrices in places where the ulceration has penetrated the skin in its entire thickness.

The chronological place of deep ecthymatous ulcerations is in the intermediary or the tertiary stage. The course of the eruption is slow, often extending over many months. It is most liable to occur in cachectic and debilitated persons, and if long continued, remittent febrile symptoms of a hectic character are apt to supervene.

DIAGNOSIS.

The superficial form of the ecthymatous syphilide bears a certain resemblance to simple ecthyma. In the latter, the suppuration is more superficial, the lesions are more inflammatory, and painful, more uniform in size, and the crust is yellowish-brown.

Deep ecthymatous ulcers occurring upon the legs bear a certain resemblance to the ulcus cruris which develops in connection with varicose veins.

THE RUPIAL SYPHILIDE.

Under the term rupia, most authors describe an ulcero-crustaceous lesion originating from a bulla, characterized by an accumulation of dirty-brown, distinctly laminated crusts covering a flat, superficially ulcerated surface.

There is no well-grounded distinction between ecthyma and rupia, except that in the latter the basic infiltration is not so elevated or pronounced, the ulceration is more superficial, its secretions contain a larger admixture of blood, giving the crusts a dark-brown or blackish color, and the crusts are more distinctly stratified and conical.

The lesion may begin as a vesico-pustule, a bulla, or a pustule surrounded by a zone of serous exudation.   The contents of the pustule usually dry into a greenish-brown or blackish crust.   The initial crust is usually quite small, but as the ulceration extends at the periphery, the crust is continually thickened by the addition of successive layers from beneath, each layer giving it a broader base while increasing its height, until finally the primitive coagulum forms the apex of a cone-like crust, which may be one to two or three inches in diameter.

Not infrequently one segment of the rupial ulcer heals, while ulceration extends at the other ; in this way, the lesions assume a reniform shape, the grayish-brown or blackish crusts, rough and furrowed upon the surface, giving them the appearance of a limpet or oyster shell.

The reparative process is announced by the fall of the crust, a modification of the base of the ulcer, which becomes covered with healthy granulations, and results in a deep red, glazed surface which later becomes white and shining.   The cicatrices are permanent and correspond in outline to the ulcerative process, which may travel over extensive tracts of skin, converting it into cicatricial tissue.

Rupia has a more general distribution than ecthyma, it may occur upon any portion of the body, it is quite common upon the face and neck and the upper extremities.   The lesions vary in dimensions ; their number is usually in inverse proportion to their size ; the ulceration is always comparatively superficial, whether the lesions be small or large.

Rupia may be ranked as a late secondary accident.   In cachectic or debilitated subjects, it may develop much earlier, within the first few months, when it is usually associated with other evidences of malignant precocious syphilis.

ANATOMY OF THE PUSTULAR SYPHILIDE.

The following description, with cut illustrating the anatomical characters of the syphilitic pustule, is taken from Kaposi.

Fig. 9.—(Hartnack, Oc. 3, Obj. 5.)—*a*, Cell infiltrated papillæ in the immediate neighborhood of a hair follicle; *b*, hair; *c*, (pus) cell heaps within the hair follicle *cc'*; *d*, *f*, *g*, normal surrounding dermal tissue; *e*, *f*, infiltrated papillæ and infiltrated corium in the centre of which is a small abscess.

The anatomical conditions which we have represented on former pages as the essential points of all the syphilitic products developing on the common integument are likewise found in the pustular syphilide.   There is a sharply limited, dense infiltration extending through the whole papillary body and into varying depths of the corium, occasionally as far as the subcutaneous cellular tissue; it consists of formed elements which, with some degree of regularity, from the older to the more recent portions progress either towards absorption or towards purulent disintegration.

In the pustular syphilide, the two modes of retrogression are combined in such a way as to give the product externally the pustular character.

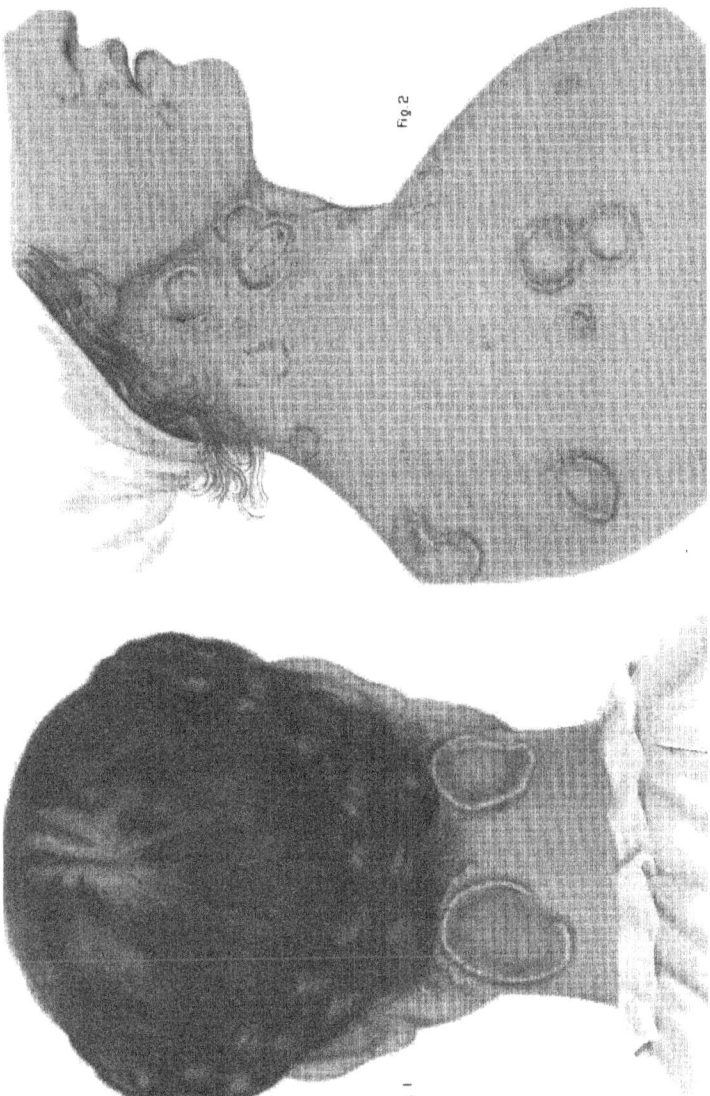

Fig 2

Fig 1

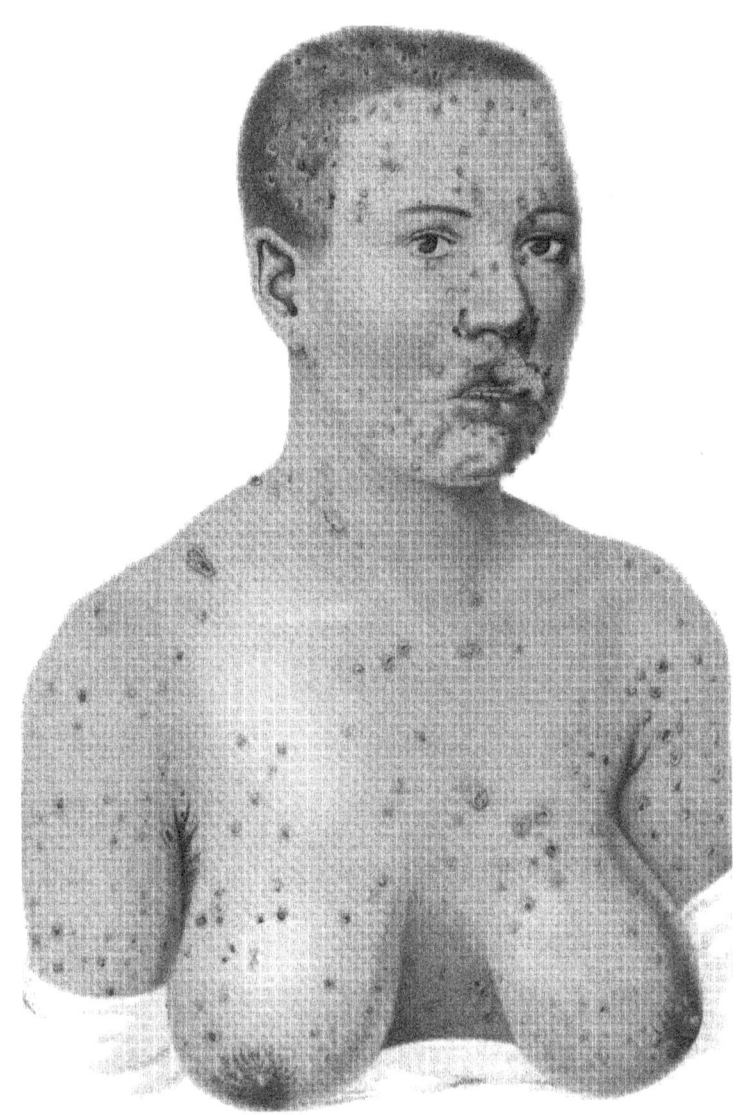

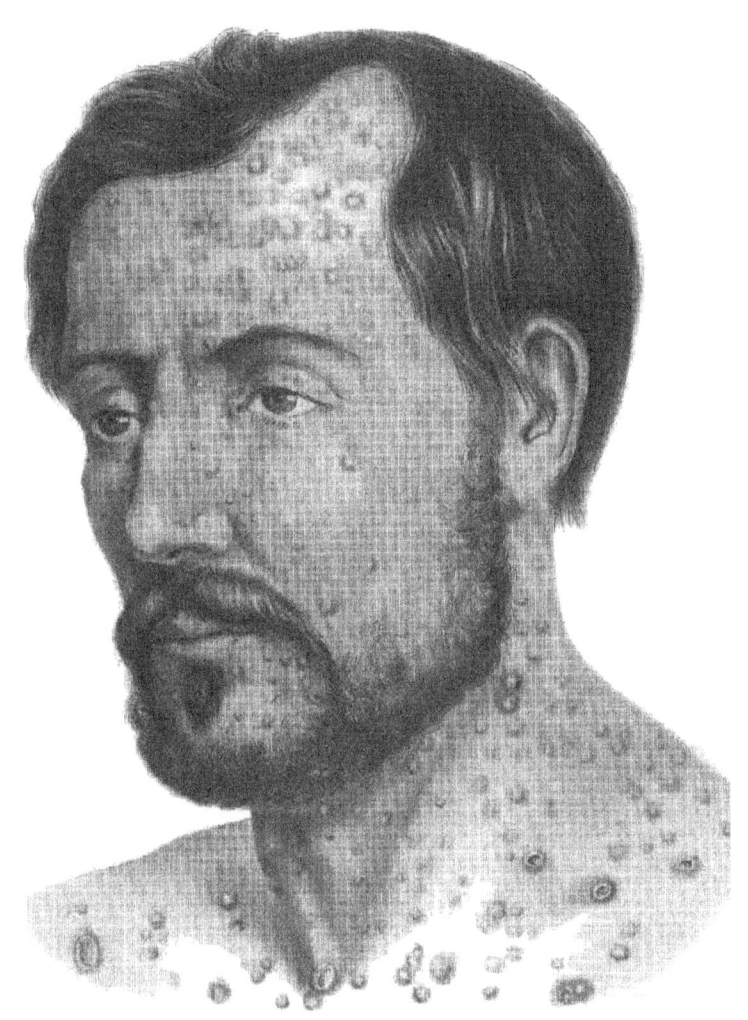

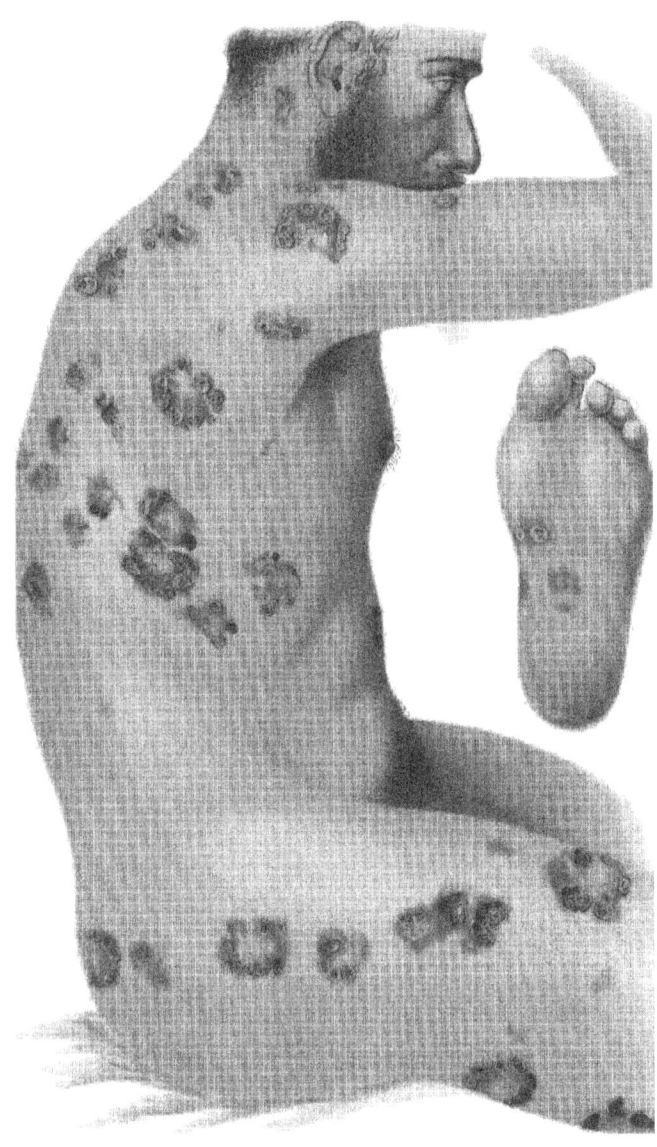

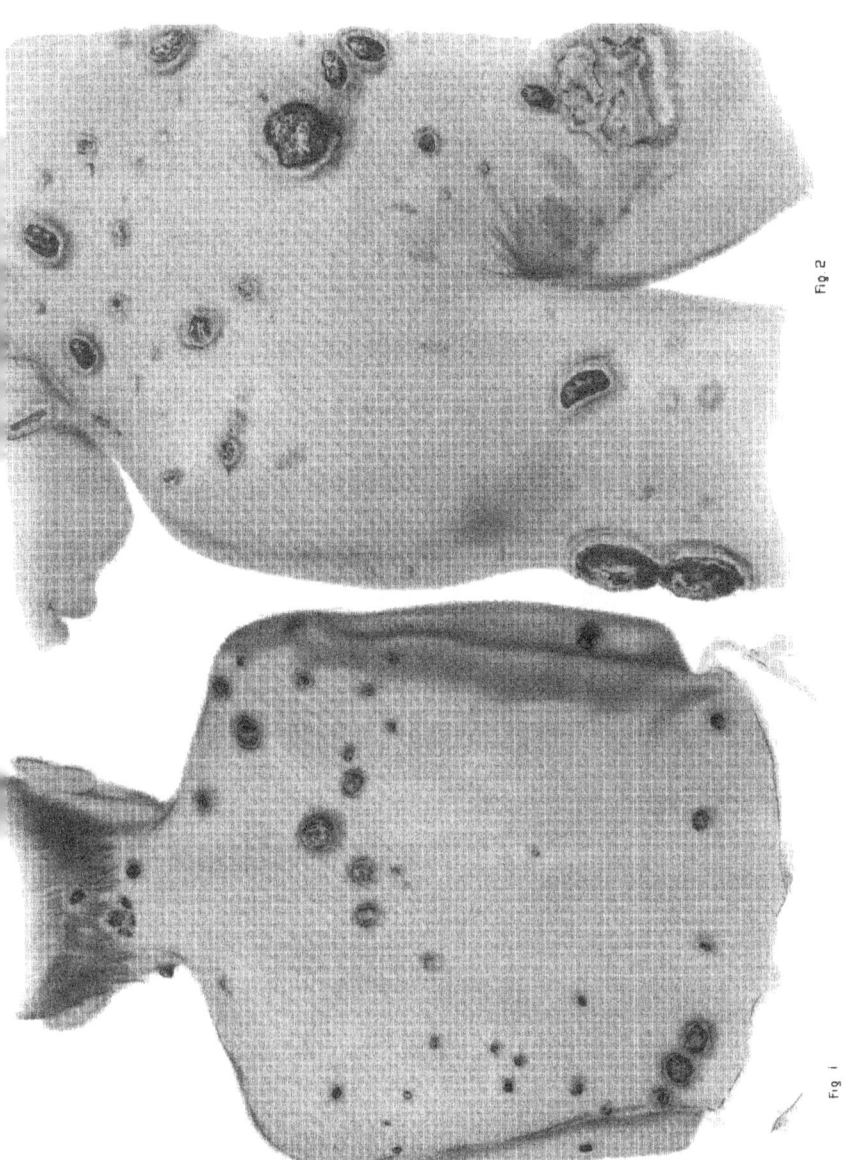

Fig 2

Fig 1

ATLAS

OF

VENEREAL AND SKIN

DISEASES

COMPRISING ORIGINAL ILLUSTRATIONS AND SELECTIONS FROM THE PLATES OF

PROF. M. KAPOSI, OF VIENNA; DR. J. HUTCHINSON, OF LONDON; PROF. I. NEUMANN, OF VIENNA;
PROFS. A. FOURNIER AND A. HARDY; AND DRS. RICORD, CULLERRIER, BESNIER, AND VIDAL, OF PARIS;
PROF. LELOIR, OF LILLE; DR. P. A. MORROW, OF NEW YORK; DR. E. L. KEYES, OF NEW YORK;
DR. FESSENDEN N. OTIS, OF NEW YORK; DR. J. NEVINS HYDE, OF CHICAGO;
DR. HENRY G. PIFFARD, OF NEW YORK, AND OTHERS.

WITH ORIGINAL TEXT BY

PRINCE A. MORROW, A.M., M.D.,

CLINICAL PROFESSOR OF VENEREAL DISEASES, FORMERLY CLINICAL LECTURER ON DERMATOLOGY, IN THE UNIVERSITY OF THE CITY OF NEW YORK;
SURGEON TO CHARITY HOSPITAL, ETC.

NEW YORK

WILLIAM WOOD & COMPANY

1888

ATLAS

OF

VENEREAL and SKIN

DISEASES

It is with special satisfaction that the publishers announce that this large and important work, which they have had in contemplation since 1883, is now ready for publication. It has long been recognized by them, from wide observation and acquaintance with similar works published in this country and abroad, that it is impossible for any one author to furnish, from his own collection of cases and illustrations, the most typical and at the same time the best and most lifelike pictures of the many peculiar forms of these diseases. Appreciating the defects and disadvantages arising from this cause, it was determined from the outset to enlist the co-operation, in the making of this ATLAS, of the leading dermatologists and syphilographers of the world. Prominent among them are Profs. M. Kaposi and I. Neumann, of Vienna. The atlas of the former, of venereal diseases, just completed, and that of the latter, of skin diseases, now being issued in parts, will be largely drawn upon in the preparation of this work, the sole right to reproduce them having been granted us by the authors.

Among other distinguished gentlemen who have engaged to contribute selections from their collections of original illustrations may now be mentioned Dr. J. Hutchinson, of London; Profs. A. Fournier and A. Hardy; and Drs. Ricord, Cullerrier, Besnier, and Vidal, of Paris; Dr. P. A. Morrow, of New York; Dr. Edward L. Keyes, of New York; Dr. Fessenden N. Otis, of New York; Dr. J. Nevins Hyde, of Chicago; Dr. Henry G. Piffard, of New York.

Other names will be added to this list as the work progresses.

The Editor of the work is Dr. Prince A. Morrow, of New York, who, in addition to plates contributed from his own remarkable collection, will write the treatise on skin and venereal diseases, which constitutes, besides the description of the plates, the text accompanying them.

In this treatise, it is aimed to include chiefly those features which are the most practical, omitting in great measure pathological and other considerations which would be more properly treated of in extended writings, rather than as the adjunct to an Atlas.

In regard to the character of the plates, it may be said, they are believed to be superior to anything of the kind heretofore produced—as accurate in drawing as photographs, and far more distinct, while the coloring faithfully represents nature.

The text is printed from new type, large, clear, and handsome, and the paper is heavy, with a highly finished surface.

Altogether, considering the reputation of the authors of the plates, the ability of the editor, the superb execution of the plates, the excellence of the presswork, the high quality of the paper of both text and plates, the large size of the page, etc., etc., this ATLAS OF VENEREAL AND SKIN DISEASES will be the most superb work in medical literature ever published in the English language.

The ATLAS OF VENEREAL AND SKIN DISEASES will be published in fifteen monthly parts, each containing five folio, chromo-lithographic plates, many of them containing numerous figures, all printed in flesh tints and colors, together with descriptive text for each plate, and from sixteen to twenty folio pages of a practical treatise upon venereal and skin diseases; the whole forming, when complete, one magnificent thick folio volume with seventy-five plates, containing several hundred figures, exquisitely printed in colors.

☞ The ATLAS OF VENEREAL AND SKIN DISEASES will be sold by subscription only, at the very moderate price of $2 per part.

WILLIAM WOOD & COMPANY, *Publishers,*

56 AND 58 LAFAYETTE PLACE, NEW YORK.

Only in the most superficial layer of the syphilitic nodule pus is produced which raises the epidermal covering in the shape of a pustule. The purulent disintegration does not progress farther into the substance of the nodule, even where it enlarges beyond its original boundaries. As in the papular (squamous) forms, the greater part of the infiltration is absorbed.

Within the confines of these general anatomical relations, two histological variations occur in the pustular syphilide.

The one corresponds to the efflorescences of the small and the large pustular syphilide, the other to the rupia type.

The efflorescences of the two first-named forms, as a rule, include a hair-follicle with its adnexa, the cellular infiltration constituting the papule being deposited in the tissue surrounding the follicle (papillæ and corium). If pus be formed in the most superficial strata and in the rete, the pustule will appear not only above, but also inside the hair-follicle; cell proliferation and exudation will take place in the region of the external root-sheath. and when excessively developed an intrafollicular abscess will result.

The process is the same as that observed in the nodule of lichen syphiliticus which likewise corresponds to a hair-follicle. A large number of transitional forms from the small-papular to the pustular syphilide are to be found.

In the larger forms of pustule leading to the development of rupia, the histological conditions are still simpler. The cellular infiltration affects a larger territory, but as a rule extends no deeper than the median layer of the corium. The other findings vary materially according to the age and the intensity of the local process. The most essential feature, again, is the occurrence of indistinctly outlined, very granular, opacified, nucleated (pus) cells and free nuclei within the uppermost stratum of the corium and papillary layer, and in the rete, inclosed in a succulent, œdematous, large-meshed tissue or even in free spaces above which the epidermis bulges (as the cover of the pustule). This condition corresponds to the acme of the process for every single point of the diseased patch. It varies, however, according to the age of the local disease. In every case, it corresponds first to the centre of the patch, and in the course of time progresses towards its periphery. At the involved points we observe an atrophied papillary body, or else the thinned corium runs in a straight line, covered with a thin, pigmented or non-pigmented mucous layer.

In vertical sections, the portion of the infiltrated spot which is in a state of purulent disintegration appears sharply demarcated externally, limited by the peripheral portion of the infiltrated tissue (papillæ).

The appearance corresponds exactly to that presented by sections of true syphilitic ulcers from which the one here discussed differs only by the shallowness of the suppurating portion.

THE TUBERCULAR SYPHILIDE.

As before remarked, syphilis is characterized by a certain definite order in the evolution of its lesions, which admits of its division into stages. The modern differentiation of the secondary and tertiary stages is based rather upon the anatomical forms or characters of the syphilitic process than upon the period at which the lesions develop. The tubercle and gumma are recognized as the essential lesions of tertiary syphilis. They possess identical histological characters, differing only in their size and depth of implantation; the tubercle is an intradermic lesion, while the gumma is hypodermic; they are both essentially chronic in their course, and may disappear either by resorption or by a process of softening and ulceration.

Tubercles may be defined as circumscribed, solid infiltrations developed within the skin or mucous membranes, but not extending into the subcutaneous or submucous tissues. The tubercular syphilide presents so many analogies with the large papular syphilide of the late secondary or intermediary stage that it is sometimes difficult to draw distinct lines of demarcation between

PLATE XXVI.

Tubercular syphilide of the face and trunk. The nodules more than pea-sized, arranged in clusters and circles. These latter surround either healthy skin, or a cicatrix which has originated from a formerly centrally situated nodule.

Over the right shoulder, a two-dollar-sized flat cicatrix, its centre traversed by telangiectases, surrounded by an outer pigmented areola—its inner surface pigmentless—the residuum of a heap of nodules which have disappeared.

AFTER KAPOSI.

them, since the one merges almost insensibly into the other.   Tubercles may thus be regarded as a magnified and exaggerated development of papules, the lesions being larger, more globular, and more firm to the feel.   The tubercular infiltration involves the entire thickness of the skin, while the papular infiltration is more superficially seated, the deeper layers of the skin escaping.   The papular syphilide is essentially resolutive, while the tendency of the tubercular deposit is to break down and become ulcerative, although, like the papule, it may disappear by interstitial absorption.

Syphilitic tubercles may appear upon any portion of the cutaneous integument.   Their seats of predilection are the face, especially about the alæ of the nose, the forehead, the lips, the ears, the back of neck and shoulders, and the inferior extremities.   When developed upon the brow and along the margin of the hairy scalp, they constitute one of the varieties of the syphilide known as the *corona veneris.*

The tubercular syphilide consists of small, rounded tumors, of a brownish-red or coppery color, varying in size from a small pea to that of a hazel-nut.   The lesions are rarely generalized or symmetrically distributed ; they may be isolated or occur in groups, and form by their confluence large nappes of infiltration.   When occurring in groups, the tubercles develop in circular or curved segments, and as they disappear by resolution or suppuration, new lesions may spring up at the periphery, resulting in variously sized circular, reniform, or serpiginous configurations.

The course of the tubercular syphilide is essentially chronic, the individual lesions are extremely persistent and slow in involution which, with the successive development of new crops, may extend its duration over a period of months or years.

According to the changes which the lesions undergo in the process of involution, they are divided into two classes, the dry or atrophic and the ulcerative.   In the former, resorption occurs without ulceration ; in the latter, the embryonic elements break down, and are eliminated by the ulcerative process.

The *dry* or *atrophic* variety of the tubercular syphilide may occur comparatively early, sometimes in the second year of syphilis, although its chronological position is from the third to the sixth year or even later.   It often develops by insensible gradations of papulo-tubercles from the papular form and in these cases the lesions are commonly more disseminated and numerous. The number of the lesions is often in inverse proportion to their size.   In the later periods, the tubercles are fewer in number, more voluminous and more apt to be isolated, and occur in groups. The face is a favorite location for this form of tubercular syphilide, the lesions being often prominent and numerous, and forming by their confluence a diffuse nodular infiltration which, with the accompanying thickening and hypertrophy of the skin, gives rise to the peculiar appearance which has been characterized as *leontiasis.*

Upon the palmar and plantar surfaces this syphilide constitutes one of the varieties of the so-called palmar or plantar psoriasis.   Like the papular syphilide of these regions, the lesions are scaly, circularly disposed, the outer borders presenting a scalloped configuration, surrounded by a coppery areola, the base consisting of confluent tubercles.

The infiltration undergoes resolution, through fatty degeneration of the embryonic cells. As this process proceeds the rounded nodules become flattened, less firm to the feel, and finally effaced.   The brownish-red coloration of the skin gradually pales, leaving a grayish pigmented spot, which may desquamate repeatedly and after a long time fades into a whitish cicatricial depression which marks the seat of the tubercle.   The formation of a cicatrix without the intervention of the ulcerative process is caused by the absorption of the normal cell tissue into which the embryonic cells have infiltrated.

When a group of tubercles undergo the retrograde metamorphosis, the older and larger central nodules first disappear, resulting in a cicatricial centre surrounded by a group of tubercles which in time undergo involution.   In this manner are produced the variously shaped cicatricial patches characteristic of this syphilide.

The Ulcerative Variety.—Softening and ulceration of the eruptive elements constitute the distinctive features of the tuberculo-ulcerative syphilide.   In the formative stage, the lesions of

PLATE XXVII.

Fig. I.—Serpiginous syphilide. Upon the left lateral and posterior surface of the neck is seen a serpiginous ulceration which has advanced in a semicircular sweep from the front of the neck backward upon the shoulders. The advancing segment shows groups of crustaceous ulcers, which have become confluent in places, forming a broken crescent of crusts. Anteriorly the surface already traversed by the ulcerative process shows as white cicatricial tissue.

Fig. II.—Serpiginous syphilide. Upon the abdomen of the same patient there is seen an irregularly oval patch, constituted by a continuous ring of crusts, of more or less uniform width and height, surrounding a pigmented cicatricial area. In this patch the ulceration has been more distinctly centrifugal in its mode of advance.

Near the larger lesions are seen two or three smaller cicatrices which mark the remains of groups of ulcerative tubercles.

Fig. III.—Tuberculo-ulcerous syphilide. Upon the back of the shoulders and trunk are seen a large number of pea-sized and larger nodules interspersed among large cicatricial patches, with numerous brownish and whitish macules which mark the seat of former tubercles. Over the large patches the crusts have become detached, showing a grayish-red cicatricial surface with still adherent crusts at portions of the circumferential borders.

Upon the summits of the shoulders are seen two perfectly white cicatrices, which have taken on a keloidal character. The cord-like, raised bands of connective tissue, which form claw-like processes, are indistinctly shown.

Fig. IV.—The bend of the right elbow of same patient is occupied by an extensive cicatricial patch, parts of which are still covered by crusts. At the lower portion of its periphery is seen a cluster of new tubercles. The white, glistening, corrugated character of the cicatrix is well shown. A band of contracting cicatricial tissue has occasioned a permanent flexure of the elbow at the angle seen in the picture.

AUTHOR'S COLLECTION.

this variety do not differ essentially from resolutive tubercles in form, volume, or the configurations they assume. The cardinal distinction is found in their terminal stage. Instead of undergoing a process of interstitial absorption, the tumor softens in the centre, the overlying skin becomes thinned, breaks down, and there is found an open ulcer, discharging a grayish-yellow gummy-like matter, which dries into dirty-yellowish or greenish-black crusts. The ulceration varies in area and depth and in the mode and rapidity of its extension ; it may become serpiginous, boring, or phagedenic.

The tuberculo-ulcerous syphilide may develop at any time from the third to the fifteenth or twentieth year of the disease, or it may occur earlier, as a manifestation of malignant precocious syphilis. According to Jullien, this variety of syphilide represents a proportion of about one-fourth of all the manifestations of tertiary syphilis.

By far the most common localization of the tuberculo-ulcerative syphilide is the region of the face. Next in point of frequency may be mentioned the legs, the neck, and scapular region, the back, chest, and anterior surfaces of the arms. Upon the face the lesions are frequently disposed in concentric rings, which may continue to enlarge by the development of new tubercles at the periphery, and invade large surfaces, presenting certain analogies in its mode of extension and cicatricial centre with the course of lupus, and on this account it has been improperly designated syphilitic lupus. When situated upon the nose, this form of syphilide often destroys the soft tissues and may perforate the cartilaginous structures, causing more or less destruction of the parts and consequent deformity.

When a tubercle becomes broken down and ulcerated, the cavity left by this loss of substance becomes covered with a crust, remains stationary for a certain period, and then cicatrizes. Most often, however, it tends to enlarge by an infiltration around the circular cavity, which in time becomes ulcerated, and this concentric destructive process may continue almost indefinitely.

In by far the larger proportion of cases, the tubercles are agglomerated or grouped in a circular or stellate fashion, the larger central one first succumbing to the necrobiotic process, and the surrounding satellite tubercles next in order. In this case the mode of extension is by the successive development of new tubercles at the periphery, with coincident cicatrization of the centre of the patch. Each ulceration is surrounded by an infiltrated areola, the outer border of the wall of infiltration being harder and more elevated, the sides perpendicular or undermined, the floor grayish, irregular, covered with disintegrated tissues, with a thick, greenish, sanious, sometimes offensive secretion.

DIAGNOSIS.

The only specific eruption with which the dry or atrophic tubercular syphilide is liable to be confounded is the lenticular or large papular syphilide. As before intimated, the difference is chiefly one of degree, the tubercle representing a deeper, larger, more solid infiltration involving the entire thickness of the skin. The papule is distinguished not only by its smaller size and its more superficial anatomical site affecting only the papillary layer, but also by its earlier appearance, its more general distribution, and its more rapid course.

The papules in the course of their involution become flattened and scaly, while the tubercles preserve their firm, globular outline until resolution takes place; they rarely become eroded or scaly. There is often, moreover, a simultaneous development of moist papules of the skin and mucous membranes, which pathological coincidence is rarely seen in the case of the tubercular syphilide, except when it is precociously developed. The differentiation of the two forms of eruption is of secondary clinical importance, since they are both the expression of the same diathesis and amenable to the same treatment.

There are a number of non-specific diseases of the skin with which the tubercular syphilide may be confounded. Chronic eczema of the palms may be mistaken for a tubercular syphilide,

In the latter, the infiltration is more distinctly demarcated, scalloped in outline, and surrounded by a coppery areola. Eczema is more apt to be characterized by fissuring and serous exudation, attended with itching, and does not respond to the influence of specific treatment.

The atrophic variety of the tubercular syphilide may also simulate psoriasis, especially when the lesions are scaly, and developed in ringed patches. In syphilis, the scales are less abundant, not so silvery white, and the outer border of infiltration is made up of closely aggregated but quite distinct tubercles.

The hypertrophic form of acne rosacea has been mistaken for the tubercular syphilide. It may be distinguished by the less distinctly demarcated outline of the lesions which gradually merge into the surrounding skin, the presence of dilated capillaries, and the accompanying hypertrophy of the skin.

Parasitic sycosis may also be mistaken for a tubercular syphilide involving the hairy regions of the face. Sycosis directly involves the hair follicles, the hairs are loosened and broken by parasitic infiltration, and the tubercles are less coppery in color, of a more intense vivid red; they readily suppurate and are limited to the beard, while syphilitic tubercles appear upon the non-hairy parts. Microscopical examination of the affected hairs would determine the question of its parasitic nature.

The tubercular syphilide may bear a marked resemblance to leprosy, especially when its lesions are hypertrophied and situated upon the brow, constituting the appearance known as syphilitic leontiasis. It may be distinguished by the conservation of the cutaneous sensibility, the absence of anæsthetic patches, of swelling of the nerve trunks, etc., the color of the tubercles, and the coincident general and local phenomena.

Lupus vulgaris is often confounded with this syphilide, especially when the tubercular infiltration is localized in the regions for which lupus shows a predilection. The regions of preference for lupus are the face, especially the nose and cheeks, and the extremities; it rarely surpasses these limits, while the tubercular syphilide may develop upon any portion of the surface. It has been observed that, when situated upon the trunk or extremities, lupus has a tendency to become serpiginous. The tubercles of lupus are pinkish, translucent, or of an apple-jelly color, more irregular in outline, and often studded, according to Besnier, with minute colloid masses resembling milium. Lupus generally appears in early life, before puberty, tubercular syphilis in persons more advanced in years. The lupus process is much slower in evolution, its sluggish development and progress, as compared with syphilis, constituting a cardinal point of distinction.

Like the atrophic tubercular syphilide, the nodules of lupus may become atrophied and gradually disappear through a process of interstitial absorption without open ulceration; also like the ulcerative tubercular syphilide, the lupus nodules may soften, break down, and result in the formation of open ulcers. Lupus ulcers are of irregular shape, not so sharply cut, the edges are softer, and readily bleed. Syphilitic ulcers are rounder, deeper, and always surrounded by a coppery pigmented areola. The secretion of lupus ulcers is less abundant, and the crusts are less bulky and do not present the brownish or greenish-black color characteristic of syphilis.

The process of cicatrization is exceedingly slow in lupus, and the scars are not thin and smooth as in syphilis, but thick, dense, hard, and puckered, and often adherent to the tissues beneath.

Notwithstanding these points of difference, it may oftentimes be extremely difficult to distinguish between lupus and syphilis, especially in the region of the nose. Both may occasion considerable destruction of tissue and consequent deformity. In lupus, the ulcerative process always proceeds from the surface to the deeper structures, and more often respects the cartilaginous and bony structures. When the alæ and tip of the nose are destroyed, these parts present the appearance as if they had been nibbled or gnawed away, and the nose is sharpened as well as shortened. Syphilitic ulceration more often begins deeply in the bony structures and extends to the superficial parts, and the organ may be destroyed in its totality.

The prompt curative influence of specific treatment in the case of syphilis, and its inefficacy against lupus, constitutes an important differential sign.

ANATOMY OF THE TUBERCULAR AND GUMMOUS SYPHILIDES.

The minute anatomical appearances of the tubercle and gumma have been carefully studied by Kaposi, and his description is here reproduced.

In view of what we have stated regarding the anatomical relations of the syphilitic products on the skin in general, and the subsequent additional remarks in connection with the several forms, little remains to be said as to the anatomical peculiarities of the tubercular syphilide.

What has been shown with regard to the histological conditions of the syphilitic papule is true likewise for the larger tubercle. It is merely the greater extent of the cellular infiltration in width and into the depth of the skin which we have to consider here. Otherwise, it is the same perishable elements which constitute the infiltration and show in the older (central) portions at the earliest period the granular opacity, an almost "dusty" appearance, while those at the periphery still permit the recognition of a nucleus which takes a distinct carmine stain and of a normally granular protoplasm (Fig. 10).

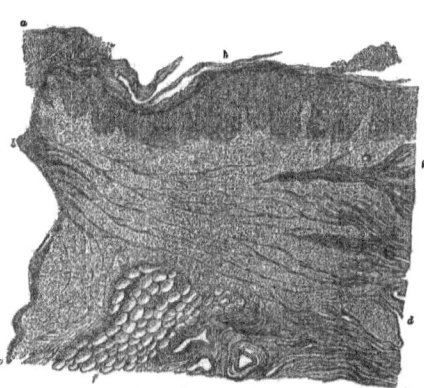

FIG. 10.

Over the last-named portions, *i. e.*, the peripheral parts of the tubercle (Fig. 10, *h c*), the papillæ are well preserved, distinctly marked from the mucous layer; the cells of the latter, besides, largely interspersed with small granular elements or, themselves enlarged, provided with several nuclei.

As the older atrophic portions are approached, and on the latter, the demarcation between rete and papillæ becomes indistinct, the penetration of the foreign elements continues from the papillæ into the former, the rete then becomes narrower, and finally is altogether absent, when the cell-infiltrated corium is laid bare: beginning of the *ulceration.*

Up to this point the appearance does not differ from that of a superficially exulcerated papilla or the chancre sclerosis.

As the ulceration progresses, there arises a loss of substance which varies in depth, but which, even in microscopic sections, reproduces the naked-eye appearance (Fig. 10, *a b*), and, with reference to its possible depth and width in general, is determined by the cellular infiltration. This, of course, in the case of a gummous tubercle, must extend into the subcutaneous cellular tissue, may closely surround and fill all the included structures, glands, and follicles, crowd in between the fat lobules (Fig. 10, *f*), enveloping the vessels, and though pretty sharply demarcated peripherally (Fig. 10, *d e*), may also reach along the vessels variable distances beyond the infiltrated focus.

The abrupt, slightly undermined border, which is raised above the level (Fig. 10, *a b*), as well as the further limiting wall (Fig. 11, *b k*), are formed by a variably thick layer of a granular, crumbly mass, whose elements differ from the pus cells of healthy granulating wounds, and behind which the cellular infiltration of the gummous node is recognizable

This layer is the expression of the advancing necrobiosis of the specifically infiltrated tissue, and gives to the surface of the ulcer the well-known " lardaceous," " unclean " macroscopic appearance.

As regards the subcutaneous gummous tubercles, the conditions are somewhat different, but, as we shall see, only in so far as the manner and the progress of their metamorphosis is determined by their deeper seat and their greater bulk, for which reason we might expect some peculiarity in comparison with the tubercle of the skin.

Repeatedly the attempt has been made to claim for " true " gummata histological qualities which were to correspond with their clinical peculiarity and, as it were, serve as a corollary, and to separate them accordingly, in view of their histological conditions, as tumors of a specific nature by a special name (syphiloma) from other syphilitic tubercular formations.

For similar reasons, *i. e.*, the microscopical structure, the condition of its constituent formed elements, others have denied the specific nature of gummous nodes, and sometimes compared them with tubercular nodes, sometimes pointed out their almost exact resemblance to the tubercles of lupus, scrofula, etc.

It is certain that the peculiar clinical behavior of the gummous tubercle is based on a special histological character which obviously can be defined with difficulty. Virchow's words, however, are quite correct: " Specific elements, and a structure so constant that in every case we would be able, with absolute certainty, to make a diagnosis from them, are not present in gummata. At all events, the structure and the general arrangement of the tubercle are peculiar in a higher degree than the single elements, in which again the perishable nature, the tendency to early disintegration, is of greater significance than the form and development of the cells themselves."

The histological composition of the tubercle, and the future fate of its constituent elements, which unquestionably manifests itself pretty clearly in their appearance, structure, and course, together give the character of the gumma, which withal, as compared with similar formations due to other causes, may be quite peculiar.

In the first place, the gummous tubercle must be considered in its recent stage, where it is still in process of formation, at all events in its peripheral portions which as yet show no tendency to retrogression.

Here I would emphasize what I have said already as to the general characteristics of the syphilitic products, that a pin-head sized nodule of " lichen syphiliticus " in its composition, course, and nature is absolutely identical with a walnut-sized gummous tubercle. Both consist of a uniform small-cellular infiltration of the affected tissue, the latter presenting by no means the appearances of inflammatory infiltration—serous succulence, marked vascular dilatation, large meshes—but, on the contrary, a dense, rather dry composition. I fully coincide with Virchow in the statement that the broad condyloma is "nothing else but a slightly developed gummous tumor."

But as the nodule, the papule in its entirety, so far as it consists of new-formed elements, disintegrates, being absorbed or thrown off, during which even the infiltrated basis substance degenerates more or less and atrophies, so does gumma. I am altogether unable to agree with some authors who maintain that the peripheral part of the gumma changes into fibrous connective tissue, into a cicatrix, while the inner portion becomes limited as a spherical tubercle, which alone is said to undergo the retrograde metamorphosis into mucous softening, fatty degeneration, or cheesy thickening. I repeat that the whole of the gumma, like the smallest syphilitic nodule, undergoes retrogression, atrophy, suppuration, or liquefaction, and never changes into permanent connective-tissue formation.

THE GUMMOUS SYPHILIDE.

The gumma is the exclusive product of syphilis and constitutes the deepest and latest, as well as the rarest of the cutaneous manifestations. Gummata rarely develop before the third or fourth year of syphilis, sometimes not until twenty, thirty, or forty years after the chancre. Fournier has reported a case of a gumma occurring in a man seventy-two years of age, whose syphilis dated back fifty-five years. On the other hand, in malignant syphilis, gummata may appear as precocious accidents, within the first year of syphilis. Mauriac has reported cases in which large nodular neoplasms with all the typical characters of gummata, which softened and were converted into deep cavernous ulcers, developed within a few months after the appearance of the chancre.

This lesion is deeply seated in the subcutaneous and submucous tissues, often involving the muscles, periosteum, and bones. The skin freely glides over the tumor, and is involved only secondarily, and always by ulceration, after preliminary softening and breaking down of the neoplastic elements. Their favorite seat is upon the lower extremities about the ankles, their next most predilected region is the face, especially over the forehead and hairy scalp. They may develop upon any portion of the cutaneous surface, except perhaps the palms and soles, which enjoy an almost absolute exemption.

Gummata consist of nodular or solid tumors, usually globular or oval, sometimes irregularly flattened, their form being determined by the anatomical relations of the tissues in which they are implanted. They are usually rounded or globular where the cellular tissue is loose and abundant, flattened upon the cranium, elongated or acorn-shaped upon the fingers. They are more or less distinctly circumscribed by the condensation of the connective tissue at their periphery which forms a limiting membrane. They vary in size from a pea or cherry to that of an egg or an orange, they are usually described as of the volume of a nut. When deeply seated or flattened, they may cause no marked projection above the surface. In number they are usually quite few, ordinarily comprised within the limits of from one to a dozen, exceptionally they may be numerous. Lisfranc counted one hundred and sixty upon the arm of a patient. As a rule, the more abundant the tissues the smaller they are, with a tendency to disappear by resolution.

Fournier reported a case in which a single tumor measured fourteen centimetres in length, eight to ten in breadth, with a thickness varying from two to six centimetres. Gummata are characterized by an exceeding slowness of evolution, they are essentially aphlegmatic and indolent, freely movable and insensitive to pressure, they are not painful except in rare cases from pressure upon a cutaneous nerve, and occasioning no marked constitutional disturbance. They may continue to recur in successive crops during a long series of years, or they may represent the awakening into activity of the syphilitic diathesis after it has remained dormant for years.

The gumma may be gradually absorbed without ulceration. This mode of involution is more apt to take place when the tumors are small, numerous, and of early occurrence. In the large proportion of cases, however, the gumma disappears by a process of softening and ulceration.

In the evolution of the gumma, three principal stages may be distinguished: the formative, the ulcerative, and the reparative. In the formative stage, the tumor grows gradually until it attains its full development, appearing as a hard, solid, hypodermic nodule, freely movable, and over which the skin freely glides. In this condition it may remain without perceptible change for weeks or months.

The stage of ulceration is characterized by a softening of the centre of the tumor, which loses its firm consistence and gives a deceptive indication of pus. Coincident with this softening of the tumor the overlying integument becomes inflamed, reddened and thin, and finally is perforated at its most prominent point. Through this circular opening exude the liquefied morbid products, consisting of a thick, viscid, gummy-like material. The sphacelated connective tissue, resembling the core of a furuncle, still remains attached to its subcutaneous connections.

PLATE XXVIII.

Fig. I.—Ulcerous syphilide. Upon the right buttock and right upper thigh of a negro patient is seen an extensive ulceration of irregular shape, quite deep in places.

The photograph from which the drawing was made was not taken until after the reparative process had begun; numerous evidences of cicatricial repair are seen in the base and margins of the ulceration.

Upon the upper portions of both buttocks, extending over the crests of the ilii and upon the right lower limb are seen cicatrices which mark the existence of ulcerations which had occurred two years previously. The cicatrices show centrally a polished white surface like old ivory, contrasting with the surrounding deep black pigmentation.

Fig. II.—Ulcero-Serpiginous Syphilide of the Inguinal Region. *Gummata exulcerata.*

Numerous ulcers, some of them extending rather deep, partly isolated and roundish, partly coalesced into larger, irregularly curved or crescentic sores. They form mainly an uninterrupted series in a curved line which runs from the symphysis along the left groin, over the inner surface of the thigh (in its upper third), and inward and upward to the attachment of the scrotum; it incloses a completely white cicatricial portion. Within the series may be recognized groups which run circularly around corresponding, partly cicatricial, partly ulcerous centres.

The convex border of the isolated ulcers, as well as that of those joined into groups and circles, is directed toward the periphery of the entire morbid patch; at the same time it is steep, sharply demarcated, covered with lardaceous deposits, and partly undermined. The adjoining skin is dark bluish-red and swollen.

The integument of the pubes is sprinkled with cicatrices having a white centre and pigmented periphery, and is denuded of hair.

FIG. I.—AUTHOR'S COLLECTION.
FIG. II.—AFTER KAPOSI.

The gummatous ulcer thus left is a circumscribed, more or less deep excavation, circular in form, with thickened and adherent borders; the walls undermined, the floor uneven, covered with disintegrated tissue, which is gradually detached and thrown off with the sero-purulent secretion secreted by the walls of the cavity in the form of a slough or shreds. Two or more contiguous ulcers may unite, the resulting ulceration exhibiting a bicyclic contour. In some cases a number of gummata are disposed in a group, each of them opening by a single orifice; as these enlarge by ulceration, the intervening borders are swept away, and the cavities unite, forming a vast excavated ulcer.

When the elimination of the necrobiotic tissue is completed, the reparative process usually begins. It is marked by a clearing up of the floor of the ulcer, which becomes covered with healthy granulations, the thickened borders become effaced, and cicatrization is effected by a filling up of the cavity. The resulting cicatrix is usually smooth, more or less depressed, white in the centre, pigmented at the periphery, circular in outline, corresponding to the area of the ulceration. The depression of the cicatrix bears a definite relation to the depth of the destructive process; it is frequently adherent to the parts beneath, especially when situated over a bony surface.

The course of the gummatous ulcer may be modified by the accident of its location and the intercurrence of certain morbid processes, such as inflammation, gangrene, phagedenism, etc. These complications are often serious in their consequences. The lower extremities constitute the seats of predilection of gummy tumors, especially the upper and middle third of the leg. Here they exhibit a greater rapidity of development than elsewhere, and are frequently the seat of inflammatory complications. They quickly break down and form open cavities, which are painful and phlegmonous, interfering with locomotion. They are attended with more or less œdema, causing an increase in the size of the limb, the integument becomes hard, brawny, and often thrown into folds about the ankles, presenting an elephantiasic appearance. Gummatous ulcers of the legs, when complicated with phagedenism, may destroy the aponeurosis of the leg, laying bare the muscles, or may penetrate more deeply, destroying all the subjacent tissues and denuding the bones.

In the groins and about the genital region, and the inner portions of the thighs, gummatous ulcers derive an additional clinical significance from the fact that they may be mistaken for chancroidal ulceration. They may cause deep and extensive destruction of important organs, erosion of important vessels, with dangerous and even fatal hemorrhage.

Upon the buttocks the ulcers are apt to be deep and of large dimensions, owing to the abundance of the connective-tissue development in this region.

Gummatous ulcers affect the posterior rather than the anterior surface of the trunk. Upon the lower abdomen they are exceedingly rare. Gumma of the female breast has been mistaken for a scirrhous tumor, but may be distinguished by the non-retraction of the nipple and the absence of enlarged glands in the axilla. Gummata of the face are often followed by deforming cicatrices, salivary fistulæ, ectropion, etc. When situated upon the forehead, they may destroy the external table of the frontal bone and involve the frontal sinuses.

Upon the hairy scalp gummy tumors may occasion considerable loss of substance. The external table or the entire thickness of the skull may become necrosed and the dura mater exposed.

DIAGNOSIS.

In the diagnosis of gummata which occur at an advanced age of the diathesis, representing the final results of the syphilitic process, the history is often obscure, and little light is thrown upon the nature of the disease by the presence of concomitant specific lesions. The patient rarely associates his existing trouble with an unfortunate experience of, it may have been, ten to twenty years before, and the occurrence of which may have been forgotten. And yet there is, perhaps,

PLATE XXIX.

Fig. I.—Serpiginous, ulcerous syphilide.

A curved line—springing from right inner canthus and passing over the malar region to the auricle, upward over the right temporal region, along the border of the hairy scalp, over the forehead to the left side, thence downward to the middle of the left upper lid, thence inward to the root of the nose and the right upper lid—is marked by a continuous series of ulcers varying in size from that of a lentil to that of a penny; they are partly covered with crusts, and either isolated or confluent. The territory thus circumscribed is sprinkled with some white and some pigmented cicatrices and smaller ulcers, while the adjoining exterior skin appears dark red for some distance. The right upper lid is œdematous and drooping.

Fig. II.—Ulcerous syphilide. On the occiput, on the right side of the head near the temple, and at the border of the hairy scalp and forehead, are three ulcers, each the size of a dollar; they are roundish and limited by steep, infiltrated, partly undermined borders; over the right parietal bone is a larger ulcer, formed by the coalescence of several others, with scalloped borders. There are, besides, single disseminated, pea-sized nodules covered with yellowish-brown crusts, and throughout the entire hairy scalp scattered reddish-brown flat tubercles and macules.

AFTER KAPOSI.

no other manifestation of syphilis in which a mistake in diagnosis has led to more deplorable results. Numerous instances are on record in which surgical interference with the knife or cautery
has been invoked to remove a gummatous lesion which would have readily and painlessly disappeared under the influence of iodide of potassium. It may, therefore, be laid down as a safe and
judicious rule, in the case of all lesions the characters of which are so doubtful as to warrant a
suspicion of their possible specific nature, to always employ a preliminary specific treatment before
resorting to severer surgical methods. Especially is this true of doubtful lesions of the face,
breast, and genital regions.

A gummy tumor is so characteristic in its mode of evolution that a mistake could by no
possibility occur if the various stages of its progressive metamorphosis came under the physician's observation. Unfortunately, however, this process is ordinarily too slow and chronic to
afford this opportunity, and serious difficulties of diagnosis may arise. In either stage, the
gumma may be mistaken for certain non-specific lesions; in the stage of tumefaction, it may
simulate various solid tumors, as lipoma, fibroma, sarcoma, etc., or an enlarged ganglion; in
the stage of softening it presents certain analogies with an ordinary abscess, a suppurating
gland, furuncle, carbuncle, etc.; in the final stage of ulceration it may bear a most deceptive
resemblance to various ulcerative lesions.

Lipoma may be differentiated from a gummous tumor by its less rounded, more flattened
and diffuse form; it is softer in consistence and more compressible, and is not so apt to be multiple. Sarcomatous tumors are less spherical, with a predilection for the trunk; the overlying
skin is changed in color, bluish or reddish-brown, and they do not disappear by absorption.

The *ulcus cruris* from varicose veins may be mistaken for a syphilitic ulcer. In the case
of the former, the existence of varicose veins as a predisposing cause may be traced, the skin is
hypertrophied from infiltration, darkly pigmented from the long-standing congestion, and often
eczematous; their favorite location is the lower third of the leg about the ankles, while syphilitic
ulcers occur most commonly in the middle or upper third.

An ulcerated gumma, especially when involving the tongue or genitals, may be mistaken
for epithelioma. Epithelioma is characterized by its development, usually from a warty base, its
slow progress, often remaining stationary for a long period. When it breaks down, it shows an
irregular, hard, granulating base, with warty, papillomatous excrescences. Gummatous ulcers are
commonly multiple, circular or ovoid in outline, deep and excavated. A carcinomatous ulcer is
single, irregular in outline, the edges hard and everted, the base fungating; the secretion is
scanty and offensive, and does not concrete into crusts. The ulceration always begins in the skin,
and extends to the deeper parts, and its superficial area is large in proportion to its depth. Implication of the neighboring lymphatic ganglia, and the cancerous cachexia which ultimately supervenes, constitute important diagnostic signs. The subjective symptoms are more pronounced,
pain of a lancinating character being a common symptom. Epithelioma is essentially a condition
of middle life or advanced age, while gummatous ulcers may occur at any age. In cases where
the differential clinical signs are doubtful, the microscope will clear up the diagnosis.

THE SERPIGINOUS SYPHILIDE.

A large number of syphilitic lesions are characterized by a peculiar creeping tendency in
their course and mode of extension. It has been seen that many of the circinate and psoriasiform
lesions of the papular type are formed by the development of new papules at the borders of a patch
while resolution occurs in the centre. In the same manner, the dry or atrophic variety of the
tubercular syphilide may creep over large surfaces. The term "serpiginous" syphilide is, however, restricted in its application to lesions whose mode of advance is by ulceration at the
periphery with coincident cicatrization of the centre. The ambulant character of the ulcerative

PLATE XXX.

FIG. I.—Syphilis cutanea ulcerosa et vegetans. Upon the right leg of a sixty-year-old man, a long, thick, dark-brown prominent crust upon an extensive, steep-edged ulcer, surrounded by a broad, red infiltrated areola. Upon the back of the foot and toes, partly red, glandiform excrescences which are arranged in heaps, and, toward the healthy skin, are limited by a border of infiltration, the ulcers partly exposed or covered with dirty dark-brown crusts.

Fig. II.—Ulcero-gummous syphilide of the left leg in a twenty-two-year-old young man, suffering with gummata upon other regions of the body. Upon a terrain traced by numerous cicatrices are found partly hazelnut-sized prominent nodules, partly round and half-moon shaped ulcers of different depths.

AFTER KAPOSI.

process, rather than the histological characters of the lesions in which it originates, constitutes the basis of its nomenclature.

Accordingly as it originates from a pustule, a tubercle, or a gumma, it has been variously designated as pustulo-ulcerous, tuberculo-ulcerous, gummato-ulcerous, etc.

The serpiginous syphilide may be superficial or deep; it may develop *d'emblee* without preceding neoplastic infiltration, or it may, and most frequently does, result from a breaking down of tubercular or gummatous deposits. Its chronological position is among the late manifestations, generally occurring from the second to the twentieth year; it may, however, develop as early as the fourth month of syphilis.

The superficial serpiginous syphilide commonly originates from a single pustule or tubercle, or a number of contiguous crustaceous pustules may run together forming a round or oval patch covered with crusts.

The mode of extension is as follows: As the ulcerative process advances at the periphery, there is formed a ring of ulceration around the encrusted centre, the purulent secretion rapidly condenses into yellowish, greenish or blackish crusts which cover the ulcerated furrow. The central portion of the crust falls off, leaving a pigmented cicatricial base surrounded by a rim of crusts, beyond which extends a coppery red infiltrated areola. This in turn becomes the seat of ulceration, and as the coincident central cicatrization keeps pace with the peripheral ulceration, we thus have a continually widening circle of ulceration inclosing a constantly increasing area of scar tissue. In this way the migratory ulceration may sweep over large surfaces.

Instead of this strictly centrifugal mode of extension, one segment of the circle may entirely heal, while the ulceration advances at the other portions of the circumferential border, producing crescentic, reniform, or horseshoe-shaped patches.

The course of the serpiginous syphilide is essentially chronic when undisturbed by treatment. A definite end of the process may be determined by the internal use of specific treatment, supplemented by appropriate local medication.

Instead of the tubercular ulcerations uniting and forming a continuous furrow of ulceration, they may remain isolated and separated by cicatricial tissue or healthy skin, forming a broken or fragmented circle. Both forms may be represented in the same patient. In Fig. I., Plate XXVII., taken from a photograph of a patient recently under my observation in Charity Hospital, there is seen upon the left lateral and posterior surfaces of the neck a number of ulcerating tubercles, forming a patch which advances from the front of the neck backward upon the shoulders in a semicircular sweep, the advancing segment shows a number of isolated and quite distinct ulcerating tubercles. In Fig. II., same patient, the patch upon the abdomen is more irregularly oval, centrifugal in its advance, and shows a ring of crusts of almost uniform width, half an inch or more in height, surrounding a vinous red cicatricial area.

The cicatrices which are left by the ulcerative process remain for a long time pigmented and finally become white. They are commonly smooth and more or less depressed, exceptionally however, they are irregular, uneven, traversed by raised bands or cord-like processes, and may be keloidal in character.

The deep serpiginous syphilide differs from the preceding variety in the deeper-seated character of the lesions which serve as the focus of ulceration and the greater depth of the destructive process. Its chronological position is in a more advanced stage of the diathesis, but since there is often a coincident development of deep ecthymatous pustules and tubercles at a late period of syphilis, it may be difficult to determine which may have been the generating lesion.

Deep serpiginous ulceration is more commonly and characteristically developed from lesions of the tubercular or gummatous type. It may have its origin in a single tubercle, or, as is more commonly the case, from a number of nodules circularly grouped. The older central nodules first undergo disintegration, suppurate, and become surmounted by a crust. As the outlying satellite tubercles in turn soften and ulcerate, they run together, forming a continuous fossa of ulceration, covered by crusts, around the central lesions which are in process of cicatrization. New nodules shoot up at the periphery, forming a belt of infiltration around the ring of crusts. This infiltrated margin is in turn ploughed up by a concentric ulcerative furrow, of more or less uniform width, appearing as if it had been dug out by a gouge. The outer wall of infiltration is steep, perpendicular, or undermined, the inner margin shallower and sloping, the base and edges secreting a puriform fluid which dries into thick, more or less elevated crusts; the patch continues to enlarge so long as new tubercles develop at the periphery.

DIAGNOSIS.

The serpiginous syphilide is so characteristic in its development and mode of extension that it can hardly be confounded with any other disease, except, perhaps, serpiginous lupus, and that form of phagedenic chancroid in which the destructive process pursues a sinuous or serpentine course.

Lupus begins in early life, and is commonly confined to the face and extremities. There is not in lupus that circular disposition of the nodular elements which is characteristic of the serpiginous syphilide, and the lupus patch is not surrounded by an coppery, infiltrated areola. The differential characters of lupus and syphilitic ulcerations have already been alluded to.

Serpiginous chancroid never occurs upon the face and certain other regions for which syphilis shows a predilection. It is only upon the genital or the perigenital region that it is liable to be confounded with the serpiginous syphilide. It may be distinguished by the fact that the ulcerative process is not preceded by neoplastic infiltration. The ulceration advances by undermining the skin and dissecting up the tissues; the secretion is less abundant, and does not form crusts. The auto-inoculability of the pus constitutes the most important differential sign.

THE VEGETATING SYPHILIDE.

This term does not indicate a distinct variety of syphilide, but is applied to certain specific lesions whose most pronounced and distinctive characteristic consists in an exaggerated papillary hypertrophy. The papillomatous element is not essentially syphilitic, since many non-specific affections—lupus, scrofulous and eczematous ulcers, etc.—may become the seat of exuberant granulations which may assume an extraordinary development. The histological characters of papillary excrescences of syphilitic origin differ in no essential particular from papillomatous productions entirely devoid of specificity. In both cases there is a hyperplasia of the papillæ, which become elongated and prominent, giving to the tumors a verrucose or mammillated aspect.

The tendency of certain lesions of the papular type, under the influence of various external causes of irritation, to assume a condylomatous character has already been referred to. Hypertrophy of the papillæ is also met with in tubercular or gummatous infiltrations with an ulcerated base.

Syphilitic lesions of the head and face are more apt to become the seat of vegetations, especially the hairy scalp and bearded regions. After the hairy parts, the preference of the vegetating syphilide is for regions where the skin is thin, delicate, and more or less humid, as about the nasal and buccal orifices, along the commissure of the lips and naso-lateral folds, often extending to the brow, cheeks, and chin. In these regions the vegetations appear as irregular, rounded protuberances of uneven elevation, of a greenish-yellow color, secreting a puriform fluid which is often offensive. The secretion may concrete into thin, lamellated crusts, which, upon being removed, disclose a rugous surface made up of villous or soft, flesh-like excrescences. Involution may occur in various ways; the mass may gradually melt away by a process of ulceration or become sphacelated.

The papillary proliferations which appear upon syphilitic ulcers of the tertiary stage often

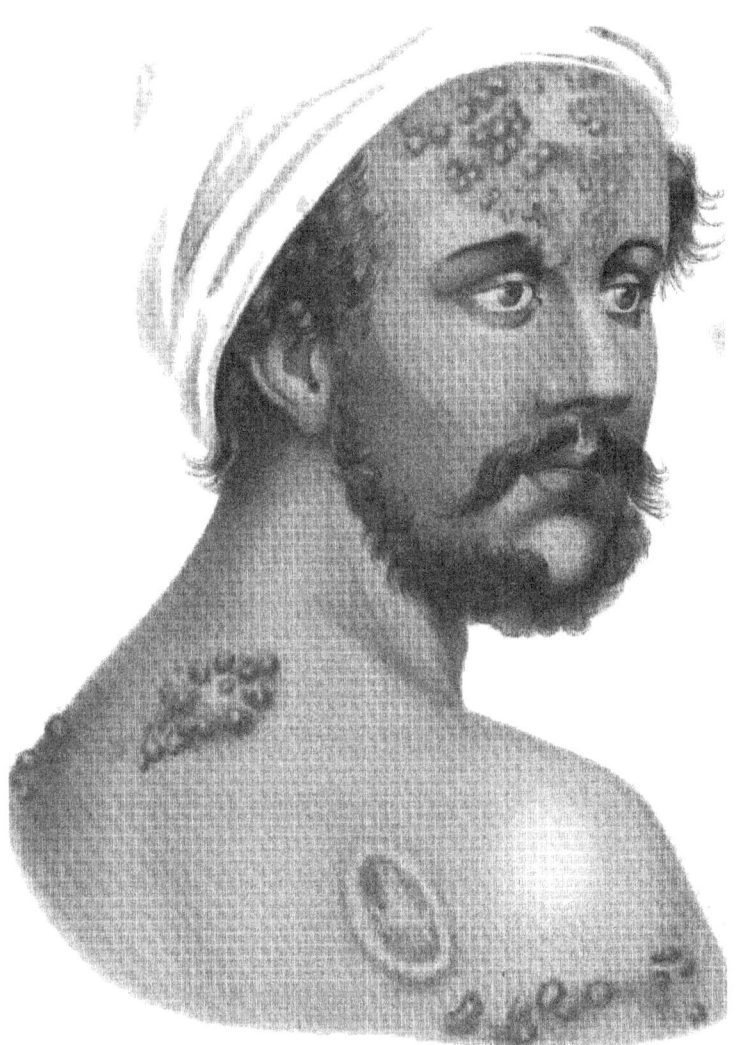

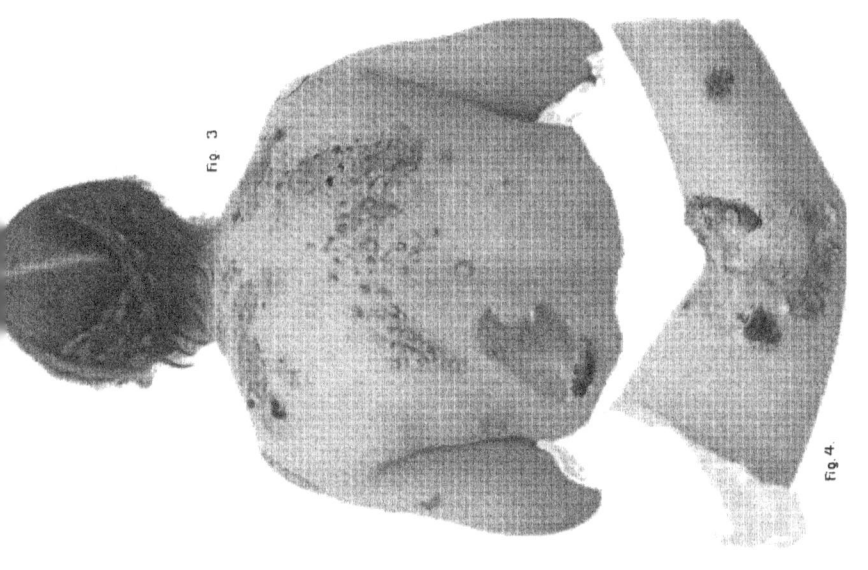

Fig. 1.

Fig. 3

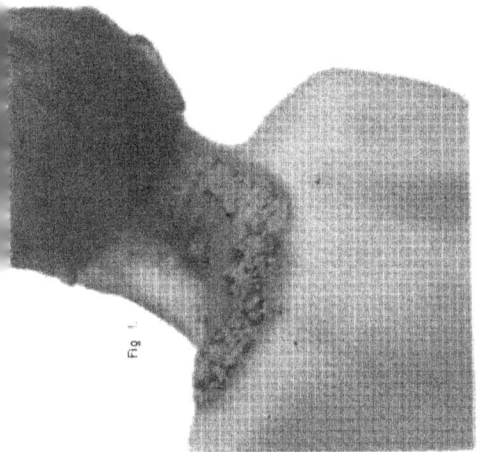

Fig. 2.

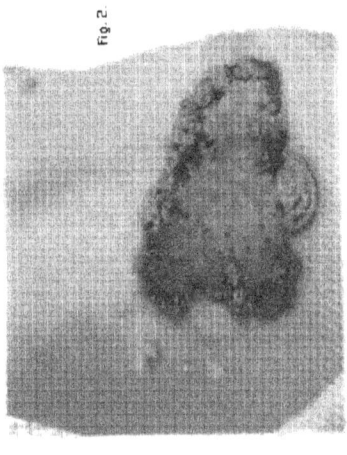

Fig. 4.

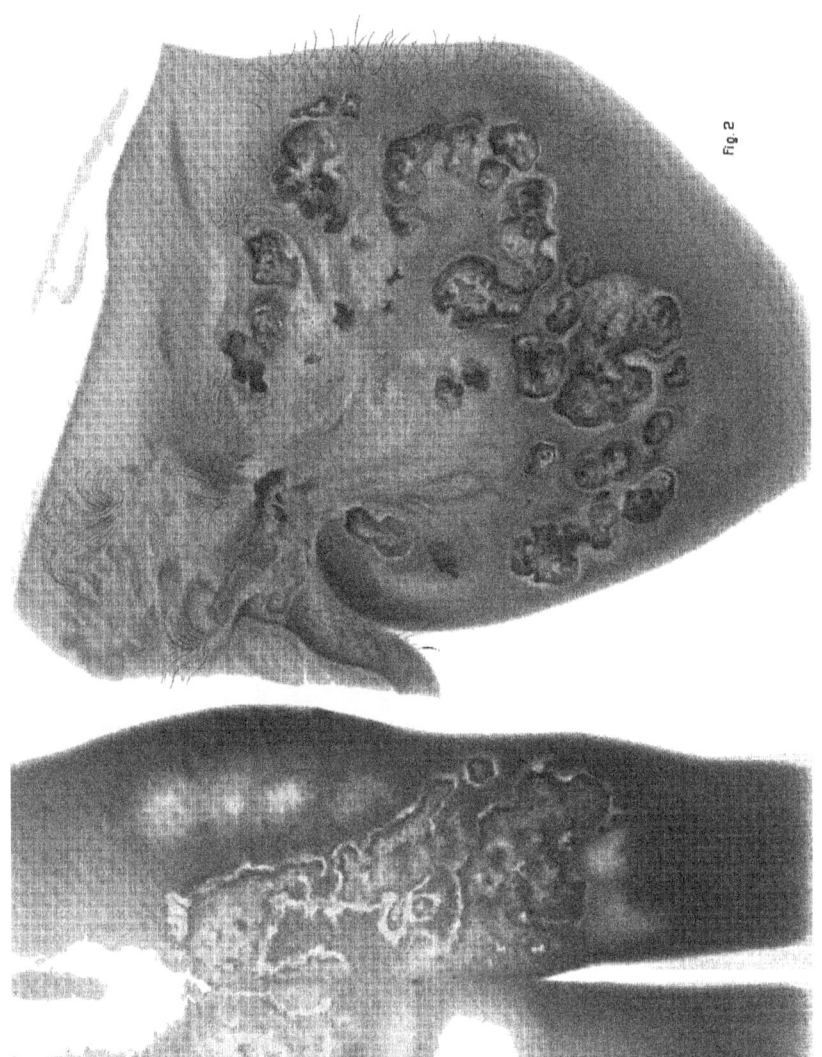

Fig 2

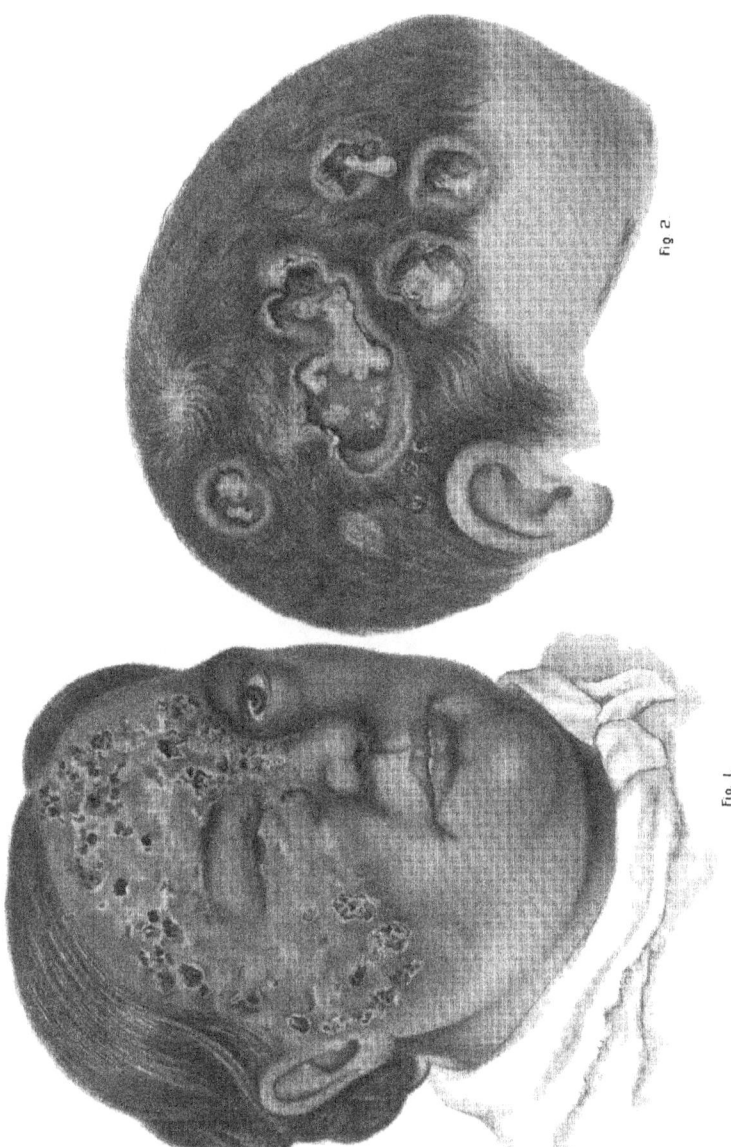

Fig 1.

Fig 2

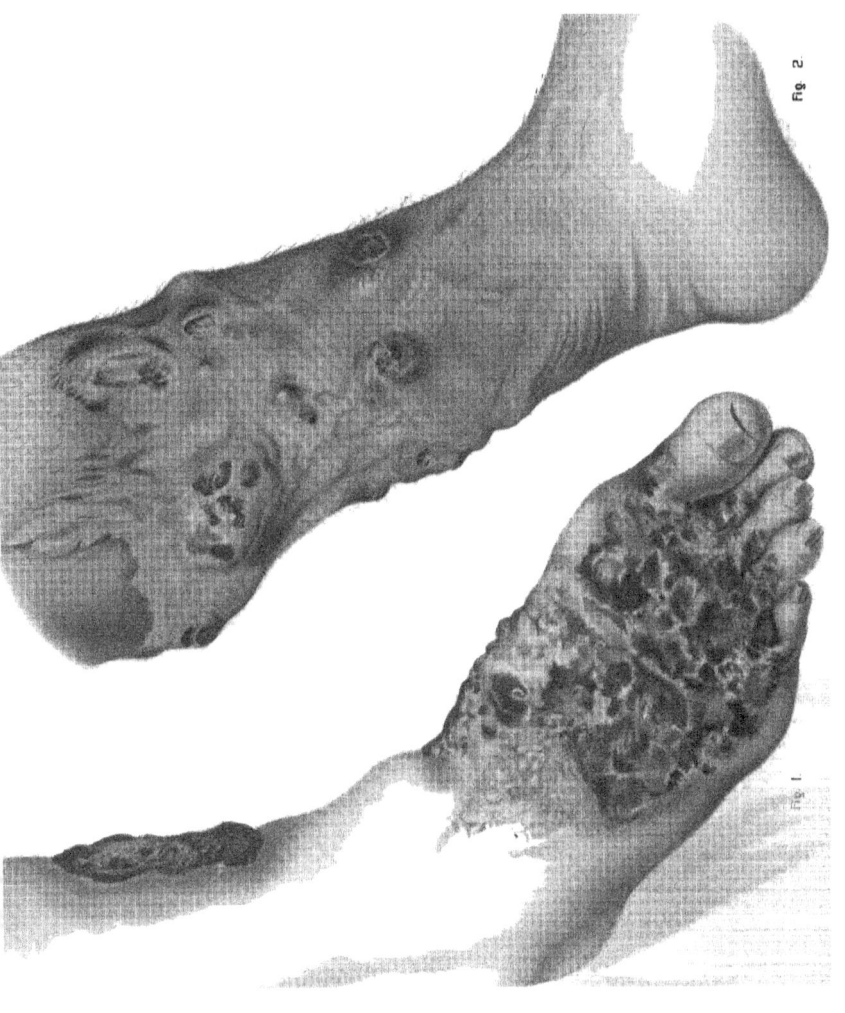

Fig. 2.

Fig. 1.

ATLAS

OF

VENEREAL and SKIN

DISEASES

COMPRISING ORIGINAL ILLUSTRATIONS AND SELECTIONS FROM THE PLATES OF

PROF. M. KAPOSI, OF VIENNA; DR. J. HUTCHINSON, OF LONDON; PROF. 1. NEUMANN, OF VIENNA;
PROFS. A. FOURNIER AND A. HARDY; AND DRS. RICORD, CULLERRIER, BESNIER, AND VIDAL, OF PARIS;
PROF. LELOIR, OF LILLE; DR. P. A. MORROW, OF NEW YORK; DR. E. L. KEYES, OF NEW YORK;
DR. FESSENDEN N. OTIS, OF NEW YORK; DR. J. NEVINS HYDE, OF CHICAGO;
DR. HENRY G. PIFFARD, OF NEW YORK, AND OTHERS.

WITH ORIGINAL TEXT BY

PRINCE A. MORROW, A.M., M.D.,

CLINICAL PROFESSOR OF VENEREAL DISEASES, FORMERLY CLINICAL LECTURER ON DERMATOLOGY, IN THE UNIVERSITY OF THE CITY OF NEW YORK;
SURGEON TO CHARITY HOSPITAL, ETC.

LIST OF PLATES IN SEVENTH FASCICULUS.

NEW YORK

WILLIAM WOOD & COMPANY

1888

ATLAS

OF

VENEREAL AND SKIN

DISEASES

It is with special satisfaction that the publishers announce that this large and important work, which they have had in contemplation since 1883, is now ready for publication. It has long been recognized by them, from wide observation and acquaintance with similar works published in this country and abroad, that it is impossible for any one author to furnish, from his own collection of cases and illustrations, the most typical and at the same time the best and most lifelike pictures of the many peculiar forms of these diseases. Appreciating the defects and disadvantages arising from this cause, it was determined from the outset to enlist the co-operation, in the making of this ATLAS, of the leading dermatologists and syphilographers of the world. Prominent among them are Profs. M. Kaposi and I. Neumann, of Vienna. The atlas of the former, of venereal diseases, just completed, and that of the latter, of skin diseases, now being issued in parts, will be largely drawn upon in the preparation of this work, the sole right to reproduce them having been granted us by the authors.

Among other distinguished gentlemen who have engaged to contribute selections from their collections of original illustrations may now be mentioned Dr. J. Hutchinson, of London; Profs. A. Fournier and A. Hardy; and Drs. Ricord, Cullerrier, Besnier, and Vidal, of Paris; Dr. P. A. Morrow, of New York; Dr. Edward L. Keyes, of New York; Dr. Fessenden N. Otis, of New York; Dr. J. Nevins Hyde, of Chicago; Dr. Henry G. Piffard, of New York.

Other names will be added to this list as the work progresses.

The Editor of the work is Dr. Prince A. Morrow, of New York, who, in addition to plates contributed from his own remarkable collection, will write the treatise on skin and venereal diseases, which constitutes, besides the description of the plates, the text accompanying them.

In this treatise, it is aimed to include chiefly those features which are the most practical, omitting in great measure pathological and other considerations which would be more properly treated of in extended writings, rather than as the adjunct to an Atlas.

In regard to the character of the plates, it may be said, they are believed to be superior to anything of the kind heretofore produced—as accurate in drawing as photographs, and far more distinct, while the coloring faithfully represents nature.

The text is printed from new type, large, clear, and handsome, and the paper is heavy, with a highly finished surface.

Altogether, considering the reputation of the authors of the plates, the ability of the editor, the superb execution of the plates, the excellence of the presswork, the high quality of the paper of both text and plates, the large size of the page, etc., etc., this ATLAS OF VENEREAL AND SKIN DISEASES will be the most superb work in medical literature ever published in the English language.

The ATLAS OF VENEREAL AND SKIN DISEASES will be published in fifteen monthly parts, each containing five folio, chromo-lithographic plates, many of them containing numerous figures, all printed in flesh tints and colors, together with descriptive text for each plate, and from sixteen to twenty folio pages of a practical treatise upon venereal and skin diseases; the whole forming, when complete, one magnificent thick folio volume with seventy-five plates, containing several hundred figures, exquisitely printed in colors.

☞ The ATLAS OF VENEREAL AND SKIN DISEASES will be sold by subscription only, at the very moderate price of $2 per part.

WILLIAM WOOD & COMPANY, *Publishers,*

56 AND 58 LAFAYETTE PLACE, NEW YORK.

form large, vegetating, verrucose masses, which present a most deceptive resemblance to the fungoid papillomatous growths of the skin known as framboesia. The clinical characteristics of the vegetating syphilide and framboesia are so nearly identical that the latter disease was for a long time regarded by many prominent authorities as a form of syphilis. At the present day, the two diseases are regarded as essentially distinct in origin and mode of evolution.

SYPHILIS OF THE MUCOUS MEMBRANES.

Syphilis produces lesions of the mucous membranes analogous to those of the skin; they are modified, however, in their forms and processes by the anatomical conditions of the soil upon which they develop. The mucous membrane manifestations of syphilis are usually of the erythematous, papular, or gummatous type; pustular lesions do not occur upon these surfaces. Like the cutaneous syphilides, the earlier lesions of the mucosa are superficial and resolutive, without destruction of tissue; the later are deep seated, chronic in character, and may occasion extensive loss of tissue with consequent scarring and deformity.

Erythema of the mucous membranes of the mouth and throat often precedes or develops coincidently with the cutaneous eruption of the same character. It is probably present in almost all cases, although it may be so slight as to escape recognition. Pillon observed it in sixty-five out of one hundred and fourteen cases of syphilis.

Upon the buccal mucous surface erythema manifests itself as a slight blush or redness, sometimes as a peculiarly livid congestion, usually most marked upon the arches of the palate and the tonsils; it may extend to the larynx or the nasal passages. The hyperæmia may be diffuse or sharply defined; it is often attended with slight swelling of the affected surfaces, and accompanied with a sensation of dryness of the throat, which is succeeded by an increased secretion, as occurs in catarrhal angina.

The internal surface of the prepuce is the occasional seat of syphilitic erythema. It is accompanied with slight swelling of the prepuce and skin of the penis with preputial catarrh, which may simulate balano-posthitis. Syphilitic erythema of the vulvar region is very infrequent; it may be attended with swelling of the labia, and become erosive with a slight secretion.

Syphilitic erythema of the mucous membranes usually disappears without causing any textural lesion; it may recur a number of times, but relapses more frequently assume the form of mucous papules.

The mucous patch is the exclusive product of syphilis, none of the ordinary dermatoses produces analogous lesions, it may therefore be regarded as pathognomonic. Of all the constitutional signs of the disease, it is the most characteristic and constant in its development. Secondary syphilis may produce no lesion of the skin; it rarely happens, however, that the mucous membranes escape its action. Mucous patches derive an additional importance from the fact that they constitute the most common and active sources of syphilitic contagion. In the immense majority of cases the secretion of these lesions is the agency by which syphilis is propagated from one individual to another.

The mucous patch is a papule occurring upon the mucous membranes, the essential characteristic of the lesion consisting in a hyperplasia of the papillæ. It may be found upon the mucous membranes of the mouth, nose, conjunctiva, throat and larynx, the genital mucous membranes of both sexes, the orifice of the anus, etc.; it does not occur upon the vaginal walls, but is found upon the vaginal portion of the cervix uteri. In women, mucous patches are more common about the vulva and around the anus; in men, their greater frequency within the mouth is probably caused by the irritating contact of tobacco and alcohol.

The typical lesion may be described as a slightly raised, circular spot of a cloudy or milky white color, formed by the thickening of the epithelium over a reddened, infiltrated surface. The papillæ in and around the follicles are ordinarily the seat of the cellular infiltration. The lesion

PLATE XXXI.

Fig. I.—*Ulcerative Cutaneous Gummata.* There is seen a destruction of tissues of end of the nose, the alæ nasi, the mucous membrane of the lip, and of the cheek as a result of the disintegration of gummata.

Fig. II.—*Syphilis Cutanea Vegetans.* (Frambœsoides; Frambœsia Syphilitica; Syphilomykes Morris Fuchs; Mykoses Syphiloides Alibert.)

Brown-red, elevated, glandular, warty, numerously clefted outgrowths of a mulberry-like granular character, united to globular excrescences, the surface partly excoriated or skinned over, partly covered with crusts.

The vegetations have as their principal localization syphilitic papules of the face, the naso-labial furrow upon and next to the lip, etc.

Fig. III.—*Frambœsia syphilitica of the soft palate.* The mucous membrane of the palatine arches and the uvula are thickly set with millet-sized, pale-red confluent excrescences, which in places are deprived of their epithelium. Similar vegetations upon the epiglottis which is swollen and shows a slight loss of substance.

FIG. I. AND III.—AFTER NEUMANN.
FIG. II.—AFTER KAPOSI.

may consist of a single rounded spot from the size of a lentil to that of a three-cent piece, or it may be a large irregular surface resulting from the confluence of a number of spots. The configuration and aspect vary according to the location and grouping of the papules, and the modifications which they undergo in the process of evolution. The patches may become eroded by the casting off of the epithelial layer, the base may become indurated and ulcerated, it may assume a diphtheritic aspect, or it may become hypertrophied, exhibiting a caruncular or condylomatous character.

The chronological limit of the mucous patch is indefinite ; it may develop coincidently with the erythematous syphilide, but it is more apt to occur in connection with papular and pustular syphilides of the integument. While it is superficial in character and of short duration, it reappears with surprising pertinacity, and its tendency is to incessant reproduction during the entire secondary stage, and sometimes as late as the fourth or fifth year of the disease.

Mucous patches rarely occasion much pain or subjective trouble, except when ulcerated. Situated in the mouth and throat, the contact of certain articles of food and drink, especially acids, may cause smarting and a burning sensation. These lesions respond readily, as a rule, to general and local treatment, the curative influence of the latter being often more marked than that of the former. As resolution takes place, the opacity and thickening gradually disappear, and the spots become covered with normal epithelial cells.

Mucous syphilides are modified somewhat in their clinical features by location. Their great frequency in the buccal region is explained by the continual friction and irritation to which these surfaces are exposed from contact of food and drink, tobacco and alcohol, the wounding of the membrane by rough and angular teeth, etc. Upon the buccal mucous membrane and arches of the palate the patches present a white, opaline appearance, as if the surface had been touched with a crayon of nitrate of silver; the surface may become slightly erosive, and the molecular detritus may give it a pseudo-membranous aspect. The tonsils are frequently the seat of mucous patches, which at first present a bluish-white, opaline covering, but later they are apt to become disintegrated, forming superficial or deep ulcerations, the base presenting a yellow pultaceous appearance. The tonsils are apt to become inflamed and enlarged, and in such cases the pain in swallowing may be severe, and sometimes propagated along the Eustachian tubes to the ears. Notwithstanding the great frequency of mucous patches in the isthmus of the fauces, they are rarely, if ever, observed upon the posterior wall of the pharynx, this remarkable immunity being due, no doubt, to the absence of papillæ.

Occurring at the angles of the mouth, the patches are often complicated with fissures, and exceedingly painful. They may be continuous with papules of the cutaneous surface, the mucous and cutaneous segments of the lesion each presenting its distinctive appearance. Upon the mucous surface the lesion is opaline, while the integumental portion is exulcerated and covered with crustaceous concretions. Mucous patches often occur at the junction of the hard and soft palate, in which location, it has been observed, they often assume a diphtheroid character.

Lingual mucous patches develop most frequently at the sides and tip of the tongue. They may be isolated and present a circular contour, but more commonly become confluent and the seat of fissures or furrows, which may give the margin of the tongue a dentated appearance, or they become converted into elongated and ragged superficial ulcers.

Upon the dorsum of the tongue mucous patches are less common, and occur in the form of circular or oval patches which may present a vivid or dark-red coloration, the surface smooth as if shaven. These round, smooth, depapillated patches, termed by Mauriac " *disques de désquamation,*" are neatly circumscribed, and, in contrast with the surrounding papillated surface, have been compared to a circle mown in a field of grain. They often enlarge at the periphery while healing in the centre, assuming an annular or horse-shoe shape. These lesions have a tendency to repeated recurrence under the irritating influence of tobacco, alcohol, etc., and they may prove the starting-point of that diffuse sclerosis known as psoriasis of the tongue.

Another rare form of lesion of the tongue, which occurs in the secondary stage of syphilis, consists of papillary overgrowths which have been described by Hutchinson as "mucous warts," and which will be found figured in Plate XXXII., Fig. 9. Their favorite location is the middle of the posterior part of the dorsum, though they may be found scattered over the surface. They are of the nature of condylomata, and consist simply in an overgrowth of the normal papillæ of the parts.

Mucous patches of the nasal fossæ, the conjunctiva, and the auditory canal are of comparatively rare occurrence, and present nothing distinctive worthy of special description. Mucous patches of the larynx are found upon the free margin of the epiglottis and upon the vocal cords; they interfere with phonation, are sometimes attended with œdema and inflammation of the larynx, and are always of prolonged duration.

Mucous patches may develop upon the genital mucous membranes of both sexes; they are much more frequent in women. They may be found upon both the internal and external surfaces of the labia, upon the cervix uteri, and upon the peri-vulvar regions. Upon the internal surface of the labia, which is their most common seat, they consist of small circular erosions or ulcerations, flat or elevated, with a moist, grayish or reddish surface, secreting a sero-purulent fluid. They may be covered with a grayish false membrane which, upon removal, exposes a raw bleeding surface. They are often attended with œdema and hypertrophy of the labia, which may be persistent for months.

Upon the cervix the patches are round or ovoid, and may be isolated or confluent; they present a dirty-gray or lardaceous appearance. In this location they are distinguished by their ephemeral character, often disappearing with surprising celerity. The vaginal walls enjoy a remarkable immunity from this and all other forms of syphilitic lesions.

Upon the free borders and external surface of the labia and peri-vulvar region mucous patches have a remarkable tendency to become hypertrophied and transformed into vegetating condylomata. The individual papules are prominent, situated upon an indurated and elevated base, and often confluent, forming nappes of infiltration intersected with rhagades and furrows. They may be superficially eroded, ulcerated, or the entire mass may become sphacelated.

Mucous patches of the anal region are also much more common in women, from the irritating contact of leucorrhœal and other secretions. They occur around the orifice of the anus, but do not extend within upon the rectal walls. They are apt to become fissured, and occasion severe pain during the act of defecation from the distention and tearing of the linear ulcerations and the passage of irritating fecal matters. The tendency of mucous papules in this region to proliferation and the formation of condylomatous masses has already been referred to. In many cases the vegetations take on an extraordinary development.

THE TERTIARY LESIONS of the mucous membranes consist of the same histological formations as are met with in the cutaneous lesions of this period; like the later syphilodermata, they are limited and localized, and attended with extensive and profound destruction of tissues. Nodes of the mucous membrane differ from cutaneous nodes in being flatter, less protuberant, and not so distinctly circumscribed, having more of the character of diffused infiltrations. Like the cutaneous lesions, they may be absorbed or break down and become ulcerative; they do not form crusts, as upon the external integument, they are situated, for the most part, upon the visible and accessible mucous membranes.

Tertiary accidents of the mucous and submucous tissues may co-exist with tubercular and gummatous manifestations upon the cutaneous system, or may constitute the sole evidences of late syphilis. They are characterized by the same tendency to relapse during months and years; they respond more or less readily to the influence of specific treatment.

Tertiary lesions of the mucous membranes consist of tubercular and gummatous deposits, which may be circumscribed or diffuse; they are modified somewhat in their evolution and general characters by the accident of location.

Their most frequent seat is upon the tonsils, the soft palate or palatine arch, the posterior wall of the pharynx, and the nasal fossæ. It has been observed that the buccal, pharyngeal, and nasal cavities are often involved simultaneously or successively. They occur less frequently upon the rectal walls, the os uteri and genitals, and still more rarely in the urethral mucous membranes.

The ramification of these mucous tracts and their close connection with important organs and cavities give tertiary lesions in these locations a grave significance. The ulcerations which result from the disintegration of the morbid infiltrations may sweep away important structures, giving rise to horrible disfigurements and mutilations, perforation of cavities, adhesions, and atresia, or complete stenosis of the tubular organs.

Upon the tonsils the lesions are usually multiple, and give rise to considerable enlargement, the swollen organs often touching each other, and interfering with the voice and deglutition, sometimes occasioning partial deafness from pressure and partial occlusion of the Eustachian tube. The nodular infiltrations may shrink or become absorbed, or, as is more commonly the case, they soften and suppurate, forming uneven, excavated ulcers, healing in places and spreading in others. If the infiltration be superficial, the ulceration creeps over the surface, leaving branching, corrugated scars. If the infiltration be of the deep, penetrating variety, the destruction of tissues is more extensive and profound; the entire palate and tonsils may be swept away in the process of ulceration. When a gumma is situated upon the uvula or the arches of the palate, the velum becomes livid, swollen, and hard, with more or less œdema of the surrounding tissues. When the infiltration breaks down, it not infrequently causes perforation of the velum, which accident results in more or less interference with the function of swallowing. The remains of the palate may be glued down by adhesions to the root of the tongue or the posterior wall of the pharynx.

Ulcerative lesions in this location are not infrequently complicated with phagedena. The sloughing process may open up large blood-vessels, producing dangerous hemorrhage; it may denude the bones, causing necrosis and horrible mutilations. The entire hard palate may be destroyed, converting the nose, mouth, and pharynx into one enormous cavity. Perforation of the hard palate most frequently occurs from an extension of the necrotic process from the nasal to the oral cavity.

Tertiary lesions of the nasal passages usually begin in the cartilages and bones, causing caries and the production of the offensive condition known as syphilitic ozæna. Perforation of the septum may occur with destruction of the nasal bones, causing a flattening or falling in of the bridge of the nose, which, with the tilting up of the apex, constitutes a characteristic deformity.

The late lesions of the tongue in syphilis occur in quite a variety of forms. The so-called "psoriasis of the tongue" is frequently of syphilitic origin. It consists of smooth grayish or silvery white plates, closely adherent to the mucous membrane, developed upon the dorsum of the tongue. The leucomatous patches are irregularly marginated, and are sometimes seen on interior of cheeks. They are due to hypertrophy and condensation of the epithelium, giving it a leathery consistence; they never become eroded or ulcerated. An illustration of leucoma due to the combined influence of syphilis and smoking is seen in Fig. 15, Plate XXXII.

The more common forms of tertiary accidents of the tongue are recognized as sclerous glossitis, which may be superficial or deep, and gummous glossitis, characterized by the production of isolated nodules identical with gummata of other organs.

Superficial glossitis more commonly affects the anterior or middle portion of the dorsum, and is characterized by a sclerosis of the mucous or submucous cellular tissue resulting in a lamellated induration which may be circumscribed in round, ovoid patches, or diffuse. The mucous membrane presents a dark-red, glossy color; it rarely ulcerates.

Deep or parenchymatous glossitis invades the muscular substance of the organ, which becomes tumefied and lumpy, and sometimes enormously hypertrophied. The surface presents an irregular, rough, lobulated appearance, quite pathognomonic. This feature is quite admirably shown in Fig. 6, Plate XXXII. The lobules are separated by deep sulci or furrows running parallel with the median raphe of the tongue. This condition may persist for years. The deep

PLATE XXXII.

Fig. I.—*Mucous patch of lower lip* (Plaque opaline). The beginning stage. The epithelium of a circumscribed space is raised above the niveau in the form of a grayish-yellow turbid patch. Near is a large pin-head-sized, superficial, sharply defined (follicular) sore.

Fig. II.—*Psoriasis lingua*, in the form of lentil-sized red, smooth, sharply defined spots upon the dorsum of the tongue which is, moreover, gray coated, rugged, deeply furrowed in the middle, and fissured upon the left margin. Papules upon the chin.

Fig. III.—*Psoriasis lingua*. Upon the posterior part of the right border of the tongue, a large bean-sized sharply defined patch, the epithelium of the inner half of which is grayish-yellow and fissured. Upon the dorsum of the tongue, bright-red, raised, pin-head-sized spots, corresponding to the fungiform papillæ. The remainder of the dorsum of the tongue gray and rough. The right corner of the mouth surrounded with a group of fissured papules.

Fig. IV.—*Syphilis ulcerosa mucosa*. A perforating ulcer the size of a split bean upon the hard palate, with partly healed, to the left and posteriorly infiltrated, reddened edges. To the right a more recent, small, not yet perforating ulcer.

Figs. V. and VIII.—*Psoriasis mucosæ oris*. Lentil to bean·sized, whitish-gray, somewhat raised collections upon the mucous membrane of the right tonsil and the posterior palatine arch. The tongue of a strawberry appearance.

Fig. VI.—Long persisting glossitis (twelve years' duration) with hypertrophy. The tongue shows general hypertrophy, with deep sulci and masses of bossy induration overhanging them. Patient has also leucomatous patches extending from angles of the mouth.

Fig. VII.—*Syphilis ulcerosa*. The posterior wall of the pharynx studded with irregular ulcerative furrows and cavities. The uvula reduced to a small stump. The remainder of the velum palati white, cicatricial.

Fig. IX.—Papillary growths in the middle of the dorsum of the tongue from a case of secondary syphilis. These mucous warts are of the same nature as condylomata, due to an overgrowth of the anatomical structures, rather than of inflammatory effusion.

Fig. X.—Perforation of the palate with ulcerative edges. The lateral margin of the uvula and the neighboring palatine arch occupied by an ulcer prolonged upon the posterior surface of the uvula which has destroyed the neck of the latter except a small pedicle, and has extended above deeply in the velum.

Fig. XI.—Deep extending ulcer of the upper lip. The cicatricial velum palati is adherent to the posterior pharyngeal wall and like a tent roofs over behind the pharyngeal space; at the dome of the tent, viz., upon the place of the destroyed uvula, is seen a bean-sized opening with cicatricial edges, through which the pharyngo-basilar cavity communicates with the pharyngo-oral cavity.

Fig. XII.—An ulcer upon the uvula, extending from the left anterior palatine arch upon the uvula. Two penny-sized ulcers of the posterior pharyngeal wall, covered with a dirty brown secretion.

Fig. XIII.—Syphilitic glossitis. The whole tongue is swollen and its tumid edges are in several parts curved upward. The papillæ are hypertrophied in parts, but glued together by the general swelling of the intervening tissues, so as to constitute a condition resembling condyloma. On some parts the papillæ have almost wholly disappeared and a smooth red area is left. There are numerous abrasions, but nowhere very deep ulceration. The appearance of the clefts is produced by the swelling of the papillæ in ridges.

Fig. XIV.—The free edge of the velum dusky red over a small zone, a deep extending ulcer upon the border of the left posterior palatine arch. The mucous membrane of the posterior pharyngeal wall traced by widened vessels. Upon the dorsum of the tongue the prominences of the fungiform papillæ recognized as red raised spots.

Fig. XV.—Chronic sclerosis of mucous membrane of tongue with very dense leucomata. Almost the whole of the anterior two-thirds of the surface of the organ is occupied by a very dense white structure which looks exactly like a thick layer of white paint. It is abruptly marginated at most parts and very irregular in outline. Over the greater portion it is smooth and not in the least papillated, but the tongue at other places is bald and fissured.

FIGS. I., II., III., IV., V., VII., VIII., X., XI., XII., XIV.—AFTER KAPOSI.
FIGS. VI., IX., XIII., XV.—AFTER HUTCHINSON.

form is also characterized by the absence of ulceration, which never occurs except from accidental irritation, as the contact of a broken tooth, etc.

Circumscribed gummatous deposits may develop in the mucous, submucous, or muscular tissues of the tongue. Superficial gummata occur as small nodules beneath the epithelium, either singly or in groups, which soften and break down into an open ulcer, as do tubercles of the skin. The deep or parenchymatous gummata are seated in the muscular substance of the organ and may cause no projection above the surface. They soften in the centre, excite absorption of the overlying tissues, and open upon the surface. Ulceration exposes a deep cavity with over-hanging sloughy walls; a number of ulcers may unite and assume a serpiginous form. After healing takes place, there remains a permanent, more or less depressed scar.

The larynx is not so apt to suffer during the secondary stage of syphilis, but tertiary lesions of this organ are more common than those of the pharynx; they consist of hyperplastic infiltrations or circumscribed gummata. By the disintegration of gummatous deposits, deep ulcers form which may sweep away the epiglottis, vocal cords, and other structures of the larynx. The ulcerative process may proceed upward to the root of the tongue and pharynx, or it may extend downward to the trachea and bronchi.

Tertiary affections of the trachea more frequently occur as a diffused infiltration of the submucous tissues. It may cause perichondritis, necrosis of the cartilaginous rings, and perforation, with a more or less permanent external opening, may occur. The most unfortunate result of syphilis of the air passages is stenosis from cicatricial contraction, producing serious and alarming dyspnœa, or a fatal result from complete apnœa.

The œsophagus, stomach, and intestinal tract in its entire extent may be the seat of tertiary lesions; the large intestine is the most frequently affected.

The tertiary affections of the rectum generally occur in the form of gummatous infiltrations in the ano-rectal walls, without special implication of the mucous membrane; circumscribed gum-mata are exceedingly rare. The neoplastic infiltration is cylindrical, involving the entire circumference of the bowel, and is limited to its lower portion, the inferior third of the rectum. This degenerates into a retractile fibrous tissue which results in a rigid, unyielding sclerotic con-dition. Sometimes ulcerations occur, and sharply cut ulcers may replace the induration. Syphi-litic ulceration of the rectum derives its chief clinical importance from the frequency with which the cicatricial contraction is followed by stricture of the rectum.

Tertiary lesions may occur upon the mucous membranes of the genital organs of both sexes. Upon the glans penis and inner surface of the prepuce they occur as hard nodules which ulcerate and may be mistaken for a chancroid or a Hunterian chancre or a commencing epithe-lioma. In the walls of the urethra they occur in the form of a urethral or peri-urethral infiltration which often simulates a peri-urethral abscess. In the process of disintegration and sloughing they may cause fistulæ, severe hemorrhage, etc. Gummy nodes also develop in the corpora caver-nosa, they are painless, indolent, and rarely suppurate; incurvation of the organ during erection generally results. Gummy tumors may be found upon the internal surface of labia majora and minora, the posterior commissure of the vulva, and more rarely upon the cervix uteri.

DIAGNOSIS.

The mucous membrane manifestations of syphilis of the erythematous type may be con-founded with non-specific affections. Syphilitic angina ordinarily develops in connection with the eruptive fever, and is contemporaneous with the erythematous syphilide of the integument; it is often accompanied with roseola of the tongue, manifest as sharply defined, circular spots, isolated or confluent. The catarrhal symptoms are not so pronounced as in ordinary angina, dryness and slight difficulty of swallowing often constituting the sole symptoms. Syphilitic angina is more persistent and resists the influence of astringents and anti-catarrhal remedies. In the production of catarrhal angina, the influence of cold as an exciting cause may often be traced.

Of all the manifestations of syphilis, mucous patches are the most characteristic in their objective appearances and their limitation to certain localities. As a rule, they are readily recognized and easily differentiated from non-specific affections of the mucous surfaces. Mucous patches of the buccal mucous membrane may be mistaken for aphthous sores. Aphthæ occur more frequently in children, they are seldom situated upon the tonsils and palate, which constitute seats of predilection for mucous patches. No matter how numerous the lesions, they never become confluent. When eroded or ulcerated, they are extremely painful.

Ulcero-membranous stomatitis may be distinguished from mucous patches by their location. Its lesions are almost exclusively confined to the gums, the mucous membrane of the lower lip and jaw, the floor of the mouth and borders of the tongue. They do not have the opaline appearance of mucous patches, but are dirty gray, the base fungous and covered with a pultaceous slough. Mercurial sloughing sores emit a most offensive odor which is quite characteristic.

The tertiary lesions of the mucous membrane often simulate most closely non-specific diseases of these surfaces, so that their differentiation may be impossible without the clinical demonstration of the existence of syphilis or the test of specific treatment. Syphilitic lingual psoriasis cannot be distinguished from arthritic psoriasis and the "smoker's tongue" by its objective characters. Etiological considerations are of more importance. The leucoma of smokers has for its seat of predilection the inner surface of lips and median portion of cheeks, it is often seen as an irregular white patch, the apex beginning at the commissures and radiating in a triangular patch upon the sides of the cheek.

Especially are gummatous infiltrations and ulcerations of the tongue difficult of differentiation from other morbid conditions of this organ. Cancerous processes in particular are most deceptively simulated by syphilis, and an error in diagnosis may lead to the most unfortunate results.

The following are the most important points of distinction between syphilis and cancer of the tongue. Cancer is essentially a disease of advanced life and may develop upon any portion of the organ, upon its inferior surface for example, where syphilis rarely does. Carcinoma is almost always unique and unilateral; ulceration begins at the surface and extends to the deeper parts, while the disorganization of a gummy tumor begins in the centre and proceeds outward. The borders of the carcinomatous ulcer are irregular, indurated, and everted, the secretion is profuse and offensive. The pain is lancinating, paroxysmal, often shooting to the ears, and there is more or less trouble in mastication and deglutition. The submaxillary and sublingual glands are hard and swollen, and at a later period a pronounced cachectic state. Cancer is aggravated by specific treatment, while a gummatous lesion readily responds to the influence of iodide of potassium. Hutchinson asserts very positively that syphilis markedly predisposes to cancer and that the latter often develops in cicatrices left by syphilitic ulcers.

Tertiary lesions of the larynx bear a close resemblance to non-specific affections of this structure—tuberculous, lupus and carcinomatous ulcers, and in many cases the differentiation is impossible. Neither the site of the ulcer, the condition of its borders and base, nor the attendant adenitis afford a positive basis of diagnosis. A satisfactory examination with the laryngoscope may be impracticable, the microscope may give deceptive indications, and the test of specific treatment may absolutely fail.

A broken-down gummy tumor of the genital organs may be mistaken for chancroid. The gumma is generally unique, essentially indolent and chronic, it disintegrates slowly and the ulceration is deeper; the chancroid is, as a rule, multiple and there are often seen a number of lesions in different stages of development from successive auto-inoculations, it is not preceded by neoplastic infiltration, and ulceration is present from the first. The secretion of the chancroid is auto-inoculable almost indefinitely; inoculation of the gummous secretion gives negative results. The characteristic inflammatory adenitis of chancroid is another important diagnostic sign. Epithelioma of the penis may be differentiated from an ulcerated gumma by the differences already indicated in the characters of the ulcerative process, the fungating papillomatous condition of the surface, its hard, everted borders, etc. The microscope aids materially in clearing a doubtful diagnosis.

SYPHILIS OF THE NAILS.

In the early stage of syphilis, the nails may become blighted and fall without any apparent local pathological change preceding or accompanying this result. Owing to some impression upon the matrix, deranging or suspending its nutrition, the secretion of the corneous elements is interfered with, and the nail loses its gloss and rosy color, it becomes dry, lustreless, and studded with white spots, with liability to easily fissure and split. Chipping and breaking of the free extremity of the nail is more common in syphilitic women.

Another form of perverted nutrition is characterized by hypertrophy of the nail substance, the nail sometimes attaining a thickness of three or four times its normal size, the surface of the nail at the same time undergoes marked alterations; it becomes bossy with longitudinal or transverse furrows, of a dirty gray or yellow color, with its free margin abruptly broken and split, and the superficial layers partly raised up. In syphilitic onychia, the morbid process may begin at the lunula or side of the nail, the posterior margin becomes thin and eroded, and terminating in a jagged edge, the nail is gradually loosened from its bed and exfoliated. Usually only three or four of the nails are the seat of trouble, exceptionally all the nails may be involved.

Paronychia often co-exists with onychia, as seen in Fig. 4, Plate XXXIII., or the morbid alteration may be limited to inflammation and ulceration of the skin surrounding the nail. Paronychia is manifest in various forms and grades of severity. Sometimes the peri-ungual redness and hardness simulates the common affection known as a "run around." In paronychia, the morbid process usually begins as a papule developed under the nail, or in the ungual fold corresponding to the lunula, or along its lateral border. The lesion may ulcerate, involving the matrix, or exuberant granulations may spring up which crowd the nail from its bed, resulting in a partial or complete loss. As a rule, only one or two nails are affected. A new nail is ultimately produced, which is apt to be misshapen or distorted. If the matrix be entirely destroyed, regeneration of the nail is not possible, and its bed is occupied by rough, irregular bands of horny substance.

The differentiation between syphilitic and non-specific affections of the nails, as eczema, psoriasis, etc., is often exceedingly difficult, and cannot be satisfactorily arrived at independent of the history and the demonstration of the etiological factor concerned.

SYPHILIS OF THE BONES.

After the cutaneous and mucous membrane manifestations, syphilitic affections of the bones are next in order of frequency and importance; they may develop at an early period, although the more marked and characteristic changes in the bones occur in the tertiary stage. In the early stage, the osseous lesions are ordinarily manifest in the form of periosteal inflammation, sometimes periosteal nodes; in the later stage, gummatous infiltrations and circumscribed deposits occcur in and beneath the periosteum and in the bone substance.

Pains in the bones have already been referred to as constituting a common and characteristic feature of the invasion period of constitutional syphilis. Ostealgia may be present without any appreciable objective phenomenon; it is most generally felt along the more superficial and prominent parts of the bony skeleton, and especially over the tendinous insertion of large muscles. The pain is rheumatoid or neuralgic in character, and is always more pronounced at night. This tendency to nocturnal exacerbation characterizes the later as well as the earlier osteocopic pains of syphilis.

In many cases, however, the pain is accompanied by appreciable lesions of the periosteum

PLATE XXXIII.

FIGS. I. and IV.—*Paronychia syphilitica.* Principally upon the ungual furrows of the fore and middle fingers, Fig. I., and also involving the matrix of the fourth toe, Fig. IV., there are seen ulcerative sores, furrowed, with the outer edges steep and serrated, surrounded by a reddened infiltrated skin. The affected phalanx thickened, the nail itself colored a dirty yellowish-brown, furrowed, opaque, and broken (onychia syphilitica).

Fig. II.—*Syphilis cutanea ulcerosa.* The nasal roof sunken in at the junction of the cutaneous and bony parts. The cutaneous portion pressed flat and broad. The right ala nasi destroyed, except a small posterior and lateral remnant, this is seen with serrated infiltrated edges with a lardaceous covering, occupied with ulcers extending upon the mucous membrane and the septum nasi, the surface of which for the most part appears covered with a crust obstructing the nasal orifice. The cutaneous covering of the septum is wanting, except an ulcerous stump below. The mucous surface of the left ala nasi occupied by sulcated ulcer. The general covering of the surrounding surface diffusely reddened.

FIG. III.—*Syphilis cutanea ulcerosa.* An irregularly rounded ulcer, surrounded by a narrow infiltrated areola, covered by a crust occluding the right nasal orifice, which extends from the upper lip upon the nasal mucous membrane, and involves the under part of the right ala nasi and the right inner surface of septum nasi.

FIG. V.—*Fissured and exulcerating papules* of the commissure of the toes. The little toe separated from the neighboring one. The exposed commissure is occupied by a shallow ulcer which extends upon the dorsum and sole of the foot, as well as upon the sides of the toes. Over the base of the ulcer is a discolored grayish-yellow detritus, partly covered with a dark-brown crust, the border of which is separated from the healthy skin by a brown-red, thick, concentric narrow wall.

In the commissure between the second and third toes are irregular, serrated, fissured ulcers with a similar condition of its edges as in the above-described ulcer.

FIG. VI.—In the plantar furrow of the second toe, one penny-sized and two larger sized round, flat elevated papules with a partly exulcerated, partly crust-covered surface.

AFTER KAPOSI.

which are manifest as rounded elevations or nodes, like inflammatory tumors, over various portions of the bony skeleton ; the cranium and the tibia are, perhaps, their most frequent seat.

The periosteal tumors are smooth, plano-convex or flattened, and somewhat elastic to the touch. They vary in size from two-fifths to an inch or more in diameter. The swellings may be quite sensitive to the touch and the pain from the pressure of the hat or the use of a comb is often insupportable. The tumors disappear by a process of resolution, often leaving no trace. Ulceration rarely occurs except in malignant precocious syphilis. When suppuration occurs, fluctuation is felt in the centre, the overlying tissues soften and break down, and the disintegrated contents are discharged through one or more openings which extend down to the bone. Caries of the bone with exfoliation of necrotic pieces may occur.

Instead of the morbid changes occurring primarily in the bones or their periosteal covering, they may be consecutive to gummatous deposits in the overlying tissues. The suppurative process, extending downward, denudes the bone, interferes with its nutrition, and results in necrosis and exfoliation of the osseous structures. The bones of the hard palate, of the nasal fossæ, the cartilages of the larynx, etc., are especially liable to secondary implication from extension of gummatous ulceration of the neighboring tissues.

The later osseous lesions of syphilis occur in the form of inflammatory effusions or infiltrations, and gummatous deposits, which may take place in and beneath the periosteum or in the bone substance. In one form, there is an infiltration of the deeper layers of the periosteum which may be partially absorbed, or transformed into bony tissue, constituting what is known as ossifying periostosis. The new deposits of bony matter become adherent to the bone beneath, forming exostoses. In syphilitic ostitis, the process begins in the bone substance, resulting in hypertrophy of the normal bone substance and the production of parenchymatous exostosis.

Circumscribed gummous deposits may also occur in the periosteum (gummous osteo-periostitis) or within the medullary canal (gummous osteo-myelitis). Upon the surface of the bones the lesions appear as rounded, hemispherical tumors of the consistence of sarcomata. They are indolent and stationary and may terminate by absorption, in sclerosis, the contents undergoing calcareous degeneration, and leaving hard, prominent masses, or more rarely in suppuration with central necrosis followed by phlegmonous inflammation of the overlying structures and exfoliation of sequestra through the fistulous openings.

Infiltrations in the cancellous structures and medullary spaces, whether diffuse or circumscribed, may undergo degeneration and absorption, or may become the seat of ossification, resulting in condensation, eburnation, or sclerosis of the bone. In what is known as rarefying osteitis, there is a destruction of the embryonal osseous tissue, resulting in the production of lacunæ and channels with increased porosity in different parts of the bones, diminishing their capacity of resistance and rendering them liable to fracture from slight external causes or even from muscular contraction.

Gummata may develop upon the external table of the skull, or the internal table and penetrate the bony substance, sometimes resulting in perforation. The frontal and parietal bones or entire surface of the cranium may be riddled with holes or pit-like depressions and tunnelled with tortuous channels. In Fig. 11 (woodcut) syphilitic lesions of the cranium are admirably portrayed. This process may occur without suppuration and has been termed dry caries. Cicatrization may be osseous or fibrous ; in the former case, the cicatricial cavity may be encased by a ragged margin of ossified matter.

Gummata of the internal table may cause meningitis or meningo-encephalitis from their presence. Various forms of paralyses, neuralgia, epileptic fits, convulsions, and disturbances of the circulation are caused by the pressure of exostoses upon the brain, cord, and nerves, or by narrowing of the bony canals through which the vessels pass. Exostoses and hyperostoses in the orbit may cause exophthalmus. Deafness and various auditory disturbances may result from ossification of the internal ear structures.

In the diagnosis of osseous affections, it may be difficult to determine whether they are syphilitic or scrofulous in their nature, since all forms of osteitis, whatever their nature, may be followed by suppuration, fistulous openings, and the discharge of sequestra. In such cases the location and form of the lesions, the demonstration of a syphilitic history, and recourse to the test of specific treatment will usually clear up the diagnosis. Syphilitic lesions of the bones, as a rule, yield with surprising rapidity to the influence of the iodide of potassium.

SYPHILIS OF THE BURSÆ.

Syphilitic affections of the bursæ must be ranked among the rare phenomena of syphilis. Fluid distentions of the bursæ may occur as a secondary accident, and are analogous to the effusions into tendinous sheaths and joint cavities which occasionally take place in the early stage of syphilis.

The tertiary lesions of the bursæ have been carefully studied by Keyes, who has furnished illustrations Figs. 14 and 15 (woodcuts). Tertiary bursitis is a comparatively late manifestation, occurring from one and one-half to eight years, on the average five years, after infection. It consists of a gummous infiltration of the bursæ and peri-articular fibrous tissues, forming a circumscribed tumor of considerable size and prominence. The bursæ may also be secondarily affected by extension of gummous infiltration of the skin or neighboring tissues. The bursæ over the patellæ are the most frequently attacked; both knees may be affected or only one. The bursæ over inner side of the knee, behind the olecranon, the tuberosity of the tibiæ, and in other situations may be involved. The course of syphilitic bursitis is exceedingly chronic and indolent. If subjected to much irritation and pressure, the surrounding tissues become inflamed, and the integument over the bursa ulcerates, the disintegrated gummous infiltration is discharged, leaving an irregular cavity. Cicatrization takes place slowly, leaving a scar which is depressed and adherent to the parts beneath.

SYPHILITIC DACTYLITIS.

An affection peculiar to the fingers and toes, originating from syphilis, is described as syphilitic dactylitis. The morbid changes are probably analogous to those occurring in the long bones, the clinical appearances being modified by the anatomical structure of the parts.

Syphilitic dactylitis is a late affection, occurring from the fifth to the fifteenth year after infection, exceptionally it may develop within the first two years.

The first form of dactylitis consists of a gummous infiltration beginning in the superficial tissues or periosteum, it may involve one phalanx or the entire member, the first phalanx being the one most commonly affected; several fingers and toes may be involved at the same time or successively. The affected member is increased in size, the integument is inflamed and bluish-red in color, the swelling more pronounced upon the dorsal surface, is hard and firm, terminating abruptly; the process is accompanied with more or less articular stiffness. The course of the disease is chronic. Effusion into the joint, disintegration of the cartilage and other joint structures, and permanent loss of motion may result.

In the second form of dactylitis, the gummous deposit is seated upon the bone underneath the periosteum or in the medullary membrane. Like the first variety, it may affect one phalanx or several, the metacarpal or metatarsal bones may be at the same time involved.

The swelling is usually fusiform or acorn-shaped, the superficial tissues are not involved except in rare cases where suppuration occurs, and the pus and gummy detritus escape through an opening in the integument. In these cases a limited necrosis may result. Most frequently involution occurs through resorption without disintegration of the gummous deposit. Atrophy and shortening of the bones or the formation of a false joint are not infrequent results.

HEREDITARY SYPHILIS.

The susceptibility of syphilis to transmission by inheritance is recognized as one of the fundamental characters of the disease. Although there is some diversity of opinion in regard to the exact measure of the syphilogenic influence exerted by the syphilitic father and mother respectively, and much obscurity as to the precise modes by which the disease passes from the parent to the offspring, yet a careful study of the facts which have been observed relative to the hereditary transmission of syphilis justifies the following conclusions:

1. A syphilitic man may beget a syphilitic child, the mother remaining exempt from all visible signs of the disease ; the transmissive power of the father is, however, comparatively restricted.

2. A syphilitic woman may bring forth a syphilitic child, the father being perfectly healthy; the transmissive power of the mother is much more potent and pronounced, and of longer duration than that of the father.

3. When both parents are syphilitic, or the mother alone is syphilitic and the disease recently acquired, the infection of the fœtus is almost inevitable ; the more recent the syphilis, the greater the probability of infection, and the graver the manifestations in the offspring.

4. While hereditary transmission is more certain when the parental syphilis is in full activity of manifestation, it may also be effected during a period of latency when no active symptoms are present.

5. Both parents may be healthy at the time of procreation, and the mother may contract syphilis during her pregnancy and infect her child *in utero*. Contamination of the fœtus during pregnancy is not probable if the maternal infection takes place after the seventh month of pregnancy.

The type of the syphilis, age of the diathesis, specific treatment, constitutional peculiarities, and other conditions imperfectly understood which influence heredity in general, modify the syphilogenic influence of both parents. Time undoubtedly exerts a marked attenuating influence upon the diathesis. As the interval between the date of parental infection and procreation increases, there is a progressive enfeeblement of the transmissive power, as shown in a series of successive pregnancies. Abortions take place at a more advanced period of fœtal development, finally cease to occur, and later pregnancies may result in a child living but syphilitic, and still later in children bearing no traces of syphilis.

The duration of the period of the transmissive power of syphilitic parents does not admit of mathematical expression. The influence of paternal heredity is rarely manifest after the tertiary stage is reached ; that of maternal heredity is much more prolonged and active, probably five or six years, and according to the researches of Kassowitz, Wiel, Hutchinson, and others, it may continue in force much longer.

Specific treatment may also hold in temporary abeyance the syphilogenic influence of both parents. Thus it has been observed that a woman may have one or more abortions from syphilis; if she be subjected to active specific treatment, and pregnancy occur, she may bring forth a healthy child ; if treatment be now discontinued, the next pregnancy may result in a syphilitic child. The modifying influence of specific treatment over syphilitic heredity is by no means constant and certain, no matter how actively it may be employed.

While originating from the same virus, and manifesting itself by lesions of the same general character, hereditary syphilis is differentiated from the acquired form by its mode of origin and certain peculiarities in its evolution. A distinguishing characteristic of hereditary syphilis is that it does not make its début by a chancre. In the acquired form of infantile syphilis, the specific primary lesion appears at the point of contagion, and the evolution of the disease does not differ materially from that of the syphilis of adults, except in an increased severity, probably because the rapidly growing infantile tissues are immature, and endowed with a feebler capacity of resistance against the action of the poison.

There is a certain definite order in the evolution of acquired syphilis which admits of its division into more or less distinct stages, it attacks first the superficial, later the deep structures; in hereditary syphilis there is a simultaneous development of superficial and deep lesions. The early cutaneous lesions of acquired syphilis are dry and plastic; in hereditary syphilis the moist or humid form predominates · vesicles and bullæ, exceedingly rare in the one, are common in the other.

The visceral lesions of acquired syphilis always mark its ultimate stage; in hereditary syphilis, interstitial hyperplasias of the internal organs may be the earliest expressions of the disease, often existing before birth. Hereditary syphilis is farther differentiated from the acquired form by certain lesions which are its exclusive product, as pemphigus, peculiar changes in the bones, dental malformations, lesions of the eye and auditory apparatus.

The influence of acquired syphilis upon mortality is restricted—it rarely causes death; the effect of hereditary syphilis upon viability is murderous; it condemns the offspring to almost certain death. The influence of syphilis upon the product of conception is manifested in various modes and in different degrees of intensity. The intra-uterine death of the fœtus is its most habitual expression. This may occur at any period of its development, and abortion result or the child may be carried to full term, but still-born; it may be born alive, with syphilis, or apparently healthy, but soon afterward give evidence of constitutional taint. Fully one-third of all syphilitic pregnancies terminate in death *in utero ;* of children born alive and viable, more than one-third die within the first six months. An analysis of statistics, carefully computed from a large number of authentic sources, shows that only one child finally survives out of every four syphilitic pregnancies.

The intra-uterine death of the fœtus is often the result of changes engendered by syphilis in the placenta. These morbid alterations may be found both in the maternal and fœtal portion. Death of the fœtus may also occur from atheromatous inflammation and occlusion of the umbilical vessels, interfering with its nutrition. When the fœtus dies *in utero* and is prematurely expelled, the skin is often found macerated, the epidermis lifted up in places, forming bullæ, or entirely wanting over large patches of the surface. If it has reached an advanced stage of development, characteristic changes are also found in the epiphyses of the long bones and the internal organs, especially the liver and lungs.

When a child, the subject of congenital syphilis, is born alive, it may be apparently healthy and present no positive evidence of specific taint. There is usually in these cases an outbreak of specific symptoms within a short period, ranging from the first two weeks to the third month, rarely delayed beyond the fourth month. If there should be no unequivocal manifestation of the disease during the first year, the probability that the child has escaped hereditary contamination is converted into an almost absolute certainty.

In some cases, the entire group of morbid manifestation is limited to mucous patches of the mouth, anus, and genitals; these may continue to recur for several months and then cease, the child afterward exhibiting no specific symptoms. The severity of inherited syphilis is generally exhausted during the first two or three years of infantile life. This period may mark the definite end of the disease or a new train of symptoms may arise in connection with the second dentition. Outbreaks of specific symptoms may not only be continued with long intervals up to the age of puberty, but evidences of the diathesis may be manifested as late as the twentieth, thirtieth, or even fortieth year. It is still a moot point whether the late lesions of hereditary syphilis may develop without having been preceded by manifestations of the disease in infancy. Hutchinson maintains that all symptoms of inherited taint may remain latent until puberty or even much later, and then unequivocal manifestations may show themselves for the first time. Positive proof of this assertion is difficult, since opportunities for continuous observation during this long period are seldom afforded.

In the majority of cases, evidences of syphilis are manifest at birth. The child is small and puny, with a peculiar aged aspect, the hair scanty, the nails undeveloped, the skin loose and wrinkled, as if it were too large for the body, and often the seat of eruptive disorder. The skin, though loose, breaks and fissures readily, especially about the natural orifices and upon the hands and feet.

One of the earliest and most characteristic symptoms is syphilitic coryza, caused by structural changes in the mucous membranes of the nasal fossæ. It is often attended with a purulent discharge, causing excoriations and fissures of the nostrils and upper lip. This condition, known as "the snuffles," is quite pathognomonic of inherited syphilis. The plugging of the nostrils interferes with breathing, and the obstruction may be so complete as to render it difficult or impossible for the child to nurse. Later, the nasal mucous membranes often become the seat of gummatous lesions, the ulcerative process may involve the cartilages of the bones and nose, resulting in destruction of the septum and bony framework, with flattening and depression of the bridge of the nose.

Most of the cutaneous eruptions described in connection with acquired syphilis are met with in the hereditary form, as erythema, papules, pustules, tubercles, etc.; in addition, vesicular, bullous, and furuncular lesions occur. Gummatous lesions are more apt to be localized in the bones or viscera; cutaneous nodes are rare in inherited syphilis; ecthymatous pustules and rupial lesions are also quite exceptional.

Erythema of the maculo-papular type is an early symptom; it may be present at birth or develop within the first few weeks. It is analogous in location and appearance to the erythematous syphilide of adults. It soon gives place to a papular eruption, the papules occur in groups about the buttocks, genitals and lower extremities, and on the palms and soles, they frequently run together, forming large, infiltrated, reddened patches. The miliary form of the papule is rarely met with. On account of the fineness and delicacy of the skin, the cutaneous papules, especially about the mouth, anus, and genitals, are quickly transformed into mucous patches. At the margin of these orifices, deep fissures and rhagades are apt to form.

Contemporaneous with the maculo-papular eruption, mucous patches are invariably present. The mucous membranes of the nose, of the mouth, especially about the commissure of the lips, of the anus and vulva, are most commonly affected; deep crevices and ulcerations occur about the angles of the mouth and upon the inner surface of the lips, these upon healing leave radiating linear scars running out into the cheeks, which afterward may prove of the utmost value in making a retrospective diagnosis.

Pemphigus is pathognomonic of inherited syphilis; it is one of the earliest manifestations, in many cases being present at birth; it is rarely delayed until after the fifteenth day. Syphilitic pemphigus begins as dark-red patches which soon become converted in flattened bullæ containing a thin sero-pus. The bullæ or pustules increase in size, sometimes becoming confluent and readily rupture, the retracted epidermis showing at the base an intensely red, shining surface, or the contents may dry up into yellowish or greenish crusts, underneath which ulceration may take place. The eruption begins on the palms and soles, but may extend up the legs and thighs, and even over the entire body. Syphilitic pemphigus always carries with it the gravest prognosis; it is usually accompanied with febrile disturbance, inability to nurse, etc., and life is extinguished by exhaustion from diarrhœa or some other intercurrent disease.

The tubercular form of syphilide is comparatively uncommon in inherited syphilis. Lesions of the gummatous type are almost always subcutaneous. The tumors follow the same evolution as in the acquired form, softening and forming abscesses. Ulcerated gummata are liable to occur upon the head and face, especially in the temporal region and about the nose, and lips. Gummata also develop on the tongue, hard palate, pharynx, and nasal fossæ.

The lesions of the bones constitute one of the most constant and characteristic features of hereditary syphilis. The long bones, particularly the tibia and the humerus, and the cranium are the most frequent seats, although the ribs, scapula, vertebra, and every part of the bony skeleton

PLATE XXXIV.

Fig. I.—*Pemphigus syphiliticus neonati.* Upon the face, the extremities, and especially upon palms and soles, variously sized bullæ, filled with a turbid fluid, surrounded by a brown-red border. Many in the centre have dried up into a crust, which seems surrounded by a bullous ring. Between the bullæ pin-head to lentil sized, brown-red glazed papules in large numbers. The integument of the trunk is free.

Fig. II.—Polymorphous syphilide of an infant regularly distributed over the entire body, appearing from lentil to penny-sized, partly macular, partly papular efflorescences, over which in numerous places the epidermis seems lifted up in the form of flat pustules. The pustules here and there are dried in the centre, or have lost their covering. Upon the palms and soles near the described forms, partly rounded, partly irregularly serrated, sharply defined, brown-red ulcerative spots deprived of epidermis and fissured.

AFTER KAPOSI.

may be involved. The morbid changes may begin as an inflammatory affection of the periosteum, or may be concentrated about the junction of the diaphysis and epiphysis of the long bones. In the former, there is a thickening of the periosteum, attended with the production of osteophytic outgrowths, which may be osteoid or spongioid in character. Both the head and shaft of the long bones may become tumefied, hypertrophied, and covered with inequalities and nodosities of the surface. A frequent result of periostitis is an overgrowth of the bone in length as well as thickness, producing a curving of the bone which was formerly thought to be peculiar to rickets. Figs. 12 and 13 (woodcuts) represent lesions peculiar to inherited syphilis.

The second form, designated as osteo-chondritis, is characterized by changes in the diaphyso-epiphysal cartilages interfering with the normal process of ossification; these consist of proliferation of the cells of the cartilage, which undergo calcareous degeneration instead of developing into true bone tissue, retardation of ossification, separation of the epiphyses, etc. The morbid process may result in inflammation, suppuration, and caries, abscesses and sinuses.

The bones of the cranium are, after the long bones, the most frequently affected. Parrot describes a gelatiniform atrophy which produces a worm-eaten appearance of the skull analogous to that resulting from the "dry caries" of acquired syphilis. Osteophytic growths not infrequently develop at the margin of the anterior fontanelle and elsewhere, more often upon the frontal and parietal bones. The fontanelle, as well as the sutures, may become obliterated by ossification, and there may result changes in the shape and dimensions of the cranium, interfering with its normal development.

Certain changes in the teeth are generally regarded as among the most trustworthy evidences of hereditary taint. The milk teeth of syphilitic children do not exhibit these specific peculiarities, although they are apt to be malformed, chalky, and lost early. This premature loss may be due to a suppurative inflammation of the tooth sacs, causing an early exfoliation of the crowns of the teeth, or, according to Hutchinson, the neck of the tooth is destroyed by caries and the crown drops off.

The peculiar changes which, when well characterized, are pathognomonic of inherited syphilis are most typically displayed in the permanent central incisors which have been denominated "syphilitic test teeth." This specific abnormality consists in the narrowing of the cutting edge of the teeth, giving them a peg-shaped form, with a single shallow crescentic notch in the middle of the cutting edge. Besides this notch, the teeth are rounder than normal, not flattened out, and so dwarfed that they do not touch each other, but have an interspace between them.

However important the value of dental malformations as indicative of hereditary syphilis, they cannot be regarded as furnishing absolutely conclusive proof. Clinical observation shows that many children undoubtedly syphilitic have perfect teeth, while almost identical peculiarities may be exhibited in the teeth of children in whom all suspicion of a hereditary taint must be excluded. Keyes has observed a most characteristic pair of perfect Hutchinsonian teeth (notched upper incisors) in a married woman who had always enjoyed perfect health until infected by her husband. The photograph, Fig. 16 (woodcut) exhibits a typical syphilitic roseola. The patient was under observation a long time, and the evolution of the symptoms was characteristic of acquired syphilis. In this case either the test teeth were not due to inherited disease, or the patient had acquired the malady over again in the ordinary way.

A hemorrhagic syphilide is also described as peculiar to inherited syphilis, consisting of small ecchymotic spots of the cutaneous surface in connection with general anasarca. Similar extravasations take place in the parenchyma of the viscera. This manifestation is rare and its occurrence has been variously explained, by a narrowing of the lumen of the arteries, by increased fragility of the blood-vessels, diminished coagulability of the blood, etc.

Lesions of the viscera, the liver, lungs, spleen, etc., may coexist with the early cutaneous manifestation of hereditary syphilis. They consist chiefly of diffused infiltrations of the connective tissue of the organs; circumscribed gummatous deposits more rarely occur.

PLATE XXXV.

FIG. I.—*Maculo-papular syphilide* of the face and hairy scalp of an infant. Upon the upper lip the papules are closely crowded and covered with crusts.

FIG. II.—Inherited syphilis.

FIG. III.—Condylomata of the anal and peri-anal regions. (Inherited syphilis.)

FIGS. IV., V., VI., VII.—Syphilitic pemphigus of the palms and soles of the new-born.

FIG. I.—AFTER KAPOSI.

FIGS. II. AND III.—SYDENHAM COLLECTION.

FIGS. IV., V., VI., AND VII.—AFTER NEUMANN.

TREATMENT OF SYPHILIS.

In the general treatment of syphilis, an immense number of agents, drawn from both the mineral and vegetable kingdoms, have been employed, but of this number only two are now regarded as possessing specific properties against the manifestations of the disease. These two drugs, mercury and iodide of potassium, which constitute the basis of all special therapeutic treatment at the present day, are classed as specifics, since when introduced into the organism they cause to disappear the organic lesions as well as the functional disorders created by the syphilitic virus. It is well to have a definite understanding of what may be accomplished by specific medication, and while appreciating the full measure of its therapeutical value, it is well also to recognize its limitations.

It can be justly claimed for mercury that it exercises a positive curative action upon the secondary manifestations of syphilis ; it abates their intensity and hastens their involution. In the treatment of erythematous, papular, and papulo-pustular eruptions, its action is usually prompt and decided, causing a much more speedy disappearance than would have taken place in the natural course of the disease. Mercury also exerts an undoubted influence upon some of the later lesions of syphilis. Iodide of potassium is, however, the remedy *par excellence* for lesions of the tertiary stage, especially those of the gummous type. The rapidity of its action in melting away gummatous deposits and in arresting ulcerative processes is often marvellous. Affections of the bones, visceral lesions, etc., also come within the range of its curative action. A combination of these two drugs, constituting the so-called "mixed treatment," is often more efficacious than either alone, especially for lesions of the intermediary stage.

But while clearly appreciating the curative action of these drugs upon syphilitic lesions, the fact must be recognized that their preventive action is much less pronounced. Mercury may modify or derange, but does not prevent the evolution of syphilis ; successive crops of accidents may continue to recur in patients under the full influence of an active mercurial treatment. It cannot be positively affirmed that mercury given continuously during the entire secondary stage will positively prevent the development of tertiary lesions ; it does not infallibly cure the diathesis or furnish an absolute safeguard against future manifestations.

While mercury still maintains its supremacy as the sovereign remedy in syphilis, after four centuries of experience, the traditional methods of its therapeutic application have been essentially modified, and the principles of treatment established on a more rational and scientific basis. The attempt is no longer made to expel the syphilitic virus from the recesses of the economy by therapeutic violence ; on the contrary, any treatment which seriously disturbs the physiological functions is regarded as positively pernicious. The genius of modern mercurial medication is in the direction of attenuation ; instead of endeavoring to overwhelm the syphilitic diathesis with a metallic mass, the treatment has been drawn out or extended to correspond to the natural life term of the malady.

There are certain principles pertaining to the use of mercury in the treatment of syphilis which large clinical experience and observation have established as fixed and definite.

Mercury should be given in moderate doses, and never pushed beyond the production of its primary physiological effects ; large doses are not necessary in order to develop the full therapeutic efficacy of the drug. Mercury judiciously administered in small doses exercises a decided curative action upon the secondary manifestations of syphilis, and its continued and prolonged use may prove inoffensive to the patient. When given in doses sufficiently large to produce severe salivation and other toxic effects, it is positively harmful. The influence of the drug upon the eruption, and the toleration of the patient's system should be the measure of the dose. The susceptibility to the action of mercury varies in different individuals within such wide limits that the exact dosage of the drug for all cases cannot be formulated with precision.

Another point of importance is that mercury should not be given indiscriminately in all cases, irrespective of the condition of the patient's general health. In weak and debilitated persons, in certain cachectic conditions, and in cases of idiosyncratic intolerance, mercury often does positive harm, and it should be employed with extreme caution or recourse be had to other therapeutic resources

As regards the proper time for beginning the general treatment of syphilis, there is a difference of opinion among authorities. Many recommend the administration of mercury upon the first evidence of induration of the initial lesion ; others counsel delay until the appearance of secondary manifestations. The latter plan is, as a rule, the most judicious ; it is not always possible to decide with absolute certainty upon the syphilitic nature of a venereal sore before secondary symptoms appear, and besides it is doubtful whether the use of mercury in the primary stage of syphilis materially modifies the evolution of the disease or diminishes the severity of constitutional accidents.

The methods of employing mercury are numerous and varied, both in respect to the activity and duration of treatment, the form of the preparation used, and the mode of its introduction into the system.

As regards the activity and duration of specific treatment, it is impossible to lay down arbitrary rules which shall apply in every case. The two principal methods of administering mercury in the treatment of syphilis are known as the "tonic treatment," by the continuous use of small doses, and the successive or "intermittent treatment." By the continuous method, the dose is gradually increased until it produces slight salivation, which quantity constitutes the "full" dose. One-half or one-third of this quantity represents the tonic dose, which is continued from two to four years, with occasional resort to the full dose when more active symptoms appear.

By the intermittent plan, the effect of the mercury is carried to the point of toleration, and its use continued for two or three months; it is now intermitted for two months, and then recommenced, intermissions alternating with periods of active treatment from two to four years. Both these methods are open to objections. The principal objection to the first is that the continuous and prolonged use of the drug may exhaust the patient's susceptibility to its influence; to the second, that the intermission of treatment may coincide with an active outbreak of the disease when the remedy is the most needed.

A broader and more rational rule is to regulate the activity and duration of the treatment by the manifestations of the disease; in other words, the treatment should be essentially symptomatic. When manifestations appear, they should be suppressed by specific treatment; when they cease, the treatment should be remitted in activity, or substituted by tonics with a view of counteracting the anæmiating and debilitating influence of the diathesis.

Metallic mercury or various preparations of its salts have been employed in the treatment of syphilis, as the chloride, the bichloride, the bicyanide, the green and red iodide, the yellow oxide, the formamide, the ammonio-peptonate, the tannate, the salicylate, etc.

Mercury may be introduced into the system through four different channels: 1. The skin (the dermic method). 2. The skin and pulmonary mucous membrane (the dermo-pulmonary method). 3. The subcutaneous tissues (the hypodermatic method). 4. The stomach (the stomachal method).

The action of the drug is essentially the same by whatever channel it is introduced. The introduction of mercury through the skin by inunction or by fumigations is lacking in precision; the quantity of the drug absorbed can only be measured by its effects upon the system. The last two are more exact—a determinate quantity of the drug is introduced each time.

THE DERMIC METHOD.—The introduction of mercury by inunctions is the oldest method of employing this drug, and still retains its popularity with many surgeons at the present day. It finds its special application in the case of children and of pregnant women, and in all cases where gastro-intestinal irritation is liable to follow the ingestion of mercury by the stomach. It is also serviceable in securing the rapid action of mercury upon lesions in the immediate locality of its application. It has the decided disadvantages of uncleanliness, proneness to produce ptyalism, and of causing cutaneous irritation.

THE DERMO-PULMONARY METHOD.—By the dermo-pulmonary method calomel or one of the oxides is usually employed, in the form of a mercurial vapor bath. The specific effect thus obtained is supposed to be due rather to the introduction of the medicated vapor through the pulmonary mucous membrane than to its absorption through the skin. Mercurial fumigations are rarely relied upon for the systematic treatment of syphilis, but serve rather as an adjuvant to other methods when it is desirable to obtain more prompt and decided effects.

THE HYPODERMIC METHOD is a comparatively recent innovation upon older and well-established methods, and of late years has made decided progress in professional favor among continental surgeons. It possesses advantages of simplicity and convenience combined with scientific accuracy, and it is less liable to produce ptyalism, stomachal or intestinal irritation. Its advocates claim that mercury introduced subcutaneously is endowed with greater rapidity and permanence of action and increased effects from a minimum dose. Despite the greatest care in the technique of the operation, inflammatory engorgements, nodular indurations, abscesses, extensive eschars, etc., are liable to result. Until these objectionable features are modified or overcome, the employment of the hypodermic method in the general treatment of syphilis is impracticable. It must be regarded as a reserve treatment to be employed in cases where, for example, the integrity of an important organ is threatened, and the necessities of the case demand a rapid and intense mercurialization, or in cases where gastro-intestinal irritation is so marked as to preclude the introduction of mercury by the stomach.

The introduction of mercury by the stomach possesses certain advantages which render it preferable to all other methods, except in cases of gastric irritability, or in rare cases when idiosyncrasy renders it objectionable. Mercury may be given in powder, in pill form, or in solution; the quantity of the drug ingested can thus be estimated with precision, and increased or diminished according to its effects upon the disease and the tolerance of the patient's system. My own preference is for the iodides of mercury which in France enjoy so much favor. Pills of the protoiodide, each containing one-sixth of a grain, may be given, one to four, three times a day after eating. If this preparation should be found objectionable on account of its tendency to produce gastro-intestinal derangement, it may be combined with opium, F. 66, 67, 68, or other adjuvants, F. 65–69. If notwithstanding the addition of these corrigents severe diarrhœa should supervene, the drug should be suspended.

Many surgeons prefer the gray powder, F. 78, or blue pill, F. 77. Bumstead and Taylor recommend pills combined with a ferruginous or vegetable tonic, F. 79. In the celebrated Dupuytren pills, the bichloride is the active ingredient, F. 72; in another excellent formula, it is combined with reduced iron, as in the following F. 76. A more stable preparation is one in which sugar of milk is the excipient.

The bichloride in pill form is liable to become decomposed and it is usually given in solution; hydrochlorate of ammonium may be added to increase its solubility, F. 52. The bichloride is the basis of Van Swieten's solution, which is so generally employed on the continent, F. 33. It may be given in bitter menstruums, as the compound tincture of gentian or cinchona, or in combination with tincture of iron, F. 35. The bichloride is objectionable on account of its tendency to gripe and purge, and it is indicated in the later forms of the disease, where active mercurial medication is productive of less benefit than a mild effect of this drug in combination with iodide of potassium.

The use of the bicyanide of mercury, the acetate, nitrate, phosphate, and sulphide salts which have been from time to time more or less in vogue, has been generally abandoned. Of the newer preparations for internal use may be mentioned the tannate, the salicylate, and the carbolate of mercury. The tannate of mercury I have used extensively, and when a tendency to gastro-intestinal irritation is marked, it is an excellent substitute for the protoiodide. Salicylate of mercury is also highly commended for its efficiency and freedom from irritating qualities.

BAD EFFECTS OF MERCURY.—There are some individuals who tolerate mercury badly ; its use in doses which are ordinarily inoffensive to the majority of patients may produce stomatitis, griping and purging, and other forms of gastro-intestinal irritation. In some cases, these ill effects may be obviated by the use of corrigents, the substitution of other preparations of the drug, or introducing it through different channels, by inunctions, fumigations, or hypodermically. There is still another class of patients who manifest an idiosyncratic intolerance of the drug to such a degree that they cannot take it in any dose without the development of toxic symptoms. In such cases, the substitution of iodide of potassium is to be recommended, since, fortunately, abnormal susceptibility to both mercury and iodide of potassium is rarely manifest in the same person.

The toxic effects of mercury upon the kidneys in the production of albuminuria and other renal disorders, its profound impress upon the central nervous system, manifest in mercurial tremor, erethismus mercurialis and other symptoms of hydrargyrism, do not belong to the domain of idiosyncrasy ; they occur, as a rule, when the drug is tolerated and taken in large doses for a long time.

MIXED TREATMENT.—Toward the close of the secondary stage and in the intermediary stage, iodide of potassium may be advantageously associated with mercury, the quantity of the iodide varying according to the ulcerative tendency of the lesions. In resorting to mixed treatment, the biniodide of mercury is generally employed ; even when the bichloride is combined with iodide of potassium, the chemical reaction results in a freshly formed solution of the biniodide, F. 36–42. The biniodide of mercury is a powerful and dangerous salt, and should be given always in combination. The syrup of the ioduretted biniodide of mercury, F. 37, and the syrup of Gibert, F. 38, are favorite prescriptions in the French hospitals.

The quantity of the iodide may be varied accordingly as the ulcerative action is more or less pronounced, as in the following formulas, F. 41, 43. Another standard formula is F. 42.

When the iodides are used in combination, it is claimed that the effect may be intensified and the tolerance of the drug increased by the addition of a little ammonia. Keyes recommends the combination of wine or arsenic in order to secure a tonic influence, F. 47, or a vegetable bitter may be used as a menstruum, F. 44 and F. 45.

THE IODIDES may be given in the form of iodide of potassium, sodium, or ammonium—the former is most generally employed. The iodide of potassium finds its special application in the tertiary stages of syphilis. In tuberculo-ulcerous lesions, serpiginous ulcerations, gummatous lesions of the subcutaneous tissues, bones, and internal organs, as well as in syphilis of the nervous system, its curative action is remarkably rapid and efficacious, but it should be understood that, while it causes tertiary lesions to disappear, it does not prevent their recurrence.

The most convenient form of administering iodide of potassium is in the form of a saturated solution, F. 48. If preferred, the iodide may be given in water, Vichy or soda, or in milk, between meals. It may be associated with a bitter infusion, with a view of assisting digestion, or with syrup of ginger or bitter orange to render it more palatable. The compounds of iodine are not so toxic in their effects as mercury, and, except in cases of idiosyncratic intolerance, the drug should be pushed, no matter how large the dose necessary to dominate the destructive action.

TOXIC EFFECTS, "iodism."—In addition to the physiological effects of iodine upon the mucous membranes and cutaneous system, it may cause a condition known as "iodism," characterized by various disturbances, due to the toxic impression of the drug upon the central nervous system, and the production of numerous forms of eruptive disorder. The symptomatology of iodic eruptions embraces a vast number of cutaneous changes, representing almost every form of lesion, as erythema, papules, tubercles, nodes, pustules, bullæ, furuncles, purpura, etc. These pathological changes may closely simulate the manifestations of the disease that the drug is intended to cure. Iodic eruptions are not always caused by large doses or long-continued use of the drug; they depend rather upon an idiosyncratic intolerance of the individual than upon the quantity ingested. Iodic, like other drug eruptions, usually disappear promptly upon the withdrawal of the offending agent. In many cases, however, the patient's condition demands the continuance of its therapeutic action, and many expedients have been suggested with a view of counteracting the ill effect while still continuing its use. Arsenic, aromatic spirits of ammonia, belladonna, sulphaniline, introduction of the drug hypodermically or per rectum, have been recommended as possessing this corrective action. When the iodine cachexia is pronounced and the system profoundly disturbed in its centres of nutrition, attended with anæmia, albuminuria, muscular tremors, paretic phenomena, etc., the continued use of the drug undoubtedly does more harm than good, and should be substituted by other therapeutic measures.

Iodoform, which is used largely as a local application in syphilitic ulcers, has also been employed internally in the systematic treatment of syphilis, F. 74. It is poorly tolerated by the majority of patients on account of its liability to cause nausea, disagreeable eructations, and even vomiting and purging. "Iodism" is peculiarly prone to occur, as might be inferred, from the large proportion of iodine, ninety per cent. it contains. Hypodermic injections of iodoform have been employed in the treatment of both secondary and tertiary accidents, but with indifferent success. The results have not been sufficiently favorable to warrant further experimentation.

Various mineral agents, as bichromate of potassium, gold, rubidium, arsenic, etc., have been recommended as highly efficacious, but experience has demonstrated their inefficacy.

Various remedies drawn from the vegetable kingdom, as guaiacum, tayuya, pilocarpine, sarsaparilla, stillingia, yellow dock, xanthoxylum, have been enthusiastically recommended and some of them are still held in high repute by many physicians. They are especially valuable as adjuvants to mercury and iodide of potassium, or as substitutes when, from idiosyncrasy or constitutional peculiarities, these drugs are not well borne by the system.

Zittman's decoction has always been held in high repute, especially in Germany, in the treatment of syphilis, either alone or as an adjuvant to mercurials. Although it contains a small amount of mercury, it owes its virtues chiefly to the vegetable ingredients which it contains. In addition to its alterative effect, it acts as a stimulant to the secretions, both as a diaphoretic and laxative. F. 57 is that described in the United States Dispensatory. A good effect may be obtained by giving the stronger decoction in wineglassful doses, several times a day. It is especially serviceable in patients exhausted by a severe course of mercury, and in whom the symptoms prove refractory to the iodide of potassium.

The combination known as McDade's formula, F. 54, has been highly recommended by the late Dr. Sims and others. Dr. Taylor recommends Coca Erythroxylon as especially valuable in the anæmia and cachexia of the secondary stage, in malignant precocious syphilis, and also for extensive gummatous lesions of the tertiary stage, F. 55 and 56.

Syphilization for the cure of syphilis is mentioned only to be condemned; the practice, quite in vogue a few years ago, is now virtually obsolete.

HYGIENIC AND TONIC TREATMENT OF SYPHILIS.

Common observation shows that syphilis is most severe in persons of delicate constitutions, in persons suffering from privation, want and misery, of intemperate habits, the scrofulous and cachectic, and persons in the extremes of life whose vital resistance is the feeblest. Since the character of syphilis, the multiplicity, severity, and duration of its manifestations, are largely the product of peculiarities of individual constitution, the obvious indications are to treat the patient as well as the disease. The hygiene of the individual, embracing all measures calculated to build up and maintain the general health at the highest possible standard, are scarcely subordinate in importance to specific treatment. The patient's food should be of the most nutritious character, his surroundings good, habits regular, overwork and exposure should be avoided, while alcoholic and venereal excesses should be prohibited. The hygiene of the mouth should be particularly attended to, by the use of astringent washes, solution of chlorate of potash, etc., which tend to prevent mercurial stomatitis when patients are under the influence of mercurial treatment. Tobacco should be absolutely interdicted as long as there is a tendency to the localization of the disease in the mouth, in the shape of mucous patches. Particular attention should also be paid to the care of the skin by frequent baths and suitable clothing, in order to maintain this organ in the best possible condition for the proper performance of its functions. Exposure to extremes of temperature, or other conditions which favor catching cold, should be guarded against.

Since the effect of syphilis is to enfeeble the organism, tonics and reconstituent remedies should be employed to counteract the anæmiating and debilitating influence of the diathesis. The ferruginous tonics should be given in conjunction with specific treatment, or during its intermissions vegetable bitters to improve the appetite. Nutritive tonics, as cod-liver oil, subserve a useful purpose in toning up the system and increasing its powers of resistance.

In cachectic individuals and in the subjects of malignant precocious syphilis, active specific treatment may do positive harm. Good food, stimulants, and all measures calculated to promote nutrition and improve the general health should first be employed.

THE LOCAL TREATMENT OF SYPHILIDES.

The local treatment of syphilis has always been regarded as merely accessory to general treatment and of secondary importance, yet direct topical applications to the seat of syphilitic lesions exert a marked influence in hastening their involution.

Ordinarily, the earlier cutaneous eruptions of the erythematous and papular type disappear with more or less promptitude under the internal use of mercury, and rarely require local treatment. When situated upon parts exposed to observation, as the hands, neck, and face, the disfiguring character of the eruption renders its speedy suppression a matter of much concern to the patient. For the purpose of hastening its involution, a number of mercurial preparations may be used, F. 91, 92, 101. The ointment should be rubbed in and allowed to remain over night, care being taken not to excite excessive irritation of the skin. A more elegant preparation is an ointment of the oleate of mercury (five to ten per cent), or a solution of the bichloride in alcohol and glycerin (five to ten grains to the ounce) may be used for the same purpose.

The unsightly pigmentations upon the face and forehead, which often remain for some time after the lesions have undergone resolution, may be painted with F. 106 as a cosmetic, or one of the following lotions may be used, F. 23, 24, 25, and 27. These lotions may be applied by means of a piece of lint saturated with the solution. For fissures and cracks of the skin, especially about the lips, nose, and ear, calomel cream is, according to Hill and Cooper, a most useful application.

For the papulo-squamous eruptions of the palms and soles, which are ordinarily characterized by an obstinacy to constitutional treatment, the white precipitate or blue ointment, or the mercurial plaster may be applied, or one of the following, F. 93, 94. The ointment should be well rubbed in at bed-time and gloved over to insure its prolonged contact. Painful fissures may be painted with mercurialized collodion, the benzoinated collodion, or the following, F. 22. A very excellent application for the so-called syphilitic psoriasis, especially where there is an abundance of thick horny cuticle, is the following, F. 17, 18, or the salicylated soap plaster may be used. Onychia and dactylitis may also be subjected to the same application, binding the ends of the fingers with lint, spread with the plaster.

In the treatment of moist lesions between the toes and under the breast, mucous patches of the integument, and condylomata about the scrotum, vulva, or around the anus, the parts should be frequently cleansed with a solution of bicarbonate of soda, permanganate of potash, or Labarraque's solution, carefully dried, and dusted with calomel, iodoform, or oxide of zinc. It is also desirable to keep contiguous surfaces separated by the interposition of dry lint or absorbent cotton. The following are excellent powders, under the influence of which condylomata rapidly melt away, F. 83, 84; dried sulphate of zinc is also a very good application. Another method is to moisten the condylomata with a solution of chloride of sodium, then sprinkle powdered calomel over them; the bichloride thus generated is, in its nascent state, less painful than a strong solution. If an ointment be preferred, the white precipitate may be used or one of the following pastes, F. 59, 60. Moist lesions may be touched with a solution of nitrate of silver (10 grs. to ʒi.), or with F. 28, 29. When the lesions are fungating and papillomatous, they may be treated with the solid nitrate of silver, the acid nitrate of mercury, or a saturated solution of the sublimate, or sublimate collodion, F. 19.

In later lesions of a pustulo-ulcerous character, in serpiginous and gummatous ulcerations, applications of iodoform powders or in paste, F. 63, or suspended in ether or collodion and painted over the surface, gives excellent results.

An ointment of calomel, the white precipitate, or the yellow oxide of mercury may be used, or Sigmund's plaster, F. 17, forms a good dressing for syphilitic ulcers.

An iodoform ointment has been found valuableas a stimulating application to tertiary ulcers, F. 103. When ulcers are indolent with hard edges, they require a more active treatment, scraping and scarification of the edges, strapping, etc.   When they take on a phagedenic action, it must be arrested by the acid nitrate of mercury, a strong solution of nitrate of silver, the Paquelin cautery, or prolonged immersion in hot water.

When papular and tubercular lesions are massed or aggregated in limited areas, forming patches, the local application of mercury by inunctions, or the hypodermic injection of calomel or bichloride in the centre of the patch, exerts a more rapidly curative action than can be obtained from internal treatment.

For mucous patches of the mouth and throat, various astringents, stimulants, and caustics have been recommended.   The patches may be touched with nitrate of silver (the solid stick or solution), tinct. of iodine, sulphate of copper, solution of chromic acid or the bichloride, or with a solution of iodo-glycerin, F. 30. The acid nitrate of mercury should be used with extreme caution ; while efficient, it is very painful.   When the lesions are more generalized, involving the mucous membrane of the tonsils and throat, and ulcerative in character, gargles of a solution of the bichloride (1 or 2 grs. to ℥ i.) or a solution of permanganate of potash or tannin may be employed.   The patient should be warned not to swallow the sublimate solution.   Spraying the throat with iodoform in solution, or touching ulcerated surfaces with a strong solution of chloride of zinc or chromic acid is beneficial.

Syphilitic affections of the nasal mucous membrane are best treated by frequently cleansing the passages with antiseptic douches, as solutions of chlorinated soda, carbolic acid, biborate of soda.   Afterward calomel or iodoform, combined with sugar of milk or bismuth, may be thrown up by means of a powder projector   The following are good combination, F. 86–88.   Gelatin bougies medicated with iodoform, hydrastis, sulphate of zinc, etc., may be inserted ; they are especially serviceable when the fetid discharges depend upon syphilitic ozæna   When the bone is necrosed and the sequestrum partially or entirely detached, it should be removed.

For painful periosteal swellings, osteocopic pains, etc., surgical interference in the way of puncturing or opening must be avoided.   Painting the surface with tincture of iodine or iodized collodion, frictions with twenty-per-cent ointment of oleate of mercury, with the addition of morphia, will frequently relieve painful symptoms.   Where the joints are affected, immobilization and the application of blisters may be employed.

TREATMENT OF HEREDITARY SYPHILIS.

The treatment of infantile syphilis, whether hereditary or acquired, demands certain modifications of the treatment best adapted for adults.   It is of the first importance that the nutrition of the child should not be impaired.   A child with congenital syphilis should always, when practicable, nurse its own mother, as the mother, though healthy, is not liable to receive the contamination from her nursing child.   On account of its tendency to produce gastro-intestinal complications, the internal administration of mercury is often contra-indicated, and the use of the drug by inunctions is preferable.   Systematic frictions with blue ointment over the general surface is often objectionable on account of its inconvenience, uncleanliness, and its tendency to cause cutaneous irritation. A better plan is to spread the mercurial ointment over the child's belly-band, and shift it from the abdomen to the back so as to avoid continuous irritation of the same surface.   The movements of the child are sufficient to cause absorption.   Mercurial baths, prepared by the addition of an alcoholic solution of the bichloride, with or without chloride of ammonium, is a cleanly and convenient, but somewhat more uncertain method of employing mercury.   The existence of large abraded or pustular surfaces would constitute a contra-indication.

The internal administration of mercury in the form of the gray powder, F. 89, or of calomel with iron, F. 90, or of the bichloride, F. 46, is well borne by some children.   Teaspoonful doses of a weak solution of the sublimate (one grain to twelve ounces of water) furnishes a convenient mode of administration, or it may be given in combination with cod-liver oil.   The systemic as well as the local effects should be carefully watched. Anæmia, stomatitis, mercurial eczema, etc., indicate a temporary remission of the treatment.

A continuous and prolonged mercurial treatment should not be employed in the case of young children, unless an unusual severity of the diathesis furnishes positive indications.   The treatment should be essentially symptomatic ; with the cessation of active symptoms mercury should be discontinued, and in the intervals between the manifestations, tonics, such as cod-liver oil, the lactate, or the syrup of iodide of iron should be given.

Iodide of potassium may be given internally or in the form of baths ; its influence is less positive and pronounced in lesions of inherited than in acquired syphilis.   When given in the early stage, it may be administered to the nursing mother and the child receives it through the medium of the milk.   It is more efficacious, however, in the later or tardy manifestations which develop at the period of the second dentition, of puberty, or even later.

APPENDIX.

TREATMENT OF SYPHILIS.

MERCURIAL INUNCTIONS.

The method of employing mercury by inunctions consists in making frictions over different regions of the body with metallic mercury or one of its salts combined with a fatty substance, as the blue ointment. From fifteen grains to one drachm of mercurial ointment should be rubbed in every day. The skin should be first thoroughly cleansed with soap and water to favor absorption. The sides of the chest and the inner sides of the arms, the internal surface of the thighs, the abdomen, and the back are the parts best adapted for this purpose. To avoid irritation, the same surfaces should not be subjected to this process at two consecutive times, but should be gone over in succession. The hands of the rubber should be encased in chamois gloves, and the friction should be gentle, and continued from ten to twenty minutes. The systemic effect of the mercury thus employed will depend somewhat upon the patient's susceptibility and the absorbing powers of his skin, also upon the thoroughness with which the ointment has been rubbed in. The skin of many patients is so exceedingly sensitive to external irritation as to render the inunction method impracticable. A modification of this method, which is especially indicated in the case of children, consists in smearing a piece of flannel or chamois with the ointment, and wearing it as a belt around the waist, or a wrapper around one of the limbs, or it may be continuously employed by spreading the ointment on a piece of flannel and wearing it inside the socks.

The oleate of mercury may be employed for purposes of inunction in the strength of five, ten, or twenty per cent. It is a more cleanly and elegant preparation than the blue ointment, but not nearly so efficient. Lanolin has also been recommended as an excipient, on account of its rapidly penetrating power, but its use has been disappointing; mercurial soap, also highly recommended, possesses no special advantage. In employing the inunction treatment, its effect should be carefully watched. Should symptoms of mercurial stomatitis be developed, the treatment must be intermitted.

MERCURIAL FUMIGATIONS.

In giving a mercurial vapor bath, heat is applied simultaneously to the drug to be volatilized, and water, so that the patient's body may be subjected to the mingled steam and vapor of the drug. Various preparations of mercury are used in fumigations, as calomel, the black and red oxides, the sulphuret, etc. Calomel is perhaps the best.

A specially constructed apparatus for volatilizing the drug with a fumigating chamber, as found in many hydropathic establishments, may be employed, or the patient closely enveloped in a blanket, over which is thrown a rubber garment, may sit over a cane-bottom chair beneath which is a spirit lamp with a tin attachment, upon which the calomel is placed. Underneath the chair is also placed a vessel of hot water so that the vapor of the calomel may be mingled with the steam. Fifteen to thirty grains is the quantity usually employed for each fumigation, the duration of which should be from fifteen to twenty minutes; profuse perspiration is usually excited. After this exposure to the vapor, the body will be found covered with a fine, white coating of calomel, which should not be removed. As the bath is usually taken in the evening, the patient may go immediately to bed.

The cutaneous application of mercury may also be made by means of an ordinary bath to which the sublimate has been added, preferably in combination with muriate of ammonia, which increases its solubility. The duration of the bath should be from one-half to one hour. This mode of administering mercury is especially adapted to persons whose skins are irritated by inunctions, and whose digestive organs will not tolerate the internal use of the drug. On this account it is particularly indicated in the treatment of syphilis in young children. For an adult, the following formula may be employed:

> ℞ Hydrarg. bichloridi............. ℈ ij.–iv.
> Spirit. odorati................... ℥ ij. to ℥ iv.
> M.

Add to bath.

The sublimate may be used in combination with chloride of sodium or sal ammonia, as in the following:

> ℞ Hydrarg. bichloridi.................. ℈ i.–ij.
> Ammonii chloridi..................... ℈ ij.–vi.
> Aq. destillat....................... ℥ vi.
> M.

To be added to ordinary bath. The quantity of the sublimate should be carefully adapted to the age of the patient. Lesions of a pustular or ulcerative character are often materially benefited by mercurial baths when other methods of employing the drug fail. On account of the difference in the absorbing power of different skins, no exact rules as to the activity and duration of this method of treatment can be formulated.

HYPODERMIC INJECTIONS.

A large number of mercurial compounds have been employed for subcutaneous injections, and numerous experiments made with a view to provide preparations which should combine facility of absorption with freedom from irritation. The following are among the numerous preparations which have been employed for the subcutaneous introduction of mercury:

1.	**2.**	**3.**
℞ Hydrarg. bichloridi............ ....grs. iv. Glycerini.............................. ℥ i. Aq. destillat......................... ℥ vij. M. Sig. 12 drops for each injection.	℞ Hydrarg. biniodidi................... ...grs. iij. Aq. destillat...................... ℥ lvss. Sodii Iodidi........................... q. s. M. Sig. 10 minims each injection.	℞ Hydrarg. bichlorid..... ....grs. xv. Sodii chloridi............... ....grs. xxx. Aq. destillat.... .. .. ℥ iij. M. Sig. 15 drops every second day.

Muriate of morphin has been combined with the bichloride in order to modify its painful effect.

4.	**5.**	**6.**
℞ Hydrarg. bichloridi............gm. iij. Morphiæ hydrochloratis ....gr. iss. Aq. destillat........................... ℥ i. M. Inject 15 to 20 drops.	℞ Hydrarg. nitratis cryst............grs. viiss. Aq. destillat......................... ℥ xv. M. Sig. 10 to 15 drops each injection.	℞ Hydrarg. bicyanidi.............grs. iv. Aq. destillat........................... ℥ ix. M. S. 7 to 15 drops each injection.

Staub, with the view of modifying the caustic action of the mercury by combining it with the white of an egg, employed the albuminate of mercury as a basis of the injections. Later, Bamberger recommended the substitution of peptone for egg albumen, forming a mercuro-peptone solution which, it is claimed, is less irritating and painful.

Martineau employs the following concentrated solution:

7.

℞ Peptone (Catillon) ....grs. xlv.
Ammonii chloridi pur .... grs. xlv.
Hydrarg. bichloridi.. ....grs. xxx.

This is dissolved in 6 drachms of pure glycerin and 2 drachms of distilled water. When required for use, 15 minims of this solution are added to 75 minims of distilled water; 15 drops of this, representing about ¼ grain of the sublimate, is injected each time.

Liebreich devised a preparation of the formamide of mercury in the proportion of one per cent. The dose is somewhat smaller than that of the sublimate. A number of advantages are claimed for it; among others, that it does not coagulate the albuminoids and is rapidly absorbed. Wolf has recommended a combination of mercury with glycocoll as superior to all other preparations for subcutaneous injections.

8.

℞ Hydrarg. ox........................... grs. viiss.
Glycocoll .... grs. xv.
Aq. destillat........................... ℥ i.
M. Sig. 15 drops for each injection.

Another preparation, Lister's sublimate serum, is made by dissolving mercury in one of the natural fluids of the body. Schutz has added to the list of injecting fluids a preparation which he claims possesses the advantages of marked efficiency and painlessness. It is prepared as follows:

9.

℞ Hydrarg bichloridi. ....grs. xv.
Aquæ destillat......................... ℥ iv.
Ureæ (pure and well dried).. ....grs. lvss.
M.

Numerous other preparations of mercury have been recommended for subcutaneous injection; each one has been enthusiastically extolled by its originator as the best. At the present time, the bichloride, the formamide, and the ammonio-peptonate, representing the group of soluble salts, and calomel and the yellow oxide, the insoluble salts, are most frequently employed. The former are introduced in a condition favorable for immediate absorption: the latter are injected, and by a process of slow chemical reaction are rendered soluble and gradually absorbed. The supply of the former must be frequently renewed, once or twice a day, on account of the rapidity of absorption and elimination, which is ordinarily effected within twenty-four hours. The latter are introduced in a relatively small quantity, and at intervals of eight to fifteen days, the slow absorption and elimination insuring an impregnation of the system with the drug during a long period.

Of the bichloride solution, a quantity representing one-twelfth to one-sixth grain is used for each injection. Of the ammonio-peptonate, which is probably the least objectionable soluble preparation yet devised, an injection of about one-sixth grain is made each day. Twenty-five to thirty injections are ordinarily considered requisite to effect a cure. Of the calomel and yellow oxide, ten centigrammes dissolved in oil of vaseline are used at each injection, and repeated three or four times at intervals of from eight to fifteen days, or one of the following:

10.	**11.**
℞ Hydrarg. chlor. mitis, Sodii chloridi...................... āā grs. xv. Aq. destill........................... ℥ iiss. Mucil. acaciæ .... q. s. M. Inject 15 to 20 minims.	℞ Hydrarg. chlor. mitis...............grs. i.–ij. Glycerinæ puris..................... ♏ xv. M. Sig. 1 injection.

The injections should be made in the buttocks and carried down into the muscular tissue, as abscesses and other local accidents are thus less liable to occur than when the injections are made in the back, sides of chest, or limbs. The needle, which should be of large calibre, is introduced vertically downward into the subcutaneous tissues, and the solution slowly forced out. During the withdrawal of the needle, pressure is made against it in order to prevent the escape of the fluid along its track and the formation of a canalicular abscess.

EMPLASTRA.

12. EMPLASTRUM MERCURIALE.	**14. EMPLASTRUM DE VIGO.**	**16.**
℞ Hydrargyri........................ ℥ i. Ol. terebinthinæ..................... ℥ ss. Emplast. plumbi..................... ℥ iv. M. Spread on linen.	℞ Hydrargyri......................... ℥ vi. Ol. terebinthini..................... ℥ i. Ceræ flavæ........................... ℥ i. Resinæ .... ℥ i. Styracis.............................. ℥ ij. Emplast. plumbi..................... ℥ iij. M. Spread on linen.	℞ Ext. belladonnæ.................... ℥ ss. Emplast. de Vigo .... ℥ i. M. Spread on linen.

13. VIDAL'S PLASTER.	**15 SIGMUND'S PLASTER.**	**17.**
℞ Hydrarg. sulphidi rubri............grs. xxlj. Plumbi oxidi....... ... .grs. xxxvij. Emplast. plumbi..................... ℥ j. M. Spread on linen.	℞ Emplast. hydrarg., Emplast. saponis , ... āā ℥ ss.	℞ Emplast. hydrag., Emplast. de Vigo.................... āā ℥ i. M. Spread on linen. For syphilitic psoriasis.

Resorcin, hydronaphthol, subiodide of bismuth, and other agents of recent introduction in combination with plaster mass (20 to 50 per cent) have been found quite as efficient as mercurials in the local treatment of syphilides.

FIXED ADHESIVE DRESSINGS.

The fixed adhesive dressings, consisting of collodion or traumaticin holding the drug in solution or suspension, are designed to afford protection as well as to maintain the remedial agent in continuous contact, and have been found of great service in the treatment of syphilitic lesions

18.

℞ Chrysarobini .... ʒ ss.
Acidi salicylici .... ʒ i.
Collodii flex .... ℥ iss.
M.

19.

℞ Hydrarg. bichloridi .... grs. xxx.
Collodii flex .... ℥ i.
M.

20.

℞ Hydrarg. bichloridi .... ʒ ss.
Ol. ricini .... ʒ ss.
Collodii .... ʒ iv.
M.

21.

℞ Hydrarg. bichloridi .... grs. iv.
Tinct. benzoin .... ℥ i.
M

22.

℞ Iodoformi .... ʒ ss.
Collodii .... ʒ v.
M.

LOTIONS.

23.

℞ Hydrarg. bichloridi .... grs. iv.
Ammonii chloridi .... grs. xij.
Spiritus odorati .... ℥ i.
Aq. destillat .... q. s. ad ℥ iv.
M. Used in syphilitic pigmentations.

24.

℞ Hydrarg. bichloridi .... grs. ij.–iv.
Spts. vini rectificati .... q. s.
Glycerini .... ʒ ss.
Aquæ .... ℥ ij.
M. To hasten the absorption of unsightly pigmentations.

25.

℞ Hydrarg. bichloridi .... grs. iv.
Glycerini .... ʒ i.
Spts. vini rectificati .... ℥ i.
Aq. aurantii flor .... q. s. ad ℥ iv.
M. Stimulant and absorbent for pigmentations.

26.

℞ Chloral. hydrat .... ʒ i.
Tinct. eucalypti .... ʒ ij.
Aq. destillat .... ℥ vi.
M. Dressing for inflamed and painful ulcers.

27.

℞ Hydrarg. bichloridi .... grs. xvi.
Zinci sulph .... ʒ i.
Plumbi acetatis .... ʒ i.
Aq. rosæ .... ℥ viij.
M. For pigmentations.

28.

℞ Acidi chromici .... grs. x.–xl.
Aq. destillat .... ℥ i.
M. For mucous patches.

29.

℞ Hydrarg. bichloridi .... grs ij.–iv.
Spts. vini rectificati .... ℥ i.
M. For mucous patches.

30.

℞ Iodi puris .... gr. i.
Potassii iodidi .... grs. x.
Glycerin .... ʒ iij.
M.

31. "Black Wash."

℞ Hydrarg. chloridi mitis .... grs. iv.
Aq. calcis .... ℥ i.
M. For initial lesion and ulcerating syphilides.

32. Yellow Wash.

℞ Hydrarg. bichloridi .... grs. ij.
Aq. calcis .... ℥ i.
M. Stimulant to chronic syphilitic ulcers.

MIXTURES.

33. Liquor of Van Swieten.

℞ Hydrarg. bichloridi .... 1 pt.
Alcohol .... 100 pts.
Aq .... 900 pts.
M. S. One teaspoonful after each meal.

34.

℞ Ammonii iodidi .... ℥ ss.
Ammoniæ carb .... ʒ iss.
Tinct. aurantii cort .... ℥ ss.
Aq. .... ad ℥ iij.
M. S. One teaspoonful three times a day, diluted.

35.

℞ Hydrarg. bichloridi .... grs. i.–ij.
Tinct. ferri chloridi .... ℥ ss.
Aq .... ad ℥ iij.
M. S. One teaspoonful diluted after each meal.

36.

℞ Hydrarg. bichloridi .... gr. $\frac{1}{16}$ – $\frac{1}{8}$.
Potassii iodidi .... grs. iij.
Tinct. cinchonæ comp .... ʒ ss.
Spts. chloroform .... ♏ x.
Aq .... ad ℥ i.
M. To be taken after each meal.

37. Syrup of the Iodurettkd Biniodide of Mercury (Paris Hospitals).

℞ Hydrarg. biniodidi .... gr. i.
Potassii iodidi .... ʒ i.
Aq. destillat .... ℥ i.
Syr. simpl .... q. s. ad ℥ vi.
M. S. Two to four teaspoonfuls.

38. Syrup of Gibert.

℞ Hydrarg. biniodidi .... gr. i.
Potassii iodidi,
Aq. destillat .... āā ʒ i.
Syr. simpl .... ℥ v.
M. S. Two to four teaspoonfuls.

39.

℞ Hydrarg. iodidi rubri .... gr. $\frac{1}{16}$ – $\frac{1}{8}$
Potassii iodidi .... grs. iij.
Tinct. cardamom. comp .... ♏ xx.
Aq .... ℥ i.
M. To be taken after eating.

40.

℞ Hydrarg. biniodidi .... grs. iij.
Potassii iodidi .... ʒ i.
Spts. vini rectificati .... ʒ i.
Syr. zingiberis .... ʒ iij.
Aquæ .... ad ℥ iss.
M. S. Twenty to thirty drops after each meal.

41.

℞ Hydrarg. bichloridi .... gr. i.–iij.
Liq. potass. arsenit. .... ♏ xij.–l.
Ferri ammonii citrat .... ʒ ss.–ij.
Aq. ammoniæ .... ʒ ss.
Potassii iodidi .... ʒ ij.–℥ i.
Syr. aurantii cort .... ℥ iss.
Aq. .... q. s. ad ℥ iij.
M. S. One teaspoonful in water three times a day.

42.

℞ Hydrarg. bichloridi .... gr. i.–ij.
Potassii iodidi .... ʒ ij.
Syr. sarsaparillæ comp.,
Aq .... āā ℥ ij.
M. S. One teaspoonful after each meal.

43.

℞ Hydrarg. biniodidi .... gr. i.–ij.
Potassii iodidi .... ʒ i., ij., iij., or iv.
Syr. aurantii cort .... ℥ ij.
Aq. destillat .... ad ℥ vi.
M. Sig. One tablespoonful three times a day, after eating.

44.

℞ Hydrarg. biniodidi .... gr. ss.–i.
Potassii iodidi .... ʒ ij.–℥ i.
Ammonii iodidi .... ℥ ss.
Syr. aurantii cort .... ℥ ss.
Tr. aurantii cort .... ʒ i.
Aq .... q. s. ad ℥ iij.
M. S. One teaspoonful in water three times a day.

45.

℞ Hydrarg. bichloridi .... gr i.–iij.
Sodii iodidi .... ʒ ij.–℥ i.
Syr. zingiberis .... ℥ ij.
Aq .... q. s. ad ℥ iij.
M. S. One teaspoonful in water three times a day.

46.

℞ Hydrarg. bichloridi .... gr. ss–i.
Potassii iodidi .... ʒ i.
Ferri et ammonii citr .... ʒ i.
Syr. simpl .... ad ℥ vi.
M. Sig. One-half to one teaspoonful three times a day. In infantile syphilis.

47.

℞ Hydrarg. biniodidi .... grs. ij.
Potassii iodidi .... ʒ iss.
Sodii arseniatis .... gr. i.
Aq. destillat .... ℥ viij.
M. Sig. Two teaspoonfuls after each meal.

48.

℞ Potassii iodidi .... ℥ i.
Aq. destillat .... ʒ vi.
M. S. Five to thirty minims or more between meals.

49.

℞ Potassii iodidi .... ʒ ij.
Syr. aurantii cort .... ℥ iv.
M. S. One to four teaspoonfuls after eating.

50.

℞ Potassii iodidi .... ʒ i.–iv
Spts. ammoniæ aromat .... ℥ ss.
Syr. aurantii cort .... ℥ i.
Decoct. sarsaparil. comp .... ad ℥ vi.
M. S. One tablespoonful three times a day.

51.

℞ Sodii iodidi .... ʒ ij.
Spts. ammon. aromat .... ℥ ss.
Aq .... ad ℥ iij.
M. S. One teaspoonful after eating.

52.

℞ Hydrarg. bichloridi,
Ammonii sesquichloridi .... āā grs. i.–ij.
Tinct. gentianæ comp .... ℥ iij.
M. S. One teaspoonful diluted in water after eating.

53.

℞ Ammonii iodidi,
Sodii iodidi .... āā ʒ ij.
Potassii iodidi .... ℥ iv.
Aq. destillat .... ℥ vi.
M. Sig. One to two teaspoonfuls, diluted, after eating.

54.

℞ Fl. ext. sarsaparillæ,
Fl. ext. stillingiæ,
Fl. ext. lappæ minor,
Fl. ext. phytolaccæ decand .... āā ℥ ij.
Tinct. xanthoxylin. carolin .... ℥ i.
M. S. One to four tablespoonfuls in water three or four times a day.

55.

℞ Fl. ext. cocæ erythrox .... ℥ ij.
Tinct. cinchonæ comp.,
Tinct. gentianæ comp .... āā ℥ i.
M. S. Two teaspoonfuls n wineglassful of water three times a day.

56.

℞ Fl. ext. cocæ erythrox .... ℥ ij.
Tinct. cinchonæ comp.,
Tinct. gentianæ comp .... āā ℥ i
Elix. calisayæ .... ℥ iv.
M. S. One tablespoonful in wineglassful of wacer one hour after each meal.

57. Zittmann's Decoction (U. S. P.)

℞ Sarsaparilla .... 12 oz.
Water .... 90 lbs.
Macerate for twenty-four hours.
Then introduce in a linen bag:
White sugar,
Alum .... āā 1½ oz.
Calomel .... ½ oz.
Prepared cinnabar .... 1 drm.
Boil until the liquor has evaporated to 30 lbs.
Remove the bag, and add to the decoction:
Anise seeds,
Fennel seeds .... āā ½ oz.
Senna leaves,
Liquorice root .... āā 1½ oz.
Press and strain; put aside the liquor under name of the *strong decoction.*
To the residue add:
Sarsaparilla .... 6 oz.
Water .... 90 lbs.
Boil to 30 lbs., and add lemon peel, cinnamon, cardamom, liquorice, of each 3 drachms.

Strain, the liquor forms the *weak decoction.*

From a pint to a quart of the strong decoction is to be taken in the morning, and the same quantity of the weak decoction in the afternoon, the dose to be regulated according to the effect upon the bowels.

PASTA.

59. PLENCK'S PASTE MODIFIED.

℞ Hydrarg. bichloridi,
Camphorae,
Aluminis,
Cera alb.,
Spts. vini,
Aceti vini............................ āā ℥ i.
M.

60.

℞ Hydrarg. ammoniati........ .. ..grs. xx.
Glycerini amyli............................ ℥ ij.
M. ft. pasta.

61. CARBO-SULPHURIC PASTE.

℞ Acidi sulphurici fort.................. ℥ i.
Carbo. ligni............ ....q. s.
M. ft. pasta.

62. VIENNA PASTE.

℞ Potass.
Calcis caust........................āā ℥ i.
Alcohol.............................q. s.
M. ft. pasta.

63.

℞ Iodoform........................ ℥ i.
Amyli glyceriti..................... ℥ ij.
M. ft. pasta.

PILLS.

64.

℞ Hydrarg. protiodidi.................grs. xv.
Ext. lactucarii ....℥ i.
M. ft. pill. No. xx. S. One to two pills three times a day.

65.

℞ Hydrarg. protiodi .... grs. x.
Ext. conii alcoholici................grs. xl.
M. ft. pil. No. xl. Sig. One pill after each meal.

66.

℞ Hydrarg. protiodidi ....5 pts.
Ext. opii.........................2 pts.
Confect. rosæ ....10 pts.
Pulv. glycyrrhizæ.................q. s.
M. ft. mass. Div. in pil. āā three grains. Sig. One pill after each meal.

67.

℞ Hydrarg. iodidi viridis ....grs. x.
Ext. lactucarii ....grs. xv.
Ext. opii.........................grs. xv.
Confect. rosæ ....āss.
M. ft. pill No. 50. S. One to two pills three times a day.

68.

℞ Hydrarg. protiodidi,
Pulv. opii ....āā grs. xv.
Sacchari lactis....................grs. xl.
M. ft. pill No. xo. S. One to two pills three times a day.

69.

℞ Pil. hydrarg ....grs. xl.
Ferri sulphatis exsiccati..........grs. xx.
Ext. opii.........................grs. v.
M. ft. pil. No. xo. S. One pill three or four times a day.

70. DUPUYTREN'S PILLS.

℞ Hydrarg. bichloridi.................grs. x.
Ext. opii ....grs. xx.
Ext. guaiac ....grs. xl.
M. ft. pil. No. 60. S. Take two to four pills each day.

71.

℞ Hydrarg. cum creta................grs. xl.
Quinine sulphatis ....grs. xl.
M. ft. pil. No. 50. S. Take two to four pills each day.

72. PLUMMER'S PILLS.

℞ Hydrarg. chloridi mitis,
Antimonii sulph ....āā ℥ i.
Pulv. guaiaci res ....℥ ij.
Ol. ricini.........................q. s.
Triturate the mercury with the antimony, then add the other ingredients, and make a uniform mass. Dose, five to ten grains.

73.

℞ Hydrarg. chlor. mit.
Gum. opii ....āā grs. xij.
M. ft. pil. No. xxxiv. S. One pill three times a day.

74.

℞ Iodoform ....grs. x-xx.
Ext. gentianæ ....q. s.
M. ft. pil. No. xx. S. One pill three or four times a day.

75. (KEYES.)

℞ Hydrarg. biniodidi................grs. iij.
Potassii iodidi ....℥ iss.
Gum. tragacanth ....q. s.
Glycerini.........................q. s.
M. ft. pil. No. 50. S. One pill after each meal.

76.

℞ Hydrarg. bichloridi.................gr. i.
Ferri reduct ....℥ ss.
Gum. tragacanth,
Glycerini.........................q. s.
M. ft. pil. No. xv. S. One pill three or four times a day.

77.

℞ Pulv. hydrarg. cum creta,
Pulv. Doveris ....āā grs. xl.
Confect. rosæ ....q. s.
M. ft. pil. No. xx. Sig. One pill after each meal.

78.

℞ Hydrarg. cum creta...............grs. x.
Pulv. ipecacuanhæ.................grs. v.
M. ft. pil. No. 20. S. Take one pill three or four times a day.

79.

℞ Mass. hydrarg...................grs. xl.
Ferri sulphatis ....grs. xl.
Quinine sulphatis ....grs. xl.
M. ft. pil. No. xx. Sig. One pill three times a day.

80.

℞ Hydrarg. ox. tannodis.............grs. v.
Gum. tragacanthi,
Glycerini.........................āā q. s.
M. ft. pil. No. 10. Sig. One to two pills after each meal.

81.

℞ Potassii bichromatis..............gr. i.
Ext. gentianæ ....q. s.
M. ft. pil. No. 100. One to four pills per meal.

POWDERS.

In the treatment of syphilitic ulcerations, vegetating condylomata, etc., calomel, naphthalin, iodoform, subiodide of bismuth, etc., in full strength or combined with some inert powder (in the proportion of thirty to fifty per cent) may be used, or one of the following.

82.

℞ Acidi salicylici....................grs. xx.
Pulv. amyli......................℥ i.
M.

83.

℞ Acidi salicylici....................grs. x
Acidi borscici.....................grs. xxx.
Hydrarg. chlor. mitis..............℥ i.
M.

84.

℞ Plumbi carb.....................℥ i.
Pulv. lycopodii....................℥ vij.
M.

85.

℞ Pulv. iodoformi,
Pulv. camphoræ ....āā ℥ j.
Bismuthi subnitr..................℥ ij.
M.

86.

℞ Pulv. zinci ox...................℥ ij.
Pulv. bismuthi subnitr ....℥ i.
Pulv. amyli......................℥ v.
M.

87.

℞ Pulv. aluminis,
Pulv. cretæ præcip................āā ℥ i.
Pulv. lycopodii...................℥ vi.
M.

88.

℞ Hydrarg. chlor. mit..............℥ i.
Zinci ox.........................℥ ij.
M.

89.

℞ Hydrarg. cum creta..............grs. ij.
Sacch. alb........................grs. xl.
M. Div ½ chart. No. 12. Seven powders three times a day for child.

90.

℞ Hydrarg. chlor. mitis.............grs. ij.
Ferri lactatis.....................grs. iv.
Sacch. alb.......................q. s.
M. Div. in chart. No. 12. S. One to four powders per day in infantile syphilis.

UNGUENTA.

91.

℞ Ung. hydrarg. nitratis.............℥ i.
Ung. zinci ox.....................℥ vij.
M.

92.

℞ Ung. hydrarg....................℥ ij.
Ung. petrolati....................℥ vi.
M.

93.

℞ Ung. hydrarg....................℥ ij.
Ol. cadini........................℥ i.
Ung. aq. rosæ....................℥ v.
M.

94.

℞ Ung. hydrarg. nitratis.............℥ i.
Ol. rusci.........................℥ iss.
Ung. zinci ox.....................ad ℥ i.
M.

95.

℞ Ung. hydrarg. nitratis.............℥ ij.
Balsami peruv.....................℥ i.
Ung. petrolati....................℥ v.
M.

96.

℞ Hydrarg. bisulphidi,
Hydrarg. ox. rubri................āā grs. x.
Creasoti.........................q. s.
Ung. simpl......................ad ℥ i.

97.

℞ Hydrarg. chlor. mitis.............℥ ss.
Pulv. zinci ox....................℥ i.
Ung. aq. rosæ....................ad ℥ i.

98.

℞ Hydrarg. ammoniati..............grs. xl.
Hydrarg. chlor. mitis..............grs. xxx.
M.

99.

℞ Ung. hydrarg.,
Ung. iodi comp.,
Ung. diachyl.....................āā ℥ ss.
M. To be rubbed over syphilitic indurations and bone lesions.

100.

℞ Acidi salicylici...................℥ ss-i.
Ol. rusci.........................℥ i.
Ung. petrolati....................℥ vi.
M.

101.

℞ Bismuthi subnitr.................℥ i.
Ung. hydrarg. nitratis.............℥ ss-v.
Ung. aq. rosæ....................ad ℥ i.

102.

℞ Pulv. zinci ox...................℥ ij.
Iodoform.........................℥ i.
Ung. petrolati....................ad ℥ i.
M.

103.

℞ Iodoformi.......................℥ ss-i.
Balsami peruv....................℥ ij.
Ung. petrolati....................℥ i.

104.

℞ Iodi............................grs. xv.
Potassii iodidi....................℥ ss.
Ung. petrolati....................℥ i.

105.

℞ Argenti nitratis cryst............grs. xv.
Balsami peruv....................℥ ss.
Ung. simpl......................℥ i.

106.

℞ Bismuthi oxidi...................℥ i.
Kaolin...........................āā ℥ ij.
Ung. petrolati....................ad ℥ i.
M.

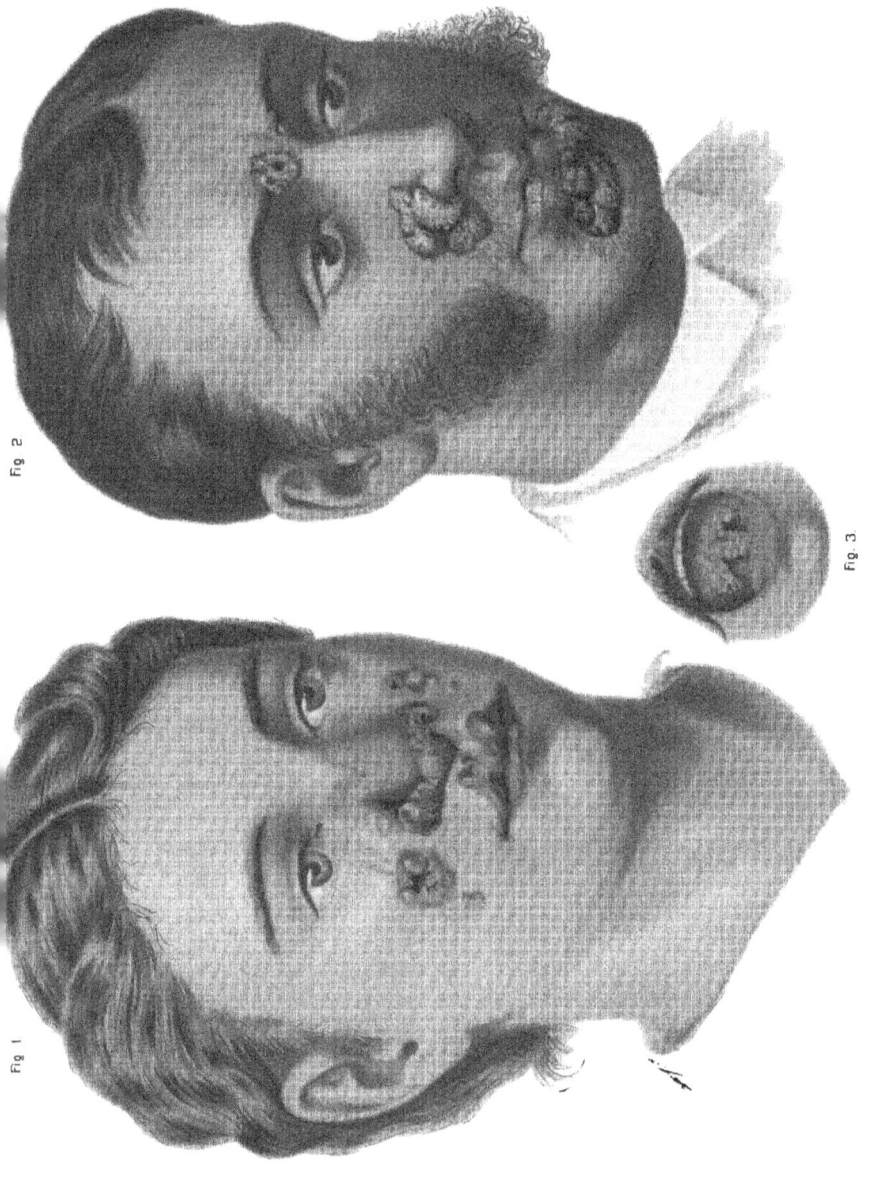

Fig. 1

Fig. 2

Fig. 3

Plate XXXII

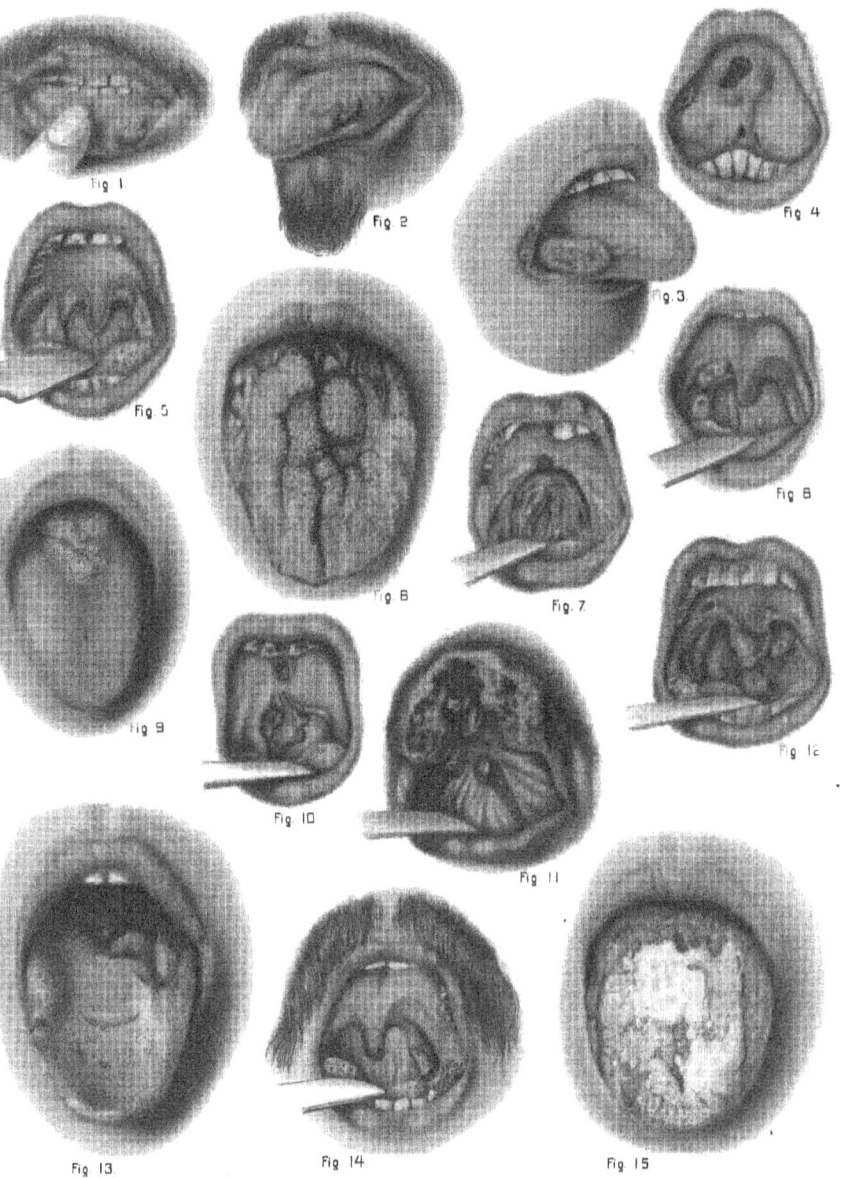

Fig 1.
Fig 2.
Fig. 3.
Fig 4.
Fig. 5.
Fig 6.
Fig. 7.
Fig 8.
Fig 9.
Fig. 10.
Fig 11.
Fig 12.
Fig 13.
Fig 14.
Fig 15.

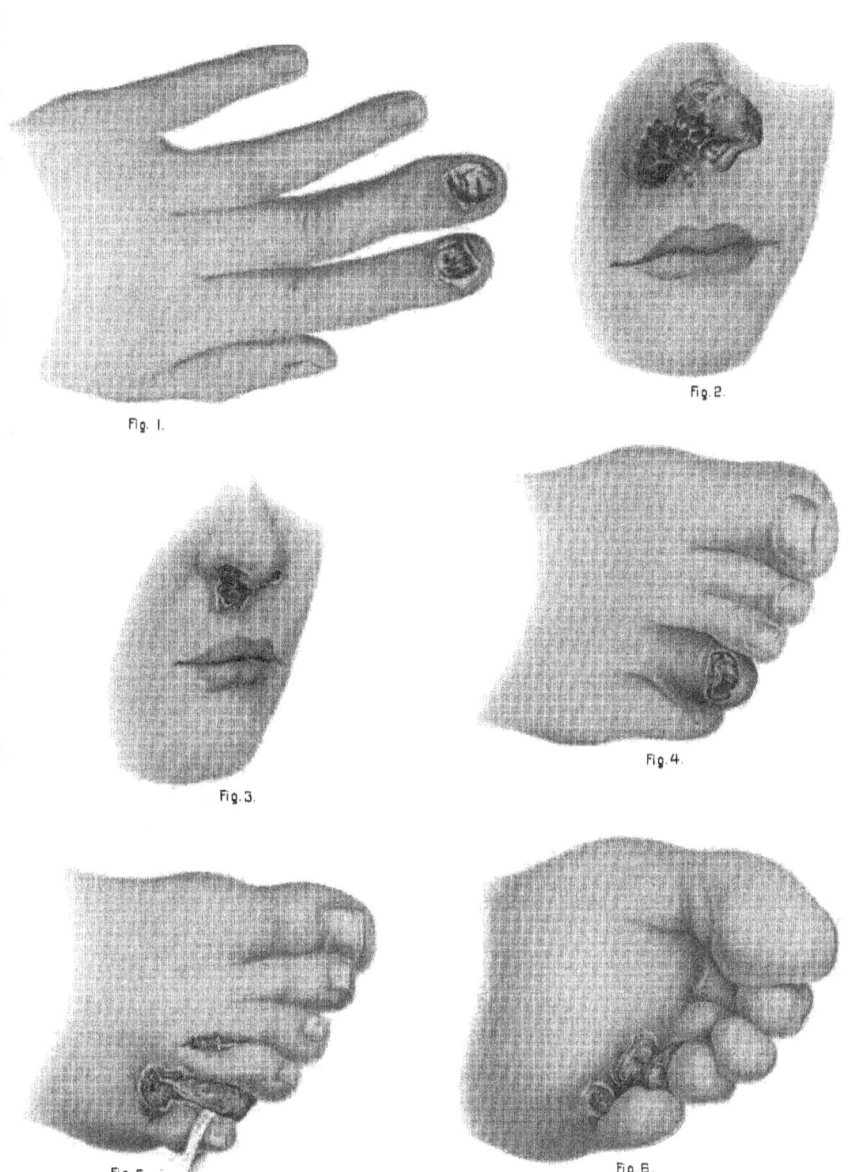

Fig. 1.

Fig. 2.

Fig. 3.

Fig. 4.

Fig. 5.

Fig. 6.

WILLIAM WOOD & COMPANY, Publishers, NEW YORK.

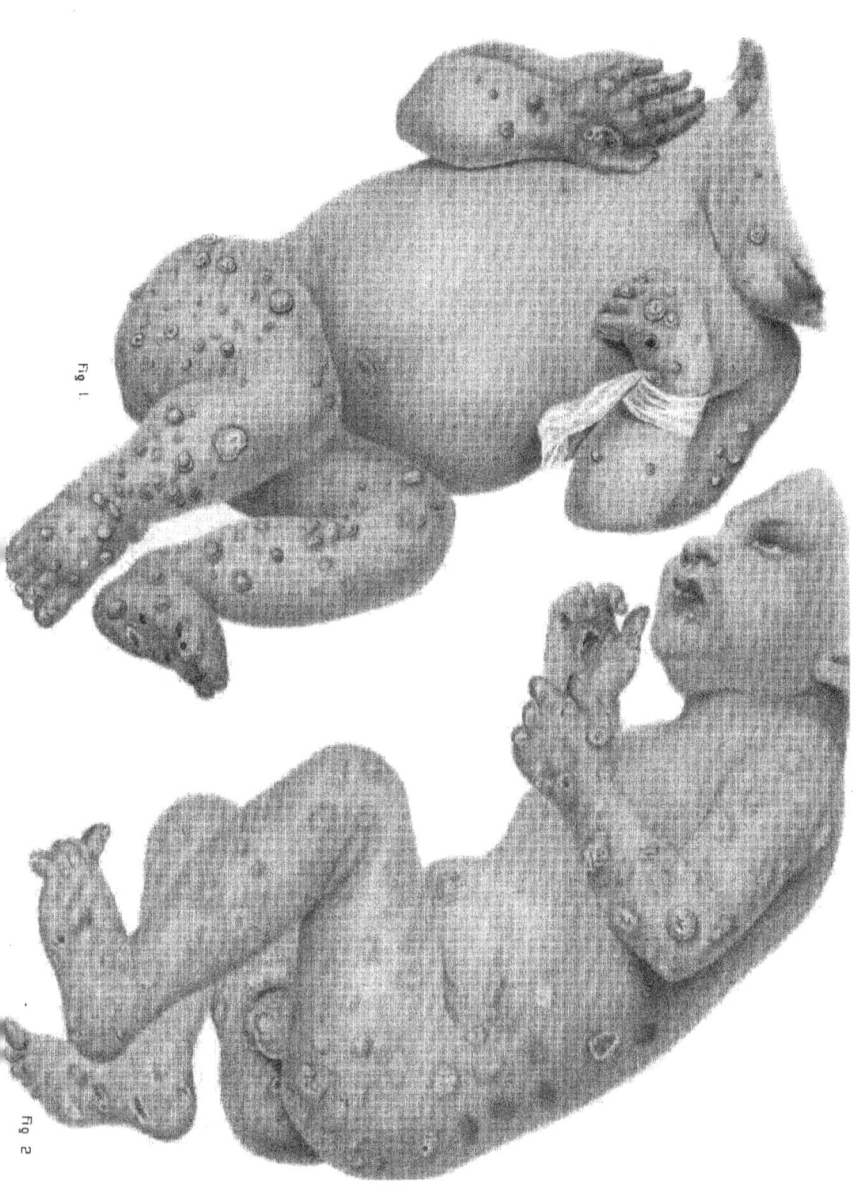

Fig 1.

Fig 2

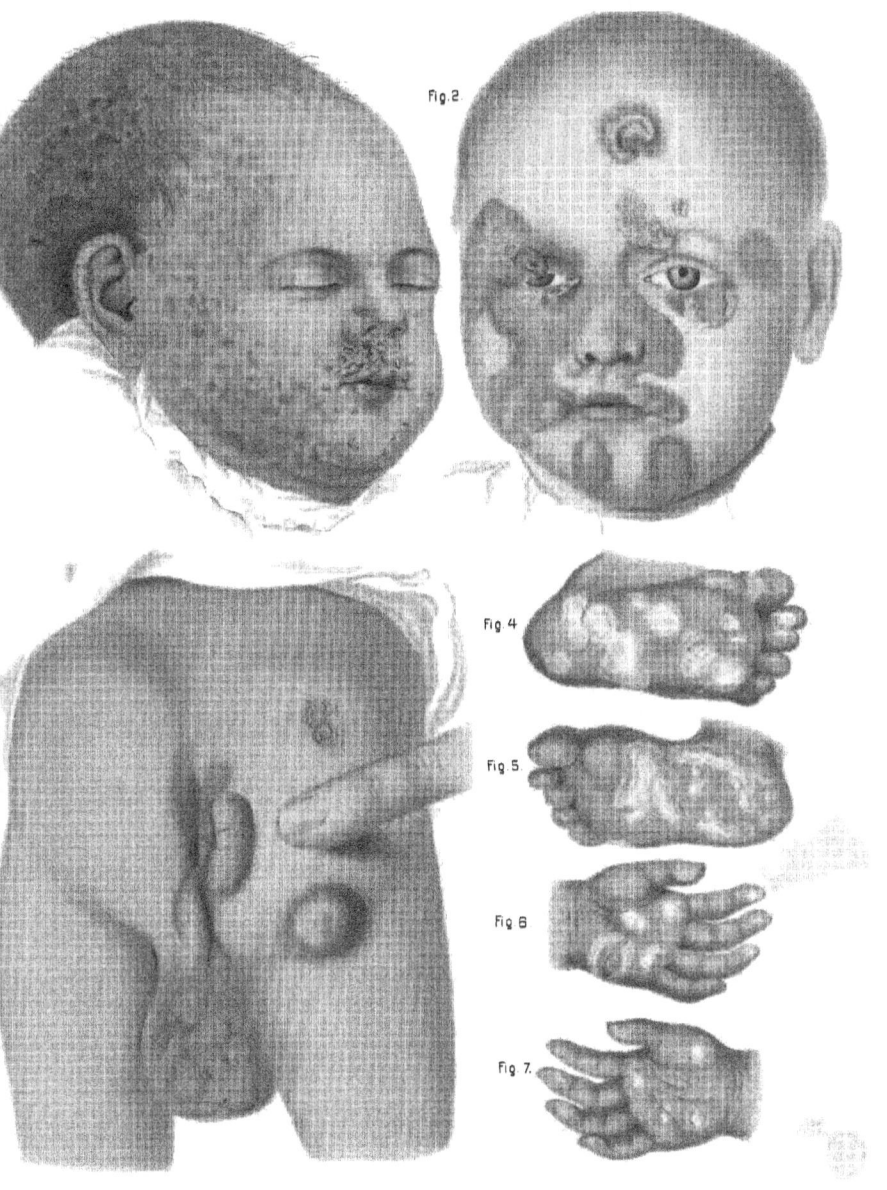

Fig. 2

Fig. 4

Fig. 5

Fig 6

Fig. 7.

WILLIAM WOOD & COMPANY. Publishers NEW YORK.

ATLAS

OF

VENEREAL and SKIN

DISEASES

COMPRISING ORIGINAL ILLUSTRATIONS AND SELECTIONS FROM THE PLATES OF

Prof. M. KAPOSI, of Vienna; Dr. J. HUTCHINSON, of London; Prof. I. NEUMANN, of Vienna;
Profs. A. FOURNIER and A. HARDY; and Drs. RICORD, CULLERRIER, BESNIER, and VIDAL, of Paris;
Prof. LELOIR, of Lille; Dr. P. A. MORROW, of New York; Dr. E. L. KEYES, of New York;
Dr. FESSENDEN N. OTIS, of New York; Dr. J. NEVINS HYDE, of Chicago;
Dr. HENRY G. PIFFARD, of New York, and others.

WITH ORIGINAL TEXT BY

PRINCE A. MORROW, A.M., M.D.,

CLINICAL PROFESSOR OF VENEREAL DISEASES, FORMERLY CLINICAL LECTURER ON DERMATOLOGY, IN THE UNIVERSITY OF THE CITY OF NEW YORK;
SURGEON TO CHARITY HOSPITAL, ETC.

NEW YORK

WILLIAM WOOD & COMPANY

1888

ATLAS

OF

VENEREAL AND SKIN

DISEASES

It is with special satisfaction that the publishers announce that this large and important work, which they have had in contemplation since 1883, is now ready for publication. It has long been recognized by them, from wide observation and acquaintance with similar works published in this country and abroad, that it is impossible for any one author to furnish, from his own collection of cases and illustrations, the most typical and at the same time the best and most lifelike pictures of the many peculiar forms of these diseases. Appreciating the defects and disadvantages arising from this cause, it was determined from the outset to enlist the co-operation, in the making of this ATLAS, of the leading dermatologists and syphilographers of the world. Prominent among them are Profs. M. Kaposi and I. Neumann, of Vienna. The atlas of the former, of venereal diseases, just completed, and that of the latter, of skin diseases, now being issued in parts, will be largely drawn upon in the preparation of this work, the sole right to reproduce them having been granted us by the authors.

Among other distinguished gentlemen who have engaged to contribute selections from their collections of original illustrations may now be mentioned Dr. J. Hutchinson, of London; Profs. A. Fournier and A. Hardy; and Drs. Ricord, Cullerrier, Besnier, and Vidal, of Paris; Dr. P. A. Morrow, of New York; Dr. Edward L. Keyes, of New York; Dr. Fessenden N. Otis, of New York; Dr. J. Nevins Hyde, of Chicago; Dr. Henry G. Piffard, of New York.

Other names will be added to this list as the work progresses.

The Editor of the work is Dr. Prince A. Morrow, of New York, who, in addition to plates contributed from his own remarkable collection, will write the treatise on skin and venereal diseases, which constitutes, besides the description of the plates, the text accompanying them.

In this treatise, it is aimed to include chiefly those features which are the most practical, omitting in great measure pathological and other considerations which would be more properly treated of in extended writings, rather than as the adjunct to an Atlas.

In regard to the character of the plates, it may be said, they are believed to be superior to anything of the kind heretofore produced—as accurate in drawing as photographs, and far more distinct, while the coloring faithfully represents nature.

The text is printed from new type, large, clear, and handsome, and the paper is heavy, with a highly finished surface.

Altogether, considering the reputation of the authors of the plates, the ability of the editor, the superb execution of the plates, the excellence of the presswork, the high quality of the paper of both text and plates, the large size of the page, etc., etc., this ATLAS OF VENEREAL AND SKIN DISEASES will be the most superb work in medical literature ever published in the English language.

The ATLAS OF VENEREAL AND SKIN DISEASES will be published in fifteen monthly parts, each containing five folio, chromo-lithographic plates, many of them containing numerous figures, all printed in flesh tints and colors, together with descriptive text for each plate, and from sixteen to twenty folio pages of a practical treatise upon venereal and skin diseases; the whole forming, when complete, one magnificent thick folio volume with seventy-five plates, containing several hundred figures, exquisitely printed in colors.

☞ The ATLAS OF VENEREAL AND SKIN DISEASES will be sold by subscription only, at the very moderate price of $2 per part.

WILLIAM WOOD & COMPANY, *Publishers*.

56 AND 58 LAFAYETTE PLACE, NEW YORK.

INTRODUCTORY.

In a work which proposes to deal chiefly with the clinical aspects of diseases of the skin, the study of the structure of this organ in a state of health, its physiology, as well as many details relating to its pathological anatomy must be omitted. The text will be devoted principally to the consideration of the nature, course, clinical features, diagnosis, and treatment of the more important dermatoses, especial attention being given to the description of the objective characters of the different diseases. Taken in connection with the plates, in which the shades of coloration of the lesions, as well as the details of their configuration and distribution are represented, it is hoped that the special nature of each eruption, and the differential characters which distinguish it from other eruptions, will be as readily recognizable as from the examination of the living subject.

OBJECTIVE SYMPTOMS.

With a view to the proper understanding of the phenomena which make up the clinical pictures of the different skin affections, it is necessary, first of all, to familiarize ourselves with the pathological alterations in the structure of the skin which are recognized as lesions.

The skin may be regarded as a composite structure, consisting of the corium, with an epidermal investment, including the hair, nails, and pigmentary structures, a glandular apparatus, vessels, and nerves. These are the elements which, under the influence of various causes, are disturbed in their vascular and nutritive relations, and enter into the production of the numerous tissue alterations, abnormalities of pigmentation and morbid growths which constitute the objective characters of all diseases of the skin.

In the complex structure of the skin, the several component parts are so intricately united and intimately related, that a disorder of one entails more or less disturbance in the others. Yet it is to be observed that in different eruptions the primary and essential changes are centered upon this or that constituent element, while alterations in the others are secondary or superadded. In some diseases the pathological changes are grouped around the blood-vessels or glands, in others the pathological process affects principally the cells of the epidermis, in others the derma proper, while in others the entire structure of the skin is implicated. The pathological changes in the skin are for the most part phenomena of inflammation, or the indirect and secondary results of that process. In many instances these changes represent different grades of the same inflammatory action, one the beginning, another a more advanced stage, and still another the acme or completion of this process. A number of elementary lesions may thus be common to the same disease, developed simultaneously or successively.

Notwithstanding the immense diversity in the external characters of different cutaneous eruptions, they are all made up of a comparatively limited number of lesions, each characterized by a definite anatomical form. The variety of aspect presented results from the different appearances of the lesions in their development and decline, and the combination of one elementary form with another.

The objective characters of skin diseases, or the signs visible upon the surface of the body, constitute the essential basis of the differentiation of one disease from another. They have been often referred to as the "alphabet of dermatology, out of which are constructed the words indicating the different diseases;" it is important then that the observer should be thoroughly familiar with the characters in order to decipher the writing.

The objective symptoms are classified as primary and secondary lesions The primary lesions are the direct results of the various morbid processes occurring in the skin. They are succeeded by the secondary lesions which result from the disintegration or metamorphosis of the products of disease.

THE PRIMARY LESIONS.

The primary lesions of the skin are nine in number: 1st, macules; 2d, erythema; 3d, wheals; 4th, papules; 5th, tubercles; 6th, vesicles; 7th, bullæ; 8th, pustules; 9th, scales.

MACULES may be defined as circumscribed alterations in the color of the skin, unattended by any marked elevation or depression, and often accompanied with changes in its texture. They may represent either the beginning stage of a disease, or the last stage in its involution, in which case they are due to the escape of the normal pigmentary matter of the blood into the rete mucosum and its subsequent metamorphosis, as may be seen in syphilis and in many long-continued congestions of the skin. Macules may result from various abnormalities of pigmentation; in vitiligo, for example, there is a deficiency of coloring matter, in lentigo and chloasma there is an excess of pigment, the macules of purpura are formed by an extravasation of blood into the cutis. As other familiar examples of this lesion may be mentioned the stains of nitrate of silver and other chemical agents, the yellowish macules of the parasitic affection known as tinea versicolor, etc.

ERYTHEMA.—This term is applied to superficial red patches, irregularly circumscribed or generally diffused over the surface. The color is of variable intensity and disappears under pressure, to return immediately when the pressure is withdrawn. Erythema may represent a simple hyperæmia of transient duration from excess of blood in the vessels, or it may be accompanied with increased heat, swelling, and other signs of active inflammation, and succeeded by secondary changes of desquamation, from suspended nutrition of the epidermis. The desquamation is usually slight and of short duration.

Erythema usually marks the beginning stage of most inflammatory diseases, it may, however, constitute the entire morbid process. It possesses *per se* little diagnostic importance; when partial or circumscribed it is ordinarily the beginning stage of a localized inflammation; when generalized and symmetrically developed, it is symptomatic of a general blood alteration, as occurs from the poison of the specific fevers.

WHEALS.—These are variably sized, rounded, oval or irregularly flat elevations produced by œdematous infiltration into the papillary layer of the corium. The swellings are solid, do not readily pit on pressure, the central portion is pale, while the circumference is reddened; they may be discrete or confluent, forming large, irregularly elevated plaques. The lesions are exceedingly evanescent, appearing and disappearing with marvellous celerity, and leaving no trace of their passage. The rapidity of involution is due to the serous quality of the exudation and its proximity to the absorbent vessels.

In one variety, known as lichen urticatus, the exudation is accompanied by a deposit of lymph, giving to the lesions a papular and more permanent form. Wheals have considerable diagnostic importance, as they are pathognomonic of urticaria; their etiology is, however, so multiple and mysterious that the ready recognition of the character of the disease rarely furnishes indications as to treatment.

PAPULES consist of circumscribed solid elevations of the skin which contain no fluid. They are ordinarily from pin-head to pea-sized, and may be acuminate, rounded or flat, discrete or confluent. Papules are produced by a variety of pathological processes, and vary not only in size and shape, but in degree of vascularity, the nature and seat of the exudation, and their persistent or transitional character. In the majority of cases, they are formed by an inflammatory process attended with an exudation into the skin with a special tendency to implication of the papillæ. In lichen there is a deposition of lymph about the follicles. The exudation may be serous, as in measles, more cellular and plastic, as in lupus and new growths. The term papule is also applied to a variety of lesions non-inflammatory in their nature; for example, to the retained recretion of the sebaceous glands as observed in milium and comedo; to the heaped up cornified sebaceous matter about the mouth of the follicles, as in keratosis pilaris; to the hypertrophy of the papillæ, as seen in verruca, etc., so that the term is thus deprived of special pathological value. Inflammatory papules are usually attended with more or less itching, and are frequently converted into vesicles or pustules.

TUBERCLES are ordinarily described as large papules or nodules, differentiated from the papule only by the difference of bulk. By later authorities, the distinction made between the papule and tubercle is a pathological one, and irrespective of size. Lesions characterized by inflammatory exudation are excluded, and the term tubercle is restricted in its application to nodules formed by a cellular infiltration into the corium, as in lupus; by a proliferation of the cells of the epidermis, as in epithelioma, or by a hypertrophy of the connective tissue, as in certain new growths.

VESICLES may be described as small, circumscribed elevations of the epidermis containing a clear or opaque fluid. Their anatomical seat is chiefly at the orifices of the follicles. Vesicles are usually, but not necessarily, of inflammatory origin, and their mode of formation is as follows: The serous fluid exuded from the capillaries readily passes through the rete mucosum, and reaches the hard, impenetrable horny layer, which is separated from its basement attachment and uplifted, forming the roof of the circumscribed collection of fluid.

Vesicles vary in size and shape; they are small in eczema, larger and more deeply seated in herpes zoster, conical or hemispherical in sudamina. The contents of the vesicle may be partially absorbed, or escape by rupture and dry up into a crust, or undergo a pustular transformation.

BULLÆ are differentiated from vesicles solely by their size, having the same anatomical seat and mode of formation. They vary in dimensions from a cherry to that of an orange, and in shape may be hemispherical, irregularly rounded, or oblong. A bulla may be formed by the confluence of vesicles, or it may develop directly from an erythematous base, as in pemphigus or syphilis, or it may be a secondary process, as in erysipelas. The contents of bullæ are usually a clear or yellowish serum, sometimes opaque and sanious, from admixture with pus or blood. The walls usually rupture, the contents escape or dry up, forming with the secretion from the excoriated surface crusts more or less thick, and gray, brownish, or black in color.

PUSTULES may be defined as circumscribed prominences of the epidermis containing pus. They usually represent a more advanced stage of development of papules or vesicles, and result from a higher grade of inflammatory action. The pustular metamorphosis is oftentimes so rapid that the primary papular or vesicular form is not recognized. They vary in size, shape, and anatomical seat; they may be acuminate, flattened, or umbilicated; they may be seated between the horny and mucous layer, upon or within the corium, or in the sebaceous and hair follicles, as seen in acne and sycosis.

The catarrhal pustule is formed simply by a transformation of the clear contents of a vesicle into an opaque or yellowish fluid without modification of its size or shape. The pock or pustule of variola represents a different mode of formation, the exudation, instead of occupying an artificial cavity between the mucous and horny layer, takes place within the cells, which are distended and the cell walls compressed, forming a network infiltrated with fluid. The pustules of syphilis, of acne, and other non-specific disease exhibit differences in their mode and rate of development. In ecthyma, the pustules are deeply seated upon a hard, red base, and their disintegration is characterized by the formation of grayish, greenish, or blackish crusts which, upon falling, leave scars.

SCALES are the lamellæ of the horny layer, separated from the surface of the skin. Since there is more or less constant shedding of the epidermis in the form of minute branny scales, the process may be regarded as physiological within certain limits. Scales may represent either a primary or secondary lesion. While in most inflammatory diseases scaling occurs secondarily, yet in certain diseases it constitutes the chief feature of the morbid process. The characteristic lesion of psoriasis consists of an accumulation of scales upon a reddened, infiltrated base. The infiltration of the derma interferes with the nutrition of the overlying cuticle, and the cell elements are imperfectly elaborated; instead of the normal process of cornification, there is simply a desiccation of the albuminoid elements. The light, silvery character of psoriasis scales are supposed to be due to contained globules of air.

The scales of seborrhœa sicca are composed of small masses of sebaceous matter and epithelial cells; they are usually small and branny; the scales of chronic eczema are larger. The cuticle may exfoliate in large lamellæ, as seen in pityriasis rubra, scarlatina, etc.

SECONDARY LESIONS.

The secondary lesions of the skin are usually the sequence of the primary, representing their terminal stage, or they may result directly from traumatism.

EXCORIATIONS.—This term is applied to the exposure of the rete mucosum by the removal of the epidermis. The loss of substance may extend deeper, and expose the true skin, in which case there is usually an exudation of blood-corpuscles with the serous fluid drying into brownish crusts.

The destruction of epidermis may be caused by effusion from beneath, as in eczema, or it may be accomplished by the nails in scratching. The linear excoriations caused by the nails in phtheiriasis, and the minute blood crusts upon the torn summits of eczema and prurigo papules are quite characteristic.

ULCERATIONS differ from the former chiefly in depth and extent of surface. The true skin as well as the subcutaneous tissue may be destroyed, and the loss of substance is replaced by cicatricial tissue.

Ulcers may result from impaired nutrition of parts, as the *ulcus cruris* from varicose veins, from suppurative inflammation, and from a retrograde metamorphosis of cell infiltration as in syphilis, tuberculosis cutis, etc. Ulcers have often an important signification from a diagnostic point of view, in their seat, shape, and depth, as well as in the characters of their edges and base. The horseshoe-shaped and serpiginous ulcers of syphilis are pathognomonic.

FISSURES (rimæ or rhagades) represent a linear lesion of continuity, which may be superficial or deep. The rent may extend only through the horny layer or penetrate deeply into the substance of the corium. Fissures are especially common about the natural orifices, between the fingers and toes, over the joints where there is much motion, and upon the palms and soles where the epidermis is thick and non-elastic. When the epidermis is thickened and infiltrated and its nutrition suspended by any chronic inflammatory process, it loses its normal elasticity, and cracks and fissures are liable to occur.

CRUSTS are secondary products, commonly caused by the drying and condensation of normal secretions or pathological fluids exuded upon the surface. They vary in size, shape, and color, depending upon the nature of the secretion, its fluidity or inspissation, and the rapidity of the exudation, etc. The crusts may be yellowish as in eczema ; grayish, brownish, greenish, or blackish as seen in impetigo, ecthyma, syphilis, etc. The thick, conical laminated crusts of rupia are quite pathognomonic. The crusts formed by dried sebaceous matter are light yellowish and greasy, and may be rolled up into a ball ; the crusts of tinea favosa are quite typical in their cup shape and sulphur-yellow color.

CICATRICES consist of new formations of connective tissue, which replace the normal tissues lost by ulceration or injury. They represent a lower organization than the true skin— they are covered by an epithelial layer and contain blood-vessels, but there is an absence of the glandular structures.

Cicatrices are white because of the absence of the pigment layer and the defective blood supply, smooth because deprived of the papillæ, and often depressed from loss of substance. The connective tissue, instead of being spread in a uniform layer, may be developed in excessive quantity and form irregular, ridge-like prominences. Cicatrices may become the seat of marked connective-tissue hypertrophy, as seen in false keloid. The contraction of an extensive cicatrix often produces marked deformity.

Cicatrices often constitute a valuable aid in making a retrospective diagnosis. Round or reniform, white cicatricial depressions surrounded with a coppery areola are generally indicative of syphilis.

SUBJECTIVE SYMPTOMS.

The symptoms appreciable to the patient himself are of far less importance, from a diagnostic point of view, than the objective characters of the eruption. Subjective sensations vary in intensity and frequency in different diseases of the skin and are sometimes altogether absent.

In acute inflammatory affections, there is usually present more or less heat and burning of the skin. The element of pain is not a common accompaniment of many skin diseases. Pain more or less pronounced usually precedes the development of herpes zoster, it may also be present in the deep ulcerations of scrofuloderma, and of syphilitic ulcers in certain locations, as the anus and toes ; the eruption of small-pox is often attended with burning pain of the face, hands, and feet.

Pruritus or itching is by far the most common and prominent of the subjective symptoms, and its presence or absence constitutes a valuable diagnostic sign. It may be tickling, from the presence of parasites, tingling as in urticaria, prickling as in lichen tropicus, while in certain forms of eczema and prurigo it may be of the most violent character, exciting the patient almost to a condition of frenzy. The physician is not always dependent upon the statement of the patient as to the existence of this symptom, since it may be revealed by the presence of scratch marks upon the body. Formication, another variety of cutaneous impression, may be mentioned, in which there is experienced the sensation as if insects were crawling over the surface.

DIAGNOSIS.

From a theoretical standpoint it would seem that no other class of diseases furnish such favorable conditions for an easy and accurate diagnosis as diseases of the skin. The morbid phenomena which form the elements of the diagnosis, instead of being concealed in organs remote and hidden from view, are spread out upon the surface and brought directly under the examination of those unerring senses, the sight and the touch. They actually obtrude themselves upon observation and the disfigurement they occasion is oftentimes the sole reason for consulting a physician.

The recognition of the character of the elementary lesions of a given eruption is, no doubt, the first step toward the establishment of a diagnosis. Very often the objective characters of an eruption are so typical that a simple inspection reveals its nature, and a correct diagnosis may be arrived at without asking the patient a single question. The dry, hard papules of lichen, the wheals of urticaria, the bullæ of pemphigus, the scales of psoriasis, etc., are peculiar to and pathognomonic of these diseases.

While it may be comparatively easy to identify the particular form of lesion as papular or vesicular, and classify the eruption in the group of papular or vesicular diseases, it must be remembered that to simply give a name to a disease is by no means the object and end of our diagnostic effects. The lesions of the skin have a definite pathological value only so far as they have a direct bearing upon the determination of the nature of the disease, and thus afford indications as to treatment. Diseases of identical character, so far as the anatomical form of the lesions is concerned, may be produced by a variety of causes of both external and internal origin. Quinine and the poison of scarlatina represent quite distinct and widely different etiological entities, yet they both produce eruptions which are quite indistinguishable in appearance. On the other hand, the same exciting cause may produce eruptions of dissimilar forms, the variable phenomena being determined by peculiarities of the individual skin. To cite a familiar example, the lesions produced by the acarus scabiei may be vesicular, pustular, or bullous in some individuals, while in another the reaction of the skin may be so insignificant as to almost escape recognition.

While it is true that many dermatoses are characterized by lesions more or less definite in type, yet in others there may be a multiplicity of eruptive forms. In eczema, for example, the lesions may be erythematous, papular, vesicular, pustular scaly, etc.; the polymorphism of dermato-syphilis is too well known to require mention.

With few exceptions, the elementary lesions have a relative, rather than an absolute value in the differentiation of one disease from another. To take, for example, the simplest form of lesion—erythema marks the beginning stage of most inflammatory diseases, it cannot therefore be considered distinctive of any ; the roseola of cholera, of variola, of scarlatina, of eczema presents the same general characters. Papules occur in a large number of skin diseases, in some as a constant element and the most distinctive feature of the eruption, in others merely as a transitional stage of one lesion into another. The same may be said of vesicles which may constitute the most essential feature of certain eruptions, in others only an ephemeral element.

In this appreciation of the value of the elementary lesions of the skin as a means of diagnosis, it is not designed to depreciate their pathological significance. As before remarked, they are the A B C of dermato-pathology and by their combinations form the external characters of all diseases of the skin. Practically, however, it will be found, in making a diagnosis, that the general character and course of an eruption, its distribution and locality, its color, configuration, the multiplicity, duration, and succession of the lesions, the history, constitutional symptoms, etc., are of far more importance than minute anatomical details.

In the examination of a patient with skin disease, a systematic course of procedure should be adopted. Every portion of the body which may be the seat of the eruption should be carefully examined, so as to get a good picture of the eruption as a whole. Upon certain parts the eruption may be so characteristically developed as to be pathognomonic, while upon others it may be entirely altered in its essential features. Generally it will be found that, in long-standing eruptions, the typical characters of the primary lesions have been modified or entirely effaced by secondary changes; in such cases it is always well to search for the more recent lesions which exemplify the simplest and least complicated characters of the eruption.

The characteristic features of psoriasis may be obliterated by time and treatment, but the discovery of a minute recent lesion covered with white silvery scales would at once resolve all doubt as to its nature.

The distribution of an eruption and the localities affected often afford valuable diagnostic indications. The partial and irregular, or the generalized and symmetrical distribution of an eruption has an important bearing upon the determination of its nature. It has been remarked that "cutaneous diseases, like plants, have their regional habitations." Many diseases manifest a preference for certain regions of the body which may be regarded as seats of predilection, upon which they first appear and from which they last recede. The preference of psoriasis for the elbows, knees, and extensor surfaces, and the predilection of eczema for the flexor surfaces, constitutes a valuable differential sign between these diseases. The knowledge that certain diseases are limited to certain localities affords positive as well as negative evidence. In the diagnosis of a scaly eruption confined to the palms and soles, psoriasis may be practically excluded, since this disease seldom affects these localities, and never without a coincident development elsewhere.

Color constitutes a conspicuous and often distinctive feature of many eruptions. The bright-red tint of most acute inflammatory lesions and the brownish-red or coppery hue of dermato-syphilis are quite characteristic. It must not be forgotten that the chronicity of an eruption, as well as the complexion of the individual, modified by racial and other peculiarities, affects the coloration of the lesion. In some diseases, an excess or deficiency of the normal pigment makes up the entire clinical picture, as in vitiligo or chloasma. For the proper appreciation of the element of color, the examination of the patient should always be made, if practicable, by daylight. Many minute characteristics of skin diseases which are vividly prominent in a natural light may be so modified by artificial illumination as to be no longer recognizable.

The form and configuration of the eruption are to be carefully noted. The butterfly shape of lupus, the round patches of ringworm, the orbicular or gyrate lesions of psoriasis, and the circinate or crescentic configurations of syphilis, etc., throw light upon the diagnosis of these diseases.

The duration, succession and multiplicity of the lesions are worthy of consideration. Some diseases are characterized by a typical mode of evolution, a series of changes follow each other successively and in a definite order; the transitional character of the eruption often furnishing a clue as to its nature. This is especially true of the acute exanthemata.

The rapidity in the evolution of the lesions of simple inflammatory diseases distinguishes them from dermato-syphilis, in which the character of the process is slow and sluggish. On the other hand, lupus is much slower in its evolution than syphilis, and the persistence for a long time in the same form of tubercular lesions, of the face for example, would exclude syphilis. The multiplicity of eruptive forms is peculiar to certain diseases, and on this account polymorphism constitutes a valuable diagnostic indication.

It is also important to inquire into the history of the patient. Age, sex, and occupation exercise a modifying influence upon the development and course of many diseases. Certain diseases are confined to childhood, while others manifest a tendency to develop at certain periods; thus acne occurs at the age of puberty; lupus erythematosus is more common in women in middle life; epithelioma is more frequent in advanced age. The occupation of the patient may be an important factor in the determination of the nature of an eruption. Finally, the condition of the patient's general health should be carefully inquired into. While many diseases of the skin are idiopathic in their nature, and cannot be considered as either the consequence or the cause of general ill-health, the larger number are essentially symptomatic, and have the closest and most intimate relations with derangements of the internal organs.

CLASSIFICATION.

It is the ambition of most writers on dermatology to put forward a new classification of diseases of the skin. The temptation doubtless arises from the recognition of obvious defects in all the systems hitherto constructed; too often, however, the result does not justify the innovation, the new classification presenting few of the advantages, with all the inconveniences of those it was intended to replace.

Classifications differ in principle and arrangement of details accordingly as the grouping of the different diseases is made upon an anatomical, a pathological, or an etiological basis. The elementary lesions were made by Plenk, and afterward by Willan, the basis of classification—the various diseases being grouped according to their anatomical forms and characters. However simple this system, and convenient as a means of assigning a name to the eruption, it took no cognizance of the pathological relationships and affinities of the different diseases, and placed in the same group diseases essentially different in their nature. The anatomico-pathological classification of Hebra is based rather upon the character of the pathological process than the anatomical form of the lesions.

In dermatology, as in other departments of medicine, a natural classification, which considers the etiological relations of diseases, is doubtless the most scientific, as well as the most practically useful, since it furnishes valuable indications as to the nature and treatment of the disease; but our present knowledge is not sufficiently complete to meet the requirements of a classification upon this basis. While we recognize that almost all diseases of the skin result from the combination of causes exterior to the organism and the predisposition of the individual, in many cases the external cause may be entirely inoperative without an aptitude on the part of the system to conceive and develop its irritant action. The predisposition may reside in the skin from functional or structural peculiarities, or the morbid process may originate in the internal economy, depending upon diathetic or other conditions. Exciting and predisposing causes are so interdependent and interactive that it oftentimes becomes impossible to resolve this etiological complex into its component parts, and assign to each factor the precise measure of its pathogenetic influence. Notwithstanding the important advances recently made in this direction, the causes of many skin diseases still escape recognition, and much more will have to be learned before a perfectly satisfactory classification of skin diseases can be made upon an etiological basis.

The order of arrangement of the different diseases of the skin, followed in this work, will be according to the classification adopted by the American Dermatological Association, with slight modifications. The propriety of the position of certain diseases in the groups to which they have been assigned in this classification is open to question, yet it can be commended for simplicity, convenience, and practicability for clinical purposes.

By this system of arrangement, cutaneous diseases are arranged in eight classes or orders:

CLASS I.—DISORDERS OF THE GLANDS.	CLASS V.—ATROPHIES.
CLASS II.—INFLAMMATIONS.	CLASS VI.—NEW GROWTHS.
CLASS III.—HEMORRHAGES.	CLASS VII.—NEUROSES.
CLASS IV.—HYPERTROPHIES.	CLASS VIII.—PARASITIC AFFECTIONS.

Class I. Disorders of the Glands.

  1. Of the Sweat Glands.
    Hyperidrosis.
    Sudamina.
    Anidrosis.
    Bromidrosis.
    Chromidrosis.
    Uridrosis.
  2. Of the Sebaceous Glands.
    Seborrhœa :
      a. oleosa.
      b. sicca.
    Comedo.
    Cyst:
      a. Milium.
      b. Steatoma.
    Asteatosis.

Class II. Inflammations.

    Exanthemata.
    Erythema simplex.
    Erythema multiforme :
      a. papulosum.
      b. bullosum.
      c. nodosum.
    Urticaria.
    Urticaria pigmentosa.
    Dermatitis :[1]
      a. traumatica.
      b. venenata.
      c. calorica.
      d. medicamentosa.
      e. gangrænosa.
    Erysipelas.
    Furunculus.
    Anthrax.
    Phlegmona diffusa.
    Pustula maligna.
    Herpes simplex.
    Herpes zoster.
    Dermatitis herpetiformis.
    Psoriasis.
    Pityriasis maculata et cir-
      cinata.
    Dermatitis exfoliativa.
    Pityriasis rubra.
    Lichen :
      a. planus.
      b. ruber.
    Eczema :
      a. erythematosum.
      b. papulosum.
      c. vesiculosum.
      d. madidans.
      e. pustulosum.

[1] Indicating affections of this class not properly included under other titles.

    f. rubrum.
    g. squamosum.
    Prurigo.
    Acne.
    Acne rosacea.
    Sycosis.
    Impetigo.
    Impetigo contagiosa.
    Impetigo herpetiformis.
    Ecthyma.
    Pemphigus.

Class III. Hemorrhages.

    Purpura :
      a. simplex.
      b. hæmorrhagica.

Class IV. Hypertrophies.

  1. Of Pigment.
    Lentigo.
    Chloasma.
  2. Of Epidermal and Papil-
      lary Layers.
    Keratosis :
      a. pilaris.
      b. senilis.
    Molluscum epitheliale.
    Callositas.
    Clavus.
    Cornu cutaneum.
    Verruca.
    Verruca necrogenica.
    Nævus pigmentosus.
    Xerosis.
    Ichthyosis.
    Onychauxis.
    Hypertrichosis.
  3. Of Connective Tissue.
    Scleroderma.
    Sclerema neonatorum.
    Morphœa.
    Elephantiasis.
    Rosacea :
      a. erythematosa.
      b. hypertrophica.
    Frambœsia.

Class V. Atrophies.

  1. Of Pigment.
    Leucoderma.
    Albinismus.
    Vitiligo.
    Canities.
  2. Of Hair.
    Alopecia.
    Alopecia furfuracea.
    Alopecia areata.

Atrophia pilorum propria.
Trichorexis nodosa.
3. OF NAIL.
Atrophia unguis.
4. OF CUTIS.
Atrophia senilis.
Atrophia maculosa et
striata.

Class VI. New Growths.
1. OF CONNECTIVE TISSUE.
Keloid.
Cicatrix.
Fibroma.
Neuroma.
Xanthoma.
2. OF MUSCULAR TISSUE.
Myoma.
3. OF VESSELS.
Angioma.
Angioma pigmentosum et
atrophicum.
Angioma cavernosum.
Lymphangioma.
4. OF GRANULATION TISSUE.
Rhino-scleroma.
Lupus erythematosus.
Lupus vulgaris.
Scrofuloderma.
Syphiloderma:
a. erythematosum,

b. papulosum.
c. pustulosum.
d. tuberculosum.
e. gummatosum.
Lepra:
a. tuberosa.
b. maculosa.
c. anæsthetica.
Carcinoma.
Sarcoma.

Class VII. Neuroses.
Hyperæsthesia:
a. Pruritus.
b. Dermatalgia.
Anæsthesia.

Class VIII. Parasitic Affections.
1. VEGETABLE.
Tinea favosa.
Tinea trichophytina:
a. circinata.
b. tonsurans.
c. sycosis.
Tinea versicolor.
2. ANIMAL.
Scabies.
Pediculosis capillitii.
Pediculosis corporis.
Pediculosis pubis,

DISEASES OF THE SKIN.

GLANDULAR DISORDERS.

The glandular apparatus of the skin consists of two distinct structures, the sebaceous and perspiratory glands, one secreting an oily, the other a watery fluid. They subserve most important and essential purposes in the economy, not only in maintaining the health and nutrition of the skin, but also in their offices as excretory organs.

The glands of the skin are subject to various functional and structural disorders, which may arise from constitutional disease, or which may be local and entirely independent of any systemic trouble; they are also incidentally involved in various inflammatory and other affections of the skin. Only the functional disorders of the glands, in which the inflammatory element is not a common or characteristic feature, will be considered in this connection.

Functional disorders may arise from an excess, a deficiency, or perversion of the normal secretion, and may be either qualitative or quantitative or both, or the entire abnormality may consist in an altered secretion within the excretory ducts, without glandular or periglandular irritation. When structural changes occur, the affection is relegated to the group of inflammatory or exudative affections.

SEBORRHŒA.

Synonyms—Acne Sebacea; Steatorrhœa.

Seborrhœa may be defined as a functional disorder of the sebaceous glands characterized by an excessive secretion of sebaceous matter. This secretion may appear in the form of minute oily drops at the glandular orifices and diffuse itself as a greasy coating upon the surface, or it may be altered in character and accumulate in the form of whitish or yellowish scales or soft friable crusts upon the skin.

Seborrhœa may occur upon any portion of the body, but it has a predilection for regions rich in sebaceous glands, as the scalp and face, the back of the shoulders, chest and the genital region. Both forms may be present in the same individual, but they are usually of separate occurrence.

In the first form, known as seborrhœa *oleosa*, the secretion exudes from the ducts, which are frequently enlarged and patulous, as oily globules which give to the affected surface a greasy, unctuous look. It is most commonly localized upon the face, especially the nose and forehead, which may present a dirty hue from the incorporation with the oily substance of minute particles of dust and dirt floating in the atmosphere. A piece of blotting paper pressed upon the surface is readily soiled by the secretion and dirt. Upon parts abundantly supplied with hair, an excessive fluid secretion is rarely observable, as it is rapidly absorbed by the hair, but upon bald individuals the scalp presents a glistening, shining appearance, as if it had just been oiled. This form of seborrhœa is comparatively rare in infancy and old age, and is most common at puberty and in adult life. It is frequently associated with other functional and inflammatory disorders of the sebaceous structures.

In the other variety, known as seborrhœa *sicca*, there is a larger admixture of the epithelial elements, giving the secretion a drier consistence, and causing it to collect in scale-like masses upon the skin. This is a much more common affection and may occur at any period of life. It is met with as a physiological condition in the *smegma* or *vernix caseosa* of the new-born. There is often a hyperactivity of the sebaceous glands, particularly of the scalp, in the early months of infantile life, and the secretion accumulates in the form of yellowish or brownish crusts, more especially localized about the anterior fontanelle and over the vertex. These pasty-like masses of scales mat the hairs together and glue them down to the scalp, giving a deceptive resemblance to eczema. This condition may also be marked upon the forehead and cheeks as well as upon the scalp.

In the adult, the disease is localized chiefly upon the scalp, brow, and nose. Upon the scalp it may occur as a thin coating of dirty white, bran-like, greasy scales, which are easily detached and which cover the entire surface, or in the form of dry, white, shining particles which fall upon the shoulders whenever the hair is brushed. This condition is known as dandriff. The accumulation of these heaped-up crusts around and between the hairs interferes with their proper nutrition and is a common cause of premature alopecia. This affection frequently extends in a diffuse form to the sides of the temples, over the ears to the neck and upon the forehead.

Upon the face, especially about the alæ of the nose, the sebaceous crusts are yellowish, greenish, or blackish in color, and are intimately adherent from the tag-like prolongations of sebaceous matter into the follicles; when removed, the gaping orifices of the follicles are distinctly visible.

There is a form of seborrhœa especially localized upon the face, which, when occurring in elderly persons, possesses a grave pathological signification. It develops in the form of patches, of hard, yellowish-brownish concretions consisting of hardened plugs of sebaceous matter rooted in the follicles and projecting above the surface. Pain and slight bleeding generally attend their removal. In old people, there is apt to be a senile degeneration of the glandular epithelium which may prove the starting-point of epithelioma.

Upon the back and shoulders the disease occurs in the form of polygonal-shaped patches of varying sizes. The crusts rarely accummulate in this locality, owing to the friction of the clothing. The orifices of the ducts are patulous and there is frequently observed a coincident development of the papules and pustules of acne vulgaris.

In seborrhœa of the chest, the patches are usually orbicular or disc-shaped, with an accumulation of greasy-like scales around the margin, which, when removed, show a reddish base. These patches may remain discrete or coalesce, forming a large, irregular patch.

Seborrhœa sicca may occur upon the genital parts of both sexes. In the male, its most frequent seat is the glans penis and sulcus, where it collects in the form of a whitish cheesy mass, its consistence depending somewhat upon whether the parts are habitually covered by the prepuce. In this location, as well as in seborrhœa of the umbilicus, there is a tendency to the rapid decomposition of the sebaceous matter and the production of an offensive odor with more or less irritation of the parts.

Little is definitely known of the etiology of seborrhœa. It is always, at least in the earlier stages, purely functional in character, but later may be attended with structural alterations, atrophy or even entire obliteration of the glands. It has been observed that it most commonly occurs in anæmic or chlorotic individuals. The skin of the affected parts, although it may appear reddened, is cold, moist and flabby, showing a deficiency in the normal blood supply. On the other hand, it may occur in persons of ordinary or even robust condition of health.

DIAGNOSIS.—Eczema is the disease to which seborrhœa of the scalp and face bears the closest resemblance, and with which it is most frequently confounded. The differential signs may be thus indicated. ,

In seborrhœa, the crusts are soft and greasy from infiltration with oily matter, and may be rolled into a ball like wax; when they are lifted up, the surface of the skin underneath is found to be pale, dry, and not inflamed; it is not, as a rule, attended with pruritic sensations. Eczema occurs in circumscribed patches; the scales are brittle, consisting almost exclusively of epithelial cells and dried albuminoid matter; the surface beneath is inflamed, infiltrated, and weeping; intense itching is a prominent and quite constant symptom. Eczema also frequently extends down behind the ears and upon other parts.

From psoriasis of the scalp, to which seborrhœa also bears a deceptive resemblance, it may be distinguished by the yellowish, fatty, crumbling character of the scales, in contrast with the whitish, more abundant, and larger scales of psoriasis. The latter occurs in the form of reddened, sharply-defined patches, which are quite characteristically developed at the margins of the hairy scalp, and the disease is usually present upon other parts of the body.

Seborrhœa of the face may be confounded with lupus erythematosus, which was formerly known as seborrhœa congestiva. The location is the same, and the sebaceous glands are involved in both diseases. Seborrhœa is not, however, so distinctly demarcated, the skin is but slightly reddened or pinkish, it is not accompanied by infiltration and thickening, nor followed by cicatrices. Lupus is distinctly marginated, the skin beneath the scales is of a dusky red or violet hue, and in places there is loss of tissue and evidences of cicatricial repair. ,

There is a rare variety of seborrhœa which is generally distributed over the surface and known as ichthyosis sebacea. The sebaceous coating is dry, adherent, blackened from exposure, and becomes cracked or fissured in the lines of the skin, forming lozenge-shaped plates. This spurious form may be distinguished from true ichthyosis by the fact that the latter is a congenital disease, the skin is dry and does not perspire, and the scale-like masses cannot be removed. In seborrhœa, the sweat glands are normal and the skin underneath the crusts is moist, soft, and supple to the feel and natural in appearance.

TREATMENT.—In the treatment of seborrhœa, any systemic disorder with which it may be associated should be corrected by means appropriate to that condition. In chlorotic and anæmic persons ferruginous and nutritive tonics will be found serviceable. A suitable diet, plenty of exercise, and all measures calculated to promote the digestion should be employed. The chief reliance must, however, be placed upon local treatment, which will vary somewhat according to the locality of the disease and the character of the incrustation. The first indication is to remove the crusts, which may be best accomplished by saturating them thoroughly with olive or linseed oil. Upon the scalp, where the hairs are matted together with heaped-up crusts, it may be necessary to use a flannel cap covered with oiled silk in order to keep up the continuous contact of the oil for a day or two. After the crusts are loosened, they may be mechanically removed, and the scalp shampooed with spts. saponis kalinus and warm water and thoroughly dried. In order to prevent the feeling of tension which follows this wash, and also with the view of preventing the reformation of the crusts, a mild astringent ointment should be immediately rubbed in. For this purpose an ointment of tannin, precipitated sulphur, or the ammoniated mercury may be employed.

The following ointment represents one of the best combinations:

℞ Acidi Tannici,	.	.	.	.	.	.	ӡ i.
Glycerini puri,	.	.	.	.	.	.	ӡ i.
Petrolati,	.	.	.	.	.	.	ӡ ij.
Ung. Aq. Rosæ,	.	.	.	.	.	.	ӡ i.
M.							

An ointment of the oleate of zinc or simple vaseline may be used to relieve the hyperæmia and tenderness.

To prevent the reformation of crusts, a sulphur ointment, about one drachm to the ounce,

PLATE XXXVI.

Fig. I.—Seborrhœa sicca.
Fig. II.—Comedo.
Fig. III.—Milium.
Fig. IV.—Sudamina (miliaria crystallina).

FIG. I.—AFTER HEBRA.
FIGS. II. AND III.—AUTHOR'S COLLECTION.
FIG. IV.—AFTER NEUMANN

of vaseline or beef marrow, to which a little almond oil or glycerin may be added, will be found of excellent service.

The following ointment, recommended by Bronson, constitutes an efficient and elegant pomade:

> ℞ Hydrarg. Ammoniati, ...   grs. xx,
> Hydrarg. Chlor. mitis, ...   grs. xl.
> Petrolati, ...   ℥ i.
> M.

This should be rubbed into the scalp every morning, and the scalp should be washed occasionally with the tincture of green soap and water, or the yolk of egg beaten up in lime water.

For seborrhea of the face, after the crusts are removed, the following will be found a most excellent application :

> ℞ Sulphuris Precipitati,
> Spiritus Odorati, ...   āā 10 parts.
> Amyli Mucilag., ...   80 parts.
> M.

To be applied at night, the following morning to be washed off, and the affected surface powdered with sulphur, 1 part, to Fuller's earth, 7 parts.

COMEDO.

Synonym—Acne Punctata Nigra.

The term comedo is applied to the small, white plugs formed by the retention and inspissation of the sebaceous matter within the excretory ducts of the sebaceous or hair follicles. The distended orifices usually project slightly above the surface in the form of minute elevations, showing in the centre a yellowish or blackish point caused by exposure of the free end of the plug to the dirt and air. Unna, who has made a special study of this disorder, regards the black point as due to pigment.

The retained secretion may be squeezed out of the follicles in the form of small, white, worm-like bodies which are commonly known as grubs. The expressed matter, which is cornified at the upper end, soft and stringy at the other, consists of epidermic cells, oil globules, and a number of spirally-coiled minute hairs. There is occasionally found a small animal parasite, the *demodex* or *acarus folliculorum*, the presence of which is, however, merely accidental and without pathological significance, as it is found in perfectly healthy sebaceous glands.

Comedo is most commonly found upon the face, especially the sides and alæ of the nose, the cheeks, brow, and chin, sometimes in the concha of the ears. It also occurs upon the back of the neck and shoulders and upper portion of the chest. The comedones may be few and scattered, or the surface may be thickly studded with them, presenting the appearance of grains of gunpowder imbedded in the skin. When numerous, they cause more or less annoyance from the disfigurement they occasion, especially when attended with seborrhœa oleosa, which imparts to the complexion a greasy, muddy appearance. They are essentially non-inflammatory, but are frequently associated with acne vulgaris and rosacea.

Comedo commonly develops at the age of puberty in connection with the increased physiological activity of the glandular apparatus manifest at this period; the condition is a sluggish one, and may continue for years. It is much more common in the male subject.

The general causes of comedo are not definitely known. It occurs more frequently in chlorotic, anæmic, and scrofulous individuals, and is associated with disorders of digestion, menstruation, derangement of the sexual apparatus, etc. The local factors concerned in the formation of comedo have been referred to an alteration in the consistence of the secretion, leading to hardening and cornification, and an atony of the muscular apparatus of the glands by which their expulsive power is arrested or impaired. An artificial comedo may be produced by tar or chrysarobin and other drugs.

DIAGNOSIS.—This condition is so common that it is well known and easily recognized by its peculiar lesions and their restriction to certain localities. From acne it may be distinguished by the absence of inflammatory symptoms. From milium by the fact that in the latter the excretory duct has been obliterated and the sebaceous concretion cannot be expressed without preliminary incision of the overlying epidermis.

TREATMENT.—The most efficient treatment of comedo consists in the expulsion of the sebaceous plug by pressure upon the surrounding parts with a watch key, or, better, a small blunt tubular instrument specially devised for this purpose, known as the comedo extractor. The slight traumatic dermatitis which follows this operation may be relieved by the application of hot water.

After the expulsion of the comedos, astringent and stimulant applications should be made to the skin in order to contract the abnormally distended ducts and increase the functional activity of the sebaceous glands. For this purpose frictions with green soap, vigorous rubbing with a rough towel, lotions of sulphur, borax, carbonate of potash, ointments of tar, sulphur, etc., should be employed. Unna recommends the following : ℞ Kaolini, ℥ss.; Glycerini, ℨ .; Aceti, ℨij. M. The eyes should be kept protected when it is applied. If the skin should become irritated or inflamed from these applications, the benzoinated zinc ointment or dusting powders should be employed until it subsides.

MILIUM.

Synonyms—Acne Albida ; Grutum.

The term milium is applied to small, isolated, millet-sized concretions of sebaceous matter situated in the skin, and covered by a tense, shining epidermis. They usually project hemispherically above the surface in the form of pearly granules, and result from the retention of altered sebaceous matter within the gland, caused by the obliteration of its excretory duct. Their favorite location is in regions where the skin is thinnest, upon the eyelids and upper part of the cheeks, sometimes upon the temples and brow, and upon the genital organs of both sexes, the penis and scrotum, and inner surface of the labia minora.

They are usually met with in adult or middle age, and are more common in women than in men ; occasionally they may be seen in early childhood. They occur quite independently of other disorders of the glandular apparatus, and are not referable to any derangement of the general health. They are not attended with inflammation, and may remain unchanged for years ; they give rise to no objective symptoms, and their sole clinical importance consists in the slight disfigurement they occasion.

When the epidermis is incised, these little bodies are easily turned out of their bed, and are found to be firm to the feel, and under the microscope are seen to consist of degenerated epithelial cells, sebaceous matter and cholesterin crystals, and, in rare cases, of calcareous matter. Similar concretions are sometimes met with at the edges of lupus cicatrices. I have seen them numerously distributed upon the chest and arms in a case of disseminated cancer of the skin ; they were not so rounded or globular as upon the face, but more elongated, suggesting in shape and size grains of wheat. On incising the summit, a comedo-like mass could be readily extruded by lateral pressure. In a case of pemphigus at present under my observation, many of the pigmented patches left by the bullæ are occupied by a number of these small whitish concretions of almost calcareous consistency.

DIAGNOSIS.—Milium can hardly be mistaken for any other affection. From comedo the

the lesions are readily differentiated by their translucent or pearly lustre and anatomical form. Unlike comedo, they cannot be pressed out without incision of the overlying cuticle. The only disease with which milium is likely to be confounded is the commencing stage of xanthelasma palpebrarum. In this affection, the lesions are softer to the feel, flattened and plate-like, and of a clear yellow color; they are more strictly confined to the eyelids.

TREATMENT.—Milium sometimes disappears spontaneously by absorption. The treatment is simple and most effective; it consists in incising the tense epidermis overlying the spherical body, which may be readily turned out by lateral pressure with the nails or a scoop-like instrument. Milia have no tendency to recur in the same anatomical site, and the more vigorous treatment recommended by some authorities, as touching the cavity after their removal with a drop of nitric acid, the tincture of iodine, or the electrolytic needle, is quite unnecessary.

SUDAMINA.

Synonym—Miliaria Crystallina.

In functional disorders of the sweat glands, the deviation from the normal state may consist in an excess or deficiency of the secretion, or in an alteration in the quality of the constituents of the sweat.

Sudamina is a non-inflammatory affection of the sudoriparous glands, characterized by an eruption of clear, discrete miliary vesicles. It is sometimes attended with slight tingling and itching, or there may be an entire absence of all subjective sensations. The vesicles form slight elevations above the surface, and appear like drops of dew standing upon the skin. They maintain their size, shape, and vesicular character throughout their entire course; they do not rupture, never become confluent, nor undergo a pustular transformation; they dry up and disappear with slight desquamation; one crop may be succeeded by another.

The eruption most frequently develops upon the abdomen and sides of the chest, but it may appear upon any portion of the body.

Much confusion exists in dermatology as to the proper nomenclature of this disease. By English and American authors, sudamina and miliaria crystallina are synonymous terms employed to indicate the same disease. By German authorities, sudamina is regarded as an entirely distinct and independent affection.

Sudamina occurs from hyperactivity of the sweat glands, superinduced by high temperature in many forms of febrile disturbance, the pathological condition consisting in minute drops of sweat which have escaped from the sudoriparous pores, and collected between the layers of the epidermis. It is a frequent concomitant of typhoid and typhus fever, acute articular rheumatism, pneumonia, puerperal fever, etc. It may be observed in conditions of debility; children with fine, delicate skins, that sweat profusely, are liable to this eruption in hot weather.

DIAGNOSIS.—Sudamina is not liable to be mistaken for any other eruption. From vesicular eczema it may be distinguished by the abundance, transparent appearance, and discrete character of the vesicles. The vesicles of eczema are smaller; they are grouped upon an inflamed surface, apt to become confluent; they are shorter in duration, readily rupture, and form excoriated surfaces. They are attended with more intense pruritic sensations than sudamina.

Sudamina may be differentiated from miliaria alba and miliaria rubra by the inflammatory element which is always present in the latter affections. The vesicles of miliaria alba undergo a milky or puriform transformation; those of miliaria rubra are each surrounded by a red areola.

TREATMENT.—The only treatment required for sudamina is the correction, as far as practicable, of the cause which occasions it. Any excess of clothing should be removed, the patient be kept cool, and the temperature subdued by antipyretic mixtures. The indications of local treatment may be summed up in protection of the surface; for this purpose any simple dusting powder will suffice. If the surface should become irritated and take on an eczematous condition, mild astringent lotions may be used.

THE ACUTE EXANTHEMATA.

In this group are included the infectious inflammations which possess certain peculiarities in their etiology, the order of their evolution, their clinical features and course. They are each caused by a specific contagion, and each exhibits a well-marked period of incubation; the cutaneous manifestations are preceded by a more or less pronounced prodromal stage, the eruption appears at a definite period, and pursues a typical course in its development and decline. The participation of the entire organism in the morbid process is shown by the fact that the eruptive phenomena are preceded or accompanied with acute febrile symptoms of a definite duration, and the occurrence of certain morbid phenomena referable to a disturbance of other organs of the body. The eruptive fevers are farther distinguished from ordinary dermatoses by the fact that one attack of the disease confers an immunity more or less absolute against succeeding attacks.

It would be manifestly out of place in a work of this nature to treat exhaustively of the entire train of constitutional accidents which make up the symptomatology of the eruptive fevers. It will be sufficient merely to outline the course of each disease with the typical morbid appearances of the skin, which shall serve for purposes of differential diagnosis. For a more detailed consideration of the constitutional phenomena, the reader is referred to standard treatises on general medicine

TYPHUS FEVER.

Synonym—Petechial Fever.

The cutaneous eruptions which occur in connection with typhus and typhoid fevers are not so constant in their development, nor do they constitute so distinctive and characteristic a feature as in the other acute exanthemata. They are, however, of the greatest importance from a differential point of view.

After exposure to the contagion of typhus, there is usually a definite period of incubation rarely exceeding twelve days. Typhus fever is usually sudden in its advent; the patient is seized, with or without premonitory symptoms, with a chill or a succession of rigors, which may extend over a period of two or three days. There is more or less vertigo, headache, restlessness, insomnia, oftentimes a mild delirium attended with muscular tremors, and a sense of lassitude and general prostration.

The eruption usually makes its appearance from the fourth to the seventh day of the fever, and is most characteristically developed upon the abdomen and sides of the chest, the axillæ and arms, it commonly spares the face and legs. The eruption consists of minute spots of irregular form, slightly raised, either isolated or grouped in patches. The coloration of the spots varies according to the stage of their development; at first it is of a dusky red or florid tint, and disappears upon pressure. After a day or two, the spots become less elevated, more dingy or reddish-brown in hue, and the color is only partially effaced under pressure. This dusky shade is gradually becomes more pronounced, and after a few days the spots assume a livid or purplish hue, caused by minute extravasations of blood in their centres resembling, flea bites. In severe cases, the spots may be distinctly petechial from the first, and this feature has given rise to the designation of typhus as *petechial fever.* The abundance of the eruption and the lividity or darkness of its color are in direct ratio to the severity of the disease.

In conjunction with these distinctly defined spots, there is an eruption of paler indistinct spots which are but faintly visible, and give to the skin a marbled or mottled aspect. This subcuticular mottling varies in abundance and in intensity of color in different cases. The eruption of typhus comes out in one crop; its duration is from seven to ten days; it gradually fades as convalescence sets in. The subcuticular mottling is more rapid in its involution than the petechial spots.

DIAGNOSIS.—The history of a known exposure to the contagion of typhus, the pronounced nervous symptoms, and the peculiar character of the eruption are the main elements of diagnosis. Murchison says: "Fortunately the eruption is rarely absent, for without it a certain diagnosis of typhus is impossible." Careful statistical observation shows that it occurs in from ninety-three to ninety-seven per cent of all cases. It is more frequently absent in children.

The disease with which the typhus eruption is most apt to be confounded is measles. The rash has been by many observers designated as rubeoloid or morbilliform, from its close resemblance to that of measles, and the similarity is heightened by the frequent development of the typhus eruption on the fourth day of the fever, as occurs in measles. The following points of distinction may be noted. The eruption of typhus is not so bright in tint, is differently distributed, rarely appearing upon the face and lower extremities, is of longer duration, and is especially characterized by a tendency to become petechial. The appearance of the eruption is not preceded by the catarrhal symptoms of measles, while the symptoms of prostation are more precocious and pronounced. Measles is, moreover, essentially a disease of childhood.

The typhus eruption has also been mistaken for purpura. Purpura is a non-febrile and non-contagious disease, the individual spots are larger, petechial from the first, and frequently accompanied with hemorrhages from the gums, nose, mouth, kidneys, and bowels. In typhus, hemorrhages from the mucous surfaces are exceptional, and occur only as complications.

The differentiation of the eruptions of typhus and typhoid fever will be considered in connection with the latter disease.

TREATMENT.—The general management of typhus fever is exhaustively considered in works on general medicine, to which the reader is referred for details of treatment. The course of the disease cannot be arrested or its duration materially shortened by any means yet discovered, so that the treatment must be mainly expectant. Strict isolation of the patient, good nursing, absolute quiet, cooling drinks, plenty of fresh air, cold spongings, affusions or immersion to keep the temperature at a moderate level, with occasional resort to quinine or other antipyretics, the use of stimulants when the strength rapidly fails, comprise the essentials of treatment. Thoracic, intestinal, and other complications should be symptomatically treated. The cutaneous symptoms do not require therapeutic intervention.

TYPHOID FEVER.

Synonym—Enteric Fever.

In this disease, the febrile movement constitutes the distinctive essential feature. Compared with typhus fever, the cutaneous changes are of minor importance and are by no means so constant in their development.

Want of space forbids the consideration of the typical temperature curve, and the characteristic intestinal lesions met with in typhoid fever. The eruption of typhoid fever appears from the seventh to the twelfth day, and is most commonly situated upon the chest, abdomen, and lumbar region. It is sometimes preceded by active hyperæmia of the entire surface of the skin, resembling a delicate scarlet rash. It consists of lenticular, rosy or pinkish spots, one to two lines in diameter, slightly elevated and distinctly circular in outline. The spots are isolated, few in number, but occasionally quite numerous, so that two or more spots may touch at their edges. They disappear upon pressure, never become petechial, are not accompanied with subcutaneous mottling and undergo no change until they fade out, which is usually in the course of three or four days; they disappear without desquamation and do not leave any trace of their existence,

PLATE XXXVII.

Fig. I.—Typhus fever. Copious mottling from a man the fifth day of the disease.

Fig. II.—Typhus fever. Numerous spots at a more advanced stage of the disease, the coloration more reddish-brown or dingy in hue, some of them showing minute extravasations of blood in the centre.

Fig. III.—Typhoid fever. Lenticular spots of enteric fever unusually numerous.

Fig. IV.—Typhoid fever. *Taches bleuatres* and lenticular spots from a case of enteric fever.

FIGS. I., III., AND IV.—AFTER MURCHISON.
FIG. II.—AFTER F. K. PRIEST.

while fresh spots continue to come out in successive crops, so that the entire duration of the eruption is from two to three weeks. The spots are apt to reappear should a relapse of the fever occur.

There is not, as in typhus, a direct relation between the abundance of the eruption and the severity of the disease; on the contrary, an unusually copious eruption is accepted by some authorities as of favorable prognostic significance.

The *taches bleuatres* which are occasionally observed as a concomitant of typhoid fever, consist of irregularly rounded spots, of a bluish tint which is unaltered by pressure. They are situated upon the abdomen, back, and thighs, and as seen in Fig. IV., Plate XXXVII., distributed along the course of the subcutaneous veins. The spots retain their size and shape and tint throughout, they are ordinarily isolated, but contiguous spots may coalesce at their margins. Their development is usually interpreted as a favorable sign.

Sudamina also occur in connection with typhoid fever, especially at the period of lysis when the perspiratory function is active. They are usually followed by desquamation.

DIAGNOSIS.—The disease with which typhoid fever is most likely to be confounded is typhus, and the cutaneous symptoms constitute the most important differential sign between the two diseases. The eruption of typhus is much more constant, being absent in only a small proportion of cases, the individual spots are of longer duration and pass through successive stages of deepening in color until they become petechial, and are often accompanied with a sub-cutaneous mottling. The eruption of typhoid comes out in successive crops, the spots are rarely numerous, fade out in three to five days, while new ones continue to develop. The diagnosis is assisted by the course of the fever, the early prostration, and the predominance of the nervous symptoms in one case, and the enteric symptoms in the other.

TREATMENT.—Experience has abundantly proved that therapeutical interference is power-less to abort the disease or abridge its duration; the indications for treatment are, therefore, essentially symptomatic. The antipyretic agencies referred to in connection with the treatment of typhus are to be employed. Especial attention should be paid to the regulation of the diet, and the essentially "typhoid" symptoms which commonly supervene at a later stage of the fever, should be combated by an abundantly nourishing and stimulating regimen.

VARIOLA.

Synonym—Small-Pox.

Although small-pox has been shorn of its terrors as one of the greatest scourges of man-kind, it still must be regarded as by far the most important of the exanthematous fevers, by reason of the severity of its constitutional symptoms, the disfigurement it occasions, and its relatively large mortality.

Small-pox may be defined as an acute, febrile infectious disease due to a specific virus, and characterized by an eruption which passes through a papular, vesicular, and pustular stage, and leaves permanent scars.

The poison of variola may be propagated by diffusion through the atmosphere, or by con-tact with the infected person, or the dead bodies of small-pox patients. The poison is more or less permanent, and clings for a long time to the clothing or any material object upon which it is deposited. Susceptibility to its influence is manifest even in embryonic life, and is continued to the most advanced age.

The period of incubation is regular and definite. From the moment of infection until the appearance of the exanthem there is an interval of fourteen days. The initial stage, which pre-cedes the outbreak of the eruption, is characterized by certain constant and well-marked symptoms. It is usually ushered in by a distinct rigor or a succession of chills, succeeded by fever, nausea

PLATE XXXVIII.

FIG. I.—Variola. Generalized eruption of small-pox

FIG. II.—Variola. Confluent eruption upon the face and neck, with tumefaction of the skin, especially marked about the lips.

FIG. III.—Variola. Discrete eruption upon the right lower extremity, the lesions showing well-marked umbilication.

FIG. IV.—Varicella. Eruption of chicken-pox upon the back, lesions unusually numerous.

FIGS. II. AND III.—AFTER C. SLOVER ALLEN.
FIGS. I. AND IV.—AUTHOR'S COLLECTION.

or vomiting, headache, severe lumbar pains, and other signs of constitutional disturbance. The temperature may rise to 102° or 104°, but subsides on the appearance of the rash.

During the initial stage, there appears, with different degrees of frequency in different epidemics, a prodromal rash which is commonly of the erythematous type, but may be hemorrhagic. The erythematous rash may be either scarlatiniform or measly, and usually appears on the second day; it is generally distributed over the covered parts, and ordinarily disappears within twenty-four hours. The hemorrhagic rash, consisting of minute punctate extravasations of blood, is most characteristically developed upon the lower abdomen, the genital region, and the inner surfaces of the thighs, and is slower in its involution.

The characteristic eruption of small-pox makes its appearance on the third day of the fever in the shape of small, hyperæmic macules, which rapidly become elevated into papules. The eruption first appears upon the scalp and face, neck and upper extremities, successively invading the trunk and lower extremities. The papules, situated about the sebaceous and hair follicles, are at first red, acuminated, and hard to the feel. On the third day, the sixth of the disease, the summit of each papule undergoes a vesicular transformation.

As the vesicular metamorphosis of the papule becomes more complete, the vesicles increase in size, become depressed in the centre, and surrounded by an inflammatory areola. The clear, serous contents become turbid or milky, and by the sixth day (ninth of the disease), the lesions are distinctly pustular.

The pustules enlarge, sometimes become globular, with more or less swelling and turgescence of the skin. Coincident with this pustular metamorphosis the temperature rises, and may attain an elevation of 105° or 106°, with an exacerbation of all the constitutional symptoms.

About the eighth day, the eleventh of the disease, the pustules attain their maximum development; they rupture, discharge their contents which concrete into scabs, or they may dry into scabs without rupture. With the desiccation of the pustules, the redness, swelling, and tenderness of the skin subside. The scabs are brownish, quite adherent, and gradually fall off, leaving pigmented depressions, oftentimes cicatrices, accordingly as the pustular process has been superficial or has affected the papillary or deeper layers of the corium. The entire process is ordinarily completed in from seventeen to twenty days.

· The mucous membranes are involved as well as the skin. The mouth and throat, as well as the conjunctival mucous membranes, may be the seat of pustules, causing more or less swelling and soreness of the throat, hoarseness, difficult deglutition, photophobia, conjunctivitis, sometimes ulceration of the cornea.

In confluent small-pox, the symptoms are more severe, the eruption is precocious, its extension over the body is more rapid, and suppuration supervenes more quickly. The papules are thickly disseminated, crowded together, and run together, forming irregularly-outlined patches; the epidermis elevated, covering large, flattened bullæ containing a sero-purulent fluid. Confluence is rarely universal. The tumefaction of the skin is much more marked in this form, especially where the connective tissue is loose, as about the eyelids and genitals. The lips are often much thickened, and the patient may be unrecognizable from the frightful swelling. The mucous membrane symptoms are also more severe and pronounced.

In the form known as hemorrhagic small-pox, the hemorrhagic element may develop either in the papular, vesicular, or pustular stage, most frequently in the latter. In these cases, there is an intensification in the gravity of the constitutional symptoms with an adynamic condition, characterized by a feeble pulse, relatively low temperature, etc. The mucous membranes are frequently occupied by livid spots, and the seat of hemorrhages from the nose, kidneys, rectum, uterus, etc. Hemorrhagic small-pox is apt to be fatal, and the gravity of this complication is in direct proportion to the precocity and abundance of the hemorrhagic element. When the hemorrhagic extravasations do not occur until late, and are few and scattered, the prognosis is proportionately more favorable.

VARIOLOID.

The term varioloid is applied to a modified form of small-pox distinguished by the mildness of its constitutional symptoms, the irregular course of the eruption, and the shortness of its duration.

The prodromal symptoms may be as severe and protracted as in true variola; ordinarily, however, the initial stage does not exceed two days. In a typical case of varioloid, the eruption usually appears on the second day; the conical papules, which are sparsely scattered, rarely abundant, rapidly become converted into vesicles; in the course of three or four days the contents of the vesicles become sero-purulent or purulent; the pustular transformation is not attended with a rise of temperature as in variola. Desiccation begins as early as the seventh day; the pustules dry up into thin, brownish scabs, which fall off with varying rapidity, leaving pigmented spots, rarely deep, permanent pitting.

Varioloid exhibits wide variations in the order and degree of development of the eruption and its subsequent involution. Some of the lesions may abort at the papular stage, or the vesicle may represent the acme of development, and there may be present at the same time abortive papules, dried up vesicles, and advanced pustules. It is rare that the eruption passes through the entire cycle of evolution typified by the true variolous process.

DIAGNOSIS.—The diagnosis of a disease which is so characteristic in its mode of invasion and so definite in the order of its evolution would seem to offer few difficulties. The initial exanthem may or may not be present, so that its inconstancy deprives it of value as a diagnostic element. In the early stage, the prodromal symptoms, especially when conjoined with a history of known exposure, are much more important from a diagnostic point of view than the eruption itself. The papular eruption of small-pox may be indistinguishable in its objective characters from a number of red papular eruptions, but in these cases the simple element of time removes all doubt, since the existence of papules which remain unchanged into vesicles longer than two days does not indicate small-pox.   ·

The eruption with which small-pox is most likely to be confounded is that of measles, especially when of the papular variety. The papules of measles are larger, softer, and darker in tint, contrasting with the paler color and hard, shotty character of small-pox papules. It is only at the onset of the eruption that such a confusion is possible; in the course of twenty-four to thirty-six hours, all doubt is removed by the further transitional change of the small-pox eruption. Independent of the character of the eruption, the most important differential signs are the absence of lumbar pain during the period of invasion of measles and the maximal development of temperature during the height of the eruption. Measles may also be confounded with a form of hemorrhagic small-pox, in which an exanthem of a measly type is succeeded by petechiæ, which may constitute the only cutaneous expression of the disease. The patient may die of small-pox without a trace of a vesicle or before any unequivocal signs of small-pox are manifest.

The resemblance of the prodromal exanthem of small-pox to scarlatina is sometimes most striking. The absence of sore throat and the typical tongue of scarlatina, taken in conjunction with the symptoms of invasion, are important diagnostic points. In hemorrhagic small-pox, the congestion of the skin, and the intense red color which sometimes precedes the hemorrhagic exanthem, may simulate a scarlatinal eruption.

The exanthem of typhus fever and of cerebro-spinal meningitis may be also mistaken for small-pox, from which they may be differentiated by the course of the fever, the date at which the eruption appears, and other concomitant symptoms.

The similitude of syphilis to variola is recognized by the term "variola-form syphilide," which is applied to one of the pustular forms of this disease. There is not only an identity of anatomical form, but also of development through the stages of papule and pustule. The similitude is heightened by the fact that in certain cases the syphilitic lesions present well-marked umbilication.

The differential points are the differences in the character of the constitutional disturbance, the more sluggish development of the syphilitic lesions, their grouping, distribution, apruriginous character, and the probable presence of other signs of syphilis. It is rare that a disease so polymorphic as syphilis does not present a number of eruptive forms at the same time. Finally, an artificial acne produced by the ingestion of drugs has been mistaken for small-pox. A number of cases of iodic acne have come under my observation which had been diagnosed as small-pox, and the patients sent to a small-pox hospital, and thence transferred to the dermatological ward of Charity Hospital.

TREATMENT.—Prophylactic measures, comprising vaccination and strict isolation of the patients, are of far more importance than the treatment. A small-pox patient is a source of danger to all with whom he may come in contact, and his prompt isolation constitutes the most efficient means at our command for circumscribing the spread of the disease. These precautionary measures should be rigidly enforced in the mildest as well as the severest cases. Varioloid possesses the same contagious activity as true variola, and a case of peripatetic varioloid may be a more dangerous agent in spreading the contagion than a case of confluent small-pox.

The modified form of small-pox pursuing a mild course rarely requires special treatment. Confinement to bed, a light diet, and inunctions with cod-liver oil or carbolized vaseline, to relieve the subjective sensations of itching, with an occasional warm bath in the declining stage of the eruption, comprise the only measures necessary.

The severer forms, on the contrary, demand active medication and the most careful and continued attention. While it is not possible to materially modify the course or severity of the small-pox eruption, much may be done to mitigate the sufferings of the patient, to guard against threatening complications, and to prevent the subsequent pitting and deformity of the face, which so often result.

The old attempts to cut short the disease by antiphlogistic and depletory treatment, and, failing in this, to bring out the eruption copiously by keeping the patient hot and profusely sweating, are now, fortunately, obsolete.

In the management of a case of small-pox, the best results are obtained by placing the patient in a large, cool, well-ventilated room, the free use of cold water, lemonade, or mucilaginous drinks, the employment of ice-cloths and compresses, or sponging with cold water to subdue pain and local inflammatory action, a light, but generous and supporting diet, and the use of such other measures as symptomatic indications call for. Good nursing and a careful attention to all details contributing to the patient's comfort, and rest are of prime importance.

Almost innumerable methods and agents have been employed with a view of aborting or modifying the development of the pustules, and thus preventing the subsequent pitting; such, for example, as painting the skin with tincture of iodine or solutions of nitrate of silver, evacuating the contents of the pustules, and cauterizing with the solid nitrate, covering the face with mercurial plaster, with lint soaked in carbolized oil or glycerin, with gutta-percha paper, traumaticin, collodion, etc. The efficacy of these expedients is of doubtful value in most cases. As Curschmann remarks: "If the pustules are superficial, their scars will be slight; if the papillæ are involved, no amount of caustic can prevent the loss of substance." Undoubtedly the best results are obtained by the use of ice-cold compresses, which relieve the swelling and inflammation, and thus have a tendency to prevent the extension in depth of the pus-formation.

When the mucous membranes of the mouth and throat are the seat of the eruption, with pain and swelling, astringent and antiseptic gargles are to be employed, as chlorate of potash, diluted chlorine water, or a weak solution of muriated tincture of iron. Œdema of the glottis is to be treated by local scarifications. Ulceration of the cornea to be touched with the point of the solid nitrate of silver; abscesses, wherever formed, should be promptly opened.

If the strength of the patient be weakened by the fever of suppuration, stimulants should be employed. When the eruption has passed through its successive stages, and the body is covered with crusts, great comfort will be derived, and the fall of the crusts hastened, by occasional warm baths. For the relief of the itching, which is often a most troublesome symptom, inunctions with fresh lard, cocoa butter, or carbolized vaseline may be employed. Complications should be treated, as they present themselves, on general principles.

The hemorrhagic and malignant forms of small-pox always carry with them a grave prognosis. Treatment is powerless to control the symptoms, and in a majority of cases the disease rapidly progresses to a fatal termination.

VARICELLA.

Synonym—Chicken-pox.

A belief in the substantial identity of this disease with variola was formerly generally entertained, and is still held by many reputable authorities. While varicella bears a certain resemblance to modified small-pox in the mode of its development and the anatomical form of its lesions, the points of distinction are so numerous and striking as to render such an opinion untenable. Neither vaccination nor a previous attack of variola protects against it.

Varicella may be defined as an acute febrile, contagious disease, characterized by a vesicular eruption and attended, as a rule, with slight constitutional disturbance. It is essentially a disease of childhood.

The period of incubation is somewhat more prolonged than that of variola or measles—from fourteen to seventeen days. The prodromic stage is not pronounced; ordinarily, there is slight systemic disturbance or none at all. The rise of temperature, if any, follows rather than precedes the outbreak of the eruption, which is often the first symptom that marks the disease. It first appears upon the upper part of the body, and is most characteristically developed upon the back, but may extend to the hairy scalp, face, and extremities.

The exanthem consists of vesicles of variable size, which rise from slightly infiltrated hyperæmic spots; they rapidly mature and attain their maximal development in twelve to twenty-four hours. The vesicles are surrounded by a slight halo, and when fully formed are globular in shape and tensely distended with a clear serous or light-yellow fluid. The lesions may be few in number and scattered, or they may be thickly disseminated over the entire body; they are generally discrete, rarely confluent. Occasionally vesicles are seen upon the mucous membranes of the fauces, the palate, and conjunctiva, and also upon the genital mucous surface.

The duration of the vesicles is brief; on the second day they rupture, or dry up in the form of yellowish or brownish crusts which soon fall off, leaving slightly reddened or darkly pigmented spots, sometimes shallow cicatrices. The individual lesions pass through their successive changes in from five to seven days. The eruption may come out in successive crops, the lesions exhibiting different stages of development.

Exceptionally, varicella is attended with a high grade of constitutional disturbance, with large, distinctly umbilicated vesicles which are deeply seated and followed by destruction of the deeper layers of the corium and permanent scar formations, as seen in variola.

DIAGNOSIS.—The disease with which varicella is most likely to be confounded is modified small-pox. The differential points have already been considered in connection with the diagnosis of small-pox. One additional point may be alluded to: since varicella is essentially a disease of childhood, occurring only with the rarest degree of frequency in adults, the diagnosis of chicken-pox may be almost certainly excluded in cases where a varicella-like eruption is met with in an adult.

The varicelliform syphilide, as the term implies, bears a certain resemblance to varicella. It is only in the early stage of the eruption and after a single examination that confusion is liable to occur. In varicella, the entire process is rapid in development and brief in duration; the eruption is bright red, the vesicles dry up within two or three days, the crusts are small, easily detached, and leave only a transient staining of the skin. In syphilis the process is more sluggish, the vesicles are grouped characteristically, each surrounded by a coppery red areola, and change into pustules. The crusts are darker, thicker, and more adherent, and upon falling leave darkly pigmented spots which are slow in disappearing.

TREATMENT.—The course of varicella is so exceedingly mild and attended with such slight constitutional disturbance that, in the large majority of cases, expectant treatment alone is indicated. A suitable regimen, rest and confinement to the house are all that is necessary ; should the itching be severe, inunctions with vaseline or an antipruritic lotion will give relief. Isolation of the patient is not required.

RUBEOLA.

Synonyms—Measles ; Morbilli.

Measles may be defined as an acute febrile, contagious disease, characterized by a papular eruption of the skin, accompanied with a catarrhal inflammation of the conjunctivæ and the mucous membrane of the upper air passages.

The contagious principle of measles is volatile and diffusible ; it never originates spontaneously, but is always derived from the secretions or emanations of a person similarly affected. The atmosphere of the sick-chamber or any object which comes in contact with the infected person may serve as the vehicle of contagion. The disease is more common in childhood, the susceptibility to its influence being modified to a certain degree by age. Second attacks are exceedingly rare, their occasional occurrence is, however, well attested by authentic observation.

The period of incubation of measles is on the average ten days, and as the prodromal symptoms extend over a period of three or four days, the interval which elapses between the date of exposure and the outbreak of the characteristic exanthem may be placed at fourteen days on the average.

In a typical case of measles the prodromal symptoms are ushered in suddenly, and consist of febrile disturbance attended with cough, sneezing, suffusion of the conjunctivæ, increased lachrymation, and photophobia. The temperature changes are more or less constant. The temperature rises to 102° or 104°, with a remission during the next two days, when it again rises, reaching its maximal elevation, 104° or 105°, on the fifth day, corresponding to the intensest development of the eruption, which usually appears on the fourth day, sometimes delayed to the morning of the fifth day, and attaining its complete development within thirty-six hours. The temperature then gradually in the next two or three days falls to the normal ; it may even be subnormal during convalescence. The exanthem makes its appearance first on the face, forehead, cheeks, chin, and nape of the neck, and gradually extends by successive advances over the trunk and lower extremities. The whole eruption is generally out within a period of three days. The duration of its acme of development is usually one-half a day, so that if its extension be slow, it begins to fade from the face before it has invaded the lower surfaces.

The efflorescence of measles consists of roundish or crescentic spots from one-twentieth to one-fifth inch in diameter, of a pinkish or bluish-red color. Their margins are defined, sometimes with offshoots into the surrounding skin. In the centre of the spots there may be sometimes seen a papule formed by an exudation around the hair follicles. The spots are usually discrete, sometimes confluent at their margins, forming irregularly circumscribed blotches upon an erythematous base. The coloration of the spots disappears on pressure, but returns immediately when the pressure is withdrawn. The hyperæmia of the skin is not universally diffused over the surface.

The retrocession of the eruption usually takes place in the order of its development ; the parts primarily attacked, as the face and upper part of the body, are the first to become normal.

PLATE XXXIX.

FIG. I.—Rubeola (measles).
FIG. II.—Rubella (German measles).

AUTHOR'S COLLECTION.

Sometimes the fading spots may become bright or vivid again under the influence of febrile exacerbation.

The spots in disappearing leave a yellowish or brownish stain, which gradually fades from view within a few days. Desquamation, in the form of fine, branny scales occurs, especially upon the exposed parts.

Measles may present certain deviations from this typical development and course; thus the catarrhal symptoms may be entirely absent, constituting what is known as measles *sine catarrho*, or the characteristic mucous membrane symptoms may be present without the typical morbid appearances of the skin; again, there may be anomalies in the character of the constitutional accidents.

In the variety known as hemorrhagic or black measles, the eruption consists of dark-red spots or papules which are due to capillary hemorrhage; the coloration of the spots is not affected by pressure. The hemorrhagic extravasations in the skin are accompanied with epistaxis and with hemorrhages from the mucous surfaces of the intestines, kidneys, uterus, etc., and parenchymatous changes in the internal organs. This malignant form usually occurs in very young children or in the weak and debilitated; it is attended with a severe grade of constitutional disturbance, and is most frequently fatal.

DIAGNOSIS.—The diagnosis of a typical case of measles is not usually a matter of much difficulty, the prodromal fever, the mucous membrane symptoms, and the character of the exanthem constitute important differential signs. There are a number of diseases attended with hyperæmia of the skin and papular eruptions with which it may be confounded.

Rötheln or German measles is distinguished by the absence of marked febrile disturbance, the development of the eruption in the form of round, rosy-red spots, which, though sometimes grouped, never become confluent, and the mild character or entire absence of catarrhal inflammation of the nasal and conjunctival membranes.

The eruption of measles sometimes bears a certain resemblance to scarlatina from which it may be distinguished by the early appearance of the scarlatinal eruption in the form of minute bright red punctate points, the more diffused redness of the surface, the presence of angina with the characteristic strawberry tongue, and the absence of the concomitant symptoms of measles.

The eruption of typhus fever has been mistaken for measles. The ordinary limitation of the typhus eruption to certain regions, as the abdomen and sides of the chest, its rare development upon the face and exposed parts, the absence of coryza and conjunctivitis, and the course of the fever are usually sufficient for a correct diagnosis.

The disease with which the papular form of measles is most often confounded is variola. It is only in the rudimentary and imperfectly developed stage of small-pox that this mistake is liable to occur. The latter may be distinguished by the intense prodromal headache and backache, sudden subsidence of the fever upon the appearance of the eruption, the hard shotty, more elevated papules, and the absence of the catarrhal symptoms characteristic of measles. In cases of doubt the element of time furnishes distinctive points of difference. Within twenty-four hours the eruption of measles will begin to fade, while the papules of variola become more protuberant and begin to undergo a vesicular transformation.

It is to be remembered that the use of certain drugs may provoke an eruption resembling measles. Antipyrine and quinine eruptions sometimes present such a striking similitude to measles that a diagnosis can only be made by an attention to the concomitant symptoms. Drug eruptions of the measly type may be differentiated by their sudden appearance, usually without fever or marked constitutional disturbance, their distribution, the intense itching they occasion, and the celerity with which they vanish so soon as the offending cause is withdrawn.

TREATMENT.—Since measles runs a definite course which cannot be interrupted, with a tendency to self-limitation, the indications of treatment are essentially symptomatic. Careful nursing and close attention directed to the prevention of the troublesome sequelæ which so often follow, are more essential than active medication.

The room should be well ventilated, the patient kept properly covered, and a light diet ordered. The light should be excluded or so tempered as to be grateful to the patient's eyes. For the relief of conjunctival symptoms, the eyes should be frequently bathed with warm water. Troublesome cough may be checked by a mild expectorant syrup. Inunctions, with vaseline or cacao butter, should be practised to allay itching. Frequent and copious inunctions have been found to lower the temperature by allaying cutaneous irritation, and also to exert a favorable influence upon the bronchial symptoms. Diluted oil of turpentine has been highly recommeded for this purpose.

The bowels should be kept open by mild laxatives. Strong cathartics are objectionable, as tending to induce diarrhœa which is often a troublesome symptom in measles. Particular care should be exercised to prevent exposure to taking cold, and thus lessen the liability to catarrhal bronchitis, which constitutes the most dangerous complication. ·

RUBELLA.

Synonyms—German Measles; Rötheln.

The distinct individuality of this disease, which was for a long time regarded as a hybrid form of measles and scarlatina, is now generally recognized. Its separate identity is proven by the fact that it does not protect against measles, nor does an attack of measles confer an immunity against the disease under consideration.

Rötheln is more essentially a disease of childhood, although it may attack adults. The duration of its incubative period and the vehicles of contagion are the same as in measles. It is not attended with complications or sequelæ.

The constitutional accidents are mild in character. Most often the eruption is the first sign of the disease, and is not preceded by fever. Exceptionally the temperature may be elevated one to three degrees the first two days, but it rapidly subsides, and does not rise again.

The eruption consists of round, rosy spots, from the size of a pin's head to that of a small pea, with tolerably distinct outlines. The spots remain discrete, but may be connected with each other here and there by delicate processes; and a number of small spots may be grouped around a larger one in a circular configuration. The spots are slightly raised, round or oval, and do not assume the crescentic shape, nor are they so crowded as in measles.

The eruption begins on the face, where it is most abundantly developed, and rapidly extends over the body. The duration of the exanthem is rarely more than two to four days. Upon its disappearance, the spots leave a slight yellowish tinge, and are not followed by noticeable desquamation.

The mucous membrane symptoms are not very pronounced as a rule, and consist of a slight congestion of the throat and conjunctivæ, attended with sneezing. The tonsils are sometimes enlarged, and may be accompanied with a moderately swollen and painful condition of the glands of the neck.

DIAGNOSIS.—The exceeding mildness or entire absence of constitutional symptoms with the peculiar character of the rash serve to differentiate rötheln from measles and scarlatina. In measles the rash is coarsely papular, with a crescentic arrangement and of a raspberry tint, in contrast with the rosy, or crimson-red, discrete spots of rötheln. In scarlatina the efflorescence is punctate, with a diffused redness, and accompanied with high temperature, difficult deglutition, and the characteristic scarlet fever tongue.

The disease is also to be differentiated from the simple erythematous eruptions symptomatic of other disorders. The rubella exanthem may be quite accurately imitated by the antipyrine eruption.

TREATMENT.—German measles is in the majority of cases a trifling complaint, unattended with subjective sensations or constitutional disorder, and active medication is rarely required.

Confinement to the house, with a light diet and ordinary care against exposure, are the only measures necessary to be observed in its management.

SCARLATINA.

Synonym—Scarlet Fever.

Scarlatina is an acute febrile, contagious disease, characterized by a more or less generalized hyperæmic exanthem, accompanied with an angina of variable intensity and various nervous phenomena.

It is due to the action of a specific poison, which may be communicated through the contagious atmosphere of the sick-room, through the medium of the clothing or other objects coming in contact with the patient, and, probably, by impregnation of milk taken as an article of food. It may occur sporadically or epidemically.

The period of incubation varies from four to seven days. The attack is ushered in by a chill or rigors, headache, and frequently, vomiting, with sore throat and a prickling sensation in swallowing. The febrile movement is quite characteristic, and is not apparently modified by the eruption. The temperature rises to 101° to 105°, and remains elevated with slight morning remissions and evening exacerbations during the entire continuance of the eruption. In malignant cases it may reach 107°.

The eruption ordinarily appears on the second day of the fever; it consists of minute red papules closely aggregated and grouped about the follicles, showing as bright red punctate spots, or rather dots. These soon become confluent, forming irregularly marginated scarlet patches, or the redness may be uniformly diffused over the surface. The color of the eruption is at first a bright scarlet, and when fully developed it has been likened to that of a boiled lobster; later it may deepen into a duskier tint, and in severe cases may become livid or even petechial in character. It first appears upon the neck and chest, and within twenty-four hours extends over the entire body. It is most intensely developed over the flexures, less prominent upon the face, the region of the mouth and chin entirely escaping, and contrasting in their pale color with the bright red of the cheeks and forehead. The eruption maintains its maximum of intensity from twelve to twenty-four hours, and then begins to decline, fading out in two or four days, so that its entire duration is from three to seven days.

The disappearance of the eruption is followed by desquamation more or less marked of the outer layers of the epidermis. In some cases it is quite slight, consisting of minute branny scales, in others more decided and pronounced, the epidermis exfoliating in large plate-like scales. In some cases the entire cuticle of the hands and feet becomes loosened and may be pulled off like a glove.

A characteristic feature of scarlet fever is the peculiar condition of the tongue, which on account of the prominence of its papillæ has received the designation of the "strawberry tongue."

The changes in the mucous membranes of the throat in scarlatina are quite as characteristic and even more constant than the cutaneous phenomena, since, exceptionally, the disease may run through its course without any trace of an eruption. The throat symptoms develop with the onset of the disease, and are characterized by congestion of the fauces, swelling of the tonsils and cervical glands, and painful, sometimes difficult deglutition.

In the higher grades of scarlatina angionosa, the throat symptoms are intensified in severity, the tonsils and mucous membranes are highly inflamed and œdematous, the inflammation extending to the posterior nares and prolonged into the Eustachian tubes. Ulceration and gangrene may occur as complications.

The numerous and varied complications of scarlatina, as parenchymatous inflammation of

PLATE XL.

FIG. I.—Scarlatina.
FIG. II.—Erysipelas.

AUTHOR'S COLLECTION

Plate XXXVI.

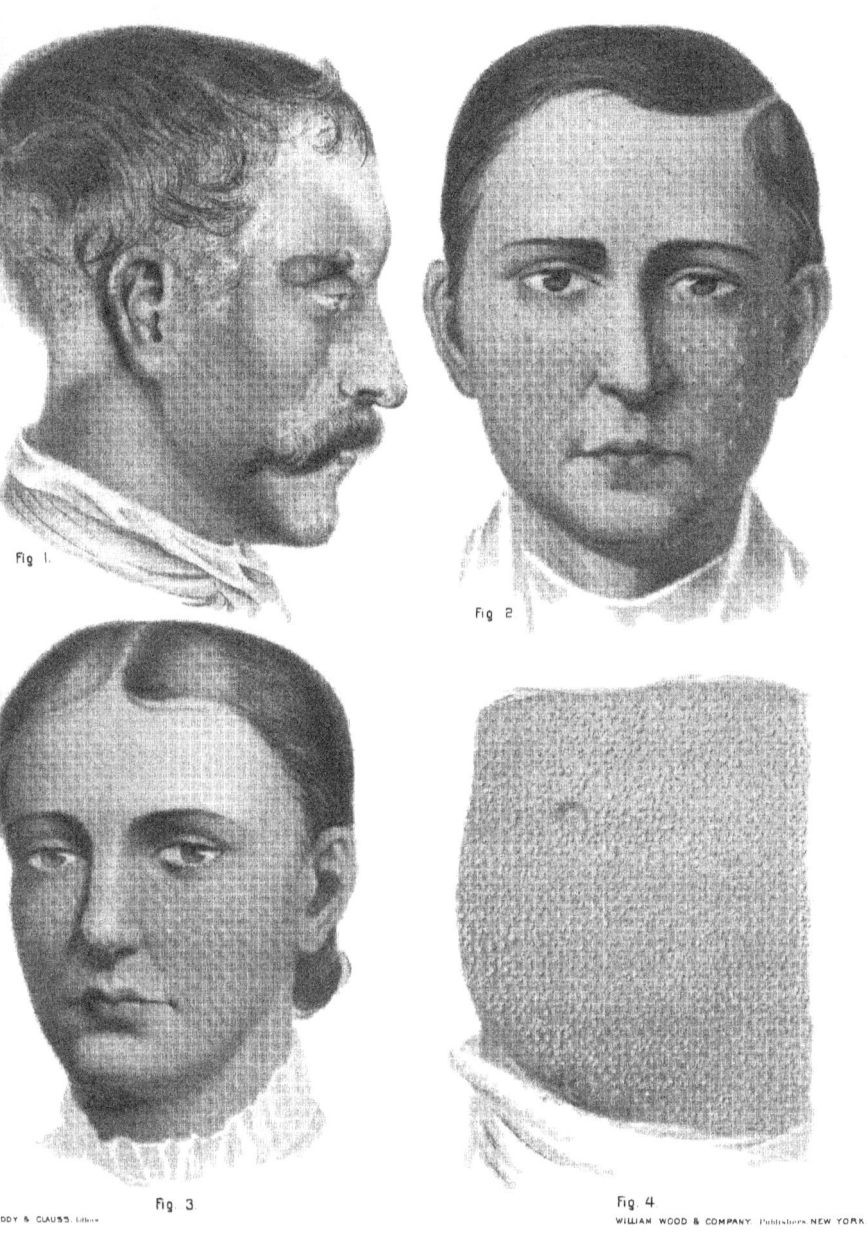

Fig 1.

Fig 2

Fig 3

Fig. 4

EDDY & CLAUSS, Lithrs.

WILLIAM WOOD & COMPANY, Publishers NEW YORK.

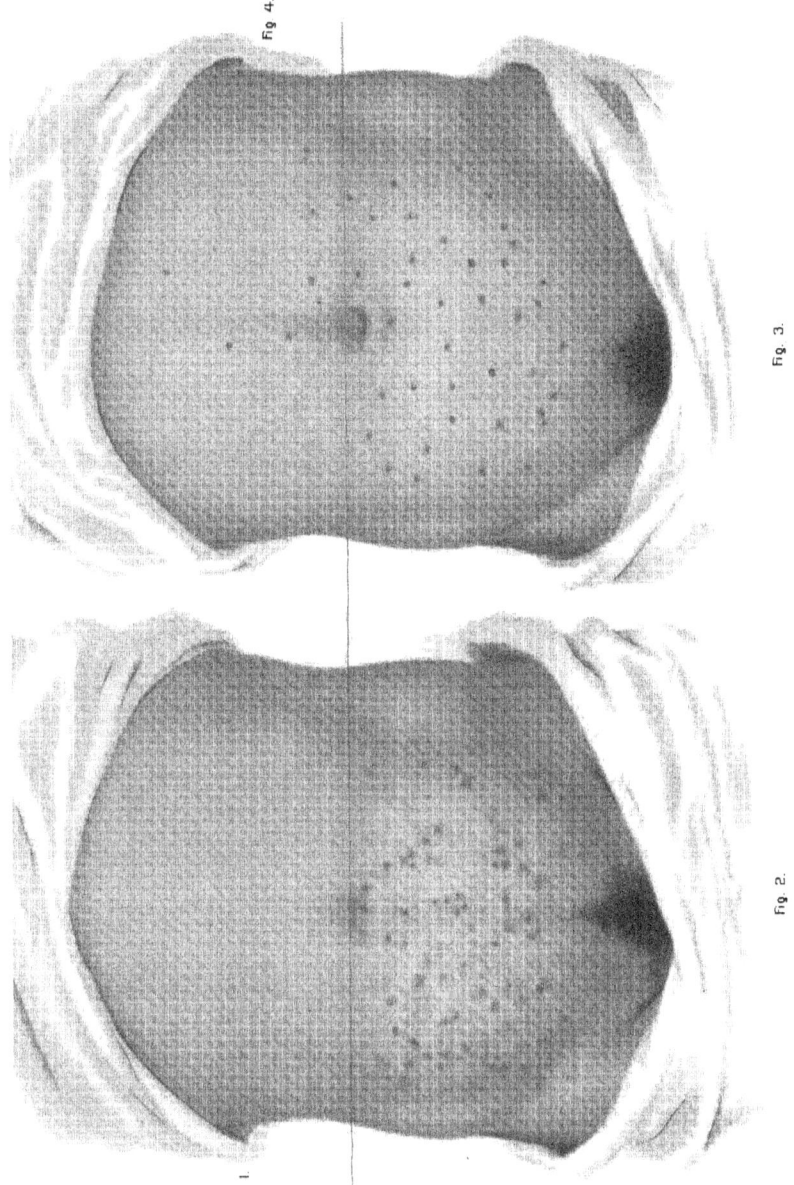

Fig. 4.

Fig. 3.

Fig. 2.

Fig. 1.

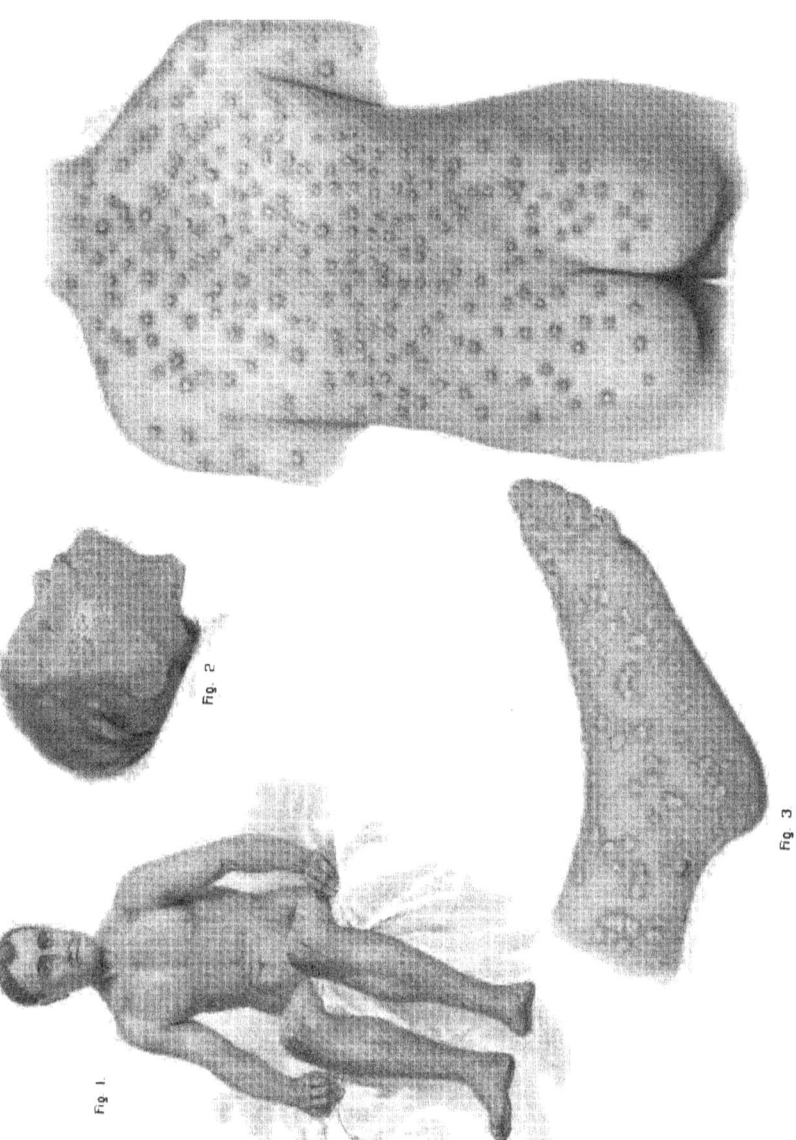

Fig. 1

Fig. 2

Fig. 3

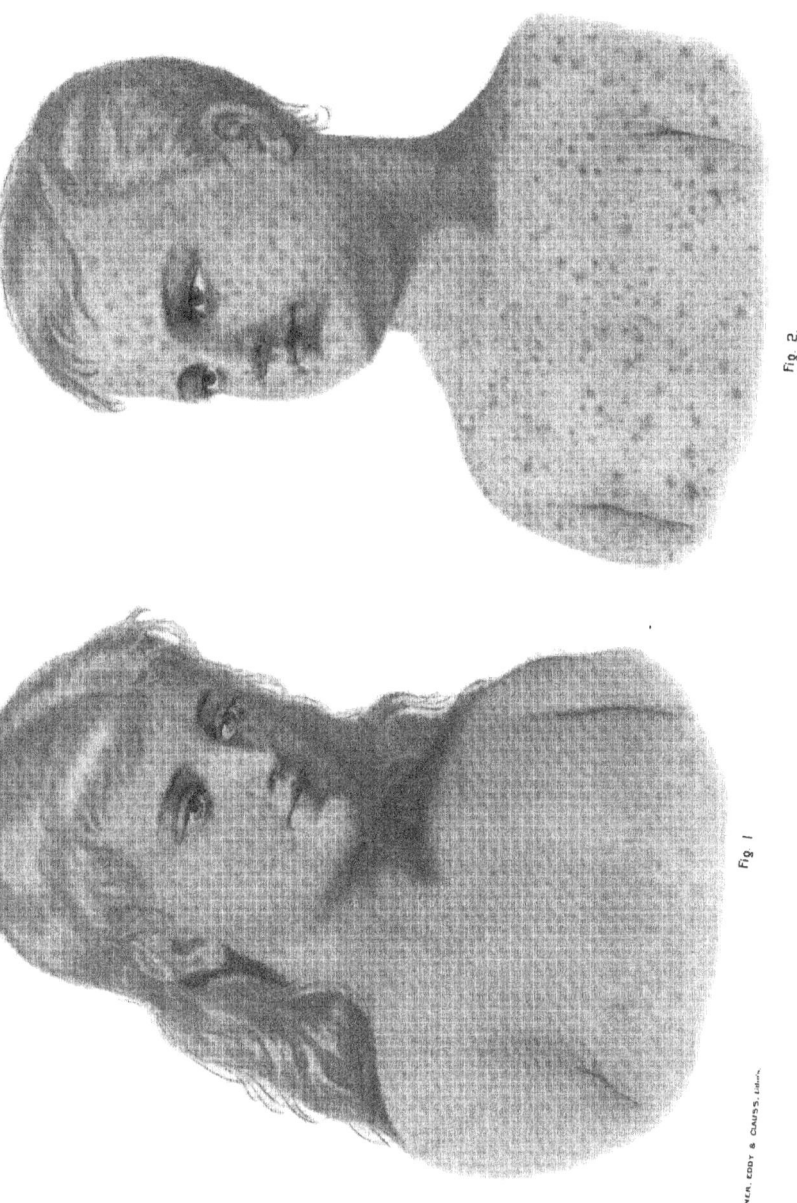

Fig. 1

Fig. 2.

UNDNER, EDDY & CLAUSS, Litho.

WILLIAM WOOD & COMPANY, Publishers, NEW YORK.

Plate XXX.

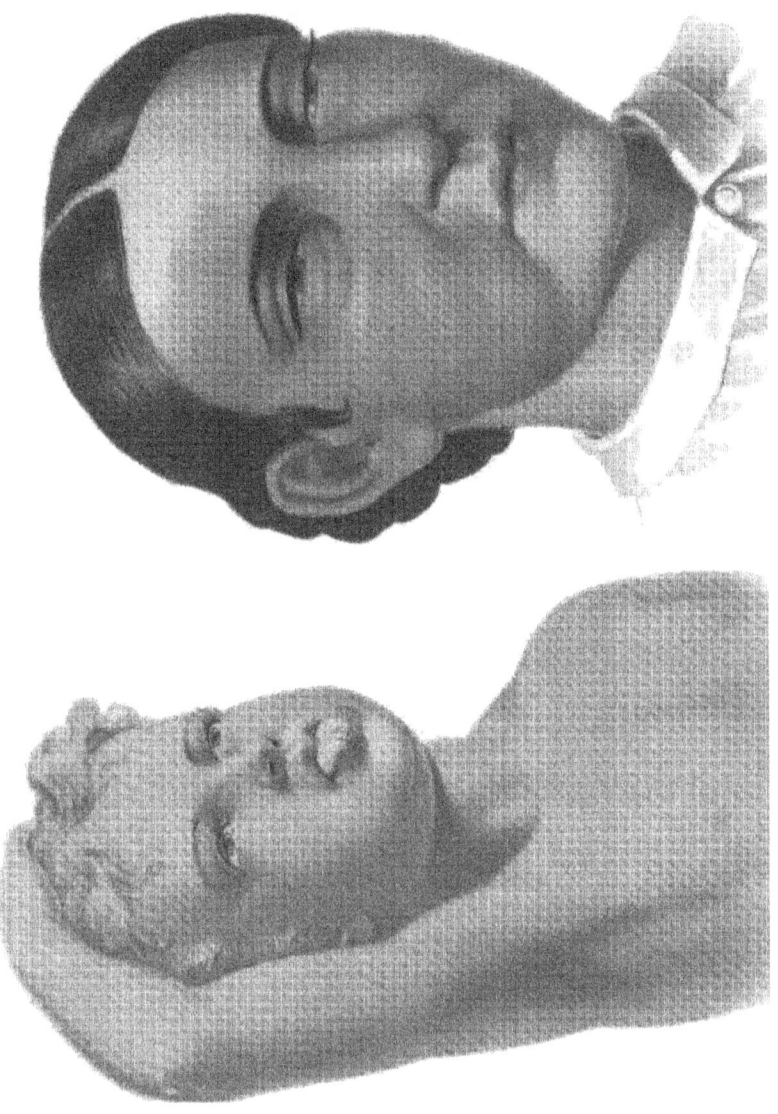

ATLAS

OF

VENEREAL AND SKIN

DISEASES

COMPRISING ORIGINAL ILLUSTRATIONS AND SELECTIONS FROM THE PLATES OF

PROF. M. KAPOSI, OF VIENNA; DR. J. HUTCHINSON, OF LONDON; PROF. I. NEUMANN, OF VIENNA;
PROFS. A. FOURNIER AND A. HARDY; AND DRS. RICORD, CULLERRIER, BESNIER, AND VIDAL, OF PARIS;
PROF. LELOIR, OF LILLE; DR. P. A. MORROW, OF NEW YORK; DR. E. L. KEYES, OF NEW YORK;
DR. FESSENDEN N. OTIS, OF NEW YORK; DR. J. NEVINS HYDE, OF CHICAGO;
DR. HENRY G. PIFFARD, OF NEW YORK, AND OTHERS.

WITH ORIGINAL TEXT BY

PRINCE A. MORROW, A.M., M.D.,

CLINICAL PROFESSOR OF VENEREAL DISEASES, FORMERLY CLINICAL LECTURER ON DERMATOLOGY, IN THE UNIVERSITY OF THE CITY OF NEW YORK ;
SURGEON TO CHARITY HOSPITAL, ETC.

NEW YORK

WILLIAM WOOD & COMPANY

1888

ATLAS

OF

VENEREAL AND SKIN

DISEASES

It is with special satisfaction that the publishers announce that this large and important work, which they have had in contemplation since 1883, is now ready for publication. It has long been recognized by them, from wide observation and acquaintance with similar works published in this country and abroad, that it is impossible for any one author to furnish, from his own collection of cases and illustrations, the most typical and at the same time the best and most lifelike pictures of the many peculiar forms of these diseases. Appreciating the defects and disadvantages arising from this cause, it was determined from the outset to enlist the co-operation, in the making of this ATLAS, of the leading dermatologists and syphilographers of the world. Prominent among them are Profs. M. Kaposi and I. Neumann, of Vienna. The atlas of the former, of venereal diseases, just completed, and that of the latter, of skin diseases, now being issued in parts, will be largely drawn upon in the preparation of this work, the sole right to reproduce them having been granted us by the authors.

Among other distinguished gentlemen who have engaged to contribute selections from their collections of original illustrations may now be mentioned Dr. J. Hutchinson, of London; Profs. A. Fournier and A. Hardy; and Drs. Ricord, Cullerrier, Besnier, and Vidal, of Paris; Dr. P. A. Morrow, of New York; Dr. Edward L. Keyes, of New York; Dr. Fessenden N. Otis, of New York; Dr. J. Nevins Hyde, of Chicago; Dr. Henry G. Piffard, of New York.

Other names will be added to this list as the work progresses.

The Editor of the work is Dr. Prince A. Morrow, of New York, who, in addition to plates contributed from his own remarkable collection, will write the treatise on skin and venereal diseases, which constitutes, besides the description of the plates, the text accompanying them.

In this treatise, it is aimed to include chiefly those features which are the most practical, omitting in great measure pathological and other considerations which would be more properly treated of in extended writings, rather than as the adjunct to an Atlas.

In regard to the character of the plates, it may be said, they are believed to be superior to anything of the kind heretofore produced—as accurate in drawing as photographs, and far more distinct, while the coloring faithfully represents nature.

The text is printed from new type, large, clear, and handsome, and the paper is heavy, with a highly finished surface.

Altogether, considering the reputation of the authors of the plates, the ability of the editor, the superb execution of the plates, the excellence of the presswork, the high quality of the paper of both text and plates, the large size of the page, etc., etc., this ATLAS OF VENEREAL AND SKIN DISEASES will be the most superb work in medical literature ever published in the English language.

The ATLAS OF VENEREAL AND SKIN DISEASES will be published in fifteen monthly parts, each containing five folio, chromo-lithographic plates, many of them containing numerous figures, all printed in flesh tints and colors, together with descriptive text for each plate, and from sixteen to twenty folio pages of a practical treatise upon venereal and skin diseases; the whole forming, when complete, one magnificent thick folio volume with seventy-five plates, containing several hundred figures, exquisitely printed in colors.

☞ The ATLAS OF VENEREAL AND SKIN DISEASES will be sold by subscription only, at the very moderate price of $2 per part.

WILLIAM WOOD & COMPANY, *Publishers*,

56 AND 58 LAFAYETTE PLACE, NEW YORK.

the kidneys with albuminuria, the affections of the joints known as scarlatinal rheumatism, the nervous phenomena and other sequelæ cannot be considered here. The character and severity of the secondary alterations vary within wide limits in different cases.

DIAGNOSIS.—The diagnosis of a typical case of scarlatina usually presents few difficulties. The three most important elements which serve as a basis of diagnosis are, the febrile movement, the punctate character of the eruption, and the appearance of the throat and tongue.

In irregular cases when the eruption is scanty, partially developed or entirely absent, the fever, throat symptoms and " strawberry " tongue may be sufficient; when an early diagnosis is impossible, the subsequent desquamation and the albuminuria will resolve all doubt.

The diseases with which scarlatina is most likely to be confounded are certain forms of erythema and measles, more particularly German measles.

The ordinary scarlatiniform erythema may proceed from a variety of causes. It is irregularly rather than uniformly diffused, and is usually slight and of transient duration, rarely lasting more than two days. The desquamation is never abundant, and it is not attended, as a rule, with fever, nor followed by sequelæ.

The erythema due to the ingestion of certain drugs as belladonna, quinine, etc., may be indistinguishable from that of scarlatina. Pathogenetic erythema is, however, not, as a rule, ushered in by high fever, the throat and tongue symptoms are not pronounced, itching is more severe, and it disappears promptly upon the cessation of action of the exciting cause. If the congestion of the skin be intense and long continued, desquamation may be abundant and several times repeated.

The rare disease, known as desquamative scarlatiniform erythema, closely resembles scarlatina in the uniform redness of the surface and in the febrile reaction. It is distinguished by its development without exposure to contagion, the absence of throat symptoms, the longer continued, more abundant lamellar-like desquamation, and its frequent recurrences.

The differentiation of scarlatina from rubeola and rubella has been already considered in connection with the diagnosis of these diseases.

In cases of malignant scarlet fever in which the system is overwhelmed by the virulence of the poison, and death takes place before the appearance of the eruption, a diagnosis can be made only upon the existence of an epidemic at the time and the history of known exposure.

TREATMENT.—In all cases of scarlatina the patient should be isolated and the strictest precautionary measures adopted against the spread of the disease. Bed clothing, towels, and other articles coming in contact with the patient should be disinfected or destroyed. The prophylactic measures employed to prevent or abort the disease, which were once held in high repute, such as belladonna, etc., are of deceptive value. When the poison has gained access to the system, the disease cannot be arrested or its natural course interfered with to advantage.

The treatment should be essentially symptomatic, the patient should be carefully watched, and unfavorable indications or threatening complications should be met as they arise by appropriate means.

In mild cases, confinement to bed in a cool, well-ventilated room, a light diet, occasional sponging of the body with tepid water, anointing with lard, cocoa butter, or carbolized vaseline to relieve the itching, the use of astringent gargles, bits of ice, or the employment of cold compresses to relieve the throat symptoms, comprise all the therapeutic measures necessary. After convalescence has been established, the patient should for some time be guarded against exposure to cold.

In severer cases, characterized by a high grade of febrile reaction, the temperature should be reduced by quinine, antipyrin, and remedies of this class, or a resort to hydro-therapeutic measures. When the scarlatinal angina takes on a diphtheritic character, it should be treated precisely as ordinary diphtheria. Scarlatinal nephritis, rheumatism, eye and ear complications should be treated upon the general principles recognized as appropriate to these conditions.

ERYSIPELAS.

Erysipelas may be defined as an acute infectious disease characterized by a peculiar creep-ing inflammation of the skin, preceded or accompanied with implication of the neighboring lymphatic system, and attended with marked constitutional disturbance.

It is due to the action of a specific poison, which is tenacious and long retains its infecting quality, it may occur sporadically or in isolated epidemics and is both contagious and inoculable.

From an etiological point of view, erysipelas has been classified as idiopathic and trau-matic; the symptomatology of the two affections is, however, essentially the same. Clinically, two varieties of erysipelas are recognized: the simple and the phlegmonous, the distinction between the two being based upon the intensity and depth of the inflammatory process. In the former, the skin or mucous membrane is affected, terminating in desquamation; in the latter, the subcutaneous cellular tissue and the fasciæ are involved, ending in suppuration with more or less destruction of tissue, cutaneous abscesses, etc.

The attack is usually ushered in by a slight chill, fever, headache, and other symptoms of constitutional disturbance. The temperature rises to 102° or even to 105°, and continues during the entire course of the dermatitis. A marked parallelism is always to be observed between the temperature curve and the local inflammatory process, the one rising or falling as the other pro-gresses or recedes.

The cutaneous inflammation ordinarily shows itself within twenty-four hours after the accession of the fever, in the form of a bright-red or rose-colored spot. It usually has for its point of departure a slight or severe lesion of the skin. Its regions of predilection are the nose, cheeks, ear or scalp, it may begin upon any portion of the body. The redness, which disappears on pres-sure, rapidly extends and is attended with œdema, giving to the skin a tense, smooth, shining appearance. The œdematous infiltration is especially marked about the eyelids, cheeks and lips, where the connective tissue is lax. The tumefaction may close the eyelids, and be so disfiguring as to render the patient unrecognizable. The inflammation rapidly invades the adjacent portions of the skin or mucous membranes, advancing by a distinctly marginated wall of redness, occa-sionally sending out tongue-like prolongations into the surrounding healthy skin.

The inflammatory process reaches its highest intensity on the second or third day, and is frequently characterized by the formation of blisters or bullæ. The active signs of inflammation then begin to disappear, the redness pales into a yellowish tinge and the cuticle desquamates in branny or membranaceous flakes. The dermatitis is usually limited to the integument of the head and face; it may, however, extend, by a series of successive morbid impulses, over the entire surface, the eruption fading from the parts first attacked as new surfaces are involved. This variety is termed erysipelas ambulans. Where the disease does not spread by continuity, but breaks out in parts remote from the surface first attacked, it is designated erysipelas erraticum.

In rare cases, erysipelas extends from the integument to the mucous membrane of the nose and throat, or the disease may begin primarily in the throat and remain limited to the mucous membrane.

The subjective symptoms vary in different cases, there is a feeling of tension which may be accompanied with sensations of burning and pain.

The duration of an ordinary attack of erysipelas rarely exceeds a week or ten days. After the subsidence of the inflammation, the skin presents a yellowish tinge, and desquamation of the epidermis takes place, leaving the skin in a normal condition. Erysipelas usually terminates in recovery, except when the brain becomes involved by extension of the morbid process.

In the phlegmonous form of erysipelas, the inflammatory process is intensified in severity, and is followed by deep-seated suppuration and the formation of sloughs, which may be extensive in depth as well as area, at times involving the periosteum and joint cavities. In phlegmonous and gangrenous erysipelas, the constitutional symptoms correspond in severity to the local inflam-. mation.

DIAGNOSIS.—The diseases for which erysipelas is most likely to be mistaken are erythema and eczema. Erythema is rarely localized exclusively upon the face, and the eruption is blotchy, and is not accompanied with elevation of temperature, pain and vesication are absent. An acute attack of eczema, especially when attended with much œdematous swelling and redness, may present a most deceptive resemblance to erysipelas. In eczema, the constitutional symptoms are less marked, the itching is more severe, the redness is not so abruptly marginated. In erysipelas, the redness has for its point of departure a single red spot, and extends from this as a centre.

Erysipelas may be differentiated from phlegmonous inflammation of the skin and diffuse cellulitis by the marked differences in its mode of origin and development.

As regards the prognosis of erysipelas, the so-called idiopathic form, attacking the face and head, almost invariably terminates in recovery. Surgical erysipelas, especially when occurring as an epidemic, the septicæmic erysipelas following vaccination, and puerperal erysipelas possess a much graver prognostic significance.

TREATMENT.—A number of remedies have been recommended as possessing specific properties against erysipelas, but careful clinical experience has not confirmed their claims. The tincture of chloride of iron has been credited with this action, and is to be given in one-half to one drachm doses every few hours; but an equally good result will probably be obtained from other tonics, since the main indications are to support the strength of the patient and treat complications as they arise.

Quinine in full doses will be found useful in reducing excessive temperature. In the sthenic forms, aconite or veratrum viride should be employed to moderate the frequency of the pulse. The administration of pilocarpine hypodermically, or the fluid extract of jaborandi by the mouth, is often followed by speedy improvement. In the asthenic forms, carbonate of ammonium and other stimulants are to be recommended. The bowels should be kept open by mild aperients during the entire course of the disease. Cleanliness, good ventilation, and isolation of the patient are measures which should always be employed.

In the local treatment of erysipelas, a great many agents have been recommended to circumscribe or abort the inflammation, such as encircling the eruption with a line traced with the solid stick of the nitrate of silver, or the entire affected surface and the sound skin for an inch beyond is painted with a strong solution of the nitrate (20 grs. to 3 i.). Painting the affected surface or its edges with collodion, tincture of iodine, a solution of camphor and tannin in ether, the fluid extract of veratrum viride, a saturated solution of picric acid, oil of turpentine, sweet spirit of nitre, iodoform, one part to ten of collodion, are among the numerous local applications which have been recommended. I have found the ordinary linseed oil, in combination with lime-water, a soothing application. McCall Anderson recommends that the surface be enveloped in cotton wool after having been dusted with the following powder:

> ℞ Pulv. zinci ox.,
> Pulv. amyli,
> Pulv. lycopodii, ... ăă ℥ ss.
> Pulv camphoræ, ... ℥ ss.
> Ol. rosæ, ... ℳ i.
> M.

Soothing ointments may also be employed with benefit.

Several years ago, Barwell suggested painting the affected surfaces with ordinary white-lead paint, with a view of exclusion of the air. It is claimed to exert an almost magical effect in some cases, promptly putting a stop to the spread of the inflammation.

Ichthyol has been highly recommended in the treatment of erysipelas. It may be used in the form of a fixed adhesive dressing to the affected surface, as in the following formula:

℞ Ichthyol,
   Ætheris, ...   ⅍   5 parts
   Collodion flex., ...   90 parts

or in the form of an ointment composed of equal parts of ichthyol and vaseline.

ERYTHEMA SIMPLEX.

Simple erythema may be defined as a circumscribed or diffuse hyperæmia, characterized by the production of variously sized and shaped, non-elevated patches of reddened skin. The redness is due to an increased quantity of blood in the cutaneous capillaries, and disappears upon pressure to reappear as soon as it is withdrawn. Simple erythema is rarely attended with symptoms of constitutional disturbance, the subjective sensations of burning and itching are trifling or altogether absent, it is transient in duration and is not, as a rule, followed by desquamation.

The causes of erythema are numerous and of the most diverse character ; according to the etiological factors concerned in its production, it has been classified as idiopathic and symptomatic erythema.

Idiopathic erythema results from the direct impression upon the skin of various external irritants. Symptomatic erythema is indicative of some disturbance of the general system ; the former is usually limited to the surface with which the irritant comes in contact, the latter is more apt to be generalized and roughly symmetrical.

Erythema caloricum is induced by extremes of temperature, as seen in the intense redness which follows the exposure of any portion of the surface to the direct rays of the hot sun or to a cold wind. If the temperature be excessive and the exposure long continued, the irritation is more intense, resulting in dermatitis and followed by desquamation.

Erythema traumaticum is applied to the hyperæmia occasioned by mechanical pressure or friction, as from tight articles of clothing, dressings, bandages, etc., or from brisk rubbing.

Erythema venenatum is caused by various chemical agencies of a mineral or vegetable nature coming in contact with the skin. As familiar examples may be mentioned, the application of mustard, various acids and alkalies, soaps, dye stuffs, the flow of irritating secretions over the skin, etc.

In all these cases, the pathogenetic mode is essentially the same : mechanical and chemical irritants act just as caloric does upon the sensory nerves of the skin, the response to the stimulus being an increased supply of blood, with redness of the surface. In general, the effect of the cutaneous irritant is limited to the vascular area supplied by the affected nerves. The irritating effect may pass beyond this limit and be reflected upon adjacent or distant regions, or it may be diffused over the entire surface. The intensity of the resulting erythema depends upon the nature of the irritant, the duration of its contact, and the sensitiveness of the skin. In persons with delicate sensitive skins, as women and children, susceptibility to irritant action is much more marked.

SYMPTOMATIC ERYTHEMA.—A superficial inflammation of the skin of the erythematous type is common to a large number of cutaneous affections. The term erythema is applied to a variety of red rashes which occur in young children from gastro-intestinal disorders, from the irritation of teething, many of which were formerly described as distinct and independent diseases, as erythema strophulus, erythema annulatus, roseola infantilis, æstiva, etc. Roseola is no longer regarded as symptomatic of any one disease, but is applied to a red rash of a fugitive character, which may result from a variety of causes. Roseola occurs in the form of pea to nail sized rose-colored patches, which often run together forming a sort of irregular network, or diffuse mottling which may be limited to certain surfaces or may spread over the entire body. It is more common in children, and occurs more frequently during the summer months, probably because of the greater tendency to disorders of the alimentary canal during this season. On account of the greater irritability of the nervous system, reflex cutaneous phenomena are much more common in children. Erythema occurs as the prodromal rash of certain eruptive fevers, as seen in the scarlatina-like efflorescence which precedes the eruption of small-pox. The poisoning of the blood in connection with diphtheria, septicæmia, vaccination, traumatism, surgical operations, is frequently manifested in the production of erythema. The infectious erythemas constitute a large and clinically important group.

An extensive mine of etiological factors in the production of erythemas has been discovered in drugs. The ingestion of belladonna, copaiba, chloral, quinine, and numerous other drugs determines in susceptible individuals an erythematous rash, which disappears promptly upon the elimination of the drug from the system.

Lastly may be mentioned erythemas due to psychical causes which are frequently observed in the examination of nervous females, *erythema pudoris.* This emotional congestion, termed " doctor's rash," is usually quite transient in duration, but may persist for several hours.

These congestions of the skin admit of a simple explanation. In many cases, they are purely reflex phenomena resulting from irritation of the gastro-intestinal mucous membrane. The larger proportion are due to the direct impression of an irritant agent circulating in the blood upon the vaso-motor centres or upon the peripheral distribution of these nerves. The emotional rashes may be regarded simply as an exaggeration of the phenomenon known as blushing, a sort of physiological angio-neurosis, and are due to an impression upon the vaso-motors emanating from the emotive centres.

DIAGNOSIS.—Erythemas are distinguished by their sudden development, usually without constitutional disturbance, the entire absence or moderate character of the subjective sensations, the bright, pinkish color of the efflorescence, and its transient duration. The presence or absence of exudation constitutes the pathological distinction between erythema and dermatitis, and as certain forms of erythema have a tendency to pass into eczema, it may be difficult to determine when the boundary line has been passed. Clinically, however, this fine differentiation is of little practical importance.

TREATMENT.—The recognition of the exciting cause of erythema is the first condition of successful treatment. In the case of idiopathic erythema, the cause is evident, and its withdrawal is followed by the prompt return of the normal condition of the skin. In symptomatic erythema, the exciting cause is usually readily traced. When dependent upon the ingestion of indigestible food, a mild purgative is often serviceable. Should troublesome itching be present, it may be allayed by a simple dusting powder, consisting of equal parts of zinc oxide, lycopodium, and starch, or protection of the surface with a bland ointment.

ERYTHEMA INTERTRIGO.

The term intertrigo indicates the seat as well as the cause of this affection; it is ordinarily limited to localities in which opposing surfaces of the skin come in contact, as between the nates, the flexures of the thighs, the axillæ, under the pendulous breasts of women, and around the neck and underneath the chin of fat babies. Intertrigo of the genital and anal regions is especially liable to occur in infants who are not properly cleansed, and from the contact of urine or leucorrhœal secretions. The irritation from the pressure and friction of the opposed surfaces, combined with the warmth and moisture from the secretions, cause congestion of the surfaces and maceration of the epidermis, accompanied with sensations of itching. The affected skin presents a shining, red, glazed appearance, and is painful to the touch, as well as upon movement. When the irritation is intense and long continued, the condition may develop into a mucoid eczema, with more or less exudation. Intertrigo is more liable to occur in young children with thin, delicate skins, during the summer months, and is apt to be more or less persistent, especially when complicated with stomach or bowel derangements, teething, worms, etc. The differentiation of intertrigo from other cutaneous affections is readily made by the form and locality of the eruption.

PLATE XLI.

FIG. I.—Erythema marginatum et gyratum.
FIG. II.—Erythema papulatum.
FIG. III.—Erythema iris et circinatus.

FIGS. I. AND III.—AFTER NEUMANN.
FIG. II.—AFTER CAZENAVE.

TREATMENT.—In the treatment of this variety of erythema, washing with cold water twice a day, the separation of the contiguous surfaces by the interposition of a piece of lint or soft linen, smeared with a bland ointment, and freedom from friction or motion are usually sufficient to effect a prompt cure.   When there is much secretion from the affected surfaces, it may be absorbed by the application of an ordinary dusting powder, as Fuller's earth, lycopodium, violet powder, or the following:

℞ Pulv. amyli, ...   ℥ ij.
   Pulv. bismuthi subnit., ...   ℥ i.
   Amyli, ...   ℥ v.
M.

Besnier recommends the following:

℞ Pulv. talc.,
   Zinci ox.,
   Amyli, ...   āā ℥ ij.
   Acidi boracici, ...   grs. v.–x.
M.

Excessive secretion may also be checked by the use of astringent lotions, the black wash, solutions of bicarbonate of soda, sulphate of zinc, grindelia robusta, etc.   Internal treatment is not required, except in cases of gastro-intestinal derangement.

ERYTHEMA MULTIFORME.

Independent of the simple active hyperæmias, there is a distinct class of erythematous in-flammations of the skin, attended with an exudation of plastic material, forming papules, vesico-papules, and tubercles, which have been grouped under the above title.   While essentially of the same nature, they exhibit polymorphic aspects, which has given rise to the designation of erythema multiforme.   According to the form and size of the lesions and the configurations they assume in the process of evolution, the following varieties are recognized: Erythema papulatum, E. tuberculatum, E. annulatum, E. iris, E. gyratum.

Erythema papulatum, which is the most common variety, usually develops in the form of irregularly rounded, flattened papules of variable size; the coloration, at first a bright red, fades as the papules grow older into a violet or purplish hue.   The papules may be discrete or confluent, their favorite location is upon the backs of the hands and wrists, the legs, and face; they may occur upon other portions of the body.   The lesions are symmetrically developed.

Erythema tuberculatum represents simply an exaggerated development of the lesions of the previous variety, having the same localization and course; the two forms often coexist.

Erythema annulatum is applied to the eruption when the patches assume a ringed con-figuration by spreading at the periphery while fading in the centre.

Erythema iris consists of a series of concentric rings, one including the other; as the rings are developed in succession, they exhibit variegated colors made up of red, purple, yellow, blue, the variations in tint resulting from the changes in the effused pigment.   Herpes iris is simply an exaggeration of this condition representing a more advanced stage, when the raised erythematous ring becomes the seat of vesicles.

Erythema gyratum is formed by the coalescence and intersection of the centrifugally spreading rings of the annular form, the inner segments of the coalescing circles fade out, leaving serpentine or gyrate bands of erythema.

Notwithstanding the diversity of appearance, these multiple forms of erythema are de-pendent upon the same pathological condition.   The different forms may pass the one into the other in the different stages of the disease, or several eruptive forms may be present at the same time in the same individual.   The disease is usually acute in its march, the lesions undergoing

PLATE XLII.

AFTER HEBRA.

spontaneous involution in the course of a few days, leaving, as a rule, slight pigmentation followed by desquamation. Fresh crops of lesions may continue to come out and the disease may thus perpetuate itself for weeks and become impressed with the character of chronicity. The subjective symptoms are not, as a rule, pronounced, itching or burning sensations are not intense or long continued, and may be altogether absent. Constitutional disturbance is usually absent or but slightly marked. Sometimes pain in the joints, a congested condition of the mouth and throat, with slight febrile reaction precedes or accompanies the eruption.

Attacks of erythema are influenced to a certain degree by seasonal conditions, they are much more common, indeed occur almost exclusively, in the spring and fall, and person subject to this eruption may have a succession of biannual attacks during a number of years. The close connection between erythemas, and hepatic and renal lesions has been pointed out by many authors.

DIAGNOSIS.—The diagnosis of erythema multiforme is rarely attended with difficulty, when its characteristic features are borne in mind. It is distinguished by the sudden and symmetric development, the peculiar coloration of the lesions, rosy red in the beginning stage, fading into a violet or purplish tint, its ordinary limitation to predilected regions, the season of its occurrence, and the absence of marked subjective symptoms.

The papular and tubercular forms are distinguished from papular eczema by the larger size and irregular form of the papules, their location, and the moderate itching. From urticaria, a disease with which it presents many analogies, by the absence of the intense itching and burning sensations, the violet tint of the lesions, and their less ephemeral duration.

TREATMENT.—The treatment of erythema multiforme is symptomatic, since the disease is essentially self-limited, with a tendency to spontaneous recovery. Many authorities assert that there is a close connection between erythema multiforme and the rheumatic diathesis. This view is strengthened by the frequent occurrence of rheumatic pains during an attack and the condition of the urine, which is often loaded with urates. In these cases the use of alkaline diuretics and saline laxatives will be found serviceable. The diet should be regulated, and intestinal derangements corrected.

Local applications are rarely required; in the exceptional cases where itching is a troublesome feature, the parts may be sponged with lotions of alcohol and water or carbolic acid, one drachm to eight ounces of water, or an antipruritic ointment may be used. Dusting powders are also serviceable in affording protection when the surface is inflamed and painful.

ERYTHEMA NODOSUM.

Synonym—Dermatitis Contusiformis.

Erythema nodosum is closely allied to erythema multiforme. It often occurs in connection with the other forms of erythema, and the opinion has been advanced that it is only a modification of exudative erythema, distinguishable by its deeper seat and greater degree ot intensity; by most authorities, however, it is regarded as a distinct and independent malady. The eruption consists of rounded or oval tumors from one-half to two inches or more in diameter. Upon their first appearance they are firm and hard to the feel, but later they are softer, with a shining, tense appearance, giving a deceptive indication of suppuration. The swellings, or "congestive tumors of the skin" as they have been termed, are due to a circumscribed inflammatory œdema, sometimes accompanied with the escape of red corpuscles into the tissues of the skin and the subcutaneous cellular tissues. The coloration is at first rosy or red, but goes through a series of chromatic changes—dark red, purplish, fading into a greenish-yellow —as seen in an ordinary bruise, hence the designation of *dermatitis contusiformis.* The lesions vary in number as well as size; their favorite location is upon the legs, between the knees and ankles; they may appear upon the arms and other regions of the body with a more or less symmetrical development. The eruption usually comes out in successive crops, so that the entire duration of an attack may extend over several weeks. The tumors are exceedingly tender and painful, but pruritic symptoms are absent; they invariably terminate in resorption. Each out-break of a crop of tumors is preceded by symptoms of constitutional disorder, lassitude, pains in the limbs, sometimes accompanied by febrile symptoms. The constitutional symptoms generally subside with the appearance of the eruption.

The disease is more common in females from the ages of fifteen to thirty, the attacks generally come on in the spring and autumn.

The etiology, as well as the pathological relations of erythema nodosum are still involved in obscurity. Many authorities regard it as an expression of the rheumatic diathesis, presenting many analogies with peliosis rheumatica, others class the affection among the angio-neuroses.

DIAGNOSIS.—The diagnosis of erythema nodosum is rarely attended with difficulty. Its limitation, as a rule, to the legs, the rounded or oval tuberosities, the series of chromatic changes presented in their involution, and the articular pains which precede or accompany their develop-ment form a sufficient basis for diagnosis. The only lesions with which the nodules of erythema nodosum are apt to be confounded are those of urticaria nodosum and syphilis, but the nodules of urticaria have no seat of predilection, they present a pale centre with a pinkish periphery, they are extremely itchy and of transient duration.

The ordinary gummatous nodes of syphilis are readily distinguishable. Mauriac has, how-ever, described, under the title of *erythème noueux syphilitique*, certain dermic and hypodermic neoplasms which in their objective characters bear a perfect resemblance to the nodes of erythema. To complete the resemblance, they are ushered in with febrile phenomena, gastric embarrassment, and rheumatoid pains. They are habitually seated upon the anterior surface of the legs and fore-arms, rarely upon the trunk, and consist of irregular protuberances, from the diameter of a small nut to that of an egg; their color is rosy at the periphery and of a sombre red, violaceous, or ecchy-motic tint in the centre, which does not completely disappear upon pressure. The ecchymotic tint pales, and becomes yellow as the tumors disappear, as they invariably do by resolution. These neoplasms develop in the early stage of syphilis, on the average about the fourth month.

The elements of diagnosis are based upon the history of the case and concomitant symptoms of syphilis. Finally, iodide of potassium may produce nut to egg-sized nodules, resembling those of nodose erythema. Pellizzari and other observers have reported such cases.

TREATMENT.—The disease usually ends in spontaneous recovery, and active constitutional treatment is rarely required beyond attention to the bowels and secretions, and the regulation of the diet. Villemin claims that iodide of potassium is a specific in this affection, although other observers have not confirmed the superior value of this drug. On account of the presumptive rheumatic relations of this form of erythema, salicin and the salicylates have been recommended. They may have a possible beneficial influence upon the articular pains, but exert no curative action upon the cutaneous lesions. Rest, preferably in the recumbent posture, should always be enjoined; the tenderness and pain may also be relieved by fomentations of alcohol and hot water, lotions of lead and opium, or belladonna ointment.

URTICARIA.

Synonyms—*Nettle Rash, Febris Urticata, Hives.*

Urticaria may be defined as an acute exudative affection characterized by the development of irregular elevations of the skin with a reddish base and whitish centre, termed wheals, and accompanied by sensations of intense prickling and burning. The typical lesion of urticaria closely resembles that produced by the stinging nettle and is commonly known as nettle rash.

The wheals vary greatly in number, size, shape, and color. The eruption may be limited to three or four lesions or there may be several hundred, thickly studding the entire surface of the body as well as the mucous membranes of the mouth and throat. The wheals are slightly elevated, firm to the feel, and vary in size from that of a split-pea to that of a silver dollar, or they may appear as large efflorescent patches formed by the coalescence of a number of individual wheals. In shape they are usually roundish or oval, but they may appear as streaks, elongated ridges, crescents, or irregular shaped patches. They are pinkish white, or pale in color, and commonly surrounded by a reddish areola.

In all cases, the subjective symptoms are quite marked, consisting of burning, stinging, and pricking sensations and the most intolerable itching. The impulse to scratch is irresistible, but the wounding of the integument only serves to increase the size and number of the efflorescences.

Of all cutaneous disorders, the eruption of urticaria is the most sudden in its outbreak, the most fugitive and capricious in character, and the most transient in its duration. It ordinarily makes its appearance without prodromal symptoms, it comes out rapidly, remains for a variable length of time, usually of short duration, and vanishes with the same marvellous celerity with which it appeared, leaving absolutely no trace of its existence. The ephemeral nature of the eruption is only equalled by the caprice of its behavior; the lesions disappear from one portion of the surface and suddenly reappear upon another part, the eruption shifting its location with extraordinary rapidity. It has no seat of predilection, but is liable to invade any portion of the general integument. The hyperæmia induced by the pressure of the clothing frequently determines its development upon the trunk and limbs. It is more common during childhood, but may occur at any period of life.

An attack of urticaria ordinarily lasts but a few hours, but there may be successive developments of new lesions which may prolong its duration several days. Exceptionally the disease may be kept up by constant relapses at regular or irregular intervals for months or years, constituting chronic urticaria. There are certain peculiarities in the anatomical form of the wheals and deviations from the typical course of the disease which constitute well-marked varieties of urticaria.

Urticaria papulosa.—This form of urticaria is almost exclusively confined to childhood. The wheals appear in the form of small acuminated papules. The apices of the papules are torn by scratching and surmounted by minute blood crusts as seen in other pruriginous conditions of the skin. After the disease has existed for a while, the clinical appearances consist of small papular wheals which come and go, interspersed with small hard reddish papules formed by a deposit of lymph, that are much more persistent, and which has led to the designation of this variety as lichen urticatus. The subjects of this variety of the affection are for the most part poorly nourished children with dry, anemic, unhealthy skins.

Urticaria hemorrhagica.—Sometimes there is an exudation of red blood-corpuscles in connection with the serous effusion constituting the variety known as purpura urticans.

Urticaria bullosa.—This term has been applied to a variety of urticaria in which the wheals are surmounted by vesicles or bullæ caused by a quite copious and at the same time superficial effusion of serum. The bullous element may be so pronounced as to suggest pemphigus.

Urticaria nodosa seu tuberosa.—This is a rare variety, commonly designated as giant urticaria. It is characterized by the production of nodules of a reddish color, varying in size from that of a small marble to that of an egg, situated in the skin and subcutaneous tissues, forming considerable elevations above the surface. They develop suddenly and usually disappear within a few hours, often leaving small ecchymotic spots.

Urticaria febrilis.—This term is applied to an attack of acute urticaria ushered in by severe febrile symptoms, with more or less marked constitutional disturbance, furred tongue, inappetence, nausea, pain in the limbs, etc., and is of comparative rare occurrence. These prodromal symptoms, after having persisted for two or three days, are terminated by the sudden outbreak of an eruption of wheals over the entire surface of the body. The eruption may occur in the form

PLATE XLIII.

FIG. I.—Urticaria—Urticaria factitia.
FIG. II.—Urticaria pigmentosa.

FIG. I.—AFTER MONTMEJA.
FIG. II.—AUTHOR'S COLLECTION.

of a diffuse red rash with much œdematous swelling of the skin, especially of the face and hands, or in the form of pea-sized efflorescences which upon the trunk and limbs may run together, forming palm-sized patches. It is attended with intense burning and itching sensations. The eruptions disappear within a few hours or may last for several days with intervals of remission and exacerbation.

CHRONIC URTICARIA, *Urticaria perstans.*—Although the distinguishing feature of urticaria is the evanescence of its lesions, yet in a certain class of cases the disease assumes a chronic form. The character of chronicity is not due to the persistence of individual wheals, but to the successive development of new crops of lesions which may continue to recur for weeks or months. The exacerbations most frequently come on at night, and, since the subjective sensations are less intense, there may be no scratch marks, excoriations, or anything discoverable, when the patient presents himself for examination, to indicate the existence of a pathological process.

ETIOLOGY.—Urticaria is remarkable for the great variety of conditions under which it develops, and the multiplicity and diversity of its causes; it may be provoked by external irritants, or the exciting cause may be found in some disorder of the general system.

The most familiar illustration of urticaria resulting from the contact of an irritant is seen in the sting of the common nettle. Among the external causes of urticaria may be mentioned the sting of certain insects, mosquitoes, bed-bugs, fleas, the acarus, the sting of certain marine animals, as the jelly fish, the star fish, etc.; the application of various chemical agents, arnica, carbolic acid, sulphur, thapsia, turpentine, etc.; extremes of temperature are also a common cause. I have observed a number of patients in whom the contact of cold water would produce an eruption of wheals; the same effect may be induced by excessive warmth. Traumatism, the puncture of a hydatid cyst, leech bites, etc., may be classed among the exciting causes. In Fig. 1, Plate XLIII., is represented a wheal upon the right chest resulting from the contact of a copper coin.

A large class of urticarias are symptomatic of internal derangements, especially gastric and intestinal disorder. Urticaria *ab ingestis* may follow the ingestion of certain articles of food, as shell fish, oysters, crabs and lobsters, fruits, raspberries, strawberries, nuts, raisins, pork, sausage, oatmeal, cheese, etc.

A vast number of drugs are capable of causing an eruption of wheals, as antipyrin, copaiba, cubebs, belladonna, the bromides, the iodides, opium, quinine, chloral, salicylic acid, etc. Urticaria may result from uterine disorders, from malaria, septicæmia, etc.; it may also develop as a concomitant in the course of many acute and chronic diseases. Finally, an attack of urticaria may result from mental emotion, as excessive joy, fright, grief, etc.

From a glance at the numerous and diverse causes of urticaria, it is evident that all of these agencies are ordinarily inoffensive to the majority of individuals. They must be regarded in the light of accidental exciting causes which would exert no pathogenetic influence whatever, were it not for a peculiar susceptibility of the skin of the individual to this form of eruptive disorder. The predisposition to urticaria resides in a peculiarity of the nervous organization, characterized by an abnormal sensitiveness of the vaso-motor system to irritant influences. The production of wheals from external irritation is a physiological property of the tissues, the normal mode of reaction of the skin against external irritation. The sting of a nettle, or a smart blow from the lash of a whip will be followed by a wheal in any individual. The condition of the skin is pathological when slight causes of irritation, not sufficient to produce this phenomenon in ordinary individuals, determines the production of wheals.

In many urticarial patients, the predisposition to the production of wheals is so constant and pronounced that merely scratching the skin or moderate pressure with a blunt instrument suffices to bring out wheals corresponding exactly to the tract of irritation; by tracing the outline of letters or figures, the characters stand out in bold relief. Both the patients figured in Plate XLIII. exhibit illustrations of urticaria factitiosa.

The pathological condition present in wheals consists in a circumscribed effusion of serum into the upper layers of the corium. The whitish aspect of the central part of the wheal, compared with its hyperæmic periphery, is due to the increased pressure of the exudation at that point driving the blood out of the capillaries from the centre to the circumference. In the pathogenesis of the wheal, it is not possible to state the precise rôle played by each constituent element of the skin, whether it is due to a spasm of the muscular fibres of the skin, to a vaso-motor contraction followed by paresis of the capillaries, or, as Unna asserts, to a spasm in the large veins of the skin, followed by a stasis in the lymphatic circulation of the skin.

The most probable explanation is that the urticarial phenomena are due to a paralysis of the vaso-motor nerves of a reflex character, the point of departure of which may be direct irritation of the sensory nerves of the skin, or of the nerves of the gastro-intestinal mucous membrane, or of other internal organs. Vaso-motor innervation may also be disturbed by emotional causes through the direct agency of the sympathetic. As a result, there is a dilatation of the cutaneous vessels, their walls become more porous and the serum or blood plasma is exuded more rapidly than can be carried away by the lymphatics, forming the raised œdematous wheals. After a variable time, when the equilibrium between the lateral blood pressure and the action of the lymphatics is re-established, this exudation is absorbed.

DIAGNOSIS.—The presence of wheals is pathognomonic of urticaria, and when they are typically developed, there is no possibility of a mistake in diagnosis. The sudden development of circumscribed solid swellings with pale centre and pink periphery, their short duration, and the intense subjective sensations of stinging, burning, and itching, which are out of all proportion to the structural change, constitute a complexus of symptoms that is characteristic of no other disease. In certain forms of urticaria which deviate from the ordinary type, the nature of the disease may not be so evident.

In lichen urticatus, the hard reddish papules may resemble the lesions of prurigo. They are, however, less persistent.

From erythema papulatum, urticaria may be distinguished by the fact that the latter develops more commonly upon the trunk, and is not localized upon backs of hands and wrists as is this form of erythema; the subjective sensations are intense in the one disease and but moderate or entirely absent in the other. When urticaria attacks the face, especially when attended with œdematous swelling of the loose cellular tissue of the eyelids and lips, it may resemble erysipelas. The skin is, however, less red and shining, and the signs of local inflammation are much less pronounced.

TREATMENT.—The multiplicity of the remedies and methods of treatment recommended for chronic urticaria attest the exceeding difficulty of its cure. It is, of course, of the first importance to determine the nature of the exciting cause, whether it be the introduction as food or medicine of some cause exterior to the organism, or whether it resides in an abnormal condition of some internal organ. In the class of urticarias associated with gout, rheumatism, malaria, etc., the remedies appropriate to these conditions will be found of the greatest service. If the source of irritation be found in some stomach, renal, or genital abnormality, this should be corrected. In cases of atonic dyspepsia, where flatulency, torpidity of the liver, constipation, and other symptoms of gastro-intestinal derangement are present, the continued use of the following tonic aperient mixture is of service:

℞ Magnesiæ sulph.,	. . . . . .	℥ i.
Ferri sulph.,	. . . .	℈ i.
Acidi sulphurici dil.,	. . . .	℈ ij.
Syr. pruni virg.,	. . . . . .	℥ i.
Aquæ, .	. . . .	ad ℥ iv.

M. S. One teaspoonful largely diluted after each meal.

Or the following:

℞ Magnesiæ sulph., ... ℥ ss.
Bismuthi carb., ... ℈ ij.
Tinct. rhei, ... ℥ i.
Syr. zingiberis, ... ℥ i.
Aquæ, ... ad ℥ iv.
M. S. One to two teaspoonfuls after each meal.

In urticarias provoked by external irritants, as well as in many urticarias *ab ingestis*, the exciting cause may be oftentimes directly traced, and subsequent attacks may be avoided. For the relief of an acute attack of urticaria resulting from indigestible articles of food, the expulsion of the offending substance by a brisk emetic, as mustard, ipecacuanha, sulphate of zinc, or apomorphia is often followed by speedy relief. If sufficient time has elapsed for the offending substance to pass into the intestinal canal, it should be evacuated by an active saline purgative, or by a full dose of castor oil, and the use of mild aperients may be continued for some days with advantage. The diet should be carefully regulated, all stimulating articles of food being interdicted. For the relief of the local symptoms, the surfaces, the seat of the eruption, may be sponged with alcohol or vinegar and water, weak solutions of carbolic acid, or the parts may be dredged with any inert dusting powder.

In a large proportion of cases of chronic urticaria, the causes escape recognition, and the treatment is therefore largely empirical. Among the numerous remedies recommended may be mentioned: sulphurous acid in drachm doses after each meal; sulphuric ether in doses of twenty to forty drops, well diluted; arsenic, the mineral acids, chloroform, belladonna, copaiba, bromide of potassium, chloral, quinine, salicin, salicylate of sodium. Of the above, the most efficient, according to my experience, are sulphurous acid, atropia, bromide of potassium, chloral and salicylate of sodium. I have used ichthyol, so highly recommended by Unna, in a number of cases, but with disappointing results. I have cured a number of cases of chronic urticaria, when ordinary means failed, by injections of a solution of sulphite of sodium.

LOCAL TREATMENT.—Probably the most efficient local means at our command for the relief of chronic urticaria are Turkish baths. These should be taken every day or every other day until the irritability of the skin subsides. When this treatment is not practicable or convenient, daily baths of warm or hot water, medicated with either sulphide of potassium, two to four ounces; bicarbonate of sodium, half a pound, or chloride of sodium, two pounds, the above designated quantity for an ordinary bath of thirty gallons of water. After the bath, the skin should be dried with a soft towel, and profusely covered with a dusting powder of oxide of zinc and starch, with a little camphor. In some cases, the intolerable itching is more promptly relieved by acid baths. For this purpose, one ounce of nitric acid, or an ounce each of nitric and muriatic acids, may be added to the ordinary bath. Should an outbreak of wheals occur, the itching may be relieved by the following lotions:

℞ Acidi carbolici, ... ℈ ss.–i.
Glyceriti cocaini (5 per cent), ... ℈ iv.
Acidi hydrocyanici diluti, ... ℈ i.
Aq. sambuci, ... ad ℥ vi.
M.

℞ Menthol, ... ℈ ss.–i.
Alcoholis, ... q. s.
Aquæ, ... ℥ iv.

Or, if more convenient, an ointment of the following composition may be ordered:

℞ Acidi carbolici, ... ℈ ss.
Glyceriti cocaini (5 per cent), ... ℈ ij.
Glyceriti amyli, vel
Ung. petrolati, ... ℥ i.
M.

A very efficient anti-pruritic ointment is one in which chloral and camphor are combined, as:

℞ Chloral hydrat.,
   Pulv. camphoræ,
   Pulv. gum acaciæ, ...   aa ℨ i.
   Ung. simplicis, ...   ℥ l.
M.

The following ointment is recommended by Jamieson:

℞ β Naphthol, ...   ℨ i.
   Lanolini, ...   ℨ ij.
   Ung. simplicis, ...   ℥ i.

Glycerite of starch in combination with five per cent of carbolic acid is an efficient application. In many cases an exclusively milk diet, change of air and scene, a sea voyage, and all measures calculated to build up the general health, are to be recommended.

In the lichen urticatus of children, especially those of a scrofulous habit, the use of cod-liver oil and other nutritive tonics is of the utmost advantage.

URTICARIA PIGMENTOSA.

Synonym—Xanthelasmoidea.

This comparatively rare variety of urticaria, which has only been recently recognized, is characterized by a tendency to the development of wheals which are unusually persistent in duration, and upon subsiding leave more less permanent pale yellowish or brownish pigmentations. It always begins in early infancy, but its duration is indeterminate, as no satisfactory conclusions upon this point have been reached in the few cases of this anomalous disease hitherto recorded.

The typical features of urticaria pigmentosa were so admirably illustrated in a case which was for a long time under my observation that a transcript from my notes, taken at the time will convey an accurate clinical picture of the disease.

A. C., first came under my observation in 1876. His mother stated that he was the youngest of nine children, none of the others ever having had any skin disease. He was vaccinated when four or five months old, and soon afterward she noticed a few small reddish spots on his back and chest, soon the entire body was profusely covered. The spots varied in size from that of a pea to a ten-cent piece, they were distinctly elevated and papular or tubercular in character, they covered the face and entire body, but were most abundant on the back and over the flexures of the joints, a few could be seen on the palms of hands and soles of the feet; ordinarily they were of a pale yellowish color, but under excitement they changed to a reddish or bright scarlet hue. The elevations could be plainly felt by the finger passed over the surface; when violently rubbed or scratched they became more marked and the surface appeared as if nettle stung.

During the next two years there was an appreciable series of changes in the physical characters of the eruption. It was marked by an obvious increase in the number of pigmented spots and the appearance successively of small crops of tubercles or nodulated masses, which were irregularly distributed, most frequently observed on the back, between the shoulders, and around the neck. These nodular masses, which varied in size from that of a coffee-grain to that of an almond, were irregular in outline, as if formed by an aggregation of small nodules. They were firm to the touch; when newly formed, they were pinkish or bright red, but as they grew older they assumed a yellowish or brownish color. They would develop suddenly, always after an urticarial attack, and remain stationary for a variable time, and then undergo a process of involution; their average duration was from one to three or four weeks. The condition in 1878 was as follows: With the exception of a limited area of healthy skin at the root of the nose and over the malar prominences, the eruption covers the entire surface of the body ; the palms and soles are profusely studded. They may be traced up into the hair, but do not occupy the superior region of the scalp ; they are most abundant over the occipital region, where the head presses the pillow in lying. A number may be seen upon the eyelid ; upon the left upper lid is seen a patch of pigmented skin strikingly suggestive both in outline and color of a patch of xanthelasma. A few may be seen upon the penis and scrotum ; they are numerous in the perineal and anal regions, extending quite to the margin of the anus. The mucous membrane of the mouth and fauces is seen to be occupied by these spots, although the yellowish hue, characteristic of the surface eruption, is wanting.

The spots upon pressure lose their reddish tinge, but the yellowish stain remains unaltered. Upon the trunk there is a decided greenish cast in the pigmentation.

Most of the spots are elevated ; some of them imparting a soft, velvety feel, like the sensation communicated to the finger when passed over the surface of a mole. Over some of the patches there is a distinct hypertrophy of the skin which seems to be punched up and lying loose. This redundant skin ordinarily lies in minute wrinkles or folds which, during the urticarial orgasm, becomes distended, forming the characteristic wheals.

The slightest irritation of the skin would develop wheals. Upon drawing the point of a blunt instrument over any portion of the surface, the following phenomena were observed : First, a slight paleness, deepening almost immediately into a deep red, spread over a broad band of hyperæmic surface. In about ninety seconds, a white welt of œdematous tissue rose in the central portion of this band, and in from two to three minutes the wheal, corresponding to the tract of irritation, was completely developed. It remained more or less distinct from thirty to forty minutes, then commenced to subside. The letters U. P., traced upon the back immediately before the patient was photographed, are shown in Fig. 11, Plate XLIII.

The wheals were also readily produced by mental emotions, as fright, anger, or through the excitement of stripping the body for examination. Occasionally, vesicular lesions, and at one time a large bulla, were observed upon the surface of the prominences.

The child's health was not materially affected by the skin disorder. He was well developed and well nourished ; he has never had any jaundice or symptoms of liver derangement.

Little is definitely known of the pathology of this affection, in which the urticarial element is the salient and distinctive feature. The hypertrophy and pigmentation of the skin are no doubt due to the frequently recurring active hyperæmia with exudation to which it had been subjected for so long a time.

TREATMENT.—The treatment of this affection has been largely empirical and of the same general character as that already described in connection with chronic urticaria. Disorders of the internal organs should be corrected, and improprieties of diet and other exciting causes of the urticarial attacks should be carefully avoided. For the relief of the subjective symptoms, antipruritics and the measures already referred to in connection with the local treatment of urticaria may be employed.

ECZEMA.

Synonyms—Salt Rheum. Moist Tetter.

Eczema, in the frequency of its occurrence, the variety of its eruptive elements, and the polymorphic aspects it assumes in its development and decline, is by far the most interesting and the most important of all the dermatoses. Under its protean forms are embraced fully one-third of all cases of skin disease, it attacks all classes and all ages and entails a vast amount of annoyance and suffering, but the darkness of the picture is relieved by the brilliant results it yields to modern treatment.

Eczema may be defined as an inflammatory affection of the skin characterized by, the

PLATE XLIV.

FIG. I.—Eczema capitis.
FIG. II.—Eczema faciei.

FIG. I.—SYDENHAM COLLECTION.
FIG. II.—AFTER NEUMANN.

production of various eruptive elements—erythema, papules, vesicles, pustules, attended with exudation, desquamation, and pruritus. As secondary products of the inflammatory process there result crusts and scales, more or less infiltration or thickening of the skin, with the formation of fissures or cracks.

In its typical course, the eruption usually passes through three stages, the acute, the sub-acute, and the chronic.

The beginning or acute stage is characterized by active hyperæmia with swelling, most marked in regions where the skin is loose, and the production of aggregated papules, vesicles, or pustules which soon give place to excoriated weeping surfaces. This stage is usually of short duration.

The second or subacute stage represents a less active inflammatory state; the surface is reddened and raw, discharging a serous gummy-like fluid which dries into thin crusts, which may be light colored or yellowish, or dark brown when the skin is torn by scratching and the exudation is mingled with blood.

The third or chronic stage succeeds when the exudation ceases, and the eruption presents the form of dry, reddened patches of skin with desquamation of the horny layer and induration. The eruption may persist in this condition almost indefinitely.

Not every eczema passes through this typical series of changes. An acute eczema may pass into the dry, scaly form without passing through the intermediary moist stage; a chronic eczema may become exacerbated and relapse into the primary acute form, or the same patient may exhibit the typical phases of the three stages in different patches of his eruption. The character of the inflammatory process, rather than the chronological element, forms the basis of the division of the different stages.

According to the anatomical characters of the primary lesions, the following six varieties of eczema are recognized: Eczema erythematosum, E. papulosum, E. vesiculosum, E. pustulosum, E. ichorosum, E. squamosum. The first two forms are characterized by hyperæmia with but slight exudation; the third, fourth, and fifth, by exudation and crusting, while desquamation constitutes the distinctive feature of the sixth form. These terms are used simply to express the predominating form of the eruptive element. The eruption may exhibit all these characters in the different stages of its development, or they may all be present at the same time.

Eczema erythematosum is characterized by an erythematous condition of the skin, the redness being diffuse or punctiform, attended with more or less interstitial exudation and swelling, which may be limited to certain regions or may occupy the entire surface of the body. On account of the exudation, there is more or less disruption of the cuticle which desquamates in fine flakes or scales. The eruption may persist in this condition or pass into other forms.

Eczema papulosum.—The essential features of this form consist in small pointed, pin-head-sized papules, usually seated upon a reddened infiltrated base, which may be grouped in patches of variable extent or irregularly scattered over the entire surface. Papular eczema is characterized by the most intolerable itching, and the summits of the papules are frequently torn by scratching and covered with a small crust. The most common location of this form of eczema is upon the inner aspect of the thighs.

Eczema vesiculosum.—This was formerly regarded as the typical expression of eczema, but it is less common than other varieties. The eruption consists of minute pin-point vesicles, closely aggregated upon a reddened surface. A number of vesicles may unite, forming larger vesicles or bullæ, particularly in regions where the epidermis is thick and resistant. The vesicles may dry and disappear with desquamation, their epidermic covering may be broken by rubbing or scratching, or they may spontaneously rupture, leaving excoriated weeping surfaces. Their favorite location is upon the face, hands, and fingers, but they may be generally distributed.

Eczema pustulosum.—This may represent a further development of the preceding variety, in which the vesicles are larger and their contents transformed into a purulent fluid or the pustules may develop *d'emblée* without a preceding vesicular stage. The pustular form, which is also de-

PLATE XLV.

Fig. I.—Eczema squamosum.
Fig. II.—Eczema papulosum, vesiculosum et impetiginosum.

AFTER HEBRA.

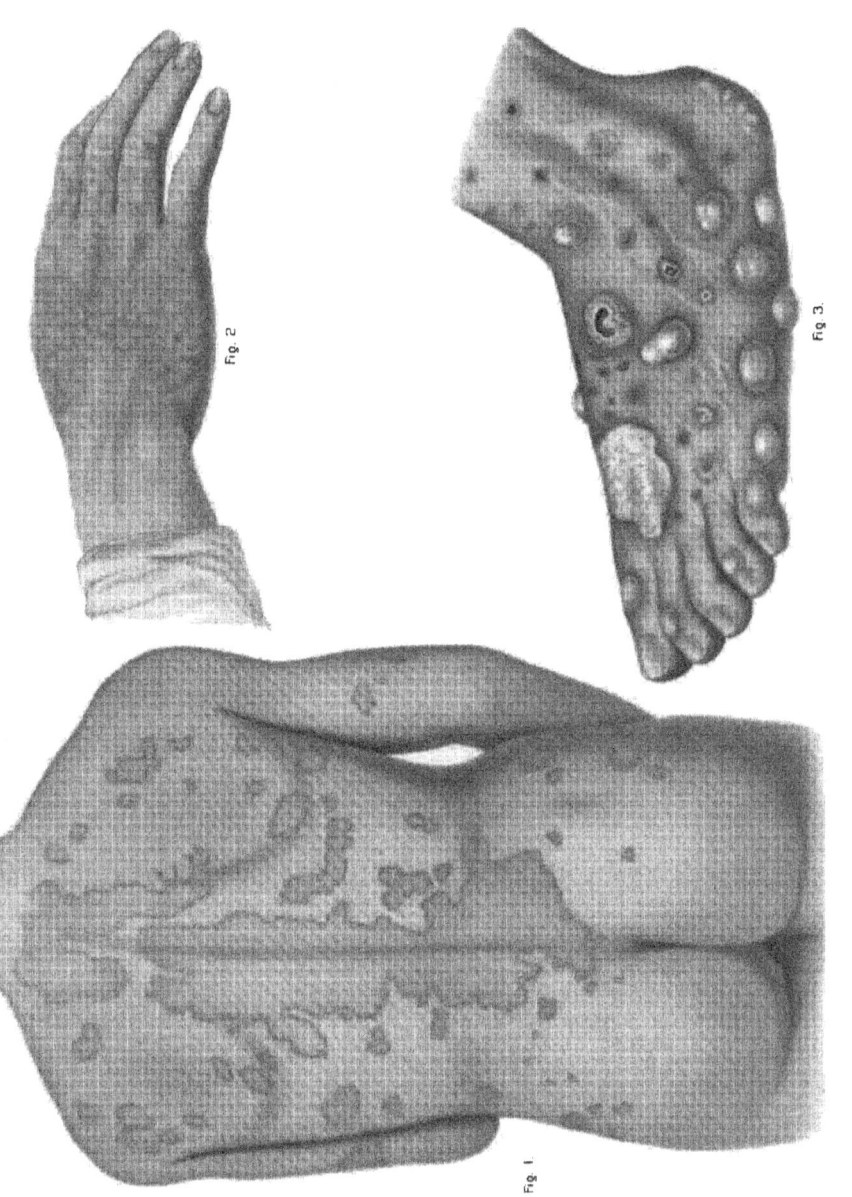

Fig. 1

Fig. 2

Fig. 3

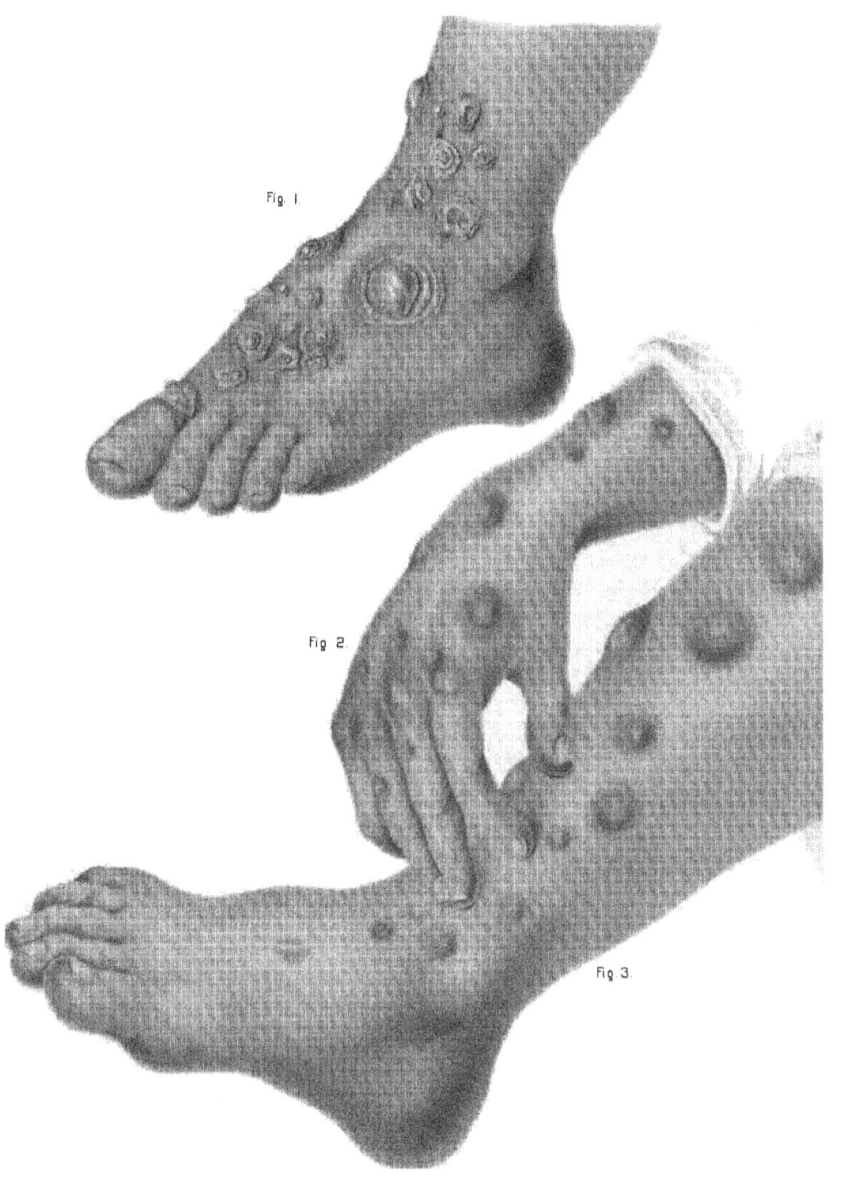

Fig. 1.

Fig. 2.

Fig. 3.

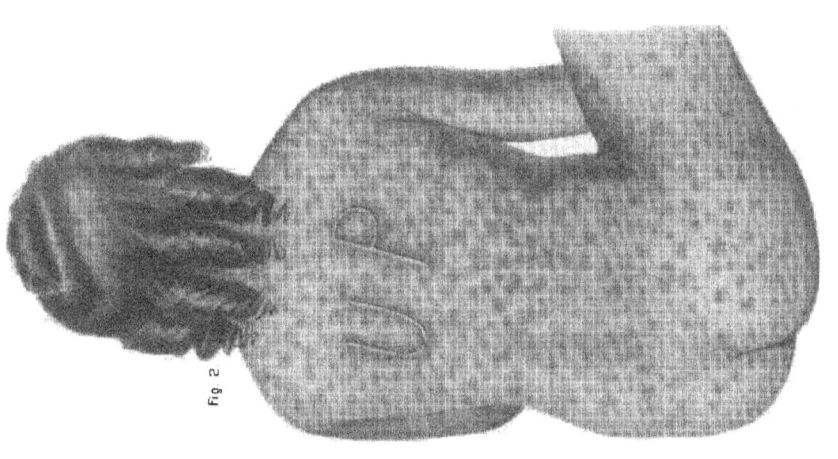
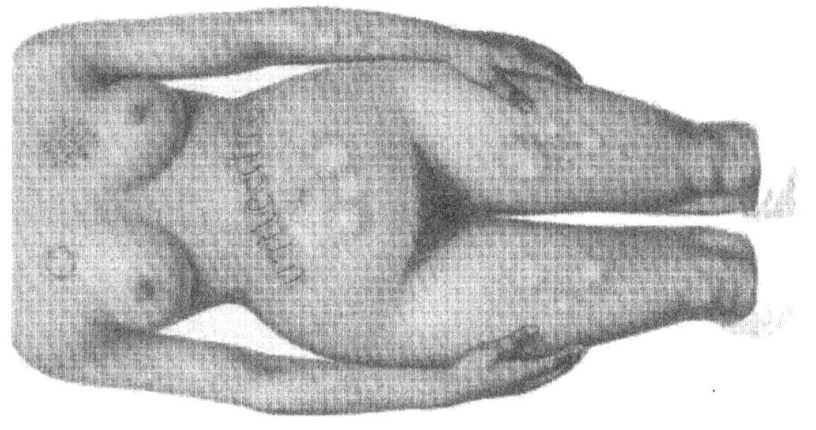

Fig 2

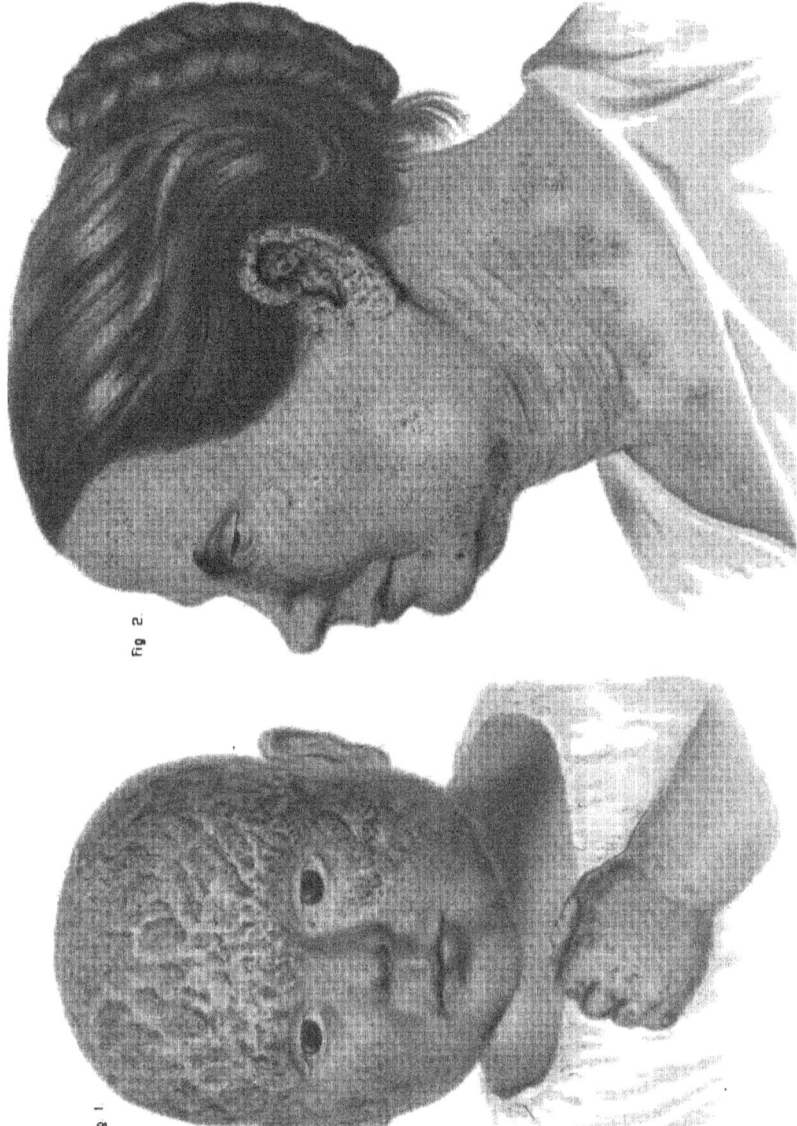

Fig 1.

Fig 2.

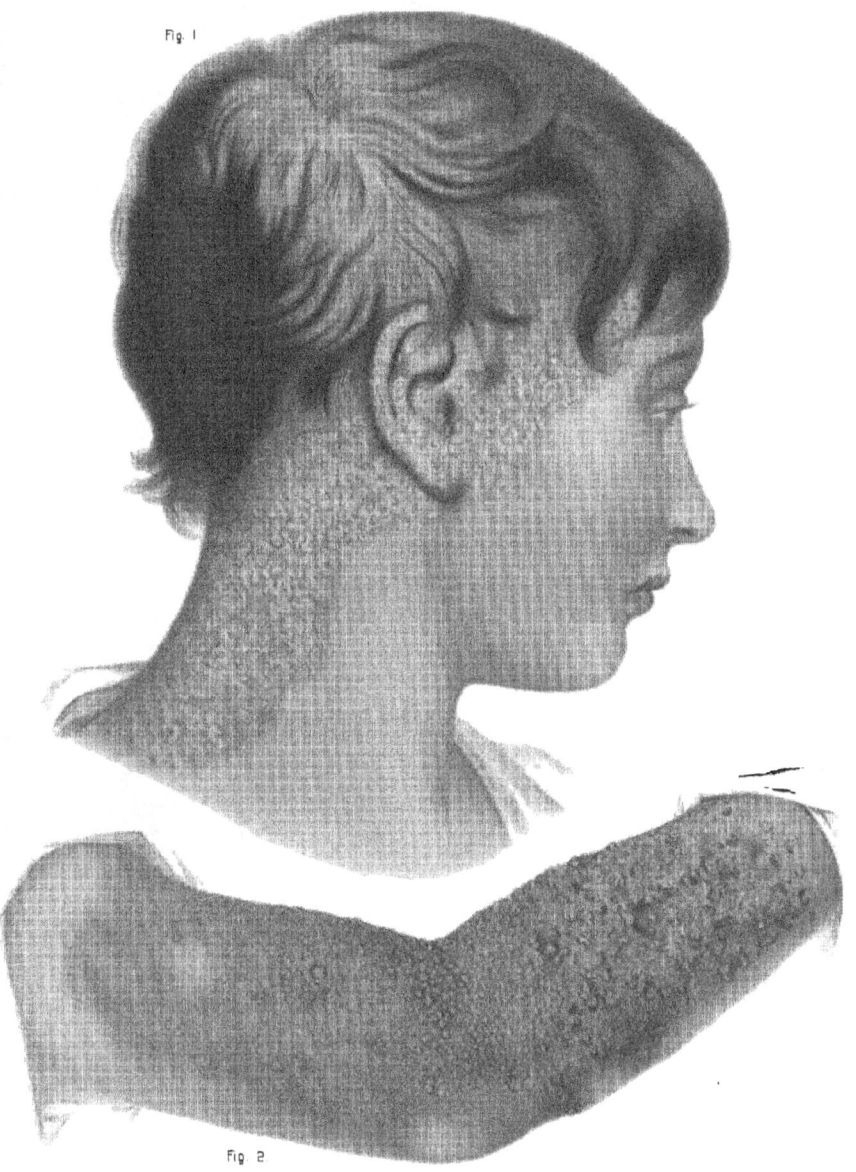

Fig. 1

Fig. 2

ATLAS

OF

VENEREAL AND SKIN

DISEASES

COMPRISING ORIGINAL ILLUSTRATIONS AND SELECTIONS FROM THE PLATES OF

PROF. M. KAPOSI, OF VIENNA; DR. J. HUTCHINSON, OF LONDON; PROF. I. NEUMANN, OF VIENNA;
PROFS. A. FOURNIER AND A. HARDY; AND DRS. RICORD, CULLERRIER, BESNIER, AND VIDAL, OF PARIS;
PROF. LELOIR, OF LILLE; DR. P. A. MORROW, OF NEW YORK; DR. E. L. KEYES, OF NEW YORK;
DR. FESSENDEN N. OTIS, OF NEW YORK; DR. J. NEVINS HYDE, OF CHICAGO;
DR. HENRY G. PIFFARD, OF NEW YORK, AND OTHERS.

WITH ORIGINAL TEXT BY

PRINCE A. MORROW, A.M., M.D.,

CLINICAL PROFESSOR OF VENEREAL DISEASES, FORMERLY CLINICAL LECTURER ON DERMATOLOGY, IN THE UNIVERSITY OF THE CITY OF NEW YORK ;
SURGEON TO CHARITY HOSPITAL, ETC.

NEW YORK

WILLIAM WOOD & COMPANY

1888

PROSPECTUS.

ATLAS

OF

VENEREAL AND SKIN

DISEASES

It is with special satisfaction that the publishers announce that this large and important work, which they have had in contemplation since 1883, is now ready for publication. It has long been recognized by them, from wide observation and acquaintance with similar works published in this country and abroad, that it is impossible for any one author to furnish, from his own collection of cases and illustrations, the most typical and at the same time the best and most lifelike pictures of the many peculiar forms of these diseases. Appreciating the defects and disadvantages arising from this cause, it was determined from the outset to enlist the co-operation, in the making of this ATLAS, of the leading dermatologists and syphilographers of the world. Prominent among them are Profs. M. Kaposi and I. Neumann, of Vienna. The atlas of the former, of venereal diseases, just completed, and that of the latter, of skin diseases, now being issued in parts, will be largely drawn upon in the preparation of this work, the sole right to reproduce them having been granted us by the authors.

Among other distinguished gentlemen who have engaged to contribute selections from their collections of original illustrations may now be mentioned Dr. J. Hutchinson, of London; Profs. A. Fournier and A. Hardy; and Drs. Ricord, Cullerrier, Besnier, and Vidal, of Paris; Dr. P. A. Morrow, of New York; Dr. Edward L. Keyes, of New York; Dr. Fessenden N. Otis, of New York; Dr. J. Nevins Hyde, of Chicago; Dr. Henry G. Piffard, of New York.

Other names will be added to this list as the work progresses.

The Editor of the work is Dr. Prince A. Morrow, of New York, who, in addition to plates contributed from his own remarkable collection, will write the treatise on skin and venereal diseases, which constitutes, besides the description of the plates, the text accompanying them.

In this treatise, it is aimed to include chiefly those features which are the most practical, omitting in great measure pathological and other considerations which would be more properly treated of in extended writings, rather than as the adjunct to an Atlas.

In regard to the character of the plates, it may be said, they are believed to be superior to anything of the kind heretofore produced—as accurate in drawing as photographs, and far more distinct, while the coloring faithfully represents nature.

The text is printed from new type, large, clear, and handsome, and the paper is heavy, with a highly finished surface.

Altogether, considering the reputation of the authors of the plates, the ability of the editor, the superb execution of the plates, the excellence of the presswork, the high quality of the paper of both text and plates, the large size of the page, etc., etc., this ATLAS OF VENEREAL AND SKIN DISEASES will be the most superb work in medical literature ever published in the English language.

The ATLAS OF VENEREAL AND SKIN DISEASES will be published in fifteen monthly parts, each containing five folio, chromo-lithographic plates, many of them containing numerous figures, all printed in flesh tints and colors, together with descriptive text for each plate, and from sixteen to twenty folio pages of a practical treatise upon venereal and skin diseases; the whole forming, when complete, one magnificent thick folio volume with seventy-five plates, containing several hundred figures, exquisitely printed in colors.

☞ The ATLAS OF VENEREAL AND SKIN DISEASES will be sold by subscription only, at the very moderate price of $2 per part.

WILLIAM WOOD & COMPANY, *Publishers,*

56 AND 58 LAFAYETTE PLACE, NEW YORK.

nominated impetiginous eczema, has for its most common seat the faces and hairy scalps of children, is characterized by the formation of greenish crusts, which often mat the hairs together and form a mask over the surface.

Eczema ichorosum.—This form of eczema represents a more advanced stage of one of the preceding varieties. It is characterized by moist, reddened surfaces, from which the epidermis has been displaced, discharging a more or less copious secretion of serum or pus, which dries into crusts or scabs, the coloration varying from a light yellow to an amber or dark brown. Its most common seat is the legs, back of ears, and the flexures of the body. This form of eczema has also been denominated eczema madidans, from the exceeding copiousness of the secretion, and also eczema rubrum, from the intensely red condition of the derma.

Eczema squamosum.—This may represent the terminal stage of any of the preceding varieties when the hyperæmia and exudation have given place to induration and thickening, its distinctive character being a constant exfoliation of the cuticle from a reddened, infiltrated surface. In rarer instances, this form may have existed from the first, the clinical features consisting only of a dry, erythematous, scaly condition of the surface, associated with more or less infiltration of the skin.

As a result of changes in the skin engendered by the eczematous process in certain localities, there may result still other modifications in the forms of the lesions.

Eczema sclerosum.—This term is applied to a form of eczema most frequently met with on the palms and soles, characterized by a thickening and condensation of the integument in circumscribed patches or over the entire surface.

Eczema rimosum seu fissum.—In this variety, fissures or cracks, superficial or penetrating, and exceedingly painful, are liable to occur, especially over the joints and the tips of the fingers, from brittleness of the infiltrated integument.

Eczema verrucosum.—This term is used to designate a condition in which there is a hypertrophy of the papillæ, giving rise to wart-like protuberances, separated by fissures, with a special tendency to localization about the ankles.

ETIOLOGY.—The French school of dermatology have always held to the view of the constitutional origin and nature of eczema, regarding the eruption as merely the outward manifestation of the dartrous diathesis. The modern German, or Hebraic school, has given special prominence to the local pathology of eczema, and has been inclined to ignore the lines which may unite the cutaneous eruption with disorders of the general system.

In endeavoring to trace the etiology of eczema, it is evident that no single diathetic condition can be recognized as the efficient cause; on the other hand, it is equally evident that the various external irritants which have been assigned as exciting causes are quite incapable of determining an eczematous eruption in a perfectly healthy individual.

Eczema originates under the combined influence of causes exterior to the organism and a predisposition on the part of the individual to this form of eruptive disorder This predisposition may be of a constitutional character, depending upon diathetic conditions or disorders of internal organs, or it may reside in structural peculiarities of the skin which dispose it to inflammatory reaction from irritation either of a direct or reflex nature.

The precise measure of pathogenetic influence exerted by these different factors cannot be definitely determined. In some cases, evidences of constitutional disorder are markedly apparent; in others, the influence of external agencies predominates.

Prominent among the constitutional causes of eczema may be mentioned disorders of the digestive apparatus manifest in impaired digestion, imperfect assimilation, and deficient excretion. Owing to imperfect oxidation on the part of the liver, the retrograde metamorphosis of waste products is not normally completed, leading to their accumulation and circulation in the blood, in the form of uric and oxalic acids, instead of their prompt elimination by the kidneys. Eczema is so frequently met with in gouty and rheumatic persons that its close connection with, and dependence upon, the uric acid diathesis cannot be questioned. Another condition of gastro-intestinal derangement, which bears a certain causal relation to eczema, is constipation. Torpidity of the bowels is an almost constant accompaniment of certain eczemas, and its correction is an indispensable requisite for their successful treatment.

The frequent occurrence of eczema in strumous subjects, especially scrofulous children, suggests the probable influence of this diathesis as a predisposing factor.

A neuropathic predisposition to eczema may also be inferred from the greater susceptibility of individuals suffering from nervous debility and the protean forms of neurasthenia.

Climatic conditions, age, sex, heredity, etc., exert a more or less marked modifying influence upon the tendency to eczema. The influence of seasonal conditions is shown in the greater frequency of eczema in winter than in summer. The predisposing influence of age is evidenced by the fact that one-fourth of all eczemas occur in children under five years of age. This is probably due to the greater delicacy and sensitiveness of the skin, its immaturity and feebler capacity of resistance against external irritants, and the greater readiness with which inflammatory fluxion is determined to the cutaneous surface by reflex causes, as gastro-intestinal disorder, the irritation of teething, vaccination, etc. Sex plays a rôle of minor importance, as a predisponent, since eczema occurs with almost equal frequency in both sexes. The slightly greater predominance among males is explained by their relatively more frequent exposure to irritant influences. On the other hand, the discharge of certain functions peculiar to women, as menstruation and pregnancy, the debility induced by lactation, the changes which take place at the menopause, favor the development of eczema.

Heredity exerts a restricted but nevertheless positive influence as a predisposing factor. In the majority of cases of eczema, inquiry into the family history fails to trace evidences of hereditary influence, but the cases in which the offspring of eczematous parents are also eczematous are too numerous to be regarded as mere coincidences.

The *local* causes of eczema are numerous and of the most varied character. Among them may be mentioned the excessive use of soap and water, the prolonged application of poultices or fomentations, the friction of coarse woollen underclothing, exposure to extremes of heat and cold, the use of certain chemical agents in the form of liniments, ointments, blisters, etc.

Eczema may arise either from the direct contact or internal administration of various drugs, as arnica, arsenic, carbolic and salicylic acid, chrysarobin, iodoform, mercury, quinine, sulphur, thapsia, turpentine, etc.; from the irritation of poisonous dyes employed in the coloring of articles of clothing. An eczematous eruption frequently follows parasitic diseases, as scabies, from the combined influence of the wounds of the insect, the scratching induced by the itching, and the irritating action of the stimulating treatment employed.

A class of eczemas, termed "eczemas of occupation," result from exposure to various acid and irritating substances; as examples may be mentioned, "washerwoman's itch," caused by prolonged contact with soap and water; "grocer's" and "baker's itch," induced by irritation of particles of flour, meal, sugar, etc.; "bricklayer's itch," from contact with particles of lime, etc.

As a necessary condition of the irritant action of all these external agencies, there must be a peculiar susceptibility of the skin to eczematous inflammation, hence it may be concluded that the most essential predisposition to eczema resides in the skin itself. This predisposition may be physiological, and may be inherent in the skin from a native debility of the cutaneous structures which renders them less resistant to irritant influences, or it may be constituted by an abnormal irritability of the sensory nerves, which disposes them to take offence at the slightest provocation. This predisposition may also be pathologically engendered by the various constitutional states with which eczema has a more or less intimate causal connection, as struma, gout, rheumatism, lithæmia, etc. These systemic conditions are all attended with general debility, in which the dermal structures participate, and they doubtless develop a morbid aptitude of the skin to eczematous inflammation by impairing the nutrition of this organ, and inducing a condition of weakness and irritability.

PATHOLOGY.—Whatever may be the cause of eczema, the pathological process consists essentially in an inflammation of the superficial layers of the skin, especially involving the papillary body; the resulting phenomena, heat, redness, and swelling, with a tendency to exudation at the surface and subsequent desquamation, are common to all simple inflammations of the skin. The redness is due to the active hyperæmia and accumulation of red globules; the continuous exudation is accounted for by the persistence of the actively congested state of the vessels, while the desquamation results from perverted or arrested nutrition of the epidermis from the vascular disturbance beneath.

The anatomical changes which take place in the different forms of eczema have been studied by numerous observers. According to Besiadecki, the papule is formed by a circumscribed infiltration of a group of papillæ, which are enlarged in breadth and length; the connective-tissue corpuscles are increased in size and number. There are also numerous spindle-shaped cells extending from the papillæ between the deepest cells of the rete mucosum, which they crowd apart. As the exudation increases from the capillary network, the serum penetrates the papillæ and elevates the epidermis, forming a vesicle.

In chronic eczema, further changes take place which result in a more marked enlargement of the papillæ and a diffuse cell infiltration, and may even extend to the subcutaneous cellular tissue. The papillæ may be so increased in size as to be visible to the naked eye. Pigment deposits may also occur in the deeper layers of the rete and the corium, especially about the dilated vessels. The lymphatics may also be enlarged, with hardening of the connective tissue and degenerative changes in the sebaceous glands and hair follicles.

The most important pathological process which occurs in eczema is the exudation, and recent researches would seem to indicate that the cells of the rete Malpighii participate more actively than was formerly supposed in its production. The exudation of eczema, it is claimed, is peculiar in its mode of origin and the morbid properties with which it is endowed. Instead of representing simply a serous exudation poured out from the vessels in consequence of over-distention, the fluid exudation of eczema may be regarded as a positive secretion from the epidermic cells, especially those of the inter-papillary spaces, which have undergone a sort of vesicular transformation. This dropsical degeneration of the cells takes place as follows: The nuclei of the cells disappear, and their protoplasm becomes transformed into a fluid substance; a number of the cells coalesce and become inclosed in a sort of reticular network formed by the remnants of the obliterated cell-walls. This secretion is constantly increased by the imbibition of serum from the vascular exudation beneath.

In the present state of our knowledge, it is impossible to state whether the changes in the epidermic cells are primary or secondary, whether they precede or follow the vascular disturbances in the papillary vessels.

Since the discovery of sensory nerves supplied to the mucous layer of the epidermis, the theory has been advanced that the pathological process in eczema is initiated by irritation of the nerves in the cells of the epidermal structures, in which irritation the adjacent vascular tissue sympathizes and responds by the phenomena of inflammation. Whatever may be the part played by the pheripheral nerves in initiating the inflammatory process of eczema, it is clearly within the sphere of the nervous system that we must look for an explanation of its morbid phenomena. The trophic changes in the integument constitute the distinctive and most essential feature of eczema, and the direct influence of the nerves in controlling and regulating nutritive processes in the skin is well established.

Whether this influence is exerted through the medium of the nerves which control the vascular supply, or through certain nerves with specialized functions, denominated trophic nerves, has not been determined. Presumptive proof of the neurotic origin and relations of eczema may also be found in the marked disorders of sensations with which it is always attended, as well as in the frequent limitation of the eruption to certain definite nerve tracts.

DIAGNOSIS.—On account of the number and variety of its lesions, and the metamorphic phases which the eruption assumes in its different stages, eczema may at some period of its course bear a most deceptive resemblance to a number of cutaneous affections. The diagnosis of a typical case of eczema is, however, rarely attended with difficulty, if its more characteristic symptoms are borne in mind. The elementary lesions possess, perhaps, the least diagnostic value, since they are common to many other dermatoses, but eczema exhibits certain features which are characteristic and pathognomonic. Prominent among these is the existence of a moist weeping surface attended with a peculiar discharge, which dries into thin, yellowish crusts. This feature is wanting in the erythematous and papular varieties, and but slightly marked in the squamous form, although in the latter a history of exudation at some previous stage may almost always be traced. The existence of congested or reddened patches gradually shading off into the healthy skin, often surrounded by outlying reddish points or papules, the more or less copious catarrhal exudation, the succeeding desquamation, the infiltration often discernible to the sight as well as the touch, make up a clinical picture presented by no other disease. Added to this, the intense itching, which is an invariable concomitant, and which serves to distinguish eczema from other eruptions presenting somewhat similar clinical aspects.

Locality is another important element of diagnosis; while eczema may occur upon any portion of the body, it has a predilection for the flexor surfaces and regions where the skin is soft and delicate, the junction of the skin and mucous membranes, around the natural orifices, etc. Finally, the very multiplicity of the eruptive forms which eczema may assume constitutes an important diagnostic sign, since polymorphism is exhibited only by a limited number of eruptions.

The diseases for which eczema is likely to be mistaken are numerous, and the differential diagnosis of many of them will be considered in connection with eczema of particular localities.

Erythema.—It is only the erythematous and papular forms of eczema that are liable to be confounded with erythema; the differential points which serve to distinguish erythema have already been referred to. The negative evidence furnished by the absence of discharge and crusting and the moderate itching of erythema are alone sufficient to exclude eczema.

Erysipelas.—An erythematous or vesicular eczema occurring upon the region of the head and face may bear a deceptive resemblance to erysipelas, especially when attended with much œdematous infiltration of the lax connective tissues about the eyelids and cheeks. Erysipelas is, however, distinguished by its origin from a single reddish spot as a centre of development, its creeping mode of extension, its uniformly diffused, never punctate redness which is always distinctly marginated, its tense, shining glazed surface, and the marked systemic disturbance, the pulse and temperature being both considerably elevated. Exudation and crusts are not present in erysipelas, except from the rupture of bullæ, and there is an absence of itching except in the terminal stage.

Herpes.—A typical eruption of herpes zoster cannot be mistaken for eczema; the vesicles of febrile herpes about the mouth and nose, when abortive or imperfectly developed, may resemble a vesicular eczema. The vesicles of herpes are flatter, and arranged in clusters or groups; they run a definite course, shrivel up in a few days, and, when ruptured, form scabs rather than crusts

Hydroa.—Hydroa is a comparatively common affection among newly arrived immigrants in this country, and may be confounded with eczema. The vesicles are larger, scattered over a larger extent of surface, and itching is not a pronounced symptom.

Impetigo bears a most deceptive resemblance to the pustular form of eczema. In impetigo, the pustules are more superficial and larger; they do not have a tendency to run together, forming patches as in eczema, but are more apt to be isolated; the crusts are thicker, and of a dark or greenish cast; the pruritus is less intense. In impetigo contagiosa, the spread of the eruption from one part to another often occurs from the transference of the pus by the finger-nails in scratching or otherwise.

Lichen Planus.—When the papules of lichen planus are discrete, they cannot be confounded with the papules of eczema, but when they are massed and closely aggregated, as frequently seen upon the arms, they present a most deceptive resemblance. Close examination will generally discover more recent isolated papules which present the angular outline, the shining flat surface with depressed centre, characteristic of lichen planus. The lesions of the latter are, moreover, chronic in their development, and, after undergoing involution, leave diffuse discolorations or stains.

Lupus.—The erythematous form of lupus has been mistaken for scaly eczema. The slower development of lupus, its limitation to the face and hands, its well-defined margins, the firm attachment of the scales by sebaceous plugs dipping down into the follicles, the existence of cicatrices, and the absence of itching suffice to differentiate it from eczema.

Pemphigus.—The foliaceous form of pemphigus may be confounded with squamous eczema. Pemphigus foliaceus usually commences on the chest and extends over the entire surface, leaving no interspace of healthy skin. The skin is red and tender, but not moist and exuding; the scales and crusts are larger, there is also an absence of itching and infiltration.

Pityriasis rubra is distinguished by a uniform intense redness, which gradually extends over the entire integument, by the abundant exfoliation of the epidermis in large, thin papery scales, and by the absence of exudation and thickening of the skin. The subjective sensations consist of superficial soreness or pain rather than pruritus.

Phthiriasis.—Lesions of the scalp from scratching, provoked by the irritation of lice, may resemble pustular eczema. The presence of pediculi, or their nits clinging to the hairs, will indicate the nature of the trouble. An intense itching, confined to the pubes or axillæ, should always lead to a careful examination for the crab-louse. The bites of the pediculus corporis, when irritated by scratching, may result in an excoriated condition of the surface closely resembling eczema. In phthiriasis corporis, the excoriations and scratch-marks are characteristic in their linear forms as well as their locality. They are usually found upon the backs of the shoulders, about the loins, and the lower limbs. An examination of the folds of the underclothing will usually reveal the cause as well as suggest the remedy for the skin lesions.

Prurigo and Pruritus.—Prurigo is a disease of such rare occurrence in this country that the points of its differentiation from eczema are of little practical import; its tendency to develop in early childhood, its primary localization upon the legs, its permanent nature and the involvement of the inguinal glands may be noted. In pruritus the subjective sensations are often paroxysmal and altogether disproportionate to the objective symptoms. The cutaneous lesions are not an essential part of the affection, but are always secondary and the result of scratching, and are usually found upon surfaces readily accessible to the nails.

Psoriasis.—A typical case of psoriasis cannot be confounded with eczema. When the lesions of psoriasis have run together forming patches, and deprived of their characteristic silvery white scales, the eruption may be mistaken for squamous eczema. The chief points of differentiation may be thus indicated: the surface of a psoriatic patch is always dry, the edges are distinctly defined and somewhat thickened or elevated, the scales are dryer, whiter and less adherent, the extensor surfaces are more commonly involved; itching is not a pronounced symptom. In squamous eczema there is commonly a history of moisture at a previous stage, the edges of an eczematous patch shade off gradually into the healthy skin, the scales of eczema are thin and closely attached, the flexor surfaces constitute the seats of predilection of the eruption.

Scabies.—Scabies is perhaps more often than any other cutaneous affection mistaken for eczema; both are polymorphous and present identical lesions, but in addition scabies is characterized by one lesion which is peculiar and always of pathognomonic value, namely, the well-known minute, black furrow in which the acarus lies imbedded; in both itching is a pronounced and prominent feature, but in scabies the itching is more intense at night and is relieved by scratching, furthermore the parasitic lesions are often masked by an artificially excited eczema.

In scabies there is usually a history of contagion, while the localities affected furnish valuable diagnostic indications. The lesions of scabies are most characteristically seen in the interdigital spaces, upon the anterior surface of the wrists, forearms and ankles, about the nipple, the axillæ, the abdomen, the penis, and the buttocks. They are rarely found upon the face and never upon the scalp

The discovery of the acarian furrow or cuniculus is the only sure means of establishing the nature of the disease.

Seborrhœa may be mistaken for eczema, especially when seated upon the face and scalp. In seborrhœa, there is neither infiltration of the skin nor exudation, only the secretion of fatty and epithelial matter which collects in the form of thick, greasy scales or crusts which may be rolled into balls. When the scales are removed, the surface is scarcely altered in hue, and the orifices of the sebaceous ducts are found patulous and prominent. In eczema, the crusts are dryer and more brittle, and when removed disclose a hyperæmic oozing surface.

Sycosis.—Eczema of the bearded portion of the face bears oftentimes a most deceptive resemblance to both parasitic and non-parasitic sycosis of the beard. In eczema the inflammation is more superficial, diffuse papules and red points appear between the pustules, and the eruption often spreads beyond the margins of the hairy parts, the hairs are not loosened and their extraction causes pain. In sycosis, the pustules are larger and more deeply situated, affecting the peri-follicular structures, the hairs are loosened and readily extracted, and the disease is confined to the hairy regions. In parasitic sycosis, there are often circumscribed indurations and large tubercular prominences which are quite disfiguring. Microscopic examination and the discovery of the tricophyton will resolve all doubt as to the nature of the disease.

Syphilis.—A number of syphilitic eruptions bear a certain resemblance to forms of eczema, but the differentiation is usually made without difficulty by the history of the patient, the presence of concomitant evidences of syphilis, the absence of itching, and the general character and course of the eruption. An exceedingly rare eruption has been described by various authors as eczema syphiliticum. It consists of minute vesicles developed upon a papular base, scattered over a limited area or collected into groups. The lesions remain small, and do not rupture, as in true eczema, but after four or eight weeks dry up, the papules assuming a coppery hue. The eruption is ordinarily limited to the face and scalp, but may extend to other parts of the body. The differential diagnosis between eczema and syphilis of the palms and soles and syphilitic ulcerations of the leg will be considered in connection with eczema of these localities.

Tinea.—Tinea circinata of the general surface of the body may be confounded with eczema, especially when the lesions have lost their distinctive ringed character from scratching and stimulating applications. Tinea is more acute in its course; the patches are more distinctly demarcated at their periphery, with a tendency to heal in the centre. A history of contagion may usually be traced in tinea, and the scales reveal the presence of its fungus.

Tinea circinata and tinea favosa of the scalp are both liable to be mistaken for eczema in this region, but the points of differential diagnosis will be more appropriately indicated in connection with eczema capitis.

PROGNOSIS.—When afflicted with a disease which causes so much annoyance and suffering, and occasions more or less disfigurement from its situation upon exposed parts, the patient is naturally solicitous for information as to its probable duration and curability. While eczema is essentially chronic in its nature, with a tendency to exacerbations and repeated recurrences, its prognostic significance, so far as ultimate results are concerned, is almost always favorable. Thanks to the new agencies and improved methods of treatment which modern advances in cutaneous therapeutics have placed at our disposal, it may always be relieved, and generally admits of permanent cure.

The prognosis of eczema is influenced largely by the character of its constitutional relations. When symptomatic of some internal disorder, as dyspepsia, derangement of the liver, kidneys, or uterus, its cure will be conditioned upon the correction of the underlying cause. When associated with a confirmed gouty or rheumatic state, while the eruption may disappear under the influence of appropriate treatment, yet it is liable to continual recurrences so long as the diathetic tendency persists. Especially in neurotic subjects is eczema impressed with the character of chronicity and obstinacy to treatment. In persons of advanced years, whose vitality is lowered, and whose nervous system is weakened beyond all possibility of restoration, senile pruritus often enters as a complicating element, and while the symptoms may be mitigated and the patient rendered more comfortable, there is little hope of a definite cure.

The relations of eczema to external causes of irritation also influence its prognosis. In eczemas of occupation, for example, there is no prospect of a cure so long as exposure to the local exciting cause continues. Eczemas depending upon varicose veins are intractable to treatment while the efficient cause continues in existence. The form as well as the locality of an eczema influences its prognosis. The erythematous and papular forms are usually more persistent than the other varieties. Eczemas of the head, face, and the hands, the anal and genital region are characterized by a peculiar obstinacy to treatment.

TREATMENT.

There is no specific for the cure of eczema and no method of treatment applicable to all cases and all stages of the disease. A knowledge of the cause of a disease is the first step toward the recognition of the therapeutical measures best adapted for its treatment. The study of the etiological factors concerned in the production of eczema shows that it results from the combined influence of external causes and individual predisposition, the latter depending upon functional disorders, diathetic conditions, or structural peculiarities of the skin. According to their etiological conception of the nature of the disease, preference is given to constitutional or local measures by different authorities. By those who regard eczema as the cutaneous expression of a systemic malady or due to a special dyscrasia, especial prominence is assigned to internal medication ; by those who believe in the essentially local nature of eczema the chief reliance is placed upon local treatment.

Leaving etiological considerations aside, clinical experience proves most conclusively that in the large proportion of cases, the best results of treatment are obtained by the judicious combination of constitutional and local measures. It is not possible to institute a strict comparison between the effects of the constitutional and local treatment of eczema, with a view to the determination of their relative value, since the one supplements and assists the other. There is no question, however, but that local treatment is far more efficacious in relieving the symptoms of most cases of acute eczema. Many cases get well under the influence of local treatment alone, without recourse to internal medication ; this is especially true of eczemas of occupation and those directly provoked by exposure to external irritants. Even in eczemas symptomatic of internal disorder brilliant curative results may be accomplished by local treatment. It is to be remembered that an eczema primarily of internal origin may persist long after the constitutional disturbance which caused it has ceased to exist, the cutaneous affection being perpetuated by a habit of the skin to eruptive disorder, or the local phenomena may be intensified and kept up almost indefinitely by the results of traumatism from friction, scratching, improper treatment, etc. On the other hand, certain forms of chronic eczema prove absolutely refractory to local therapy, they are deeply rooted in the system, and defy dislodgment until the constitutional vice is corrected.

CONSTITUTIONAL TREATMENT.—The first indication in the treatment of eczema is to determine the nature of the constitutional disturbance with which it may be associated. In certain cases, no doubt, such causal connection will elude our search ; the most careful and rigid investigation will fail to discover any derangement of the internal organs. The general health of the patient may appear perfectly good, his appetite and digestion unimpaired, with no recognizable abnormality in his assimilative and excretory functions. In the large proportion of cases, however, departures from the standard of perfect health are unmistakably present, impairment of the digestive functions, torpidity of the liver, constipation, lithæmia, or the existence of some special dyscrasia, as rheumatism, struma, or neurasthenia may be detected. While eczema cannot be considered a common or specific product of any of these internal disorders, yet their pathogenetic influence is well established. They may affect the skin by reflex irritation or by inducing a condition of general debility in which the skin participates.

The clinical features of eczema point to faulty innervation and defective nutrition as the most essential elements of the pathological process, and the rational indications are to regulate the functions of the body, and to employ such measures as are best adapted to give energy and strength to the constitution. The nutritive debility which in many cases lies at the root of the disease should be corrected by tonics and reconstituent remedies, by diet and suitable hygiene, and by all measures calculated to improve the tone of the general health. In cases in which a diathetic tendency is manifest, the obvious indications are to employ a treatment appropriate to the special dyscrasia.

For the successful management of eczema, the diet of the patient, both as regards the quantity and quality of the food, should be carefully regulated. The diet of an eczematous patient should be light and unstimulating, but nutritious and of good quality. Pastries, fried dishes, all articles of food which the patient finds difficult of digestion, the free use of condiments and alcoholic drinks of all kinds should be interdicted. The excessive use of nitrogenous articles of food should be prohibited as tending to augment the amount of urates circulating in the blood, and thus favoring the increase of the cutaneous excitement. The free use of milk, butter, and fatty articles of food should be encouraged.

In many cases of eczema, torpidity of the liver and constipation are almost constant conditions. The functional activity of the liver should be stimulated by cholagogues, as podophyllin, irisin, calomel, etc., and the bowels kept freely open. The use of laxative mineral waters, as Friedrichshall, Hunyadi Janos, the Carlsbad salts, etc., is often of efficient service. An admirable tonic aperient is the following mixture:

R Magnesiæ sulphatis, ...   ℥i.
   Ferri sulphatis, ...   ℨi.
   Acidi sulphurici diluti, ...   ℨiss.
   Syr. zingiberis, ...   ℥i.
   Aquæ, ...   q. s. ad ℥iv.
M. Sig. One teaspoonful largely diluted after each meal.

In many cases in which constipation is a constant element, the use of the ordinary mixture of rhubarb and soda yields excellent results:

R Pulv. rhei, ...   ℨi.-ij.
   Sodii bicarb., ...   ℨij.
   Aq. menthæ piperit., ...   ℥iij.
M. Sig. One to two teaspoonfuls after each meal.

Many eczemas owe their cause and continuance to a deficient excretion of excrementitious principles by the kidneys and consequent impurification of the blood; the kidneys should therefore be stimulated to the proper performance of their excretory functions by alkaline diuretics. For this purpose, there is no combination better than the following:

R Potassæ acetatis, ...   ℨv.
   Spts. ætheris nitrosi, ...   ℨiij.
   Aq. camphoræ, ...   ad ℥iv.
M. S. Two teaspoonfuls after each meal.

In many cases, the judicious use of depurative remedies and alkaline diuretics comprise all the general measures necessary in the treatment of eczema.

While there is no drug yet discovered which exercises anything of the nature of a specific curative action upon eczema, yet there are certain remedies which experience has proven of value in modifying its course and symptoms.

Arsenic has long been reputed to possess specific properties against eczema through its selective action upon the skin, but careful clinical experience has tended to singularly modify the classic conception of its therapeutic worth. Arsenic is unquestionably of benefit in certain chronic forms of eczema, but the common practice of administering it indiscriminately in all cases, irrespective of the stage or character of the disease, is positively pernicious. Arsenic should never be given in the acute inflammatory stage, as it intensifies the cutaneous congestion and agravates all the symptoms. It is also contra-indicated in cases attended with disorders of the digestive system, because of its tendency to produce gastric irritability. In the chronic stage, when the exudation has ceased and the squamous element is pronounced, its judicious use often yields excellent results.

In neurotic eczemas attended with impaired cutaneous innervation, the undoubted virtues of arsenic as a neuro-tonic may be utilized. Its effects should be carefully watched, and its pathogenetic action upon the stomach or kidneys should be accepted as a signal for its discontinuance. As regards the preparation of the drug, it may be most conveniently employed in the form of Fowler's solution, but many prefer the Asiatic pills as more effective.

Strychnia is another drug which is highly recommended in neurotic forms of eczema attended with much pruritus. It may be given in combination with phosphoric acid. The syrup of the hypophosphites is also highly spoken of in this class of cases.

In anemic and chlorotic persons, iron may be advantageously given in the form of Blaud's pills, containing one and a half grains each of sulphate of iron and carbonate of potassium. The iron in this form is readily assimilable, and rarely produces anorexia or headache. Iron may also be administered in the syrup of the iodide, the tincture of the chloride, or in the compound mixture of the Pharmacopœia.

Cod-liver oil is one of the most valuable of the internal remedies, especially in strumous subjects and in young children manifesting evidences of imperfect nutrition.

Viola tricolor is a remedy which has always enjoyed a high repute among the French school of dermatologists on account of its marked diuretic and depurative action. It may be given in the form of the fresh infusion, of the fluid extract, either alone or in combination with senna.

Calx sulphurata is another remedy reputed to be of great benefit in certain forms of eczema, especially in eczema rubrum attended with much infiltration, and in the pustular variety.

Jaborandi has been recently recommended on account of its marked influence upon the sweat glands of the skin. The clinical observations thus far recorded have not been sufficiently extensive to justify positive conclusions as to its value.

Various remedies of the narcotic class, as opium, chloral, bromide of potassium, etc., are mentioned only to be condemned. They exert a more or less disturbing effect upon the general system, and the relief of the subjective symptoms which they propose can best be effected by local measures.

LOCAL TREATMENT.—Although the constitutional relations of eczema have been fully emphasized, the fact remains that it is for the relief of the local affection, rather than the constitutional disorder with which it may be associated, that the patient applies for treatment. The localization of the morbid changes would naturally suggest the direction in which our therapeutic efforts should be applied. The ready accessibility of the affected organ fortunately facilitates the fulfilment of this indication. Rest, avoidance of irritation, protection of the suffering surface, and measures of stimulation comprise the local treatment of eczema.

The topical applications must be modified to meet the indications furnished by the character of the inflammatory process, the type of the eruption, and the different stages through which it passes in its development and decline. Local measures which would be admirably adapted to the acute stage of the disease would prove absolutely inert in the chronic stage, while the subacute stage, which marks the transition from an active to a passive inflammatory condition, requires still another class of remedies. Again it will be found that the medication must be modified to suit the peculiarities of different skins: a treatment which yields excellent results in one case will prove inefficient or injurious in another.

In the early acute stage, characterized by redness and tumefaction, but without transudation at the surface, the best applications are lotions continuously applied, which allay irritation by abstraction of the heat, or the use of carbolized oil, which relieves the tension of the skin and diminishes cutaneous evaporation.   Later, when disruption of the epidermis takes place, with exposure of the sensitive corium to the influence of the atmosphere and other external irritants, the suffering surface should be protected by dusting powders or soothing ointments.   In a more advanced stage, when exudation and crusting have taken place, the indications are to soften and remove the crusts, and to keep the surface under the continuous shelter of a non-irritating ointment until regeneration of the epidermis is effected.   When the discharge is copious, astringent lotions or absorbent powders are to be preferred.   In the chronic or scaly stage, alterative or stimulating agents which excite the reparative process and modify the vital action of the tissues are indicated.

In chronic eczemas, attended with much thickening of the skin, strong stimulants or irritants are to be employed, with a view of converting the passive into an active inflammation, thus favoring the absorption of the infiltrated products, and restoring the diseased tissues to a condition in which they are more amenable to the curative influence of the remedies appropriate to the acute stage.

Ordinarily the eczematous patient does not come under treatment until the exudative stage is reached, when the parts are covered with an accumulation of secondary products, in the form of crusts and scales.   The removal of these pathological products is of the first importance, in order to enable the physician to examine the condition of the diseased surface and to determine the remedies best adapted to its treatment.   This procedure is, moreover, an essential preliminary to the successful action of topical applications, which should be brought into direct contact with the diseased surface.

The removal of the crusts is oftentimes attended with difficulty, especially when seated upon parts covered with hair.   The crusts may be saturated with almond, olive, or linseed oil, and washed off with soap and water.   A poultice of starch, or bread and milk, lotions of bicarbonate of soda, covering the parts with thin vulcanized rubber, are excellent means for softening and detaching crusts.   When the surface is thoroughly cleansed and fully exposed to view, the remedies appropriate to the inflammatory condition present are to be employed.

The agencies employed in the local treatment of eczema are numerous, and embrace a wide range of therapeutic properties; they may be classed as emollients, sedatives, astringents, stimulants, and alteratives.   They are employed in the form of lotions, powders, ointments, oleates, pastes, soaps, plasters, collodions and other fixed adhesive preparations.   It will be convenient, in describing these various preparations, to indicate the form or stage of the disease to which they are specially applicable.

LOTIONS of a sedative nature are employed in the acute stage of eczema to lessen the inflammation and cool the surface by abstraction of the heat, and also to allay the pruritic irritation. For this purpose, dilute alkaline lotions may be employed, as the bicarbonate or biborate of soda, one to two drachms to a pint of water; the sulphite or the hyposulphite of sodium may be used in the same proportion.   The following formula is recommended:

> B Sodii hyposulphitis, ...   ℥ ij.–iv.
> Glycerini, ...   ℥ ss.
> Aquæ, ...   Oi.
> M. S. Apply with compresses dipped in the lotion, and frequently renewed.

When the inflammatory action is high, accompanied with much heat and tension of the skin, lotions of dilute lead-water and opium, of lime-water, or of dilute hydrocyanic acid and glycerin, one drachm of each to four ounces of water, are valuable sedatives.   The use of the lotio nigra or black wash is most highly recommended, also carbolic acid, one drachm to the pint, with an ounce of glycerin.   Jamieson recommends the following:

℞ Lotionis nigræ,
Liquoris calcis, ... ᴀᴀ ℥ iv.
Mucilaginis tragacanthæ, ... ℥ i.
M.

The antipruritic virtues of hot water may be utilized by wringing out cloths steeped in boiling water, and applying them to the parts. The affected surfaces may also be painted with a two-per-cent solution of cocaine once or twice a day.

For purposes of protection, lotions may be used holding in suspension a powdery substance, which is deposited upon the inflamed surface, excluding the air. The calamine lotion is one of the best known for this purpose, prepared by adding half an ounce of finely levigated calamine powder, two drachms of oxide of zinc, two drachms of glycerin, to six ounces of water. This should be applied with a sponge, allowing the powder to collect upon the skin.

Stimulant lotions are often employed with service in the chronic forms of eczema attended with infiltration. For this purpose, the spiritus saponis kalinus of Hebra is generally preferred. Anderson recommends the following combination:

℞ Acidi hydrocyanici diluti, ... ♏ xl.
Saponis mollis, ... ℥ iss.
Aquæ destillatæ, ... ℥ iij.
Olei rosamarini, ... ℥ i.
M. Sig. Dip a piece of flannel in the solution, and rub firmly night and morning.

Carbolic acid, with alcohol and glycerin, in water, may be used for the same purpose, the strength to be regulated according to the effect desired to be produced. After the use of a stimulant lotion, a soothing ointment, the diachylon or zinc ointment, is generally employed.

POWDERS.—In the acute stage of erythematous or vesicular eczema, various inert powders are employed as a protection to the inflamed surface. Dusting powders of lycopodium, starch, French chalk, the carbonate, oxide, or oleate of zinc, bismuth subnitrate, Pear's Fuller's earth, either alone or in various combinations, may be employed. I frequently employ the following: Five drachms of powdered starch, two drachms of oxide of zinc, and one drachm of subnitrate of bismuth, to which half a drachm of powdered camphor may be added, to allay the itching. The application of the powder should be copious and continued; an occasional sprinkling does little good. Preliminary to the application of the powder, it may be advantageous to smear the surface lightly with some unctuous substance, cold cream, or oxide of zinc ointment, so that the powder may more readily adhere to the surface. In eczema intertrigo, Unna recommends the use of powder bags, which are quilted across to prevent the powder from shifting from one part to the other. These bags are placed between opposing surfaces, and maintained in position continuously.

OINTMENTS are generally regarded as the most universally applicable and efficient means at our command for the local treatment of eczema. They constitute a convenient vehicle for the application of the various soothing and astringent remedies indicated in the different forms and stages of the eruption. A great deal of care is required in their preparation, as otherwise they are liable to aggravate the symptoms they are intended to relieve. They should be made of fresh materials, and the active ingredients employed in their composition should be finely powdered and thoroughly incorporated. The lard, which forms the basis of many ointments, should be free from rancid and irritating qualities; mollin and lanoline have been recommended as ointment bases, but they present no special advantages over lard and vaseline.

Soothing ointments are employed in the acute stage of eczema, for the purpose of softening the dried products of exudation and protecting the inflamed parts by exclusion of the air. For purposes of protection, the benzoinated zinc ointment is probably the most universally applicable. Of other sedative applications of this class may be mentioned the *unguentum diachyli alba* of Hebra, and the oleate of zinc and oleate of bismuth ointments. As these latter are not officinal, their composition may be given. The formula of the "unguentum zinci oleatis," as recommended by Dr. Crocker, is as follows:

> ℞ Zinci oxidi, ... ℥ i.
> 　Acidi oleici, ... ℥ viij.
> 　Vaselini, ... ℥ ix.
> 　M.

I have found this ointment of especial value in eczemas of the face and head.

The oleate of bismuth ointment was introduced by Dr. McCall Anderson; its composition is as follows:

> ℞ Bismuthi oxidi, ... ℥ i.
> 　Acidi oleici, ... ℥ viij.
> 　Ceræ albæ, ... ℥ iij.
> 　Vaselini, ... ℥ ix.
> 　Olei rosæ, ... ♏ v.
> 　M.

The relative quantity of the white wax may be increased or diminished to adapt its consistency to the temperature of different seasons.

Jamieson recommends as a cooling salve the following formula:

> ℞ Aquæ rosamarini,
> 　Olei amygdalæ, ... āā 10 pts.
> 　Ceræ albæ,
> 　Cetacei, ... āā 1 pt.
> 　M.

Another excellent soothing ointment is the following:

> ℞ Zinci carbonatis,
> 　Zinci oxidi, ... āā ℈ ss.
> 　Unguenti aquæ rosæ, ... ad ℥ i.
> 　M.

When a marked sedative effect is desired, the extract of belladonna or stramonium may be added in the proportion of five to ten grains to the ounce. Ointments are open to the objection that they are easily rubbed off or absorbed by the clothing, and to secure their most efficient action they should be spread evenly upon thin pieces of linen, and maintained in position by careful bandaging. The salve muslins introduced by Unna are exceedingly convenient. They consist of thin woven fabric, with wide meshes, impregnated with various ointments. The salve muslins may be cut in any desired shape or size, and fitted to the surface.

Stimulant ointments are indicated in a more advanced stage of eczema, when there is more or less infiltration, with a dry, scaly surface. The ammoniated mercurial ointment is an excellent preparation in certain forms of eczema, but it is rarely judicious to use it in full strength, especially over extensive surfaces. It may be used in combination with unguentum aquæ rosæ, or the zinc ointment, in the proportion of one part of the former to two or four of the latter. The tarry preparations are of especial utility in the chronic stages of eczema. The unguentum picis liquidæ, or ointments composed of oleum cadini or oleum rusci, one drachm to the ounce, are often followed by brilliant curative effects.

Sulphur, chrysarobin, naphthol, ichthyol, resorcin, and other remedies of recent introduction have been used in the form of ointments for chronic eczema, but their superiority over the better known agents has not been established by clinical experience.

Ointments are also serviceable applications for the relief of pruritus. An ointment of carbolic acid, ten to thirty grains to the ounce, often controls the itching. Still more effective is an ointment composed of gum camphor and hydrate of chloral, of each one-half to one drachm to the ounce, or the following combination:

℞ Acidi carbolici, ... 3 ss.
　Glyceriti cocaini (5 per cent), ... 3 ij.
　Unguenti petrolati, . ad ℥ i.

PASTES.—The principal objection to ointments as ordinarily prepared is that they do not possess sufficient solidity or consistency for exclusion of the air and complete protection of the surface. This indication is better fulfilled by pastes, which are dryer and adhere more firmly.

Lassar's paste is the best known and most valuable of this class of preparations. Its composition is as follows:

℞ Acidi salicylici, ... grs. x.
　Zinci oxidi,
　Pulveris amyli, ... āā 3 ij.
　Unguenti petrolati, ... ad ℥ i.
M.

This may be smeared over the surface, or spread upon lint and kept in position by bandages. The salicylic acid may be omitted if the surface is sensitive.

Ihle's paste has the following formula:

℞ Resorcini, ... grs. x.–xx.
　Zinci oxidi,
　Pulveris amyli,
　Lanolini,
　Vaselini, ... āā 3 ij.
M.

A large number of active ingredients may be conveniently used in the form of pastes.

FIXED ADHESIVE DRESSINGS.—The introduction of this class of preparations marks a decided advance in cutaneous therapeutics, especially in chronic eczemas when the lesions are circumscribed and limited to certain localities. They consist of glycerin jelly medicated with oxide of zinc, or any active ingredient desired, collodion or traumaticin combinations, in which the drug is held in liquid suspension, and adhesive plasters, the basis of which is gutta percha, combined with emollients or stimulants in any desired proportion. The plaster may be cut into any shape, and is especially convenient of application in eczemas so situated that accurate adjustment of a dressing to the affected parts is difficult, as about the fingers and interdigital spaces, as well as in eczemas of the anus, the genital regions, the crease of the thighs, etc.

Klotz has recently devised a compound salicylated plaster which he highly recommends in the non-inflammatory scaly forms of eczema. The following is the formula for its composition:

℞ Emplastri diachyli,
　Emplastri saponis, ... āā 40 pts.
　Petrolati, ... : 15 pts.
　Acidi salicylici, ... 5 pts.
M.

This is spread on linen or muslin.

The formula for Unna's glycerin jelly is as follows:

℞ Gelatinæ, ... 15 parts.
　Zinci oxidi, ... 10 parts.
　Glycerini, ... 30 parts.
　Aquæ, . . . 40 parts.

The ingredients are melted and carefully combined, and poured into any suitable vessel. When desired for use, the mass is liquefied by heating, and with a flat brush is painted over the surface, forming a thin, adherent, and pliable coating. This combination is peculiarly serviceable in chronic eczemas, characterized by thickening and induration of the skin, with excessive pruritus. Even in acute cases, when the skin is actively congested and sensitive, with exudation, it may be employed with benefit.

Collodion or traumaticin, medicated with five to ten per cent of chrysarobin, iodine, or salicylic acid, will be found serviceable in removing dry, thickened, scaly patches of eczema. Cantharidal collodion may also be conveniently employed in chronic, localized, very obstinate eczemas, where blistering of the affected surface is indicated.

Crocker has recently recommended blistering over the back and spine for the relief of certain cases of chronic eczema. Several years ago I called attention to the efficacy of this method of treatment for eczemas of the anus and genital region.

SOAPS.—There are a variety of soaps employed in the local treatment of eczema, including soda, potash, and tar soaps. The soda soaps are milder in their action, and are employed chiefly for detersive purposes where there is an accumulation of crusts and scabs, preliminary to the use of other remedies. Of the soft potash soaps, the sapo viridis is the most efficient in its action and the one most generally employed. It special utility is found in eczema rubrum and localized patches of squamous eczema with thickening and induration and persistent pruritus. Its action is to clear away the dead epidermis, give exit to the ichorous fluid imprisoned beneath, stimulate the circulation, and thus promote the absorption of the infiltrated products, besides affording relief from the intolerable itching. To obtain its full therapeutic efficacy, it is necessary that it should be thoroughly rubbed into the skin and its application continued for some time. The amount of infiltration present and the sensitiveness of the skin should be the measure of the activity and duration of its employment. After each application the surface should be dressed with some soothing ointment, as the *unguentum diachyli,* which should be thickly spread upon muslin cut to fit the parts, and retained in position by means of strips of cloth or a roller bandage. This procedure should be repeated once or twice daily until a healthy reaction is established. Fox has recommended as a substitute for the green soap, a soft olive soap, such as is used in the manufacture of silk and other delicate fabrics.

Tar soaps are indicated only in the chronic scaly stage of the eruption. The susceptibility to the action of tar varies in different skins, and its reactionary effect should be first tested over a small area before it is applied to a large eczematous surface.

In chronic and obstinate patches of eczema, it may be necessary to have recourse to a more powerful irritant than soap. A strong alkali, such as liquor potassæ or caustic potash in the proportion of from ten grains to half a drachm to the ounce, or a solution of nitrate of silver, sixteen grains to the ounce of nitrous ether, or even the solid nitrate may be brushed over the surface, followed by the application of a sedative emollient ointment.

MECHANICAL MEANS.—In the local therapy of certain eczemas, especially infiltrated eczemas of the hands and lower extremity, mechanical compression by the agency of vulcanized india-rubber constitutes a most useful means. The close contact of the rubber dressing serves to moisten and macerate the thickened epidermis, while the continuous pressure favors the absorption of the infiltrated products.

In chronic eczemas which prove refractory to the ordinary means of treatment, it may be necessary to resort to severer surgical methods, such as puncturing, scarifying or curetting the affected surfaces. These vigorous procedures, by modifying the nutrition of the diseased tissues, and favoring the elimination of exuded products, may effect a cure when milder means fail.

INFANTILE ECZEMA.—Eczema represents a large proportion of the cutaneous diseases incident to childhood. The greater comparative frequency of the disease in children is due to the delicacy of the skin, its feebler capacity of resistance to external irritants, the exceeding sensitiveness of the nervous system, and the facility with which disorders of the internal organs are reflected upon the external integument. While eczema presents the same general characters as are seen in the adult skin, it is peculiar in its predilection for certain regions, as the scalp, forehead, cheeks, nose and chin, and in the predominance of the moist and impetiginous forms of the eruption.

The most common and typical expression of infantile eczema is seen upon the head and face in the form of crusta lactea or milk crust, which consists of thick, yellowish, gummy masses of dried exudation covering the features like a mask, beneath which there exists a reddened, swollen, and excoriated surface.

The location and configuration of the lesions in different cases is often quite similar, and although all forms of eczema may be found, generally when the patient first comes under observation the disease presents the characteristics of eczema rubrum. When vesicles exist as a primary lesion, they are of short duration; their delicate walls quickly suffer destruction by rubbing or scratching. The actual skin lesions will, in the majority of untreated cases, be found hidden beneath a glue-like coating of the dried secretion of the patch, or a mass of thick, grayish, yellowish or dark colored crusts, varying in hue as they become mixed with dirt from the outside or with blood from the torn and excoriated parts beneath.

Pustules often occur upon the hairy scalp in infantile eczema, and the crusts which result from their rupture mat the hairs together, and are often separated by a layer of pus and foul secretions from the underlying reddened skin which they conceal. The pustular form of eczema is more commonly associated with subcutaneous abscesses about the posterior aspect of the head and neck than are the other varieties. These abscesses occur for the most part in poorly nourished or scrofulous children, and have the characteristics of a gradually thinning wall of bluish color which is easily ruptured and gives exit to a thin grumous pus.

Though the head and face are the regions of predilection for infantile eczema, other parts of the body may be primarily affected, or the eruption may spread over almost the entire body. The ears are quite constantly implicated, and the ciliary borders of the eyelids are often so affected that the lids are found glued together in the morning. The ano-genital region rarely escapes, for here, beside the natural heat and moisture of the parts, the constant contact of urine and fæces is productive of considerable irritation in many cases, and in others the careless washing to which the child is subjected does not tend to ward it off.

Eczema intertrigo in the fold of the groin is rarely covered with crusts, and the constant rubbing of the parts together causes much suffering to the little patient. In eczema occurring upon the trunk or general surface of the body, thin scales rather than crusts are apt to form.

The usual time for the first appearance of an eczema in infancy is at about the age of four or six weeks.

A raw and exuding surface is first noticed as a rule, although papules and vesicles may coexist with it or appear subsequently.

The patch is excessively itchy and the child, if permitted, will scratch and rub it with the hands, or by rubbing the cheeks, scalp, or other portion of the body affected against the pillow or clothing will effect the same purpose. The extra amount of exudation and perhaps bleeding provoked by this scratching proves a further source of irritation and tends to increase the area of the eruption by causing the coalescence of adjacent patches. Later on, the exudation becomes more opaque and perhaps contains pus, and the crusts become thicker and amber colored. If pustules appear in the vicinity, a so-called impetiginous variety of eczema is produced, and in severe cases the whole face, and perhaps a greater portion of the head as well, becomes covered with thick crusts.

Whenever the posterior portion of the head is affected, we find the lymphatic glands enlarged, either the post-auricular, the occipital, or the cervical or all of them together, and in eczema of the back of the head excited by the presence of pediculi capitis this is quite constantly the case.

Itching is the all important subjective symptom; it is worse at night, rendering the child at times almost frantic.

As a patch of eczema rubrum improves either under its own crust or under treatment, the fiery redness disappears and the surface becomes smooth and shiny; an untreated patch may become transformed into one of eczema squamosum. In fact, one variety may merge into another or several varieties may exist together.

ETIOLOGY.—Heredity seems to exercise a certain influence in the production of eczema; still we often find but one child affected in a family, and this child will usually be found to suffer from some symptom of mal-assimilation. Insufficient or improper nourishment, or imperfections on the part of the digestive apparatus will, in almost all cases, be found at the root of the evil. Unna distinguishes a nervous, a tuberculous, and a seborrhœal variety of infantile eczema.

The nervous, which is typified in the eczema of dentition, or that in which the eruption of the teeth acts as an exciting cause, is found to occur upon the cheeks or forehead, and at the same time upon the radial side of the backs of the hands and wrists in a symmetrical manner. The eruption is extremely itchy, occurs upon previously healthy skin, and the stronger the child, and the more healthy the epidermis, the greater is the itching. It is due to reflex irritation, and is found upon the forehead and cheeks more particularly because, by reason of their natural hyperæmia, they offer a favorable soil. Though the eruption may spontaneously disappear, it is apt to recur.

Slight irritation of almost any kind seems, in some children who appear healthy, to act as an exciting cause and call forth an eruption of eczema. Exposure to cold wind, excessive bathing with soap and water, the bites of pediculi, flannel worn next the skin, constipation, diarrhœa, acrid urine are a few of the common exciting causes. Vaccination has been assigned as a prolific cause of the development of eczema in children. The frequent occurrence of eczema after vaccination is due, no doubt, to the constitutional disturbance or febrile movement determined by the vaccine virus circulating in the blood, in which vascular disturbance the cutaneous tissues sympathize, and respond by phenomena of inflammation.

A seborrhœa of the scalp, existing almost from birth, is in many cases an important etiological factor in the production of the seborrhœal variety. This eczema takes on a moist character, and spreads from the scalp over the ears, forehead, and cheeks, maintaining a seborrhœal nature. Upon the shoulders and arms it spreads as scaly and more or less fatty patches, and usually extends to the lower extremities. It itches less than the nervous variety, but more readily becomes generalized. The tuberculous form is the least itchy of all.

The DIAGNOSIS of infantile eczema is not difficult when the characteristic mucilaginous exudation is present, but there are a number of diseases to which it bears a more or less deceptive resemblance.

It is to be distinguished from impetigo, which is an inoculable disease, having a more rapid course and whose crusts are thicker, softer, of a deeper yellow color, and less adherent.

In simple seborrhœa, the crusts are of a waxy nature and can be rolled into a ball, which is not the case in eczema. Again, in the former, the region of the nose is affected, and in the latter the ears.

In trichophytosis, which is a contagious disease and of rarer occurrence, we have more uniform circular patches upon the scalp, covered with brittle hair, and itching less than patches of eczema.

In favus, the crusts are of a sulphur-yellow color, rounded, cup-shaped, and each pierced with a hair. Beside this, there is an odor of mice, not common to eczema, and the disease is very rare in infancy. If necessary, the microscope will readily distinguish these two affections from eczema.

In psoriasis, which is rare in young children, the margin of the patches is abrupt; they are dry, covered with whitish scales, and do not itch.

Eczema of dentition resembles herpes zoster in its groups of vesicles upon a reddened base, but zoster is not symmetrical, its duration is limited, and it does not recur.

Scabies does not occur upon the face, and furrows are found upon the fingers, wrists, and ankles.

TREATMENT.—Before speaking of the management of eczema in the infant, a word may be said about the advisability of treatment. It has been a common belief held by many of the laity, and even by some physicians as well, that milk crust and salt rheum at this age should be left alone, for fear of internal disorders resulting from its cure. Such a belief is quite groundless, and is controverted by the facts of every-day experience.

The same general principles of treatment apply to infantile eczema as to the disease in adult life. It is to be remembered, however, that we have here a more delicately structured and highly sensitive skin to deal with, and that, as a rule, soothing applications are more needed than the stronger astringent and stimulating applications employed in the adult.

As before said, mal-assimilation will be found at the bottom of many cases. It may be that the breast milk the infant receives is not of proper quantity or quality, and it may become necessary to change the nurse or to substitute artificial nourishment. It is common to find older children given the freedom of the table, and not only allowed all kinds of improper food, but beer and tea as well. Minute instruction should be given regarding a proper diet and the proper intervals at which it should be taken. In strumous and pale children cod-liver oil may be added to the dietary with advantage, and weak children given meat juice. Beside the matter of dietetics, attention to hygiene is important.

Bathing is a matter demanding consideration. Most children with eczema are bathed entirely too much. Plain water and common soap should never be used while the eruption is present, and only the amount of bathing employed which is necessary to keep the parts freed from extraneous matter. Starch can with much benefit be added to the water in the proportion of an ounce or more to a gallon, and if an alkali is desired, from two to four teaspoonfuls of bicarbonate or biborate of soda. In eczema of the face, it is only necessary to wash the region of the eyes, nose, and mouth, which are usually free from eruption. About the pudendal regions, bathing with pledgets of absorbent cotton, as often as necessary to remove the excreta, is required, but must be carefully done not to injure the highly inflamed tissues.

As regards internal treatment authorities differ, but there is no doubt that in many, if not all cases, remedies internally administered do much good.

If the skin be flabby, the limbs thin, and the body ill nourished, it is probable that a change of diet and the addition of oil, pepsin, etc., will be of much benefit. Arsenic has a tonic effect in young children and is especially well supported. Wilson considered it a specific in infantile eczema.

Alkaline waters, as Vichy or small doses of potash or soda salts, may be added to the milk with advantage in some cases. Where there is acidity of the stomach, the rhubarb and soda mixture in small doses will benefit. Anderson is very warm in his praise of calomel in dose of a grain to a child one year of age twice a week or oftener, and in some cases it has a most pleasing effect.

Local treatment to be effective must be thorough, and much pains and patience are required on the part of physician and nurse. First of all, the crusts should be softened and removed from the scalp by applying some bland oil, and covering with an oiled-silk cap. The medicated dressing may then be applied directly to the diseased skin.

Tar is one of the best external remedies, and Hebra considered it nowhere so useful as in infantile eczema of the scalp. In public practice the pix liquida is mostly used, but the oleum cadini or oleum rusci or Goudron are to be preferred. One part of oil of cade to five or seven of almond oil makes an excellent dressing. Ointments will be found treated of elsewhere, but nowhere is it so important that they should be freshly and carefully prepared, with freedom from all acrid or irritating qualities, as in the treatment of infants.

Pastes are more easily retained in contact with eczematous surfaces than ointments, and for the face a mask covering a thick paste is probably the best dressing. Two parts of salicylic acid to a hundred of starch paste, with the addition of eight parts of zinc oxide, makes a much prized dressing. The oleate of zinc is an excellent application in eczema capitis. The oleate of bismuth also acts well, but is not so good a face dressing, as it is apt to discolor the skin.

In a more chronic stage when the inflammatory action has subsided, ointments made with tannin or calomel and vaseline, or dilute ammoniated mercury ointment act beneficially. In seborrhœal eczema, sulphur preparations are recommended; sulphur and zinc act well together.

LOCAL VARIETIES OF ECZEMA.

The appearance and course of eczema in different localities are modified by the anatomical peculiarities of the tissues, their exposure to irritant influences, and the more or less close sympathetic relations of different surfaces to disorders of the internal organs.   Eczema of the palms and soles, for example, exhibits certain peculiar phases on account of the thick resistant epidermis and the constant motion and pressure to which these surfaces are exposed.   Eczemas of the face are peculiarly prone to be sympathetically affected by disorders of the digestive organs, besides being constantly exposed to atmospheric influences.   Eczemas of the anus have a close relation with disorders of the hepatic system, constipation, etc.; they are aggravated by contact of opposing surfaces, maceration of the epidermis from moisture and pressure and passage of fecal matter.   Eczemas of the lower extremities are markedly influenced by their location.   The existence of varicose veins, stasis of the blood, etc., etc., constitute potential factors in their causation and perpetuation.

ECZEMA OF THE HEAD (*Eczema Capitis*).—In this location eczema may occur as an erythematous, dry, scaly eruption, or it may assume a moist or pustular form.   Eczema of the scalp is incomparably more frequent in children, in whom it generally exhibits the characters of a pustular eruption.   The contents of the ruptured pustules, mingled with the sebaceous secretions, form crusts which mat the hairs together.   These thick masses of agglutination constitute a favorable nidus for the development of pediculi; many cases of eczema capitis, especially among illy cared for or neglected children, will be found to be complicated with pediculosis.   Furuncles and subcutaneous abscesses are frequent phenomena of infantile pustular eczema of the scalp, and swelling of the post-cervical glands is a very common concomitant, especially in scrofulous children.

Erythematous eczema occurs in the form of irregular red patches, which may become generalized over the entire scalp.   It is excessively itchy and attended with fine branny desquamation. Squamous eczema may develop from the erythematous form, or represent the final stage of the pustular variety.   The scalp is red, scaly, and infiltrated, and the eruption often passes beyond the limits of the hairy scalp upon the forehead, or extends over and down behind the ears and upon the nape and sides of the neck.

DIAGNOSIS.—There are a number of eruptions occurring upon the scalp with which eczema may be confounded.   In seborrhœa the crusts are thinner, more greasy to the feel, with a pasty consistence from the larger admixture of sebaceous matter; after their removal, the surface is seen to be pale and smooth, non-infiltrated and non-excoriated, itching sensations are not marked. The crusts of eczema are thicker, more brittle, and after removal the scalp appears reddened, thickened, and moist, exuding serum or pus.

In psoriasis, the edges of the patches are more circumscribed and defined, and the eruption is most characteristically developed along the margin of the hairy scalp.   The patches are covered with grayish-white dry scales, which are heaped up and quite adherent.   Their removal discloses a reddened and thickened, sometimes bleeding base.   The eruption is not itchy and is commonly associated with psoriasis of other parts, which may be so characteristically developed as to leave no doubt as to the diagnosis.   In tinea tonsurans, the patches are circular, the hairs are stubbly, as if nibbled off, easily extracted, and often loaded with the parasite.   Ringworm of the scalp often co-exists with typical tinea patches upon other parts of the body; in the adult it is so exceedingly rare that it may be practically eliminated as an element of diagnosis.   Microscopic examination of the affected hairs would resolve all doubt.

Tinea favosa.   The sulphur-colored, cup-shaped crusts of favus, when typically developed, cannot be confounded with any other eruption.   It is only at a later stage, when the crusts are removed, leaving a thin, shining or powdery epidermis with occasional pustules, that it bears any resemblance to eczema.   As in the previous disease, the microscope may be relied upon to clear up the diagnosis.

Eczema of the scalp may be differentiated from the so-called syphilitic eczema, by the circumscribed deeper ulcerations of the pustular syphilide, its more frequent occurrence in adults, and its association with other signs of syphilis.

TREATMENT.—In eczema of the scalp, the crusts should be softened by soaking in almond or linseed oil, and after washing the surface with soap and water, they should be loosened and separated from the hairs and carefully removed by means of a comb. When the crusts are thick and tenacious, it may be necessary to envelop the scalp for a night or two in a thin rubber cap. If pediculi are present, the hair should be thoroughly saturated with crude petroleum, either pure or mixed with olive oil. After the scalp has been thoroughly cleansed, the surface may be treated with an ointment of the oxide or oleate of zinc, or simply carbolized vaseline. An ointment of iodoform or iodol, five or ten grains to the ounce of vaseline or lard, is recommended in pustular eczema of the scalp. In many cases, the application of mild astringent lotions serves a useful purpose. In the chronic, scaly stage, stimulant applications should be employed. An ointment of the oil of cade, the oleum rusci, ammoniated mercury or tannin—either of the above ingredients in the proportion of twenty to sixty grains to the ounce is recommended. In inveterate cases attended with much infiltration, good results are obtained by painting the affected surfaces with strong stimulant lotions, such as solution of the nitrate of silver, five to fifteen grains to the ounce of nitrous ether, tincture of iodine, a solution of resorcin one drachm to one ounce of glycerin, or a lotion of liquor carbonis detergens. Schwimmer recommends the following:

℞ Acidi salicylici, . . .	10 parts.
Liquoris ammonii acetatis, ...	25 "
Glycerini, ...	100 "
M.	

After the requisite degree of irritation has been determined, one of the above-mentioned soothing ointments may be employed with advantage.

ECZEMA OF THE FACE (*Eczema Faciei*).—Eczema of the scalp is frequently associated with an eczematous eruption of the face, especially in children, in whom it commonly assumes the moist or pustular form, attended with the production of crusts. In adults the erythematous form predominates and is usually chronic in character. The skin is red, dry, more or less infiltrated, rough and harsh to the feel, and the seat of a fine branny desquamation. Moisture is rarely present, the eruption maintaining its erythematous character throughout. It is attended with intense pruritic sensations, and the integument frequently cracks and fissures in the lines of natural motion. The integument over the eyelids, the brow, and the infra-orbital regions, and about the sides of the nose is most frequently attacked, but the entire face may be involved. Eczema of the face is especially common in cooks, firemen, and engineers, whose occupation exposes them to heat and draughts.

There are a number of eruptions in this locality from which the erythematous form of eczema should be differentiated. Rosacea may be distinguished by the absence of heat and active congestion, the skin being cool and smooth to the feel, with no roughness or desquamation. Rosacea is much more frequent in women, and commonly occurs at the time of puberty or the menopause. Lupus erythematosus of the nose and cheeks bears a certain resemblance to eczema, but it may be readily distinguished by its well-defined margins, its symmetrical distribution, the absence of subjective sensations, its more sluggish evolution, and the presence of its characteristic thin cicatrices.

TREATMENT.—It is of the first importance to correct the digestive disturbances with which eczema in this locality is so frequently associated. The diet should be carefully regulated and the bowels kept open by saline aperients. In the local treatment, the avoidance of soap and water cannot be too strongly insisted upon. For cleansing the face, a small quantity of almond flour in water, sufficient to render the water bland and soothing, should be employed. At night the face should be smeared with a mild ointment of the oleate, oxide, or carbonate of zinc. Calamine liniment, composed of prepared calamine, two scruples; oxide of zinc, one-half drachm; lime-water and olive oil, each one ounce, is another excellent application. When the patient can remain in-doors, the face may be enveloped in a mask freely smeared with Lassar's paste, which may be worn continuously until the tenderness and irritation subside. The addition of oil of cade to the zinc ointment, in the proportion of one drachm to the ounce, often has an admirable effect in relieving the pruritus and modifying the infiltration.

ECZEMA OF THE BEARD (*Eczema Barbæ*).—Eczema of the beard ordinarily assumes the pustular form; it may be superficial or extend down into the follicles. The pustules dry up, forming small crusts which may run together, forming large irregular crusts covering the entire hairy surface. When the inflammation is deep-seated and chronic, it not unfrequently leads to obliteration of the follicles and permanent alopecia. It is attended with intense itching and burning sensations.

Eczema of the beard is difficult of distinction from both non-parasitic and parasitic sycosis. In non-parasitic sycosis, the follicles are primarily and chiefly involved, and the eruption is strictly limited to the hairy parts, tubercles and small abscesses frequently occur; in eczema, the eruption often extends to the adjacent parts not covered with hair, and there is more discharge and crusting. In parasitic sycosis, there is frequently a history of contagion, and ringed patches characteristic of tinea are frequently detected upon other parts of the body. In ringworm of the beard, tubercles and nodules forming large brawny indurations are a prominent feature, the hairs are brittle and twisted, and their extraction is easy and often painless; in eczema, the hairs are healthy and their extraction is exquisitely painful, unless deep suppuration has occurred. In cases of doubt, microscopic examination may reveal the presence of the fungus.

TREATMENT.—As a preliminary to successful treatment, the beard should be removed and the face kept closely shaven; in cases where the inflammation has extended deep down into the hair follicles, it may be necessary to resort to epilation. After this process the surface should be dusted with a protective powder, or a soothing ointment applied. Auspitz recommends that the pustules be opened and the surface scraped with a scoop, especially devised for this purpose. This procedure is to be repeated every few days, and diachylon ointment continuously applied in the intervals of the operations. After the pustular element has been eliminated, and there remains a dry, reddened, scaly condition of the surface, a resort to more stimulating applications, as the citrine ointment or the ammoniated mercurial ointment, often suffices to effect a cure. A weak sulphur ointment, twenty grains to the ounce, may also be employed with benefit.

ECZEMA OF THE EDGES OF THE EYELIDS (*Eczema tarsi*).—Eczema of the edges of the eyelids is of comparative common occurrence in strumous subjects, especially scrofulous children, in whom it is generally associated with ophthalmia and conjunctivitis. The glandular structures are principally involved, the eruption occurring in the form of small pustules at the orifices of the hair follicles, which burst and form crusts or scabs which glue the eyelashes together. The edges of the lids are reddened, infiltrated, often excoriated; the upper and lower lids become agglutinated by the dried secretion, so that it is impossible to open them without softening and removing the crusts. The persistence of this condition may cause obliteration of the follicles and permanent loss of the lashes. Not infrequently there is excessive lachrymation and the integument of the lower lid and the upper portion of the cheek becomes red, swollen, and eczematous from the irritation caused by constant flowing of the tears over these surfaces.

TREATMENT.—As this affection ordinarily occurs in weak and strumous children, the internal treatment should be directed to the improvement of the general health by the use of cod-liver oil and other nutritive tonics. In the local treatment, cleanliness is of the first importance; the crusts should be softened by the application of warm milk or hot water by means of a fine sponge; the addition of a little bicarbonate of sodium to the water will increase its solvent and soothing properties. After the crusts have been removed, the use of a mildly stimulating ointment, such as the dilute citrine or the red oxide of mercury, generally suffices to effect a cure. In obstinate cases, attended with much infiltration, it may be necessary to lightly brush the edges of the lids with a weak solution of nitrate of silver, or potassa fusa, preparatory to the use of the ointment.

ECZEMA OF THE NOSTRILS (*Eczema narium*).—Eczema of the nostrils may occur in connection with eczema of the face, but it most commonly owes its origin to an acute or chronic rhinitis, the continual irritation from the discharge causing an eruption of pustules, with excoriations and rhagades, and more or less hyperplasia of the upper lip. Not infrequently the disease is associated with an inflammation of the vibrissæ, resulting in a suppurative folliculitis. The external integument, as well as the mucous lining of the nostrils, becomes hot, congested, and swollen, the increased secretion dries into crusts, which may block up the nares, and impede the nasal respiration. As the crusts are removed by the nail or by violent blowing, the mucous membrane underneath becomes exulcerated, and if this process is continually repeated, the ulceration may increase in depth until perforation of the septum takes place. When associated with suppurative folliculitis, which condition is considered by many authorities as pathologically and clinically distinct from eczema of the nares, the skin of the nose is apt to become red and inflamed, and sometimes the seat of erysipelas.

Eczema narium may be mistaken for lupus, as in both diseases perforation of the septum may occur. The course of lupus is more sluggish, the subjective symptom of itching is absent, and lupus nodules may generally be seen at the orifice of the nares or upon the neighboring integument. Syphilitic affections of the nares may also produce destructive perforation of the septum, but there are usually concomitant evidences of the disease upon other portions of the body, and the existence of a specific history.

TREATMENT.—The successful treatment of eczema of the nostrils requires much care and attention to minute details. The patient should be enjoined against forcible removal of the scabs or crusts by picking them with the nail or violent blowing. The crusts should be first softened by the application of oil or an emollient ointment, as the oleate of zinc. Hebra's diachylon ointment, or the ammoniated mercurial ointment may be applied on a pledget of cotton and rubbed in thoroughly. Pencilling the surface with strong solutions of nitrate of silver, or sulphate of zinc, are useful applications when stimulation is required. Nasal suppositories, variously medicated with zinc, opium, belladonna, form a convenient and useful mode of application. When a smarting, burning pain is complained of, relief may be had by the application of a small pledget of cotton soaked in strong solution of morphine in glycerin, or the glycerite of cocaine. Hardaway has recommended in suppurative folliculitis fomentations of hot water, the use of sulphide of calcium, one-tenth grain every third hour, epilation of the hairs, and the application of glycerole of subacetate of lead, ʒij. to the ounce of glycerin.

When there is much hyperplastic swelling of the upper lip, puncturing and scarifications may be employed with advantage.

ECZEMA OF THE EARS (*Eczema aurium*).—Eczema of the auricle commonly occurs in connection with eczema capitis by extension of the eruption from contiguous parts. The space between the auricle and scalp is most frequently affected, but the entire surface may be involved. The integument presents a reddish, raw, infiltrated appearance, the exudation forming thick yellowish crusts or scabs. Not infrequently the whole ear becomes swollen and distorted, the peculiar disfigurement being occasioned by the projection of the ear forward and outward from the head.

Eczema of the ears requires no modification in the treatment best adapted to eczema of other surfaces. When the posterior auricular surface is involved, as well as the contiguous region over the mastoid, constituting a variety of eczema intertrigo and frequently attended with fissuring of the post-auricular sulcus, the surfaces should be separated by the interposition of lint smeared with a mild astringent ointment or the calamine liniment.

In many cases, eczema is confined to the external auditory canal, one or both, and is apt to be chronic in character and peculiarly obstinate to treatment. The canal may be occluded from swelling, and the meatus blocked up with the dried exudation. Itching is a most troublesome symptom, and the attempt to relieve it by picking or boring in the ear with the point of the finger or an instrument serves to aggravate the condition.

TREATMENT should be directed first to the removal of the crusts. After softening with glycerin, oil, or warm milk, they may be washed out, and the surface treated with astringent lotions of carbolic acid or sulphate of zinc in the proportion of two to five grains to the ounce, with the admixture of a small quantity of glycerin. It is important that the lotions should be weak and used with care, to prevent injury to the membrana tympani. Boracic acid is a favorite remedy with many surgeons, it may be used either in the form of a lotion, or the powder may be thrown into the canal by means of the ordinary powder blower. Another excellent application is the glycerole of the subacetate of lead, one part to four.

In chronic eczema attended with thickening of the walls of the canal, fissuring, and desquamation, stronger applications are requisite. I have always obtained the best results by painting the surfaces with a strong solution of carbolic acid in glycerin (℥ij. to the ounce), carefully absorbing any excess of the solution, and then applying an ointment of the oleate of bismuth. The glycerite of tannin or an ointment of tannin (ℨi. to the ounce) is also highly recommended.

ECZEMA OF THE FLEXOR SURFACES OF THE JOINTS (*Eczema articulorum*).—The flexor surfaces of the joints constitute seats of predilection for eczema. The axillæ, groin, elbows and knee joints, the wrists and ankles are favorite locations, the eruption often being limited to one or more of these regions. The eruption is almost invariably symmetrical, and it has been observed that there is commonly a coincident implication of the elbow and popliteal spaces, also that when the anterior aspects of the wrists are involved, the front of the ankles is apt to be at the same time the seat of the eruption.

Eczema of the flexures exhibits certain peculiarities in its appearance, from the greater thinness of the skin, the contact of opposing surfaces, and the mobility of the parts. The epidermis is frequently macerated and removed, leaving excoriated raw surfaces; the skin is thickened and infiltrated, losing its natural elasticity, fissures form in the natural furrows, and movement of the joints becomes restricted and painful.

TREATMENT.—The treatment is not essentially modified by the accident of location. Rest and the avoidance of unnecessary movement should be enjoined. In the acute stage, soothing; and in the chronic stage, astringent and stimulating applications are indicated. The Lassar paste is an excellent soothing and protective dressing. When there is much infiltration and scaling, the tarry and mercurial ointments may be applied. Fixed adhesive dressings are of admirable service, since they admit of accurate adjustment to the diseased surface, and may be maintained in continuous and prolonged contact, thus securing permanence of action.

ECZEMA OF THE BREAST (*Eczema mammæ*).—Eczema occurring under the pendulous breasts presents the same clinical features and demands the same treatment as eczema intertrigo of other regions.

Eczema of the nipples, though not peculiar to nursing women, so commonly results from the irritation induced by lactation that its occurrence in a non-nursing woman should always suggest a suspicion of scabies. The nipples become chapped and fissured and bleeding, more or less retracted, and frequently encrusted. The treatment consists of absolute cleanliness, carefully drying the nipple, after which it should be coated with a soothing protective dressing. For this purpose Unna recommends a paste composed of white sugar, oxide of zinc, mucilage of acacia, and glycerin, equal parts. The fissures may be touched with a solution of nitrate of silver, or painted with the compound tincture of benzoin. It will be found advantageous in most cases to use a nipple shield or breast pump, thus protecting the nipple from the suction and the irritating secretions of the child's mouth.

Eczema of the nipple has an important clinical significance in connection with "Paget's disease of the nipple," to the beginning stage of which it bears a close resemblance.

This form of superficial epithelioma, according to Paget, presents a florid red, raw surface, finely granular, appearing as if the whole thickness of the epidermis had been removed, with a copious, clear, viscid exudation, and attended with intense itching and burning. Later the ulceration extends in depth as well as area, and assumes the characteristics of rodent ulcer. It may be distinguished from eczema by its occurrence in persons after the climacteric period, its abrupt well-defined margins, and its proving refractory to the ordinary topical remedies to which eczema readily yields.

ECZEMA OF THE GENITAL ORGANS (*Eczema genitalium*).—Eczema of the genitals is more common in females owing to the anatomical conformation of the parts, their exposure to leucorrhœal and other secretions, uterine derangements, pregnancy, and consequent congestions of the genital organs. Ordinarily the labia majora are primarily and principally affected; they become hot, swollen, and œdematous, with all the signs of active inflammation; the opposing surfaces may be glued together by the dried exudation. In the chronic form, there is marked induration, the surfaces presenting a dry, fissured, rough, or scaly appearance. The eruption may extend to the mons veneris, the perineum and the inner surfaces of the thighs.

In the male, eczema may affect the penis alone, or with it the scrotum, which, owing to its copious lymphatic supply, may become enormously swollen. The integument is red, shining, often raw in places, the exudation drying in thin crusts or scales. The eruption often extends to the adjacent surfaces.

In a more chronic stage, the natural furrows of the scrotum are deepened, fissures form, with marked thickening and induration of the skin, simulating elephantiasis. The itching is most intense, causing the patient to pinch, rub, or tear the parts in order to obtain relief.

TREATMENT.—In the treatment of eczema of the genitals in both sexes, the antipruritic virtues of hot water should be utilized. After bathing the affected parts for five or ten minutes with water as hot as can be borne, they should be dried with a soft towel and a protective ointment, such as the unguentum diachylon or the zinc ointment, should be applied upon lint and retained in position by means of snugly-fitting cotton drawers. During the day-time, an ointment of the oil of cade may be used. In eczema affecting the penis and scrotum, it will generally be found that the under surface of the penis and the portion of the scrotum with which it lies in contact are most actively inflamed. I am, therefore, accustomed to order a suspensory bandage, such as actors wearing tights or bathers use, which keeps the penis elevated upon the abdomen and thus prevents the irritation from heat and friction with the scrotum. In the dry, scaly form, more stimulating applications may be required. According to Jamieson, Ihle's paste acts in many cases like magic. After the use of the hot water, the paste is smeared over the surfaces, and the spaces between the penis and scrotum and between the latter and the thighs are packed with cotton-wool, which is retained in position by cotton drawers. Painting the labia with a solution of nitrate of silver, potassa fusa, or carbolic acid, often affords relief. The black wash is also an excellent application.

It is to be borne in mind that glycosuria is a most prolific cause of eczema of the genitals in both sexes, and when sugar is found in the urine, the constitutional remedies appropriate to diabetes should be employed.

ECZEMA OF THE ANUS (*Eczema ani*).—Eczema of the anus is a comparatively common affection, most frequently occurring in persons of sedentary habits. The disposition of the veins of the hemorrhoidal plexus, and their anatomical relations with the portal circulation, explain the causal connection of torpidity of the liver, constipation, etc., with eczema of this region. As local determining causes may be mentioned, the passage of fæcal matters, the free acid perspiration, the contact of opposing surfaces, and other irritating agencies to which the parts are subjected. Eczema may be confined to the orifice of the anus or extend to the perineum and genitals. The parts are reddened and infiltrated, deep fissures form in the anal folds, and the stretching of the parts incident to defecation often causes the most intense pain. Itching, which is more or less teasing or tormenting during the day, becomes most violent and atrocious at night; the scratching and tearing of the surfaces aggravates and perpetuates the eruption.

TREATMENT should first of all be directed to the correction of the digestive disorder with which it is so commonly associated. The bowels should be kept freely open, the diet carefully regulated, and proper exercise ordered. The local measures consist in bathing the parts in hot water, followed by a soothing ointment as recommended in eczema genitalium. Fissures and

PLATE XLVI.

FIG. I.—Psoriasis diffusa of the palm.
FIG. II.—Eczema of the palm.
FIG. III.—Eczema rubrum of the leg.

FIGS. I. AND III.—SYDENHAM COLLECTION
FIG. II.—AFTER HEBRA.

itchy painful patches should be touched with a solution of caustic potash, ten grains to the ounce, or carbolic acid, one to two drachms to the ounce.

ECZEMA OF THE LEGS (*Eczema Crurum*).—The surface of the legs is a common seat of eczema, especially in persons of advanced years, in whom the eruption often occurs in an aggravated and refractory form. A number of predisposing causes favor the production of eczema in this locality; the pressure of tight garters, the presence of varicose veins, the existence of old ulcers, the natural dependent position of the parts, all tending to induce passive hyperæmia from interference with the return circulation. The eruption usually begins upon the anterior aspect of the legs in the form of erythematous patches, which become actively inflamed, extend, and coalesce until they involve the entire surface.

Eczema of the legs most commonly assumes the ichorous form; upon no other region of the body is eczema rubrum so characteristically and typically developed. The surface presents a deep red coloration, raw in places, exuding a copious exudation of serum or pus, sometimes mingled with blood, which dries in thin dark crusts. It is attended with the most atrocious itching, causing the sufferer to tear and lacerate the tissues in the effort to secure relief. As a result of scratching and the long-continued congestion, there is often an increased deposit of pigment in the rete mucosum; this brownish pigmentation is apt to be quite persistent, even after the eczematous affection is cured.

Another clinical manifestation of eczema of this region is in the form of circumscribed dry scaly patches, with more or less thickening of the skin. In long standing cases, the infiltration may be so marked as to suggest elephantiasis. The verrucose form of eczema is most often seen about the ankles in connection with eczematous ulcers.

Syphilitic ulcers of the leg are often mistaken for varicose ulcers, which may precede or follow the eczematous process. The former are distinguished by their distinctly circular contour, deep punched out edges, dirty grayish floor, and the surrounding coppery induration. They are more commonly seated upon the posterior surface, and in the middle or upper third of the legs. Varicose ulcers most frequently develop on the anterior or lateral aspect of the legs just above the malleoli.

TREATMENT.—Rest in the horizontal position is a very important element in the treatment of eczema of the legs, with a view of counteracting the stasis of the blood incident to their dependent position. Support to the relaxed vessels and tissues may also be effected by means of bandages or vulcanized rubber cloth. Martin's pure rubber bandages are most valuable adjuvants in the treatment of chronic eczema of the leg, especially when there is much infiltration. The rubber bandage admits of smooth and accurate adjustment, it exerts a constant and equable compression, and thus favors the absorption of the inflammatory products. In cases where the skin is tense, shining, and smooth, without copious exudation, the fixed medicated gelatin dressings, already referred to, constitute an admirable mode of treatment.

Apart from the methods in which mechanical compression enters as a factor, the local treatment is essentially the same as that indicated in eczemas of other regions. In acutely inflamed conditions, ointments of the oxide of zinc or Lassar's paste may be employed. In chronic, infiltrated conditions, stimulating applications are necessary. For this purpose, the tarry preparations, as the oil of cade or the ammoniated mercurial ointment, naphthol ointment, etc., may be employed. The treatment of varicose ulcers is that appropriate to ulcers in general; the healing process may be stimulated by balsam of Peru, iodoform, powdered subcarbonate of iron, by scarifying or deeply incising the edges, strapping, etc.

ECZEMA OF THE HANDS AND FEET (*Eczema manuum et pedum*).—Eczema is often limited to the hands and feet, more often to the former on account of their greater exposure to the action of local irritants. On this account, the so-called "eczemas of occupation" are commonly confined to the hands and forearms, as they are brought into immediate contact with irritating agencies.

The appearance of eczema of the palms is somewhat modified by the anatomical structure of the parts and their constant movement. In the vesicular variety, on account of the thick, resistant character of the epidermis, the vesicles are deeper seated, larger, and more persistent. Eczema rimosum is most commonly and characteristically seen on the palms and soles. The epidermis loses its elasticity from the infiltration and impaired nutrition, and deep cracks or fissures form in the natural lines of motion, which are exceedingly painful and restrict the movement of the parts.

The eruption may occur in the form of circumscribed patches, affecting the centre of the palm or the entire surface, extending over the palmar surface and sides and back of the fingers. The epidermis is dry, rough, and horny, and scales off in the centre of the patch, with an epidermic fringe uplifted, but adherent at the margins.

The diagnosis of an eruption localized upon the palms lies between eczema, psoriasis, and syphilis. Psoriasis may be practically eliminated, since its occurrence upon the palms is of extreme rarity, and always coincident with the appearance of patches of the disease upon other portions of the body.

The differentiation between eczema and syphilis of the palms is extremely difficult, and oftentimes impossible in those cases where the palmar lesions constitute the sole sign of the disease, and a definite history of syphilis cannot be obtained. The test of specific treatment unfortunately cannot be relied upon, since syphilis of the palms proves refractory to internal medication, while both syphilis and eczema may improve under the topical application of mercurials.

Syphilitic affections of the palms usually begin as a small papule, or a patch of papules in the centre of the palm; as these flatten and heal in the centre, the disease spreads by the development of new lesions at the periphery, but not with concentric regularity, so that the patch presents a scalloped wavy outline, with an abruptly marginated border, surrounded by a coppery wall of infiltration. Eczema of the palms, while often presenting a sweeping circinate outline, is not distinctly demarcated, but shades off insensibly into the surrounding skin. Moreover, the eruption creeps over the back of the fingers and in the interdigital spaces, while syphilis is rarely seen upon the dorsal surfaces of the fingers.

TREATMENT.—In eczemas of occupation involving the hands, the first essential is to remove the exciting cause, either by a change of occupation or by absolute protection of the surfaces from exposure to contact with the irritating agents. The fulfilment of this latter indication is sometimes practicable by means of rubber or chamois gloves.

Eczema of the palms most often presents itself in the form of dry, scaly patches, with occasional deep-seated vesicles. The treatment should be essentially stimulating, the masses of dead and partly detached epidermis should be removed, either by rubbing with prepared pumice stone, fine sand-paper, or by vigorous frictions with green soap. This should be continued until the surface is smooth and the epidermal covering of the vesicles is removed and their contents evacuated. The hands should be bathed in hot water for a few minutes, softly dried, and the surface enveloped with strips of prepared lint thickly smeared with diachylon or zinc ointment. As this procedure is most conveniently employed at night before retiring, the dressings should be kept on until morning; they may be retained in position by a bandage or by drawing over them a loose pair of cotton gloves. The next morning the excess of ointment may be wiped off with a dry towel, or the hands may be washed with tar soap. Through the day the hands should be protected by thin gloves, or if the eczema affects the fingers alone, rubber stalls may be worn. A most excellent application for eczema of the hands is the oleate of bismuth ointment, it imparts pliancy and smoothness to the skin, and is most grateful to the patient in relieving the dryness and disagreeable feeling of tenseness almost invariably present. Ointments of tar, oleum rusci, the ammoniated mercury, balsam of Peru, boracic acid, etc., have been recommended. The salicylic acid plaster in any desired strength from five to forty per cent, accurately adjusted to the surface and kept constantly applied, is a most efficient means of removing the thickened epidermis. The salicylic acid constitutes an excellent preparatory of the surface for the curative action of the mild or astringent ointments above mentioned. In eczema of the soles attended with marked thickening of the epidermis, the salicylic acid plaster should be continuously worn until the rough, hardened cuticle peels off, leaving the surface soft and pliant.

Eczemas of the tips of the fingers and the nails are best treated by protecting them with stalls of india-rubber, or the application of lead, tar, or salicylic acid, either in the form of ointment or plaster. Shoemaker recommends the oleate of tin, one to two drachms to the ounce.

SEBORRHŒAL ECZEMA.

Eczema seborrhoicum is a term by which Unna has designated and described a particular variety of eczema which, while possessing an almost endless variety of forms, presents the characteristic features of oiliness, itchiness, a peculiar circinate configuration of lesions, a yellowish color, crumbling fatty crusts, etc. The term includes many cases formerly recognized as seborrhœa sicca. It attacks by preference the scalp, face, inter-scapular and sternal regions, but may affect any region of the body. Although the qualifying term seborrhœal is employed to designate the affection, Unna believes that the disease is due to changes, not in the sebaceous, but in the sweat glands.

An almost unnoticeable eczematous condition of the scalp which may have existed for years as a scaly, dry, slightly itching condition is the starting point for almost all cases of seborrhœal eczema. The eyelids or the cruro-sacral fold may be coincidently affected. There is present a latent catarrh, causing a faulty secretion of fatty matter, and an agglutination of the epidermic scales into lamellæ. The hair becomes dry because of the occlusion of the orifices of the hair follicles.

One of the three following conditions may now exist: *the scaly form;* in which there is an increase in whitish epidermic scales, a moderate amount of fatty material, and gradually increasing baldness. The scalp becomes less movable. The scaliness decreases, complete baldness ensues, and a condition of hyperidrosis oleosa. In other words, we have a simple pityriasis capitis leading to alopecia pityrodes.

The crusty form; in which heaps of fatty crusts and falling of the hair are the predominant symptoms. There is present a *corona seborrhoica* at the edge of the hair. The eruption extends to the temples, the ears, and the neck, or these regions may escape, and the nose and cheeks become affected.

The moist form; in which there is weeping, and the catarrhal appearances are the most noticeable symptoms. It may consist of a pityriasis with redness, in which the fatty scales have disappeared, and the horny layer become exposed; in case excessive exudation has occurred, erosions have been produced, and the rete made visible. This group comprises various chronic eczemas of the scalp. Starting from the scalp, seborrhœal eczema tends to spread downward over the body. Upon bearded portions of the face it appears as dry, scaly, or as red itchy patches, and as slightly elevated yellowish patches about the cheeks, naso-labial fold, and forehead in women. Unless cured, a true rosacea may result, and Unna believes that it constitutes the most frequent cause of this affection in women.

The moist form of seborrhœal eczema is frequently found upon the face of children, the red base being covered with crumbling fatty crusts.

The external auditory canal is almost without exception dry, scaly, and itchy. The most characteristic feature of the disease is observed upon the chest. Here the crusty form is found almost to the exclusion of other varieties, although the scaly form is now and then seen but the moist only when a generalized eczema rubrum is present.

The appearances of the lesions, as they occur upon the chest and inter-scapular regions, have been described by Wilson as *lichen annulatus serpiginosus*, and by French writers as *eczema marginatum.* The chief characteristic is an annular or circular spot, or horseshoe-shaped segment of a circle, with a sharply defined outer border. Sometimes the spot is bow-shaped. The color is a yellowish one, due to crumbling, fatty scales. In the axillæ are found the moist form and also

PLATE XLVII.

FIG. I.—Eczema seborrhoicum of the breast and arms; dry scaly form.
FIGS. II. AND III.—Eczema seborrhoicum universale; mixed wet and dry forms.

AFTER UNNA.

upon the backs of the fingers, while the crusty form occurs upon the flexor surfaces of the arms. That it occurs upon the palms and soles would indicate that it is independent of the sebaceous glands. The epidermis exfoliates in considerable areas, but no weeping takes place. There are found here also heaped up masses of fatty scales, corresponding to the openings of separate sweat glands.

Upon the lower portion of the trunk and upon the buttocks, the crusty form is met with, and here too, at times, are to be seen the same characteristic ring-formed patches. Where two opposing surfaces touch, and especially if sudoriparous glands are abundant in the parts, this form of eczema is frequent. Undoubtedly many cases which pass for the eczema marginatum of Hebra are only instances of this form of eczema in the cruro-scrotal fold.

The differential diagnosis lies between these forms just described and other clinical manifestations of chronic eczema. It must be distinguished from seborrhœa, especially seborrhœa of the scalp, in which are found fatty crusts upon a non-inflammatory and non-itching base. But especially must seborrhœal eczema not be confounded with psoriasis.

Eczema seborrhoicum begins so habitually upon the scalp and spreads downward, and the distribution upon the chest and back, mostly in the middle line of the body, is so striking and characteristic, that these features may be regarded as pathognomonic. The lesions are stationary, but in chronic cases the ringed appearance is lost in a general eczema of the whole body, which may closely resemble a pityriasis rubra, but is to be distinguished from it by the lack of odor, the yellow crumbling crusts, and its more benign course.

The diagnosis of a patch upon the lower extremities must be made from co-existing lesions upon the scalp or upper portions of the body.

TREATMENT.—Sulphur is the remedy which has given the best results. It may with advantage be combined with zinc in an ointment. In the scaly and crusty forms, chrysarobin, resorcin, and pyrogallol act, perhaps, more promptly, and salicylic and boracic acids are recommended in combination. The scalp must be treated after a cure is effected, to maintain it in a healthy condition, and prevent recurrences.

IMPETIGO.

Impetigo is a term which was formerly very indefinitely applied to any pustular eruption. At the present time most authors regard the conditions thus designated as pustular eczemas; still by many the term is employed to designate an acute inflammatory condition of the skin in which discrete, rounded, firm, deep-seated pustules, from the size of a pea to that of a filbert, appear as the primary lesions. They are elevated above the level of the skin, have a slight areola at first, but no surrounding infiltration of the tissues and do not itch.

Though the pustules do not tend to rupture, many authorities describe an *impetigo figurata* in which the pustules run together, rupture, and cover more or less extensive areas, usually upon the face. Such a case is illustrated in Fig. I., Plate XLVII.

IMPETIGO CONTAGIOSA.

Synonym—Porrigo contagiosa.

The disease to which the name impetigo contagiosa was given by Dr. Tilbury Fox, who first described it in 1863 and gave an account of its occurrence in small epidemics, differs in several essential features from the impetigo of previous writers. In the first place, it occurs almost exclusively in children, as a rule under ten years of age, and mostly in those of the lowest classes encountered in dispensary practice. The patients are usually poorly nourished, and show evidences of little attention having been paid to their care and cleanliness, though children previously in perfect health may also acquire the disease. The eruption is preceded by pyrexia which,

PLATE XLVIII.

FIG. I.—Impetigo figurata.
FIG. II.—Impetigo contagiosa.

FIG. I.—AFTER HARDY.
FIG. II.—SYDENHAM COLLECTION.

although at times marked, may in other cases be so slight as to escape notice altogether, indicating that there is a systemic disturbance present before the skin lesions appear. The eruption is confined almost exclusively to the face and head, but is sometimes found upon the legs, back, neck, and hands. In fact it may begin upon the fingers, especially upon the dorsal aspect of the phalanges near the nail, and simulate a burn. The lesions are very superficial and consist primarily of vesicles, at times no larger than the head of a pin, which soon become bullæ by spreading at the periphery until they reach the size of a finger-nail. The contents of the lesions soon become purulent, resulting in vesico-pustules and veritable pustules. They are more flattened than those of impetigo previously described, and sometimes are umbilicated; and, although not deeply seated in the skin, they do not tend to rupture, but rather to increase in diameter and then dry into crusts. The eruption is uniform in distribution, occurring mostly upon the unprotected parts, and especially about the mouth and nose. It is supposed to be spread from one part to another by scratching, but lesions are found upon parts of the back not accessible to the fingers.

That transference does take place between subjects of the disease and healthy individuals is abundantly proven by clinical observations and inoculative experiments.

Various observers have found in the pus and crusts vegetable fungi and micrococci, but none has yet been proven conclusively to be the real growth to which the contagiousness is due.

Mr. Hutchinson, from whose collection Fig. II., Plate XLVII. is taken, says, "the theory is that this eruption is due to the transplantation of pus-cells by the patient's fingers from one part to another. It is believed to be contagious, not only to different parts of the skin of the same patient, but also to other persons. It may originate from any cause which induces the formation of pus, such, for instance, as a scratch." In the case from which the drawing is taken, it resulted from the suppuration beneath the scab left after vaccination. It will frequently be possible to trace a case or an epidemic of the disease to a more or less recent vaccination. Piffard claims that the fungus growth found in the crusts and those found in vaccine crusts are identical, and, indeed, in some instances, the eruption itself resembles that of vaccinia. In other cases a scratch, an irritated insect bite, an otorrhœa, a nasal discharge, or the presence of pediculi capitis would appear to be the *fons et origo mali.*

The lesions appear more or less in successive crops for about a week. The crusts which result from the drying up of the pustules and their contents are thin, flat, yellowish, or straw colored, but at times brownish, dry, granular, or gummy and are not firmly attached to the skin, but appear as though "stuck on." Beneath the crust the surface is excoriated, superficially ulcerated, or the reddened skin is covered with a layer of aplastic lymph, or the skin is dry and glazed. Though usually discrete, the crust may become more or less confluent upon the face. Lesions may appear upon the mucous membrane of the nose, eyes, and mouth.

Fox found that pediculi capitis were usually absent in the cases observed in England, but in this country they are, as a rule, present.

In fact, the disease, as observed here, may differ somewhat from the original description, and present irregular and atypical features. The crusts are not found so uniformly of a straw-yellow color, but have a brownish tinge. In adults an abortive form has been observed.

DIAGNOSIS.—Subjective symptoms may be very slight or altogether absent. Chilliness or fever, together with slight malaise, may precede the outbreak. Very slight itching may accompany the first eruption, or this may be occasionally quite a noticeable symptom at night. Kaposi has found a marked swelling of the submaxillary glands to accompany the eruption upon the face.

In impetigo simplex, the eruption is pustular from the very first, while here vesicles are first present. Furthermore, in the contagious variety, a definite course is run, and adults are rarely affected. The diagnosis must often be made from the appearance of the crusts, as at the time the case comes under observation the primary lesions may have entirely disappeared.

The differential diagnosis is to be made from scabies, ecthyma, syphilis, varicella, vaccinia, impetiginous eczema, etc.

PLATE XLIX.

Varicella is closely simulated, when, as is sometimes the case, the lesions do not tend to spread at the periphery.

Impetiginous eczema may be simulated when the eruption is confluent in patches, but the clinical history is different and cure is much more rapid.

Syphilis is distinguished by the history and concomitant signs of this disease.

In pemphigus, the bullæ are larger, more distended, become less pustular, the disease is neither contagious nor inoculable, and crusts are absent.

Ecthyma occurs oftener in adults, the lesions are attended with more surrounding induration, and occur chiefly upon the lower extremities. The crusts are heaped up, darker in color, and more adherent.

Scabies is distinguished by the lesions upon the hands, papules upon the body, and furrows of the acarus in certain regions.

TREATMENT.—The disease being self-limited, very active treatment is not called for. Tonics and salines may be given in the early and febrile stage in debilitated subjects, but local applications are, as a rule, alone required.

The virulence of the pus should be destroyed as speedily as possible by antiseptic applications.

The crusts should be first removed with care, and such an ointment as the one of the ammonio-chloride of mercury (gr. v. to ʒi.) applied directly to the secreting surface. A five-percent solution of naphthol in oil also acts well.

Should any local cause, such as pediculi or otorrhœa, be discovered, it should be corrected by appropriate treatment.

DERMATITIS EXFOLIATIVA.

Synonym—Pityriasis Rubra.

The term dermatitis exfoliativa is applied to an inflammatory affection, the most essential features of which consist of an intense redness of the skin, attended with an abundant exfoliation of the epidermis in large flakes or lamellæ. The eruption may be limited to certain localities, but more commonly involves the entire cutaneous surface.

Much confusion exists in dermatology as to the proper position of this dermatosis in the nosological category, as well as its etiological and pathological relationships. It has been confounded with desquamative scarlatiniform erythema, pemphigus foliaceus, generalized squamous eczema, diffuse psoriasis, and certain drug exanthems. The frequent development of exfoliative dermatitis as a primary process, and the fact that it exhibits in many cases a special physiognomy with well-defined clinical characteristics, would seem to indicate that it possesses a distinct individuality.

The propriety of including exfoliative dermatitis and pityriasis rubra in the same category has been questioned by many authorities. There would seem to be no well-grounded basis for the establishment of the theory of the separate identity of the two diseases, since they possess identical clinical features and are apparently expressions of the same morbid process.

The term dermatitis exfoliativa should be applied to acute attacks of the disease with a tendency to spontaneous limitation, while pityriasis rubra should include those cases impressed with the character of chronicity, in which the exfoliation is continuous and persistent for months and years and usually associated with marasmus and deep-seated constitutional disorders.

An attack of dermatitis exfoliativa is usually sudden in its outbreak, it may commence with or without constitutional symptoms; ordinarily, there is an elevation of the temperature and other symptoms of systemic disturbance. The eruption appears either in the form of red, itchy patches or as a diffuse redness. It may first develop upon the chest, the lower extremities, or upon any portion of the surface. The redness gradually spreads, sometimes with great rapidity, until the entire cutaneous envelope is invaded; the face, hands, and feet are usually the last to become affected. Exfoliation rapidly succeeds the redness, the epidermis fissures, and becomes separated from its subcuticular attachment in thin scales or flakes of various sizes and shapes. The desquamation may be branny, or the epidermis may peel off in pieces as large as the palm of the hand. The size of the scales varies in different regions; upon the brow, face, and neck, they are fine and small; upon the trunk and extremities, they are larger and coarser. Upon the palms and soles, the epidermis is often detached *en masse;* the entire horny layer may be stripped off like a glove, forming a complete cast of the parts.

The scales are frequently adherent in the centre or at one extremity, the free edge curling over and disclosing beneath an intensely red, angry surface; they may present an imbricated arrangement, overlapping each other like the scales of armor. The scales are easily brushed off by the hand or friction from the clothing, but they rapidly reform, so that a considerable quantity may be collected within twenty-four hours.

When the scales are removed, the skin appears red, dry, shining, and non-infiltrated. Although the eruption is essentially dry and non-exudative, slight moisture or weeping may occasionally occur in the beginning stage. I have observed three cases in which distinct vesicular and pustular lesions were present. One was a psoriatic patient, an attack of exfoliative dermatitis substituting, so to speak, the psoriatic outbreak, which the patient had been accustomed to experience for several successive years with the approach of cold weather. Cases have been observed in which the skin became fissured, ulcerated, and the seat of pemphigoid bullæ. The perspiratory function is commonly partially or completely suppressed.

The mucous membranes, especially the buccal, may be involved by an extension of the process from the skin, and also become the seat of aphthous sores or pseudo-membranous formations. The nails not infrequently participate in the morbid process, becoming opaque; uneven, brittle, sometimes hypertrophied and loosened from their beds by the accumulated epithelium beneath. The hairs may also fall and general alopecia result.

The subjective symptoms consist of sensations of heat and pain, often of a lancinating character, worse at night, which may prevent sleeping. Itching is rarely present. Patients are exceedingly sensitive to cold, and often complain of sensations of chilliness during the first few days of the attack.

In the chronic and graver form of the affection, designated as pityriasis rubra, the exfoliative process is more persistent and continuous. The skin is of an intense dark red color, sometimes cyanotic or purplish in color, without notable infiltration. Upon pressure, the redness fades into a yellowish pigmentation. The scales are small at the beginning, but later become larger; upon the palms and soles the dry epidermis may accumulate in successive layers of exfoliation forming thick masses, as seen in Figs. I. and II., Plate XLIV.

The duration of the chronic form may be prolonged for years; the skin gradually loses its elasticity, secondary changes, as fissures, ulceration, or gangrene occur, and a condition of marasmus or general debility may supervene, terminating fatally, or the patient may die from some intercurrent disease, as phthisis, nephritis, etc.

The nature of this affection is obscure, and its etiology unknown. Unquestionably there is impairment of the nutrition of the skin, resulting probably from an impression made upon the nerve centres or the vaso-motor system. Hutchinson assumes that the changes in the skin are due to a degeneration of the spinal cord.

DIAGNOSIS.—There should be little difficulty in the diagnosis of the acute form; the suddenness of the outbreak, the universality of the skin inflammation, the absence of fluid exudation, and the abundant and continuous exfoliation of dry, thin, papery scales are pathognomonic. The chronic form may be mistaken for psoriasis, eczema, pemphigus foliaceus, or lichen ruber.

Psoriasis is rarely so universal; the scales are smaller, heaped up on a thickened base, more adherent, and minute bleeding points result from their detachment.

In eczema, the redness is rather punctate than uniform, desquamation is not so copious, it is generally preceded by a moist stage, and itching is a pronounced feature. Pemphigus foliaceus may be distinguished by its flaccid bullæ, the ill-smelling secretion, and the existence of moist eroded patches which mark the seat of the lesions. Chronic lichen ruber is rarely so generalized; the presence or previous existence of a papular element would alone serve to distinguish it, as the elementary lesion of pityriasis rubra is always an erythema.

TREATMENT.—The acute form has a tendency to spontaneous recovery, and external treatment is of most importance in relieving the pain and discomfort. The surface should be constantly protected by oily or emollient applications. I am accustomed to direct the patient to be enveloped in sheets saturated with linseed oil. The use of vaseline, the glycerole of the subacetate of lead, or an ointment of the oxide of zinc has been found serviceable.

In the early stage, diuretics, saline aperients, and the use of quinine have been recommended. Especial attention should be paid to the condition of the general health, and any systemic disorders should be corrected.

In the chronic form, when the patient is losing flesh and strength, cod-liver oil, iron, and a most nutritious diet should be ordered. Arsenic and mercury have proven unreliable, and rather pernicious than useful. Kaposi reports the cure of one case from the internal administration of carbolic acid, when other means had failed.

DERMATITIS MEDICAMENTOSA.

Synonym—Drug Eruptions.

Under the general designation of drug eruptions are included all congestive and inflammatory changes in the skin caused by the external or internal use of drugs. These eruptive phenomena are of the most varied and diverse character; every possible lesion of the skin—macules, papules, wheals, tubercles, vesicles, bullæ, pustules, furuncles, ulcerations, gangrene, etc.—have been observed as the direct result of the use of drugs. In their clinical appearances they may simulate most closely the eruptive fevers as well as idiopathic affections of the skin, and on this account a knowledge of the drugs capable of causing cutaneous disorder, the typical features they present, and the differential signs which distinguish them from the ordinary dermatoses, is of the utmost practical importance.

While it is not possible to formulate with absolute precision the distinctive characters of drug eruptions, or indicate definite features by which they may be in every instance recognized and differentiated from ordinary affections of the skin, yet they exhibit certain special attributes which stamp them as a separate clinical class. Certain common characteristics may be briefly referred to. The length of time which intervenes between ingestion of the drug and the first appearance of the eruption varies according to the nature of the drug, the quantity administered, and the sensitiveness or predisposition of the individual. The erythematous and exudative forms of inflammation may appear within a few minutes, or not until after some hours, while others may require the long-continued use of the offending agent to develop its irritant effect upon the skin. In a great many cases, the quantity of the drug employed bears no relation to the severity of the lesions, the effects being due rather to the susceptibility of the individual. The eruptions differ greatly in form and intensity; those caused by many drugs have a peculiar configuration, not absolute and unvarying, but sufficiently constant and regular to be considered as typical, while other drugs may each produce a variety of eruptive forms.

The course of the eruption varies; in some cases it persists in a certain form, in others it becomes intensified if the use of the drug be continued; thus a drug eruption of the erythematous type may, under the prolonged continuance of the exciting cause, be developed into a papular, vesicular, or bullous eruption, while in other cases the indefinitely prolonged use of the drug will be unattended with any essential change in the character of the eruptive element; the acnei-

PLATE L.

FIG. I.—Bullous eruption of the hands produced by iodide of potassium.
FIG. II.—Ulcerating hydroa from bromide of potassium.

FIG. I.—AUTHOR'S COLLECTION.
FIG. II.—SYDENHAM COLLECTION.

Plate XXXXVI

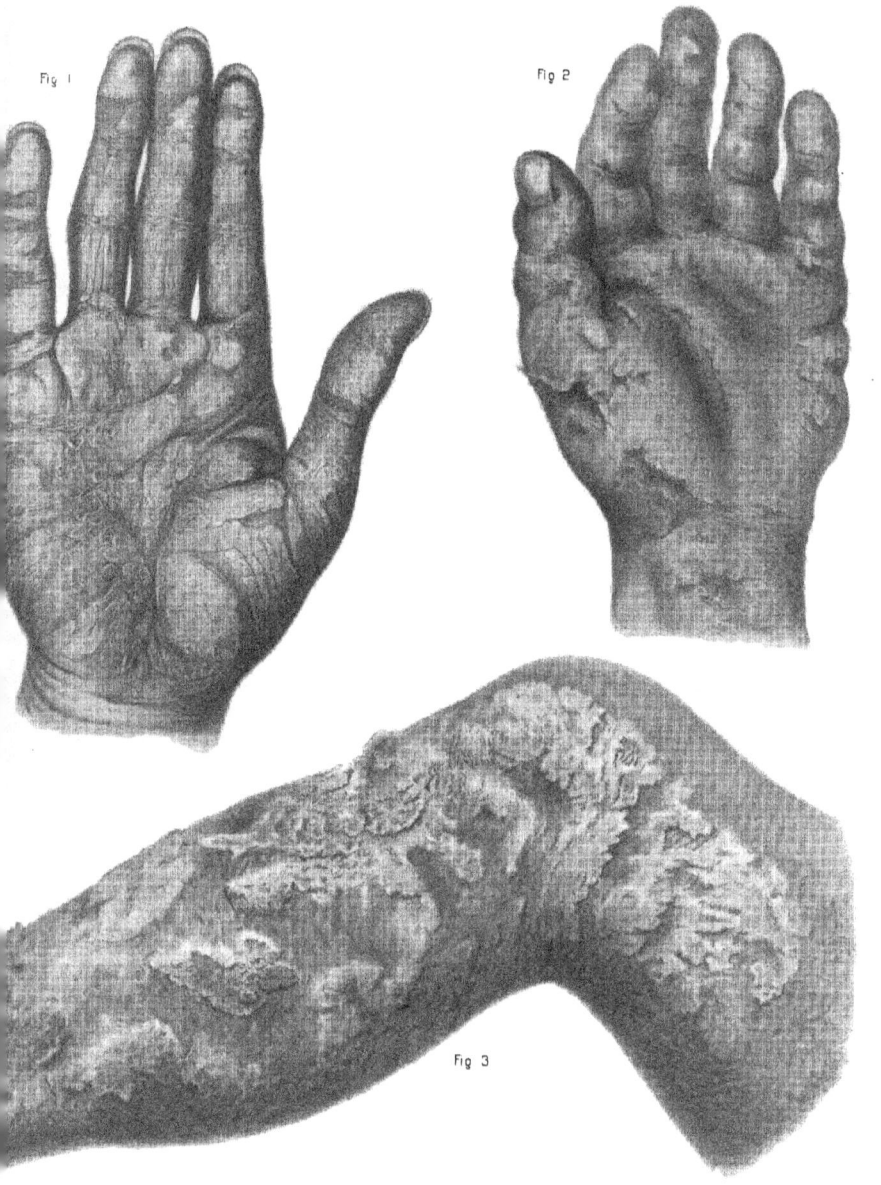

Fig 1

Fig 2

Fig 3

WILLIAM WOOD & COMPANY   NEW YORK

Plate XXXXVII

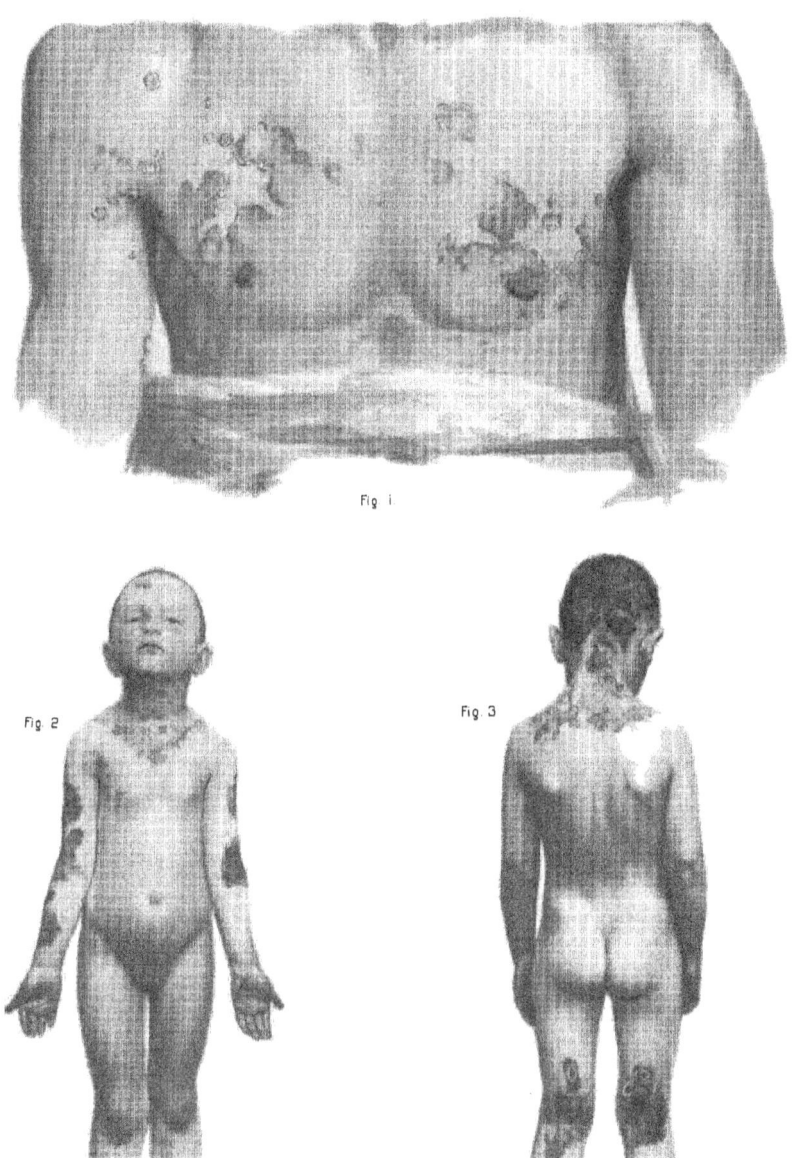

Fig. 1

Fig. 2

Fig. 3

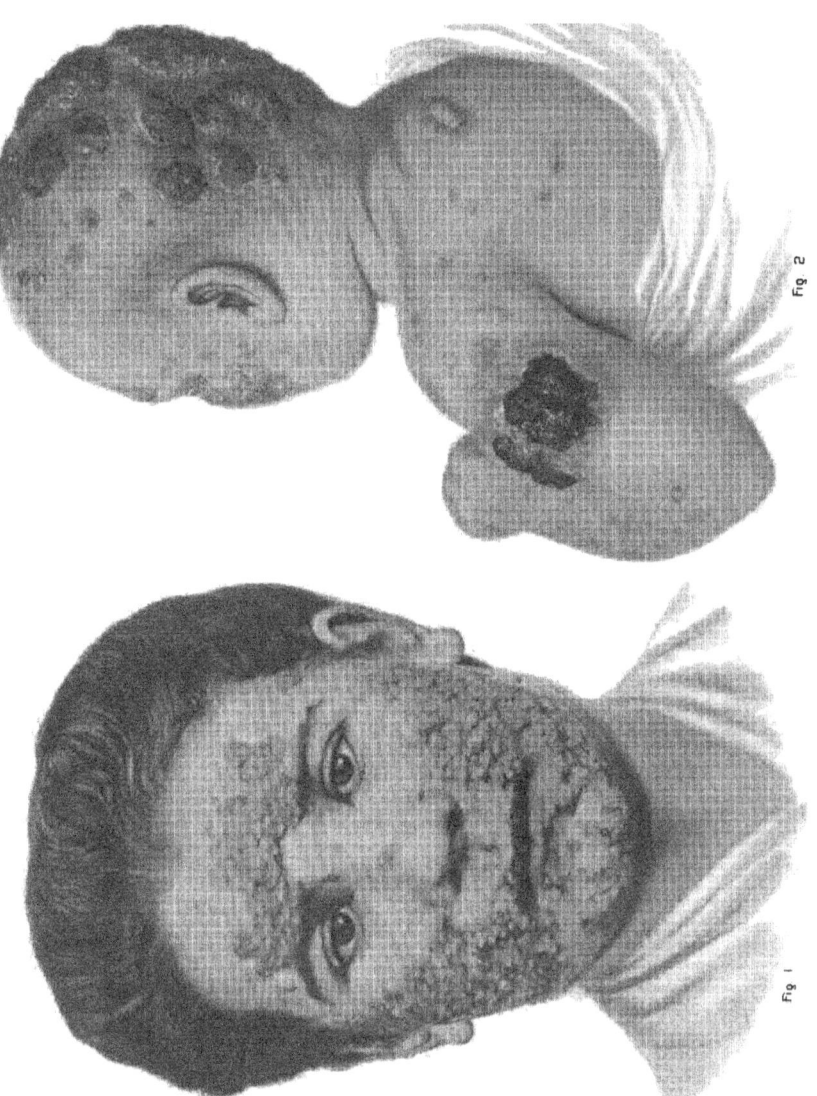

Fig 2

Fig 1

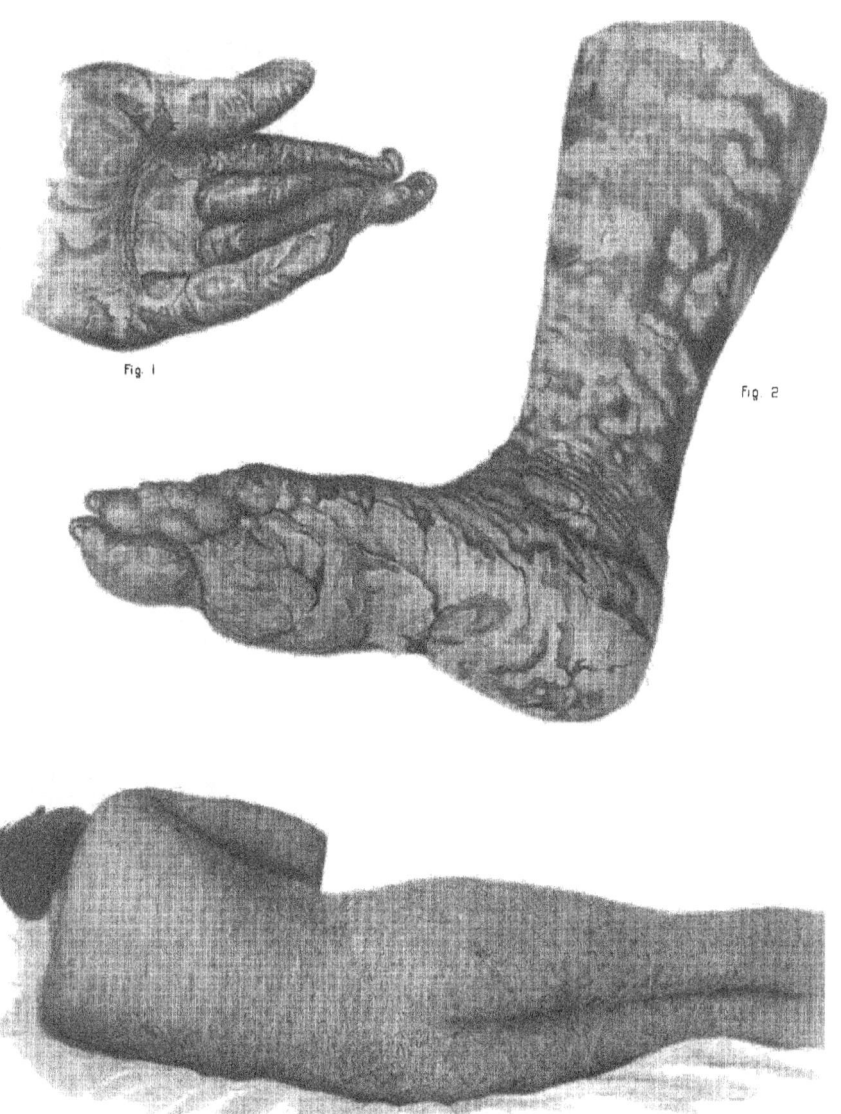

Fig. 1

Fig. 2

Fig 3

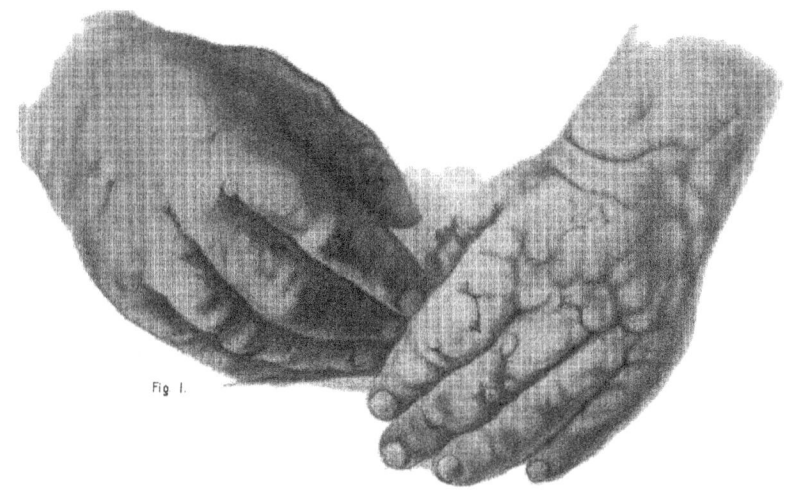

Fig 1.

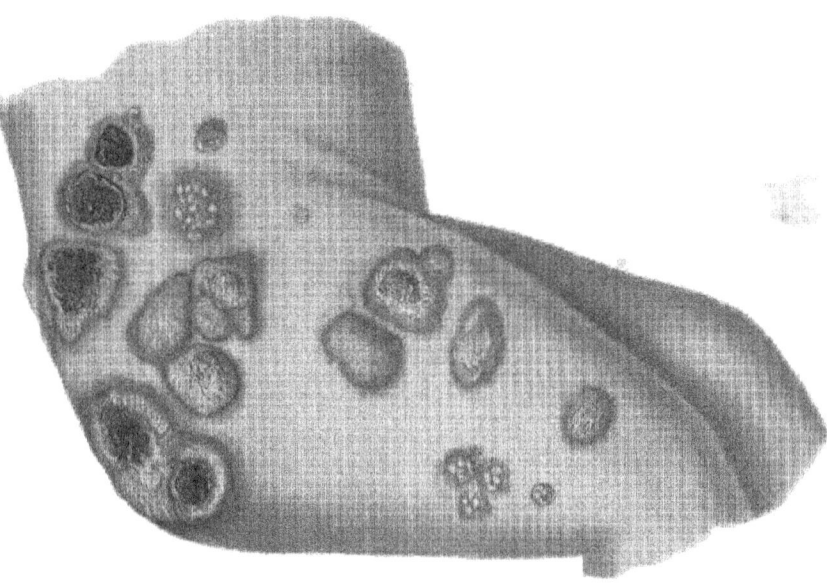

Fig 2

ATLAS

OF

VENEREAL AND SKIN

DISEASES

COMPRISING ORIGINAL ILLUSTRATIONS AND SELECTIONS FROM THE PLATES OF

Prof. M. KAPOSI, of Vienna; Dr. J. HUTCHINSON, of London; Prof. I. NEUMANN, of Vienna;
Profs. A. FOURNIER and HARDY ; and Drs. RICORD, CULLERRIER, BESNIER, and VIDAL, of Paris;
Prof. LELOIR, of Lille; Dr. P. A. MORROW, of New York; Dr. E. L. KEYES, of New York;
Dr. FESSENDEN N. OTIS, of New York; Dr. J. NEVINS HYDE, of Chicago;
Dr. HENRY G. PIFFARD, of New York, and others.

WITH ORIGINAL TEXT BY

PRINCE A. MORROW, A.M., M.D.,

CLINICAL PROFESSOR OF VENEREAL DISEASES, FORMERLY CLINICAL LECTURER ON DERMATOLOGY, IN THE UNIVERSITY OF THE CITY OF NEW YORK
SURGEON TO CHARITY HOSPITAL, ETC.

LIST OF PLATES IN ELEVENTH FASCICULUS.

NEW YORK

WILLIAM WOOD & COMPANY

1889

ATLAS

OF

VENEREAL AND SKIN

DISEASES

It is with special satisfaction that the publishers announce that this large and important work, which they have had in contemplation since 1883, is now ready for publication. It has long been recognized by them, from wide observation and acquaintance with similar works published in this country and abroad, that it is impossible for any one author to furnish, from his own collection of cases and illustrations, the most typical and at the same time the best and most lifelike pictures of the many peculiar forms of these diseases. Appreciating the defects and disadvantages arising from this cause, it was determined from the outset to enlist the co-operation, in the making of this ATLAS, of the leading dermatologists and syphilographers of the world. Prominent among them are Profs. M. Kaposi and I. Neumann, of Vienna. The atlas of the former, of venereal diseases, just completed, and that of the latter, of skin diseases, now being issued in parts, will be largely drawn upon in the preparation of this work, the sole right to reproduce them having been granted us by the authors.

Among other distinguished gentlemen who have engaged to contribute selections from their collections of original illustrations may now be mentioned Dr. J. Hutchinson, of London; Profs. A. Fournier and A. Hardy; and Drs. Ricord, Cullerrier, Besnier, and Vidal, of Paris; Dr. P. A. Morrow, of New York; Dr. Edward L. Keyes, of New York; Dr. Fessenden N. Otis, of New York; Dr. J. Nevins Hyde, of Chicago; Dr. Henry G. Piffard, of New York.

Other names will be added to this list as the work progresses.

The Editor of the work is Dr. Prince A. Morrow, of New York, who, in addition to plates contributed from his own remarkable collection, will write the treatise on skin and venereal diseases, which constitutes, besides the description of the plates, the text accompanying them.

In this treatise, it is aimed to include chiefly those features which are the most practical, omitting in great measure pathological and other considerations which would be more properly treated of in extended writings, rather than as the adjunct to an Atlas.

In regard to the character of the plates, it may be said, they are believed to be superior to anything of the kind heretofore produced—as accurate in drawing as photographs, and far more distinct, while the coloring faithfully represents nature.

The text is printed from new type, large, clear, and handsome, and the paper is heavy, with a highly finished surface.

Altogether, considering the reputation of the authors of the plates, the ability of the editor, the superb execution of the plates, the excellence of the presswork, the high quality of the paper of both text and plates, the large size of the page, etc., etc., this ATLAS OF VENEREAL AND SKIN DISEASES will be the most superb work in medical literature ever published in the English language.

The ATLAS OF VENEREAL AND SKIN DISEASES will be published in fifteen monthly parts, each containing five folio, chromo-lithographic plates, many of them containing numerous figures, all printed in flesh tints and colors, together with descriptive text for each plate, and from sixteen to twenty folio pages of a practical treatise upon venereal and skin diseases; the whole forming, when complete, one magnificent thick folio volume with seventy-five plates, containing several hundred figures, exquisitely printed in colors.

☞ The ATLAS OF VENEREAL AND SKIN DISEASES will be sold by subscription only, at the very moderate price of $2 per part.

WILLIAM WOOD & COMPANY, *Publishers,*

56 AND 58 LAFAYETTE PLACE, NEW YORK.

form eruption of bromide of potassium, for example, may continue practically unchanged for months. Habituation does not come into play; on the contrary, each new exhibition of the drug seems to cause a more prompt irritation of the skin.

The duration of the eruption usually depends upon the continuance of the exciting cause. As a rule, the eruption disappears with the same celerity with which it appeared. The prompt return to a normal state of the skin, so soon as the offending drug is withheld, constitutes the most distinctive and differential sign of this class of eruptions. Sensations of burning, tingling and intolerable itching are generally present, especially preceding the outbreak of the eruption, and during its acute stage in some cases the eruption is completely indolent and causes scarcely any subjective disturbance.

Drug eruptions are often accompanied by the ordinary physiological effects of the drug; in the majority of cases, however, the effect upon the skin seems to be merely incidental, and not a constant expression of the drug's action.

The list of drugs capable of causing cutaneous disorders is very long, embracing many drugs not in common use, and a consideration of their irritant action upon the skin would be lacking in practical value. The drugs in more general use will be taken up in alphabetical order, and the cutaneous phenomena exhibited by each briefly referred to in succession.*

ACIDUM BENZOICUM.—Eruptions of an erythematous, maculo-papular, and urticarial character have been observed from the internal use of benzoic acid.

ACIDUM BORACICUM.—An erythematous type of eruption has been observed from the use of boracic acid; also an eruption consisting of scaly patches quite characteristic of psoriasis. These rashes were distributed over the face, trunk, and extremities.

ACIDUM CARBOLICUM.—The general employment of carbolized dressings in the antiseptic treatment of wounds has produced a variety of eruptive disturbances. The most common form is an erythema manifest upon surfaces where the skin is fine and delicate. The inflammatory reaction may proceed to the formation of vesicles and even a production of gangrene of the skin. The eruption may extend from the region of application over contiguous surfaces and become generalized. It is frequently followed by desquamation, with albumin in the urine, resembling in many particulars scarlatina

ACIDUM PYROGALLICUM.—The local use of pyrogallic acid occasions inflammatory disturbances varying from a slight dermatitis to a destruction of the skin followed by ulceration and sloughing. Its most common and characteristic effect upon the skin is the production of an erythemato-vesicular eruption.

ACIDUM SALICYLICUM, SODII SALICYLAS.—The local application of salicylic acid as an antiseptic in the treatment of wounds is frequently attended with the production of a vesicular eruption, usually limited to the surface covered by the dressing. Numerous forms of eruptive disturbances—erythematous, urticarial, vesicular, pustular, and petechial—have been observed from the internal use of both salicylic acid and salicylate of sodium. Herpetic and pemphigoid eruptions, and in one case gangrene of the lower extremities, have been observed from its use. The erythematous form of eruption produced by salicylic acid and its salts bears a more or less marked resemblance to scarlatina and measles.

ACIDUM TANNICUM.—An erythematous eruption affecting the face and neck has been observed from the use of tannic acid.

ACONITUM.—Congestion, redness, and an eruption of itching vesicles, also an erysipelatous inflammation, have been observed from the external application of aconite. Vesicles, pustules, and bullæ have also been noted from the internal use of this drug.

AMYGDALA AMARA.—Erythematous and urticarial eruptions have resulted from the external application, as well as the ingestion of bitter almonds.

---

* For a more extended description of the irritating effects of drugs upon the skin, see author's work on "Drug Eruptions," Wm. Wood & Co., Publishers, New York, 1887.

ANACARDIUM.—The oil of the cashew-nut is extremely irritant to the skin, producing dermatitis, characterized by papules, vesicles, pustules, and bullæ. The inflammatory disturbance is most frequently of the erysipelatous type, attended with œdema, and may extend to parts distant from the point of application.

ANTIMONIUM.—The external application of tartarized antimony produces an eruption resembling variola in the anatomical form and mode of development of its lesions. Pustular eruptions not infrequently develop on parts distant from the original point of application. Urticarial and vesiculo-pustular eruptions have also been observed from the internal use of antimony.

ANTIPYRIN.—The type of the antipyrin eruption is erythematous, and bears a marked resemblance to the eruption of measles. It is frequently attended with profuse sweating and occasionally followed by desquamation. It is most marked upon the chest, abdomen, and back, but may also occur upon the extremities ; the extensor rather than the flexor surfaces are affected. Urticarial, furuncular, and purpuric eruptions have also been observed from the internal use of this drug.

ARGENTI NITRAS.—A peculiar bluish-gray and grayish-black discoloration, most marked on the face and flexor surfaces, may be occasioned by the prolonged ingestion of nitrate of silver. Argyria derives a certain clinical importance from the fact that it may be mistaken for Addison's disease. An erythematous and papular eruption has also been observed from the continuous use of this drug.

ARNICA.—The strong tincture of arnica causes eruptive disturbances of various form and degrees of severity. The most common form of arnica dermatitis is an erythemato-vesicular eruption which presents a certain resemblance to the poison-oak eruption. Numerous cases have been reported in which large bullæ and blisters running into gangrene and causing partial destruction of the tissues have been caused by the tincture of arnica. Purpuric eruptions have also been recorded. Violent erysipelatous inflammation ending in death has resulted from the application of arnica.

ARSENICUM.—The cutaneous eruptions which follow either the external or internal use of arsenic are similar in character. The application of arsenic to the skin in the form of ointments or pastes, of lotions or dusting powders, as well as its contact from various industrial pursuits in which arsenic is used, may produce inflammatory redness, vesicles, pustules, erysipelatous swellings, and blisters which may be followed by suppurative action or sloughing. The following forms of eruptive disturbances have been observed from the internal use of arsenic: erythematous, papular, urticarial, vesicular, erysipelatous, pustular, and petechial eruptions. Boils and carbuncles occasionally follow a course of arsenical treatment. Gangrene also may occur, especially about the genitalia. Among the incidental effects of arsenic upon the skin may be mentioned certain grayish or brownish discolorations which are especially liable to occur upon the face and various parts of the body after its prolonged use. This pigmentation is comparable to the staining of nitrate of silver, and the bronzed appearance of the skin is similar to that of Addison's disease. Alopecia areata has been developed by the prolonged internal use of arsenic.

BALSAMUM PERUVIANUM.—Erythematous, urticarial, and eczematous eruptions have been observed from the application of balsam of Peru.

BELLADONNA, ATROPINA.—The exanthem produced by the external or internal use of belladonna is usually erythematous in character, and strikingly suggestive of the rash of scarlatina. It is generally confined to the face and neck, but may extend to the upper portion of the chest, and become generalized over the surface. The scarlatiniform eruption may be accompanied with lesions like those of papular erythema and also vesicles. Erythema and partial gangrene of the scrotum have been observed from the internal use of belladonna. The topical use of belladonna may also produce a scarlatina-like exanthem. An herpetic eruption with an erysipelatous inflammation about the lids and face has been observed from a solution of atropine used as an eye wash.

BROMUM AND BROMIDES.—The most common and characteristic manifestation of the irritant effect of bromine upon the skin consists of papulo-pustular lesions which have been termed, from their resemblance to the lesions of acne vulgaris, "bromic acne." As in acne vulgaris, there are associated papules, tubercles, and pustules, affecting by preference regions rich in sebaceous glands. While it manifests a preference for parts where hairs abound, the eruption may surpass these habitual limits and be generally distributed. Erythematous, urticarial, furuncular, and anthracoid, and also vesicular and bullous forms of eruption may occur. Ulcerative forms of lesions, consisting of large, irregular, ulcerated raised patches, denominated ulcera elevata, have also been observed. Papillary hypertrophies and wart-like prominences may result from the long-continued use of bromide of potassium. The severer forms of bromide eruption are often associated with other symptoms of bromism. Numerous observations have shown that the bromide of ammonium exhibits this pathogenic influence upon the skin in the highest degree. The bromide of potassium is less irritant in its effects, and still less so is the bromide of sodium.

CALX SULPHURATA.—The internal use of the sulphide of calcium may produce lesions of a vesicular, pustular, or furuncular character. I have observed a petechial eruption, consisting of a scattered eruption of pin-head to pea-sized petechiæ localized upon the lower extremities, from the internal use of sulphide of calcium in small doses.

CANNABIS INDICA.—An extensive eruption, covering the scalp, face, ears, neck, trunk, and extremities, including palms and soles, consisting of thickly disseminated vesicles, has been observed from the use of cannabis indica.

CANTHARIS.—Vesicular, pemphigoid eruptions may develop upon the skin around a blister caused by cantharides, and extend over the entire surface of the body. Ulceration, anthrax, furuncles, even gangrene of the affected surface, have been observed. Pereira mentions a case in which the application of blisters to the pectoral region caused the development of ecthymatous pustules over the entire body. Erythematous and papular eruptions may follow the internal use of cantharides.

CAPSICUM.—The rubefacient and irritant effect of capsicum, when locally applied, is well known. Erythematous and papulo-vesicular eruptions have been recorded from its internal use.

CHLORAL.—The type of the chloral rash is erythematous, and the inflammatory redness is strikingly suggestive of the scarlatina exanthem. A variety of eruptive phenomena have been observed from the use of chloral—papular, urticarial, vesicular, and petechial eruptions, also deep ulcers with formation of blisters.

CHRYSAROBINUM.—The application of chrysarobin causes an irritation which varies with the strength of the preparation and the susceptibility of the patient. The following forms of inflammatory disturbance have been observed: Hyperæmia with a peculiar purplish discoloration of the skin; erythematous, papular, pustular, and furuncular forms of eruption. An erysipelatous condition has been observed in connection with the use of this drug, causing considerable swelling and puffiness of the face, sometimes leading to closure of the eyes. Chrysophanic conjunctivitis not infrequently follows the application of this agent to the face and scalp.

CINCHONA, QUININÆ SULPHAS.—Various forms of cutaneous disturbance result from the external contact or internal use of cinchona and its preparations. The eruptions which follow the ingestion of quinine are multiform in character. The prevailing type of the quinine exanthem is erythematous, but almost every form of elementary lesion has been observed as the direct result of the administration of this drug. Erythematous, urticarial, papular, vesicular, petechial, bullous, and gangrenous forms of eruption have been observed. The quinine exanthem derives its chief clinical importance from its close resemblance to the rash of scarlatina. This resemblance is rendered more striking from the congestion and swelling of the mucous membrane of the throat and fauces, and the subsequent desquamation which may last from a few days to several weeks. In some cases, exfoliation of the epidermis in large flakes or lamellæ, giving a complete cast of the fingers like a glove, has been recorded.

CONIUM.—Erythematous or papular and erysipelatous eruptions may follow the internal use of this drug.

COPAIBA AND CUBEBS.—The disturbances caused by these two drugs are generally classed together under the name of the "balsamic" eruptions. They manifest a predilection for the wrists, ankles, knees, hands and feet, breast, and abdomen, though occasionally they are generalized. The rash may assume different forms, such as the erythematous, papular, urticarial, vesicular, bullous, and petechial, and derives its chief clinical importance from its resemblance to the erythematous syphilide and the rash of the eruptive fevers.

DIGITALIS.—The external application of this drug may cause an erythema or a papular eruption; its ingestion may produce macular and maculo-papular eruptions, and an erysipelatoid affection of the face followed by desquamation. I have observed an erythematous efflorescence changing into an urticarial eruption of the entire surface, followed by desquamation and albuminuria.

DULCAMARA.—Erythematous, urticarial, and red scaly eruptions have been recorded from the use of this drug

ERGOT.—"Ergotism" may result from the internal administration of the drug. A vesicular eruption with petechiæ has been observed; also a pustular and furuncular inflammation; circumscribed gangrene may occur on the extremities. Hypodermic injections of ergotin may cause painful black swellings and even a phlegmonous inflammation.

FERRUM, IODIDE OF IRON.—An acneiform eruption is the most common cutaneous disturbance, appearing mostly upon the face, breast, and back. The iodide may cause erythematous, papular or urticarial, eczematous and pustular eruptions. (See Iodine.)

HYDRARGYRUM, MERCURY.—The application of mercurial ointment to the skin may cause, according to its concentration, an erythematous or vesicular eruption, sometimes intense dermatitis and sloughing. The use of corrosive sublimate dressings has been followed by a papulo-vesicular eczema and a general erythema. A peculiar roseolous rash has been observed after the use of sublimate irrigations. Calomel, the proto-iodide, and other preparations may be followed by a scarlatiniform eruption succeeded by desquamation. Urticaria, herpes, impetigo, purpura, furuncles, and ulcerative lesions have also been recorded as due to the internal administration of this drug.

HYOSCYAMUS.—The most common form of eruption is erythematous, with œdema and sometimes urticarial wheals. A purplish rash, especially on the face and neck, attended with great swelling, has been reported; also scarlatinal, pustular, and purpuric eruptions.

IODUM, IODIDES.—The local effects of iodine are well known: a yellow stain becoming brownish and followed by desquamation; papular, pustular, and even bullous eruptions may co-exist on distant parts of the body. The internal use of the iodides may give rise to almost any form of cutaneous lesion: erythematous, papular, urticarial, vesicular, bullous, papulo-pustular, anthracoid, petechial, nodular, and polymorphous eruptions have been recorded. The most common form of iodic eruption is the papulo-pustular which presents certain analogies with the acneiform eruption produced by the bromides. It is most habitually seated upon the face and back of shoulders, and in regions where sebaceous glands are abundant. Sometimes it surpasses these limits and is generally distributed. The bullous form of eruption may be ranked among the rarer cutaneous manifestations of the iodides; the bullæ vary in size, and are often commingled with vesicles and pustules, not infrequently they run together, forming lesions of enormous dimensions. The bullous form of eruption is usually limited to the face, forearms, and hands. Cardiac and renal complications have been noted in many cases.

IODOFORMUM.—The external application of this agent may cause an erythematous, papular, urticarial, or eczematous eruption which may develop into vesicles and bullæ.

IPECACUANHA.—The local use, if prolonged, causes irritation and the formation of papules, vesicles, and pustules. Internally, the same drug may give rise to an erysipelatous eruption over the whole surface of the body.

NUX VOMICA, STRYCHNINE.—Formication, pruritus, a miliary eruption, and a scarlatinoid exanthem have been recorded from the internal administration of strychnine.

OLEUM CADINI.—Oil of cade, when applied to the skin, often causes an erythematous and papular eruption which may involve a large surface and assume an erysipelatous form. An affection resembling tar acne has also been described.

OLEUM MORRHUÆ.—The internal use may give rise to a miliary, eczematous, or acneiform eruption.

OLEUM RICINI.—Pruritus and erythema have been reported from the ingestion of castor oil.

OLEUM TIGLII.—The local application of Croton oil causes redness and papules rapidly changing into vesicles and pustules. A secondary vesicular dermatitis may appear upon the face and genitals.

OPIUM, MORPHINA.—A scarlatinoid erythema, accompanied by intense itching and followed by desquamation, has been observed from the ingestion of opium. Morphine may produce similar effects; also an exudative erythematous eruption; red wheals with œdema of the face and eyelids, vesicles, pustules, furuncles and carbuncles, and multiple ulcerations have been reported.

PHOSPHORUS, ACIDUM PHOSPHORICUM.—Flushings, and a bullous, purpuric, or pemphigoid eruption may develop from the use of this drug.

PIX BURGUNDICA.—The prolonged application may cause a vesicular, pustular, or eczematous eruption.

PIX LIQUIDA, TAR.—The external application of tar may cause an erythematous, papular, vesicular, or pustular eruption; the most common form is tar acne: an inflammation of the hair follicles which may end in sloughing. The internal use may cause an erythematous, rubeoloid, and urticarial eruption.

PLUMBUM, PLUMBI ACETAS, PLUMBI CARBONAS.—The external application of these preparations sometimes produces brownish or blackish discolorations of the skin. The internal use may be followed by an erythematous or petechial rash.

PODOPHYLLUM PELTATUM.—Workers in this drug suffer from irritation of the skin and mucous membranes, especially of the genital organs. Topical applications produce rubefacient and vesicant effects.

POTASSII BICHROMAS.—The use of this agent in the industries causes papular and pustular eruptions on the exposed parts of the body, deep ulcers and sloughs, ulcerations of the mucous surfaces, and perforation of the septum nasi.

POTASSII CHLORAS.—An erythematous and papular eruption has been reported from the internal use of chlorate of potassium.

RHUS TOXICODENDRON, RHUS VENENATA, RHUS VERNIX.—Some persons are peculiarly susceptible to the toxic action of Rhus. The eruption is usually of an eczematous type, associated with burning and itching, and the formation of vesicles which run together into large blebs. Œdema and erythematous swelling are not uncommon. Exfoliation of the skin may occur, and an eruption of papules and pustules has been observed. Similar disturbances may follow the internal use of the drug.

SANTONINUM, SODII SANTONAS.—Urticarial and vesicular eruptions, followed by slight desquamation, have been reported from the internal use of these preparations.

SINAPIS.—Redness, burning, vesication, ulceration, and even pustules and violent erysipelatous inflammation may result from the long-continued external application of mustard.

STRAMONIUM.—An erythematous, scarlatiniform or petechial eruption and an erysipelatoid inflammation have been observed from the internal use of this drug.

SULPHUR.—Redness, papules, vesicles, and an eczematous eruption may result from the use of a strong ointment, lotion, or the vapor of sulphur. The sulphide of potassium may cause a violent inflammation with pustules, dermic abscesses, and phlegmons. The internal use of the drug often produces a dark coloration of the skin, an eczematous, papular, or scarlatinoid eruption, and even boils and carbuncles.

TANACETUM, TANSY.—A varioliform eruption has been observed from the ingestion of the oil of tansy.

THAPSIA.—This drug, in the form of a plaster, causes rubefaction, sometimes an intense miliary or erysipelatous eruption. I have observed a pustular eruption on the face from the application of the plaster to the chest.

TURPENTINE, OLEUM TEREBINTHINÆ.—The external application of turpentine causes pain and redness, vesicles, blisters, and dermatitis which is often rebellious to treatment. From the internal use, erythema, a papular and later vesicular and pustular eruption of an eczematous type may result. An erythematous, urticarial, and scarlatinoid eruption have also been reported. Terebene may produce a similar effect.

VERATRINA, VERATRUM VIRIDE.—Used locally as an ointment, according to its concentration, veratrine and veratrum viride may cause burning, smarting, erythema, and even pustular and petechial eruptions. The latter drug, internally, sometimes occasions erythema, pain, and a pustular eruption of the face. Hypodermically, the drug may be succeeded by painful swellings and the formation of an abscess.

The large proportion of drugs above enumerated neither commonly nor specifically produce eruptive disorders, their irritant effect upon the skin being manifest only in certain individuals; it is evident, therefore, that the determining cause must reside in the individual rather than in the drug. So far as we can apprehend the nature of this physiological predisposition, it may inhere in the skin from some structural peculiarity, or it may depend upon a condition of nervous organization, characterized by an abnormal sensitiveness of the vaso-motor system to irritant influences.

Various hypotheses have been advanced in explanation of the mechanism of drug eruptions. The most satisfactory theory is based upon the assumption of the essentially neurotic character of these phenomena. Certain drug eruptions are reflex in their nature, and result from irritation of the sensory nerves of the skin or of the gastro-intestinal mucous membrane, while those which are consecutive to the absorption of drugs are doubtless due to the direct impression of the irritant agent, circulating in the blood, upon the vaso-motor centres.

DIAGNOSIS.—The diagnosis of eruptions produced by the external use of drugs is generally easy, since the irritation is usually limited to the surface exposed to direct contact, and the links in the chain between cause and effect are directly traceable.

The eruptions caused by the internal use of many drugs, especially those of the erythematous or erythemato-papular type, often present a deceptive resemblance to the eruptive fevers. Generally, however, it will be found that the cutaneous symptoms caused by drugs present certain points of dissimilarity with the clinical features of ordinary eruptions. They develop suddenly, usually without febrile or other constitutional disturbance; the subjective sensations are rarely severe, and they rapidly disappear upon cessation of action of the exciting cause. Other diagnostic distinctions may be drawn from the configuration and grouping of the eruption, its limitation to certain predilected parts, and its clinical behavior and course.

In cases of doubt, when a certain drug is suspected to be the offending agent, its presence may often be detected in the urine, sweat, or saliva, since most drugs are eliminated by the kidneys, and a few in part through the salivary and sweat glands.

TREATMENT.—In the majority of cases the morbid changes in the skin originated by drugs have a tendency to spontaneous recovery; the first, and oftentimes the only, indication is to suppress the exciting cause. It may be desirable in some cases to stimulate the functional activity of the kidneys, and thus increase their eliminating capacity, by the free use of diuretics.

In the local treatment of drug dermatitis, the soothing and protective measures already referred to in connection with acute eczematous inflammation may be employed. The surface should be covered with a simple dusting powder, to which a little powdered camphor may be added, if itching be present. If the subjective sensations of itching and burning are pronounced and severe, the various antipruritic agents already recommended will be found serviceable. In the treatment of the severer bullous, pustular, and ulcerative lesions, dressings of carbolized vaseline or of powdered iodoform will materially hasten the reparative process.

HERPES.

The term herpes has been used by writers to designate a variety of different skin lesions, some of which are parasitic and some not. At the present time it is employed chiefly in a generic sense, and includes the benign acute inflammatory diseases whose predominant eruptive element is a vesicle containing a clear fluid. Besides this use of the word, we find *herpes circinatus* and *herpes tonsurans* at times still employed in describing tricophytosis or ringworm; likewise *herpes iris* for the condition treated of in this work under erythema annulatum; *herpes impetiginiformis*, a rare and often fatal affection occurring in the puerperal state, and more properly called impetigo herpetiformis; and *herpes gestationis*, also met with in pregnant women. The last two conditions will be found elsewhere described.

HERPES FEBRILIS.

Under this designation are included several forms of acute outbreaks of vesicles in groups, attended with inflammatory symptoms, and more or less associated with pyrexia and rigors. The individual vesicle is small, and though at times remaining distinct in the group, more commonly they coalesce, forming a patch which soon becomes covered with a crust. There may be one or more such groups upon a given region. The eruption is usually associated with some febrile complaint, and hence is popularly known as feversore when it appears upon the lips, or cold sore when associated with a catarrhal condition. An herpetic eruption is also seen at times in the early stages of pneumonia, in pleurisy, and in the fever following operations upon the urethra. In some instances the eruption comes in apparent perfect health, and, as febrile symptoms are absent, the term would here seem inappropriate. There is no preceding neuralgic pain, as a rule, but rather a burning or tingling sensation in the part, and sometimes tumefaction, before the vesicles appear. Coincident with the eruption there may be itching, and if the vesicles are early ruptured the patch may become painful. This form of herpes has a decided tendency to recur, and in some individuals the intervals between the attacks are quite regular.

The eruption is not confined to the skin, but may occur upon the mucous membranes, and we have *herpes buccalis*, *herpes laryngis*, *herpes linguæ*, etc. It may also affect the uvula, soft palate, pharynx, and other parts. Here crusts will not form and an erosion succeeds the vesicle, producing the subjective symptoms of any excoriation subject to the irritating influences of spiced and acid food, tobacco, etc. The diagnosis is to be made from croup when affecting the larynx, and from aphthæ when in the mouth.

HERPES FACIALIS.—Although herpes febrilis is not confined to the face, it is most frequent in this region, and indeed *herpes labialis* is the name under which it is commonly described, so often is it limited to the lips. As is shown in the plate, the ala nasi may be coincidently affected, or there may be a single rounded patch of vesicles upon the cheek or several such patches may co-exist, but the groups are not so regularly distributed as in herpes zoster, and often coalesce. Recovery is more rapid. Ulceration does not take place and no cicatrices remain. There is a marked tendency to recurrence.

HERPES PROGENITALIS includes both *herpes præputialis* of the male and *herpes vulvæ* of the female. It is a comparatively frequent form of vesicular eruption and occurs upon the prepuce and sometimes the glans and skin of the male organ, and upon the labia of the female. It is much more common in the uncleanly and in those having uncleanly intercourse in both sexes, but is in nowise limited to this class. So often is it seen to follow venereal excess that it has been thought to be due to contagion, and attempts have been made to inoculate the fluid contents of the vesicles and with some success.

PLATE LI.

AFTER HEBRA.

Still this eruption is seen in the most cleanly and independent of any mal-use of the organs. It is usually, like herpes zoster, a unilateral affection, being strictly confined to one side of the organ, but unlike it has a most decided tendency to recur, and is not attended with the neuralgic pain so marked in many cases of zoster. In exceptional instances, the vesicles and the small circular eroded spots resulting from their rupture exist around the whole circumference of the penis, or upon both sides of the vulva and pubic region. The vesicles, which are the size of a pin's head or larger, have been ruptured, as a rule, before the patient comes under observation.

DIAGNOSIS, from the characters presented alone, is, therefore, at times difficult. The erosions have the appearance of having been punched out, being round and well defined. They are very superficial, of a bright red color, discrete or confluent, and often within a few days become covered with a yellowish crust. Ulceration sometimes takes place, a whitish deposit forms over the sore, and a superficial cicatrix results from the healing. The condition must not be confounded with chancroid or chancre, although the poison of these diseases becomes at times inoculated upon the herpetic base. In case of doubt, time will decide the question, for a simple herpes will recover within one or two weeks, while the induration of the chancre will be absent, as well as the tendency to spread usually seen in the chancroid.

Leloir has suggested the following means of diagnosis between chancre and herpes. If a specific sore is pressed between the fingers, little or no secretion comes to the surface, while in herpes repeated pressure will produce a drop of secretion a great number of times in succession.

Itching and burning in the part are symptoms which usually precede the outbreak of herpes.

ETIOLOGY.—Herpes progenitalis occurs for the most part in those who have had some previous venereal disease, and appears to depend largely upon some form of genital irritation. It is frequently observed in men who have an elongated prepuce, and in some cases follows every coitus. Though herpes vulvæ is frequent in prostitutes, it also occurs in those having no connection, the eruption appearing for a season before or after each menstrual epoch. When associated with disorders of the genital system, it is often preceded by increased sensibility and congestion of the parts.

By some herpes is regarded as essentially a neurosis, by others as of traumatic origin. Epstein believes that a relatively slight nerve lesion is sufficient to call forth the eruption on regions covered by delicate skin. He cites a case of recurrent herpes of the index finger the former site of a specific sore.

TREATMENT, in the forms of herpetic disease which we have considered, is mostly symptomatic. The burning and irritation may be relieved by any bland ointment, such as that of zinc oxide, or dusting powder, such as bismuth. If the vesicles have not ruptured, they should be carefully protected. Herpes upon the face may be painted over with a benzoated or otherwise medicated collodion. This is of especial advantage if done early. An ointment of red oxide of mercury, one grain to the drachm, is praised by some. Camphor ice and cold cream are much used popular remedies for cold sores. In treating herpes progenitalis, cleanliness is of the utmost importance. Here, too, the vesicle, if possible, must be protected, and borated or other variety of absorbent cotton should cover the parts which have been previously dusted with some bland powder. A wash of zinc sulphate (gr. v. to ʒi.) may be used if there be much congestion and œdema. To prevent repeated attacks of herpes preputialis, the application of a tannin ointment or wash, or the free use of alcohol to the prepuce is recommended. At times circumcision is resorted to when an abnormally long prepuce favors frequent recurrences.

HERPES ZOSTER.

Synonyms:—Zoster; zona; cingulum; Ignis sacer; shingles. Ger., Feuergürtel.

The features of this variety of herpes are, that it is an acute inflammatory disease, in which the vesicles are tense, firm, and situated upon a more or less highly inflamed or congested base,

PLATE LII.

Fig. I.—Herpes zoster.

AUTHOR'S COLLECTION.

It is unilateral, the groups of vesicles being limited to one side of the body and following the distribution of the nerves; it occurs but once, as a rule, runs a regular course of from two to four weeks, is attended with pain of a neuralgic character, and may leave cicatrices.

The vesicles are closely packed together and grouped into more or less rounded patches upon an erythematous base. They are first filled with a clear or yellowish fluid which may soon take on a milky or greenish-yellow appearance from the production of pus-corpuscles. These fluid contents dry into dark-colored or even blackish crusts, and when they become bluish from being mixed with altered blood, as in the hemorrhagic form occasionally met with, the crusts are quite black. The number of groups varies. There may be only one or two upon the trunk, or so many as to thickly cover the affected region. The latter condition is well illustrated in the plate which was drawn from a typical case in the author's service at Charity Hospital.

These lesions become confluent, bullæ are formed, and at times we find large patches of epidermis raised by the fluid. Where only one or two groups of vesicles are seen, they are situated upon the course of a nerve, and usually near the point of exit of the nerve from the spine or near its ganglion, and also at the extreme point to which the nerve is distributed.

The groups may not all come out at once, but a few be seen at first, and new ones appear as these are beginning to dry up, the process extending over a week or more. The individual vesicles of a group, however, all appear at the same time. By the end of the second week usually all the lesions are covered with dry brown or dark crusts which by the end of another week fall off, leaving behind at times quite marked permanent cicatrices, especially if the vesicles have been ruptured. Pain is a characteristic feature of zoster. It usually precedes the appearance of the early erythematous spots and subsequent eruption of vesicles by some days, and it may be, in individual cases, by some weeks. It is of a neuralgic character and often very severe, and may persist for a variable time after the lesions have disappeared. The older and the more debilitated the patient the longer is the pain apt to last. In rare cases pain is scarcely complained of, the eruption being the first symptom noticed, and the attack ending with the fall of the crusts. In children the pain is, in my experience, often very slight.

The typical zoster occupies one side of the trunk, including an area supplied by several of the spinal nerves. The most usual form is *zoster pectoralis*, which extends from the middle of the back to the median line in front, and has a breadth equal to that of several ribs, corresponding to the region supplied by two or three intercostal nerves. Here the pain preceding the vesicles and the difficulty of breathing may simulate pleurisy. Almost any region of the body may, however, be the seat of a zoster which then takes the name of the part affected. Thus a zoster whose groups begin upon the upper portion of the back and shoulders, and extend down the arm, following the nerve distribution, is called *cervico-brachialis*. In such a case observed by myself, vesicles extended to the finger-tips. One starting out from the region supplied by the sacral nerves, and distributed over the lumbar region, thigh, genitals, etc., is known as a *zoster lumbo-femoralis*. The lesions may be limited to the buttock, or extend to the popliteal space and calf. Upon the anterior surface of the leg they may reach even to the toes. In *zoster ophthalmicus*, or as it is commonly called *zona*, we have one of the most serious varieties. It is not only extremely painful both before and after the eruption, but is attended with great danger to the integrity of the eye. Conjunctivitis is usually present, and there may be iritis, keratitis, glaucoma, and even destruction of the globe.

The eruption here occupies the supra-orbital region, passing upwards over the forehead and scalp. When the forehead alone is affected, it is called *zoster frontalis*. A *zoster capitis* may begin upon the posterior portion of the scalp and pass forward, the lesions being scattered beneath the hair. Thus, as is seen, the disease may take a name from any region it may occupy, but I will only speak of one other form, *zoster faciei*, which has been observed several times as a bilateral affection. Hebra saw it twice affecting both sides of the face, as is portrayed in the plate taken from one of his cases. This illustration would pass equally well for a case of simple *herpes facialis* in which often a bilateral eruption is present. This variety has occasionally been noticed to be associated with or followed by paralysis of the face, usually of the parts supplied by the second division of the fifth nerve.

Strübing has recorded a case in which exposure to a strong draught was followed by severe pain in the left side of the face for three days, and then an eruption of herpes upon the lobe of the ear, cheek, jaw, chin, front and back of neck.   Upon the seventh day the whole side of the face became completely paralyzed.   The orbicularis did not contract, the eyelids remained open and tears flowed over the cheek.   The author believes there was primary inflammation of the sensory branches of the trigeminus which extended to the twigs of the facialis.   Zoster situated in other parts has illustrated the fact that nerves may be affected in their motor functions as well as in their sensory or trophic fibres.   Dr. Gibney, of this city, observed a case of zoster brachialis in a boy to which there succeeded a paralysis of the muscles of the arm.   A number of similar cases are on record.

ETIOLOGY.—The remote causes which may determine an attack of zoster are not always clear.   It is, however, a well-established fact that pathological changes in the nerve centres, ganglia, nerve trunks or branches lead to the outbreak.   The ganglia have been usually found inflamed or otherwise abnormal, and in rare instances disease of the brain and spinal cord has been observed.   In other cases there seems to be only an alteration in the course of the sensitive nerve from its ganglion to the periphery, and this may result from traumatism or disease.

A history of injury is only occasionally found, but neuralgia often precedes the eruption It has been considered by some that zoster has an infectious origin, and they thus account for its being more prevalent at certain times.

Hutchinson and others have reported zoster as a result of arsenical treatment.

Attacks are occasionally observed to follow sudden cold, moral impressions, shock, checking of the perspiration, inflammatory diseases, as pneumonia or pleurisy, as well as direct injury to the nerve.

Gerhardt has advanced the theory that the compression which nerves suffer in passing through bony canals, by the expansion of adjacent blood-vessels, causes sufficent injury to produce zoster.

PATHOLOGY.—Various observers have studied the nerve lesions in patients who have died during or after an attack of zoster, and Bärensprung's view that the disease was one of the ganglionic system has been abundantly confirmed.   Among others, Wyss, in a case of zoster of the face, found the ganglion Gasseri large, succulent, and light red, also a red mass on its inner side, caused by an ecchymosis.   A similar condition was noticeable in the part of the ganglion whence arises the first branch of the fifth.

Kaposi has found destruction of ganglion cells from extravasation of blood.   Pitres and Vaillard found in a case of zoster (the patient having died of pleuro-pneumonia of the same side) that the intercostal nerves showed fragmentation, disappearance of the myeline and complete atrophy of the nerve tubes.   The sixth dorsal ganglion presented an evident diminution of the nerve tubes.   They believe with others that zoster may depend upon alterations of the peripheric nerves, with or without concomitant lesions of the ganglia and corresponding roots.

Lesser believes that a partial tissue necrosis takes place in the skin through failure in functional activity of the nerve, caused remotely by disease of its ganglion, or by an injury which the nerve may sustain in its course from the ganglion to the minute ramifications in the skin.   In rare instances disease of the brain or spinal cord has been noted, and the ganglia appeared to be only secondarily affected.

Nys has studied zona as occurring in tuberculous subjects, having found twenty-five instances on record.   Raymond thinks these cases easily explained by the hypothesis of a central lesion, produced by a meningo-myelitis under the form of isolated tumors, or of diffuse nodular or infiltrated lesions.

DIAGNOSIS is easy in zoster extending half-way around the body in an interrupted band limited to one side of the chest or abdomen.   Zona ophthalmica or that of the head may not be so readily recognized as many lesions are covered by the hair. In atypical cases with scanty eruption, we must be guided by the history of preceding pain, the absence of itching, the febrile disturbance, the grouping upon a hyperæmic base of tense vesicles in circular clusters, which are at first clear and may become opaline or purulent and dry into brown crusts. It is to be distinguished from other forms of herpes by the unilateral distribution of eruption, and its tendency to occur but once in an individual, though cases are on record in which it has appeared a second time and even oftener. Likewise it may affect both sides of the body in exceptional cases; even a one-sided zoster may pass for a limited distance beyond the median line. In zoster of the arm or leg, as elsewhere, the nerve supply can at times be distinctly traced in the distribution of the lesions and this may aid greatly in making a diagnosis. From eczema it is distinguished by the larger-sized vesicle, which does not rupture and exude, by the grouping, and heat, burning, or pain instead of itching. In erysipelas there is a deeper red color, and a line of demarcation, as well as more severe constitutional symptoms.

Rare forms, such as *zoster hæmorrhagicus* and *zoster gangrenosus*, are occasionally encountered, and though not so readily diagnosed, the main general characteristics will be present. Leloir describes a case of "black herpes" over the crest of the ilium in a pregnant woman. It began as a bluish patch two or three inches in diameter which became gangrenous.

Prognosis as to severity depends upon the age and general condition of the patient, and the region affected. An ordinary case will recover spontaneously in from ten days to three weeks. The pain may persist for several months. In the region of the eye, grave results may follow, and death has been known to occur after the destruction of the globe from subsequent phlebitis and pyæmia. If the vesicles are ruptured, ulceration may take place and pitting scars be produced.

Treatment.—Being, as we have seen, a self-limited disease, the neuralgic pain is the symptom requiring the most attention, and aside from this the prevention of rupture of the vesicles is all that is required unless the patient from his general condition stands in need of a tonic course. The pain may be relieved by internal remedies or by local applications. Opium or morphine may be given by the mouth, or hydopermic injections may be made in the painful region. Thompson has recommended the phosphide of zinc in one-third of a grain dose every there hours. Great relief follows arsenious acid combined with quinine and bromide of potash and given in $\frac{1}{16}$ grain dose, three times daily in severe cases.

The salicylate of soda has been recommended by several French observers. Duhring has used with advantage the fluid extract of Grindelia robusta as a lotion. Anodyne ointments and washes containing opium, belladonna, etc., are advised by some. Others prefer, as I myself do, dusting powders. These may consist simply of buckwheat flour, corn-starch, the subnitrate of bismuth or other bland powder, to which may be added camphor or morphine if desired. This is to be dusted thickly over the groups of vesicles and intervening sound skin, and a wide bandage or pillow-case, also dusted with the powder, snugly applied about the part. Individual groups may with advantage be painted with flexile collodion in which morphine (gr. v.-x. to ʒi.), benzoin, menthol or other medicament is dissolved. The application of the constant galvanic current often gives great relief. Five or more cells are required, and the electrodes should be held upon the course of the nerves for fifteen minutes each day, or the negative pole placed over the spine, and the positive wet electrode over the seat of pain. It is possible thus not only to relieve the pain, but to arrest the development of vesicles if employed early. If the after-pains do not give way to electricity, the Paquelin cautery may be used to "fire" the region of the spine from which the affected nerves originate.

PLATE LIII.

Fig. I.—Dermatitis herpetiformis.
Fig. II.—Dermatitis herpetiformis (back view).

AFTER ROBINSON.

DERMATITIS HERPETIFORMIS.

Synonyms.—Dermatitis multiformis. Fr., Dermatite polymorphe prurigineuse chronique.

In 1884, Dr. Duhring described a remarkable and rare disease of the skin having multiform lesions, running a very chronic course, attended with much itching and subsequent pigmentation of the skin, which, because of the almost constant eruption of vesicles in more or less distinct groups, he has classified under the comprehensive term of *Dermatitis Herpetiformis*, including with it a variety of ill-defined affections hitherto known under other names.

A variety of symptoms and lesions with irregular evolution characterize the disease, one form of which had been previously described by Hebra under the name *impetigo herpetiformis.* This Duhring regards as a severe pustular form of the same general process, and thinks there is no doubt of the relationship between it and dermatitis herpetiformis. In like manner are included the conditions formerly known under such titles as *herpes circinatus bullosus, herpes chronicus, pemphigus pruriginosus, pemphigus circinatus, herpes phlyctenodes,* and *herpes gestationis.*

SYMPTOMS.—In severe cases, more or less malaise and febrile symptoms have been observed at the onset of an attack, followed by an eruption which may appear upon any portion of the body. It may be either erythematous, papular, vesicular, bullous, or pustular, or several different forms of lesion are found combined. It may resemble erythema multiforme, or the pigmented skin may cause it to simulate the first stage of confluent small-pox. The vesicles vary from the size of a pin-head to that of a pea.

They may be angular or of irregular outline, and their fluid is pale yellow; they are often disseminated, and, unless closely grouped, are without areola. Bullæ may reach the size of a hen's egg and be distended with fluid similar to that found in pemphigus. The pustules begin as such, are at first small and flat, but increase to the size of a pea in from two to six days, and have a deep red areola. They may appear in clusters just as the vesicles do. As the original pustules crust over, a circle or segment of a circle of new ones appears immediately around them, and the whole patch becomes covered with a greenish or dark-colored flat crust. Large patches may thus be formed. No definite sequence of eruption is observed. An erythema may pass into any one of the other forms of eruption, and within a year all the varieties may have been present. Where recurrences take place, this multiformity becomes more apparent, but the herpetic character usually remains more or less pronouced throughout, or is marked from time to time. Pigmentation is usually present even before the process has become very chronic and thickening of the skin has occurred. Besides the itching, sensations of burning or prickling are also complained of with each eruption of new lesions. Attacks may occur every few months or once or twice a year for a number of years in succession, and during the intervals the skin may be quite free. Or, in the form previously known as:

HERPES GESTATIONIS, the eruptive phenomena may be observed only with each successive pregnancy. This latter variety of herpetic disease was first described by Milton in 1872. It is a rare form, occurring in the puerperal state. Other lesions, such as erythematous spots, papules, and bullæ may be present, but the vesicle is the lesion usually succeeding the erythema. It occurs chiefly at first upon the extremities, but has also been observed about the umbilicus, and may remain local or become a generalized eruption. The same sensations of irritation, burning, pruritus, etc., are experienced as in other forms of dermatitis herpetiformis. The bullæ are rarely observed to become purulent. The lesions may disappear shortly after delivery, or persist for a month or more or pass into a chronic state. In some instances they do not make their appearance until after delivery.

A number of dermatologists do not agree with Duhring that herpes gestationis and Hebra's impetigo herpetiformis should be included as varieties of dermatitis herpetiformis.

ETIOLOGY.—The cause of the affection is still obscure, but it appears to depend upon à variety of distinct pathological conditions, without bearing any constant and characteristic etiological relation to any one definite morbid process. Probably grave nervous disorders are present in many cases.

Besides the neurotic origin and reflex nervous disturbances, we may have a septicæmic condition to account for the severe and sometimes fatal pustular forms observed in the parturient state, while the variety last described appears to depend upon the gravid uterus. The disease occurs mostly in middle adult life, and men and women are equally subject to it. Dr. Sherwell has found diabetes associated with the eruption, and in a case of Dr. Bulkley, generalized sarcoma was discovered at the autopsy, and it is probable that, as our knowledge of the pathology increases, we will find severe internal disorders having this dermatitis as an outward expression.

DIAGNOSIS.—In no other skin affection are such varied combinations met with. Besides the primary lesions, excoriation from scratching and dirty yellow variegated pigmentation and thickening of the skin are usually present. The diagnosis is not always easy in the first attack, but it would not readily be taken for an eczema. Pemphigus is simulated when the bullous form exists alone, but the general health is not so affected. Herpes iris or erythema bullosum is a more benign and acute affection. In the bullous form of urticaria, wheals are present or can be produced by irritation. Prurigo is an affection beginning more constantly in early life, and has peculiar features which would serve to distinguish it as well as impetigo, ecthyma, herpes, scabies, and dry eruptions from the disease under consideration.

TREATMENT.—The disease has so far appeared to be little influenced by treatment. If the morbid condition upon which the eruption depends can be discovered and removed in any given case, recovery from the skin lesions will naturally follow. Large doses of arseniate of soda have acted well in the experience of some; it should be given in moderate dose at first and rapidly increased. Brocq advises hydrobromate of quinine, thirty to sixty centigrams a day, with from five milligrams to three centigrams of ext. belladonnæ.

Aside from the treatment by drugs, the use of coffee, tea, alcoholics, tobacco, and indigestible articles of food should be forbidden, and the functions should be kept normal. Tonics containing strychnia may be given in some cases with benefit; also cod-liver oil and nerve sedatives.

Local applications of carbolic-acid lotion, naphthol dissolved in oil, sublimate solution, or hydrocyanic acid in a wash will relieve the itching and heat of the skin. Vaseline, glycerole of starch, or dry dusting powders will be found better suited to some cases.

The case represented in the plate occurred in the practice of Dr. Robinson, of this city. As an exception to the rule, the patient was a boy only ten years of age, who had suffered from a similar eruption three years before. This attack had existed for two months. The groups and rings of vesicles and bullæ are seated upon an inflamed base. A collection of serum has occurred in the apex of papular lesions, vesicles have formed and increased in size by peripheral extension, the centre gradually becoming normal, thus producing a condition resembling ringworm. Bullæ with clear contents are also present, surrounded by a red areola; new bullæ have occurred about the original in annular form. These secondary bullæ are marked on the anterior surface of the abdomen and thorax. Small vesicles can be observed at the periphery of the patches. Neighboring patches coalesce to form excoriated areas which might resemble eczema rubrum. There are also to be seen isolated bullæ resembling those of pemphigus or varicella. Intense itching and marked pigmentation characterized the eruption, the individual lesions of which lasted for two or three weeks. Treatment consisted in the administration of nine drops of Fowler's solution three times each day, under which the eruption disappeared in about two weeks.

PEMPHIGUS.

Pemphigus is a term signifying a *bulla*, and it is employed to-day to indicate an acute or chronic inflammatory process attended with the production of various-sized, more or less rounded blebs upon the skin, and occasionally the mucous membranes. The eruption of bullous lesions is usually a successive process, sometimes attended with fever, and the fluid contents of the bullæ may be either clear serous, or may become purulent or hemorrhagic. It is one of the rarer forms of skin disease. Two distinct varieties are encountered: pemphigus vulgaris and pemphigus foliaceus. The former may run either an acute or a chronic course, while the latter is always chronic, and often fatal.

PEMPHIGUS VULGARIS

Represents the more typical and common disease. It may have such prodromal symptoms as chills, fever, and headache; or the bullæ may arise upon the normal skin of an apparently healthy person; or bright-red, erythematous spots may precede the first as well as subsequent crops of blebs. The lesions occupy either a limited area or are scattered over the whole surface. They are tensely distended with fluid at first, but are usually soon ruptured, or the walls shrivel up as the contents evaporate or become absorbed; and if the epidermis, of which the walls are composed, becomes detached, the surface beneath is found to be bright red, but the discharge from it soon dries into a crust. When this in turn falls off, a red spot is left which becomes pigmented and may remain so for a long time. In size, the bullæ vary from that of a pea to that of a goose egg, and are discrete or more or less grouped. They develop quite suddenly, and before a given crop has run its course of from a few days to a week, new bullæ appear, and thus the disease is protracted and large patches of denuded corium may be produced by the coalescence of old and new lesions. Cicatricial tissue, however, does not result. There is often more or less disturbance of the general health. Besides fever, there may be diarrhœa, prostration, and loss of appetite. The course may be acute or chronic.

PEMPHIGUS ACUTUS.

The acute form of pemphigus is by far the least common, and many dermatologists of large experience have never observed it, while others recognize it only as occurring in childhood. Lepoise described it as early as 1618, and Willan collected cases and gave an account of it. Cazenave has also given a description of the acute disease. Gilibert wrote upon the subject, considering it as a fever accompanied by derangement of the nervous and digestive systems. A sufficient number of carefully studied cases have now been reported to place the question beyond doubt that the acute disease now and then attacks adults as well as children. In the accompanying plate is represented a well-marked case of pemphigus vulgaris running an acute course which occurred in my service at Charity Hospital. The patient, aged thirty-three, had yellow fever ten years ago, and has since had intermittent fever, pneumonia, and rheumatism, but never any previous eruption, and had been well for some time prior to this attack. On Jan. 10th, an intense itching was first noticed, followed on the 12th by a chill, malaise, nausea, restlessness, cessation of pruritus, and an eruption of small bullæ upon the parts which had been most itchy. The following day new bullæ appeared, and the first crop increased in size. Febrile symptoms, extreme weakness and prostration with dry and thickly coated tongue were present for the next few days, when a dozen or more large-sized bullæ were found upon the chest, back, and arms. Such lesions continued to appear almost daily, springing from healthy-looking skin as a rule, and not from preceding erythematous spots, until Jan. 24th, and a continuous fever ranging at times over 104.5° persisted for nearly a month. The corium became exposed over almost the whole of the back from decubitus, and rupture of the separate lesions upon the front of the body was followed by bright-red, excoriated, moist or glazed surfaces. Though no preceding erythema was noticed excepting in the lesions upon the forehead which ruptured and resulted in a denuded patch, almost all the bullæ were surrounded by a faint areola. Upon the shoulders and upper chest small bullæ were grouped together. The fluid in the blebs, while at first usually clear or

PLATE LIV.

FIG. I.—Pemphigus vulgaris.
FIG. II.—Pemphigus foliaceus.

FIG. I.—AFTER ALLEN.
FIG. II.—SYDENHAM COLLECTION

light colored and of alkaline reaction, soon became acid and of opaline, milky, yellow, and even greenish hue, and a few were hemorrhagic. The crusts which formed were at first yellowish, but soon became dark brown and crumbly. The patient remained under observation for several months after recovery and showed no signs of recurrence, and nine months later reported himself well. The situation of each lesion was plainly marked by a dark-red pigmented spot.

TREATMENT.—Quinine and tonics containing bark and strychnia, liberal diet, ale, wine, etc. Antipyrin to reduce the temperature. Arsenic in gradually increasing doses up to fifteen drops of Fowler's solution three times daily.

Local treatment consisted in carefully puncturing the larger bullæ and evacuating the contents without removing the bleb wall, and then applying a protective antiseptic paste made with starch and bismuth.

Acute pemphigus in children is more frequent than in adults. The bullæ arise upon the extremities, most noticeably upon the backs of the feet and hands. Favorable cases recover in three weeks or a month, but sickly children may die, especially if the eruption is abundant or hemorrhagic.

PEMPHIGUS NEONATORUM is usually an acute disease. It does not appear at birth, but, as a rule, at least nine days later, or perhaps only after the lapse of several months. Clear bullæ which do not readily become pustular occur upon the neck, shoulders, and trunk. The palms and soles escape or are but slightly implicated. It is thus distinguished from the bullous form of hereditary syphilis which is often a strictly congenital lesion, bullæ being present at birth or occurring within a few days, especially upon the palms and soles. In pemphigus neonatorum, there is usually no fever, and the eruption runs a favorable course of from a week to three weeks' duration.

Severe cases may be attended with diarrhœa, aphthæ, emaciation, and end fatally.

Payne, Legg, and others have reported pemphigus beginning shortly after birth, and running a chronic course extending over several years.

PEMPHIGUS CHRONICUS.

Much the more usual form in which pemphigus vulgaris is encountered, runs a course extending over years, during which successive outbreaks of bullæ occur. If the patient's general condition and surroundings are good and the type of disease be mild, recovery will take place. If opposite conditions prevail and the type be malignant, with production of large and numerous bullæ, the course will be unfavorable. Most cases are benign and the number of lesions limited, but each attack may last for several months, and recurrences be more or less frequent, with corresponding effect upon the general health. The bullæ are the same as those of acute pemphigus and run their course in from two to eight days, being succeeded by new crops. Itching and burning may precede and accompany the eruption. Pruritus is at times quite severe, and the patient may so injure the lesions by scratching as to cause ulceration, and thus decrease the chances of recovery. Instead of clear or purulent fluid, the bullæ may have hemorrhagic contents in debilitated subjects. Intercurrent disease often terminates the patient's life, the eruption having disappeared when the incidental affection began. Pemphigus recurring at each menstrual epoch, and with each successive pregnancy, has been frequently reported. Many such cases would undoubtedly now be classed with dermatitis herpetiformis (*herpes gestationis*).

PEMPHIGUS FOLIACEUS.

This name was given by Cazenave to a very rare and severe variety of bullous eruption, because, instead of being tense, the bullæ contain but little fluid and their walls soon become flaccid, and dry with the secretion into thin, flaky crusts. The epidermis appears as though undermined, and shreds or scales of whitened cuticle lie upon the red, excoriated, or superficially ulcerated base, giving the appearance of a scald. The corium is laid bare, and does not tend to heal. The scales are constantly being detached and new ones produced. New blebs form about those first appearing, and readily coalesce by peripheral extension until large areas are affected. The disease is very chronic and may last for years, the whole body becoming gradually implicated and the general health undermined. The hairs fall in the late stages, the nails become brittle, ectropion occurs, the whole surface becomes more or less denuded; febrile attacks, loss of appetite, diarrhœa, and a condition of extreme pain and misery succeeds, from which the patient usually finds relief in death. The lesions may appear first upon a mucous membrane, and the skin be subsequently affected. Cases beginning as a pemphigus vulgaris with tense bullæ have occasionally been observed to change to the foliaceous type, and in well-marked cases of the latter, the formation of typical tense blebs now and then would indicate a close connection between the two.

ETIOLOGY.—Little exact knowledge is possessed regarding the cause of pemphigus. Generally there is some systemic derangement, and nerve changes may be made out. It often occurs in the spring time, and is seen in children after measles, typhoid, pneumonia, etc. Most cases of acute pemphigus occur in children under the age of four years. Colrat, Spillman, Gibier, Riehl, and others have found micro-organisms within the bullæ of acute pemphigus, and, indeed, instances have been reported which would make it appear to be contagious under certain circumstances. Thus parents and attendants of children with pemphigus have in several instances developed bullous eruptions upon the breast, lips, and fingers. It has also been observed to occur in small epidemics, and among children attended by the same midwife. The bacteria described by different observers are not identical, those of Gibier being in series of from two to twenty joints arranged in chaplets. Thin failed to find them. Riehl, on the other hand, found fungous elements and clusters of conidiæ resembling those of tricophyton, which he believes produce the bullæ. Inoculations have, however, been unsuccessful. Many observers have found disturbances of the nerves in chronic pemphigus, especially of the vaso-motor system. Ferraro and others describe alterations in the nervous system in pemphigus foliaceus, consisting of atrophy of the nerve-cells in the posterior horns of the cord, inflammatory lesions of the nerves, and sometimes of the ganglia. The primary cause of these lesions, it is thought, may be attributable to infectious elements of parasitic nature. This would seem probable from what we know of bullous eruptions in lepra subsequent to nerve changes and presumably due to the lepra bacillus. Acute febrile pemphigus, from its stages of invasion, eruption, efflorescence, and decrustation, resembles the exanthemata.

Uterine disorders and pregnancy are causative agencies in a recurrent form of bullous eruption which has been described. Heitzmann and Duhring were led to regard pemphigus and impetigo herpetiformis as kindred diseases.

ANATOMY.—In the formation of bullæ which are superficially situated, the lower cells of the rete are separated, the upper layers are flattened. The papillæ are enlarged, as are also the blood-vessels. Hence the hyperæmia at times present before the fluid is exuded. The bleb-wall is composed of the corneous layer of the epidermis and the upper portion of the rete. The fluid is alkaline at first, and may become acid, as instanced in my case of acute pemphigus in the adult.

DIAGNOSIS.—We must not confound with pemphigus other diseases in which bullæ occur, such as herpes, urticaria bullosa, erysipelas, eczema, impetigo, scabies, pompholyx, erythema bullosum, hydroa, drug eruptions, feigned eruptions (pemphigus hystericus) from pressure and the application of cantharides and other drugs; solitary bullæ, especially on the hands and feet, due to pressure, cold, heat, etc.; and the bullous eruptions of syphilis and lepra. The bullæ of syphilis dry into thick dark or greenish crusts, beneath which are excoriations or ulcerations. Other signs of syphilis are often present. Pemphigus foliaceus must further be distinguished from dermatitis exfoliativa and pityriasis rubra.

TREATMENT.—Besides the general line of treatment indicated for acute pemphigus, dusting powders of any inert substance can be applied. In chronic pemphigus, the continuous bath has been resorted to with benefit. If pruritus is marked, some preparation of tar will be found service-able. Antiseptic absorbent cotton applied to all regions affected will absorb the discharge, and give a certain amount of comfort and protection. In the chronic form, all means to preserve the strength are indicated: generous diet, wines, iron, quinine, strychnine, bitter tonics, and mineral acids. Here, as in the acute form, arsenic exercises the most beneficial influence, and in some cases acts almost as a specific. The dose must be large and long continued. In pemphigus folia-ceus, arsenic does not act so favorably. Dr. Sherwell, of Brooklyn, has used with much success topical applications of linseed oil, wrapping the patient up in cloths saturated with it. He also praises the free use of the oil as an internal remedy. In most cases, treatment will be simply pal-liative. Powders and antiseptic cotton may also be here employed as dressings, while all hygienic and supporting means are being carried out.

PURPURA.

The essential character of this disease is the spontaneous development upon any part of the body, but especially the lower extremities, of hemorrhagic spots or patches, which do not dis-appear under pressure. Various forms have been described, but the two varieties of purpura ex-isting as an independent disease, under which all others may be included, are, *purpura simplex* and *purpura hæmorrhagica*. In many cases we must look upon the skin lesions rather as symptom-atic of other disease, sometimes of a severe nature, and it is probable that several affections of dif-ferent nature have been included under *purpura rheumatica*, *purpura contagiosa*, etc. Stephen Mackenzie looks upon all purpura as a symptom, and suggests its division into vascular, toxic, mechanical, and neurotic forms.

PURPURA SIMPLEX

Is the more common variety, in which cutaneous hemorrhage occurs as a primary lesion. Small round or oval purplish-red spots or petechiæ occur, symmetrically distributed over the body, but especially over the lower extremities. Constitutional symptoms are absent, with the possible ex-ception of a general debilitated condition, and subjective symptoms are likewise wanting. Its dura-tion is from one to three weeks, and may be prolonged even beyond this by successive out-breaks, and recurrences may take place at intervals over a period of years. It is more frequent in middle life and old age than in the young, and more prone to attack those who are in one way or another debilitated. In women coincident menstrual derangement is often complained of. Hardy says this variety may be transformed into the hemorrhagic. The vast majority of cases, however, terminate favorably. The diagnosis is easily made, but it may be mistaken for the result of flea-bites. These, however, have a central puncture mark to indicate their origin.

The eruption has been attributed to fatigue, mental worry and emotions, damp dwellings, insufficient nourishment, and spanæmia, or poverty of the blood in its coagulating qualities. Rheu-matism does not appear to be a cause, or the eruption would be more frequent in true rheumatism, whereas it scarcely ever occurs with marked attacks of this disease The muscular and articular pains associated with so-called *peliosis rheumatica* must be looked upon as a complication of the purpura. Pains are complained of in various regions of the body, but more particularly about the joints of the lower extremities. They may precede the eruption by several days. There is fever, and the eruption may be raised above the surface in spots as large as the finger-nail. Many of these cases are in reality instances of erythema multiforme or erythema nodosum, and possibly not a few cases of scorbutus have been described under this heading, as well as purpuric eruptions due to toxic and septic influences.

TREATMENT.—Faulty hygienic conditions should be corrected, and the patient sent where he could have sunlight and pure air. The diet should consist of fresh meat, fresh vegetables, and wine. Fatigues and worriment should be avoided. Iron, quinine, bitter tonics, acids, and ergot

PLATE LV.

Fig. I.—Purpura simplex.
Fig. II.—Purpura thrombotica.

FIG. I.—AUTHOR'S COLLECTION.
FIG. II.—SYDENHAM COLLECTION.

will usually be found of benefit. In recurrent cases, change of occupation, of dwelling, or of climate will alone cause the outbreaks to cease. Sulphur, salt, or plain cold baths, with friction of the body, often do much good.

PURPURA HÆMORRHAGICA.

Synonym.—Morbus Maculosus Werlhofii.

This more severe form of purpura is distinguished by its tendency to produce hemorrhagic lesions upon the serous and mucous membranes as well as upon the cutaneous surface. It has much more marked general symptoms preceding and accompanying the eruption, and the individual lesions are larger and more generally distributed over the surface. Hemorrhages from the various orifices of the body are a marked feature of the affection which may be accompanied by fever and end in collapse and death. In many cases, however, extravasation of blood beneath the skin, into solid organs, as well as upon mucous and serous membranes, is due to serious diseases, such as variola, typhus, scorbutus, leukæmia, idiopathic anæmia, diseases of the liver and kidneys, as well as to the action of certain poisonous substances.

It is at times difficult to separate such symptomatic cases from true idiopathic purpura, and so frequently are the effects of drugs and these grave organic changes found to account for the eruption that purpura hæmorrhagica becomes less and less to be regarded in all cases as a morbid entity.

The course of the disease in benign cases is from two to four weeks, but the staining remains until the hæmatin has undergone such changes as permit of its being again absorbed, in which process it passes through the varied shades of color so noticeable in a common bruise. The extravasated blood may be confined to the layers of the epidermis, or it may occupy the connective tissue of the corium or the papillæ. Albumin is often present in the urine.

ETIOLOGY.—To ascertain the cause of the skin lesions in purpura is of the utmost importance, both for diagnosis and treatment, as the lesions themselves require little care. A satisfactory explanation of purpura simplex is difficult to find. It occurs in young and old; in those of apparent good health, also in the ill-nourished, but in common with the hemorrhagic form seems to be favored by such circumstances as cause debility. In some cases, there is a diminution in the number of red corpuscles and the solid constituents of the blood. Stasis favors it. Fatty and waxy degeneration of the vessels has been theoretically regarded as a cause, and in some cases lardaceous and inflammatory changes in the vascular walls have been found. Some cases appear to be of neurotic origin, as they follow violent emotions, neuralgias, ataxia, etc. The most frequent direct cause found in recently investigated cases is a thrombosis of the capillary arteries, and consequent diapedesis or passage of blood-elements through the vessels' walls. In a number of instances as the apparent cause of the thrombosis, the capillaries have been discovered plugged by bacilli with colonies of organisms in the effused blood. In another case, Watson-Cheyne found streptococci in long chains coiled into masses which blocked the capillaries. These cases might be called:

PURPURA THROMBOTICA,

Which is the name given by Hutchinson to a variety of purpuric eruption usually affecting women, accompanied by rheumatic pains and invariably occurring at first upon the legs. An exaggerated example of the affection is seen in the plate. The patient was a girl of nineteen years. Blood was passed per rectum, and albumin and blood-casts were found in the urine. The lesions are bright red at first, rarely round in form and never abruptly marginated, but shade off gradually into the surrounding skin. Like other forms of purpura, the color is not diminished by pressure. It has been found to be due to thrombosis of the capillaries, and Hutchinson says is closely allied to erythema nodosum and erythema multiforme.

DIAGNOSIS.—The lesion of purpura presents no difficulties to the student. The macule or staining may be at first bright red, but it soon changes to a purplish hue, or at times takes on a brownish tinge. It is, however, not always such an easy matter to decide upon the variety of purpura present or the conditions upon which it depends. Purpura simplex begins upon the legs; purpura hæmorrhagica may first appear upon the arms. Great care must be exercised not to make the serious mistake of regarding as purpura, cases of hemorrhagic small-pox. *Purpura variolosa* I regard as a faulty and misleading term. Serious epidemics have occurred from failure to distinguish " black small-pox " from this disease. Sudden fall in temperature, coincident with the eruption, is a valuable sign which is absent in purpura. Scarlatina and measles are sometimes attended with a purpuric eruption, and typhus also has petechiæ. Another important disease having a purpuric eruption, and very apt to lead into error, is *scorbutus* or scurvy. It, however, does not often occur in isolated cases, but attacks many living under the same unhealthy conditions, as in ships' crews, prisons, etc. Slight hemorrhages about the hair follicles cause a goose-flesh-like purpura of the extremities and, at times, of the trunk. Large ecchymoses are also produced, chiefly upon the legs, which may leave lasting dark pigmentation and thickening of the tissues, as I have seen in an epidemic which occurred during my term of service at the Work-house on Blackwell's Island. The gums become spongy, grow up over and between the teeth, and bleed most readily. The teeth become loose, and even necrosis of the jaw has been known to follow. The condition may last for several months unless fresh vegetables and vegetable acids, limes, lemons, vinegar, and the like can be supplied. It is most important to exclude the purpuric eruptions following the ingestion of various drugs. Iodic purpura is the one which has attracted most attention, but quinine, phosphorus, arnica, and arsenic are said to be capable of producing purpuric lesions. Guntermann has reported a case of purpura hæmorrhagica from swallowing two tablespoonfuls of coal-tar. *Petechiæ* have also been known to follow the inhalation of chloroform, epilepsy, fits of coughing, as in pertussis, and mountain climbing with low atmospheric pressure. They are also a feature of hereditary hæmophilia. Finally syphilis, tuberculosis, cancer, ergotism, and alcoholism may at times be attended with purpura-like lesions, and the venom of snake bites may also cause them.

TREATMENT.—Successful treatment depends in a great measure upon removal of the cause. Besides the treatment already mentioned for purpura simplex, we must secure proper rest and diet; in purpura hæmorrhagica, ergot will be required much more than in the simple form. From one to five grains of ergotin hypodermically every four hours is recommended; also the oil of erigeron in five or ten drop dose upon loaf sugar; fluid extract of hamamelis virginica in half-drachm doses; tincture of the chloride of iron, twenty or thirty drops; turpentine, acetate of lead, etc. Externally, sponging with vinegar, tannin, and other astringents, is advised. Diet is of much importance, and food rich in fatty matter, together with plenty of milk and cream, should be given. Hemorrhages from the mucous membranes are to be treated by the usual means, and during convalescence tonics and change of air are required.

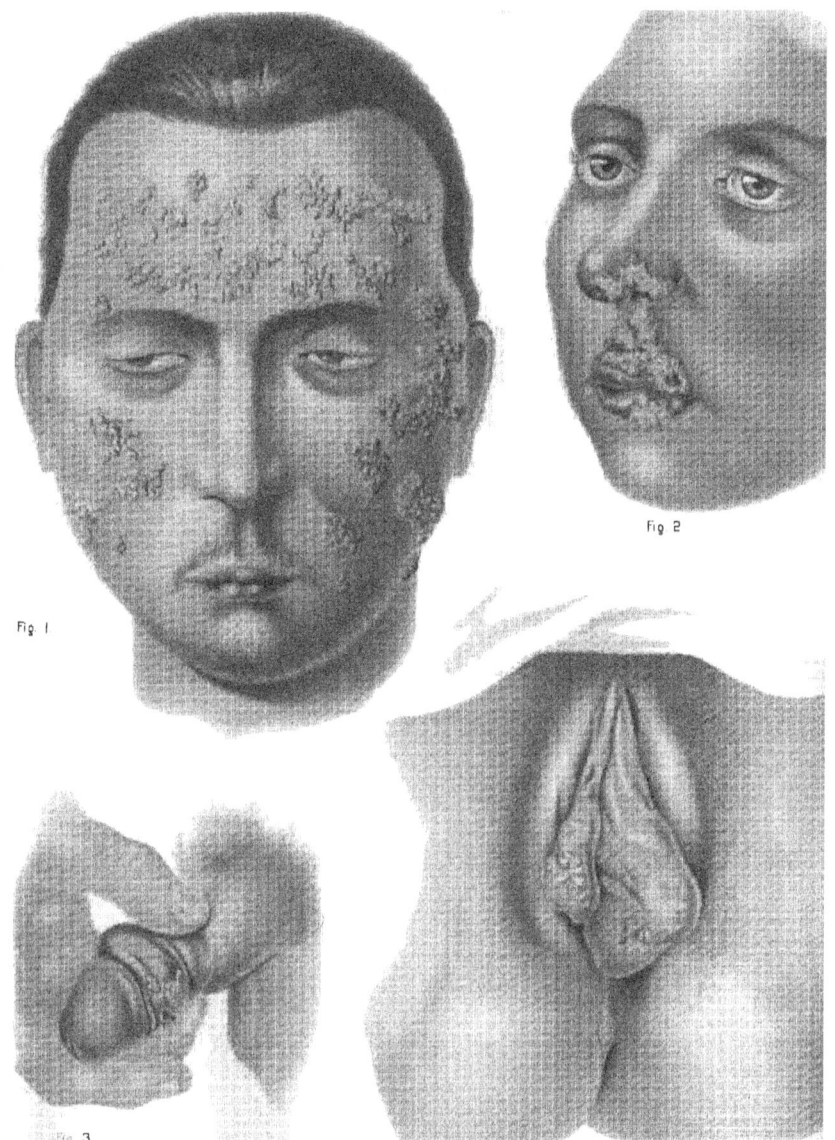

Fig 1

Fig 2

Fig 3

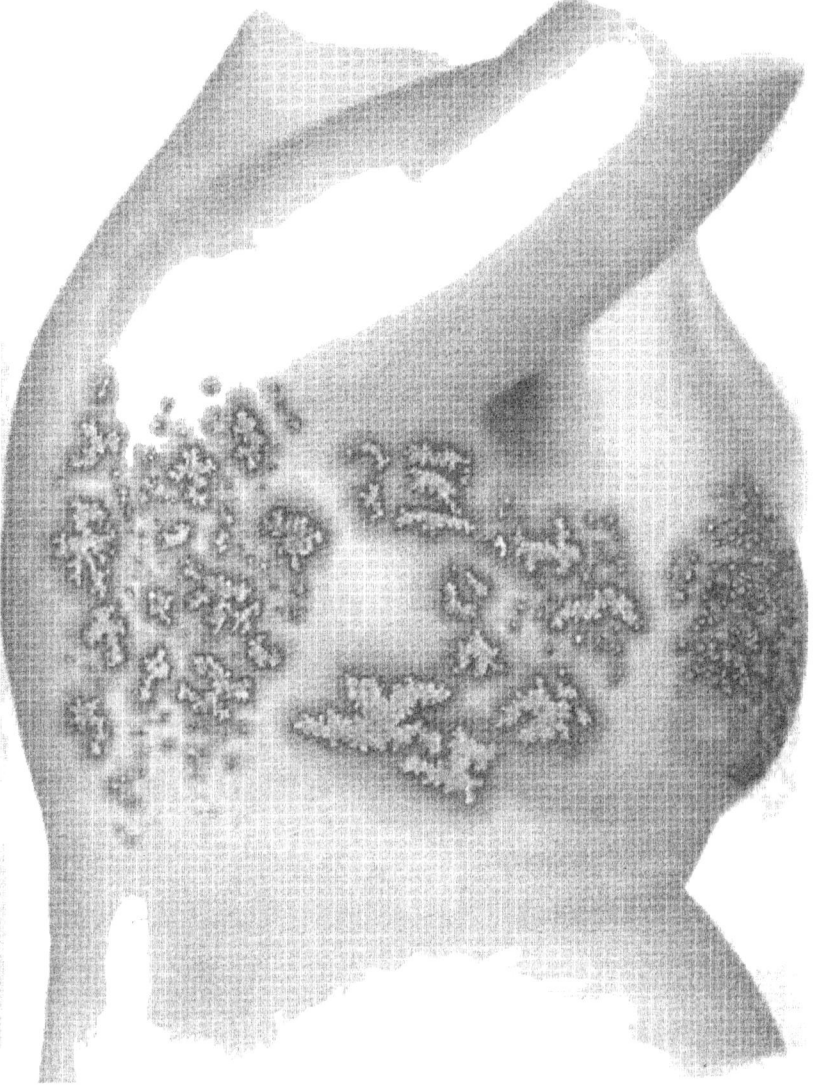

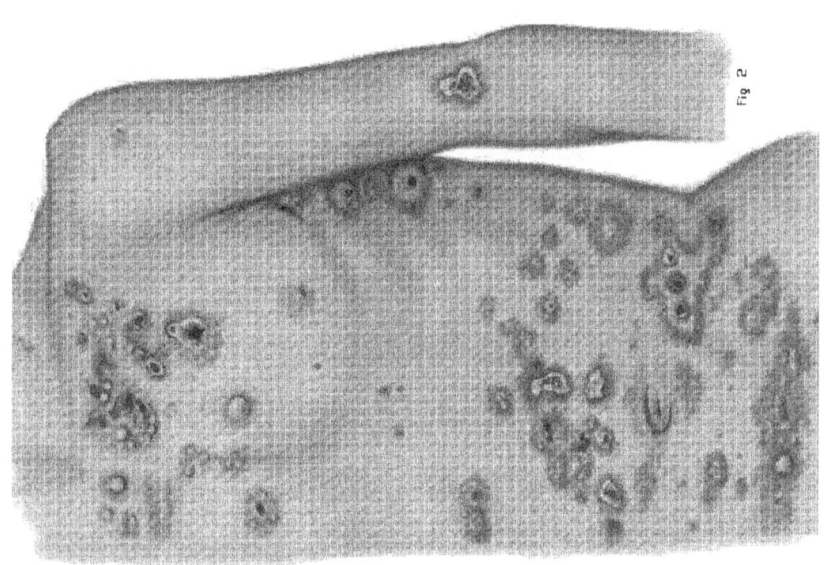

Fig 2

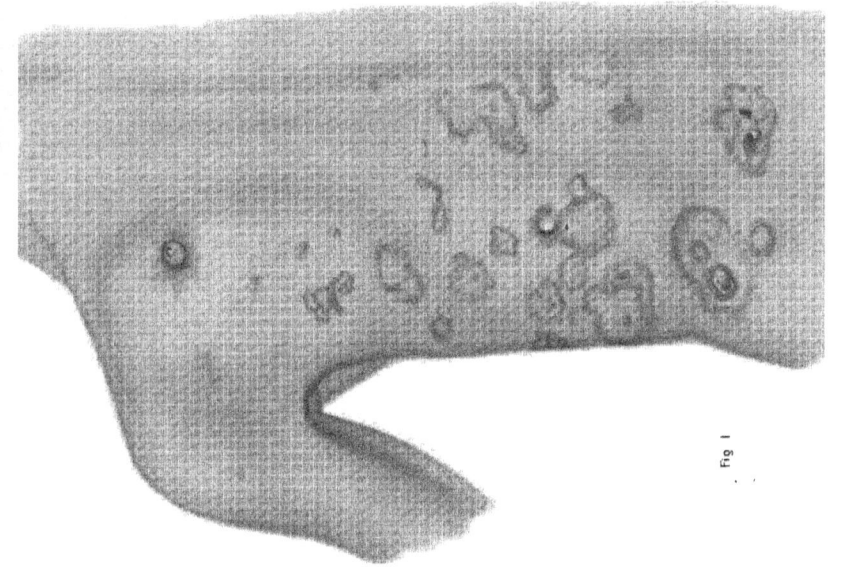

Fig 1

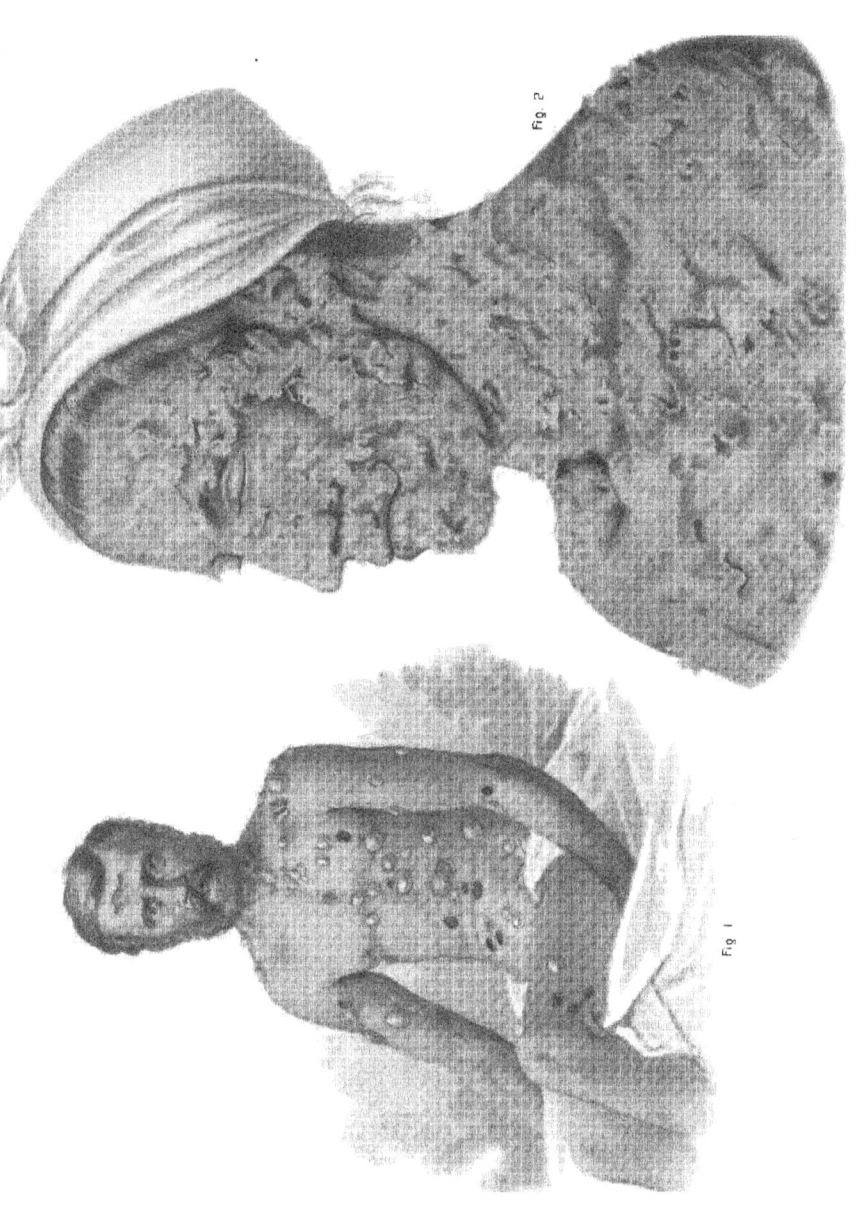

Fig 1

Fig 2

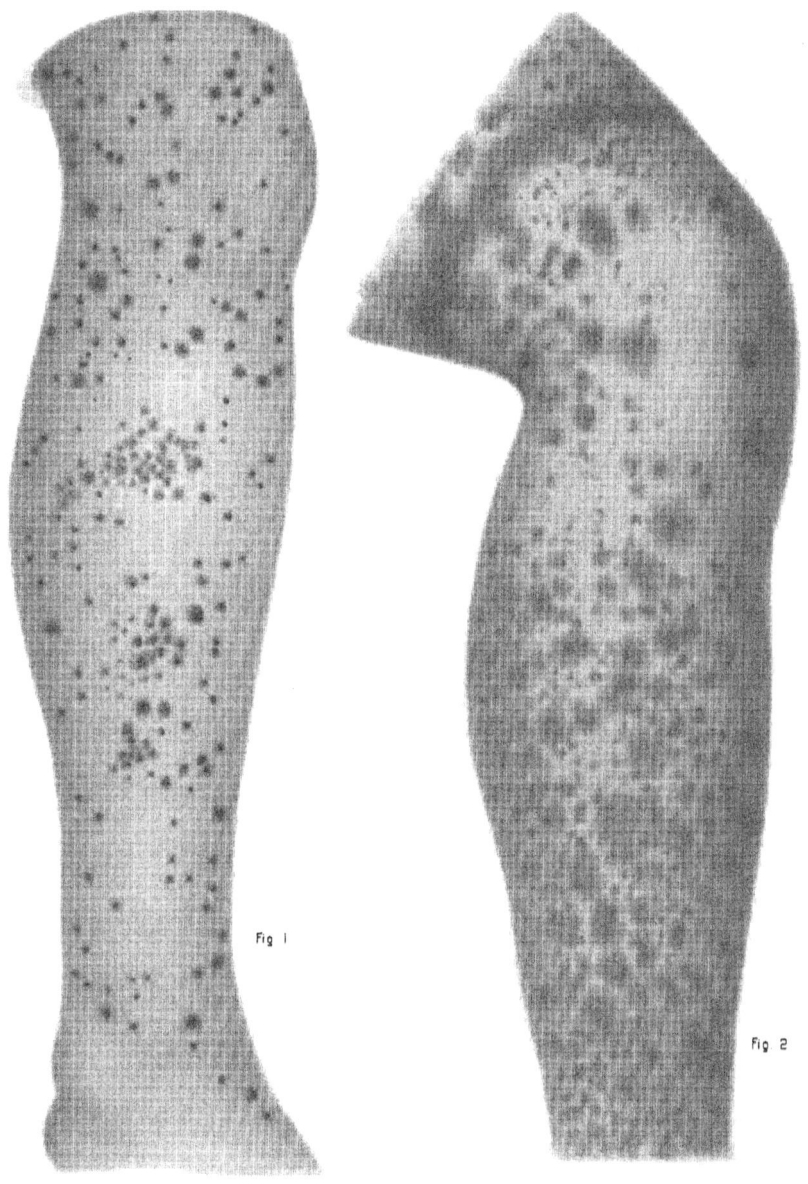

Fig 1

Fig 2

WILLIAM WOOD & COMPANY, Publishers NEW YORK

ATLAS

OF

VENEREAL AND SKIN

DISEASES

COMPRISING ORIGINAL ILLUSTRATIONS AND SELECTIONS FROM THE PLATES OF

Prof. M. KAPOSI, of Vienna; Dr. J. HUTCHINSON, of London; Prof. I. NEUMANN, of Vienna; Profs. A. FOURNIER and HARDY ; and Drs. RICORD, CULLERRIER, BESNIER, and VIDAL, of Paris; Prof. LELOIR, of Lille; Dr. P. A. MORROW, of New York; Dr. E. L. KEYES, of New York; Dr. A. R. ROBINSON, of New York; Dr. J. NEVINS HYDE, of Chicago; Dr. HENRY G. PIFFARD, of New York, and others.

WITH ORIGINAL TEXT BY

PRINCE A. MORROW, A.M., M.D.,

CLINICAL PROFESSOR OF VENEREAL DISEASES, FORMERLY CLINICAL LECTURER ON DERMATOLOGY, IN THE UNIVERSITY OF THE CITY OF NEW YORK
SURGEON TO CHARITY HOSPITAL, ETC.

NEW YORK

WILLIAM WOOD & COMPANY

1889

ATLAS

OF

VENEREAL AND SKIN

DISEASES

It is with special satisfaction that the publishers announce that this large and important work, which they have had in contemplation since 1883, is now ready for publication. It has long been recognized by them, from wide observation and acquaintance with similar works published in this country and abroad, that it is impossible for any one author to furnish, from his own collection of cases and illustrations, the most typical and at the same time the best and most lifelike pictures of the many peculiar forms of these diseases. Appreciating the defects and disadvantages arising from this cause, it was determined from the outset to enlist the co-operation, in the making of this ATLAS, of the leading dermatologists and syphilographers of the world. Prominent among them are Profs. M. Kaposi and I. Neumann, of Vienna. The atlas of the former, of venereal diseases, just completed, and that of the latter, of skin diseases, now being issued in parts, will be largely drawn upon in the preparation of this work, the sole right to reproduce them having been granted us by the authors.

Among other distinguished gentlemen who have engaged to contribute selections from their collections of original illustrations may now be mentioned Dr. J. Hutchinson, of London; Profs. A. Fournier and A. Hardy; and Drs. Ricord, Cullerrier, Besnier, and Vidal, of Paris; Dr. P. A. Morrow, of New York; Dr. Edward L. Keyes, of New York; Dr. Fessenden N. Otis, of New York; Dr. J. Nevins Hyde, of Chicago; Dr. Henry G. Piffard, of New York.

Other names will be added to this list as the work progresses.

The Editor of the work is Dr. Prince A. Morrow, of New York, who, in addition to plates contributed from his own remarkable collection, will write the treatise on skin and venereal diseases, which constitutes, besides the description of the plates, the text accompanying them.

In this treatise, it is aimed to include chiefly those features which are the most practical, omitting in great measure pathological and other considerations which would be more properly treated of in extended writings, rather than as the adjunct to an Atlas.

In regard to the character of the plates, it may be said, they are believed to be superior to anything of the kind heretofore produced—as accurate in drawing as photographs, and far more distinct, while the coloring faithfully represents nature.

The text is printed from new type, large, clear, and handsome, and the paper is heavy, with a highly finished surface.

Altogether, considering the reputation of the authors of the plates, the ability of the editor, the superb execution of the plates, the excellence of the presswork, the high quality of the paper of both text and plates, the large size of the page, etc., etc., this ATLAS OF VENEREAL AND SKIN DISEASES will be the most superb work in medical literature ever published in the English language.

The ATLAS OF VENEREAL AND SKIN DISEASES will be published in fifteen monthly parts, each containing five folio, chromo-lithographic plates, many of them containing numerous figures, all printed in flesh tints and colors, together with descriptive text for each plate, and from sixteen to twenty folio pages of a practical treatise upon venereal and skin diseases; the whole forming, when complete, one magnificent thick folio volume with seventy-five plates, containing several hundred figures, exquisitely printed in colors.

☞ The ATLAS OF VENEREAL AND SKIN DISEASES will be sold by subscription only, at the very moderate price of $2 per part.

WILLIAM WOOD & COMPANY, *Publishers*,

56 AND 58 LAFAYETTE PLACE, NEW YORK.

PSORIASIS.

An hyperplastic outgrowth of the epithelial layers of the skin characterizes this disease. The scales, which form a prominent feature of the spots and patches, are silvery white or lustrous, dry, adherent, and laminated. The base upon which they rest is raised above the surface, circumscribed, rounded, of a deep red color, and bleeds from numerous small points when scraped. It is a chronic affection, beginning as small papules, which soon become scaly at the summit, and increase at the periphery, until various-sized lesions are produced. A number of different names have been employed to designate the form which these lesions assume. Thus we find described *psoriasis punctata*, when their size does not exceed a pin's head ; *guttata*, when the appearance presented is that of drops of mortar scattered over the surface ; *nummularis*, when the lesions have the size of small coin ; *circinata*, when rings have been formed by extension at the periphery while the centre of the patches grows smooth ; *gyrata*, when these rings join each other and form, by their coalescence, segments of circles and gyrate forms ; *diffusa*, when the patches become of irregular size and of wide distribution ; *geographica*, if very large patches resemble the map of a

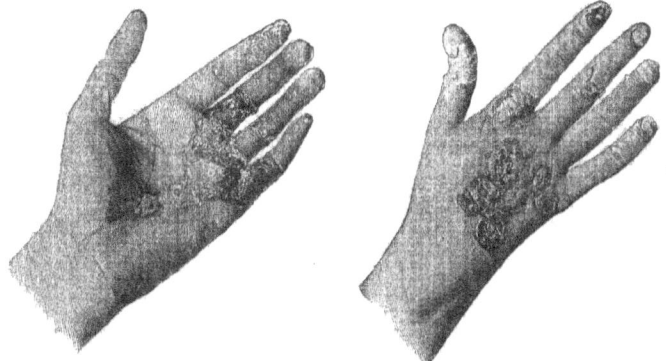

continent ; and finally *universalis*, if no portion of the integument has escaped. The disease, however, is always the same process, the lesions possess identical features, and in the same individual may show themselves as different forms in successive outbreaks, or in any given attack may become transformed from one variety into another.

It is one of the most frequent skin eruptions, occurring generally before puberty, but may appear first in old age. It is also occasionally observed in the first years of life, and has even been reported in infancy. It attacks those as a rule who are in apparent good health, and even the robust. Males and females are equally subject to it. The first attack may last for years, new lesions constantly appearing, and the primary ones persisting, or there may be a spontaneous disappearance of the eruption in part or in whole, preceded by a diminution in the quantity of scales and a flattening of the patches. This process of involution is the same as that which takes place when the eruption is disappearing under appropriate treatment. Scars are not produced, but the skin is left normal. Symptoms of burning and itching

PLATE LVI.

Fig. I.—Psoriasis of body.
Fig. II.—Psoriasis of hand and arm.

AUTHOR'S COLLECTION.

are often complained of, especially in the early stages, and if there be much inflammatory irritation of the skin present. Scratching readily causes the lesions to bleed, but cases of long standing do not itch. No region is exempt, but the eruption is especially prone to become localized about the knees and elbows. This is especially true of women, while about half the men show lesions in this situation. The eruption may appear first about the point of the elbow or below the patella, and may persist here long after other regions have recovered. Localized patches of psoriasis, symmetrically situated, may occupy certain regions for a lengthy period, while no other part of the body shows any sign of the disease. An example of this is seen in the accompanying woodcuts from the author's collection representing the lesions confined to the back of the hands and palms in a case of psoriasis which he presented at the New York Dermatological Society in February, 1883. There were no nails, except rudimentary ones, upon either hand. The lesions were mostly confluent, scaly, and infiltrated. A similar instance occurred in a boy nineteen years of age, who has just been discharged from Charity Hospital, cured by the application of a ten-per-cent solution of chrysarobin in liquid gutta-percha. The patches in his case were located upon the dorsum of both hands, had a peculiar square configuration, and were much thickened. They had existed for five years, and had persisted after the cure of a few round psoriatic spots upon the legs. At the date of discharge the skin appeared perfectly normal, but a course of arsenic was advised as an after-cure. The palms and soles are rarely affected in psoriasis, compared with the scaly forms of syphilis and eczema in these situations. Still, undoubted cases do occur, as illustrated in Fig. 2 of Plate LVI., and the eruptions may for a time even be exclusively limited to these regions. Distinct lesions may form beneath the nail and destroy a portion of the matrix, and in severe forms the whole nail is affected, becoming brittle, uneven, transversely ridged or worm-eaten in appearance, and may be thrown off. A few only or all of the nails, both of the hands and feet, may be implicated. The scalp often has an abundance of psoriatic spots or patches upon it, but the hair does not suffer any alterations, and is seldom lost to any great extent, and never permanently.

The face usually escapes entirely or with a sparse eruption of small-sized lesions. Mucous membranes, as well as the internal organs, are never affected.

ETIOLOGY is very obscure, and a diversity of opinion exists concerning the causes which produce it. Heredity seems occasionally to play a part. A few cases are of the type which might be called scrofulous, while others seem to depend more or less upon a rheumatic or gouty diathesis. It must, however, be remembered that the great majority of individuals affected appear otherwise perfectly free from disease, and can give no definite data pointing to heredity. The attack itself will often be precipitated by debilitating influences, such as lactation, insufficiency of food, or a too exciting diet, with excesses in alcohol, etc. It occurs most frequently in winter, and is modified by summer weather. It has occasionally been observed to follow vaccination, scarlatina, and such irritation of the skin as produces hyperæmia and proliferation of the rete cells. Syphilis is never a direct cause, and it is improbable that it has any indirect or remote influence upon its production. Certain cases closely resemble eczema, and it is probable the one affection modifies the other when, as sometimes happens, a tendency to both exists in the same individual.

It is not contagious. Eklund and Lang have found micro-organisms, differing somewhat from each other, but attempts to produce psoriasis by their inoculation have so far failed.

ANATOMY.—Psoriasis consists in a hyperæmic state of the upper portion of the derma and an excess of epidermic scale formation. According to Dr. A. R. Robinson, the rete mucosum shows marked hyperplasia in recent lesions, while the corneous layer is found but slightly changed. In the papillæ and superficial part of the corium, the blood-vessels are enlarged and the surrounding tissues contain many white blood-corpuscles. The deeper parts of the cutis appear normal, and the sebaceous and sweat glands are not affected. All the inflammatory changes in the cutis are secondary to hyperplasia of the rete, the cells which lie next the derma taking the first step in the diseased process. Thin found the interpapillary projections of the rete increased in depth, while the part over the papillæ was much thinner than in normal epidermis. The thicker the epidermis the greater will be the amount of scaling. Thus fewer scales are found upon the flexor surfaces and in women.   According to Rindfleisch, the peculiar whiteness of the scales is due to air between the dried epithelial cells.

DIAGNOSIS.—Psoriasis is throughout a dry and scaly eruption.   Any vesicles, pustules, or other lesions which may be present, will be due to some incidental affection.   It is to be especially differentiated from a papulo-squamous syphilide, which it often closely resembles in its distribution and form of lesion.   In doubtful cases, where the hands, palms, and nails are affected, if syphilitic the fingers will be found club shaped, while in psoriasis they are more tapering.   Other signs of syphilis will usually be present, but if the palms or soles be alone affected, it is much more likely to be syphilis.   Eczema squamosum is most likely to be confounded with psoriasis, and indeed some cases are extremely puzzling.   In the case of eczema, however, there are apt to be evidences or history of moisture ; the itching is more pronounced ; the elbows and knees are more apt to be spared ; the thickening of the patch is more marked in the centre, while in psoriasis the periphery shows more infiltration ; the scales are less abundant, more loosely attached, and not so lustrous; and upon scraping them off, instead of minute bleeding points we get a more general oozing of a sero-sanguineous fluid.   In eczema seborrhoicum we often have circular or rounded lesions, raised above the surface, and covered with scales, which closely resemble a psoriasis, but the scales are finer, smaller, more oily, and the scalp and middle regions of the body are more implicated than in psoriasis.   It may resemble dermatitis exfoliativa in advanced cases with extensive involvement of the skin.

Pityriasis rubra never occurs before puberty ; the scales are thin, large, and loosely attached ; an exudation is present, and it may prove fatal.

Ringworm is distinguished by its non-symmetrical distribution on the body, and by the looseness and thinness of its scales.   The parasite too is readily found.

Lupus erythematosus could only be mistaken in its earliest stage for psoriasis.

Upon the scalp psoriasis is limited to distinct areas, while seborrhœa may involve the whole surface, and the scalp is not infiltrated.

Ringworm and favus of the scalp show peculiar changes in the hair, and the microscope reveals the parasite.

TREATMENT.—Psoriasis may be cured if treatment is begun early and persistently carried out.   Though usual, relapses are not inevitable, and are much more frequent in neglected cases.   The first thing to accomplish in treating a case of psoriasis, is to remove the scales as a preparatory step to the removal of the lesions.   This is readily effected by means of soapy lotions, frictions with green soap, and simple or alkaline baths.   The following ointment may be rubbed in twice daily when the scales are very thick :

R	Ammon. carbonat.,	.	.	,	.	,	.	10 grams.
	Lanolini,	.	.	.	.	.	.	25 "
	Ung. aquæ rosæ,	.	.	.	.	.	.	50 "

Dr. Fox has recommended a two-per-cent solution of salicylic acid in castor oil.

Having removed the scales and prepared the lesions for local treatment, it is usual to apply some preparation of chrysarobin as being the most efficacious drug we now possess for the purpose.   It may be dissolved in chloroform, liquid gutta-percha, collodion, or incorporated in an ointment with lard or lanolin, in strength of from ten to thirty grains to the ounce, or the drug may be applied to the separate lesions in a moist state, or in a fifteen-per-cent chloroform solution and a coating of collodion or traumaticine painted over it with a separate brush.   Its application is not without danger.   A dermatitis of the surrounding skin may be and usually is produced, unless means are employed to limit its action to the diseased areas.   Severe general toxic symptoms, and even death, have been known to follow its free use.   This is equally true of pyrogallol, a drug which has given very good results in some cases.   It does not possess the staining properties of chrysarobin, and does not cause the same dermatitis, but may produce extensive destruction of tissue, and hence must be used with care and applied only to diseased tissue.   It can be used as an ointment in strength of ʒi. to ℥i. or dissolved in collodion or traumaticine. Anthrarobin, which has recently been introduced as a substitute for chrysarobin, while possessing the advantages of not discoloring the clothing as chrysarobin does, and of not producing dermatitis, still in my hands falls below the latter drug in therapeutic properties. In France, tarry preparations are much employed, some preferring oil of cade in strength from ten to fifty per cent, while others use ointments made with goudron, pix liquida, oleum rusci, etc. Where it is desirable not to discolor the clothing and skin, and where the odor of tar is disagreeable, or is not well borne, a mercurial ointment may be used as a substitute. Thus citrine ointment, ʒi. or ℥ij. to an ounce of lard or lanolin, or fifteen grains of proto-iodide to the same quantity of base, or ointment of white precipitate or red oxide of mercury may be rubbed into small areas of eruption. Vidal prefers the Vigo plaster applied to a limited region at a time. Hebra's " tinct. saponis viridis cum pice " makes an efficacious application when rubbed well into the patches night and morning after a tepid bath.

It has the following composition :

℞ Saponis mollis,
Picis liquidæ.
Spt. vini rectificati, ... āā ℥i.

Baths may often be ordered with great advantage. If the patches are inflamed and itchy, a simple hot bath, or with the addition of four or six ounces of starch or a pound of gelatin, may be given. The wet pack for several hours each day has been followed with success, even in non-inflammatory cases. If the patient's circumstances will permit, a course of baths at such a resort as Leuk or Kreuznach in Europe, or a season spent at some of our own watering-places, will be of great benefit, not only from the effect of the waters, but from the change of air, etc.

Local treatment alone is sufficient to remove the lesions, but it cures only the attack, and does not influence the predisposition or prevent recurrences. Internal treatment thus becomes a necessity, and some rely upon it almost to the exclusion of local measures. Arsenic is the drug which has been found to possess the greatest worth in this disease, having almost a specific effect. It is usually best to combine it with alkalies, such as the acetate of potash and sweet spirits of nitre, well diluted. If the urine is found filled with urates, and especially if the patient has a tendency to gout or rheumatism, colchicum may also be given with great advantage. In the young, better results are obtained when Donovan's solution is conjointly administered, while in old cases arsenic acts better alone, or in the combination above mentioned, to which may be added the necessary quantity of liquor potassæ arsenitis to suit each case. Besides Fowler's solution, which is the preparation commonly employed, other forms of arsenic may be given, such as Pearson's solution or arsenious acid in the so-called Asiatic pill : ℞ Acidi arseniosi, gr. iv.; Piperis nigri, ʒiv.; Pulv. glycyrrhizæ rad., ʒiv. M. ft. in pil. no. 80 div. S. One or more pills after each meal. To secure the most rapid effect, arsenic must be given in increasing doses until the limit of toleration is reached, and this maximum dose maintained until the lesions disappear. It is well to begin with a full dose, gradually decrease it for a few days, and then little by little increase the quantity until the full effect of the drug is secured. When the disease begins to disappear, the dose is to be gradually diminished, or if the drug disagrees, omitted for a few days, but it will seldom be found necessary to stop it altogether.

The use of arsenic should not be altogether discontinued with the disappearance of the eruption, but persisted in for several weeks. In patients who have frequent recurrences of psoriasis, it is well to give a course of arsenical treatment as a prophylactic measure, after the eruption has been cured by external means. Hardy discovered by accident that balsam of copaiba causes the eruption of psoriasis to disappear. It may be given in capsules or in combination with liquor potassæ and mucilage of acacia, so that twenty minims are taken thrice daily.

Before beginning any course of internal treatment, the exciting cause of the attack must be sought for, and if possible removed. Though the patient may appear otherwise perfectly healthy, some disorder can usually be found.   It may be only of a moral nature and due to worry or grief, or there may be an excess of urates found in the urine.   Indigestion may be present, with acidity of the stomach and deposit of lithates in the urine.   In this case, the administration of twenty-minim doses of liquor potassæ or other alkali will be of benefit, combined with appropriate diet. If the patches show signs of inflammation, an unstimulating diet should be ordered.   As a rule the dietary should exclude pork, game, salt meats, spiced dishes, fish and shell-fish, alcohol, and coffee.

Cases have been cured by an exclusive animal diet, but this regime does not always succeed. In alcoholics, ten-grain doses of carbonate of ammonia are advised.   If scrofulosis be an element, cod-liver oil, general tonics, and a sojourn at the seashore will be beneficial, and change of air will be found a valuable adjunct to any course of treatment.   The iodide of potassium has been employed by some with happy results.   Iron is sometimes indicated, especially in nursing women or those whose eruption succeeds some debilitating influence. '

In psoriasis of the face and scalp, local treatment must be somewhat modified.   Here it will not do to apply chrysophanic acid, because of the danger of irritation extending to the eyes. The compound tincture of green soap, as in the formula above given, will be found an excellent preparation for friction of the scalp, and may of itself remove the lesions, which are in these situations not so obstinate.   Beta-naphthol, in strength of ʒ ss. to ʒ i., has also here given good results. Localized cold packing has an application in limited patches, as upon the extremities.   Many cases will be found quite refractory to treatment, and recurrences will be frequent; but persistent and well-directed effort will bring its reward.   Local treatment should be persisted in until no trace of the lesions is left upon any part of the body, and I believe it a wise course to continue internal treatment for several weeks later, and where recurrences are anticipated to give arsenic, and possibly alkalies, in the intervals of eruption.

LICHEN.

In the present acceptation of this term, we are to understand a skin disease whose only lesion is a papule standing out upon the skin, and during its whole evolution never changing into any other lesion, such as a tubercle, pustule or vesicle, but which may and usually does become scaly, and often forms patches by the fusion of separate, but closely aggregated lesions.

It is confusing to apply the term, as some older writers have done, to all papular eruptions, and at the present day *lichen simplex* is usually regarded as a papular eczema, *lichen urticatus* as a papular form of urticaria, and *lichen lividus* as a purpura.   *Lichen tropicus* (prickly heat), *lichen scrofulosus*, and *lichen pilaris* are, however, terms which it is still expedient to retain, although the last-named affection is more appropriately termed keratosis pilaris.   Much discussion has recently taken place relative to the identity or non-identity of two important varieties of lichen, viz.: *lichen planus* and *lichen ruber:* the Vienna school still holding to Hebra's teaching that lichen planus is only a variety of lichen ruber, while in this country the majority of dermatologists believe that the former, more common and less severe affection differs so from lichen ruber in its course, amenability to treatment, histology, and termination that the diseases should be regarded as distinct processes.

Kaposi, on the other hand, says that they are often combined upon the same subject; lichen planus lesions existing upon the palms and soles, for example, while upon the trunk the eruption is that of lichen ruber acuminatus.   Besnier regards this as demonstrative of the identity, while recent authors in this country hold that the diagnosis cannot be made from the form of lesion alone in all cases, that a few scattered lesions resembling those of lichen planus may exist in lichen ruber, that the one does not change into or succeed the other, that excepting in possibly rare instances they never co-exist upon the same individual, and that, even if shown to co-exist, it does not prove that they form one and the same process, any more than that syphilis or psoriasis is identical with lichen because either of these diseases may occur in a patient affected with lichen.

LICHEN PLANUS.

The eruption in this, the more common but still comparatively rare affection, first described by Wilson, consists of disseminated or aggregated firm papules of a peculiar and characteristic appearance which may occupy a limited region only or cover a large extent of surface, but are often found situated just above the wrists upon the flexor surface of the forearm.

The papules are rounded at first and without scales, but when fully formed have a wax-like appearance, and differ from those of other affections in being for the most part angular or polygonal at the base, and flattened at the summit as though by pressure or from being shaved off. The top is shiny, smooth or horny, and many of the lesions show a central depression or umbilication.

The color is a dull or yellowish red, which in larger papules may be more of a crimson with a suffused violaceous or lilac tinge. This latter appearance is characteristic, especially in recent lesions. When patches have formed, and especially in old ones, the color becomes more dusky.

In size, the papules vary from a mustard seed or even much smaller to a lentil, and are somewhat elevated above the skin level. When newly formed they are round, but soon take on the quadrangular outline, and show from the first a decided tendency to group, form patches, and occur in lines. The horny summit does not scale off. The papule never changes into any other lesion, such as a vesicle or pustule, and it does not increase in size to any great extent by peripheral extension, but the constant formation of new lesions finally produces a patch, the separate lesions being bound together by an infiltrated and inflamed base. These thickened patches are sharply defined, raised above the skin level, of a dark red, bluish or violet color, become scaly, horny, with an irregular surface which has been aptly compared to a nutmeg-grater. In patches of long standing, small white masses of dried epithelium can be dug out here and there, leaving little cups. The French call this inveterate form of scaly patches which exists principally upon the anterior aspect of the legs *lichen planus cornée*. They usually have the size of a silver dollar or are as large as the palm, and may vary in color from a bluish red to dark brown or black.

The spread of the patch takes place by the formation of papules at the periphery, and it is indeed by these new lesions that a diagnosis can often be made with certainty. Small flat patches surrounded by papules have been compared to dark-colored gems set around with pearls. In rare instances, old and large patches become smooth or depressed in the centre from atrophy, and a ringed or gyrate form of eruption presents itself. Though having, as we have seen, a predilection for the forearms, still we may find lichen planus papules and patches upon many other parts. The calves and front of the legs, as well as about the knee, are common locations in which to discover it, and it may develop upon the abdomen, penis, palms, soles, and even mucous membranes. It is usually symmetrical.

Though tending to final spontaneous disappearance, the lesions run a very chronic course, and remain for a long time unaltered. The tendency to become generalized is not very marked.

Upon disappearing, a red, purplish, or dark pigmentation remains behind. The general health is not affected. No period of life is wholly exempt. It is, however, not common in childhood. Lavergne has described an acute lichen planus in which the papules originate and develop with extraordinary rapidity, and form large red patches within a few days or weeks, or the eruption becomes generalized and presents the aspect of an exfoliative dermatitis. This acute form terminates after a variable time in resolution and cure more or less complete.

ETIOLOGY.—Little is known of the cause of the disease. Digestive derangements and constitutional disturbances are usually to be found, but it also occurs in well-nourished strong individuals. There seems to be some connection with the nervous system, and neuralgias at times

PLATE LVII.

Fig. I.—Lichen planus.
Fig. II.—Lichen planus.

AFTER ROBINSON.

accompany the skin lesions. Besides this, certain cases develop lesions along nerve tracts, are symmetrical, and in very rare instances a zoster-like distribution is observed.

ANATOMY.—The pathological distinction between lichen planus and lichen ruber has been clearly demonstrated by Robinson, and confirms the clinical observations and results of treatment which also point to the non-identity of the two affections. The papule of lichen planus results from a primary hyperæmia of the papillæ and an inflammatory process attended with round-cell infiltration in the upper part of the corium. This cell infiltration presses upon the papillary blood-vessels, and by interfering with the circulation permits red blood-corpuscles to pass out. As a consequence of this extravasation, pigmentation remains after the papules have disappeared. In old lesions the epidermis is hypertrophied, but changes in both the rete and corneous layers are secondary to the changes of nutrition. The hair follicles play no part in determining the situation of the papules. The small central umbilication Robinson finds due to the sweat-duct, and the depressed centre to a fatty degeneration of the round-celled infiltration and a flattening of the rete. He has as yet found no abnormal condition of the nerves nor micro-organisms.

DIAGNOSIS.—Lichen planus is not readily mistaken for other affections, because of its characteristic papule with irregularly angular or polygonal base, flat and shiny top, depressed centre, and its peculiar course. In doubtful cases the whole evolution must be taken into account, for the papule may be rounded, obtuse, without central depression, and resemble more the small lesions of molluscum contagiosum, while, on the other hand, in papular eczema we find occasional umbilicated papules. In eczema, the papule is bright red, more acuminate, varies more in size, is much more itchy, tends to disappear sooner, and leaves less pigmentation behind. In psoriasis, the small early lesions have more scales, and extension at the periphery takes place rapidly. In syphilis, the papule is not covered with a horny adherent scale, is not, as a rule, flattened, and the eruption does not itch. The similarity in color between a papular syphilide and a lichen planus is often very striking. It is distinguished from lichen ruber by its appearance upon the extremities, and not upon the whole surface of the body; by the nails remaining unaffected, and by its tendency to spontaneous disappearance, and by the therapeutical test of arsenic, which drug has but little effect upon it unless very large quantities be taken, while lichen ruber (the severer affection) is greatly benefited by arsenic. Again, the iodide of potassium is curative in some cases of lichen planus and of no value in lichen ruber.

In the absence of isolated lesions about a thickened scaly patch of lichen planus, it becomes most difficult to distinguish it from a chronic psoriasis or eczema squamosum.

TREATMENT must be both internal and external to secure the most speedy removal of the lesions and prevent recurrences. Derangements of the digestive system, and symptoms referable to the nerves, will often be found and must be remedied. Hygienic measures are often called for, and such drugs as alkalies, mineral acids, iron, quinine, mercury, and arsenic, together with cod-liver oil, will each be found beneficial in individual cases in which they are indicated.

Alkalies do most good where there is most hyperæmia. Robinson prefers acetate of potash with sweet spirits of nitre, while Taylor has found rapid improvement to follow twenty-grain doses of chlorate of potash in four ounces of water, given fifteen minutes after meals, and followed in fifteen minutes by twenty drops of dilute nitric acid in a wineglassful of water.

Local treatment is of great importance. The ointment recommended by Unna, which consists of 1 part corrosive sublimate, 20 parts carbolic acid, and 500 parts of benzoated zinc ointment, has been used with the most satisfactory results. It must be well rubbed into the lesions night and morning, after which the parts are covered with cotton-wool, and the patient remains in bed. Vidal recommends glycerole of starch, twenty parts, and tartaric acid, one part. In chronic horny or inveterate patches, soap plaster, iodine, pure carbolic acid, or ten-per-cent pyrogallol may be used, or the patch can be scraped out with a sharp spoon (raclage).

LICHEN RUBER.

Under this name Hebra first described a disease characterized by an eruption of small, firm, acuminated, distinct, dark-red papules, having a slight epidermic scale at their summit. It is an extremely rare disease, regarding which the following are the generally accepted views in this country. The papule never increases by peripheral growth, but remains unchanged through the whole course of its existence. The eruption of acuminate papules may be acute, following chilly sensations, itching of the skin, and perspiration; beginning in fact like an exanthem, or prodromal symptoms are wholly absent. The eruption has three periods or stages of existence. In the first, the miliary papules are discrete. In the second, they are fully formed, and become clustered or united into patches which are always of a decided red color and covered with fine epidermic scales. By scraping away the scales, dilated hair follicles, about which the lesions form, are brought into view. In the third stage, the whole skin becomes reddened and thickened, and the papular element becomes entirely lost. The eruption generally begins upon the trunk and thence extends to the extremities, and the whole surface of the body may become involved, including the face, and the skin attain twice its normal thickness; this is especially noticeable upon the palms and soles. In consequence of the thickening of the corneous layer, the fingers and toes may become widely separated, semiflexed, and transverse fissures are often produced over the articulations, which cause bleeding with every attempt at walking or using the hands. The nails are almost invariably affected, and often become twice their normal thickness, brittle, opaque, of a rough appearance, and yellowish-brown color, or a thin horny plate may alone grow out from the matrix.

The general health at last suffers, and malnutrition, with loss of flesh, leads to a condition of marasmus, and in severe cases the patient dies after perhaps several years' duration of the disease. The hair of the scalp, pubes and axillæ remains unaffected, but that upon other portions of the body takes on the condition of lanugo. Though itching is a marked symptom, lesions resulting from scratching are exceptional. In the early stages, while yet the papules are scanty, the general health is but little affected, and even after the whole surface becomes involved the changes in nutrition go on slowly.

It is a disease rarely seen in this country, in England, or in France, but appears to be somewhat more frequent in Germany and Austria, where, too, a more severe and fatal type seems to exist. Still seven cases were reported at the last meeting of the American Dermatological Society as having occurred of late years in this country.

In three years Kaposi saw sixty-six cases, four only of which were pure lichen ruber acuminatus; a few he considered as mixed, and the rest as lichen planus. It would appear that the features of the disease change somewhat in different countries and climates.

Still severe cases, such as the fourteen fatal ones first described by Hebra, do not appear to occur so frequently now even in Vienna. This may be due to improved methods of early treatment, or the proportion may be small because lichen planus is now included, as it was not in Hebra's early cases, Wilson having subsequently described it. Recurrences may take place several times in succession, after the eruption has been wholly cured.

Etiology is quite as obscure as in the case of lichen planus. Nervous debility, overwork, anxiety, and depression seem to favor the outbreak. There is a tendency to attribute the lesions to the presence of micro-organisms, although demonstration is as yet wholly lacking.

Diagnosis.—Lichen ruber must first of all be distinguished from other forms of lichen, including lichen planus. The form of the lesion must not be exclusively relied upon for the diagnosis, for although it is always acuminate or conical at first, becoming later on obtuse, and finally flat, and there is as a rule a slight desquamation; the surface being smooth with a small amount of central depression, still such lesions may occur in lichen simplex, pilaris, or scrofulosorum. When papules fully formed become clustered and very numerous, they resemble for the time being the eruption of lichen planus. Some points of diagnosis given by authors are that the distribution is symmetrical, spreading from the upper parts of the body downward, and may rapidly invade the whole surface, large patches being formed by the fusion of papules of uniform size, while patches of lichen planus may remain localized for years. The color of the papule is at first yellowish, or brownish-red, or of a waxy appearance, becoming later on of a uniform deeper color, differing from the lilac hue of lichen planus.

In the chronic stage all traces of the papule become lost, and the surface has a roughened feel. The palms and soles are invaded, and the nails are hypertrophied or have their nutrition impaired, and may even be destroyed. Impairment of nutrition affects the hairs upon the regions implicated. Emaciation and death from exhaustion result in severe cases, all of which are changes not found in lichen planus.

It is further to be distinguished from eczema, psoriasis, pityriasis rubra, pityriasis pilaris, and syphilis. In eczema the papule is larger, and not, as a rule, flat or umbilicated, much more itchy, of a redder color, and exudation and crusting are apt to be present. In exceptional cases, the eruption of papular eczema (lichen simplex) closely resembles that of lichen ruber, and the absence of vesiculation should not exclude the former. Psoriasis, when universal, resembles this disease in a slight degree, and in the disseminate form lichen ruber might readily pass for psoriasis punctata. Pityriasis rubra is often universal, but the color is much brighter, the primary lesion is an erythema and not a papule, and the epidermis exfoliates in large flakes, while the infiltration of the skin is very slight. Pityriasis pilaris is an affection, described by Devergie, having a peculiar horny cone surrounding the exit of the hairs. It is also called Lichen pilaris. The skin is not thickened, though diffusely red and itchy. It is readily cured, and may get well spontaneously. In syphilis, the papules are large, never confluent or universal, and rarely possess many of the characters of the lichen papule. In the matter of diagnosis it is important to bear in mind the stage in which the lichen ruber is observed.

ANATOMY.—The pathological change begins in the corneous layer of the epidermis, and is not an inflammatory process, but a parakeratosis or hypertrophy of epidermis, associated with an inflammatory exudation in the papillæ and corium. The corneous cells digress from their normal process of transformation, many remaining incompletely changed and preserving their nuclei, especially about the hair follicles. Hypertrophy of the unstriped muscles of the skin has been demonstrated. In the inveterate cases seen in Germany, the whole thickness of the skin becomes inflamed and infiltrated, and the surface becomes extremely harsh. Hebra and Kaposi found the principal seat of the disease in the hair follicles and neighboring perifollicular tissue.

TREATMENT.—Under appropriate treatment, thoroughly carried out, an attack of lichen acuminatus can surely be cut short and the lesions removed more promptly than those of lichen planus. Arsenic has been found to possess wonderful curative properties in this affection, but, at times, when given by the mouth, its action is very slow, and when given hypodermically, as Köbner has advised, its action is too painful. The Asiatic pill, for which Kaposi's formula is:

℞ Arsenici albi,	.	.	.	.	.	.	.	.	0.75
Pulv. piper. nigri,	.	.	.	.	.	.	.		6.
Gummi arab.,	.	.	.	.	.	.	.	.	1.5
Rad. althææ pulv.,	.	.	.	.	.	.	.	.	2.
Aqu. font.,	.	.	.	.	.	.	.	.	q. s.
M. f. pilul. No. 100 ;									

is probably the best way to administer the drug, as the dose can be conveniently increased, as it must be to be of service, until the point of toleration has been reached.

Kaposi begins with three pills a day, and increases the dose by one pill every fourth or fifth day. A maximum dose of eight or ten pills is kept up until involution takes place in the eruption. This may occur only after several months of treatment, and possibly only after from

PLATE LVIII.

Fig. I.—Lichen ruber.
Fig. II.—Lichen ruber moniliformis.

AFTER NEUMANN.

one to two thousand pills have been taken. The arsenic should be continued for a time after the eruption has disappeared.

In small children it is well to begin with a mild dose of Fowler's solution, say one or two drops, and gradually increase it just as the Asiatic pills are increased in the adult, until a maximum dose is reached, at which the patient can be kept for several months.

To Unna is due the credit of having introduced an external means of treatment which is both effective and of rapid action. It is his zinc-carbolic-sublimate-inunction cure, for which the formula is given under lichen planus, and to which an increased percentage of corrosive sublimate may be added until each ounce contains from two to ten grains or even more, and Hebra's unguentum diachylon may be substituted for the zinc oxide. The patient is rubbed with the ointment twice daily, and must, of course, be carefully watched for symptoms of mercurial poisoning. While internal and external treatment is being carried out, the general nutrition of the body must be maintained by all possible means and a diet rich in starchy food has been advised, with plenty of milk and cream.

LICHEN MONILIFORMIS.

The term *lichen ruber moniliformis* was applied by Neumann to a very striking case which occurred in the practice of Kaposi, and which is beautifully illustrated in Plate LVIII. The name was chosen from the resemblance which the lesions bore in their configuration to strings of coral beads, or to a nun's rosary. Upon the sides of the neck and throat, as well as upon the flexor surfaces of the arms, are seen symmetrically distributed hypertrophies presenting the appearance of cicatrices from a burn, or keloid-like bands of thickened skin. The lesions, disposed like strings of pearls or corals, also occupied the upper arms and shoulder, as well as the thighs, in which latter situation they often crossed each other. They were of a yellow or pale red color; had a wax-like shiny appearance; were of firm consistence, and sensitive to pressure. Numerous small flat papules from the size of a poppy seed to that of a mustard grain, and of a brownish-red or dark-brown color, were scattered over the body, especially upon the parts surrounding the bead-like lesions. They were rounded, firm, polygonal, having facets, wax-like, with smooth top, showing for the most part a central pit, as though dug out with a needle point. Here and there are scattered points or diffuse areas of pigmentation of the skin. Kaposi regarded the case as one of lichen ruber planus. Dr. Fox recently presented a case of this variety of lichen before the New York Dermatological Society, in which the appearances were much the same as those presented in the plate, but in a less marked degree; the papules forming a number of long, scaly, bead-like ridges upon the arms and other portions of the body, crossing each other in many instances, and giving the impression that the skin had at some time been deeply scratched in these regions. With the exception of two members present who thought it a mixed form, this case was regarded as one of lichen ruber, having none of the elements of lichen planus. The condition is so rare and remarkable that further observation is required to make its exact position clear.

ACNE.

Synonyms.—Acne Vulgaris; Acne Simplex; Acne Juvenilis.

Acne is a disease of the sebaceous system of a purely inflammatory nature, but the term includes that condition due to an accumulation of sebaceous material within the sebaceous ducts by which they are occluded, and which is known as *comedo.* This is in reality the first stage of acne, in the majority of cases, and is very properly otherwise called *acne punctata.* Acne may, however, occur in the absence of comedones. Of all skin diseases it is the most common, and it is probable that few persons of either sex escape having at least a few "blackheads" or "pimples" before or about the time of puberty, and a large percentage of men and women pass

PLATE LIX.

Fig. I.—Acne vulgaris.
Fig. II.—Acne rosacea.

FIG. I.—AUTHOR'S COLLECTION.
FIG. II.—AFTER HEBRA.

through a more or less severe attack of acne vulgaris before reaching adult life. The sum total of mental distress and the amount of disfigurement (at times permanent from scarring) which is caused by acne makes it most important that the general practitioner should understand well the management of this affection, and should not regard its early stage as trivial and beneath his attention.

The characteristic early lesion of acne is a red papule which begins about the orifice of a sebaceous follicle, and involves the surrounding tissue in an inflammatory process. Tubercles are also often present and both forms of lesions rapidly change into pustules. The eruption is located chiefly upon the face, but may occur upon the neck, shoulders, back and chest, at the same time, or independently. It is rarely seen upon other parts, though occasionally upon the extremities, and it may occur upon any region supplied with sebaceous glands. Though the disease tends to chronicity, the individual lesions run an acute course, acquiring almost at once their full size and within a few days undergoing a process of self-cure by becoming pustular, and in the suppurative stage throwing off the plug of sebum or comedo, which usually occupies the centre of the lesion, where it acts like a foreign body, and excites a perifolliculitis. In a typical aggravated case, such as is presented in Plate LIX., Fig. 1, lesions in various stages of development are to be seen. There are comedones appearing as small black dots upon the surface with little or no surrounding redness; simple red papules from the size of a mustard seed to that of a pepper; papulo-pustules and pustules of the same size or somewhat larger; tubercles from the size of a split pea to that of a large bean; subcutaneous indurations about the glands, dermic abscesses, and, in long-standing cases, pits or scars resulting from preceding lesions of a similar nature. The pustules are usually rounded or acuminate, and attended with more or less surrounding inflammation. When not ruptured, a process of desiccation sometimes takes place and a loosely attached, small crust remains for a short time upon the lesions. The lymphatics of the neck are often markedly enlarged, especially in strumous subjects. Acne is essentially a disease of youth, beginning as the age of puberty approaches, and the glandular systems become active, and disappearing, in the rule, with the attainment of mature development. It is common to both sexes, but somewhat more frequent in men.

ACNE INDURATA is the term we apply to those inveterate cases in which hard nodules, as well as indurated tubercles, are thickly scattered over the cheeks, and, perhaps, the neck. They usually have a pustular apex, or contain a drop of watery pus in their interior, which a deep puncture or incision brings to light, but, if left untreated, may result in a subcutaneous abscess. The base is always hard, and the surrounding skin is often dense, red, infiltrated, and painful on pressure. This variety occurs mostly in those who may be called of a lymphatic temperament. Upon disappearing, the lesions leave behind more or less indelible cicatrices, and the whole face may be left pitted in much the same way as from small-pox. A hypertrophic variety is also described by some writers, in which a connective-tissue new growth takes place, and remains as a permanent disfigurement. It occurs only late in life, and principally among drunkards. Red or violaceous nodules or tumors surrounded by dilated veins are present upon the cheeks and forehead, but more especially upon and about the nose. This organ is enlarged to possibly double its natural size, the skin is red and thickened, and the orifices of the sebaceous follicles are wide open. There is no pain or itching present, but at times a sensation of heat. This condition is more properly called rosacea, and will be treated of in the next chapter. Acne-like eruptions produced by medicinal substances taken internally or applied upon the surface have been treated of in the chapter on Drug Eruptions. They differ in their development and course from acne proper, and usually disappear soon after the cause has been removed.

ANATOMY.—Retention of sebum in the follicle is the first stage of the pathological changes in acne. Hyperæmia and exudation soon follow, suppuration occurs, and, if the inflammation is severe, the gland is destroyed, sometimes by changes occurring without much perifollicular inflammation.

ETIOLOGY.—A great variety of different causes may operate to determine an eruption of acne. These may be external, and in a measure mechanical, and result from such influences as cause retention and hardening of the natural flow of sebum. The muscular apparatus of the skin, connected with the sebaceous glands, may act imperfectly. Again when acne has once begun, each lesion acts injuriously upon neighboring glands and ducts, by pressure and extension of surrounding inflammation, and excites to new outbreaks.

Although the *Demodex folliculorum* often exists in the sebaceous plug, it does not appear to take any active part in inflammatory changes which attend the transformation of the comedo into acne. The comedo, however, swarms with micro-organisms, which in all probability do produce putrefactive changes, making the previously inoffensive mass a source of irritation, and causing the inflammation of the acne pustule. Lanugo hairs are often found coiled up in the plug, and are sometimes very long. I am inclined to believe that they play a part in causing the retention and inspissation of the gland secretion.

The internal causes are quite as important as the local, and foremost among them stand the conditions peculiar to the changes which take place in the system at puberty. It is at this time that the natural hair growth takes on increased activity, and the sebaceous glands, so intimately associated with the hairs, have their physiological functions so altered that it amounts at times to disorder or disease, resulting in the production of acne. Disturbances of the digestive or genito-urinary functions are present in almost every case, and dyspepsia, constipation, uterine disorder, or abuse of sexual function can usually be discovered. Hardy believes that continence plays an important etiological rôle, and cites in confirmation the great prevalence of acne among the theological students in France, between the ages of fifteen and twenty-five. Bazin looked upon the indurated form as an indication of scrofula, but this view does not hold good for all cases. A tendency to acne may be transmitted by heredity.

DIAGNOSIS.—Acne is recognized almost at a glance, and the diagnosis is easily established. Still a papulo-pustular syphilide is at times readily mistaken for it, and vice versa. Examination of the whole surface of the skin, and the glands typically enlarged in syphilis, will make clear the lesions upon the face. It must further be differentiated from the drug eruptions, rosacea, variola, papular eczema, impetigo, and lupus disseminatus.

Acne and rosacea often coexist, but they have been shown to be distinct processes. The presence of comedones will aid greatly in making a diagnosis, especially when they are seen to occupy the centre of the papule or pustule. Variola is attended with fever and pains, while eczema itches. In impetigo the pustules are larger, and in lupus disseminatus they are absent.

TREATMENT.—Though constitutional means of cure are not to be neglected, we must constantly bear in mind that the condition to be relieved is one due to a local inflammation of the sebaceous follicles, and that in the comedo we often find the exciting cause of this inflammation.

Operative interference, before the inflammatory stage comes on, thus becomes of great prophylactic importance, and indeed by carefully removing the sebaceous plugs from their ducts with a suitable instrument, such as the straight silver tube devised by Bulkley, a watch-key-like expressor with blunt edges, or the spoon-shaped instrument recently introduced by Piffard, we may prevent the occurrence of a more serious condition. When painful inflammation is present, this pressing out of comedones must be done with the utmost care, or deferred for a time, lest injury be inflicted upon the already over-inflamed structures. Hot water as a local application has great worth in the therapy of acne, especially where there is much redness and congestion or inflammation about the lesions, and after the operation of removing the comedones. It should be applied night and morning, as hot as can be borne, by means of a sponge or cloth held for a few moments against the various affected regions in succession. Hardy has suggested as a wash a teaspoonful of one of the following solutions, added to a glass of the hot water:

℞ Hydrarg. chl. corros.,	gram.	2.
Alcohol.,	"	10.
Aq. destil.,	"	300.

℞ Potass. sulphuret, ... gram.   4.
 Tinct. benzoin., ...   "   2.
 Aq. destil., ...   "   300.

In the indurated form, and where dermic abscesses form deep in the skin, opening the separate lesions by means of a sharp pointed lance-shaped instrument will be necessary before the hot water and medicated washes or ointments are applied.   In the aggravated and indolent cases attended with a low grade inflammatory process and abscess-formation, with involvement of the lymphatic glands, such as are termed strumous cases, it often becomes necessary to scrape out the lesions with a Volkmann's sharp spoon, at the same time that an active internal treatment is being carried out by means of cod-liver oil, iodide of iron, phosphorus, and, if much suppuration is present, sulphuret of calcium.

In any severe case of acne, a more prompt result may be obtained by the following somewhat harsh treatment, if the patient will submit to it.   The whole face is to be scraped over at intervals of four or five days with a large spoon-shaped curette, in such a way as to remove the tops of the papules and pustules, and cause free bleeding and extrusion of the sebaceous plugs, cheesy masses, pus, and other contents of the lesions.   The immediate effect of course is quite disfiguring, but ultimately the result is eminently satisfactory, and permanent cicatrices, far from being caused by the treatment, are prevented.   Vidal's scarifying knife is often of much value in the treatment of obstinate cases of acne indurata, multiple incisions being made through the hardened tissues, and carried down to the level of the healthy skin, especially through the centre of the lesions.   In the indurated cases local operative measures of some kind are almost absolutely necessary to effect a cure, for all internal measures fail if alone relied upon.   Puncturing to the centre of each tubercle with a sharp instrument, so as to cause bleeding, and favoring the flow of blood by the application of hot water has long been a favorite procedure, and one followed after several sittings by very marked improvement.   Stelwagon has employed with success pure carbolic acid applied to each lesion separately every third or fourth day in patients who will not submit to instrumental treatment.   Touching the summits with acid nitrate of mercury is a mode of treatment which has been employed, but which I cannot recommend.

Electrolysis has been used by some, but it is painful and not as effective as punctured scarification or scraping.

Frictions with a coarse towel, sand, or, better still, flannel wet with compound tincture of green soap for several minutes each night, until an inflammatory action takes place, and the skin is caused to peel, is often highly beneficial where the lesions are numerous.   Soothing applications must follow this as well as any other course of harsh treatment.

Sulphur is probably the most useful drug we possess in the local treatment of acne, but its employment must be combined with the procedure already mentioned, or it will often fail to bring about a cure.   Its action is to increase the circulation by stimulating the surface vessels to carry off the blood from the passively congested parts.

No two cases require the same management; so in beginning treatment we must decide whether the case comes under the so-callled strumous variety, or if it is due to local vascular disturbance, or to internal disorder.   We must search diligently for the cause upon which the eruption may depend, directing our investigations toward the digestive and genito-urinary systems. Uterine disorder is, undoubtedly, a common source of acne in women, and where this is incurable the acne will also be found little influenced by treatment.   There are few drugs which have a direct action upon acne when taken internally ; two, however, do appear to act with much benefit—they are the sulphuret of calcium and ergot.   The former has a decided effect upon the suppurative process when given in frequent small doses, say one-twentieth to one-tenth grain every two hours.   The latter in half-drachm dose of the fluid extract, or ergotin in three-grain pill, thrice daily, has an effect upon the capillary vessels according to some observers, and in the opinion of Denslow and others it acts upon the arrectores pilorum muscles of the skin, causing contraction.

PLATE LX.

Figs. I. and II.—Molluscum epitheliale.
Fig. III.—Verruca senilis.

FIGS. I. and II.—SYDENHAM COLLECTION.
FIG. III.—AUTHOR'S COLLECTION.

Fox has found it of most benefit in lymphatic subjects with thick pasty skin and sluggish circulation.

Neither of these drugs will act well unless by dietary, hygienic, and treatment by other drugs we have removed those conditions which, by reflex action, produce constantly recurring hyperæmia of the face. Alcohol, tea, coffee, hearty meals, hepatic torpor, constipation, and faulty menstruation may be mentioned as common causes of flushing of the face. In women, acne is often noticeably aggravated just before the menstrual epoch, and at the time of the menopause an eruption sometimes appears, especially about the chin and those portions of the face where at this time, too, an increased hair growth is very noticeable in some women. In strumous subjects with clay-colored, pasty or flabby skin, malt preparations given with the meals, iron just after eating, and cod-liver oil half an hour later, is a course of treatment advocated by Stelwagon. A restricted and plain diet is advisable in almost every case of acne. Pastry, buckwheat cakes, cheese, gravies, hot fats, fried meats, and high-seasoned dishes in general are to be forbidden.

Besides the local use of hot water already spoken of as such an excellent adjuvant to treatment, Turkish baths can be taken by most patients several times a week with great benefit to the face, as well as to the general system. Sprays of hot water, medicated or plain, can be directed against the face with good effect.

ROSACEA.

Synonym.—Acne Rosacea.

This is a chronic inflammatory disease of the face, beginning as hyperæmic or red blotches upon the skin of the cheeks, nose, and chin, due to dilatation of the capillary vessels, and accompanied or succeeded by soft, red, acne-like papules and hypertrophy of tissue. At first the redness is simply congestive, and is increased with each sudden afflux of blood to the face, but later on it becomes permanent, the small veins become dilated, tortuous, varicose, and appear as little wavy lines of red or blue beneath the skin.

SYMPTOMS AND COURSE.—Heat in the skin of the nose and other hyperæmic portions of the face is complained of, and symptoms of cerebral congestion, such as ringing in the ears and dizziness, may accompany the flushed condition of the face, which takes place from time to time, especially in sudden changes from heated apartments to the cold outside air, and vice versa; also after hearty eating or excesses in drink. There is a quasi stasis in the capillaries of the parts affected, and the surface becomes cold, and in cold weather the previously red color of the skin becomes more or less blue. The border of the patch is not abrupt, but fades off gradually into surrounding normal skin. If the disease is not cured in this stage, the dilatation of the vessels spoken of takes place, usually beginning upon the nose and the adjacent portion of the cheek, and the tendency is for them to become permanent, and to increase in size, causing at times marked disfigurement. At this time also the papules and tubercles appear in limited numbers, and small branches of cutaneous blood-vessels can often be seen upon their surface. These are soft, dark-red lesions, some of which may become pustular. This condition may last for years, varying in intensity with the patient's general health and habits, almost disappearing at times, only to assume more distressing proportions under conditions favorable to its increase. Finally hypertrophy of the connective tissue and sebaceous glands of the part takes place, the nose becomes nodular and as though covered with small tumors, which in the very aggravated and rare form, known as *rosacea hypertrophica*, may become of a size equal to that of a hen's egg. In old age these masses of hypertrophied tissue, which have lost in a great measure their red or blue color, may overhang the mouth. This condition is commonly known as "wine nose" or "brandy nose," and is more common in wine-growing countries than here.

DIAGNOSIS is easy. Rosacea is distinguished from acne vulgaris by its onset, course, and form of lesion. The papules are not of glandular origin, and the pustules are rounded at the summit, and have no central comedo. Tubercles and abscesses are also present, but are situated upon an inflamed or hyperæmic base, unlike the same lesions in acne, and the former are larger and slower of formation. There is absence of secretion, and no itching is present as in eczema. The eruption has a characteristic limitation to the middle region of the face, occupying the centre of the forehead, the nose, and adjacent portion of the cheeks and the chin. The rest of the face is usually free, and unless acne complicates the disease, as it sometimes does, there are no outlying comedones or pustules. In occasional instances rosacea spreads to the whole face, but this is exceptional.

ETIOLOGY.—Rosacea is most common between the ages of thirty and fifty, and may be said never to appear before puberty. Some authors consider it more frequent in women, especially those of a nervous or sanguine temperament, while others believe that men are more often affected. The tendency to it at times appears to be transmitted by heredity. Affections of the digestive tract and of the uterine organs are etiological factors of great importance, just as in acne. Dysmenorrhœa is a symptom frequently associated with rosacea in women. Cold feet and constipation are almost always present. Occupations which necessitate exposure to excesses of heat and cold, and sudden changes from the one to the other, and work which causes the head to be bent or held low, favor greatly the occurrence of rosacea. Thus, cooks and coachmen are especially prone to it. Drinking of spirits and beer has a marked influence on its production, and when, as often happens, the last two conditions coexist, the eruption is very apt to follow. Coachmen are especially liable to go from heated rooms into cold and stormy weather when the vessels of the face are congested with drink, and after exposure to enter and drink again.

TREATMENT is pre-eminently local, but just as in acne the cause must be sought for, and, if removed, the disease will often disappear of itself, especially if still in its early stages. The same general rules for constitutional treatment, diet, and hygiene apply to rosacea as were given for acne. Here, too, ergot is of much value, and if suppuration is present, we may give calx sulphurata in the same dose as for acne.

In the early stage, and in mild forms, the application of Vleminckx's solution, diluted according to the amount of stimulation thought necessary, has been used by a number of dermatologists. The solution, as modified by Hebra, is made by boiling one part of quicklime and two parts of sublimed sulphur in twenty parts of water. This is to be boiled down to about twelve parts, cooled and filtered. Diluted four or five times with water, and applied each night, this solution has given good results. Other preparations, such as sublimed sulphur ten parts, and spirits of lavender ninety parts, or green soap, nightly applied with friction, act well. If many tubercles are present, emplastrum hydrargyri will cause them to disappear. The dilated vessels can be treated by multiple puncture or scarification at various points along their course, or they may be destroyed by the electrolysis needle. I have had good results in several cases of disfiguring "red nose," by making numerous punctures with the acne lance, encouraging bleeding with hot water, and painting over the parts a solution of ergotine ℥i. in collodion flex. ℥i., and keeping it applied for several days or a week, when the operation is gone through with again, and so on until the parts assume a normal appearance. When much hypertrophied tissue has been formed, it can only be removed by some operation.

Hot water is of as great value in rosacea as in acne, and may be applied in the same way. Its first effect is to increase the redness by dilating the vessels, but they afterward contract, and pallor of the parts succeeds.

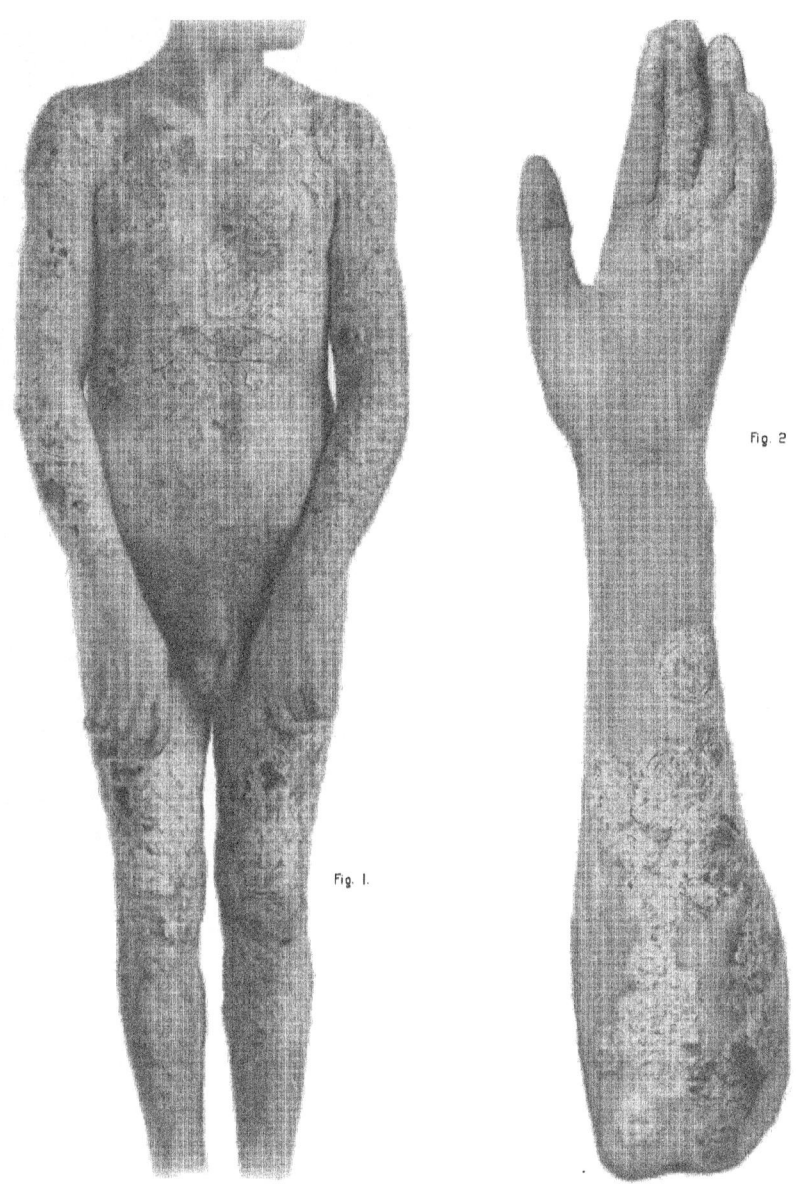

Fig. 2

Fig. 1.

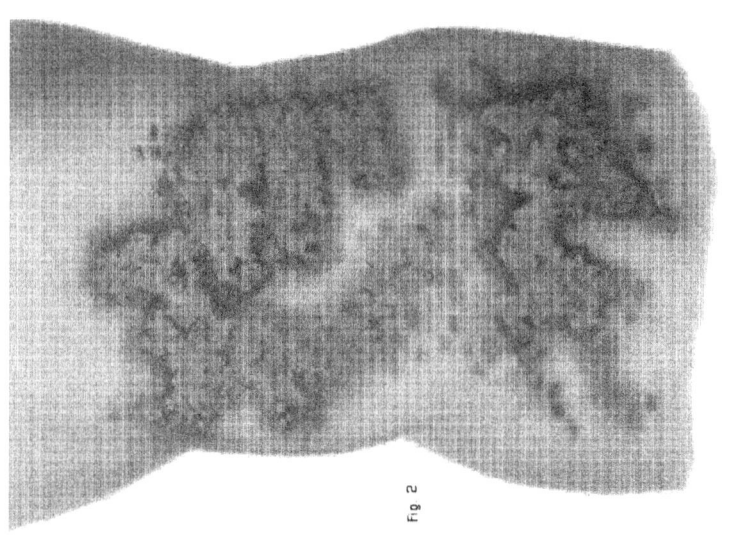

Fig 1

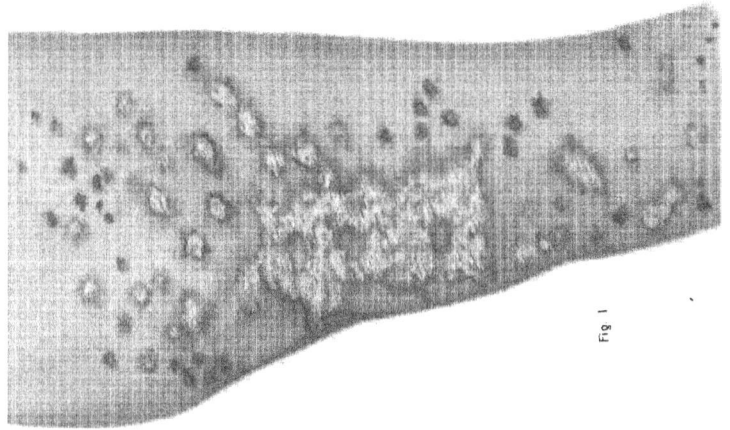

Fig 2

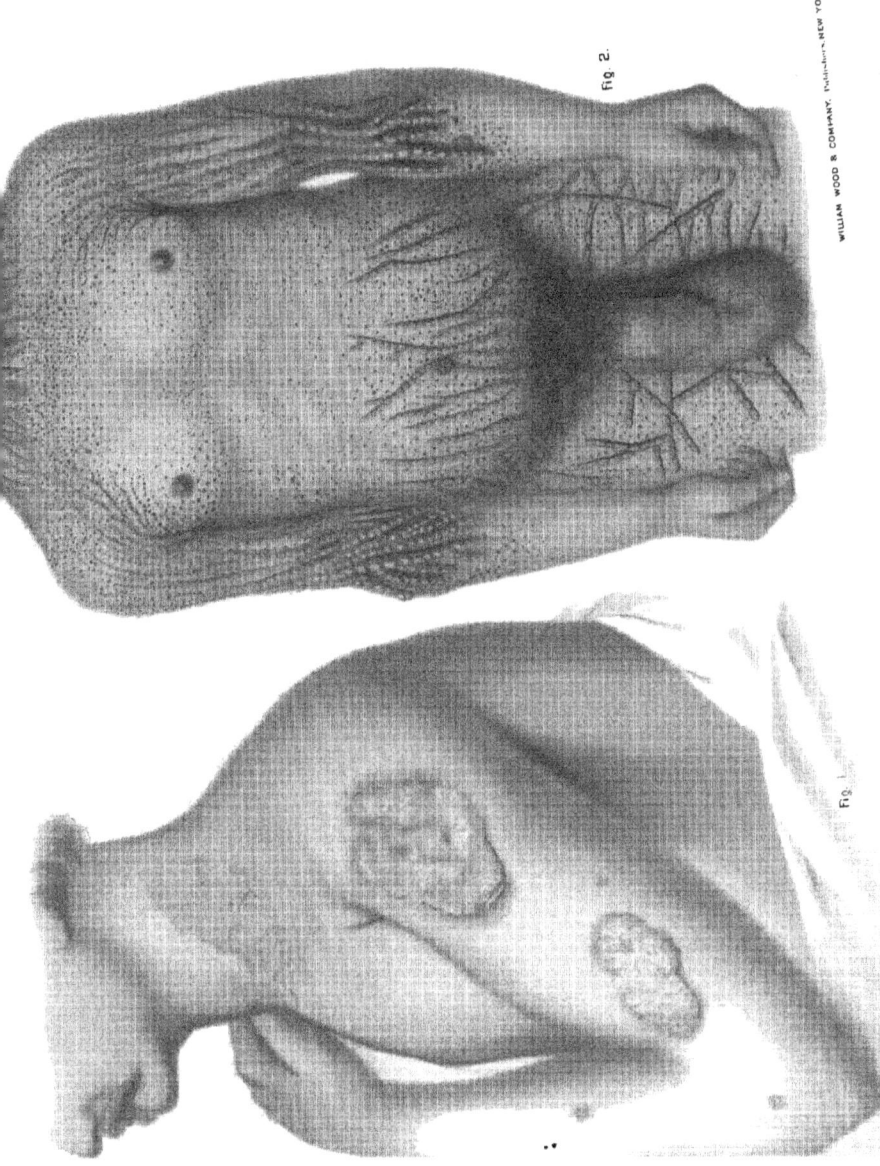

Fig. 2.

Fig. 1.

WILLIAM WOOD & COMPANY, Publishers, NEW YORK

Fig 1

Fig 2

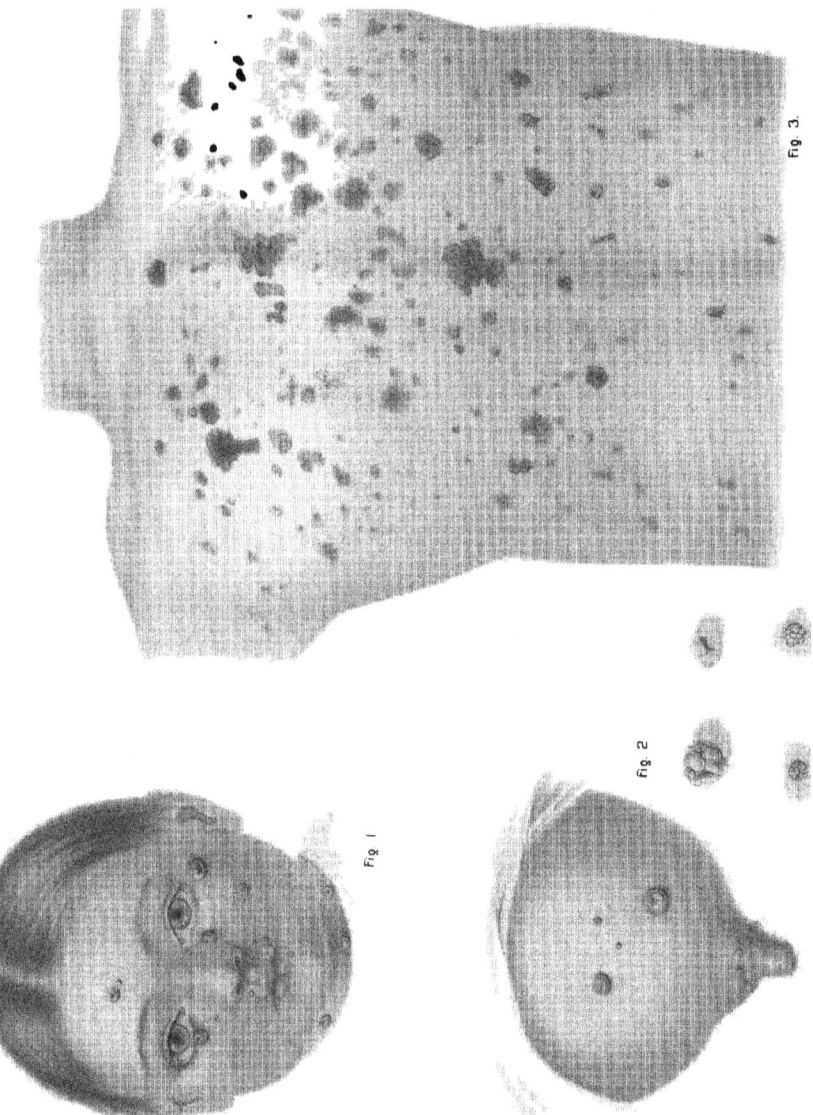

Fig. 1

Fig. 2

Fig. 3.

FASCICULUS XIII.

ATLAS

OF

VENEREAL AND SKIN

DISEASES

COMPRISING ORIGINAL ILLUSTRATIONS AND SELECTIONS FROM THE PLATES OF

Prof. M. KAPOSI, of Vienna; Dr. J. HUTCHINSON, of London; Prof. I. NEUMANN, of Vienna;
Profs. A. FOURNIER and HARDY ; and Drs. RICORD, CULLERRIER, BESNIER, AND VIDAL, of Paris;
Prof. LELOIR, of Lille; Dr. P. A. MORROW, of New York; Dr. E. L. KEYES, of New York;
Dr. A. R. ROBINSON, of New York; Dr. J. NEVINS HYDE, of Chicago;
Dr. HENRY G. PIFFARD, of New York, and others.

WITH ORIGINAL TEXT BY

PRINCE A. MORROW, A.M., M.D.,

CLINICAL PROFESSOR OF VENEREAL DISEASES, FORMERLY CLINICAL LECTURER ON DERMATOLOGY, IN THE UNIVERSITY OF THE CITY OF NEW YORK,
SURGEON TO CHARITY HOSPITAL, ETC.

NEW YORK

WILLIAM WOOD & COMPANY

1889

ATLAS

OF

VENEREAL AND SKIN

DISEASES

It is with special satisfaction that the publishers announce that this large and important work, which they have had in contemplation since 1883, is now ready for publication. It has long been recognized by them, from wide observation and acquaintance with similar works published in this country and abroad, that it is impossible for any one author to furnish, from his own collection of cases and illustrations, the most typical and at the same time the best and most lifelike pictures of the many peculiar forms of these diseases. Appreciating the defects and disadvantages arising from this cause, it was determined from the outset to enlist the co-operation, in the making of this ATLAS, of the leading dermatologists and syphilographers of the world. Prominent among them are Profs. M. Kaposi and I. Neumann, of Vienna. The atlas of the former, of venereal diseases, just completed, and that of the latter, of skin diseases, now being issued in parts, will be largely drawn upon in the preparation of this work, the sole right to reproduce them having been granted us by the authors.

Among other distinguished gentlemen who have engaged to contribute selections from their collections of original illustrations may now be mentioned Dr. J. Hutchinson, of London; Profs. A. Fournier and A. Hardy; and Drs. Ricord, Cullerrier, Besnier, and Vidal, of Paris; Dr. P. A. Morrow, of New York; Dr. Edward L. Keyes, of New York; Dr. Fessenden N. Otis, of New York; Dr. J. Nevins Hyde, of Chicago; Dr. Henry G. Piffard, of New York.

Other names will be added to this list as the work progresses.

The Editor of the work is Dr. Prince A. Morrow, of New York, who, in addition to plates contributed from his own remarkable collection, will write the treatise on skin and venereal diseases, which constitutes, besides the description of the plates, the text accompanying them.

In this treatise, it is aimed to include chiefly those features which are the most practical, omitting in great measure pathological and other considerations which would be more properly treated of in extended writings, rather than as the adjunct to an Atlas.

In regard to the character of the plates, it may be said, they are believed to be superior to anything of the kind heretofore produced—as accurate in drawing as photographs, and far more distinct, while the coloring faithfully represents nature.

The text is printed from new type, large, clear, and handsome, and the paper is heavy, with a highly finished surface.

Altogether, considering the reputation of the authors of the plates, the ability of the editor, the superb execution of the plates, the excellence of the presswork, the high quality of the paper of both text and plates, the large size of the page, etc., etc., this ATLAS OF VENEREAL AND SKIN DISEASES will be the most superb work in medical literature ever published in the English language.

The ATLAS OF VENEREAL AND SKIN DISEASES will be published in fifteen monthly parts, each containing five folio, chromo-lithographic plates, many of them containing numerous figures, all printed in flesh tints and colors, together with descriptive text for each plate, and from sixteen to twenty folio pages of a practical treatise upon venereal and skin diseases; the whole forming, when complete, one magnificent thick folio volume with seventy-five plates, containing several hundred figures, exquisitely printed in colors.

☞ The ATLAS OF VENEREAL AND SKIN DISEASES will be sold by subscription only, at the very moderate price of $2 per part.

WILLIAM WOOD & COMPANY, *Publishers*,

56 AND 58 LAFAYETTE PLACE, NEW YORK.

MOLLUSCUM EPITHELIALE.

Synonyms.—Molluscum contagiosum ; molluscum sebaceum ; molluscum verrucosum ; epithelioma contagiosum. Fr. *acné varioliforme.*

The rather striking form of eruption which Bateman described in 1817, and to which he gave the name molluscum contagiosum, consists in the development upon delicate skins, and especially in children, of rounded, soft or moderately firm, waxy-looking translucent new growths, which stand out like warts. The color of these nodules is that of the surrounding skin or somewhat paler, and when their full development has been attained they assume a pinkish hue, from the ramification of small blood-vessels over their sides, or they may become even red, but there is little redness about the base. The form is rounded or spherical, the surface smooth and shiny, and the summit somewhat flattened, and there is a depression in the centre. Upon close inspection a small opening is discovered at this point, which at a little distance appears like a black spot. The epidermic covering of the growth appears to terminate abruptly upon the summit at some distance from the central opening, especially in the larger lesions, thus presenting a rough or warty surface, and even a horny appearance may be produced in some lesions by the drying and extrusion of this central portion.

The number of molluscum tumors present in any case is usually limited to less than a dozen, and it is common to find only one or two : still, a great number may co-exist, as in Ebert's case, where 108 were counted upon the face of a fourteen-year-old girl. Though much more prone to develop upon the face than elsewhere, still they may grow upon almost any portion of the skin's surface. In nursing women they often occur about the breasts, and in both men and women the genital region furnishes a favorite location for their growth. Out of 133 mollusca removed by myself in an epidemic at an infant asylum, 51 had occupied the eyelids and the immediate neighborhood of the eyes, and 73 other portions of the face and neck, while 4 only were found upon the hands, and one each upon the chest, back, arm, knee, and leg. The tendency to occur in epidemics, attacking many of the children in a school or public institution, is a noteworthy feature of the affection, while in the family several children, and possibly the mother, may have molluscum at the same time. The early appearance of the nodular growth is such as to attract little or no attention unless it has its situation upon the eyelids, as is usually the case.

I have a number of times seen them upon the forehead, nose, or lips of infants or young children in this early stage, before they had been noticed even by the parents. At first they do not project at all beyond the skin level, but they soon increase in size until they are as large as a pepper. Between this volume and that of a lentil, or even a cherry, there are all gradations, and I have found single lesions more than once which measured quite a centimetre in the long diameter. When this extreme development takes place, suppurative inflammation is apt to occur in and about the lesion, or there is gangrene of the mass and the growth is cast off in several successive attempts and self-cure is effected.

Though the growths are usually sessile, now and then one is seen more or less constricted at the skin level, or it may be distinctly pediculated, and such lesions may after a time drop off. When pressed between the fingers, a small quantity of sebaceous-like milky material can be forced out of the central opening. When this substance is placed under the microscope and examined with an ordinary power, besides epidermic cells, numerous large ovoid bodies are observed which have a peculiar glimmer, are without nucleus, some free, and some wholly or in part covered with an epidermic-like envelope. These are the *molluscum corpuscles.*

ETIOLOGY.—Bateman's original idea, which he indicated in naming the disease, was that it was capable of transmission by contagion. Though this view has been opposed by many authorities, the weight of evidence from clinical observations is so strong that to-day few are outspoken in their belief to the contrary. It has repeatedly happened that epidemics have occurred from the introduction of a child with molluscum into a hospital ward, school, or asylum. I have reported one such outbreak in which nearly fifty children became affected, and have more recently observed another instance of its spread in an institution where the same history of origin was given. Numerous instances are recorded in which mothers who nursed children affected with molluscum have shown the same growths upon their breasts. Such an instance is beautifully illustrated in the plate taken from a case under the observation of Jonathan Hutchinson. The child was eighteen months of age and had not been weaned, and the mother's breast became affected, evidently by direct contagion. I, myself, have seen in Dr. Bulkley's clinic a typical group of molluscum tumors on the side of a mother's neck, corresponding to the place where her child's face, which was affected, habitually rested when being carried. For a long time inoculation experiments were all unsuccessful, and this gave color to the theory of the non-contagionists; but now a sufficient number of successes have been recorded to show that the disease is capable of being transmitted by inoculation. Paterson, Retzius, Haab, Vidal, Wigglesworth have all reported positive results from inoculation experiments.

As yet all attempts to discover, isolate, and cultivate a micro-organism on which its contagious property depends have been fruitless, but I am inclined to attribute this more to faulty methods of research than to absence of the germ.

DIAGNOSIS.—It is scarcely probable that any one who had read an accurate description of molluscum epitheliale would mistake a case for any other disease, and surely not after he had studied so excellent a plate as that here presented, taken from the Sydenham Society's collection. The eruption, however, was thought by Bazin to resemble so much that of small-pox as to deserve the appellation *Acné varioliforme,* a name still adhered to by French writers, although it has been pretty clearly shown that the disease bears no relation to acne, and that the lesion is not a dilated sebaceous gland, as has been erroneously supposed. Small sebaceous cysts are now and then seen upon the face, but more especially upon the genitals, which resemble in a measure this affection.

Molluscum has often been allowed to pass with a diagnosis of verruca by superficial observers, and the laity usually speak of the growths as "warts."

Molluscum fibrosum occurs upon the body, is more common in adults, the tumors are firm, and have no central opening.

Subjective symptoms are entirely wanting.

PATHOLOGY.—The tumors are superficially situated in the skin, and when pressed out or removed with a scoop, they present the gross appearances of a small brain or rounded gland-like structure. When opened, a cavity is found filled with the milky substance described, and the mass of the growth is seen to be composed of a thickened wall to this cavity, having an acinous formation, and convolutions which produce the brain-like appearance of the outer surface. A section through the whole substance of the growth shows a number of acini separated from each other and bound together by connective tissue, and made up of rete cells more or less transformed from those of the mucous layer from which they arise by a process of proliferation.

Virchow found, and others have confirmed his work, that the disease begins in the hair follicles, and a growth of epidermis takes place downward into the cutis. The folded-in appearance of the wall is due to hyperplasia of the lining epithelium of the hair follicle, and not to sebaceous gland structure, as some maintain. The soft white contents of the tumor consist of changed rete cells, mostly without nuclei, and those peculiar bodies already mentioned, which are known as molluscum corpuscles or globules.

These were first described by Henderson, nearly fifty years ago, but their exact nature is still in doubt, and Kaposi believes that they are to be found in other conditions, such as comedo, epithelioma, and situations where epithelium lies quiet for a long time.

Neisser regards them as the coverings or shells of collections of parasites (*Gregarinen* of Bollinger), while most authorities agree with him that they are formed from rete cells which have undergone peculiar changes.

In a recently published article, Neisser describes the changes which take place in a cell cast off from the Malpighian layer which is destined to become a molluscum globule. First there appears alongside of the nucleus a granulated body in the protoplasm of the cell which presses the nucleus to the cell-wall, where it becomes half-moon shaped. This protoplasmic mass finally fills the cell completely, and divides into shining bodies separated by open spaces in such a way as to suggest "spores." This is in the main the same account of the changes undergone which Thin gave some years ago, stating, however, that the nucleus of the original cell becomes lost, while Neisser says proper staining makes it visible afterwards. In the final stage Thin, too, says the molluscum substance may fall out, leaving an empty capsule.

Hyde says, in his recent work on Dermatology, "At present we must be content with recognizing the molluscous corpuscle as the result of a transformation undergone by the prickle-cell," while Robinson dismisses the subject with the statement that "the exact nature of the transformation is not known."

TREATMENT.—Simple mechanical treatment is all that is required to effect a permanent cure in most cases; for once thoroughly removed, new lesions cease to appear. While still small, the growths can be pressed out between the finger nails. When large, a curette or sharp spoon will be required, unless an incision is first made through the walls of the tumor. There is usually considerable bleeding from the operation. The base may be cauterized with nitrate of silver, but if removal has been thorough this will be unnecessary, excepting perhaps in the larger lesions. When the growth is constricted at the base or pediculated, it may be cut off with curved scissors, and any part remaining behind can then be pressed out.

As a prophylactic measure, all children entering public institutions should be examined for molluscum, and isolated until cured. Removal of early lesions appears not only to prevent spread to others, but also the development of new lesions upon the person affected.

VERRUCA SENILIS.

Synonyms.—Verruca plana; Keratosis pigmentosa.

This variety of benign warty growth is, as its name implies, peculiar to the aged. It occurs as compact, soft, flat, indolent growths of a dirty brown color, varying in size from a split pea to a one-cent piece, located upon the face, body, or arms. They are often numerous, especially upon the back, develop quite rapidly at times, and coalesce forming patches. The chief importance attached to verruca senilis is that it may become the starting point of an epithelioma, especially if subjected to irritation. The growth consists mainly of hypertrophied epidermis and can be readily removed by scraping. This procedure occasions some bleeding, there being a hypertrophic papillary body brought to view by the removal of the growth.

ELEPHANTIASIS.

Synonyms.—Elephantiasis Arabum; Barbadoes leg; Pachydermia; Lymph-Scrotum; Eléphancie.

Elephantiasis of the Arabs is an affection of the skin and subjacent tissues, characterized by a chronic hypertrophic process which, in many cases, leads to enormous increase in the size of the affected parts; and when, as is usually the case, the lower extremities are implicated, the deformity produced is very suggestive of an elephant's legs, whence the affection derives its name.

It is a disease much more frequently observed in tropical regions, but cases are not rarely encountered in this country, as well as in other temperate climes the world over. Although the legs and feet are the seat of disease in the great majority of instances, the upper extremities, face, breast, and other parts may occasionally suffer, and the scrotum in the male and the labia in the

PLATE LXI.

Fig. I.—Elephantiasis of leg.
Fig. II.—Elephantiasis of scrotum.

FIGS. I. and II.—AFTER ARAUJO.

female not infrequently become greatly enlarged, and the genitals gradually disappear within the hypertrophic mass, as illustrated in the plate. Such a scrotal tumor may attain a weight of over a hundred pounds. Lymph scrotum is only another phase of the same general pathological process, and may exist alone or be associated with other evidences of the disease. In rare instances, the abdomen, breasts, face, or other portions of the body are affected.

SYMPTOMS AND COURSE.—Strictly speaking, the condition is not a skin disease, for the subcutaneous tissues are more decidedly implicated than the derma, and the great deformity resulting from the œdema and infiltration of the tissues beneath the skin, together with the concomitant lymphangitis, are disproportionate to the thickening of the true skin and epidermis. The earliest manifestation of the disease is an attack of fever resembling a severe intermittent, attended or soon followed by localized inflammation, lymphangitis, with enlarged and tender glands. The parts affected become œdematous, and as the febrile symptoms disappear this œdema persists. After an interval of some weeks, or perhaps months, the patient has a repetition of his fever, and the local manifestations are now, perhaps, more severe than before, though possibly not so painful; and as they subside, the tissues are found still further increased in volume and more indurated. Thus successive attacks finally result in an enormous hypertrophy of the limb or scrotum in some instances, while in others the lymphatic inflammation becomes arrested earlier, and the resulting deformity is not so great. The marked skin changes proper show themselves after the active stage of the disease is passed, and we then get, in a certain proportion of cases, pigmentation, fissures, warty growths, an eczematous condition with scales and crusts, and subsequently ulceration. In other cases, the skin assumes a livid or dark color. The lymphatics become often prominent and tortuous. Vesicles form in the substance of the skin, and, when ruptured, exude great quantities of lymph. The decomposition of the discharges from an elephantiasis in this stage, especially when fissured and ulcerating, is often offensive beyond description. Fortunately, a chronic hypertrophy without exudation characterizes many cases, and it must be acknowledged that some cases are chronic from the first, and give no history of lymphangitis. When the leg is the part affected, the tissues above the ankle often present a succession of rolls or superimposed masses of thickened and darkened skin. The general health is but little affected in some cases after the inflammatory stage is passed, but constitutional symptoms may be so severe as to cause death, especially in lymph-scrotum.

ETIOLOGY.—Climate has much to do with the prevalence of the disease, and it is much more frequently seen in Brazil, for example, than in any part of the United States. Tropical countries furnish the necessary conditions for its development and existence as an endemic disease. Malaria, poverty, and bad hygienic surroundings have been looked upon as causes of the affection, whose victims are, as a rule, those in the lower walks of life. Heredity plays no part in its production, and it is not contagious. It may begin at any age. Moncoro has observed it twenty-four times in infancy; once at the age of fifteen days, and once at four months.

Lymphatic obstruction occasions the inflammatory symptoms, and in many cases, if not in all true instances of elephantiasis and lymph-scrotum, this occlusion results from the presence of the filaria sanguinis hominis. Both conditions are closely allied to chyluria, in which disease Wucherer found the embryo of this parasite in 1866, since which time the male and female worms have been repeatedly found in elephantiasis. In an excellent description of the filaria and its life-cycle, by Dr. Christie in McCall Anderson's recent work, he says "the female worm is a long, slender, hair-like animal quite three inches in length." When embryos issue from the parent in the lymphatics, "by vigorous movements they pass the parenchyma of the gland, and emerging into the afferent vessels, are borne along the current till, having traversed gland after gland, they pass into the thoracic duct, and finally into the blood itself." Dr. Manson thinks undeveloped ova may become arrested in minute branches and produce embolus, and thus be the immediate cause of elephantiasis within the endemic area of this disease; but when the disease occurs outside of this area, where the filaria does not exist, then some other cause for the impaction of the lymphatics must be sought for. Within the human body the filaria is encased, as it were, in a sac and undergoes no change. The female of a species of mosquito has been found to act as intermediate host, by sucking from the blood of the affected person the filaria, which becomes liberated when the mosquito dies, and finds its way into water, which being drunk by a human being reproduces the affection. Syphilis may occasion vascular obstruction and lead to elephantisis, but otherwise has no influence on its production.

PATHOLOGY.—All the tissues of an affected region are found hypertrophied as a result of inflammation and occlusion of the lymphatics, with coagulation of retained lymph. The skin is thickened, the papillæ enlarged, and the elastic areolar and fatty tissues increased in amount. Bands of connective tissue resist the knife on section of the part, and enlarged lymphatics are abundant.

Robinson says there is "a true lymphatic œdema, and the abundant active leucocytes it contains not only directly become connective-tissue corpuscles, but induce also a hyperplasia of the fixed cells already present." There is hypertrophy of the lymphatic ganglia, and dilatation of the vessels. Endo- and peri-arteritis and phlebitis may be present, the nerves hypertrophied, and the muscles in a state of fatty degeneration.

PROGNOSIS depends upon whether the inflammatory process becomes early arrested or undermines the health by repeated attacks, and causes at the same time great enlargement and much hardening of the tissues. In some cases the weight of the mass is the only complaint, and the patient may live many years. A patient in Charity Hospital some years ago was over seventy years of age. The harder the tissues the graver the prognosis. Suppuration in lymph scrotum is often speedily fatal, especially if the patient be of feeble constitution. Removal of the scrotal tumor is usually successful.

DIAGNOSIS.—The disease is entirely distinct from leprosy, though occasionally lepers acquire it. It may be confounded with simple hypertrophy, hard œdema, and excessive thickening of the leg seen in some chronic cases of eczema, ulcer and cellulitis of the leg, associated with varicose veins, and giving rise to a pseudo-elephantiasis. In the same way an enlarged scrotum from mechanical or inflammatory blocking up of the lymphatics might be mistaken for lymph-scrotum due to the presence of filaria ova, and it might be confounded with an exaggerated case of molluscum fibrosum, nævus lipomatodes, or dermatolysis.

TREATMENT.—The onset is to be met by complete rest, antipyretics, and local antiphlogistics, and the recurrent attacks of lymphangitis treated in the usual way. After the acute symptoms have passed, the patient must be sent, if possible, to a dry, healthy region where the disease is not endemic.

Various plans of treatment have been employed, but those which give the best results are ligature of the artery supplying the part, the careful application of the elastic bandage, and electricity. Elevated position of the part must be maintained, and inunction with iodine and mercurial preparations may be added with benefit. Silva Aranjo, of Rio de Janeiro, whose observations extend to over four hundred cases, has obtained excellent results from electrolysis. He first used the induction current of electricity in treating a case of lymph-scrotum in 1877 with such success that he was led to give it further trial. In this country, Beard and Rockwell had previously employed electricity in treating this disease, but Dr. Aranjo appears to have used it before knowing that others had worked in the same field, and, together with Dr. Moncorvo, has given it extensive trial. His manner of applying electrolysis is as follows : He inserts from three to five needles into the most resistant part of the hypertrophy, which has previously been benumbed by the application of salt and ice or some local anæsthetic. The needles are attached to the negative pole of a continuous current battery, while the positive pole is applied to some other part of the body. To avoid the possibility of exciting a lymphangitis, the needles are anointed with an antiseptic ointment after Lister's method. To begin with, six elements are used, and increased up to sixty, according to the necessities of each case. The number of sittings varies greatly. One case of cure is reported after fifteen applications, but the method must be persisted in patiently even for many years, until the benefit is obtained. It is well to practise massage and apply a rubber bandage in the intervals while electrolysis is being used. Its mode of action seems to be by quickening the circulation of the lymph, combating the paralysis of the lymphatics, and causing absorption of the hypertrophied tissues.

Ligature of the artery supplying the limb has been practised with success by Carnochan, of this city, as early as 1851, and Leonard has collected sixty-nine cases thus treated, with forty recoveries and thirteen improvements; but in tropical countries the benefit seems to be only of a temporary nature. Elephantiasis of the scrotum and of the labia majora may be removed by operation, and, as a last resort, a limb may be amputated. In a severe case at Charity Hospital, where operation became necessary on account of extensive ulceration, copious discharge, and great pain, the disease appeared in the opposite leg soon after amputation.

Plate LXI. is taken from a photograph, kindly furnished by Dr. Aranjo, of a patient whom he subsequently treated by electrolysis with great benefit. The man was thirty-five years of age, and the disease had existed for nine years. One year after treatment was begun, the size of the foot was reduced almost to the normal, and the circumference of the calf had been decreased one-half or more.

LEUCODERMA.

Synonym.—Vitiligo.

An acquired whitening of the skin in one or more rounded patches is the condition to which the names leucoderma and vitiligo have been given. The patches have a sharply defined margin, which is usually convex, and, as they increase in size and coalesce, a patch with irregular outline may be formed. The skin of these whitened areas, aside from the loss of pigment, appears quite normal. There is no scaliness, atrophy, or change in sensation, and no alteration excepting that of pigment deficiency is shown by the microscope. The skin immediately surrounding the white spots becomes more darkly pigmented in most instances, making a striking contrast, and giving the impression that the pigment has been pushed ahead of the creeping patch. Dark-skinned races are more subject to this deformity than others, and negroes who are gradually turning white are not uncommonly seen in this country, while instances of the affection in so-called "leopard boys" are usually to be found in some of the dime museums of this city. It is a very chronic affection, and may spread gradually over a greater portion of the body in the course of years.

There are usually no subjective symptoms, though itching has in some instances been said to precede it, and an excess of pigment has also been noted before the whitening.

ETIOLOGY.—The affection appears to be of nervous origin, depending in some cases upon perverted innervation of the sympathetic, and occasionally follows some severe constitutional disease or local injury. It is more common in those having a dark skin, being frequent in the tropics, and in white races is said often to begin near a pigmentary mole. In summer it becomes more conspicuous because of the darkening of the neighboring skin. In this country it is observed in about the proportion of one to four hundred skin cases.

It occurs in the lower animals as well as in man. Kaposi speaks of it in the horse, and it appears that the piebald appearance of a "white" elephant recently exhibited here was due to a similar loss of pigment.

DIAGNOSIS is not very difficult. It usually has a symmetrical distribution, and may occur upon any part of the body. Chloasma, with which it may be confounded, is due to an excessive deposit of pigment in the skin, but here it is the border of the dark patch, and not the white, which is convex. In lepra the patches are not so round nor so white, and are apt to be anæsthetic and atrophic, or else thickened. In pityriasis versicolor there are scales which can be scraped off, and in which the parasite can be found. This differs, too, from leucoderma in being slightly itchy at times, and in the fact that it can be readily cured. In morphœa there are changes in the skin's structure, causing a thinning and parchment-like condition, which distinguish it.

PLATE LXII.

FIG. I.—Leucoderma.
FIG. II.—Alopecia areata.

FIG. I.—AFTER NEUMANN.
FIG II.—AUTHOR'S COLLECTION.

Albinism is also a disease common in dark races, and when partial might readily be regarded as leucoderma, but it is due to a congenital lack of pigment in the tissues and is often called congenital leucoderma. The borders of the patch are here never more strongly pigmented as is the case in the acquired form.

Syphilis, especially in women, not infrequently produces spots like vitiligo, especially about the neck, with increased pigmentation surrounding them and such spots may remain after other lesions have disappeared. Finally, white spots may be left upon the skin either for a short time or permanently as a result of burns, injury, or disease. In psoriasis for example, the site of the spots is often left white for a time after the lesions have been removed, and if chrysarobin has been used the contrast is more noticeable.

PROGNOSIS.—As regards any effect upon the constitution, or even upon the skin itself, leucoderma must be looked upon as a most innocent disease. In rare instances the skin may regain its natural color, but as a rule the patches remain white and tend to spread over large areas, until at times almost the whole body becomes involved. .

TREATMENT.—Unless upon parts exposed to view, treatment is scarcely necessary, for the most that can be done is to remove or modify the surrounding excess of pigment by applying acids, a strong solution of corrosive sublimate, bismuth, or some other remedy used in curing chloasma. Negroes often take it much to heart that they are turning white, and demand energetic treatment. Blisters may be applied to the spots of leucoderma and may have the effect of causing a deposit of pigment, but as a rule it soon disappears again. Internally nerve tonics with strychnia, but especially arsenic long continued, is the course of treatment which offers the best results. The spots, if disfiguring, may be stained with walnut juice or other pigment, and where the hair has become white in patches from extension of the disease to the scalp, some dye may be used to restore the color. Spontaneous arrest of the process may take place, but most instances of improvement or supposed cure are due to a disappearance of surrounding pigmentation, or to the lack of contrast from the whole surface becoming uniformly white.

ALOPECIA AREATA.

Synonyms.—Alopecia Circumscripta ; Area Celsi. Fr. *Pelade.*

In alopecia which occurs in well-defined areas, for the most part round, appearing suddenly and leaving the surface smooth and free from any sign of eruption, we have one of the most interesting and striking affections of all dermatology. Though the bald spots are produced mainly upon the scalp, they are not infrequently seen upon the bearded part of the face, and they may be found upon any hairy region. The whole surface may in fact become involved in the shedding of the hair, and I have seen a patient on whose entire body scarcely a hair could be found. In other cases, a strip of bare scalp may be discovered extending across the head, in a serpentine course, or gradually the greater portion or the whole of the scalp may become bald. Usually, however, the number of spots is limited to two or three upon the top, back, or sides of the head, as shown in the plate. The whiteness of the bald spot is sometimes almost like that of chalk ; in other cases like ivory, and the smoothness has suggested that of a billiard ball. A woman with complete alopecia of the scalp, now on exhibition in this city, is in fact advertised as "the human billiard ball." · The marked contrast between the white areas and the remaining hair, firmly rooted and healthy at the very margin of the patch which has ceased to spread, makes the condition conspicuous and remarkable. For this reason most patients affected come under treatment, and they are found to furnish about two per cent of all skin diseases. It is, however, more common in France than here. As there are no subjective sensations, the patient may be unconscious of his sudden loss of hair, but it occasionally happens that the hair becomes loosened over a considerable area, and comes out in quantities at the slightest touch.

Though, as I have said, there are no subjective symptoms, tenderness on pressure over the spot is at times acknowledged; sometimes there is anæsthesia. After a variable time, lanugo hairs appear upon the bald spots, and after attaining a certain development they, too, are shed, and thus several crops may grow and fall off before permanent healthy hairs are produced. The first crop of stout hair is apt to be devoid of pigment, and we have the smooth spots replaced by patches of white hair. In time, these, too, are shed, and a growth of normal color finally appears. In the very severe universal form of alopecia, a permanent new growth cannot always be obtained even after most energetic treatment. These cases begin as circular areas of baldness, which extend, coalesce, and finally implicate the whole surface, or the hair is lost from all parts simultaneously. Relapses are not common, but Dr. Hardaway has reported two cases in which the alopecia recurred each spring for a number of years in succession.

ETIOLOGY.—Though much has been written upon the cause of this affection, authors are by no means in accord. It has been usual to regard it as a tropho-neurotic disease and in many instances preceding neuralgias, shock, injury to the head and nerve lesions have been shown. Cases of universal alopecia in which the whole body rapidly becomes devoid of hair, especially after mental shock, seem properly to be looked upon as tropho-neuroses, and it is difficult to assign any other reason for a certain class of cases which come on after an injury to a nerve or follow a blow upon the head, although it is possible that, parasites being present, the injury may but serve to call them into activity. On the other hand, there is an abundance of clinical evidence pointing to contagion. The affection has occurred repeatedly in quasi-epidemic form among soldiers, in schools, and in various members of a family. I have treated two brothers who slept together and developed alopecia at about the same time, in whose history there was complete absence of anything pointing to the nervous system as a cause, and I could not believe that heredity played any part. Hillier reports an instance strongly confirmatory of the parasitic theory, in which no less than forty-three girls in a large parochial school suddenly affected after a single case had been known to exist for some time. It was limited to girls between the ages of seven and fourteen. Gruby first advanced the parasitic theory in 1843, and gave to the parasite which he discovered the name *Microsporon Audouini*. Since then Bazin has found and described the *Microsporon decalvans*, and Thin, von Sehlen, Robinson, and others have been rewarded in their investigations by the discovery of still other micro-organisms supposed to bear a causative relation to the disease. Unfortunately for the theory, which I believe to be the correct one, so far as a large class of cases of true alopecia areata is concerned, the micro-organisms described are not identical, nor has the observation of any one investigator been properly confirmed or the disease been artificially reproduced. On the other hand, alopecia areata, or at least a falling of the hair which closely resembles it, can be produced by nerve injury. Max Joseph has caused such an effect in cats by removing the spinal ganglion of the second cervical nerve.

The micrococci which Robinson has described are deeply situated in the corium, mostly in the lymph spaces, but also seen in the lymph-vessels and blood-vessels, both of which may be obstructed by them and thus lead to coagulation of fibrin and other changes not otherwise easily explained. The cocci are regarded by Thin as identical with those described by himself as present in the hairs of alopecia areata. The extension of the patch is explained by their travelling in the lymph spaces, and their deep situation would account for the rarity of contagion, and the slight effect of those remedies which do not penetrate deeply. In the series of cases examined by Robinson the cocci were constantly present. It seems probable that there are two varieties of alopecia, showing a tendency to develop in areas, one being contagious and presumably parasitic, and the other capable of being produced through nerve influence, such as the generalized alopecia following shock. Whether any micro-organism so far discovered has an etiological worth, or if the true one has yet to be discovered, remains to be seen.

ANATOMY.—Atrophy of the hair bulb and of the surrounding tissues is always present. There is usually also atrophy of the corium and epidermis in long-standing cases, destruction of sebaceous glands, and a diminution of pigment. Sometimes the hair shaft appears broken.

DIAGNOSIS is rendered easy by reason of the sudden and complete falling of the hair, and the well-defined limits of the bald spots. From ordinary baldness, or alopecia prematura, it is distinguished by these features, and by the more favorable prognosis. Congenital absence of hair from the whole head is distinguished from alopecia areata by the history.

The disease most likely to be mistaken for alopecia is a rare form of tricophytosis of the scalp, in which the round patches are left quite smooth, or show but few broken hairs upon the surface. It is quite common to find a few hairs, either broken or of normal length, or a tuft of hair still growing from the white spot in alopecia areata, and in all doubtful cases the microscope should be used to make the matter of diagnosis positive. It is quite probable that some cases of alopecia reported as showing marked contagious properties have been due to tricophyton disease producing these alopecia-like smooth areas. When the hairs have grown in white, as they sometimes do, the patch may resemble vitiligo, but in the latter the hairs are of normal size, while in alopecia they are finer, shorter, and weaker than those beyond the patch. Occasionally the disease is associated with vitiligo.

PROGNOSIS for final recovery is good in the alopecias of rounded area; a new growth of hair usually appearing in the course of a few months. In universal forms of tropho-neurotic origin, in which oftentimes the nails too are affected, all treatment may fail to produce any amelioration of the unfortunate condition, and the deformity remains a permanent one. Recurrence is rare.

TREATMENT.—Those who believe in the neurotic theory of the disease advise internal treatment and nerve tonics. These certainly find their use in those acknowledged cases of tropho-neurotic origin, but in all others, unless the general health requires attention, most reliance must be placed upon external remedies. There is a great variety of these which have been in favor at different times, and the great number of methods advanced indicate how little efficacious any one of them is. Repeated blistering of the patch is probably the procedure which has been looked upon with most favor for patches of limited area. Cantharidal plaster or collodion is usually employed; but to secure good results, prevent spreading, and hasten recovery, it should be applied so as to overlap the margin of the hairless patch, and a new blister must be produced as soon as the last one has healed, and this kept up for some time or until new hair begins to grow. Schachmann reports twenty-nine cases so treated, with a favorable result in each instance inside of three months. Croton oil has been successfully employed in sufficient strength to create a decided dermatitis. In obstinate cases, 50% strength may be required, but as a rule one part to five of olive oil will suffice. Robinson believes that any irritant must be strong enough to cause a sufficient exudation of white blood-corpuscles into the lymph channels to destroy the micrococci there present. Drugs having marked antiparasitic properties have been found of much value when applied in sufficient strength and with sufficient persistence. Of these, chrysarobin, sulphur, mercurial preparations, and naphthol may be mentioned. In a series of fifteen cases, Thin obtained uniformly good results from the use of sulphur ointment well rubbed in. Chrysarobin produces a dermatitis of the scalp, and is also an excellent parasiticide, whose use has been followed by the most favorable results in recent cases. An ointment of ʒi. to ʒi. of lard, or lard and lanoline, should be applied with friction morning and night, care being taken not to allow the effect to extend to the region of the eyes. Pyrogallic acid I have found of value in some cases, and naphthol has appeared to exert a beneficial influence in others. In one case the hair began to grow shortly after the patient had, by mistake, begun to rub in the pure beta-naphthol crystals.

Of mercurial preparations, either an oleate of from two to twenty per cent strength, or the corrosive chloride from one to five grains to the ounce can be used. In Vienna, the expressed oil of mace is a favorite application. In England, much has been claimed for strong spirits of ammonia applied by means of a flannel mop until the spots become sensitive, and for spirits of turpentine rubbed in with a sponge twice daily.

Pilocarpine injections have been somewhat successfully employed. One-thirtieth of a grain or more of the hydrochlorate may be injected into a patch twice a week, but I have seen very disagreeable effects; profuse perspiration, weakness, vomiting, and diarrhœa follow within a short time after larger doses.

Finally, electricity is recommended for cases of long standing, and cutaneous faradization appears to be as appropriate a mode of treatment for the late as the antiparasitic is for the early stage. It is applied by brushing over the bald spot daily with a wire brush, while the opposite moist sponge-electrode is held by the patient. The scalp and wire brush must both be quite dry, and the movements be slowly made until the patch has become red. Whatever method of treatment may be chosen, it must always be borne in mind that in time the affection tends to spontaneous recovery, and we must not always attribute the cure to the last means employed.

KELOID.

Synonyms.—Cheloid; Keloid of Alibert.

This disease, which Alibert first described under the name of cancroid, and afterwards called kelis, is a fibro-cellular new-growth which begins as a cell infiltration about the vessels in the corium, and produces a circumscribed tumor of a pinkish hue and cicatricial aspect raised above the skin level, over which the epidermis appears tense, giving the surface a smooth, shining appearance, the whole having the form of a crab with claws extending into the surrounding healthy skin. Its usual situation is upon the chest, though any region of the body may be affected.

At first, one or more small nodules are noticed, and by a gradual increase in size, perhaps extending over several years, a tumor from an inch in length to the size of the palm may be produced. Once having attained its greatest development, the growth remains stationary, perhaps for a life-time, or it may undergo a retrograde metamorphosis and disappear, leaving behind a whitened, depressed cicatrix. This is the history of so-called spontaneous keloid; it may come without an assignable cause, and disappear in the same way. There is, however, a form of keloid which is due to injury, and which is known as *false keloid* or *scar keloid.* It develops upon cicatricial tissue, and is prone to occur in the pits of small-pox, to follow lesions of syphilis, to produce nodules in the lobe of the ear after piercing, and to result from surgical operations, injuries, and especially burns. This spurious keloid is very frequent in the negro, and the color of the tumor is apt to be several shades darker than the surrounding skin. The distinction between the idiopathic and the cicatricial forms of keloid are not marked, and the history of preceding ulcerative process and scar-formation must be elicited. While true keloid is at times attended with symptoms of burning, pain, and itching, especially at night, it is said that false keloid does not itch, and the pain is not apt to be so marked. Scar keloid differs from hypertrophic scar in its ability to pass beyond the limits of the cicatrix in which it develops, while the latter never does. Addison's keloid, usually called morphœa, is an entirely distinct disease.

ETIOLOGY.—Doubt has been expressed as to the spontaneous development of keloid in any case, as it is known to follow at times such slight lesions as those produced by leech bites, acne, herpes, excoriations, blisters, etc. The frequent location over the sternum, a situation much exposed to blows and often subjected to irritant application and pressure, is advanced in support of this theory. A predisposition to keloid appears to exist in certain families, but why one individual or one variety of scar tissue should show a tendency to keloidal formation has not yet been discovered. Dénériaz in a recent thesis has suggested that as the disease always begins as a hyperæmic nodule, it might be due to the presence of microbes, especially as giant cells are found, and these usually form about foreign bodies, and particularly where micrococci exist.

TREATMENT.—Excision and caustic applications are unsatisfactory, for the growth almost invariably returns in the scar because of the diathesis. If excision is practised, the incision should be made as far as practicable from the margin of the growth. Guyard has secured excellent results from multiple scarifications at regular intervals as recommended by Vidal, having treated seven cases by this method. The scarifications must be continued until all indurated tissue entirely disappears.

Hardaway has reported some good results from electrolysis in keloid, as well as in hypertrophic scars, but so far the experience of others who have tried the method has not been uniformly favorable. In view of the occasional spontaneous disappearance of the growth, some advise that no active treatment be undertaken, but that application of an anodyne and antipruritic nature be used to relieve the symptoms which in some cases are quite distressing.

FIBROMA.

Synonyms.—Molluscum fibrosum ; Fibroma Molluscum.

This affection is characterized by the presence of tumors upon the surface of the body varying in size from the smallest nodules which can be felt beneath the skin to growths weighing many pounds. They are for the most part round, pyriform or polypoid, indolent, soft, with usually a lax covering of the color of the surrounding skin, and not prone to ulcerate. They are of hereditary origin and may be thickly disseminated over the surface, as nodules imbedded in the skin and pedunculated growths standing out upon it. Bateman was the first to accurately describe the disease, and most authors have followed his description, ascribing to the growths a slight degree of sensibility and an elasticity due to its fibrous nature. It is essentially a benign formation, unattended by any symptoms save those due to the weight of the growths when large, but occasionally becomes the seat of more serious neoplastic formation, and thus we find *Sarcomatous Molluscum* described by Malassez, and carcinomatous and epitheliomatous changes reported by others. The affection is not at all common here, but is more frequent in eastern countries. Dr. Hashimoto, of Japan, showed a patient, at a recent meeting of the Tokio Medical Society, upon whose body were counted no less than 4,503 tumors of various sizes, which had been in process of development for forty-two years, one having reached a diameter of 39 centimetres. The patient's father and sister were similarly affected. Dr. Ledeard reported in the *Lancet*, II. 63, 1887, a case in which the body was covered with molluscum, and a pendulous fibroma which had existed from birth hung down like a satchel from the left iliac crest, and, when removed, was found to weigh six pounds.

PATHOLOGY.—Fibrous connective tissue forms the principal part of the structure of these tumors. It probably arises from the deeper layers of the corium and subcutaneous tissues, although Von Recklinghausen sought its origin in the nerve connective tissue, while Fagg and Hawse believe it to arise from the connective tissue of the hair sac. Spindle-shaped, oval and round cells are also found. On section of a tumor a homogeneous white or yellowish substance, soft at the periphery and more dense towards the base, is observed. On pressure a thick white liquid can be squeezed out, and in some instances the soft contents of the tumors become absorbed and an empty sac is left, but in most cases the tendency is towards an increase in size. Pendulous folds of skin and sac-like masses attached by a rather broad base, while occurring mostly in association with smaller fibromata, sometimes exist in their absence. This condition is known as dermatolysis, which means laxity of the skin, or, it is more properly called, *fibroma pendulum*. It may affect the side of the head, as in a patient, familiar to many, who has been an inmate of Bellevue Hospital for many years. In this case, great masses of skin hang down from the side of the scalp and brow, while upon the body are many Molluscum tumors. In other cases the region of the buttocks or hips is most affected. The majority of patients with fibroma are found to be stunted in physical development and of slight mental capacity.

ETIOLOGY.—As already mentioned, the affection is usually of hereditary origin, and sometimes congenital. A form of localized fibroma occurring after injury has been mentioned by Schwimmer. Taylor, who has also studied this subject, presented a patient at the New York

PLATE LXIII.

Fig. I.—Keloid.
Fig. II.—Fibroma.

FIG. I.—AFTER HYDE.
FIG. II.—AFTER OUCHTERLONY.

Dermatological Society in 1887 upon whose shoulder were a number of soft fibromata said to have resulted from a human bite. Von Recklinghausen believes in a close connection between the nerves and the development of fibroma in a part, having found the co-existence of fibroma and neuroma on post-mortem examination. Atkinson had, previous to this observation, noted the existence of these two forms of tumor in a case which he reported. Taylor thinks that nerve injury offers the only explanation of the origin of his cases which conforms to the history of injury and the shape of the patch. We might designate this variety, which is consecutive to injury of the part false fibroma, just as we have a variety of false keloid. It is apparently a local affection.

DIAGNOSIS is not attended with any difficulty. The condition most closely resembling it is one of single fibroma occupying the head or back, mostly seen in elderly persons. Soft moles might also mislead, but here, as well as in the later form of new-growth, the epidermis is usually altered, while in molluscum it is not. Neuroma follows the course of nerves, and the tumors are apt to be painful. Lipoma makes a lobulated tumor in the skin which does not become pedunculated. Multiple sarcoma is also a widely disseminated form of tumor, often pigmented, however, and coming on suddenly in adult life.

TREATMENT consists in removal by operation when, on account of the size or deformity, this is deemed advisable. Very large growths have been successfully operated, and no recurrence has taken place; but to secure this result the removal must be complete. Pedunculated tumors are readily operated upon by ligature or the galvano-cautery, which are preferable to the knife or scissors because of the danger from hemorrhage.

XANTHOMA.

Synonyms.—Xanthelasma ; Vitiligoidea.

The designation which Rayer first gave to this affection, *plaques jaunâtres des paupières*, indicates the appearances usually presented, for in the great majority of cases the first if not the only lesions present consist in yellow patches upon the eyelids. A connective-tissue new-growth of benign nature having a marked predilection for the upper lids, though occasionally seen elsewhere, and occurring in soft velvety patches like chamois leather inserted into the skin, constitutes the disease now usually called xanthoma. It may be met with under two forms, *Xanthoma planum* and *Xanthoma tuberosum*, and may again be single or multiple, being limited in the one instance to the region of the eyes (*Xanthoma palpebrarum*), and in the other appearing upon the trunk and extremities. The plain variety projects but slightly above the skin level, the xanthomatous tissue being situated in the corium. The conformation of the patch is usually oval with its long diameter corresponding to that of the lid, or it may be arched and the margins are abrupt. To the touch it is smooth and soft; painless and unaltered by pressure. In individual cases the tint is very light, being cream-colored or light buff, while in others it is a deep orange or bronze. At the onset the lesion is only of a pin-head size, but usually it is not discovered until it has attained a considerable length; it may be after several years of gradual growth. In multiple xanthoma, involving various regions of the surface, there is as a rule jaundice, and the flexures of joints, palms, soles and genitals are the parts most likely to become involved, though mucous and serous membranes do not always escape, and in a few instances a rapid spreading to the whole body has been noted. In a number of instances it has been seen upon the elbows, knees and other parts while the region of the eyes remained free. A zoster-like distribution has also been reported by Hardaway suggestive of nerve origin.

The tubercles of xanthoma tuberosum vary in size from a pin's head to that of a bean. They may be diffuse or aggregated into patches, forming lesions which are more prominent to the view and touch and of firmer consistence than those of the plain variety. This tuberculated form may be found associated with the latter. There are no subjective symptoms excepting in

PLATE LXIV.

Figs. I., II., and III.—Xanthelasma.
Fig. IV.—Rhinoscleroma.

FIGS. I., II., and III.—AFTER HUTCHINSON.
FIG IV.—AFTER NEUMANN.

tubercular xanthoma when pain is occasionally complained of, especially when the palms and soles are involved, or from kneeling when the knees are affected.

ETIOLOGY.—Women are more frequently affected than men, and children rarely suffer, though it is at times congenital, and appears to differ little in infantile life from the disease as observed in adults. It is usually not met with before middle life. An hereditary tendency seems to exist; at least in some instances a family predisposition is manifest. Those having much pigmentation about the eyes are more prone to it, and half of Hutchinson's cases suffered from migraine. Probably more patients showing xanthoma are subject to jaundice or some form of liver derangement than any other disorder to which the lesions could be attributed. Hebra and Kaposi found icterus in fifteen out of thirty cases collected. Some observers regard jaundice as a secondary condition due to a xanthomatous affection of the liver or bile ducts, and in a certain number of cases the jaundice first appears long after the lesions of xanthoma. Diabetics now and then develop xanthoma. According to Crocker this is a form which should be considered as distinct from the usual varieties, because it is generally papular, occurs suddenly, affects the elbows, knees, etc., and not the eyelids, and after a time gets well, tending to undergo involution, at times quite rapidly.

PATHOLOGY.—Connective tissue forms the basis of this neoplasm, but fatty degeneration readily takes place in the growth, and in the meshes are to be found besides fat cells large epithelioid and infiltrated cells, and brownish or yellow pigment is present in the rete. The firmer the tubercle the greater the connective-tissue growth, and the softer the patch the more has fatty degeneration occurred. Xanthoma giant cells have also been described by Touton. It is believed by some that xanthomatous degeneration may take place in various new-growths not originally xanthoma.

DIAGNOSIS.—The only affection which one is likely to mistake for xanthoma is that known as milium. When aggregated about the eyes, the appearances presented by the latter may be quite similar to it, but upon pressure the contents of the milium papule can be removed and the nature of the growth thus made evident.

PROGNOSIS.—Spontaneous disappearance is as rare as it is a fortunate occurrence. In diabetes involution takes place, especially if the disease is improving under treatment. Degeneration into malignant growth has not been recorded. After attaining a certain size, the patches remain stationary, perhaps for many years, and unless removed by treatment, last during the patient's lifetime.

TREATMENT.—Excision, scraping out with the curette, or removing with the cutaneous punch are the favorite means of treatment.

In operation about the lids, the danger of producing ectropion must not be forgotten. Co-existing disorders of the hepatic system, diabetes, etc., should be sought for and treated.

RHINOSCLEROMA.

By the formidable appellation of rhinoscleroma, Hebra described an equally formidable, but fortunately rare disease of the nose and adjacent parts, which usually begins in the skin of the upper lip or first shows itself within the nostril, starting from the septum or one of the alæ nasi. The mucous membranes, soft tissues, and even, in rare instances, cartilage and bone, become implicated, and the disease is capable of perforating the soft palate and extending to the pharynx, and even to the larynx. It is a chronic disease of very slow evolution, and never, upon the skin at least, subject to ulceration or involution. There is a gradual thickening of the tissues, due to a formation within the corium of small-celled granulation tissue producing a tumor or a plaque by the aggregation of flat tubercles. These plaques are extremely hard to the touch, painless excepting on firm pressure, have sharply defined margins, are reddish brown or the color of the healthy surrounding skin, having, however, enlarged vessels over the surface, which is usually smooth and shining.

But when the epidermis becomes tense and dry, fissures are apt to form, and give rise to an offensive secretion which dries into adherent crusts.

ETIOLOGY.—Until recent years, little has been known of the nature of this affection. Indeed, it was only in 1870 that Hebra and Kaposi first described it, and opportunities for study are rare either here or in Europe. Kaposi regarded the disease as closely allied to the small-celled sarcoma. The pathological changes are almost wholly confined to the corium, where a dense infiltration of small cells is present, and in the mucous and submucous tissues there is also a connective-tissue new-growth. Frisch discovered and described a bacillus having a special form, being short, thick, and ovoid, possessed of a hard hyaline capsule, staining only at the ends, and occurring in groups both in and out of cells. This bacillus, supposed to be peculiar to rhinoscleroma, has been found by a number of other competent observers, and being quite constantly present in recent and old cases, furnishes strong presumptive evidence of the parasitic nature of the disease. Furthermore, rhinoscleroma exists almost endemically in certain parts of Central America and elsewhere, which would favor such a view.

DIAGNOSIS.—Though little difficulty will be encountered, the condition must be differentiated from a variety of others. Rhinophyma, which is a form of rosacea of an aggravated type, resembles it; but here the enlargement of the nose is soft, vascular, and a glandular condition is evident, while rhinoscleroma has an ivory-like hardness. Tubercular syphilis is also not so hard, tends to ulcerate, and improves under specific treatment.

Tubercular lupus and tubercular lepra, as well as scrofula, may be suggested by this condition.

Keloid is rare in this situation, and being of fibrous structure, an excised piece under the microscope would decide the question.

Epithelioma rarely affects the upper lip and alæ nasi primarily, ulcerates early, and shows outlying pearls. Sarcoma, also, would not remain hard and free from ulceration.

TREATMENT.—Excision appears to be of no avail, as the growth promptly returns. As the nares often become occluded, dilatation by sponge tents or laminaria, or boring through the diseased tissue with caustics, or some operation becomes necessary to facilitate breathing, and give temporary relief. Improvement has been reported by Crocker from salicylic acid applied in various ways externally, and given in ten-grain doses three times daily for a long period. Dr. Alvarez has succeeded in securing cicatricial tissue and improving the patient's condition by the combined use of the knife and the actual cautery, and Dr. Davies has also given one patient much relief by ablation of a portion of the growth followed by the thermo-cautery. This is a method of treatment which might succeed while the growth is still in its early stages.

XERODERMA PIGMENTOSUM.

This dermatosis, which the work of Hebra and Kaposi brought to the knowledge of the profession in 1870, and which the latter eminent dermatologist described at greater length in 1882, has now been studied by a number of observers and over forty cases have been recorded, eleven of these in this country, of which seven were seen by Taylor, two by White, and one each by Duhring and Heitzmann. Though the term xeroderma pigmentosum is now generally employed, authors have suggested almost as many designations as there have been separate observations of the disease; thus Taylor and Duhring, who first described cases in this country in 1877 and 1878, called it *xeroderma of Hebra*, and Taylor subsequently suggested the name *Angioma pigmentosum et atrophicum*. Vidal honored its discoverer by introducing the name *Dermatose de Kaposi*. Pick calls it *Melanosis lenticularis progressiva;* Neisser, *Liodermia cum melanosi et telangiectasia*, while Crocker prefers *atrophoderma pigmentosum*, because xeroderma, meaning parchment skin, is employed for a mild grade of ichthyosis. These various designations indicate the characteristic features of the affection, for we find melanosis, superficial atrophy of the skin, and vascular new-growths or telangiectases in the early stages, but there are important later changes which are not suggested by them. It is a disease of the family, appearing in early life, usually in the second year, and affecting a number of the children, especially those of the same sex. Those portions of the child's skin which are usually exposed to the sun's rays are in the great majority of instances alone implicated; the face and neck much more so than the hands, and the feet and legs least of all. The early lesions are in thé form of erythematous spots like small sun-burns or an eruption of measles, which are succeeded by pigmented spots, but in some instances rounded or irregular freckle-like deposits of pigment are the first symptoms noted. These pigmentary stainings are at first light brown, but gradually become darker, and by coalescing may form patches the size of small coin. This constitutes what may be regarded as the first stage. In the course of a few months, or by the end of the first year, a peculiar dryness of the skin has occurred, and it becomes thinned, stretched, glossy, and cicatricial-like, and irregularly dotted here and there with small bright telangiectases between the pigmentations. Or, as some maintain, the atrophic condition of the skin is subsequent to the angiomatous formation. Furfuraceous desquamation takes place, the skin becomes harsh, and in the course of a few years, or in rare instances only after many, during which the lesions come and go, the patient's general condition meanwhile remaining good, the last stage is entered upon. Now papillary or epitheliomatous growths resembling at times keratosis senilis, at others warty, fungoid, or vegetative lesions appear, sessile or pedunculated tumors form, the eyelids become ectropic, stenosis of the nose may occur, and the face presents a deformed appearance. Those lesions at the junction of mucous membranes are especially apt to take on malignant action, and in some cases all the tumors are clearly carcinomatous, while in others, at least for a time, they remain papillomatous. Ulceration finally takes place, and the patient falls into a marasmic condition and dies.

Little is known of the etiology of xeroderma, but the chief factor appears to be the effect of sun-light upon the skin of a child having an innate tendency to the affection. In a number of instances a family predisposition to cancer has been found, and some have looked upon xeroderma as a congenital variety of epithelial carcinoma.

As regards the pathology, Kaposi thinks the alterations begin in the papillary body and epidermis, and spread thence to the true skin. His examinations showed true epitheliomatous nests in the excised growths.

DIAGNOSIS.—The early stage is most likely to be regarded as a case of lentigo or freckles, but the preceding erythema, if noticed, and not confounded with measles, together with the subsequent white atrophy, will aid in making the distinction. The early stage is also not to be confounded with urticaria pigmentosa, likewise a disease beginning in infancy, not, however, limited to the face and hands. The telangiectases might be regarded as nævi. Lupus might suggest itself by the cicatricial-like skin, and the presence of crusts upon the ulcers of the last stage. Generalized scleroderma and macular or pigmentary leprosy have been mentioned as diseases necessary to distinguish from this condition.

TREATMENT must be for the most part palliative. The pigmentary growths should be excised or scraped out early before they show signs of carcinomatous nature or ulcerate, but new ones soon form. All sources of irritation should be removed. Conjunctivitis, which is usually present, should be carefully treated, as the secretions from the eyes may aid in causing ulceration. No cures have been reported and no line of treatment has given any very favorable results, so that about all that can be done at present is to treat symptomatically.

In the plate, which is taken from one of Vidal's five cases, the affection is represented in the second stage. Brown spots were first noticed upon the patient's face in the summer time at about the age of two and a half years. In six months' time these had covered the whole face. Eighteen months after the first symptoms the skin became dry, harsh, and was the seat of a desquamation. The picture represents the patient at the age of five years. For a year the skin of the neck has been covered with brown patches, and upon the face are small, warty elevations just beginning to appear; horny vegetations are seen upon the nose, right cheek, and upper lip. The mother could not tell just when the hands and forearms began to become pigmented.

PLATE LXV.

Figs. I. and II.—Xeroderma pigmentosum.

FIGS. I. and II.—AFTER VIDAL.

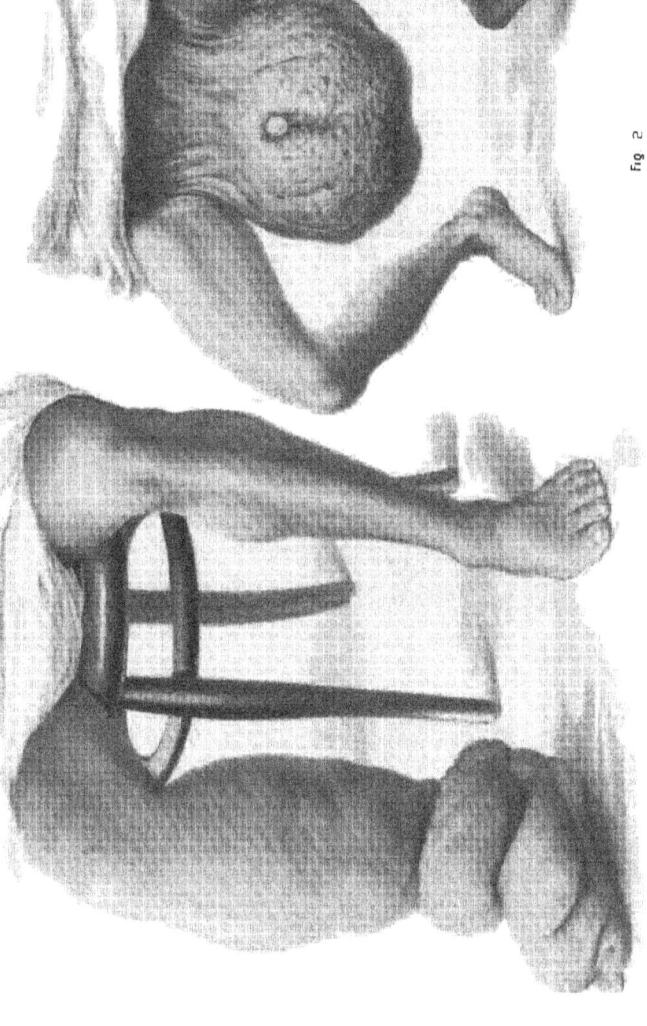

Fig 1

Fig 2

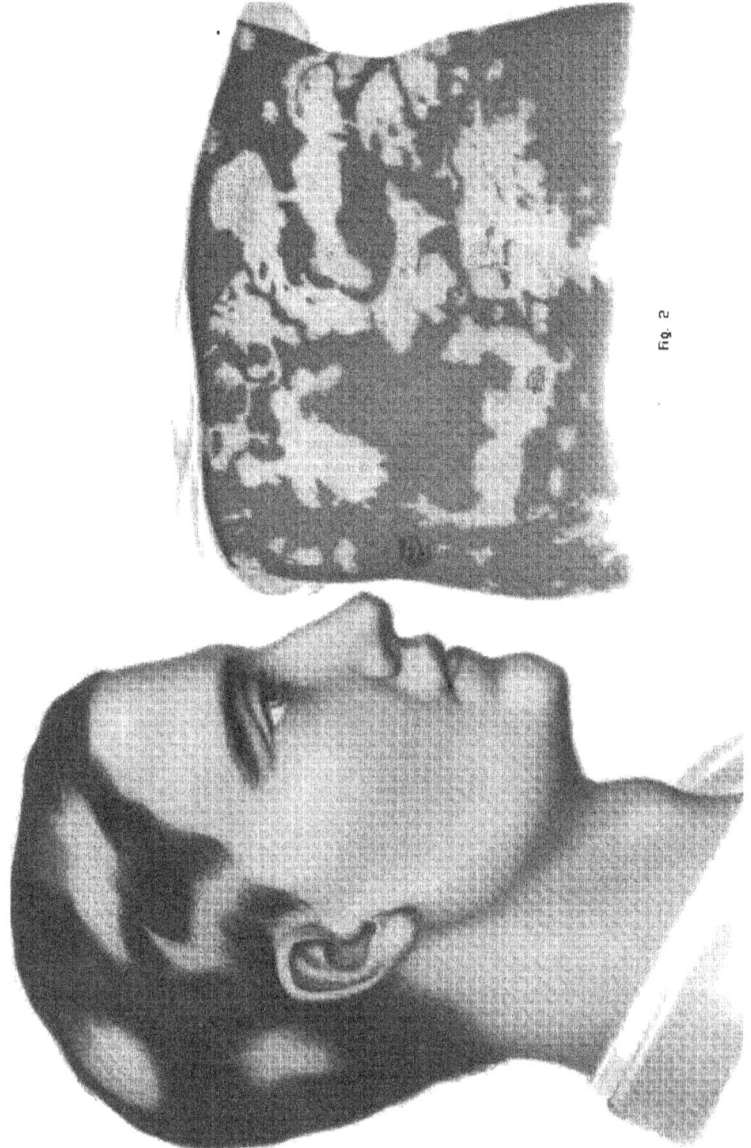

Fig. 2

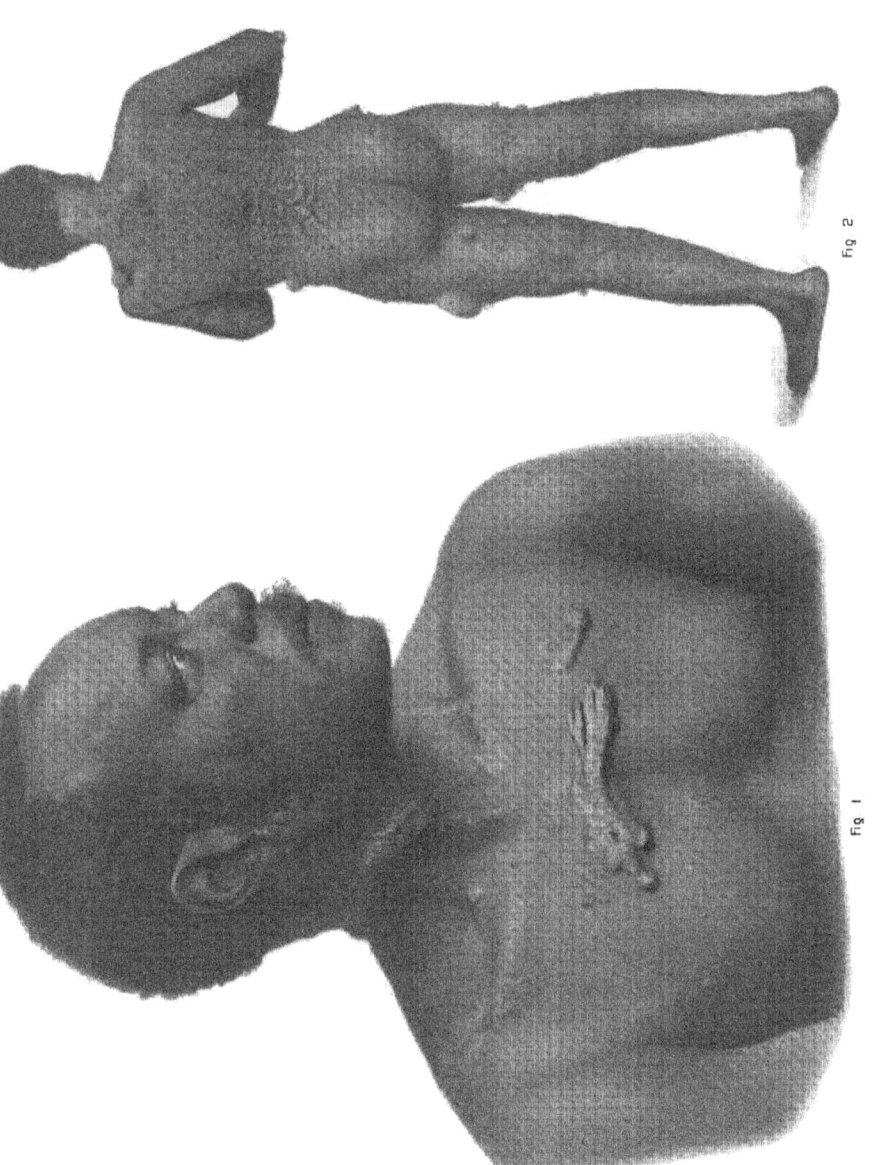

Fig 2

Fig 1

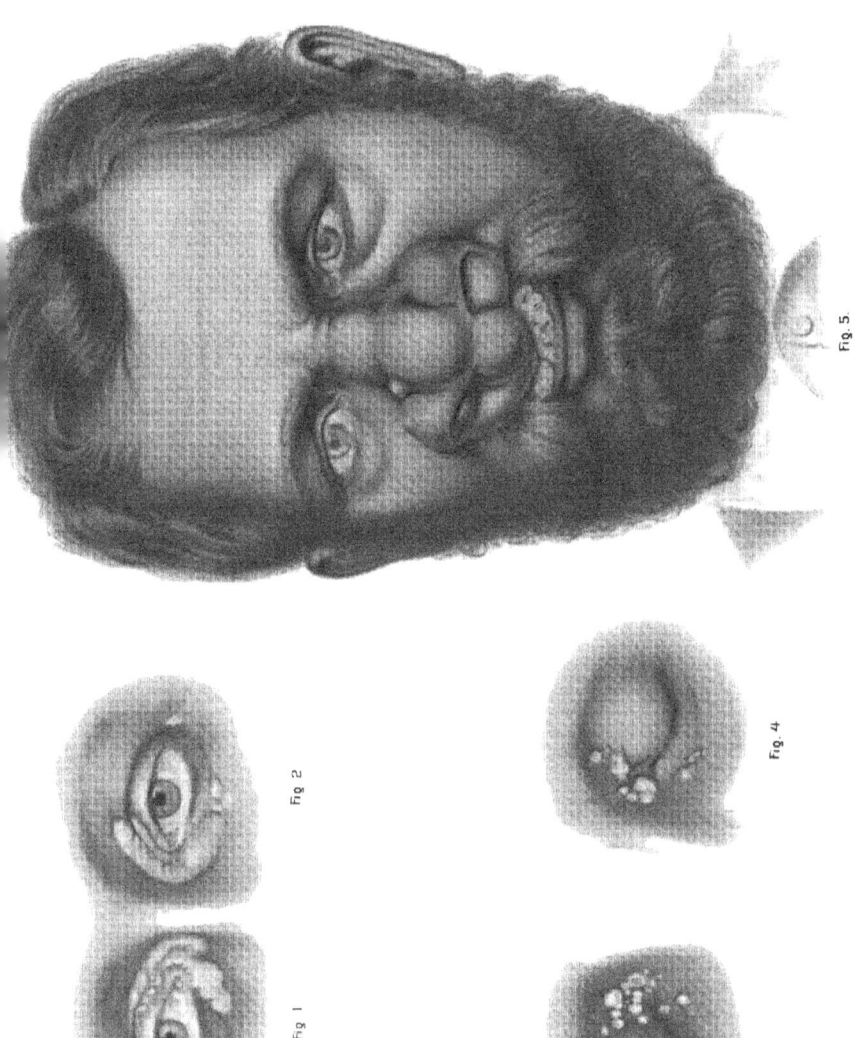

Fig 1

Fig 2

Fig. 3

Fig. 4

Fig. 5

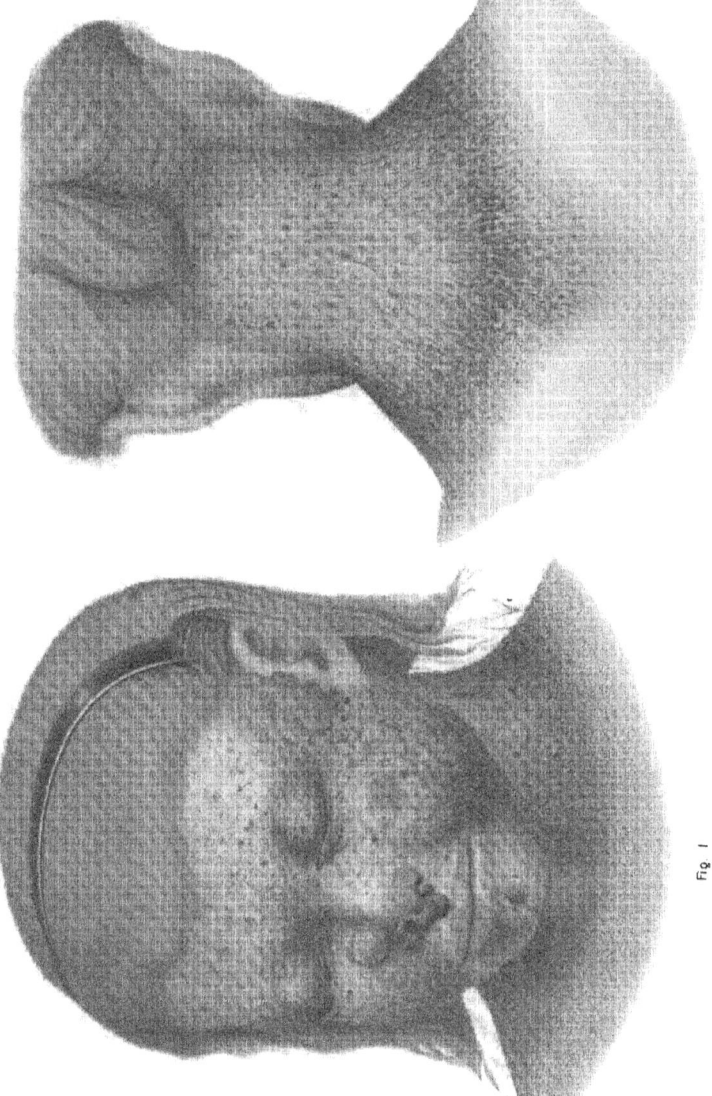

Fig. 1

Fig. 2

ATLAS

OF

VENEREAL AND SKIN

DISEASES

COMPRISING ORIGINAL ILLUSTRATIONS AND SELECTIONS FROM THE PLATES OF

Prof. M. KAPOSI, of Vienna; Mr. J. HUTCHINSON, of London; Prof. I. NEUMANN, of Vienna;
Profs. A. FOURNIER and HARDY; and Drs. RICORD, CULLERRIER, and VIDAL, of Paris;
Prof. LELOIR, of Lille; Dr. UNNA, of Hamburg; Dr. SILVA ARAUJO, of Rio Janeiro;
Dr. P. A. MORROW, of New York; Dr. E. L. KEYES, of New York; Dr. A. R.
ROBINSON, of New York; Dr. J. NEVINS HYDE, of Chicago;
Dr. HENRY G. PIFFARD, of New York, and others.

WITH ORIGINAL TEXT BY

PRINCE A. MORROW, A.M., M.D.,

CLINICAL PROFESSOR OF VENEREAL DISEASES, FORMERLY CLINICAL LECTURER ON DERMATOLOGY, IN THE UNIVERSITY OF THE CITY OF NEW YORK,
SURGEON TO CHARITY HOSPITAL, ETC.

NEW YORK

WILLIAM WOOD & COMPANY

1889

PROSPECTUS.

ATLAS

OF

VENEREAL and SKIN DISEASES

It is with special satisfaction that the publishers announce that this large and important work, which they have had in contemplation since 1883, is now ready for publication. It has long been recognized by them, from wide observation and acquaintance with similar works published in this country and abroad, that it is impossible for any one author to furnish, from his own collection of cases and illustrations, the most typical and at the same time the best and most lifelike pictures of the many peculiar forms of these diseases. Appreciating the defects and disadvantages arising from this cause, it was determined from the outset to enlist the co-operation, in the making of this ATLAS, of the leading dermatologists and syphilographers of the world. Prominent among them are Profs. M. Kaposi and I. Neumann, of Vienna. The atlas of the former, of venereal diseases, just completed, and that of the latter, of skin diseases, now being issued in parts, will be largely drawn upon in the preparation of this work, the sole right to reproduce them having been granted us by the authors.

Among other distinguished gentlemen who have engaged to contribute selections from their collections of original illustrations may now be mentioned Dr. J. Hutchinson, of London; Profs. A. Fournier and A. Hardy; and Drs. Ricord, Cullerrier, Besnier, and Vidal, of Paris; Dr. P. A. Morrow, of New York; Dr. Edward L. Keyes, of New York; Dr. Fessenden N. Otis, of New York; Dr. J. Nevins Hyde, of Chicago; Dr. Henry G. Piffard, of New York.

Other names will be added to this list as the work progresses.

The Editor of the work is Dr. Prince A. Morrow, of New York, who, in addition to plates contributed from his own remarkable collection, will write the treatise on skin and venereal diseases, which constitutes, besides the description of the plates, the text accompanying them.

In this treatise, it is aimed to include chiefly those features which are the most practical, omitting in great measure pathological and other considerations which would be more properly treated of in extended writings, rather than as the adjunct to an Atlas.

In regard to the character of the plates, it may be said, they are believed to be superior to anything of the kind heretofore produced—as accurate in drawing as photographs, and far more distinct, while the coloring faithfully represents nature.

The text is printed from new type, large, clear, and handsome, and the paper is heavy, with a highly finished surface.

Altogether, considering the reputation of the authors of the plates, the ability of the editor, the superb execution of the plates, the excellence of the presswork, the high quality of the paper of both text and plates, the large size of the page, etc., etc., this ATLAS OF VENEREAL AND SKIN DISEASES will be the most superb work in medical literature ever published in the English language.

The ATLAS OF VENEREAL AND SKIN DISEASES will be published in fifteen monthly parts, each containing five folio, chromo-lithographic plates, many of them containing numerous figures, all printed in flesh tints and colors, together with descriptive text for each plate, and from sixteen to twenty folio pages of a practical treatise upon venereal and skin diseases; the whole forming, when complete, one magnificent thick folio volume with seventy-five plates, containing several hundred figures, exquisitely printed in colors.

☞ The ATLAS OF VENEREAL AND SKIN DISEASES will be sold by subscription only, at the very moderate price of $2 per part.

WILLIAM WOOD & COMPANY, *Publishers,*

56 AND 58 LAFAYETTE PLACE, NEW YORK.

LUPUS ERYTHEMATOSUS.

Synonyms.—Lupus sebaceus; Seborrhœa congestiva; Scrofulide erythemateuse; Erythème centrifuge.

Lupus erythematosus may be defined as a chronic disease, characterized by the production of variously sized and shaped erythematous patches, covered with thin, closely adherent scales.

The proper position of this disease in the nosological category was for a long time indeterminate. In its clinical aspect and course it presents the features of a chronic inflammation of the skin, and it was first described by Biett as an erythema centrifugum. From its marked tendency to involvement of the sebaceous follicles it was classed by Hebra as seborrhœa congestiva, and still later Cazenave, recognizing its close anatomical relations with lupus, identified it as a superficial form of this disease. The lesions consist of circumscribed cellular infiltrations into the corium, which are followed by degeneration and a tendency to atrophic changes. Analogies with lupus vulgaris are so many and striking that it cannot properly be considered as a distinct and independent disease.

Lupus erythematosus usually begins in the form of small, pin-head-sized, slightly elevated spots, of a reddish color which disappears upon pressure. These spots are isolated or grouped about the sebaceous follicles, each covered by a small scale with an epidermic prolongation into the follicle beneath. By a coalescence or an aggregation of these spots there is formed a patch, roundish or irregularly circular in shape, the surface covered by a layer of grayish or yellowish, closely adherent scales. When the scales are forcibly detached the under surface presents small epidermic plugs or conical processes which dip down into the dilated and patulous follicles beneath.

By the coalescence of contiguous patches, or the development of new foci of aggregated cells in the intervening spaces, the disease advances, forming larger patches with a slightly elevated, well defined border. Coincident with this peripheral extension a tendency to atrophic change and cicatrization is observed in the centre of the patch. The central area becomes thinner, slightly depressed, and the patch finally presents a dry, shining centre with a peripheral border brighter in hue, clearly defined, and slightly elevated; upon this raised border the presence of comedones, as well as the thread-like, sebaceous plugs depending from the scales, show the participation of the glandular structures in the morbid process.

After complete involution the diseased areas are occupied by scars which are thin, white, and indelible; they may in some cases be so slight and superficial as to be scarcely noticeable.

This circumscribed form of the disease, characterized by peripheral morbid extension with coincident central atrophy, has been designated as *lupus erythematosus discoides.* A number of discs or patches may be present at the same time; their favorite seats are upon the nose and cheeks, but they may occur upon the eyelids, ears, and scalp, more rarely upon the fingers and toes. When the patches are limited to the nose and cheeks, there is often a symmetrical development, presenting the form of a butterfly with outstretched wings. When the scalp is involved by the morbid process, permanent alopecia of the affected surface results.

The disease is essentially chronic, remaining stationary or slowly spreading during months and years, and is usually unaccompanied by any appreciable impairment of the general health. It is much more common in women than in men, and in some cases it is associated with derangement of the digestive and uterine systems. The subjective sensations are usually slight or nil; sometimes itching, rarely pain is complained of. It is essentially a disease of adult life, seldom developing before the thirtieth year.

Under the title of *lupus erythematosus disseminatus,* Kaposi and others describe a disseminate form of the disease, never met with in this country, which is much graver in type and more malignant in its effects than the circumscribed or discoid variety. The disease does not spread by

PLATE LXVI.

FIG. I.—Lupus Erythematosus.
FIG. II.—Lupus Vulgaris.

FIGS. I. and II.—AUTHOR'S COLLECTION.

extension or coalescences of the primary patches, but multiplies by successive outbreaks of the disease in new localities, until not only the face and scalp are involved, but also the extremities and trunk, and in rare cases it becomes generalized over the entire surface. The extension of the morbid process may occur gradually or in the form of an acute febrile eruption, associated with severe constitutional disturbance, such as osteocopic pains, effusion into the joints, erysipelatous swellings ; a typhoid condition may supervene. A fatal result occurs in quite a proportion of cases.

The mucous membranes of the nostrils, gums, and cheeks may be invaded by the lupus process, by extension from the contiguous cutaneous surface. Sometimes lupus affects the mucous surfaces primarily, and entirely independent of cutaneous complications. The spots or patches are usually of a yellowish red or grayish color, and sometimes excoriated and bleeding from desquamation of the thickened epithelium.

DIAGNOSIS.—The clinical features of erythematous lupus are in general sufficiently typical to render its diagnosis easy. The localization of the disease, the symmetrical development, the circumscribed reddish patches with raised edges and atrophic centre, the involvement of the sebaceous glands, the intimately adherent scales, and its slow course, are quite characteristic. It bears certain clinical resemblances to lupus vulgaris, the points of differentiation from which will be considered in connection with the diagnosis of the latter disease.

In the beginning stage, and in cases where the eruption is less characteristically developed, erythematous lupus may be confounded with other forms of cutaneous disease.

Chronic erythema of the face may be mistaken for this variety of lupus. The tint of erythema is brighter; its edges are not elevated nor so distinctly demarcated, and fade more gradually into the surrounding skin; the sebaceous structures are not involved, and cicatricial changes do not occur.

From rosacea it may be distinguished by the absence of capillary dilatation, of papules, pustules, and scales, and the presence of atrophic changes in the centre of the patches.

The erythematous syphilide has been confounded with lupus, but the lesions of the former are less vascular, not so apt to be localized upon the places of predilection for lupus, and are commonly associated with specific manifestations upon other parts of the body. They run a much more rapid course and do not leave scars.

TREATMENT.—The assumed relationship of lupus to struma has led to the employment of many internal remedies appropriate to that diathesis, such as cod-liver oil and other nutritive tonics. Phosphorus has also been highly recommended on the assumption that it produces fatty degeneration of the infiltration. Hutchinson speaks favorably of the value of arsenic as a curative agent. Iodine is another remedy which has been employed in various forms and combinations. McCall Anderson claims remarkable results from the use of the iodide of starch in doses of from one to four drachms three times daily. In my own experience and that of others who have given this remedy a faithful trial, the results have been disappointing. In general, it may be said, the results of internal treatment are far from satisfactory. There is no drug that appears to exert anything in the shape of a specific or direct action in causing to disappear the local manifestations of lupus.

Since the disease is in some cases associated with digestive and menstrual derangements, and oftentimes with an impaired or depraved condition of the general health, the indications are to correct existing complications and invigorate the general health by tonics, nutritious diet, change of air, scene, etc.; but all such measures will be found subordinate in importance to local treatment as a curative agent.

LOCAL TREATMENT.—In all cases hygiene of the skin should receive strict attention ; the affected parts should be protected against extremes of heat and cold, and exposure to all external irritants carefully avoided. The nature and strength of the topical applications will depend somewhat upon the stage, development, and location of the disease. The obvious indications are to promote the absorption of the infiltrated products by the use of irritant or caustic applications, but it is to be borne in mind that the scars left in the spontaneous cure of erythematous lupus are generally superficial, and often scarcely noticeable, and any treatment is to be condemned which results in scars more disfiguring than the disease itself. In lupus of the extremities or upon non-exposed parts, the character of the resulting cicatrix is of less importance.

Among stimulating applications no agent is more serviceable than the common soft or green soap. It may be applied by means of frictions with a piece of flannel, or it may be spread upon a piece of muslin and maintained in continuous contact. Tar, or oil of cade, with equal parts of rectified spirits and glycerin, as recommended by Anderson; resorcin collodion, 10 per cent; sulphur in the form of Hebra's modification of the Wilkinson ointment; tincture or glyce-rite of iodine, the compound iodine ointment, chrysarobin, pyrogallol, or naphthol in a ten to a twenty-per-cent ointment, have all been employed with results more or less favorable. If excessive inflammation should be occasioned by the use of stimulating applications, a soothing lotion or ointment should be employed until it subsides.

Mercurial, hydronaphthol, and salicylic plasters of varying strength are also recommended. Among the severer measures may be mentioned blistering by cantharidal collodion or a fly-blister, the surface subsequently dressed with diachylon or some other mild ointment. Painting the surface with pure carbolic acid often constitutes one of the most efficient modes of treatment. Among other caustic agencies may be mentioned a solution of caustic potash, glacial acetic acid, ethylate of sodium, nitrate of silver, chromic and nitric acids. The employment of any of these caustic agencies should be followed by soothing applications.

The purely mechanical methods of treatment by punctate or linear scarifications, the actual or the galvano-cautery, etc., which will be described in connection with the treatment of lupus vulgaris, do not give such brilliant results as in the latter form of the disease.

LUPUS VULGARIS.

Synonyms.—Lupus exedens; Noli-me-Tangere; Scrofulide tuberculeuse.

Lupus vulgaris consists of a cellular infiltration into the tissues of the skin or mucous membranes, characterized by the production of tubercles, papules, and flat patches of variable size and shape, and presenting a reddish or brownish color. It is chronic in its course, the patches spread by peripheral extension, and undergo involution by a process of interstitial absorption or ulceration followed by cicatrization.

The primary and characteristic lesions of lupus vulgaris consist of pin-head to millet-seed-sized nodules of a yellowish-brown or reddish hue, slightly translucent, compared to a drop of apple jelly inserted beneath the epidermis. The nodules are slightly elevated, soft in consistence, and easily penetrated by a stick of nitrate of silver or any blunt instrument, in marked contrast with the firm and resistant character of the surrounding normal tissue. By the coalescence of contiguous nodules yellowish-brown or violaceous patches of variable extent and configuration are formed. The surface of the patches may be smooth or slightly scaly, with a glossy or glistening aspect.

The disease progresses by the development of new nodules in the periphery of the patch, which may thus assume an irregularly circular, distinctly marginated outline. Coincidently with the peripheral extension of the patch, the central infiltration gradually undergoes involution by a process of fatty or caseous degeneration, with or without ulceration, resulting in cicatrization. In the further course of its development a lupus patch presents a more or less pigmented centre, depressed here and there with distinct evidences of scarring, and a brighter, slightly elevated margin, often studded with new nodules.

According to the depth of the infiltration into the papillary body or connective tissue, the tendency to resorption or necrobiosis of the infiltration, and the general march of the morbid process, the disease assumes a variety of aspects and forms.

Lupus exfoliativus has been applied to that form of the disease characterized by a marked tendency to superficial desquamation, with constant reformation of the epidermis. The lupus nodules become atrophied, the surface depressed, sometimes rough and fissured, and the seat of an exfoliation of thin, papery scales. This desquamative process continues, the pigmentation gradually disappearing and resulting ultimately in a thin, white scar.

Lupus exedens.—In this variety the nodules often form by their coalescence pea-sized tubercles, which are disintegrated by transformation into a soft, cheesy mass which is eliminated by ulceration. These ulcers become covered with brownish crusts, beneath which ulceration proceeds; the removal of the crusts discloses a granular fungating base, which bleeds easily. The disease advances by the development and breaking-down of new nodules, and the ulcerating process may extend over considerable surfaces. The destruction of tissue is apt to be especially marked about the orifices of the nostrils, the alæ presenting thin, eroded edges, as if "nibbled." The cicatrices which follow the reparative process are often dense, puckered, and uneven. In the form known as *lupus terebrans*, the destructive process, instead of spreading superficially, may penetrate profoundly, the loss of tissue causing more or less disfigurement.

Lupus serpiginosus.—This form presents certain analogies with the serpiginous syphilide in its peripheral mode of extension, and its tendency to creep over considerable areas of surface. New nodules develop at the circumference of the parent patch, coincident with the retrogressive changes which take place in the centre. The disease thus spreads in circles or segments of circles, the circular ulcerating surface in advance, with the formation of scar-tissue in its wake. The cicatrices are apt to be firm, uneven, or distorted, with more or less tendency to retraction; not infrequently they cause considerable deformity, producing eversion of the lower lids, dragging down the corner of the mouth, or otherwise distorting the features into an almost unrecognizable shape. The cicatrices may become the seat of deposit of lupus nodules, and these fresh foci of disease constitute the points of departure of new circles of ulceration.

Owing to the chronic nature of the disease, and the slow, sluggish course of its evolution, lupus often presents a polymorphic aspect. One may observe in the same patient the various phases which the lesions present in the different stages of their development and decline; side by side in the same patch may be seen the primary efflorescence, papules, tubercles, scales, crusts, ulcers, with atrophied and cicatricial tissue, exhibiting the variable color peculiar to the age of the process. Hypertrophic lupus is applied by some authors to an exaggerated development of the lupus nodules in which the tubercles are of large size, salient, and prominent. This term is more properly used to designate a metamorphic phase of lupus vulgaris.

According to the more or less active participation of the pars papillaris or the connective tissue of the skin, there results, under the influence of long-continued irritation, a papillary proliferation or a connective-tissue hyperplasia in the form of exuberant growths.

Lupus papillaris is characterized by warty formations or excrescences more or less elevated, showing upon the surface distinct evidences of papillary structure. Fig. I., Plate 67.

Lupus is essentially a disease of early life, generally developing before the twenty-fifth year, and is far more frequent in females than in males. Its seats of election are the face, especially the nose and cheeks; it may appear upon the extremities, the trunk, and upon the ano-vulval region.

When lupus affects the mucous membranes, it is usually by extension of the disease from the adjacent skin. Sometimes, however, it develops primarily upon a mucous surface and involves the cutaneous structures secondarily. It is to be borne in mind that lupus may attack the mucous membranes exclusively and be unassociated with any lesions upon the skin.

Upon the mucous membranes lupus usually appears in the form of grayish or opaque patches, covered with a thickened epithelium, which when removed may show an excoriated, fissured, or ulcerated surface. The ulcers are exceedingly persistent and apt to become the seat of proliferating granulations. Lupus of the nasal mucous membrane may destroy the cartilaginous septum, as well as cause perforation of the palate, leaving unsightly and deforming cicatrices.

In the case, Fig. II., Plate 66, representing an extensive lupus of the face, the disease began primarily in the nostrils, and resulted in complete destruction of the septum with commencing caries of the nasal bones.

DIAGNOSIS.—The diagnosis of a typical case of lupus vulgaris offers few difficulties. The age at which it begins, its location, its yellowish-brown patches with pigmented, cicatricial centre and brighter, somewhat elevated, clearly demarcated margin, its slow progress, and the absence of subjective symptoms, make up a clinical picture which is quite characteristic.

The macular form of lupus vulgaris in its early stage of development bears a certain resemblance to lupus erythemadotes. In some cases the clinical features of the two diseases seem to be separated by slight and almost insensible shades of difference. Lupus erythematosus is a disease of adult life, and may be distinguished by its flatter, less infiltrated, more superficial character, its tendency to symmetrical development, its absence of nodules and ulceration, its adherent scales with its tag-like plugs dipping down into the sebaceous follicles, and its thinner, atrophic scars.

A tubercular syphilide may be mistaken for lupus. Syphilis is more apt to be met with in adult life; it is more destructive in its action, and runs comparatively a rapid course; it effects more destruction of tissue in weeks than lupus would in months and years. The syphilitic ulcer is painful; it presents a punched-out appearance with an infiltrated margin, an ashen-gray floor; the secretion is more abundant, and the crusts are thicker and greenish. There is usually a history of acquired syphilis, and evidences of the disease are commonly traceable upon other parts of the body. Finally it yields with more or less promptitude to specific treatment. The serpiginous form of lupus, as already intimated, presents many close analogies with the serpiginous syphilide in its progressive character and its creeping mode of advance.

Epithelioma, which may be confounded with ulcerous lupus, may be distinguished by its almost invariable occurrence in advanced life. It usually develops from a single hard nodule or warty growth. The ulceration of epithelioma is greater in depth compared with its superficial area; the ulcer is painful, with hard, everted margins, and the secretion is scantier and more offensive. Epithelioma is often attended with glandular complications and evidences of impairment of the general health, and after ulceration occurs its course is relatively much more rapid.

The possibility of the transformation or degeneration of long-existing lupus into epithelioma is to be borne in mind.

TREATMENT.—Lupus is generally regarded as the local manifestation of a constitutional disorder closely analogous to, if not identical with, tuberculosis. By most authorities at the present day it is classed as a tuberculosis of the skin. Notwithstanding its diathetic relations, experience proves that constitutional treatment fails to materially modify the development and course of the disease, while a judicious local treatment is almost invariably successful. The conditions of successful treatment are that it should be instituted sufficiently early, energetically carried out, and adapted to the particular variety and stage of the morbid process. After local destruction or removal of the infiltration, constitutional measures are undoubtedly of great value in delaying or preventing recurrences. The internal remedies recommended in connection with the treatment of lupus erythematosus may be employed with advantage in this variety of the disease. Of especial value are ferruginous and nutritive tonics, as iron and cod-liver oil; nerve tonics, as quinine and strychnia; and all hygienic measures calculated to improve the general health. In strumous children, the syrup of the iodide of iron may be given with benefit.

LOCAL TREATMENT.—The local agencies and methods which have been employed in the treatment of lupus are numerous and varied. The object in view is twofold: 1st. To remove or cause the absorption of the lupus infiltration. 2d. To secure a good cicatrix. The importance of this latter indication will be appreciated when it is remembered that lupus is essentially a disfiguring disease; and since it is almost invariably situated upon the face, hands, or exposed parts, cosmetic considerations should enter largely into the appreciation of the applicability of any proposed method of treatment. The essential conditions of a good cicatrix are that it should be superficial, smooth, supple, and non-contractile, not restricting the mobility of feature which contributes so materially to the appearance and expression of the face.

A variety of irritant substances have been employed with a view of determining in the diseased tissues an inflammatory reaction which favors the resorption of the lupus infiltration. Various chemical agents have been recommended with this view, the energy of whose irritative action varies, such as green soap, tincture or glycerite of iodine, iodoform, iodide of sulphur, mercurial and other plasters. These various resolvent applications are, as a rule, disappointing in their effects, and, while failing to remove the morbid growth, may do harm by stimulating the morbid process to renewed activity. Many of them are, however, excellent adjuvants to more radical methods, and their chief value lies in this direction. Exception may, perhaps, be made to the hydronaphthal plaster in the strength of ten to twenty per cent, recommended by Piffard, who claims brilliant results from its use.

Far more efficient results are obtained from the use of caustics, which destroy the diseased tissue. Destructive cauterization may be effected either by potential caustics or by the actual or galvano-cautery. The chemical agents most generally employed are arsenic, chloride of zinc, caustic potash, the Vienna paste, Llandolfi's paste, Canquoin's paste, the solid stick of nitrate of silver, and nitrate of mercury; or various acids, as acetic, carbolic, chromic, lactic, pyrogallic, salicylic acid, etc.

The arsenical and other pastes are most active agents in the destruction of the diseased tissue, but they possess certain disadvantages: the pain is usually severe and prolonged, the depth and extent of their destructive action cannot be accurately limited, and the cicatrices are not as a rule good. Among the acids, pyrogallic, lactic, and salicylic acids are most generally employed. Pyrogallic acid suspended in ether or traumaticin was a few years ago in high repute, but its tendency in some cases to produce gangrene of the tissues and other disagreeable accidents has led to its abandonment in a great measure. Schwimmer claimed remarkable results from the following treatment: Pyrogallic, ten to twenty per cent, was used two or three times daily for a week, then a mercurial plaster was applied; this procedure to be repeated until no more tubercles appear. Lactic acid has been especially extolled for its virtues in searching out and destroying only the diseased tissue, and on the same ground salicylic acid has been highly recommended; but there is no good basis for the belief that either of these agents has an elective affinity for lupus tissue. Salicylic acid may be conveniently employed according to Treves' method, which consists in the addition of sufficient acid to glycerin to form a paste. Creasote or carbolic acid, in the proportion of one drachm to the ounce, may be added with the object of annulling the pain. The pain of the application may also be mitigated by preliminary painting the surface with a twenty-per-cent solution of cocaine.

Unna claims most remarkable curative results from the employment of a twenty-five to fifty-per-cent salicylated plaster, to which an equal or double percentage of pure creasote is added to deaden the pain. He claims that thus used the salicylic acid searches out and destroys the lupus nodules as if a punch had been employed.

The hot iron or thermo-cautery is more prompt in its action, but it is open to the objection that the pain is quite severe, usually necessitating an anæsthetic; besides, most patients naturally shrink from the application of so formidable an appliance.

When the entire surface of a lupus infiltration is cauterized, destruction of the sound tissue included within this area is inevitable. This objection has been to a certain extent overcome by the employment of discrete or interstitial cauterization. The caustic agent may be introduced into the diseased tissue on the point of a lancet, by acupuncture instruments, or by boring into the lupus nodules with the solid stick of nitrate of silver or potassa fusa. Practically these procedures are found to be slow in action, quite painful, and apt to leave deforming cicatrices.

The galvano-cautery constitutes, perhaps, the best agent for practising punctate scarifications. By means of ingenious instruments devised by Besnier, in the shape of points, buttons, and blades, accurate limitation of the destructive action to lupus nodules may be obtained. The small nodules may be destroyed by a single puncture with the galvano-cautery needle or button, or a lupus patch may be thickly studded or tattooed with punctures. A cherry-red heat is preferable to a white heat; local anæsthesia is rarely necessary. After the operation the surface is covered with a dry dressing or a mercurial plaster. The operation is repeated about every eight days until every trace of the lupus tissue is destroyed. This method is especially applicable in lupus of the eyelids, and of the buccal, pharyngeal, and nasal mucous membranes.

The method of treatment by excision of the entire morbid growth is available only when the lupus is favorably situated and of limited extent. If applied to an extensive infiltration, it is apt to leave a deep, unsightly, and contractile cicatrix. A modification of this method by raclage or scraping with the Volkmann spoon or dermal curette is much to be preferred. The softened, diseased tissue may easily be scraped away, while the firm, healthy tissue resists the action of the curette. After thorough scraping, the wound may be treated with iodoform or a mild caustic to destroy any remaining lupus products.

The treatment which at the present day appears to give the best results, both from a curative and cosmetic point of view, is the method of linear scarifications, the object of which is to divide and obliterate the cutaneous capillaries, cutting off the blood-supply to the lupus tissues and thus destroying them by inanition. The same object was formerly attempted by multiple punctures with a sharp-pointed instrument.

The method of linear scarifications was introduced by Balmanno Squire, but it has been developed and perfected by Vidal, of Paris. Parallel linear incisions are made over the entire diseased surface, and these crossed at right angles or obliquely by another series of incisions. The cuts are made as closely together as possible, and of sufficient depth to penetrate to the base of the lupus infiltration. Care should be taken not to go too deeply, as the resulting cicatrix would not be so good. A practical knowledge of the technique of the operation, and thoroughness and efficiency in its application, are essential to success. The pain is more or less marked, according to the sensitiveness of the region affected and the depth of the incisions; bleeding is usually slight and readily arrested by pressure. After the operation, the surface is sprayed with an antiseptic solution and a dry dressing employed. The little wounds heal readily, leaving no trace, and in the course of a week the operation may be repeated. In the interval between the operations, the red cinnabar plaster, mercurial or hydronaphthol plaster may be applied. Treatment by this method has the advantage of giving a more uniform, superficial, and supple cicatrix, and one which more nearly approaches the normal skin in appearance and texture. Linear scarifications may also be made with the galvano-cautery knife devised by Besnier.

No one method of treatment is applicable in every case of lupus; it must be modified to suit the variety and stage of the disease, its location, and the morbid conditions present; in some cases a combination of methods gives better results than one alone. Relapses are liable to occur after any method of treatment, and even when the disease is in process of cure, isolated yellowish brown nodules may appear here and there in the cicatrix or margin of the patch. In the destruction of these minute points of infiltration, excellent results are obtained by the use of the pyramidal double-threaded screw devised by Malcolm Morris, which is inserted into each nodule, and twisted round and round until the morbid infiltrate is broken up and destroyed. For the same purpose Fox recommends the use of a certain small instrument employed in dental practice, and known as the dental hook, which is introduced with the least possible injury to the epidermal covering, and the nodule is broken up by a series of rapid revolutions.

TUBERCULOSIS PAPILLOMATOSA CUTIS.

Under this title I have described * a form of disease which presents many clinical analogies with the *lupus verrucosus* of McCall Anderson, the *lupus sclereux* of Vidal, and that form of tuberculosis of the skin described by Riehl as *tuberculosis verrucosa cutis.* In this case, figured in Plate LXVII., Fig. 2, the typical papillomatous features presented a more exaggerated development than has been observed in the verrucose forms of lupus.

As regards the relationship of lupus to tuberculosis, many of the leading authorities at the present day recognize lupus as a form or "partial manifestation" of tuberculosis, while others believe in the distinct and independent nature of the two diseases. Proof of the substantial identity of lupus and tuberculosis is based upon the discovery of the bacillus of Koch in lupus products, the pathological anatomy of the lesions, their evolutive characters, the results of inoculative experiments, and, finally, the observation of the clinical fact that a high percentage of deaths from tuberculosis of other organs occurs among those affected with lupus.

In my case the first manifestation of the disease was in the form of a verrucose tubercle upon the side of the nose, and was probably the result of auto-inoculation from a tubercular osteitis of the bones of the metacarpus and forearm which necessitated amputation at the elbow. The papillomatous proliferations developed without any pre-existing ulceration. The lesions appeared at disseminated points as small, pin-head-sized papules, with a large base upon apparently normal skin; as the papules enlarged, the epidermis disrupted in the centre, and small, pea-sized vegetations sprouted forth. The disease advanced both by continuity of tissues at the periphery and by the development of fresh foci at points distant from the central disease. The morbid process was essentially slow and sluggish in its evolution: more than two and one-half years after its first development upon the face it presented the appearance seen in the illustration. The lesions consist of an exuberant growth of papillary excrescences, closely pressed together, forming for the most part a uniformly lobulated surface. The papillary elevations were for the most part club-shaped, a few nipple-shaped or distinctly acuminate, and were separated at their free extremities by minute, decussating fissures, through which exuded a thick, puriform, very concrescible fluid. The elevation of the surface varied from one to three centimetres, being most marked on the outer margins of the patch.

The papillary growths were of a soft, fleshy consistence, of a bright red to a deeper raw-flesh tint; they were extremely vascular, readily bleeding. The subjective sensations of itching and pain were marked.

In addition to the papillomatous lesions, the patient exhibited a number of rounded protuberances—the *gommes tuberculeuses* of the French—in the right cervico-maxillary region, extending in a vertical series from the lobe of the ear to the root of the neck. They were soft and fluctuating, and varied in size from a hazel-nut to an English walnut, gradually increasing in size along the descending line. The appetite and general health of the patient were good; no impairment of the pulmonary organs. Microscopic examination of sections made from the lesions upon the face showed the presence of tubercle bacilli.

DIAGNOSIS.—Exuberant papillomatous growths, presenting similar or identical clinical characters, occur in connection with a variety of pathological conditions, and their differential diagnosis is by no means easy. This case was at first regarded as a condylomatous or vegetating syphilide, from which it was differentiated by its more sluggish course, the absence of ulceration and destruction of tissues, and by the failure of specific treatment. The presence or absence of tubercle bacilli would, of course, settle the question of its tubercular nature.

TREATMENT.—The most efficient treatment consists in the removal of the papillomatous

* Journal of Cutaneous and Genito-Urinary Diseases, October and November, 1888.

PLATE LXVII

proliferations by mechanical means, as excision or scraping. In an extensive vascular surface the accident of profuse hæmorrhage must be guarded against ; remarkable curative results have been claimed from the employment of injections of iodoform in oil of vaseline. The general health of the patient should be improved by nutritious diet and the constitutional measures appropriate to the tuberculous diathesis.

SARCOMA.

Sarcoma of the skin is a malignant disease which in its evolution produces various clinical forms, of which fleshy tumors in the derma are the predominating lesions. It occurs either as an idiopathic condition or as the result of metastasis ; lymphatic glands or internal organs being first affected. Until recent years sarcoma was not regarded as a distinct cutaneous affection, and until Kaposi wrote upon the subject in 1870 its importance was not recognized, although both Köbner and Korte had reported cases a year before Kaposi brought the subject prominently before the medical world. Perrin has collected fifty-four cases which, together with two personal observations, form the basis of an excellent monograph on the subject, published in Paris in 1886 ; and Funk, of Warsaw, has recently made an excellent clinical study of the disease.

Sarcoma of the skin first appears either as macules of a color varying from yellowish to bluish red, or as small, discrete nodules or tumors upon any portion of the surface, varying in size from a bird-shot or small pea to a grape, and these gradually becoming larger. They are imbedded in the skin proper, and in many instances are dermic infiltrations rather than distinct tumors. The skin is movable over them when they develop in the hypoderm, but as they grow they are found to be firm, smooth, flattened or even depressed in the centre, and may be attached firmly to the skin, while the epidermis becomes scaly. Softening may occur, but ulceration is exceptional. The growths are inclined to rapid multiplication, and in spreading to other regions increase in size and number. When single the surface may be warty and the base fungating. It seems proper, in the present state of our knowledge, to make two principal divisions according to the presence or absence of pigment : *melanotic sarcoma* being the more frequent and forming a group by itself, while the *non-melanotic* may occur either as a primary or a secondary affection. Pathologically the growths may be divided into round-celled and spindle-celled sarcoma.

MELANOTIC or pigmentary sarcoma is usually multiple, idiopathic, and of the fusiform or spindle-celled variety of new growth—though round cells may be present—and, having its origin in the pigmentary layer of the skin, contains more or less brownish or black pigment granules, or a substance called melanin, which produces a color varying from a tawny yellow to a blue. In form the tumors are spherical or oval, and rarely exceed the size of a large nut. The limits of the growth are at times not well defined, and the surrounding parts may appear infiltrated. There is usually no pain felt in the tumors, but they may be both painful and tender. They usually occur upon the hands and feet at first, and spread to other parts. Though as a rule sessile, now and then a pedunculated tumor may be observed, and an idiopathic form of solitary sarcoma often develops upon a congenital pigmentary mole or nævus which has been irritated in some way, and is followed by metastatic growths in other organs. Ulceration may occur and a black liquid like Indian ink be discharged, and a small quantity of such liquid may be found on section in the centre of tumors which have softened. · These melanotic growths are but slightly vascular, differing from the non-melanotic, which often bleed readily. The whole skin may become melanotic, as in Addison's disease, the urine dark colored, and granular pigment may be found in the blood. Cachexia soon shows itself, and, at the end of two or three years at most, the patient dies. Sex does not appear to influence this form as much as the other, though few cases of sarcoma occur in women. No treatment has been at all successful, and surgical interference may be of injury. Dissemination through the lymphatics and blood-vessels is often more rapid if the primary growth is excised.

The NON-MELANOTIC form has its anatomical seat in the derma, and the epidermis usually

PLATE LXVIII.

is healthy. The small tumors, from the size of a millet-seed up, are at first discrete, but may soon become confluent and form patches of large size. The feet and hands may become deformed from the presence of the new growths, the toes and fingers separated, and neighboring lymphatic ganglia enlarged. Upon disappearing, as some lesions do, while new ones appear, depressed pigmented spots are left. The epidermis may become scaly over the growths, and even show a tendency to horny transformation. It is rare for this disease to appear idiopathically in the skin, but it may do so and be a local or a generalized condition, lasting possibly for many years before involving other organs. Secondary sarcoma of the skin, due to metastasis, is more common. After a certain time the health fails, cachexia, œdema, and spontaneous ecchymoses occur, and the patient dies.

PATHOLOGY.—According to Cornil and Ranvier, the tumors consist of pure embryonic tissue, either as such or in the process of transformation into adult tissue. They distinguish three varieties : round-celled, spindle-celled, and melanotic. The cells of the first are no larger than white blood-corpuscles; masses of these cells are separated by connective tissue bands, producing the so-called alveolar sarcoma. In the second are seen bundles of fusiform or spindle cells. While in the last variety, which is also usually of the spindle-celled variety, the tumor is of a blue or black color from the presence of melanin.

The first form is more apt than the second to become softened and discolored by interstitial hæmorrhage. The spindle-celled variety is not so likely to be followed by sarcoma of internal organs.

ETIOLOGY.—No causes excepting those ascribed to other forms of cancer are known. The first twenty-five cases reported by Kaposi occurred in men, and only three women are found in Perrin's fifty-four cases. It is usually encountered between the ages of forty and sixty, though young adults may have it, and it may occur in infancy.

DIAGNOSIS.—Sarcoma in its varied manifestations is to be distinguished from syphilis, lupus, lepra, cysticercus tumors, neuromata, fibromata, carcinomata, etc. The peculiar blue color will often serve to distinguish it. Carcinoma is harder and undergoes more rapid evolution, ulcerates earlier, and is usually consecutive to cancer of other parts. Mycosis fungoides of Alibert, or the "inflammatory fungoid neoplasm of the skin" of Duhring and Geber, has been regarded as another form of sarcoma, while some make of it a distinct infectious skin disease. Perrin makes a pseudo-mycosic variety of primitive generalized sarcoma.

It is probable that many fungoid neoplasms and pigment diseases now little understood may be properly included in the sarcomata.

TREATMENT.—Single tumors may be excised, though the probabilities of return are very great, and the advisability of interference is questioned. Hæmorrhage may be severe, ulcerated sarcoma often bleeding at the slightest touch. The only treatment which offers any chances of success is that of arsenic injected beneath the skin. Several cases have been reported cured by this method, the arsenic being injected into the gluteal region, and continued for several months. Köbner in 1882 reported a case cured by daily injections of from six to nine drops of a one-percent solution of arseniate of soda continued for a month. ·

Iodoform ointment is recommended for ulcerative lesions.

EPITHELIOMA.

Epithelial tumors of the skin of a malignant nature have been at different times designated *epithelial* or *skin cancer, cancroïde, rodent ulcer, noli-me-tangere*, etc. At the present day the term *epithelioma* is universally applied to a cancerous tumor or ulcer of the skin which, though presenting certain marked characteristics, may occur under a variety of forms.

There is in all cases an infiltration of the skin with epithelial elements analogous with those of normal tissue, and recent lesions, either in beginning epithelioma or surrounding a patch of long standing, occur as sago-grain nodules or transparent, pearl-like globules imbedded in the

PLATE LXIX.

Fig. I.—Epithelioma.
Fig. II.—Rodent Ulcer.

FIG. I.—AFTER UNNA.
FIG. II.—AFTER HUTCHINSON.

skin. When grouped together these pearls may present a wart-like appearance. Usually at the very onset there is a superficial infiltration followed by ulceration, or an excoriation covered with a crust or an adherent scale. This may occur upon the free surface of the skin or upon a warty growth, mole, or patch of seborrhœa of the horny type often seen upon the faces of elderly persons. It is an insidious process, and the ulcer does not heal under any ordinary form of treatment, and yet does not tend to enlarge with any degree of rapidity. The favorite site for such a new growth is some portion of the face, and especially the eyelids, at the inner canthus, upon the cheek, bridge of the nose, or lower lip.

Although the process of development is essentially the same in all, three varieties of epithelioma of the skin are described: the *superficial*, the *deep*, and the *papillary*. Rounded ulcerating epithelioma of a superficial kind, of slow progression and of slight malignancy, has been called rodent ulcer; but this name was never used in this country as much as in England, and has now been dropped almost entirely. It is now pretty generally conceded that rodent ulcer is but a variety of epithelioma, starting as a rule from the external root-sheath of the hair follicles, and occasionally from the sebaceous glands, and differing in the development of its cell-growth. This variety of cancer is so likely to become aggravated by superficial cauterization, and applications which act upon it only as irritants, that the older authors advised that no treatment at all be used, and applied to it the warning name of *noli-me-tangere*. Though superficial in its early stages, and often existing for several years before its nature is discovered, it may finally, by slowly creeping from one tissue to another, invade and destroy muscle, cartilage, and bone. The eyelid, cheek, and side of nose may in turn be eaten away, and the unfortunate victim, with teeth, eye-ball, and nasal cavity exposed, may present the horrible spectacle of a death's-head in life. Fortunately this does not always happen, and even spontaneous cure may occur. The ulcer begins usually upon the upper half of the face, but when the region of the mouth is reached the epitheliomatous nature is more manifest and the lymphatics become involved. The centre of an ulcer may now and then be seen to cicatrize, and outlying nodules to disappear without treatment. Furthermore, active and properly directed treatment in the early stage may result in permanent removal of the growth. As a rule the general health remains unaffected, and the lymphatics do not become implicated. In the deep variety, which develops from the interpapillary layer of the rete, tubercles from pea to bean size, hard and semi-transparent, often extend down to the subcutaneous connective tissue, and a number of such growths may be closely packed together. This form of epithelioma may also be elevated above the skin or exist as a diffuse infiltration. As the growth advances the surface becomes hard and waxy, and blood-vessels radiate over it. Spontaneous atrophic changes with depression of the centre now and then occur. When ulceration takes place the margins are perpendicular. The lymphatics become involved in this deep form, and, within a few years at most, a fatal result ensues. This variety is the one which occurs usually upon the lower lip, whence it may spread rapidly to the mouth and tongue.

The third subdivision, or papillary epithelioma, is the most malignant and fatal, often running a rapid course. This malignant papilloma is often wart-like or raspberry-like from the first, and when it occurs, as it frequently does, upon the genitals, bears a close resemblance to a venereal wart. After a time a viscid secretion is discharged from its surface or from fissures which not uncommonly form, and this, together with dried epidermis, makes a yellowish crust. New granulations spring up about the original tumor, which breaks down, and form an ulcer.

PATHOLOGY.—This varies somewhat in the different varieties and stages of the process, but in general there are epithelial prolongations downward from the rete mucosum into the connective tissue, attended with great proliferation of cells and the formation of cell-nests. The cells are of the pavement variety, and compact masses of them are formed by pressure into globes or stratified bodies like the layers of an onion, and constitute the cell-nests or globules, which are, however, not constantly present. The epithelial cells in the centre of these bodies become horny, while the outer layers remain flattened. Instead of these nests with their attendant horny changes, there may be tube-like collections of epithelial structure extending into the deeper tissues.

In severe cases these conical prolongations penetrate in all directions, pressing upon all the surrounding tissues. Inflammatory changes and infiltration of round cells also take place in the neighboring structures, and the blood-vessels are constantly found enlarged. When, however, the nutrition is cut off from the centre of the growth by pressure of the cells, degeneration occurs and ulceration takes place, while at the margin proliferation remains active.

ETIOLOGY.—At times an hereditary predisposition to cancerous affections can be made out, and it is quite well determined that certain abnormal conditions of the skin, such as warty growths, lupus, xeroderma, pigmented moles, and senile changes, predispose to malignant growths of epithelial structure. Mechanical irritation, as from the pressure of eye-glasses, the habitual holding of a pipe-stem in the corner of the mouth, the accidental injury to a benign growth, etc., often acts as the determining cause of malignant action. Age is an important etiological factor, for, although epithelioma may occur in the young and even in children, it is not usually found before about the fortieth year of life.

A superficial variety upon the prepuce and scrotum has been called chimney-sweeper's cancer, because thought to be due to that occupation; but the same variety occurs in those otherwise engaged, just as the so-called "smoker's cancer" is not always due to smoking.

DIAGNOSIS should be made early, for then alone are the chances of permanent cure favorable. Epithelioma should be suspected when a cluster of waxy or colorless nodules or points of infiltration exist for any length of time upon the face, or when a superficial ulceration covered with a crust or scale refuses to heal under ordinary treatment, especially if the margin is hard or button-like. It may closely resemble an ordinary wart, but the latter does not desquamate or ulcerate. The papillary variety, when occurring upon the genitals, must be distinguished from a venereal wart and from the initial lesion of syphilis, especially when situated upon the glans. The age of the patient and the nature of the margin of the ulcer will aid in distinguishing from these lesions. Tertiary syphilitic ulceration is known by its more rapid evolution, and lupus by its being often multiple, more extensive, and attended with a more abundant puriform discharge. Lupus may be succeeded by epithelioma, or the two diseases may co-exist.

PROGNOSIS depends upon the variety of the disease, the age of the patient, and the location of the lesion. The superficial may remain almost stationary for years, or may go over into the deep, or possibly spontaneous cure may occur; though internal organs are not usually involved, it becomes a very grave disease, and, if operated upon, recurrences are apt to follow. The deep variety often proves rapidly fatal, sometimes within a year or two; secondary growths appear in the lymphatic glands, and death is due to the involvement of a vital organ or to septicæmia following ulceration.

TREATMENT.—Internal medication appears to be of little or no direct benefit, and treatment resolves itself into the use of the knife or a caustic. When superficial and not too near a mucous membrane, the latter is perhaps preferable, or the growth may be scraped or cut away and a caustic then applied. Some authors prefer the caustic-potash stick, which is followed by an eschar in about two weeks; others use Marsden's paste, composed of equal parts of white arsenic and powdered acacia made into a paste with sufficient water at the time of using. This is left on for twelve to twenty-four hours and the part poulticed until well. Pyrogallic acid in twenty-per-cent strength, or even weaker, has at times acted favorably. It is often well to apply it after the diseased tissue has been thoroughly scraped out with a dermal curette.

When the growth is so situated that the operation can be done, as upon the lip, it is best treated by free excision.

LEPROSY.

Synonyms.—Elephantiasis Græcorum ; Lepra ; Leontiasis.

Leprosy may be defined as a chronic infectious disease of parasitic origin, characterized by the production of new cell formations in the cutaneous and mucous surfaces, in the connective tissue of the nerves, the lymphatic ganglia, and in certain viscera. The disease is constitutional in its nature, slow in its development and course, and progresses almost invariably to a fatal termination.

The history of leprosy is coeval with that of the human race. Records of its existence in India, China, Egypt, and other Eastern countries date back from the earliest historical times. It was prevalent in Greece in the last century before Christ; it had gained a foothold in Italy in the second century of our era, and was thence introduced into the greater part of Europe along the routes of the Roman armies. Its thorough dissemination throughout Christendom was materially influenced by the Crusaders.

The spread of leprosy has always followed the great human currents of military and commercial movements, and its disappearance has always been in direct ratio to the measures taken to prevent the contact of the afflicted with the healthy.

The Mosaic prescriptions contained in the Levitical law for the suppression of leprosy by enforced isolation constitute one of the most interesting chapters of ancient sanitation. The order of St. Lazarus, entered into by those who devoted their services and lives to the victims of leprosy, was instituted in the eighth century, and lazar-houses were established throughout all Europe for the reception of lepers. In the twelfth century, the number of lazarettos in France alone was 2,000, and it was estimated that there were not less than 19,000 in Europe. In the fifteenth century the disease began to decline, and by the end of the seventeenth century it had become practically extinct in Europe.

At the present day leprosy has quite an extensive geographical distribution. It is found in India, China, Egypt, Palestine, Turkey, the Grecian islands, the Mediterranean ports, the West Indies, Spain, Portugal, Norway, Russia, Iceland, Brazil, Central America, Mexico, Africa, Mauritius, New Zealand, and the Hawaiian Islands. In North America it is found in Canada, in Louisiana, in the Scandinavian colonies of Minnesota, Iowa, and Wisconsin, and along the Pacific coast among the Chinese residents. Sporadic cases occasionally occur in other parts of Europe and in the United States.

The lesions of leprosy consist of inflammatory new formations containing bacilli, and, according to the localization of these lesions and their subsequent development, it has been divided into two principal forms which, while pathologically similar, are clinically distinct. When the morbid deposits occur upon the skin and mucous membranes in the shape of macules and nodules, the form of the disease is termed *tegumentary* or *tubercular ;* when they are centred upon the peripheral nerves, it is termed *tropho-neurotic* or *anæsthetic.* In a certain proportion of cases there is an admixture of both forms in the same individual, the lesions peculiar to one or the other predominating; and this combination constitutes what is known as the *mixed type* of leprosy.

TUBERCULAR LEPROSY.—The evolution of leprosy is not sufficiently regular and constant to admit of its division into stages, yet there are certain prodromal symptoms which commonly precede the outbreak of the characteristic manifestations. The first evidences of leprous infection of the system consist of general debility, noticeable in weariness after slight exertion, a sense of depression, heaviness, and a tendency to sleep. Oftentimes there is an eruption of erythematous spots, which may come and go a number of times before becoming persistent. The febrile symptoms, which are a quite constant feature of the prodromic stage of tubercular leprosy, are usually preceded by sensations of chilliness or a well-defined rigor. The pyrexia is commonly of the

PLATE LXX.

intermittent type, the rise of temperature being succeeded by profuse perspiration ; vertigo and epistaxis are frequent accompaniments.

Among the cutaneous changes may be mentioned a heightening of the color of the skin over the malar prominences, which gives it a shining, glossy appearance; the secretory function of the sebaceous and sudatory glands is increased ; the skin has an unctuous, greasy feel, and the sweat is abundant and profuse. In rare cases there is, instead of this increased functional activity of the cutaneous glands, a suppression of their secretions, which may be general or localized in certain areas. At the same time there is often a falling of the hair, especially of the eyebrows and lashes.

Subjective sensations of various kinds are among the prodromal symptoms ; itching and burning of the skin is complained of, and the skin, upon examination, may show scratch-marks. Rheumatoid pains, cramps in the lower limbs, and various algias are complained of, and are accompanied by sensations of numbness or deadness, and a sense of weight or heaviness, especially in the lower limbs. These symptoms are none of them invariably present, and all of them more or less intermittent. They vary in intensity and duration ; they may be so slight as to escape attention, or their significance may not be recognized until unmistakable evidences of the disease declare themselves.

The prodromic symptoms continue for a variable time, often extending over a period of many months, and are succeeded by the phenomena peculiar to what is termed the eruptive stage. The first cutaneous manifestations of the tubercular form consist of an eruption of erythematous spots or blotches, which may appear and disappear a number of times before the characteristic tuberculation develops. The places of predilection for the eruption are the face, hands, and feet, but it may appear upon any portion of the trunk or limbs. The macules are usually oval or circular in shape, of a reddish-brown or coppery color fading into a dirty yellow, suggesting patches of chromo-phytosis. Sometimes they present a purplish or vinous tint resembling port-wine discolorations. They are slightly elevated, distinctly demarcated from the sound skin, more pigmented in the centre. The skin, especially of the face, is more or less thickened and swollen, and presents an œdematous appearance. The circumscribed patches may coalesce, forming extensive diffuse infiltrations, which, instead of undergoing resolution, may remain permanent and become elevated into tubercular excrescences, or the tubercles may develop upon new surface without preceding infiltration.

The tubercles vary in size from a pea to that of a walnut or larger, and by this aggregation may form elevated masses of considerable size. The regions most affected are the forehead, nose, lips, chin, cheeks, and ears, the hands and forearms, especially the extensor surfaces. Any portion of the surface may be the seat of tubercular deposits, except, perhaps, the scalp.

The course of the tubercles and infiltrations varies. They may remain stationary for months and years with but little change, the surface desquamating slightly, and the color changing into a yellow or dark brown. They may gradually undergo involution, leaving pigmented stains or atrophied scars. The disappearance of one crop is succeeded by the development of another after a more or less prolonged interval, and generally in the same region. Instead of being resorbed, the tubercles may soften, disintegrate, and break down, forming shallow, indolent ulcers, the granulating base secreting a yellowish, thin, somewhat offensive discharge. Ulceration is more liable to occur in lesions upon the extremities. They may usually be healed in the earlier stages by strapping and dressing.

The most marked and characteristic development of tubercles ordinarily occurs upon the face. In a more advanced stage, the integument of the forehead may be infiltrated to such a degree that it presents the appearance of prominent bosses or ridges divided by deep furrows corresponding to the natural lines of the skin. The bulging out of the frontal and supra-orbital folds, upon which are superimposed nodular masses, gives a leonine appearance to the face, from which the disease received the designation of leontiasis. The cheeks, especially over the malar prominences, are often enormously tumefied, forming cushion-like or pillowy protuberances. The ears are almost always affected : they are greatly exaggerated in size; the lobe is especially liable to be hypertrophied, and may hang down in a flabby, pendulous mass, almost touching the shoulder. The alæ of the nose are swollen and broadened, which, with the flattening or sinking-in of the bones of the nose, the loss of the eyebrows and lashes, and the conjunctival and corneal lesions, adds to the hideous deformity.

The mucous membranes are also the seat of infiltrations and node formations, which usually break down and form ulcers, and result in more or less destruction of tissue. The conjunctival, nasal, buccal, and pharyngeal are most commonly involved. Lesions of the visual organs may occur as flat deposits, like pannus, producing opacity of the cornea, interstitial keratitis, sometimes perforation of the lens, and resulting in partial or total blindness. One of the earlier symptoms of leprosy is a snuffling nasal respiration from obstruction of the naso-pharyngeal tract by infiltration and thickening, followed by ulceration and still later by absorption of the nasal septum and bones, producing the characteristic flattening or sinking-in of the nose. The naso-laryngeal lesions cause hoarseness and difficulty of speech, and impart to the voice that peculiar harsh, croaking, raucous quality which is quite characteristic.

Enlargement of the lymphatic glands, especially marked in the cervical and inguinal regions, is a constant concomitant of the surface lesions. The testicles often atrophy, and in an advanced stage sexual desire, as well as power, is lost. When the disease occurs at an early age, physical development is retarded, and at puberty a condition of infantilism exists.

The duration of the tubercular type of leprosy varies from one to twelve years, sometimes, but rarely, longer—on the average, eight years. Death generally ensues from pulmonary, renal, or intestinal complications, marasmus, and what is termed leprous exhaustion.

Anæsthetic Leprosy.—The symptoms preceding the outbreak of this form of leprosy vary in kind and degree, but they are distinguished from the prodromata of the tubercular form in their marked neurotic character, which plainly indicates the active participation of the nervous system in their production. Febrile symptoms are absent in many cases, but there is a general feeling of malaise, with occasional sensations of chilliness. The subjective symptoms are quite pronounced, and often of the most distressing character, such as extreme itchiness and burning of the skin. The hyperæsthesia is not confined to the skin, but tenderness and pains of a lancinating, boring character are felt in the deeper structures. To these succeed sensations of numbness or deadness, and later an entire loss of sensation in spots or limited areas, especially in the regions supplied by the ulnar and peroneal nerves. At quite an early stage the ulnar nerve may be felt hypersensitive and distinctly enlarged.

The cutaneous changes consist of dryness and scaliness of the skin, with an eruption of pemphigoid blebs, most commonly upon the fingers and toes. The bullæ are of variable size, with their walls containing a clear, yellowish serum; they spontaneously rupture after a few hours, and their flaccid walls may be brushed or wiped away, showing excoriations like superficial burns or scalds, which upon healing leave pigmented stains. The eruption may successively develop upon one portion of the body after another. The more characteristic eruption appears in the form of small circular or oval patches of a reddish-brown color, which may remain discrete or spread peripherally, and by their confluence form large gyrate patches with a distinctly raised, clearly defined reddish margin. The centre of the patch becomes thin, white, atrophic, and wrinkled, and usually denuded of hair. This process of blanching may affect the greater portion of the body. The atrophic patches are usually devoid of sensation. The anæsthesia is, however, by no means confined to these limited areas, but spreads irregularly, and may be manifest over an entire region —as, for example, the upper or lower extremity. A patient often receives a severe injury or burn unconsciously, and such an accident may first direct attention to the nature of the trouble. Another symptom of comparatively early occurrence is the plantar ulcer, which is especially common in those accustomed to walk barefoot. It is, however, not peculiar to anæsthetic leprosy, but may be observed in the tubercular form.

Paralysis of certain nerves, with atrophy of the muscular tissues which they supply, is

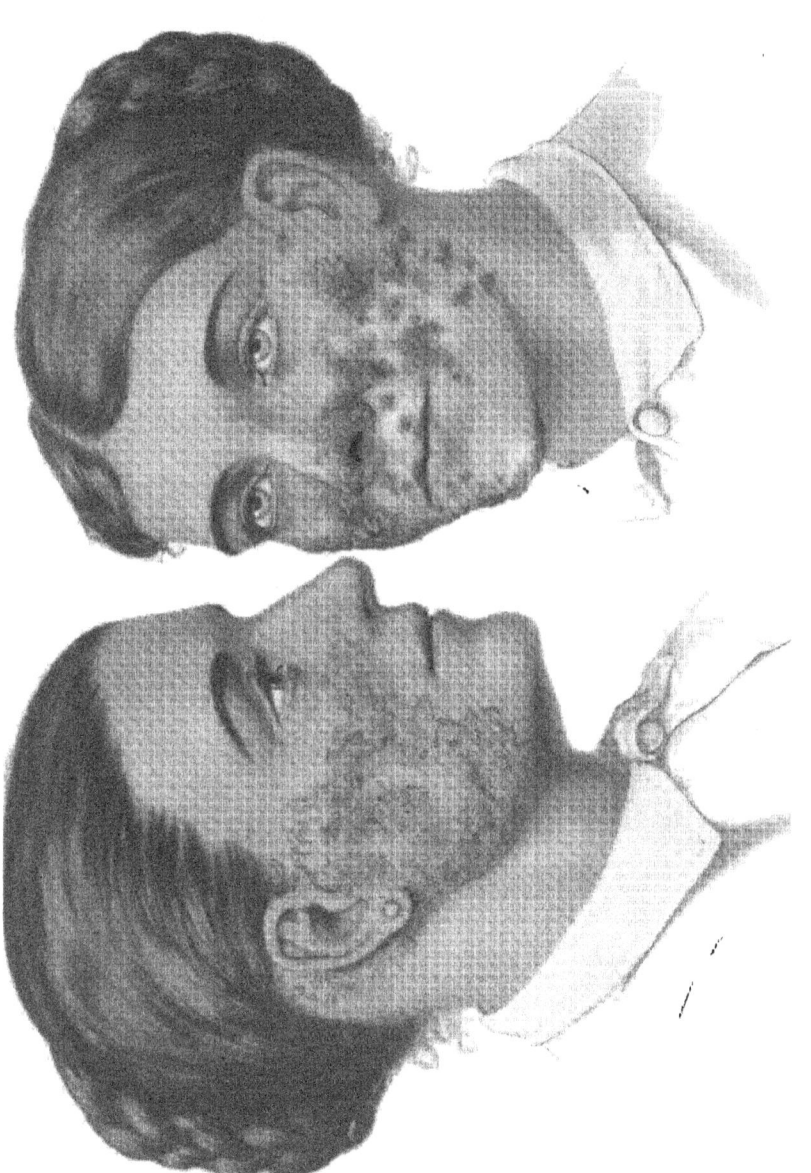

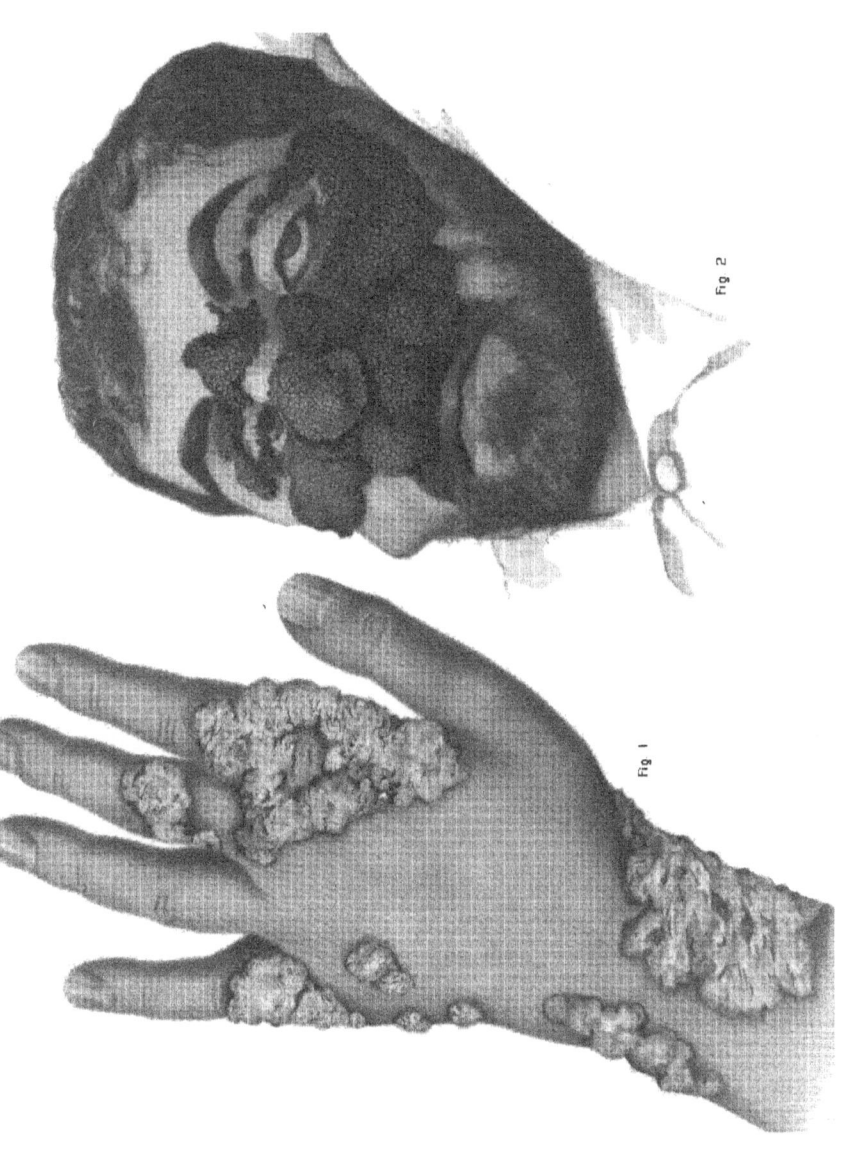

Fig 1

Fig 2

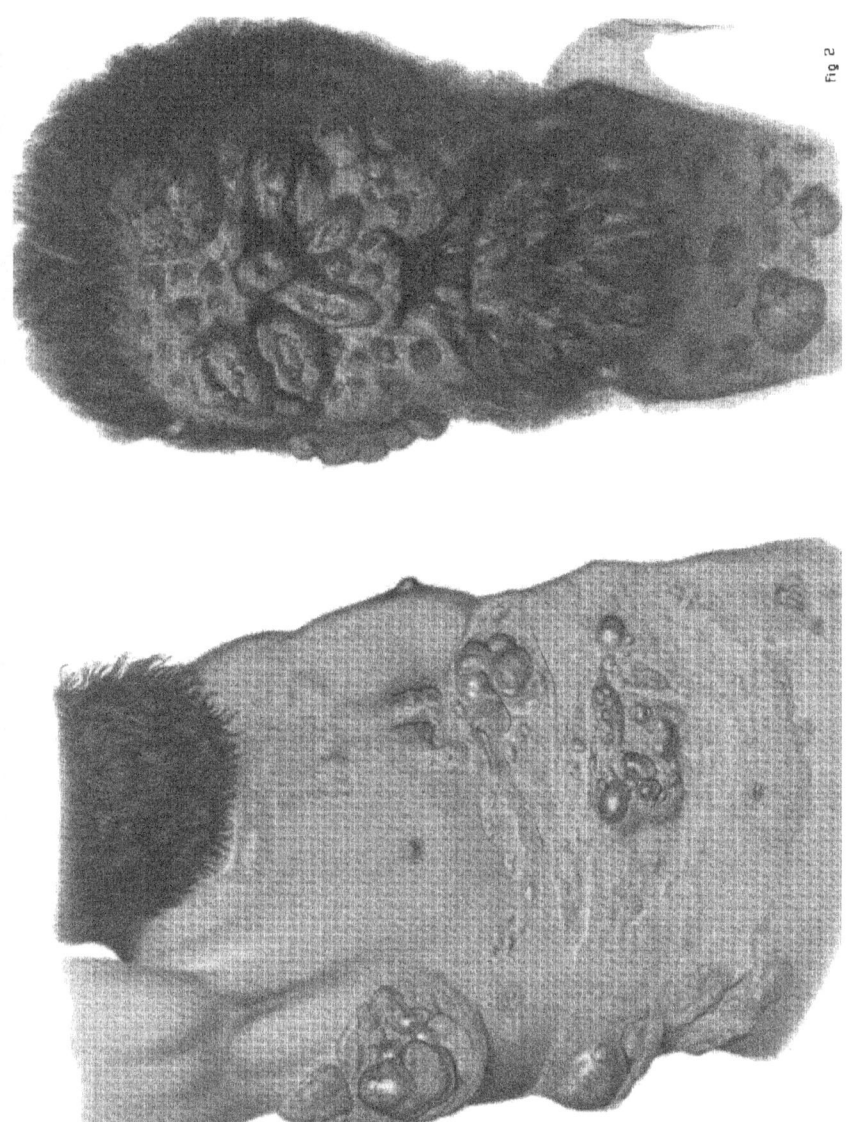

Fig 2

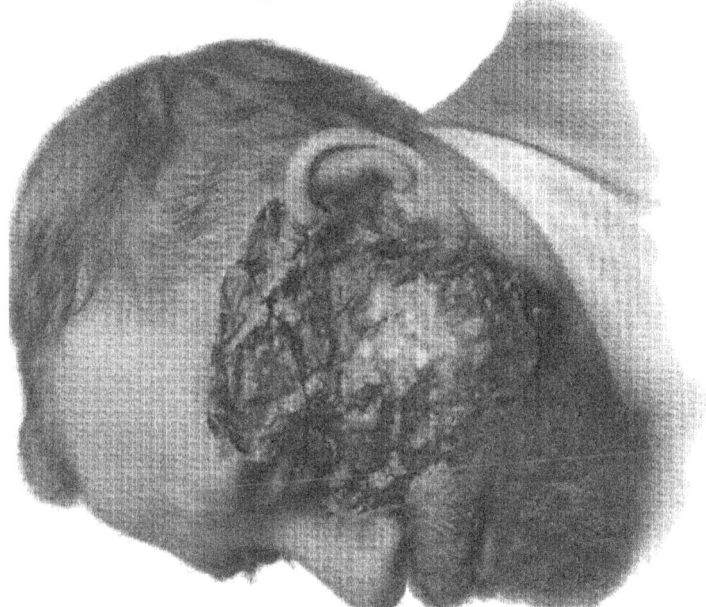

Fig 1

Fig 2

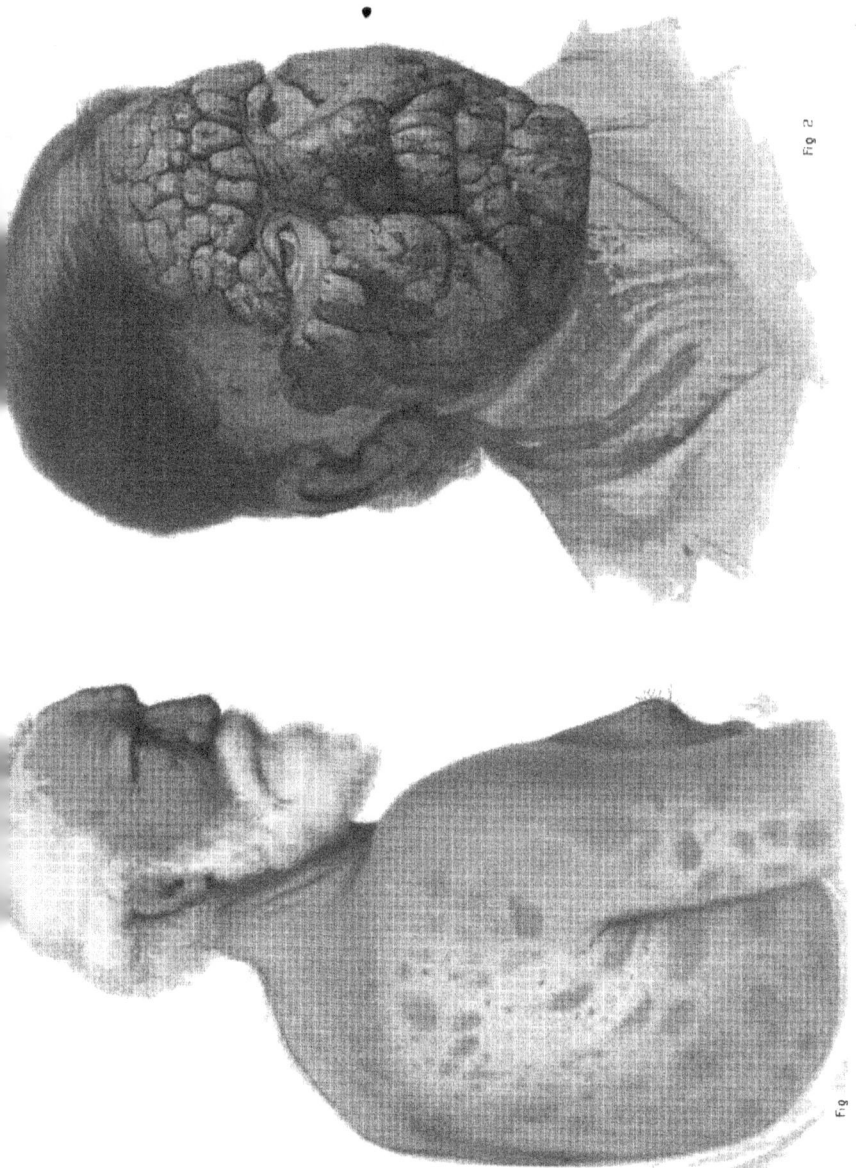

Fig 2

Fig

ATLAS

OF

VENEREAL AND SKIN

DISEASES

COMPRISING ORIGINAL ILLUSTRATIONS AND SELECTIONS FROM THE PLATES OF

Prof. M. KAPOSI, of Vienna; Mr. J. HUTCHINSON, of London; Prof. I. NEUMANN, of Vienna;
Profs. A. FOURNIER and HARDY; and Drs. RICORD, CULLERRIER, and VIDAL, of Paris;
Prof. LELOIR, of Lille; Dr. UNNA, of Hamburg; Dr. SILVA ARAUJO, of Rio Janeiro;
Dr. P. A. MORROW, of New York; Dr. E. L. KEYES, of New York; Dr. A. R.
ROBINSON, of New York; Dr. J. NEVINS HYDE, of Chicago;
Dr. HENRY G. PIFFARD, of New York, and others.

WITH ORIGINAL TEXT BY

PRINCE A. MORROW, A.M., M.D.,

CLINICAL PROFESSOR OF VENEREAL DISEASES, FORMERLY CLINICAL LECTURER ON DERMATOLOGY, IN THE UNIVERSITY OF THE CITY OF NEW YORK,
SURGEON TO CHARITY HOSPITAL, ETC.

NEW YORK

WILLIAM WOOD & COMPANY

1889

PROSPECTUS.

ATLAS

OF

VENEREAL AND SKIN

DISEASES

It is with special satisfaction that the publishers announce that this large and important work, which they have had in contemplation since 1883, is now ready for publication. It has long been recognized by them, from wide observation and acquaintance with similar works published in this country and abroad, that it is impossible for any one author to furnish, from his own collection of cases and illustrations, the most typical and at the same time the best and most lifelike pictures of the many peculiar forms of these diseases. Appreciating the defects and disadvantages arising from this cause, it was determined from the outset to enlist the co-operation, in the making of this ATLAS, of the leading dermatologists and syphilographers of the world. Prominent among them are Profs. M. Kaposi and I. Neumann, of Vienna. The atlas of the former, of venereal diseases, just completed, and that of the latter, of skin diseases, now being issued in parts, will be largely drawn upon in the preparation of this work, the sole right to reproduce them having been granted us by the authors.

Among other distinguished gentlemen who have engaged to contribute selections from their collections of original illustrations may now be mentioned Mr. J. Hutchinson, of London; Profs. A. Fournier and A. Hardy; and Drs. Ricord, Cullerrier, and Vidal, of Paris; Prof. Leloir, of Lille; Dr. Unna, of Hamburg; Dr. Silva Araujo, of Rio Janeiro; Dr. P. A. Morrow, of New York; Dr. Edward L. Keyes, of New York; Dr. J. Nevins Hyde, of Chicago; Dr. Henry G. Piffard, of New York.

Other names will be added to this list as the work progresses.

The Editor of the work is Dr. Prince A. Morrow, of New York, who, in addition to plates contributed from his own remarkable collection, will write the treatise on skin and venereal diseases, which constitutes, besides the description of the plates, the text accompanying them.

In this treatise, it is aimed to include chiefly those features which are the most practical, omitting in great measure pathological and other considerations which would be more properly treated of in extended writings, rather than as the adjunct to an Atlas.

In regard to the character of the plates, it may be said, they are believed to be superior to anything of the kind heretofore produced—as accurate in drawing as photographs, and far more distinct, while the coloring faithfully represents nature.

The text is printed from new type, large, clear, and handsome, and the paper is heavy, with a highly finished surface.

Altogether, considering the reputation of the authors of the plates, the ability of the editor, the superb execution of the plates, the excellence of the presswork, the high quality of the paper of both text and plates, the large size of the page, etc., etc., this ATLAS OF VENEREAL AND SKIN DISEASES will be the most superb work in medical literature ever published in the English language.

The ATLAS OF VENEREAL AND SKIN DISEASES will be published in fifteen monthly parts, each containing five folio, chromo-lithographic plates, many of them containing numerous figures, all printed in flesh tints and colors, together with descriptive text for each plate, and from sixteen to twenty folio pages of a practical treatise upon venereal and skin diseases; the whole forming, when complete, one magnificent thick folio volume with seventy-five plates, containing several hundred figures, exquisitely printed in colors.

☞ The ATLAS OF VENEREAL AND SKIN DISEASES will be sold by subscription only, at the very moderate price of $2 per part.

WILLIAM WOOD & COMPANY, *Publishers*,

56 AND 58 LAFAYETTE PLACE, NEW YORK.

another pathognomonic feature, and is most characteristically displayed in the regions supplied by the ulnar and peroneal nerves, as also by the third and seventh pair. The interossei and the extensor muscles of the hand and forearm are wasted, rendering them incapable of extension, and resulting in wrist-drop and a peculiar claw-like contraction of the fingers. The lower lid may become pendulous and everted, rendering it impossible to close the eyes. The paralysis may affect the muscles of the face, drawing the face to one side and constituting a characteristic deformity.

Another characteristic feature of anæsthetic leprosy is mutilation of the hands and feet. The bones of the fingers and toes may be lost, without ulceration, by a process of osseous absorption affecting one phalanx after another, the tissues retracting and the nail retreating backward until it may cap the first phalanx or the terminal extremity of the metacarpal bone; or the fingers and toes may become the seat of gangrene, which extends until a line of demarcation is formed and the member is spontaneously amputated, painlessly and perfectly; the reparative process is prompt and complete, the stump healing neatly. After partial loss of the phalanges the stumps stand out at every conceivable angle, and often in the most distorted and grotesque positions.

The course of anæsthetic leprosy is much slower than that of the tubercular form; its duration is ordinarily from ten to eighteen years, but instances are on record where it has been prolonged to twenty, thirty, or even forty years, the patients preserving a fair degree of good general health. Contrary to what is observed in the tubercular form, the sexual power is unimpaired, and in an advanced stage may approach the condition of satyriasis. Death most often occurs from marasmus or exhaustion supervening upon enteric complications.

Mixed Leprosy.—Under this designation are included those cases which exhibit the characteristic lesions of both the tubercular and anæsthetic forms. Although the symptoms peculiar to the latter usually predominate in the earlier stages, yet in the course of time the disease becomes stamped with the impress of tuberculation and correspondingly intensified in severity. The progress of the disease is, however, less progressively active than that of the pure tubercular type, the average duration of life being considerably longer. Taking my observations of 1,050 lepers at Molokai as a basis of comparison, I should say that among this number nearly one-half were tubercular, one-third anæsthetic, and the remainder of the mixed type. The proportion varies in different countries, and in the same country under different conditions. As the virulence of the disease becomes attenuated, the proportion of tubercular cases progressively diminishes.

In addition to the two typical forms of leprosy, and the series of symptoms common to both which make up the mixed form, certain writers have described a macular form of the disease. There is, however, no well-founded basis for this farther division; macular lesions may be met with in any of the forms of leprosy, but they represent simply a phase in the evolution of the disease, and should be classed in the same category as the bullous, ulcerative, and mutilating lesions. These pigmentary changes, moreover, vary greatly in color, extent, and duration, and their coloration is also materially influenced by the complexion of the individual.

A variety of eruptions may occur in connection with leprosy which are not an essential part of its cutaneous manifestations, but merely incidental thereto. The possible co-existence of syphilis, eczema, herpes, scabies, and the vegetable parasitic diseases should always be borne in mind. This latter class of affections are frequently met with in leprous patients, especially in tropical climates, and their presence may introduce an element of confusion in the diagnosis.

In the later stages, a variety of internal complications or intercurrent diseases may develop, as pneumonia, enteritis, nephritis, etc., which materially hasten the fatal termination.

ETIOLOGY.—While at the present day there is a general consensus of opinion among authorities as to the pathogenetic influence of the lepra bacillus in the propagation of leprosy, much confusion still exists as to the predisposing causes. Climate, race, soil and food, bad hygiene, malaria, etc., are considered as important factors in the development and spread of the disease.

As regards climate and race, a glance at the geographical distribution of the disease, which

embraces every variety of climate, from the tropics to the Arctic regions, and the most diverse nation-
alities, must convince any one that these agencies cannot be invoked as efficient causes.   The
same may be said of the soil, since the disease is prevalent in countries characterized by the greatest diversities of soil and geological conformation, embracing both marshy and mountainous
regions.

A prominent importance has been ascribed to the influence of food as a factor in the production of leprosy, especially the consumption of fish.   This view has gained support from the
fact that along the coast of Norway and other maritime regions where leprosy is endemic, raw or
partially decayed fish is a principal article of diet; but leprosy flourishes in countries where no fish
is eaten, and there is no well-grounded evidence that the consumption of fish excites or predisposes to leprosy.   In the Sandwich Islands, vegetables and fish have always been the staple
articles of diet, and yet leprosy was unknown among the inhabitants until within the last forty
years.   It has been assumed that the soil, food, and water may serve as receptacles for the
germs of leprosy, and that in these media they pass through a condition of spore life before they
attack the human tissues; this view is altogether fanciful and may be dismissed as untenable.

Bad hygienic conditions, privation, want, and misery, and certain diathetic conditions, as
syphilis, scrofula, etc., undoubtedly act as predisponents, just in that degree in which they lower
the general health and enfeeble the capacity of resistance to the germs of the disease.

CONTAGION.—There is at the present day by no means a unanimity of opinion as to the contagious activity of leprosy.   In 1867 the Royal College of Physicians of London formulated the
opinion that leprosy was not contagious, but recent clinical observations strongly negative this
view.   The history of the development of leprosy in the Sandwich Islands furnishes the most
abundant and conclusive proof of the eminent contagiousness of the disease.   The rapid spread
of the disease, affecting as it does at the present time more than five per cent of the entire native
population, besides many foreigners in whom no hereditary disposition can possibly be alleged,
can be explained on no other ground than that the disease is propagated from one individual to
another by direct contagion.

As regards the modes of contagion, our knowledge is by no means definite.   It is probable that in the immense majority of cases the disease is propagated by inoculation through direct
contact, as in sexual intercourse or through abraded surfaces.   It may possibly be inoculated by
punctures of mosquitoes and other insects, or by animal parasites, as the acarus scabei.   There
is also a strong probability that the contagion may be conveyed in the process of vaccination.
Inhalation is another assumed mode of infection, but it rests upon presumptive rather than positive proofs.

The influence of heredity in the transmission of leprosy must still be regarded as an open
question.   So far as has been observed, the disease is never congenital, and it is probable that a
predisposition to the disease rather than the actual germs are transmitted from parent to offspring.

PATHOLOGY.—The discovery of a micro-organism in the products of leprous infiltration
by Hansen, and its subsequent confirmation by the researches of Neisser and others, effected a
revolution in our views of the pathology and etiological relations of the disease.   At the present
day the lepra bacillus is generally recognized as the efficient cause of leprosy, which is classed in
the same category with tuberculosis and other bacillary diseases.

The bacilli lepræ are exceedingly minute rods tapering at both ends, about one-half to
three-quarters the diameter of a red blood-corpuscle in length, and about one-eighth to one-fif-
teenth of this diameter in breadth.   The spores form knob-like expansions, and are situated upon
one or both extremities of the bacillus.

The bacilli occur in all forms and all stages of leprosy; they are found in the diffuse and
nodular infiltrations of the skin and mucous membranes, in the lymphatic glands, in the interstitial connective tissue of the peripheral nerves, in the cornea, the cartilages, and in the spleen, liver,
and testicles.

They are endowed with extraordinary vital resistance, and present many analogies with the bacillus of tuberculosis.

The microscopic appearance of sections of a lepra tubercle resemble those of tuberculosis, and the two processes are in their beginning scarcely to be differentiated. The principal changes which take place in the corium consist of an accumulation of exudation-cells, which at first show a great tendency to arrange themselves about the blood-vessels. In size they vary from that of the ordinary lymph-cell to the so-called " lepra-cell," up to the multi-nucleated or " giant cell "; these latter are much less numerous than in tuberculous tissue.

The blood-vessels, about which the embryonic cells have a great tendency to group themselves, are dilated ; the walls are thickened. This thickening affects not only the external coat of the vessels, but often the internal as well; in which case, instead of being dilated, the lumen of the vessel is contracted.

The vascular lesions explain in part the disturbances of the circulation so pronounced on the surface of the lepra infiltration, in particular those on the extremities.

It is remarked that the eruption is often highly vascular from the dilated and varicose blood-vessels. In time, as a part of the leprous tissue becomes absorbed and eliminated, a sclerosis of a part of the tumor, or rather of the surrounding tissues, is produced. This formation of sclerotic tissue is especially marked about the nerves. The vascular lesions explain the frequency of the *taches ecchymotiques* in the leprous infiltrations, and the brown tint which the skin presents after the eruption has disappeared without ulceration.

In non-tuberculated lepra, foci of exudation-cells penetrate the externa. nerve sheath and pass between the fibres, pressing upon them and producing at first pain and hyperæsthesia; later, when the pressure is greater, anæsthesia. The fact that individual nerve fibres are pressed upon and destroyed explains the localized spots of pain and hyperæsthesia, and later anæsthesia.

Some difference of opinion exists in regard to the minuter distribution of the bacilli in the tissues. It was until recently held by nearly all observers that the chief seat of the micro-organisms was in the so-called " lepra-cells." Unna, however, disputed this general belief, and claimed to have demonstrated that the lymph-vessels of the skin are the principal abode of the bacilli. He asserts that by means of the ordinary coloring methods a great many of the bacilli are not stained and escape observation. He sought by means of his method to avoid the use of alcohol and oil in the after-treatment of stained sections. His cuts after being stained in the ordinary aniline water, gentian violet solution, and passed through a twenty-per-cent nitric acid solution, were washed in water and dried over a flame. Such specimens, after being inclosed in balsam and examined, are claimed by Unna to demonstrate that the masses of bacilli, which were formerly supposed to be inclosed in cells, are in reality quite independent of them, and are contained in dilated portions of the lymph-vessels.

Subsequent investigators, however, claim that Unna by his method has destroyed the normal tissue picture, and that his dilated lymphatics are artificial products without signification.

It can scarcely admit of doubt that the chief situation of the micro-organisms is the lepra-cells, although they are also encountered free in the tissues.

DIAGNOSIS.—The premonitory symptoms of leprosy are so indefinite in character and so lacking in constancy and regularity of development that, except in countries where the disease is endemic or where there is a known history of exposure to contagion, attention would not likely be directed to their true nature ; but when the eruptive stage is reached and the cutaneous lesions are fully developed, they are pathognomonic and cannot be confounded with those of any other disease.

The earlier macular eruption bears some resemblance to simple or exudative erythema, but the latter is more sudden in its development and more acute in its course; its localization is different, and it is not accompanied by the peculiar subjective sensations of leprosy.

Syphilitic roseola can hardly be confounded with the erythematous patches of leprosy. The lesions differ greatly in their extent, localization, and duration. The tubercular syphilide may bear a deceptive resemblance to tuberculated leprosy. The syphilitic neoplasms are, however, differently grouped; the infiltrations are less diffuse, they are more circular in outline, coppery in hue, and are more rapid in their involution. After their absorption or elimination by ulceration, characteristic cicatrices remain. The frequent co-existence of leprosy and syphilis in the same subject should be borne in mind. Leprosy should not be confounded with vitiligo, morphœa, or scleroderma. An attention to the minute clinical features of these eruptions would readily eliminate any possible source of error in the diagnosis.

An eruption of pemphigoid blebs, unaccompanied, as it often is, by any other cutaneous manifestations of leprosy, may simulate ordinary pemphigus, but the primary localization of the bullæ, always few in number, upon the extremities, and their successive development upon other parts of the body, and the concomitant disorders of sensation, should serve to differentiate them. Very often in the early stage of anæsthetic leprosy there is a painful swelling of the ulnar and peroneal nerves, with anæsthesia and commencing atrophic changes in the regions they supply.

TREATMENT.—The cure of leprosy still remains, as it has been in all ages, the despair of medical science. The disease, when once developed, progresses almost invariably to a fatal termination, and the resources of medical art chiefly comprise measures of prevention and of palliation. The experience of centuries has proven that the isolation of lepers constitutes the most effective means for the suppression of the disease, and its good results are directly proportioned to the strictness and completeness with which segregation is carried out.

Hygienic measures, comprising an abundance of animal food, warm clothing, and freedom from exposure to damp and cold, with frequent bathing and care of the skin, have a favorable influence upon the progress of the disease.

Palliative treatment is both constitutional and local. While no remedy has yet been discovered which exerts anything like a specific action in radically curing leprosy, yet there are certain drugs which seem to modify the manifestations of the disease and render its course less progressively active. Of the numerous remedies recommended, chaulmoogra oil, expressed from the seeds of the gynocardia odorata, and gurjun oil, derived from depterocarpus lævis, have given the best results. Under the prolonged use of chaulmoogra oil there is a notable amelioration of the symptoms, the leprous products undergo involution, the disorders of sensibility are corrected, and the general health is improved. To secure the best results of the remedy, it should be given in sensible doses. We should begin with doses of five minims after each meal, preferably given in capsules or in emulsion with milk to obviate the unpleasant taste, and increase it according to the effect produced and the toleration of the patient. In many cases the dose may be increased to sixty minims or more three times a day with advantage.

At the same time the remedy may be used externally in the form of an ointment of gyno-cardic acid, or as a liniment in the proportion of one part of the oil to five or fifteen of olive oil; or the gurjun oil may be used instead as a local application in the form of the "gurjun ointment," consisting of one part of gurjun oil to three parts of lime water or olive oil.

In India the gurjun oil has a high repute as an internal remedy. It is given in an emulsion, equal parts of the oil and lime water, of which the dose is from two to four drachms. In conjunction with the external use of the gurjun ointment, baths should be administered twice a day. Cod-liver oil or linseed oil may be used in the same way. Other remedies have been highly recommended, among which may be enumerated hoang-nang, strychnia, salicylate of soda, creasote, carbolic acid, iodide of potassium, sulpho-ichthyolate of sodium, etc.

Unna claims remarkable curative results from the external use of certain reducing agents, as resorcin, ichthyol, chrysarobin, pyrogallol, etc. He regards them most efficacious when employed in a weak form, "in that they compete with the micro-organisms for the acid, and in strong applications, besides this action, they produce an inflammation of the skin which effects an elimination of the organisms." He gives the following formulæ: Chrysarobin or pyrogallol, five parts; ichthyol, five parts; salicylic acid, two parts; simple ointment, one hundred parts; M. Also; Resorcin, five parts; ichthyol, five parts; salicylic acid, two parts; simple ointment, one hundred parts;

M.   For the lepra nodes plaster mulls are recommended, containing each forty parts of salicylic acid and creasote.

The ulcers and sores of the extremities, which interfere so seriously with the patient's comfort and locomotion, should be treated on surgical principles.   The gangrenous flesh should be cut away, necrosed bones removed, and the sores dressed with iodoform and boracic acid lint or with a simple ointment.

The ulcerations of the nose, mouth, and throat, the secretions from which emit a most offensive odor and poison the patient from their constant swallowing, should be treated with medicated sprays and antiseptic douches or with caustics.   The ocular lesions of leprosy may be treated by cauterization of the cornea and conjunctiva around the tubercles, which limits or arrests their extension.   Various delicate operations have been successfully made with the object of correcting the epiphora and other disagreeable symptoms which result from inability to close the eyelids. Electricity has been found serviceable in restoring impaired sensibility to anæsthetic areas or extensive regions, while massage and nerve-stretching often overcome contraction of the muscles and result in a return of motion.   When the tubercles are localized upon the face and cause much deformity, they may be removed by excision, by destructive cauterization with the thermo-cautery, or by interstitial injections of antiseptic liquids, as alcohol, carbolic acid, etc.

The complications of leprosy which are more apt to supervene at an advanced stage, such as diarrhœa, bronchial and renal disorders, should be symptomatically treated.

SCABIES.

Synonym—The Itch.

Scabies is a contagious animal parasitic disease, characterized by a peculiar lesion caused by the burrowing of the acarus in the cutaneous tissues, the irritation from which results in the production of secondary lesions in the form of papules, vesicles, and pustules.   The intensity of the secondary eruptive phenomena varies in different individuals, according to the severity and extent of the local irritation and the reaction of the tissues.

The female acarus penetrates beneath the skin and burrows in a tortuous or curled canal termed a cuniculus.   In this canal she deposits from a dozen to fifty eggs, which, after about a week's incubation, are hatched.   The young female acari come to the surface, are impregnated, and in turn repeat the process of burrowing and propagation.   The cuniculus, the track of which may be seen as a sinuous or tortuous beaded or blackish line on the surface, varies in length from one-third of an inch to two, three, or four inches; if the canal be carefully opened up, the acarus may be lifted out from the end of the furrow on the point of a needle, visible to the naked eye as a minute white speck.   The female acarus is about twice the size of the male; the latter does not burrow, but wanders over the surface, and may occasionally be found under scales and crusts.

The irritation excited by the presence of the mites in the skin gives rise to intense pruritus, and provokes scratching with consequent lesions of various kinds.   When fully developed the eruption of scabies is essentially polymorphous; the skin becomes the seat of burrows, papules, vesicles, pustules with torn summits, blood-crusts, excoriations, and scratch-marks, the artificial dermatitis resembling eczema.   When the disease is of long standing, bullæ with ulcerations and furuncles may develop, which, with the infiltration and pigmentation of the skin, may entirely mask the primary and more characteristic lesions.

The itching is always more severe at night, and may become so intolerable that patients scratch and tear the integument in a most frightful manner in the effort to obtain relief.

In some cases the subjective sensations are mild, and the penetration of the acarus causes scarcely any reaction of an inflammatory nature, so that secondary lesions from scratching are entirely absent.

PLATE LXXI.

Scabies.

The places of election for the burrowing of the acarus are in regions where the skin is thin, delicate, and easily penetrable, as between the fingers and toes ; the flexor surfaces of wrists and axillæ, the mammæ and penis, and the anterior aspect of the thighs ; sometimes the eruption overspreads its regions of predilection and becomes almost universal, sparing only the neck and face.

As the itch-mites are transferred to new surfaces by the nails in scratching, the accessibility of parts to the fingers, as well as the character of the clothing and pressure, affect the distribution of the eruption. In adults, the anterior surface of the trunk between the nipples and knees, and the buttocks, are the regions of predilection.

Scabies varies in frequency in different countries, its prevalence being influenced by conditions of climate, uncleanliness, and social habits. It is much more common in Europe than in this country, its relative proportion to the sum total of skin diseases being only one per cent in the United States.

DIAGNOSIS.—The presence of the acarian furrow is the diagnostic mark of scabies, and in cases where this can be distinctly made out there is no possibility of error. The cuniculus may often readily be traced as a sinuous, punctated line, which, as pointed out by Hebra, becomes all the more distinct when the surface is painted with ink and allowed to dry. A good lens will also serve as an efficient aid in the investigation. But the absence of the furrow, or rather the inability to detect it, does not necessarily exclude scabies. Very often when the patient comes under treatment its characteristic features are effaced by time or masked by an artificial eczema, and in such cases the polymorphous character of the eruption, and its localization in parts which have already been described as the favorite habitat of the parasite, will furnish indications as to its nature. In many cases the diagnosis may be cleared up by the history of contagion, from some member of the family or bedfellow

As before intimated, a secondary eczema frequently masks scabies, but ordinary eczema does not exhibit a predilection for the favorite seats of the acari; the vesicles are smaller and grouped, instead of being large and scattered, and there is more exudation and crusting.

Phthiriasis may be distinguished from scabies by its different localization, upon the shoulders and back and the outer aspects of the limbs. An attention to the minute clinical features of the two diseases, the absence of furrows, and the presence of the pediculus, will obviate any mistake.

TREATMENT.—There are a vast number of agents which are destructive to the itch-mite, but in the selection of the agent, its strength and mode of application, due regard should be had to the irritative condition of the skin, which may be present from secondary eczema. The sensitiveness of the individual skin must also be respected; a treatment which might be admirably adapted to an adult would be too irritating to the delicate skin of an infant. Then, again, a treatment which would be indicated in hospital practice might be objectionable to a private patient. Fortunately the number of efficient parasiticides at our command is sufficiently large and diversified to fulfil any or all of these indications.

Sulphur is a time-honored parasiticide, and in the promptitude and efficiency of its action it cannot be surpassed. In the St. Louis hospitals, a two-hours treatment is regarded as quite sufficient for an ordinary case of itch. The patient is washed with black soap and bathed for half an hour. Then, during another half-hour, he is thoroughly anointed with the following ointment: Sulphur. puriss., 2 parts; potass. sub. carb., 1 part; and adipis, 8 to 12 parts. This is left on for a while, and a final cleansing bath is given, which terminates the treatment, in two hours.

Hebra's modification of Wilkinson's ointment: Flor. sulp., ol. cadini, āā 40 parts; sapon. virid., adipis, āā 80 parts ; cretæ. alb. pulv., 15 parts, is equally efficacious.

An ointment of ten to twenty per cent of sulphur in lard is quite efficient, only requiring a somewhat longer time to effect a cure.

Preliminary to the application of the parasiticide, the patient should take a soap bath, which softens the skin and facilitates the penetration of the ointment, which should be thoroughly rubbed in, and the procedure repeated in twelve to twenty-four hours. Two to four days of this treatment usually suffice to effect a cure.

In many cases the skin is too irritable to tolerate this treatment, and milder, more soothing applications are indicated until the eczematous inflammation subsides.

Among the recently introduced remedies, naphthol possesses certain advantages over sulphur from its lack of odor and tendency to irritate the inflamed skin. It may be used in the form of a simple ointment of from five to ten per cent, or combined in the following proportions after Kaposi's formula: Naphthol, fifteen parts; sapo. virid., fifty parts; pulv. cretæ alb., ten parts; axung., one hundred parts. Naphthalin, ten to twenty per cent solution, in linseed oil, has also given satisfactory results.

McCall Anderson prefers styrax, in the proportion of one ounce to lard two ounces, to all other remedies. Balsam of Peru, either alone or in combination with other remedies, is a most efficient and pleasant preparation. A vast number of remedies—tar, the ethereal oils, petroleum, infusions of black hellebore, staphisagria, sublimate solutions—have been recommended. Whatever remedy is used, especial care and attention should be paid to the mode of its employment. An eczematous eruption may be perpetuated almost indefinitely by the continued use of preparations which are too strong and irritating.

PEDICULOSIS.

Synonym.—Phthiriasis.

There are three varieties of pediculi, or lice, which infest the human skin, and which, according to their habitat, have been termed pediculus capitis, pediculus corporis, and pediculus pubis. The peculiar lesions which they occasion, both primary and secondary, will best be described under each of the species named.

PEDICULUS CAPITIS.—The head-louse is much more common .n children than in adults, on account of their close association in schools, asylums, and other crowded institutions, and its principal habitat is the occipital region and top of the hairy scalp. The bite of the insect causes more or less irritation of the scalp, accompanied by intense itching, in the effort to relieve which by scratching the parts are wounded, and excoriations, pustules, and scabs result; the hairs often become matted together by the effusion of a serous or sero-purulent discharge. When the disease is of long standing and the lice numerous, the entire scalp may be the seat of these lesions, the condition resembling that seen in impetigo contagiosa. Not infrequently, in young children, the glands of the neck become swollen and inflamed, and may finally suppurate. Vesicular and pustular eruptions of an eczematous character may spread from the scalp over the adjoining surface of the neck and back.

The eggs or nits are deposited on the hair shafts near the roots, and a number of them may be attached to a single hair. They adhere closely by a glutinous material, and are with difficulty detached.

PEDICULUS CORPORIS.—The body-louse—or more properly the *pediculus vestimentorum*, since the insect lives in the clothes and seeks the skin only for nourishment—is similarly shaped but larger than the head-louse. It is more common in the old, feeble, and cachectic who are filthy in their habits and seldom change their clothing.

The bite of the insect is followed by a hæmorrhagic spot or elevated wheal at the seat of puncture, accompanied by considerable itching, and in the endeavor to allay this by scratching, the summit of the wheal or papule is torn and a drop or two of blood exudes upon its surface, forming a crust.

The bite of the insect, as well as its movements over the skin, excite a sensation of creeping or formication which spreads over a large surface, and the patient frequently scratches parts distant from the points of injury.

Secondary eruptions are produced in the form of excoriations, pustules, furuncles, ecthymatous lesions, and cutaneous ulcerations, with more or less thickening and pigmentation of the skin. The scratch-marks are usually in parallel lines, and are most marked upon the backs of the shoulders, the clavicular region, the region of the loins, and the outer aspects of the thighs and legs. They may be found upon all parts of the skin accessible to the nails.

PEDICULUS PUBIS.—The crab-louse—so named from its resemblance to a crab—has for its chief habitat the hair of the pubes, but exceptionally it may be found upon the eyelashes, the beard, and the hairs of the chest, axillæ, and abdomen.

Its bite causes an intense irritation, and the scratching gives rise to an eruption of papules, vesicles, or pustules resembling eczema. Crab-lice are ordinarily communicated during sexual intercourse, and are rarely seen upon persons before the age of puberty; they may, however, occur in children from transmission through the medium of clothing or the bedding.

DIAGNOSIS.—The localities affected, and the easily demonstrated presence of pediculi or their ova, render the diagnosis easy.

In *pediculosis capitis* the nits may be seen firmly agglutinated to the shaft of the hair, and most abundant in the occipital region. When eczema of the scalp exists, the lice may be hidden among the crusts and matted hairs, but they are usually discovered by careful investigation. The existence of occipital eczema should always direct suspicion to pediculosis as the probable cause.

In *pediculosis corporis* the existence of hæmorrhagic spots, blood crusts, and parallel linear streaks made by the nails in characteristic locations, as the clavicular and scapular regions, will suggest the nature of the trouble. As the pediculi only utilize the skin for a feeding ground, they should be sought for in the folds and seams of the undergarments. The disease is readily differentiated from papular or pustular eczema, urticaria papulosa, and senile pruritus of a neurotic character.

Pediculosis pubis is frequently mistaken for eczema, but the limitation of the itching and eruptive phenomena to the pubes, or the other hairy regions infested by the crab-louse, is unusual in eczema. The presence of the nits, which appear as minute dots or specks closely adherent to the base of the hairs, will establish the diagnosis.

TREATMENT.—The treatment of pediculosis is extremely simple and efficacious. The first object is to destroy the pediculi with their ova, and then cure the secondary eczema which is generally present. For the destruction of the head-louse a thorough application of petroleum is sufficient. It may be used pure or with equal parts of balsam of Peru. If the hair is to be preserved, some difficulty will be experienced in getting rid of the nits, which adhere closely. Sponging the affected hairs with alcohol, vinegar, or solutions of soda will gradually effect this purpose. In long-standing cases where the hairs are matted together by crusts, it may be desirable to cut the hair close, thus removing the mass of nits which it contains, and facilitating the application of remedies to the eczematous surface. Naphthol, a solution of corrosive sublimate, or the ammoniated mercurial ointment will also be found efficient parasiticides.

In the treatment of pediculosis corporis, the first step is to remove the clothing which harbors the parasite. The garments should be destroyed, or thoroughly baked in a hot oven before being again used. The irritative condition of the skin will subside spontaneously with the removal of the offending parasite. Soda baths, followed by inunctions of carbolized oil or vaseline, will assist the reparative process.

In the treatment of pediculosis pubis, blue ointment and the white precipitate ointment are time-honored remedies. They are objectionable from their tendency to aggravate the existing eczema, or to provoke an eczematous eruption where none was present. Petroleum, with balsam of Peru, ether, or one of the ethereal oils, is far preferable.

PLATE LXXII.

Pediculosis Corporis.

SYDENHAM COLLECTION.

CHROMOPHYTOSIS.

Synonym.—Tinea Versicolor.

Chromophytosis may be defined as a vegetable parasitic disease affecting the superficial layers of the epidermis, and characterized by brownish or fawn-colored patches of variable size and shape. It is but feebly contagious, and its distribution is limited almost exclusively to the trunk, rarely affecting the extremities or exposed parts.

The disease first appears as pin-head to pea-sized spots, roundish in outline, which may remain stationary or enlarge into dollar or palm-sized patches. The spots may remain discrete, with a tendency rather to increase in number than to aggregate into large patches, as seen in Fig. 2, Plate LXXIII. In the farther course of their extension, these patches often run together, forming by their coalescence large, irregularly marginated tracts. Their peculiar configuration gives to the surface a mapped appearance, the marginated outlines inclosing extensive areas or islands of skin, which may remain unaffected or appear dotted here and there with isolated spots.

The entire surface of the trunk may be the seat of the eruption; sometimes it may extend down the thighs or over the arms, but rarely beyond the knees and elbows. With the exception of one or two cases, its presence has never been recorded upon parts habitually exposed, as the hands and face.

The surface of the patches is usually the seat of a slight furfuraceous desquamation. When the affected skin is moist and sweaty, the scales may be readily scraped off by the finger nail, and are usually found loaded with the fungus. The color varies from a light fawn to a brown or even blackish tint, depending upon the complexion of the individual: the more pigmented the skin, the darker the coloration of the patches.

The subjective sensations consist of a slight pruritus, which becomes more pronounced when the body is warm and perspiring; the patches sometimes assume an inflamed or eczematous appearance from the irritation caused by scratching.

Chromophytosis is essentially a disease of adult life, but it may develop before puberty, and still more rarely at an advanced age. Its contagious character is but slightly marked, but, nevertheless, definitely proven in the case of persons occupying the same bed, one contracting it from the other. A condition of contagion would seem to be malnutrition or debility of the cutaneous tissues. The skin of persons the subjects of the syphilitic or tuberculous diathesis furnishes a most congenial soil for the growth of the fungus. Its very frequent association with phthisis has been generally remarked.

DIAGNOSIS.—There are a number of cutaneous discolorations with which the patches of chromophytosis may be confounded.

Chloasma may be distinguished by the fact of its common occurrence upon the hands and face. These pigment spots are not the seat of desquamation, nor are they attended with subjective disorders.

Chromophytosis has been mistaken for a macular syphilide, on account of its color and distribution upon parts habitually covered by clothing. The color of the syphilide is more coppery in hue, less scaly, not itchy, and its presence is usually accompanied by other signs of syphilis. It is well to bear in mind the occasional association of the two diseases in the same subject.

Chronic scaly erythema may be differentiated by its non-limitation to the places of predilection for chromophytosis, the presence of inflammatory evidences, the brighter red color of the patches, and the differences in the character of the desquamation.

TREATMENT.—The treatment of chromophytosis is simple and more promptly efficacious than that of other vegetable parasitic diseases of the skin. The disease is situated in the superficial layers of the epidermis, and easily accessible to parasiticidic agents, which destroy the spores or cause exfoliation of the epidermic structures in which they find a lodgment. The skin should

PLATE LXXIII.

Chromophytosis.

AFTER PIFFARD.

be thoroughly washed with soft or green soap to remove the greasiness and allow the more ready penetration of the parasiticide. Sometimes vigorous scrubbing with spiritus saponis kalinus will alone be sufficient to completely clear the skin; but in order to destroy any remaining spores, which might serve as germs for future development, it is well to follow it with the application of a more active agent.

A most excellent parasiticide is the hyposulphite of soda, 1 to 2 drachms to the ounce, with a little glycerin. This preparation has the recommendation of being unirritating to the skin.

Applications of sulphurous acid, diluted to one-half strength, painting with a solution of the bichloride of mercury, 2 grs. to the ounce of tincture of benzoin or myrrh, tincture of iodine, or a strong solution of sulphate of copper, or the use of chrysarobin or salicylic acid, 5 to 10 per cent in traumaticin, will be found equally efficacious.

It is desirable to continue the treatment or keep the patient under observation for some time after apparent cure, in order to guard against recurrences from the development of deep-seated spores which may have escaped destruction.

TRICOPHYTOSIS.

Synonyms.—Ringworm ; Tinea Tricophytina; Herpes Tonsurans.

Of the group of vegetable parasitic diseases included under the class of tineas, tricophytosis is the most frequent and, clinically, the most important. The presence of the tricophyton in the tissues gives rise to phenomena of irritation which vary in intensity and severity according to the region affected. These clinical variations, determined by modifications in the mode of reaction of the tissues in which the fungus finds lodgment, were formerly regarded as distinct diseases, but now their pathological identity is clearly demonstrated. They are all distinguished by their circinate character and their tendency to centrifugal extension, the margins of the patches showing the most active and characteristic signs of the proliferation of the fungus.

According to their location and the anatomical peculiarities of the tissues, the lesions of tricophytosis assume different aspects in different regions of the body. The disease may be most conveniently described under the following regional forms :

> Tricophytosis Corporis—Tinea circinata.
> Tricophytosis Cruralis seu Axillaris—Eczema marginatum.
> Tricophytosis Capitis—Tinea tonsurans.
> Tricophytosis Barbæ—Tinea sycosis.
> Tricophytosis Unguium—Onychomycosis.

All of these forms are eminently contagious, and, with the exception of sycosis, are more frequent in children. Tinea capitis is of such rare occurrence in adults that this circumstance constitutes a valuable differential sign between ringworm and favus.

TINEA CIRCINATA affects principally regions of the body provided with fine lanugo hairs. The disease begins in the form of a small, erythematous, slightly scaly spot, presenting a circular, well-defined, slightly elevated border, which may be either papular or vesicular. As the patch extends at the periphery, the centre clears up, becomes less pigmented and the seat of a branny desquamation. Sometimes the central portion of the patch becomes quite normal ; the sharply defined erythematous circle presents a distinctly annular outline. In rare cases, concentric rings, three or four in number, are formed in the evolution of the disease. Ordinarily a number of circular patches develop from separate foci. After attaining a certain size, they undergo involution or coalesce with contiguous rings, forming large patches with irregular outlines. In tropical climates especially, there is a tendency to rapid and exaggerated development of the rings.

Ringworm of the body is more common upon the face, neck, arms, and exposed parts, but may occur upon the trunk.

ECZEMA MARGINATUM is exaggerated in its clinical features by the accident of location in the genito-crural region. The conditions of warmth, moisture, and friction here present not only favor a more luxuriant growth of the fungus, but an inflammatory element is added which imparts to the eruption the characteristics of an eczema. The primary rings coalesce and form large patches with festooned or scalloped outline, which may extend down the thighs or up over the abdomen. In Mexico and the Sandwich Islands, I have observed this exaggerated development of the eruption, creeping over large areas in the form of immense gyrate circles.

TINEA TONSURANS.—This form of tricophytosis occurs almost exclusively in children. It begins as small, circular, reddish spots, which are sometimes the seat of vesicles. The fungus gradually penetrates the hairs and hair follicles, and as the patch increases in size the hairs become dry, brittle, and break off near the surface. The broken hair stumps are surrounded with white, powdery scales loaded with the fungus, and the surface of the patches presents an appearance as if covered with a mealy powder. After the disease has existed for some time, the color of the affected patches becomes bluish or slate colored, which contrasts markedly with the hue of the healthy scalp.

In exceptional cases an inflammatory process resembling a pustular folliculitis develops. There are circumscribed infiltrations in the subcutaneous cellular tissue, which give a deceptive indication of suppuration; the whole scalp may present a boggy, fluctuating feel. The hairs loosen and fall out, and through the patulous orifices a thick, glairy mucus of the consistence of honey exudes. Such rare conditions have been described as kerion celsi.

SYCOSIS PARASITICA.—The beginning stage of barber's itch presents the same phenomena as ringworm of the scalp. In its further course inflammatory implication of the deeper structures more commonly occurs. Dusky-red papules, pustules, and deep nodular indurations develop. There is more or less discharge of a yellow, gluey fluid from the dilated follicles, which forms crusts. In neglected or improperly treated cases, furuncular lesions and large subcutaneous abscesses may also form, and in the submaxillary region papillomatous proliferations with mulberry or fig-like masses develop. In the process of involution, cicatrices with permanent spots of baldness result. The upper lip is seldom implicated in the process.

ONYCHOMYCOSIS.—Tinea of the nails is a quite rare affection, and its occurrence is almost always in connection with ringworm of other portions of the body. One or several nails of either the fingers or toes may be attacked. The nail becomes opaque, with irregularly distributed, grayish-white spots, more or less thickened, brittle, and friable. The free edges of the nails become fissured and split, or the nail itself may become raised from its bed. Examinations of the splinters or scrapings of the diseased nail show the plentiful presence of mycelia.

DIAGNOSIS.—As the various forms of tricophytosis just described are due to the same pathogenetic agent, microscopical examination will constitute an efficient aid in establishing the diagnosis. This is, however, not always practicable, and in long-standing cases it may be difficult to detect the parasite. The clinical features of *tinea circinata* are often sufficiently characteristic to render it easy of recognition. The diseases with which ringworm of the body is most apt to be confounded are eczema seborrhoicum, psoriasis, and the circinate syphilide. The orbicular patches of seborrhœic eczema are not so distinctly circular, the edges shade off into the surrounding skin without the elevated, abrupt margin of ringworm, nor do they show the same tendency to heal in the central portion of the patch.

Patches of psoriasis deprived of scabs and in process of cure may simulate ringworm. They are characteristic in their location, more apt to be symmetrical, and are further distinguished by their more abundant, whiter scales.

The circinate syphilide is distinguished by its coppery color, its pigmented or atrophic centre, and differences in its peripheral infiltration.

The differential diagnosis between *eczema marginatum* and eczema of the genital and perigenital region may sometimes be difficult, as their clinical appearances are almost identical. Eczema marginatum affects more particularly the inside of the thighs, while eczema involves the entire scrotum and penis, often extending along the perineum and around the anus. The curved, sweeping outlines of the tricophyton rings constitute a valuable diagnostic sign.

Tinea capitis may resemble favus, psoriasis, and squamous eczema. The differential features of favus and ringworm of the scalp have already been considered. In psoriasis the hairs are unaffected in shape and length, and there is a greater accumulation of mortar-like scales. It is more characteristic developed around the margin of the hairy scalp. Evidences of the disease will also be seen upon other portions of the surface.

Patches of dry, scaly eczema are distinguished by the presence of moisture and crusts, and the entire absence of the stumpy hairs projecting through the white, powdery débris of the fungus.

Ringworm of the beard often presents a most deceptive resemblance to idiopathic sycosis, but the course of the latter is less acute, the inflammation is more superficial in character, and it is usually confined to the production of pustulation about the hairs. Non-parasitic sycosis frequently attacks the upper lip, while tinea sycosis is rarely observed in this location. Tubercular syphilis occurring upon the hairy regions of the face may simulate sycosis, but the nodules of the former are more circumscribed and coppery in tint, the crusts are more abundant and greenish, and the hairs are unaffected.

Onychomycosis may be mistaken for eczematous, psoriatic, and syphilitic affections of the nails. The differential diagnosis is extremely difficult, and can only be definitely determined with the aid of the microscope.

TREATMENT.—All rational treatment of the present day has for its object the destruction of the offending parasite by topical means, and varies only in the choice of the agents used and in the mechanical details of its execution.

In the treatment of tinea circinata, in which the epidermic structures and shallow follicles are principally involved, the treatment is promptly curative. Energetic washings with the tincture of green soap, followed by applications of pure sulphurous acid, or salicylic acid, one drachm to the ounce, painting the affected surfaces with chrysarobin in traumaticin (ten per cent) or iodized collodion (tincture of iodine and collodion, equal parts), will be found efficient. The use of the bichloride in tincture of benzoin is also a convenient and effective mode of treatment.

In the treatment of tineas affecting the hairy regions, more particularly the scalp, the problem is complicated by causes purely physical. Instead of the spores being confined to the superficial epidermis and readily accessible to our remedies, they have penetrated to the depths of the hair follicles and even into the substance of the hairs themselves, and within this secure retreat they vegetate into luxuriant growth and defy dislodgment. The disease is obstinate to treatment on account of the mechanical difficulty of bringing parasiticidal agents into immediate contact with the parasite, to overcome which various measures have been employed.

The first step is the removal of all crusts or scales from the affected surfaces. This may be accomplished by a thorough soaking with olive or linseed oil, or the application of emollient poultices. After removal of all extraneous matters and thorough cleansing of the affected surfaces with soap and water, the hairs should be cut, either with the scissors or a pair of barber's clippers. The razor should never be used, as, according to Besnier, it is the frequent cause of auto-inoculation.

The next step in the treatment is the extraction of all the hairs in the area of the diseased patches. Although many authorities depreciate the importance of epilation, or reject it altogether as an unnecessary, painful procedure, yet it must be regarded as a most essential part of the treatment, especially in advanced or chronic cases. It subserves the double purpose of removing the mass of spores contained in the diseased hairs, while leaving the orifices of the follicles open, and thus furnishing a more ready entrance to the parasiticidal agent.

For this procedure a good epilating forceps with smooth blades should be employed. The use of the calotte or the epilating sticks is too barbarously painful to be recommended. In ringworm of the scalp, the texture of the hairs is so altered, from the abundant infiltration of their substance with the fungus, that they easily break off, and frequent repetition of the epilation over

PLATE LXXIV.

Tricophytosis and Favus.

AFTER HEBRA.

the same area may be necessary. It is always well to remove the healthy hairs in a narrow zone immediately surrounding the patches, thus limiting their peripheric extension. In order to accelerate the spontaneous elimination of the diseased hairs by provoking a certain amount of irritation, M. Feullard, in his recent work, " Teigne et Teigneux," recommends touching the diseased patches with a little crystallizable acetic acid, pure or mixed with chloroform. The applications are to be made with care and at sufficiently long intervals, so as not to cause too much irritation.

Immediately after epilation, the parasiticidal preparation should be applied. A vast number of agents have been recommended for this purpose, as bichloride and sulphate of mercury, iodine, naphthol, thymol, acetic, boracic, carbolic, chrysophanic, pyrogallic, pyroligneous, salicylic, and sulphurous acids, oil of cade, oil of turpentine, croton oil, etc., etc. Success depends, however, less upon the choice of the agent than upon the thoroughness with which the details of treatment are carried out. Equally numerous have been the preparations employed, as aqueous, alcoholic, ethereal solutions, ointments, oleates, collodion and traumaticin combinations, etc.

One of the most efficient parasiticides is a lotion of corrosive sublimate (one or two grains to the ounce), which may be applied by means of a small brush or a piece of flannel dipped in the solution. At night the scalp should be washed with the tincture of green soap and warm water. Should the treatment provoke pustular or other irritation, it must be suspended and emollient applications, or a lotion of hyposulphite of soda (thirty grains to the ounce of water, with a little glycerin), be employed until the irritation subsides. After a few days of this treatment, ointments, or other forms of application, may, with advantage, be substituted for the lotion.

. Hardy recommends frictions, night and morning, with an ointment of thirty to forty grains of flowers of sulphur and fifteen grains of camphor to the ounce of lard. Bazin prefers an ointment of fifteen to thirty grains of turpeth mineral to the ounce. Fox uses, after epilation, a two to five per cent solution of salicylic acid in alcohol or castor oil. Lailler recommends the continuous applications of compresses saturated with sublimated glycerin.

According to my experience, an ointment of chrysarobin, ten per cent, and salicylic acid, five per cent, is one of the most efficient topical applications. I prefer to use these drugs, singly or in combination, in collodion or traumaticin, forming a fixed, impermeable dressing which may be renewed whenever it begins to crack or lift up from the surface. This dressing possesses the advantage of maintaining the active agent in continuous contact, while excluding the air; a supply of oxygen being regarded as essential to the life of a vegetable parasite. Used in this way, general staining of the hair, the production of chrysophanic conjunctivitis from transference of particles of the drug to the eyes, and other attendant disadvantages, are obviated. Pyrogallic acid, five per cent; iodine, five to ten per cent, and other active agents, may be employed in these combinations. Coster's paste (iodine, з i., to colorless oil of tar, з iv.) and an ointment of the oleate of mercury, five to ten per cent, are also efficient as parasiticides.

Active treatment should be suspended from time to time in order to ascertain whether a cure has been effected. Should clinical or microscopic evidences of the disease be again manifest, a second or even third series of epilations, followed by parasiticide applications, should be employed until a complete cure is obtained.

As a general rule, it will be found that the readiness with which the disease responds to treatment is directly proportionate to its chronicity and the consequent deep diffusion of the spores.

As before intimated, there is a wide field for the selection of remedies. Experimentation has not only been active in testing their parasiticidal action, but also in devising expedients for bringing them in direct contact with the microphyte. Ether has been recommended as a menstruum on account of its property of dissolving fatty matter; chloroform on account of its power of penetration; lanolin on account of the facility with which it is absorbed, etc. Harrison has recently recommended iodide of potassium in liquor potassæ for softening the hairs, and the subsequent application of a mercuric bichloride solution, on the theory that it readily penetrates to the roots of the hairs, and a chemical action takes place, resulting in the formation of the biniodide of mercury, which destroys the fungus.

One caution should be observed in the selection of a parasiticide, which is, that it should never be of such strength as to cause destruction of the tissues themselves. The intense derma-titis determined by certain irritants may produce a permanent alopecia, which tinea tonsurans never occasions. Ladriet's treatment of tinea with croton-oil pencils, which has for its object the production of an artificial kerion by setting up a suppurative inflammation of the hair follicles, is on this account to be condemned. Cramoisy's treatment by pyroligneous acid, the use of glacial acetic acid, blistering the scalp, and other severe measures, are likewise objectionable. It is well, also, to remember that the susceptibility of the scalp to irritants varies in different individuals, and the strength of the application in each case should be measured by the reaction produced.

In the treatment of tinea affecting the beard, the same general principles of treatment obtain. Epilation, with the use of an ointment of iodide of sulphur (thirty or forty grains to the ounce), I have found most serviceable. Good results may also be obtained from the use of an ointment of the oleate of copper or mercury (ten per cent).

In the treatment of onychomycosis, mechanical or chemical means for the removal of the nail substance infiltrated by the fungus should be employed, and the nails dressed with an ointment of iodide of sulphur or ammoniated mercury.

FAVUS.

Synonyms.—Tinea Favosa; Teigne Faveuse.

Favus is a contagious vegetable parasitic disease characterized by the development of sulphur-colored, cup-shaped crusts. It affects chiefly the hairy scalp, but may occur upon other regions of the body.

The disease first appears in the form of small, inflammatory puncta or reddish, scaly spots situated about the hair follicles, which soon enlarge into yellowish discs, and in a further stage of their development assume the characteristic cup-shaped contour and sulphur-yellow color of the typical favus crusts. Ordinarily each crust is perforated by one or more hairs; the centre is depressed, with elevated margins, giving it a concave or umbilicated appearance. The crust may be dug out or uplifted from its bed, showing its under surface convex and leaving a pit-like depression in the scalp. The crusts are extremely friable, and may be readily crumbled or pulverized between the fingers. They are fungous masses formed by the proliferation of the fungus, which penetrates into the hair shaft and follicles and the surrounding epidermis.

The nutrition of the hairs in the affected area suffers from the presence of the parasite and the pressure of the crusts upon the follicles and papillæ; they become dry and brittle, and finally fall out, leaving bald spots. Itching, more or less pronounced, is a constant feature.

Upon the general surface of the body occupied by the lanugo hairs, where the follicles are more shallow, the fungus does not take such deep root and proliferate so abundantly. Occasionally, however, the crusts or scutula are persistent for years, and take on an exaggerated development. The crusts, instead of remaining discrete, become attached at their margins or aggregate into elevated, yellowish-white masses, in which the circular contour of the component cups may be distinctly seen.

Favus of the body and the scalp sometimes coexist, as in the case illustrated in Fig. 2, Plate LXXV., in which the disease was distributed over the head, left upper arm, lateral surface of thighs and legs below the knee, and the internal surface of the buttocks. It had existed nine years. Scattered over almost the entire hairy scalp are numerous variously sized, cup-shaped, yellow crusts, the depressed centres perforated by hairs. Over the vertical region are two or three irregu-larly shaped concretions, formed by the coalescence of the favi, which still retain their cup-shaped contour. The ridgy borders of these patches are elevated one-half inch or more above the surface, the centres somewhat hollowed. The hair is quite thin, and in many places, especially over the vertex, there is complete alopecia. The peculiar "mousey" odor exhaled by the crusts is quite pathognomonic.

Over the left deltoid region, at the insertion of the deltoid, and on the lateral and posterior surface of the arm, extending nearly to the elbow, are a number of rounded, irregularly shaped concretions formed by the fusion of contiguous scutula which have lost their distinctive shape, constituting the condition known as favosa squamosa. The lateral borders of these crusts are firm and unbroken, rising fully one inch above the niveau, and of a clear, sulphur-yellow color. On the surface the crusts are fissured and disintegrated and somewhat friable, presenting the appearance of whitish-yellow mortar. The patches on the lower extremities present the same general characters, but are of much smaller dimensions.

Sometimes ulceration occurs beneath the crusts, obliterating the follicles and leaving a thin, atrophied scar, dead white and glistening, and presenting the appearance of a tensely drawn piece of parchment. The affected area may be completely bald or occupied by a few scattered hairs.

Favus may also affect the nails, but tinea favosa unguium is of quite rare occurrence, and usually secondary to the development of the disease upon other surfaces. The characteristic yellow deposits may be seen at the free edge of the nails, sometimes in the centre. The nail first appears opaque, thickened, and crossed with intersecting furrows; later it becomes soft, friable, and thinned in places.

Favus is much common in childhood, but may develop at all ages. Piffard recently presented before the New York Dermatological Society a case of favus occurring in an infant six weeks old. The geographical distribution of favus is influenced not only by conditions of climate, but also by the habits of the people as regards cleanliness, care of the person, etc. It is quite common in Poland and Southern Europe, of much rarer occurrence in Northern Europe, and comparatively infrequent in this country. It is to be remembered that favus affects certain animals, as rabbits, cats, mice, and dogs, and they not infrequently serve as the agents of the transmission of the disease to their human associates.

DIAGNOSIS —The diagnosis of a recent case of favus should admit of no mistake. The sulphur-colored, cup-shaped crusts, most typically developed as a rule around the anterior margin of the hairy scalp, and the peculiar mousey odor, are most characteristic. When the disease is of long duration, and the typical features are obliterated by the breaking down or removal of the crusts, confusion may arise, but even in these cases the existence of a recent characteristic scutulum will reveal the nature of the affection. Microscopic examination of the fungus should clear up the diagnosis.

Patches of tinea tonsurans may resemble those of favus deprived of crusts, but in ringworm the hairs are broken off short, and the hirsute patches present a short, stumpy appearance, with more or less white, powdery scaliness in the centre; while in favus the hairs are unchanged in length, and the surface is of a dull red hue.

When a favus surface is irritated, by scratching or otherwise, into an eczematous condition, it may be mistaken for impetiginous eczema. In the latter disease the hairs are unaffected, or simply glued together by the discharge, and there is more or less excoriation and crusting.

In seborrhœa the surface is pale, smooth, and of a normal color; the scales are greasy and may be rolled into balls.

Psoriasis presents a certain resemblance to the mortar-like masses which are present in many cases of favus, but the scales of psoriasis are whiter, and the skin beneath is reddened with a number of bleeding points.

TREATMENT.—The object of treatment being to destroy the fungus, measures should be taken to bring parasiticides into immediate contact with the offending parasite. If the favus be situated upon the general surface of the body, the removal of the crusts and the subsequent employment of any of the numerous parasiticides already referred to usually suffice to promptly effect a cure.

PLATE LXXV.

FIG. I.—Eczema Marginatum.
FIG. II.—Favus.

FIGS. I. AND II.—AUTHOR'S COLLECTION.

When situated upon the hairy scalp, other means are to be brought into requisition. The spores, instead of being confined to the superficial epidermis or shallow follicles, have penetrated to the depths of the hair follicles and are inaccessible to these remedies. The treatment of favus and ringworm of the hairy scalp does not differ essentially in principle or detail, and the preliminary measures to be taken in preparing the patch, in order to insure the thorough penetration of the parasiticide to the depths of the hair follicle, are just as essential in the treatment of the one disease as in the other. In favus the hairs are firmly implanted, and the epilation is often quite painful. After epilation the surface should be treated with an application of the corrosive sublimate in alcohol, one or two grains to the ounce, or the following ointment may be rubbed in: ℞ Acidi salicylici, ʒi.; chrysarobin, ʒi.; pulv. cretæ, ʒiss.; lard, ʒi. M. F. ung. Ointments of oleate of mercury and oleate of copper are also highly recommended. A vast number of parasiticides have been used in the treatment of favus, the most valuable of which have been mentioned in connection with the treatment of tinea tricophytina. After the surface has been subjected to this treatment for three or four weeks, and evidences of the disease are still present, epilation should again be practised with subsequent use of the parasiticides, and continued until a cure is effected. The patient should be kept under observation for some time after the hair is allowed to grow, in order that any remaining vestiges of the disease may be early recognized and promptly destroyed.

INDEX.

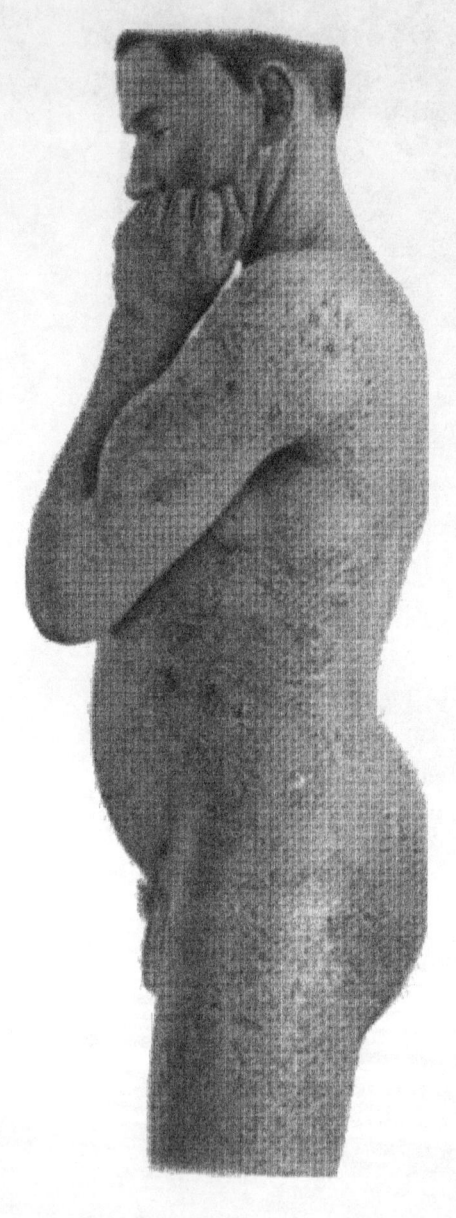

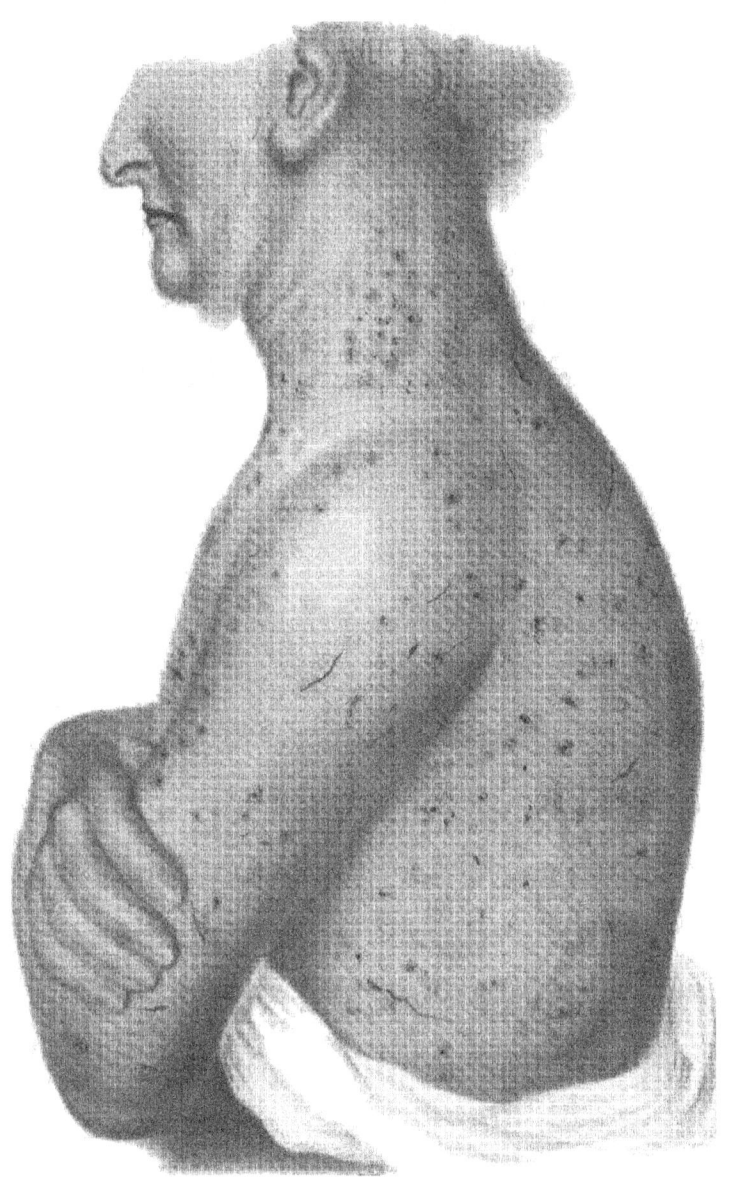

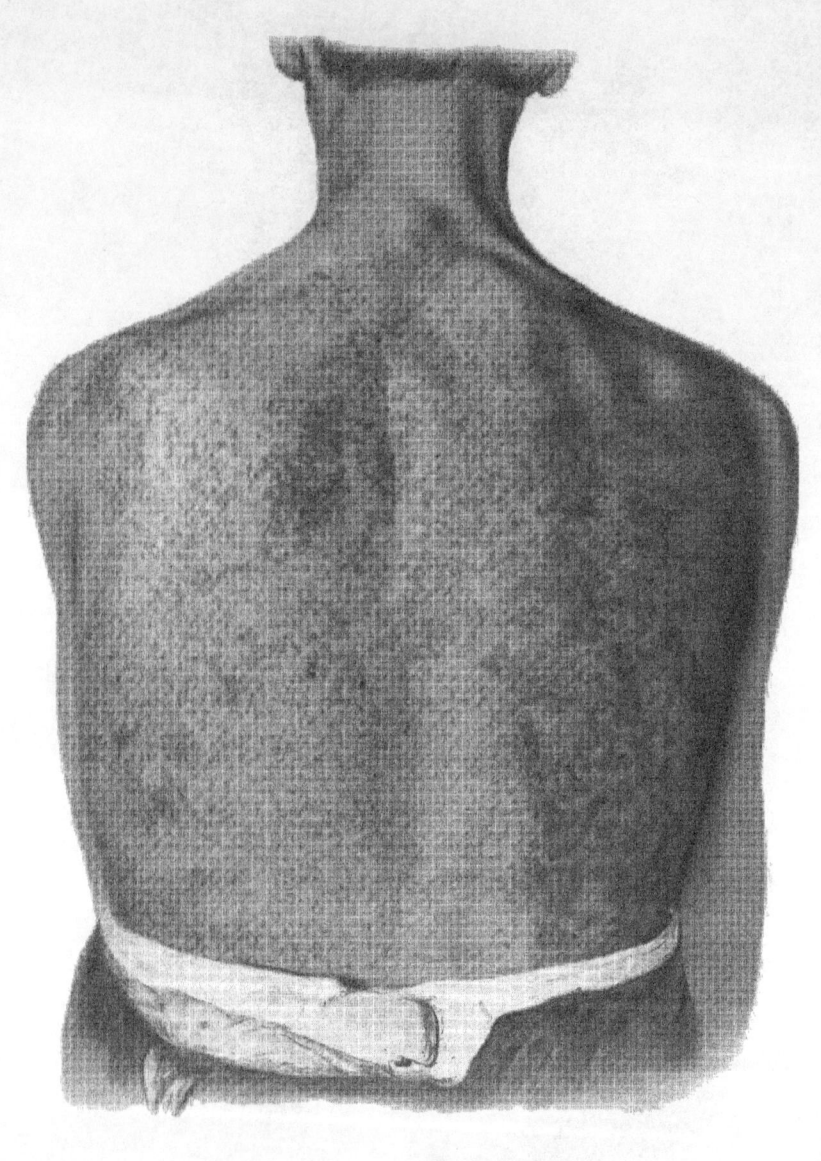

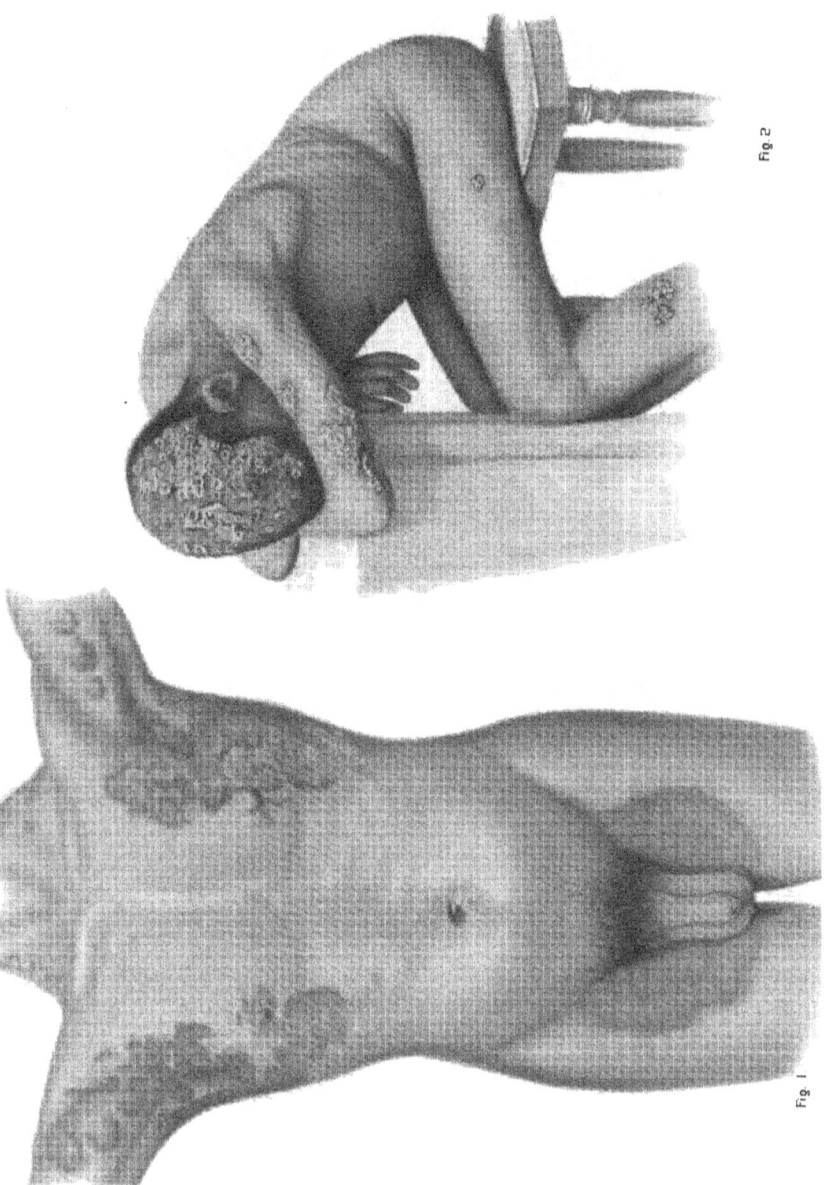

Fig. 1

Fig. 2

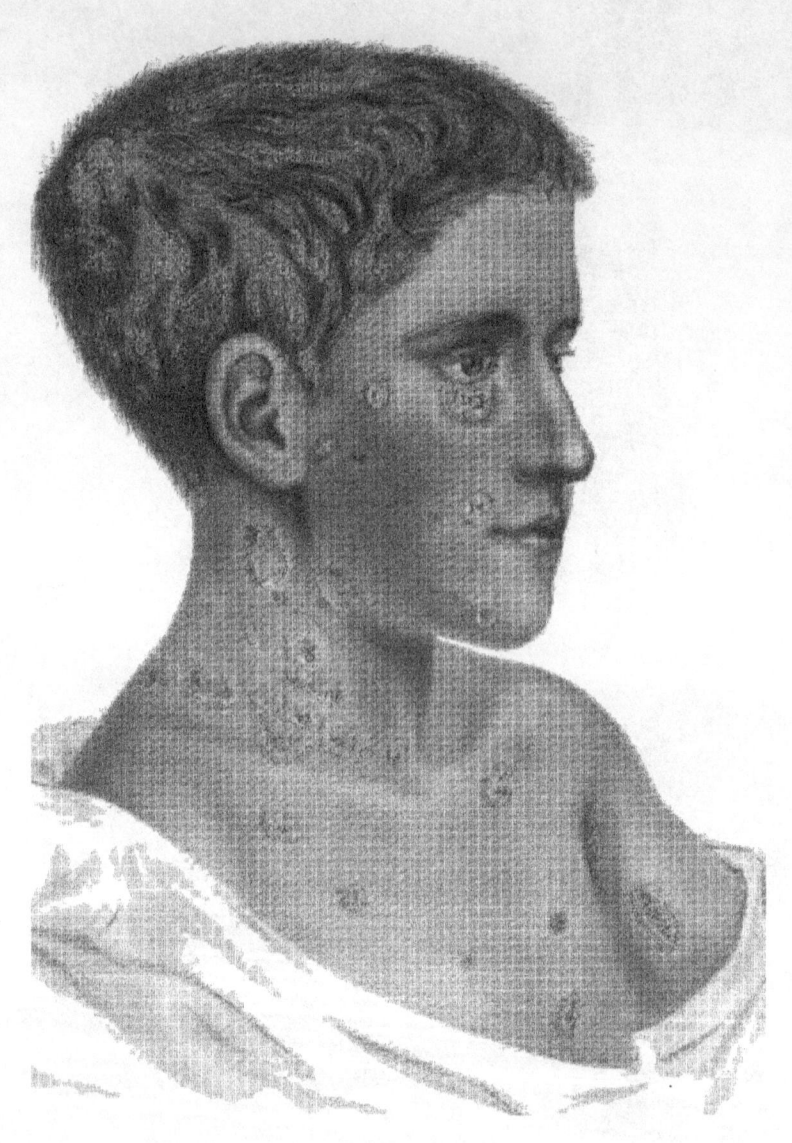